The Editors

GREGORY EISELEIN is Associate Professor and Director of Graduate Studies in the Department of English at Kansas State University, where he teaches American literature and cultural studies. He is the author of *Literature and Humanitarian Reform in the Civil War Era* and editor of *Emma Lazarus: Selected Poems and Other Writings* and *Adah Isaacs Menken:* Infelicia *and Other Writings*. With Anne K. Phillips, he coedited *The Louisa May Alcott Encyclopedia*.

ANNE K. PHILLIPS is Associate Professor and Assistant Department Head in the Department of English at Kansas State University, where she teaches children's and adolescent literature and American literature. She is a coauthor of *Resources for Teaching the Bedford Introduction to Literature* and coeditor of the annual *Children's Literature 21*. With Gregory Eiselein, she coedited *The Louisa May Alcott Encyclopedia*.

A NORTON CRITICAL EDITION

Louisa M. Alcott
LITTLE WOMEN
OR
MEG, JO, BETH AND AMY

AUTHORITATIVE TEXT
BACKGROUNDS AND CONTEXTS
CRITICISM

Edited by

ANNE K. PHILLIPS
KANSAS STATE UNIVERSITY

GREGORY EISELEIN
KANSAS STATE UNIVERSITY

W. W. NORTON & COMPANY
New York • London

W. W. Norton & Company has been independent since its founding in 1923, when William Warder Norton and Mary D. Herter Norton first published lectures delivered at the People's Institute, the adult education division of New York City's Cooper Union. The Nortons soon expanded their program beyond the Institute, publishing books by celebrated academics from America and abroad. By mid-century, the two major pillars of Norton's publishing program—trade books and college texts—were firmly established. In the 1950s, the Norton family transferred control of the company to its employees, and today—with a staff of four hundred and a comparable number of trade, college, and professional titles published each year—W. W. Norton & Company stands as the largest and oldest publishing house owned wholly by its employees.

Every effort has been made to contact the copyright holders for each of the selections. Rights holder of any selections not credited should contact W. W. Norton & Company, Inc., 500 Fifth Avenue, New York, N.Y. 10110, in order for a correction to be made in the next reprinting of our work.

The text of this book is composed in Fairfield Medium
with the display set in Bernhard Modern.
Composition by PennSet, Inc.
Manufacturing by the Courier Companies, Westford.
Book design by Antonina Krass.
Production Manager: Ben Reynolds.

Library of Congress Cataloging-in-Publication Data

Alcott, Louisa May, 1832–1888.
    Little women, or, Meg, Jo, Beth, and Amy / Louisa M. Alcott ; edited
by Anne K. Phillips, Gregory Eiselein.
        p. cm.
    "Authoritative text, backgrounds and contexts, criticism."
    Includes bibliographical references (p.   ).

ISBN 0-393-97614-9 (pbk.)

    1. March family (Fictitious characters)—Fiction. 2. Alcott, Louisa May,
1832–1888. Little women. 3. Mothers and daughters—Fiction. 4. New
England—Fiction. 5. Young women—Fiction. 6. Sisters—Fiction. I. Title:
Little women. II. Title: Meg, Jo, Beth, and Amy. III. Phillips, Anne K.
IV. Eiselein, Gregory, 1965– V. Title.

PS1017.L5 2003
813'.4—dc21

                                                            2003054123

W. W. Norton & Company, Inc., 500 Fifth Avenue, New York, N.Y. 10110
www.wwnorton.com

W. W. Norton & Company Ltd., Castle House,
75/76 Wells Street, London W1T 3QT

1 2 3 4 5 6 7 8 9 0

Contents

Criticism

Illustrations

Illustrations on pages 3 and 67 and images of the original title pages on pages 5 and 187 appear
courtesy of the Harry Ransom Humanities Research Center, the University of Texas at
Austin. All other illustrations are courtesy of the Louisa May Alcott Collection, Hale Library
Special Collections, Kansas State University.

Illustrations

Preface

Louisa May Alcott's *Little Women* (1868–69) is one of the most loved and widely read classic American novels. Meg, Jo, Beth, and Amy remain a part of American cultural consciousness, and new generations of readers continue to cherish their story. Increasingly, *Little Women* has attracted attention from scholars in a variety of fields, including American literature, American studies, children's literature, critical theory, history, and women's studies. This recent critical notice, along with the novel's enduring popularity, has made *Little Women* an increasingly familiar presence in college curricula.

An abiding artifact of American popular and now academic culture, *Little Women* is not merely a novel, it is a phenomenon. One of the world's most widely translated pieces of writing, it continues to inspire countless discussions and cultural reproductions, including several Hollywood films; television, radio, and cable productions; postage stamps; cartoons; dolls; lesbian theater; musical theater; opera; and much more. Moreover, the history of its reception reveals that *Little Women* has always managed to appeal to and resonate meaningfully with different kinds of audiences—the middle class and the working class, the native born and immigrants, teenagers and college students, intellectuals and professional writers. Long regarded as a significant exploration of the processes of becoming a woman, the novel acknowledges the various conflicts inherent in the girls' artistic ambitions and societal expectations as well as the evident tensions between their attachments to each other and their attractions to the world beyond the March family home. Unlike other mid-nineteenth-century fiction for girls, such as Susan Warner's *The Wide, Wide World* and Martha Finley's *Elsie Dinsmore*, *Little Women* portrays distinct, fascinating, but flawed girls who inhabit a riveting but recognizably ordinary world. Suffused with imaginative play, self-centered behaviors, enduring friendships, and memorable scenes, from Christmas theatricals and the pickled lime debacle to literary triumphs and the French Riviera romance, the novel continues to attract, entertain, and enlighten its readers.

Little Women is an ideal text for the Norton Critical Edition series. The novel appeared in two tangibly different versions, the first in 1868–69, the second in 1880. This Norton Critical Edition provides both a critically established first edition text as well as a list of the significant changes included in what became known as the "regular edition." There is also a rich selection of biographical, literary, and contextual documents here that enable readers to study the relationship between Alcott's life (as revealed in journals, correspondence, and memoirs) and her fiction. Because the novel makes regular reference to literary classics by Bunyan, Goethe, and Edgeworth, as well as to Alcott's own juvenile productions, this Norton Critical Edition supplies the original sources for a number of these allusions, offering readers the opportunity to gain a richer understanding of the novel, its traditions, and its contexts. Finally, *Little Women* has generated a wide range of critical and cultural responses. In addition to reprinting a wealth of contemporary reviews, this edition incorporates critical commentary about the novel from the flapper era to the present, demonstrating the depth and diversity of contemporary theoretical approaches to what might be the most beloved novel in American literary history.

Acknowledgments

We extend our heartfelt gratitude to Madeleine B. Stern, Christine Doyle, and Joel Myerson, our advisors and mentors, for their generosity and encouragement. We are indebted to Melea Seward for getting us started and to Carol Bemis for her support throughout the development of this edition. Ann Tappert's careful and impressive copyediting made this edition better and more accurate, and we appreciate her contribution. Kansas State University has always been an intellectually exciting and enjoyable place to work. We are especially grateful for travel grants, in particular a University Small Research Grant and a Big Twelve Faculty Fellowship, that enabled us to spend time at Harvard's Houghton Library and the University of Texas's Harry Ransom Humanities Research Center. At Harvard, Susan Halpert and Elizabeth Falsey were professional and dedicated, just as Margaret Tufts Tenney's help made our work at the Ransom Center pleasant and quite productive. The support of the English Department and our head, Larry Rodgers, was crucial; and Dana Reinert's year of meticulous collation, proofreading, and collaboration has been more valuable than we could have expected or imagined. We thank the staff of Kansas State's Interlibrary Loan department—Kathy Coleman, Lori Fenton, Cherie Geiser, Bernie Randall, and Sharon Van Rysselburghe. We also want to express our appreciation to Roger C. Adams, rare books librarian at Kansas State University's Hale Library, for his dedication to Kansas State's Louisa M. Alcott Collection and his passion for this project. For encouragement or support at key moments, we thank Bob Hirst, Sarah Elbert, and Sara Wege. Finally, we would also like to thank our American literature and children's literature students for sharing with us their responses, insights, and enthusiasm.

In addition to these professional recognitions, we offer the following personal thanks. Eric and Wesley Danielson and Patricia and David Phillips continue to serve as the most generous of Alcott cohorts. For their Joian sense of adventure and good cheer while Greg was in the vortex, thanks to Michele Janette and Linda Brigham.

Abbreviations

Cheney: Ednah D. Cheney, ed., *Louisa May Alcott: Her Life, Letters, and Journals* (Boston: Roberts Brothers, 1889)

Journals: Joel Myerson, Daniel Shealy, and Madeleine B. Stern, eds., *The Journals of Louisa May Alcott* (Boston: Little, Brown, 1989)

Letters: Joel Myerson, Daniel Shealy, and Madeleine B. Stern, eds., *The Selected Letters of Louisa May Alcott* (Boston: Little, Brown, 1987)

The Text of
LITTLE WOMEN
or
Meg, Jo, Beth and Amy

They all drew to the fire, mother in the big chair, with Beth at her feet; Meg and
Amy perched on either arm of the chair, and Jo leaning on the back.—PAGE 16.

"What do you want now?" she asked, looking sharply over her spectacles; while the parrot, sitting on the back of her chair, called out, "Go away; no boys allowed here."—PAGE 145.

LITTLE WOMEN

OR,

MEG, JO, BETH AND AMY

BY LOUISA M. ALCOTT

ILLUSTRATED BY MAY ALCOTT

BOSTON
ROBERTS BROTHERS
1868

CONTENTS.

PREFACE.

"Go then, my little Book, and show to all
That entertain, and bid thee welcome shall,
What thou dost keep close shut up in thy breast;
And wish what thou dost show them may be blest
To them for good, may make them choose to be
Pilgrims better, by far, than thee or me.
Tell them of Mercy; she is one
Who early hath her pilgrimage begun.
Yea, let young damsels learn of her to prize
The world which is to come, and so be wise;
For little tripping maids may follow God
Along the ways which saintly feet have trod."

ADAPTED FROM JOHN BUNYAN.[1]

---

1. Cf. John Bunyan, "The Author's Way of Sending Forth His Second Part of the Pilgrim," in *The Pilgrim's Progress* (1684), excerpted in this Norton Critical Edition on p. 447.

CHAPTER I.

PLAYING PILGRIMS.

CHRISTMAS won't be Christmas without any presents," grumbled Jo, lying on the rug.

"It's so dreadful to be poor!" sighed Meg, looking down at her old dress.

"I don't think it's fair for some girls to have lots of pretty things, and other girls nothing at all," added little Amy, with an injured sniff.

"We've got father and mother, and each other, anyhow," said Beth, contentedly, from her corner.

The four young faces on which the firelight shone brightened at the cheerful words, but darkened again as Jo said sadly,—

"We haven't got father, and shall not have him for a long time." She didn't say "perhaps never," but each silently added it, thinking of father far away, where the fighting was.[2]

Nobody spoke for a minute; then Meg said in an altered tone,—

"You know the reason mother proposed not having any presents this Christmas, was because it's going to be a hard winter for every one; and she thinks we ought not to spend money for pleasure, when our men are suffering so in the army. We can't do much, but we can make our little sacrifices, and ought to do it gladly. But I am afraid I don't;" and Meg shook her head, as she thought regretfully of all the pretty things she wanted.

"But I don't think the little we should spend would do any good. We've each got a dollar, and the army wouldn't be much helped by our giving that. I agree not to expect anything from mother or you, but I do want to buy Undine and Sintram[3] for myself; I've wanted it *so* long," said Jo, who was a bookworm.

"I planned to spend mine in new music," said Beth, with a little sigh, which no one heard but the hearth-brush and kettle-holder.

"I shall get a nice box of Faber's drawing pencils;[4] I really need them," said Amy, decidedly.

"Mother didn't say anything about our money, and she won't wish us to give up everything. Let's each buy what we want, and have a little fun; I'm sure we grub hard enough to earn it," cried Jo, examining the heels of her boots in a gentlemanly manner.

"I know *I* do,—teaching those dreadful children nearly all day, when I'm longing to enjoy myself at home," began Meg, in the complaining tone again.

---

2. United States Civil War, 1861–65. The novel opens in December 1861.
3. Pair of tales by German romantic writer Friedrich de la Motte Fouqué (1777–1843). *Undine* (1811) is a fairy tale about a water sprite; *Sintram und seine Gefährten* (1815), an allegory inspired by Albrecht Dürer's famous engraving *Knight, Death, and Devil* (1513). Jo is probably referring to the popular American edition and translation *Undine, and Sintram and His Companions* (1845).
4. Famous pencil brand known for high quality. A. W. Faber pencils were first sold in the United States in 1843.

"You don't have half such a hard time as I do," said Jo. "How would you like to be shut up for hours with a nervous, fussy old lady, who keeps you trotting, is never satisfied, and worries you till you're ready to fly out of the window or box her ears?"

"It's naughty to fret,—but I do think washing dishes and keeping things tidy is the worst work in the world. It makes me cross; and my hands get so stiff, I can't practise good a bit." And Beth looked at her rough hands with a sigh that any one could hear that time.

"I don't believe any of you suffer as I do," cried Amy; "for you don't have to go to school with impertinent girls, who plague you if you don't know your lessons, and laugh at your dresses, and label your father if he isn't rich, and insult you when your nose isn't nice."

"If you mean *libel* I'd say so, and not talk about *labels*, as if pa was a pickle-bottle," advised Jo, laughing.

"I know what I mean, and you needn't be 'statirical' about it. It's proper to use good words, and improve your *vocabilary*," returned Amy, with dignity.

"Don't peck at one another, children. Don't you wish we had the money papa lost when we were little, Jo? Dear me, how happy and good we'd be, if we had no worries," said Meg, who could remember better times.

"You said the other day you thought we were a deal happier than the King children, for they were fighting and fretting all the time, in spite of their money."

"So I did, Beth. Well, I guess we are; for though we do have to work, we make fun for ourselves, and are a pretty jolly set, as Jo would say."

"Jo does use such slang words," observed Amy, with a reproving look at the long figure stretched on the rug. Jo immediately sat up, put her hands in her apron pockets, and began to whistle.

"Don't, Jo; it's so boyish."

"That's why I do it."

"I detest rude, unlady-like girls."

"I hate affected, niminy piminy chits."

"Birds in their little nests agree,"[5] sang Beth, the peace-maker, with such a funny face that both sharp voices softened to a laugh, and the "pecking" ended for that time.

"Really, girls, you are both to be blamed," said Meg, beginning to lecture in her elder sisterly fashion. "You are old enough to leave off boyish tricks, and behave better, Josephine. It didn't matter so much when you were a little girl; but now you are so tall, and turn up your hair, you should remember that you are a young lady."

"I ain't! and if turning up my hair makes me one, I'll wear it in two tails till I'm twenty," cried Jo, pulling off her net, and shaking down a chestnut mane. "I hate to think I've got to grow up and be Miss March, and wear long gowns, and look as prim as a China-aster. It's bad enough to be a girl, any way, when I like boy's games, and work,

---

5. See Isaac Watts, Song 17 ("Love between brothers and sisters"), in *Divine Songs for Children* (1715). Verse 2 reads: "Birds in their little nests agree; / And 'tis a shameful sight, / When children of one family / Fall out, and chide, and fight."

and manners. I can't get over my disappointment in not being a boy, and it's worse than ever now, for I'm dying to go and fight with papa, and I can only stay at home and knit like a poky old woman;" and Jo shook the blue army-sock till the needles rattled like castanets, and her ball bounded across the room.

"Poor Jo; it's too bad! But it can't be helped, so you must try to be contented with making your name boyish, and playing brother to us girls," said Beth, stroking the rough head at her knee with a hand that all the dish-washing and dusting in the world could not make ungentle in its touch.

"As for you, Amy," continued Meg, "you are altogether too particular and prim. Your airs are funny now, but you'll grow up an affected little goose if you don't take care. I like your nice manners, and refined ways of speaking, when you don't try to be elegant; but your absurd words are as bad as Jo's slang."

"If Jo is a tom-boy, and Amy a goose, what am I, please?" asked Beth, ready to share the lecture.

"You're a dear, and nothing else," answered Meg, warmly; and no one contradicted her, for the "Mouse" was the pet of the family.

As young readers like to know "how people look," we will take this moment to give them a little sketch of the four sisters, who sat knitting away in the twilight, while the December snow fell quietly without, and the fire crackled cheerfully within. It was a comfortable old room, though the carpet was faded and the furniture very plain, for a good picture or two hung on the walls, books filled the recesses, chrysanthemums and Christmas roses bloomed in the windows, and a pleasant atmosphere of home-peace pervaded it.

Margaret, the eldest of the four, was sixteen, and very pretty, being plump and fair, with large eyes, plenty of soft brown hair, a sweet mouth, and white hands, of which she was rather vain. Fifteen-year old Jo was very tall, thin and brown, and reminded one of a colt; for she never seemed to know what to do with her long limbs, which were very much in her way. She had a decided mouth, a comical nose, and sharp gray eyes, which appeared to see everything, and were by turns fierce, funny, or thoughtful. Her long, thick hair was her one beauty; but it was usually bundled into a net, to be out of her way. Round shoulders had Jo, big hands and feet, a fly-away look to her clothes, and the uncomfortable appearance of a girl who was rapidly shooting up into a woman, and didn't like it. Elizabeth,—or Beth, as every one called her,—was a rosy, smooth-haired, bright-eyed girl of thirteen, with a shy manner, a timid voice, and a peaceful expression, which was seldom disturbed. Her father called her "Little Tranquillity,"[6] and the name suited her excellently; for she seemed to live in a happy world of her own, only venturing out to meet the few whom she trusted and loved. Amy, though the youngest, was a most important person, in her own opinion at least. A regular snow maiden, with blue eyes, and yellow hair curling on her shoulders; pale and slender, and

6. Cf. *Journals*, 163.

always carrying herself like a young lady mindful of her manners. What the characters of the four sisters were, we will leave to be found out.

The clock struck six; and, having swept up the hearth, Beth put a pair of slippers down to warm. Somehow the sight of the old shoes had a good effect upon the girls, for mother was coming, and every one brightened to welcome her. Meg stopped lecturing, and lit the lamp, Amy got out of the easy-chair without being asked, and Jo forgot how tired she was as she sat up to hold the slippers nearer to the blaze.

"They are quite worn out; Marmee must have a new pair."

"I thought I'd get her some with my dollar," said Beth.

"No, I shall!" cried Amy.

"I'm the oldest," began Meg, but Jo cut in with a decided—

"I'm the man of the family now papa is away, and *I* shall provide the slippers, for he told me to take special care of mother while he was gone."

"I'll tell you what we'll do," said Beth; "let's each get her something for Christmas, and not get anything for ourselves."

"That's like you, dear! What will we get?" exclaimed Jo.

Every one thought soberly for a minute; then Meg announced, as if the idea was suggested by the sight of her own pretty hands, "I shall give her a nice pair of gloves."

"Army shoes, best to be had," cried Jo.

"Some handkerchiefs, all hemmed," said Beth.

"I'll get a little bottle of Cologne; she likes it, and it won't cost much, so I'll have some left to buy something for me," added Amy.

"How will we give the things?" asked Meg.

"Put 'em on the table, and bring her in and see her open the bundles. Don't you remember how we used to do on our birthdays?" answered Jo.

"I used to be *so* frightened when it was my turn to sit in the big chair with a crown on, and see you all come marching round to give the presents, with a kiss. I liked the things and the kisses, but it was dreadful to have you sit looking at me while I opened the bundles," said Beth, who was toasting her face and the bread for tea, at the same time.

"Let Marmee think we are getting things for ourselves, and then surprise her. We must go shopping to-morrow afternoon, Meg; there is lots to do about the play for Christmas night," said Jo, marching up and down with her hands behind her back, and her nose in the air.

"I don't mean to act any more after this time; I'm getting too old for such things," observed Meg, who was as much a child as ever about "dressing up" frolics.

"You won't stop, I know, as long as you can trail round in a white gown with your hair down, and wear gold-paper jewelry. You are the best actress we've got, and there'll be an end of everything if you quit the boards," said Jo. "We ought to rehearse to-night; come here, Amy, and do the fainting scene, for you are as stiff as a poker in that."

"I can't help it; I never saw any one faint, and I don't choose to make myself all black and blue, tumbling flat as you do. If I can go down easily, I'll drop; if I can't, I shall fall into a chair and be graceful; I don't care if Hugo does come at me with a pistol," returned Amy, who was not gifted with dramatic power, but was chosen because she was small enough to be borne out shrieking by the hero of the piece.

"Do it this way; clasp your hands so, and stagger across the room, crying frantically, 'Roderigo! save me! save me!' " and away went Jo, with a melodramatic scream which was truly thrilling.

Amy followed, but she poked her hands out stiffly before her, and jerked herself along as if she went by machinery; and her "Ow!" was more suggestive of pins being run into her than of fear and anguish. Jo gave a despairing groan, and Meg laughed outright, while Beth let her bread burn as she watched the fun, with interest.

"It's no use! do the best you can when the time comes, and if the audience shout, don't blame me. Come on, Meg."

Then things went smoothly, for Don Pedro defied the world in a speech of two pages without a single break; Hagar, the witch, chanted an awful incantation over her kettleful of simmering toads, with weird effect; Roderigo rent his chains asunder manfully, and Hugo died in agonies of remorse and arsenic, with a wild "Ha! ha!"

"It's the best we've had yet," said Meg, as the dead villain sat up and rubbed his elbows.

"I don't see how you can write and act such splendid things, Jo. You're a regular Shakespeare!" exclaimed Beth, who firmly believed that her sisters were gifted with wonderful genius in all things.

"Not quite," replied Jo, modestly. "I do think 'The Witch's Curse, an Operatic Tragedy,'[7] is rather a nice thing; but I'd like to try Macbeth, if we only had a trap-door for Banquo. I always wanted to do the killing part. 'Is that a dagger that I see before me?' " muttered Jo, rolling her eyes and clutching at the air, as she had seen a famous tragedian do.[8]

"No, it's the toasting fork, with ma's shoe on it instead of the bread. Beth's stage struck!" cried Meg, and the rehearsal ended in a general burst of laughter.

"Glad to find you so merry, my girls," said a cheery voice at the door, and actors and audience turned to welcome a stout, motherly lady, with a "can-I-help-you" look about her which was truly delightful. She wasn't a particularly handsome person, but mothers are always lovely to their children, and the girls thought the gray cloak and unfashionable bonnet covered the most splendid woman in the world.

"Well, dearies, how have you got on to-day? There was so much to do, getting the boxes ready to go to-morrow, that I didn't come home

---

7. See the Alcott sisters' juvenile drama *Norna; or, The Witch's Curse* (reprinted in this Norton Critical Edition on p. 471), written between 1847 and 1849 and first published in *Comic Tragedies* (1893). See also Stern, p. 436 in "Backgrounds and Contexts."
8. *Macbeth* 2.1.33. The "tragedian" is probably the well-known American actor Edwin Forrest (1806–1872) whom Alcott had seen in 1855. In a 28 November 1855 letter to her father, she wrote: "Forrest does not act Shakespere well. . . . I can make up a better Macbeth & Hamlet for myself than Forrest with his gasping & shoutings can give me" (*Selected Letters*, 14).

to dinner. Has any one called, Beth? How is your cold, Meg? Jo, you look tired to death. Come and kiss me, baby."

While making these maternal inquiries Mrs. March got her wet things off, her hot slippers on, and sitting down in the easy-chair, drew Amy to her lap, preparing to enjoy the happiest hour of her busy day. The girls flew about, trying to make things comfortable, each in her own way. Meg arranged the tea-table; Jo brought wood and set chairs, dropping, overturning, and clattering everything she touched; Beth trotted to and fro between parlor and kitchen, quiet and busy; while Amy gave directions to every one, as she sat with her hands folded.

As they gathered about the table, Mrs. March said, with a particularly happy face, "I've got a treat for you after supper."

A quick, bright smile went round like a streak of sunshine. Beth clapped her hands, regardless of the hot biscuit she held, and Jo tossed up her napkin, crying, "A letter! a letter! Three cheers for father!"

"Yes, a nice long letter. He is well, and thinks he shall get through the cold season better than we feared. He sends all sorts of loving wishes for Christmas, and an especial message to you girls," said Mrs. March, patting her pocket as if she had got a treasure there.

"Hurry up, and get done. Don't stop to quirk your little finger, and prink over your plate, Amy," cried Jo, choking in her tea, and dropping her bread, butter side down, on the carpet, in her haste to get at the treat.

Beth ate no more, but crept away, to sit in her shadowy corner and brood over the delight to come, till the others were ready.

"I think it was so splendid in father to go as a chaplain when he was too old to be drafted, and not strong enough for a soldier," said Meg, warmly.

"Don't I wish I could go as a drummer, a *vivan*[9]—what's its name? or a nurse, so I could be near him and help him," exclaimed Jo, with a groan.

"It must be very disagreeable to sleep in a tent and eat all sorts of bad-tasting things, and drink out of a tin mug," sighed Amy.

"When will he come home, Marmee?" asked Beth, with a little quiver in her voice.

"Not for many months, dear, unless he is sick. He will stay and do his work faithfully as long as he can, and we won't ask for him back a minute sooner than he can be spared. Now come and hear the letter."

They all drew to the fire, mother in the big chair with Beth at her feet, Meg and Amy perched on either arm of the chair, and Jo leaning on the back, where no one would see any sign of emotion if the letter should happen to be touching.

Very few letters were written in those hard times that were not touching, especially those which fathers sent home. In this one little was said of the hardships endured, the dangers faced, or the homesickness conquered; it was a cheerful, hopeful letter, full of lively de-

---

9. Vivandière, a civilian woman who accompanies armies to provide provisions.

scriptions of camp life, marches, and military news; and only at the end did the writer's heart overflow with fatherly love and longing for the little girls at home.

"Give them all my dear love and a kiss. Tell them I think of them by day, pray for them by night, and find my best comfort in their affection at all times. A year seems very long to wait before I see them, but remind them that while we wait we may all work, so that these hard days need not be wasted. I know they will remember all I said to them, that they will be loving children to you, will do their duty faithfully, fight their bosom enemies bravely, and conquer themselves so beautifully, that when I come back to them I may be fonder and prouder than ever of my little women."

Everybody sniffed when they came to that part; Jo wasn't ashamed of the great tear that dropped off the end of her nose, and Amy never minded the rumpling of her curls as she hid her face on her mother's shoulder and sobbed out, "I *am* a selfish pig! but I'll truly try to be better, so he mayn't be disappointed in me by and by."

"We all will!" cried Meg. "I think too much of my looks, and hate to work, but won't any more, if I can help it."

"I'll try and be what he loves to call me, 'a little woman,' and not be rough and wild; but do my duty here instead of wanting to be somewhere else," said Jo, thinking that keeping her temper at home was a much harder task than facing a rebel or two down South.

Beth said nothing, but wiped away her tears with the blue army-sock, and began to knit with all her might, losing no time in doing the duty that lay nearest her, while she resolved in her quiet little soul to be all that father hoped to find her when the year brought round the happy coming home.

Mrs. March broke the silence that followed Jo's words, by saying in her cheery voice, "Do you remember how you used to play Pilgrim's Progress[1] when you were little things? Nothing delighted you more than to have me tie my piece-bags on your backs for burdens, give you hats and sticks, and rolls of paper, and let you travel through the house from the cellar, which was the City of Destruction, up, up, to the house-top, where you had all the lovely things you could collect to make a Celestial City."

"What fun it was, especially going by the lions, fighting Apollyon, and passing through the Valley where the hobgoblins were," said Jo.

"I liked the place where the bundles fell off and tumbled down stairs," said Meg.

1. March (and Alcott) family game based on John Bunyan's *Pilgrim's Progress* (1678, 1684). In part 1 of Bunyan's narrative, Christian, with a burden on his back, leaves home to flee the City of Destruction. On his way to the Celestial City, he travels to a variety of allegorical places such as the Slough of Despond, where a character called Help rescues him; a wicket gate where he meets Good-will; the Palace Beautiful, which is guarded by lions; the Valley of Humiliation, where he encounters the enraged dragonlike monster Apollyon; the Valley of the Shadow of Death, where demons beleaguer him; the Delectable Mountains; and more. Conducted by the Shining Ones, Christian eventually reaches the Celestial City. Part 2 continues the allegory: Christian's wife, Christiana, and their children set out on the road to salvation, encountering similar difficulties but receiving help from allegorical figures such as Great-heart.

"My favorite part was when we came out on the flat roof where our flowers and arbors, and pretty things were, and all stood and sung for joy up there in the sunshine," said Beth, smiling, as if that pleasant moment had come back to her.

"I don't remember much about it, except that I was afraid of the cellar and the dark entry, and always liked the cake and milk we had up at the top. If I wasn't too old for such things, I'd rather like to play it over again," said Amy, who began to talk of renouncing childish things at the mature age of twelve.

"We never are too old for this, my dear, because it is a play we are playing all the time in one way or another. Our burdens are here, our road is before us, and the longing for goodness and happiness is the guide that leads us through many troubles and mistakes to the peace which is a true Celestial City. Now, my little pilgrims, suppose you begin again, not in play, but in earnest, and see how far on you can get before father comes home."

"Really, mother? where are our bundles?" asked Amy, who was a very literal young lady.

"Each of you told what your burden was just now, except Beth; I rather think she hasn't got any," said her mother.

"Yes, I have; mine is dishes and dusters, and envying girls with nice pianos, and being afraid of people."

Beth's bundle was such a funny one that everybody wanted to laugh; but nobody did, for it would have hurt her feelings very much.

"Let us do it," said Meg, thoughtfully. "It is only another name for trying to be good, and the story may help us; for though we do want to be good, it's hard work, and we forget, and don't do our best."

"We were in the Slough of Despond to-night, and mother came and pulled us out as Help did in the book. We ought to have our roll of directions, like Christian. What shall we do about that?" asked Jo, delighted with the fancy which lent a little romance to the very dull task of doing her duty.

"Look under your pillows, Christmas morning, and you will find your guide-book," replied Mrs. March.

They talked over the new plan while old Hannah cleared the table; then out came the four little work-baskets, and the needles flew as the girls made sheets for Aunt March. It was uninteresting sewing, but to-night no one grumbled. They adopted Jo's plan of dividing the long seams into four parts, and calling the quarters Europe, Asia, Africa and America, and in that way got on capitally, especially when they talked about the different countries as they stitched their way through them.

At nine they stopped work, and sung, as usual, before they went to bed. No one but Beth could get much music out of the old piano; but she had a way of softly touching the yellow keys, and making a pleasant accompaniment to the simple songs they sung. Meg had a voice like a flute, and she and her mother led the little choir. Amy chirped like a cricket, and Jo wandered through the airs at her own sweet will, always coming out at the wrong place with a croak or a quaver that

spoilt the most pensive tune. They had always done this from the time
they could lisp

"Crinkle, crinkle, 'ittle 'tar,"[2]

and it had become a household custom, for the mother was a born
singer. The first sound in the morning was her voice, as she went
about the house singing like a lark; and the last sound at night was the
same cheery sound, for the girls never grew too old for that familiar
lullaby.

CHAPTER II.

A MERRY CHRISTMAS.

JO was the first to wake in the gray dawn of Christmas morning. No
stockings hung at the fireplace, and for a moment she felt as much
disappointed as she did long ago, when her little sock fell down because it was so crammed with goodies. Then she remembered her
mother's promise, and slipping her hand under her pillow, drew out a
little crimson-covered book. She knew it very well, for it was that
beautiful old story of the best life ever lived, and Jo felt that it was a
true guide-book for any pilgrim going the long journey.[3] She woke Meg
with a "Merry Christmas," and bade her see what was under her pillow. A green-covered book appeared, with the same picture inside,
and a few words written by their mother, which made their one present very precious in their eyes. Presently Beth and Amy woke, to rummage and find their little books also—one dove-colored, the other
blue; and all sat looking at and talking about them, while the East
grew rosy with the coming day.

In spite of her small vanities, Margaret had a sweet and pious nature, which unconsciously influenced her sisters, especially Jo, who
loved her very tenderly, and obeyed her because her advice was so
gently given.

"Girls," said Meg, seriously, looking from the tumbled head beside
her to the two little night-capped ones in the room beyond, "mother
wants us to read and love and mind these books, and we must begin at
once. We used to be faithful about it; but since father went away, and
all this war trouble unsettled us, we have neglected many things. You
can do as you please; but *I* shall keep my book on the table here, and

---

2. Ann Taylor and Jane Taylor, "Twinkle, Twinkle, Little Star," in *Rhymes for the Nursery*
   (1806).
3. Some critics have argued that the life mentioned here is Christian's and the guidebook *The
   Pilgrim's Progress*. Others believe that Marmee gives the girls copies of the New Testament
   and that "the best life ever lived" refers to Jesus Christ. The latter position is supported by
   reference to the book's chapters (see p. 134 [part 1, chap. 16]); the New Testament is divided into chapters, whereas *The Pilgrim's Progress* has no such divisions. For more on the
   critical debate, see Anne K. Phillips, "The Prophets and the Martyrs: Pilgrims and Missionaries in *Little Women* and *Jack and Jill*," in Little Women *and the Feminist Imagination: Criticism, Controversy, Personal Essays*, ed. Janice M. Alberghene and Beverly Lyon Clark (New
   York and London: Garland, 1999), 213–36, esp. 222–23, 235 nn. 21–23.

read a little every morning as soon as I wake, for I know it will do me good, and help me through the day."

Then she opened her new book and began to read. Jo put her arm round her, and, leaning cheek to cheek, read also, with the quiet expression so seldom seen on her restless face.

"How good Meg is! Come, Amy, let's do as they do. I'll help you with the hard words, and they'll explain things if we don't understand," whispered Beth, very much impressed by the pretty books and her sisters' example.

"I'm glad mine is blue," said Amy; and then the rooms were very still while the pages were softly turned, and the winter sunshine crept in to touch the bright heads and serious faces with a Christmas greeting.

"Where is mother?" asked Meg, as she and Jo ran down to thank her for their gifts, half an hour later.

"Goodness only knows. Some poor creeter come a-beggin', and your ma went straight off to see what was needed. There never *was* such a woman for givin' away vittles and drink, clothes and firin'," replied Hannah, who had lived with the family since Meg was born, and was considered by them all more as a friend than a servant.

"She will be back soon, I guess; so do your cakes, and have everything ready," said Meg, looking over the presents which were collected in a basket and kept under the sofa, ready to be produced at the proper time. "Why, where is Amy's bottle of Cologne?" she added, as the little flask did not appear.

"She took it out a minute ago, and went off with it to put a ribbon on it, or some such notion," replied Jo, dancing about the room to take the first stiffness off the new army-slippers.

"How nice my handkerchiefs look, don't they? Hannah washed and ironed them for me, and I marked them all myself," said Beth, looking proudly at the somewhat uneven letters which had cost her such labor.

"Bless the child, she's gone and put 'Mother' on them instead of 'M. March;' how funny!" cried Jo, taking up one.

"Isn't it right? I thought it was better to do it so, because Meg's initials are 'M. M.,' and I don't want any one to use these but Marmee," said Beth, looking troubled.

"It's all right, dear, and a very pretty idea; quite sensible, too, for no one can ever mistake now. It will please her very much, I know," said Meg, with a frown for Jo, and a smile for Beth.

"There's mother; hide the basket, quick!" cried Jo, as a door slammed, and steps sounded in the hall.

Amy came in hastily, and looked rather abashed when she saw her sisters all waiting for her.

"Where have you been, and what are you hiding behind you?" asked Meg, surprised to see, by her hood and cloak, that lazy Amy had been out so early.

"Don't laugh at me, Jo, I didn't mean any one should know till the time came. I only meant to change the little bottle for a big one, and I gave *all* my money to get it, and I'm truly trying not to be selfish any more."

As she spoke, Amy showed the handsome flask which replaced the cheap one; and looked so earnest and humble in her little effort to forget herself, that Meg hugged her on the spot, and Jo pronounced her "a trump," while Beth ran to the window, and picked her finest rose to ornament the stately bottle.

"You see I felt ashamed of my present, after reading and talking about being good this morning, so I ran round the corner and changed it the minute I was up; and I'm so glad, for mine is the handsomest now."

Another bang of the street-door sent the basket under the sofa, and the girls to the table eager for breakfast.

"Merry Christmas, Marmee! Lots of them! Thank you for our books; we read some, and mean to every day," they cried, in chorus.

"Merry Christmas, little daughters! I'm glad you began at once, and hope you will keep on. But I want to say one word before we sit down. Not far away from here lies a poor woman with a little new-born baby. Six children are huddled into one bed to keep from freezing, for they have no fire. There is nothing to eat over there; and the oldest boy came to tell me they were suffering hunger and cold. My girls, will you give them your breakfast as a Christmas present?"

They were all unusually hungry, having waited nearly an hour, and for a minute no one spoke; only a minute, for Jo exclaimed impetuously,—

"I'm so glad you came before we began!"

"May I go and help carry the things to the poor little children?" asked Beth, eagerly.

"I shall take the cream and the muffins," added Amy, heroically giving up the articles she most liked.

Meg was already covering the buckwheats, and piling the bread into one big plate.

"I thought you'd do it," said Mrs. March, smiling as if satisfied. "You shall all go and help me, and when we come back we will have bread and milk for breakfast, and make it up at dinner-time."

They were soon ready, and the procession set out. Fortunately it was early, and they went through back streets, so few people saw them, and no one laughed at the funny party.

A poor, bare, miserable room it was, with broken windows, no fire, ragged bed-clothes, a sick mother, wailing baby, and a group of pale, hungry children cuddled under one old quilt, trying to keep warm. How the big eyes stared, and the blue lips smiled, as the girls went in!

"Ach, mein Gott! it is good angels come to us!" cried the poor woman, crying for joy.

"Funny angels in hoods and mittens," said Jo, and set them laughing.

In a few minutes it really did seem as if kind spirits had been at work there. Hannah, who had carried wood, made a fire, and stopped up the broken panes with old hats, and her own shawl. Mrs. March gave the mother tea and gruel, and comforted her with promises of help, while she dressed the little baby as tenderly as if it had been her

own. The girls, meantime, spread the table, set the children round the
fire, and fed them like so many hungry birds; laughing, talking, and
trying to understand the funny broken English.

"Das ist gute!" "Der angel-kinder!" cried the poor things, as they ate,
and warmed their purple hands at the comfortable blaze. The girls had
never been called angel children before, and thought it very agreeable,
especially Jo, who had been considered "a Sancho"[4] ever since she was
born. That was a very happy breakfast, though they didn't get any of it;
and when they went away, leaving comfort behind, I think there were
not in all the city four merrier people than the hungry little girls who
gave away their breakfasts, and contented themselves with bread and
milk on Christmas morning.

"That's loving our neighbor better than ourselves,[5] and I like it," said
Meg, as they set out their presents, while their mother was up stairs
collecting clothes for the poor Hummels.

Not a very splendid show, but there was a great deal of love done up
in the few little bundles; and the tall vase of red roses, while chrysanthemums, and trailing vines, which stood in the middle, gave quite an
elegant air to the table.

"She's coming! strike up, Beth, open the door, Amy. Three cheers for
Marmee!" cried Jo, prancing about, while Meg went to conduct
mother to the seat of honor.

Beth played her gayest march, Amy threw open the door, and Meg
enacted escort with great dignity.

Mrs. March was both surprised and touched; and smiled with her
eyes full as she examined her presents, and read the little notes which
accompanied them. The slippers went on at once, a new handkerchief
was slipped into her pocket, well scented with Amy's Cologne, the rose
was fastened in her bosom, and the nice gloves were pronounced "a
perfect fit."

There was a good deal of laughing, and kissing, and explaining, in
the simple, loving fashion which makes these home-festivals so pleasant at the time, so sweet to remember long afterward, and then all fell
to work.

The morning charities and ceremonies took so much time, that the
rest of the day was devoted to preparations for the evening festivities.
Being still too young to go often to the theatre, and not rich enough to
afford any great outlay for private performances, the girls put their wits
to work, and, necessity being the mother of invention, made whatever
they needed. Very clever were some of their productions; paste-board
guitars, antique lamps made of old-fashioned butter-boats, covered with
silver paper, gorgeous robes of old cotton, glittering with tin spangles
from a pickle factory, and armor covered with the same useful diamond-
shaped bits, left in sheets when the lids of tin preserve-pots were cut
out. The furniture was used to being turned topsy-turvy, and the big
chamber was the scene of many innocent revels.

4. In Miguel de Cervantes's *Don Quixote* (1604, 1614), Sancho Panza is Don Quixote's comical but faithful squire.
5. Cf. Luke 10.27.

No gentlemen were admitted; so Jo played male parts to her heart's content, and took immense satisfaction in a pair of russet-leather boots given her by a friend, who knew a lady who knew an actor. These boots, an old foil, and a slashed doublet once used by an artist for some picture, were Jo's chief treasures, and appeared on all occasions. The smallness of the company made it necessary for the two principal actors to take several parts apiece; and they certainly deserved some credit for the hard work they did in learning three or four different parts, whisking in and out of various costumes, and managing the stage besides. It was excellent drill for their memories, a harmless amusement, and employed many hours which otherwise would have been idle, lonely, or spent in less profitable society.

On Christmas night, a dozen girls piled on to the bed, which was the dress circle, and sat before the blue and yellow chintz curtains, in a most flattering state of expectancy. There was a good deal of rustling and whispering behind the curtain, a trifle of lamp-smoke, and an occasional giggle from Amy, who was apt to get hysterical in the excitement of the moment. Presently a bell sounded, the curtains flew apart, and the Operatic Tragedy began.

"A gloomy wood," according to the one play-bill, was represented by a few shrubs in pots, a green baize on the floor, and a cave in the distance. This cave was made with a clothes-horse for a roof, bureaus for walls; and in it was a small furnace in full blast, with a black pot on it, and an old witch bending over it. The stage was dark, and the glow of the furnace had a fine effect, especially as real steam issued from the kettle when the witch took off the cover. A moment was allowed for the first thrill to subside; then Hugo, the villain, stalked in with a clanking sword at his side, a slouched hat, black beard, mysterious cloak, and the boots. After pacing to and fro in much agitation, he struck his forehead, and burst out in a wild strain, singing of his hatred to Roderigo, his love for Zara, and his pleasing resolution to kill the one and win the other. The gruff tones of Hugo's voice, with an occasional shout when his feelings overcame him, were very impressive, and the audience applauded the moment he paused for breath. Bowing with the air of one accustomed to public praise, he stole to the cavern and ordered Hagar to come forth with a commanding "What ho! minion! I need thee!"

Out came Meg, with gray horse-hair hanging about her face, a red and black robe, a staff, and cabalistic signs upon her cloak. Hugo demanded a potion to make Zara adore him, and one to destroy Roderigo. Hagar, in a fine dramatic melody, promised both, and proceeded to call up the spirit who would bring the love philter:—

> "Hither, hither, from thy home,
> Airy sprite, I bid thee come!
> Born of roses, fed on dew,
> Charms and potions canst thou brew?
> Bring me here, with elfin speed,
> The fragrant philter which I need;

> Make it sweet, and swift and strong;
> Spirit, answer now my song!"

A soft strain of music sounded, and then at the back of the cave appeared a little figure in cloudy white, with glittering wings, golden hair, and a garland of roses on its head. Waving a wand, it sung:—

> "Hither I come,
>   From my airy home,
> Afar in the silver moon;
>   Take the magic spell,
>   Oh, use it well!
> Or its power will vanish soon!"

and dropping a small gilded bottle at the witch's feet, the spirit vanished. Another chant from Hagar produced another apparition,—not a lovely one, for, with a bang, an ugly, black imp appeared, and having croaked a reply, tossed a dark bottle at Hugo, and disappeared with a mocking laugh. Having warbled his thanks, and put the potions in his boots, Hugo departed; and Hagar informed the audience that, as he had killed a few of her friends in times past, she has cursed him, and intends to thwart his plans, and be revenged on him. Then the curtain fell, and the audience reposed and ate candy while discussing the merits of the play.

A good deal of hammering went on before the curtain rose again; but when it became evident what a masterpiece of stage carpentering had been got up, no one murmured at the delay. It was truly superb! A tower rose to the ceiling; half-way up appeared a window with a lamp burning at it, and behind the white curtain appeared Zara in a lovely blue and silver dress, waiting for Roderigo. He came, in gorgeous array, with plumed cap, red cloak, chestnut love-locks, a guitar, and the boots, of course. Kneeling at the foot of the tower, he sung a serenade in melting tones. Zara replied, and after a musical dialogue, consented to fly. Then came the grand effect of the play. Roderigo produced a rope-ladder with five steps to it, threw up one end, and invited Zara to descend. Timidly she crept from her lattice, put her hand on Roderigo's shoulder, and was about to leap gracefully down, when, "alas, alas, for Zara!" she forgot her train,—it caught in the window; the tower tottered, leaned forward, fell with a crash, and buried the unhappy lovers in the ruins!

A universal shriek arose as the russet boots waved wildly from the wreck, and a golden head emerged, exclaiming, "I told you so! I told you so!" With wonderful presence of mind Don Pedro, the cruel sire, rushed in, dragged out his daughter with a hasty aside,—

"Don't laugh, act as if it was all right!" and ordering Roderigo up, banished him from the kingdom with wrath and scorn. Though decidedly shaken by the fall of the tower upon him, Roderigo defied the old gentleman, and refused to stir. This dauntless example fired Zara; she also defied her sire, and he ordered them both to the deepest dungeons of the castle. A stout little retainer came in with chains, and led them away, looking very much frightened, and evidently forgetting the speech he ought to have made.

Act third was the castle hall; and here Hagar appeared, having come to free the lovers and finish Hugo. She hears him coming, and hides; sees him put the potions into two cups of wine, and bid the timid little servant "Bear them to the captives in their cells, and tell them I shall come anon." The servant takes Hugo aside to tell him something, and Hagar changes the cups for two others which are harmless. Ferdinando, the "minion," carries them away, and Hagar puts back the cup which holds the poison meant for Roderigo. Hugo, getting thirsty after a long warble, drinks it, loses his wits, and after a good deal of clutching and stamping, falls flat and dies; while Hagar informs him what she has done in a song of exquisite power and melody.

This was a truly thrilling scene; though some persons might have thought that the sudden tumbling down of a quantity of long hair rather marred the effect of the villain's death. He was called before the curtain, and with great propriety appeared leading Hagar, whose singing was considered more wonderful than all the rest of the performance put together.

Act fourth displayed the despairing Roderigo on the point of stabbing himself, because he has been told that Zara has deserted him. Just as the dagger is at his heart, a lovely song is sung under his window, informing him that Zara is true, but in danger, and he can save her if he will. A key is thrown in, which unlocks the door, and in a spasm of rapture he tears off his chains, and rushes away to find and rescue his lady-love.

Act fifth opened with a stormy scene between Zara and Don Pedro. He wishes her to go into a convent, but she won't hear of it; and, after a touching appeal, is about to faint, when Roderigo dashes in and demands her hand. Don Pedro refuses, because he is not rich. They shout and gesticulate tremendously, but cannot agree, and Roderigo is about to bear away the exhausted Zara, when the timid servant enters with a letter and a bag from Hagar, who has mysteriously disappeared. The latter informs the party that she bequeaths untold wealth to the young pair, and an awful doom to Don Pedro if he doesn't make them happy. The bag is opened, and several quarts of tin money shower down upon the stage, till it is quite glorified with the glitter. This entirely softens the "stern sire;" he consents without a murmur, all join in a joyful chorus, and the curtain falls upon the lovers kneeling to receive Don Pedro's blessing, in attitudes of the most romantic grace.

Tumultuous applause followed, but received an unexpected check; for the cot-bed on which the "dress circle" was built, suddenly shut up, and extinguished the enthusiastic audience. Roderigo and Don Pedro flew to the rescue, and all were taken out unhurt, though many were speechless with laughter. The excitement had hardly subsided when Hannah appeared, with "Mrs. March's compliments, and would the ladies walk down to supper."

This was a surprise, even to the actors; and when they saw the table they looked at one another in rapturous amazement. It was like

"Marmee" to get up a little treat for them, but anything so fine as this was unheard of since the departed days of plenty. There was ice cream, actually two dishes of it,—pink and white,—and cake, and fruit, and distracting French bonbons, and in the middle of the table four great bouquets of hot-house flowers!

It quite took their breath away; and they stared first at the table and then at their mother, who looked as if she enjoyed it immensely.

"Is it fairies?" asked Amy.

"It's Santa Claus," said Beth.

"Mother did it;" and Meg smiled her sweetest, in spite of her gray beard and white eyebrows.

"Aunt March had a good fit, and sent the supper," cried Jo, with a sudden inspiration.

"All wrong; old Mr. Laurence sent it," replied Mrs. March.

"The Laurence boy's grandfather! What in the world put such a thing into his head? We don't know him," exclaimed Meg.

"Hannah told one of his servants about your breakfast party; he is an odd old gentleman, but that pleased him. He knew my father, years ago, and he sent me a polite note this afternoon, saying he hoped I would allow him to express his friendly feeling toward my children by sending them a few trifles in honor of the day. I could not refuse, and so you have a little feast at night to make up for the bread and milk breakfast."

"That boy put it into his head, I know he did! He's a capital fellow, and I wish we could get acquainted. He looks as if he'd like to know us; but he's bashful, and Meg is so prim she won't let me speak to him when we pass," said Jo, as the plates went round, and the ice began to melt out of sight, with ohs! and ahs! of satisfaction.

"You mean the people who live in the big house next door, don't you?" asked one of the girls. "My mother knows old Mr. Laurence, but says he's very proud, and don't like to mix with his neighbors. He keeps his grandson shut up when he isn't riding or walking with his tutor, and makes him study dreadful hard. We invited him to our party, but he didn't come. Mother says he's very nice, though he never speaks to us girls."

"Our cat ran away once, and he brought her back, and we talked over the fence, and were getting on capitally, all about cricket, and so on, when he saw Meg coming, and walked off. I mean to know him some day, for he needs fun, I'm sure he does," said Jo, decidedly.

"I like his manners, and he looks like a little gentleman, so I've no objection to your knowing him if a proper opportunity comes. He brought the flowers himself, and I should have asked him in if I had been sure what was going on up stairs. He looked so wistful as he went away, hearing the frolic, and evidently having none of his own."

"It's a mercy you didn't, mother," laughed Jo, looking at her boots. "But we'll have another play some time, that he *can* see. Maybe he'll help act; wouldn't that be jolly?"

"I never had a bouquet before; how pretty it is," and Meg examined her flowers with great interest.

"They *are* lovely, but Beth's roses are sweeter to me," said Mrs. March, sniffing at the half dead posy in her belt.

Beth nestled up to her, and whispered, softly, "I wish I could send my bunch to father. I'm afraid he isn't having such a merry Christmas as we are."

CHAPTER III.

THE LAURENCE BOY.

Jo! Jo! where are you?" cried Meg, at the foot of the garret stairs.

"Here," answered a husky voice from above; and running up, Meg found her sister eating apples and crying over the "Heir of Redcliffe,"[6] wrapped up in a comforter on an old three-legged sofa by the sunny window. This was Jo's favorite refuge; and here she loved to retire with half a dozen russets and a nice book, to enjoy the quiet and the society of a pet rat who lived near by, and didn't mind her a particle. As Meg appeared, Scrabble whisked into his hole. Jo shook the tears off her cheeks, and waited to hear the news.

"Such fun! only see! a regular note of invitation from Mrs. Gardiner for to-morrow night!" cried Meg, waving the precious paper, and then proceeding to read it, with girlish delight.

" 'Mrs. Gardiner would be happy to see Miss March and Miss Josephine at a little dance on New-Year's-Eve.' Marmee is willing we should go; now what *shall* we wear?"

"What's the use of asking that, when you know we shall wear our poplins, because we haven't got anything else," answered Jo, with her mouth full.

"If I only had a silk!" sighed Meg; "mother says I may when I'm eighteen, perhaps; but two years is an everlasting time to wait."

"I'm sure our pops look like silk, and they are nice enough for us. Yours is as good as new, but I forgot the burn and the tear in mine; whatever shall I do? the burn shows horridly, and I can't take any out."

"You must sit still all you can, and keep your back out of sight; the front is all right. I shall have a new ribbon for my hair, and Marmee will lend me her little pearl pin, and my new slippers are lovely, and my gloves will do, though they aren't as nice as I'd like."

"Mine are spoilt with lemonade, and I can't get any new ones, so I shall have to go without," said Jo, who never troubled herself much about dress.

"You *must* have gloves, or I won't go," cried Meg, decidedly. "Gloves are more important than anything else; you can't dance without them, and if you don't I should be *so* mortified."

"Then I'll stay still; I don't care much for company dancing; it's no fun to go sailing round, I like to fly about and cut capers."

6. Among the most popular British novels of the nineteenth century, Charlotte M. Yonge's *Heir of Redclyffe* (1853) is a romantic tale of devotion and self-sacrifice. The hero, the virtuous if imperfect Guy Morville, dies an early death.

"You can't ask mother for new ones, they are so expensive, and you are so careless. She said, when you spoilt the others, that she shouldn't get you any more this winter. Can't you fix them any way?" asked Meg, anxiously.

"I can hold them crunched up in my hand, so no one will know how stained they are; that's all I can do. No! I'll tell you how we can manage—each wear one good one and carry a bad one; don't you see?"

"Your hands are bigger than mine, and you will stretch my glove dreadfully," began Meg, whose gloves were a tender point with her.

"Then I'll go without. I don't care what people say," cried Jo, taking up her book.

"You may have it, you may! only don't stain it, and do behave nicely; don't put your hands behind you, or stare, or say 'Christopher Columbus!' will you?"

"Don't worry about me; I'll be as prim as a dish, and not get into any scrapes, if I can help it. Now go and answer your note, and let me finish this splendid story."

So Meg went away to "accept with thanks," look over her dress, and sing blithely as she did up her one real lace frill; while Jo finished her story, her four apples, and had a game of romps with Scrabble.

On New-Year's-Eve the parlor was deserted, for the two younger girls played dressing maids, and the two elder were absorbed in the all-important business of "getting ready for the party." Simple as the toilets were, there was a great deal of running up and down, laughing and talking, and at one time a strong smell of burnt hair pervaded the house. Meg wanted a few curls about her face, and Jo undertook to pinch the papered locks with a pair of hot tongs.

"Ought they to smoke like that?" asked Beth, from her perch on the bed.

"It's the dampness drying," replied Jo.

"What a queer smell! it's like burnt feathers," observed Amy, smoothing her own pretty curls with a superior air.

"There, now I'll take off the papers and you'll see a cloud of little ringlets," said Jo, putting down the tongs.

She did take off the papers, but no cloud of ringlets appeared, for the hair came with the papers, and the horrified hair-dresser laid a row of little scorched bundles on the bureau before her victim.

"Oh, oh, oh! what *have* you done? I'm spoilt! I can't go! my hair, my hair!" wailed Meg, looking with despair at the uneven frizzle on her forehead.

"Just my luck! you shouldn't have asked me to do it; I always spoil everything. I'm no end sorry, but the tongs were too hot, and so I've made a mess," groaned poor Jo, regarding the black pancakes with tears of regret.

"It isn't spoilt; just frizzle it, and tie your ribbon so the ends come on your forehead a bit, and it will look like the last fashion. I've seen lots of girls do it so," said Amy, consolingly.

"Serves me right for trying to be fine. I wish I'd let my hair alone," cried Meg, petulantly.

"So do I, it was so smooth and pretty. But it will soon grow out again," said Beth, coming to kiss and comfort the shorn sheep.

After various lesser mishaps, Meg was finished at last, and by the united exertions of the family Jo's hair was got up, and her dress on. They looked very well in their simple suits, Meg in silvery drab, with a blue velvet snood, lace frills, and the pearl pin; Jo in maroon, with a stiff, gentlemanly linen collar, and a white chrysanthemum or two for her only ornament. Each put on one nice light glove, and carried one soiled one, and all pronounced the effect "quite easy and nice." Meg's high-heeled slippers were dreadfully tight, and hurt her, though she would not own it, and Jo's nineteen hair-pins all seemed stuck straight into her head, which was not exactly comfortable; but, dear me, let us be elegant or die.

"Have a good time, dearies," said Mrs. March, as the sisters went daintily down the walk. "Don't eat much supper, and come away at eleven, when I send Hannah for you." As the gate clashed behind them, a voice cried from a window,—

"Girls, girls! *have* you both got nice pocket-handkerchiefs?"

"Yes, yes, spandy nice,[7] and Meg has Cologne on hers," cried Jo, adding, with a laugh, as they went on, "I do believe Marmee would ask that if we were all running away from an earthquake."

"It is one of her aristocratic tastes, and quite proper, for a real lady is always known by neat boots, gloves, and handkerchief," replied Meg, who had a good many little "aristocratic tastes" of her own.

"Now don't forget to keep the bad breadth out of sight, Jo. Is my sash right; and does my hair look *very* bad?" said Meg, as she turned from the glass in Mrs. Gardiner's dressing-room, after a prolonged prink.

"I know I shall forget. If you see me doing anything wrong, you just remind me by a wink, will you?" returned Jo, giving her collar a twitch and her head a hasty brush.

"No, winking isn't lady-like; I'll lift my eyebrows if anything is wrong, and nod if you are all right. Now hold your shoulders straight, and take short steps, and don't shake hands if you are introduced to any one, it isn't the thing."

"How *do* you learn all the proper quirks? I never can. Isn't that music gay?"

Down they went, feeling a trifle timid, for they seldom went to parties, and, informal as this little gathering was, it was an event to them. Mrs. Gardiner, a stately old lady, greeted them kindly, and handed them over to the eldest of her six daughters. Meg knew Sallie, and was at her ease very soon; but Jo, who didn't care much for girls or girlish gossip, stood about with her back carefully against the wall, and felt as much out of place as a colt in a flower-garden. Half a dozen jovial lads were talking about skates in another part of the room, and she longed to go and join them, for skating was one of the joys of her life. She telegraphed her wish to Meg, but the eyebrows went up so alarmingly

7. Very nice, very clean.

that she dared not stir. No one came to talk to her, and one by one the group near her dwindled away, till she was left alone. She could not roam about and amuse herself, for the burnt breadth would show, so she stared at people rather forlornly till the dancing began. Meg was asked at once, and the tight slippers tripped about so briskly that none would have guessed the pain their wearer suffered smilingly. Jo saw a big red-headed youth approaching her corner, and fearing he meant to engage her, she slipped into a curtained recess, intending to peep and enjoy herself in peace. Unfortunately, another bashful person had chosen the same refuge; for, as the curtain fell behind her, she found herself face to face with the "Laurence boy."

"Dear me, I didn't know any one was here!" stammered Jo, preparing to back out as speedily as she had bounced in.

But the boy laughed, and said, pleasantly, though he looked a little startled,—

"Don't mind me; stay, if you like."

"Shan't I disturb you?"

"Not a bit; I only came here because I don't know many people, and felt rather strange at first, you know."

"So did I. Don't go away, please, unless you'd rather."

The boy sat down again and looked at his boots, till Jo said, trying to be polite and easy,—

"I think I've had the pleasure of seeing you before; you live near us, don't you?"

"Next door;" and he looked up and laughed outright, for Jo's prim manner was rather funny when he remembered how they had chatted about cricket when he brought the cat home.

That put Jo at her ease; and she laughed too, as she said, in her heartiest way,—

"We did have such a good time over your nice Christmas present."

"Grandpa sent it."

"But you put it into his head, didn't you, now?"

"How is your cat, Miss March?" asked the boy, trying to look sober, while his black eyes shone with fun.

"Nicely, thank you, Mr. Laurence; but I ain't Miss March, I'm only Jo," returned the young lady.

"I'm not Mr. Laurence, I'm only Laurie."

"Laurie Laurence; what an odd name."

"My first name is Theodore, but I don't like it, for the fellows called me Dora, so I made them say Laurie instead."

"I hate my name, too—so sentimental! I wish every one would say Jo, instead of Josephine. How did you make the boys stop calling you Dora?"

"I thrashed 'em."

"I can't thrash Aunt March, so I suppose I shall have to bear it;" and Jo resigned herself with a sigh.

"Don't you like to dance, Miss Jo?" asked Laurie, looking as if he thought the name suited her.

"I like it well enough if there is plenty of room, and every one is lively. In a place like this I'm sure to upset something, tread on people's toes, or do something dreadful, so I keep out of mischief, and let Meg do the pretty. Don't you dance?"

"Sometimes; you see I've been abroad a good many years, and haven't been about enough yet to know how you do things here."

"Abroad!" cried Jo, "oh, tell me about it! I love dearly to hear people describe their travels."

Laurie didn't seem to know where to begin; but Jo's eager questions soon set him going, and he told her how he had been at school in Vevey, where the boys never wore hats, and had a fleet of boats on the lake, and for holiday fun went walking trips about Switzerland with their teachers.

"Don't I wish I'd been there!" cried Jo. "Did you go to Paris?"

"We spent last winter there."

"Can you talk French?"

"We were not allowed to speak anything else at Vevey."

"Do say some. I can read it, but can't pronounce."

"Quel nom à cette jeune demoiselle en les pantoufles jolis?" said Laurie, good-naturedly.

"How nicely you do it! Let me see—you said, 'Who is the young lady in the pretty slippers,' didn't you?"

"Oui, mademoiselle."

"It's my sister Margaret, and you knew it was! Do you think she is pretty?"

"Yes; she makes me think of the German girls, she looks so fresh and quiet, and dances like a lady."

Jo quite glowed with pleasure at this boyish praise of her sister, and stored it up to repeat to Meg. Both peeped, and criticised, and chatted, till they felt like old acquaintances. Laurie's bashfulness soon wore off, for Jo's gentlemanly demeanor amused and set him at his ease, and Jo was her merry self again, because her dress was forgotten, and nobody lifted their eyebrows at her. She liked the "Laurence boy" better than ever, and took several good looks at him, so that she might describe him to the girls; for they had no brothers, very few male cousins, and boys were almost unknown creatures to them.

"Curly black hair, brown skin, big black eyes, long nose, nice teeth, little hands and feet, tall as I am; very polite for a boy, and altogether jolly. Wonder how old he is?"

It was on the tip of Jo's tongue to ask; but she checked herself in time, and, with unusual tact, tried to find out in a roundabout way.

"I suppose you are going to college soon? I see you pegging away at your books—no, I mean studying hard;" and Jo blushed at the dreadful "pegging" which had escaped her.

Laurie smiled, but didn't seem shocked, and answered, with a shrug,—

"Not for two or three years yet; I won't go before seventeen, any way."

"Aren't you but fifteen?" asked Jo, looking at the tall lad, whom she had imagined seventeen already.

"Sixteen, next month."

"How I wish I was going to college; you don't look as if you liked it."

"I hate it! nothing but grinding or sky-larking; and I don't like the way fellows do either, in this country."

"What do you like?"

"To live in Italy, and to enjoy myself in my own way."

Jo wanted very much to ask what his own way was; but his black brows looked rather threatening as he knit them, so she changed the subject by saying, as her foot kept time, "That's a splendid polka; why don't you go and try it?"

"If you will come too," he answered, with a queer little French bow.

"I can't; for I told Meg I wouldn't, because—" there Jo stopped, and looked undecided whether to tell or to laugh.

"Because what?" asked Laurie, curiously.

"You won't tell?"

"Never!"

"Well, I have a bad trick of standing before the fire, and so I burn my frocks, and I scorched this one; and, though it's nicely mended, it shows, and Meg told me to keep still, so no one would see it. You may laugh if you want to; it is funny, I know."

But Laurie didn't laugh; he only looked down a minute, and the expression of his face puzzled Jo, when he said very gently,—

"Never mind that; I'll tell you how we can manage: there's a long hall out there, and we can dance grandly, and no one will see us. Please come."

Jo thanked him, and gladly went, wishing she had two neat gloves, when she saw the nice pearl-colored ones her partner put on. The hall was empty, and they had a grand polk, for Laurie danced well, and taught her the German[8] step, which delighted Jo, being full of swing and spring. When the music stopped they sat down on the stairs to get their breath, and Laurie was in the midst of an account of a student's festival at Heidelberg, when Meg appeared in search of her sister. She beckoned, and Jo reluctantly followed her into a side-room, where she found her on a sofa holding her foot, and looking pale.

"I've sprained my ankle. That stupid high heel turned, and gave me a horrid wrench. It aches so, I can hardly stand, and I don't know how I'm ever going to get home," she said, rocking to and fro in pain.

"I knew you'd hurt your feet with those silly things. I'm sorry; but I don't see what you can do, except get a carriage, or stay here all night," answered Jo, softly rubbing the poor ankle, as she spoke.

"I can't have a carriage without its costing ever so much; I dare say I can't get one at all, for most people come in their own, and it's a long way to the stable, and no one to send."

"I'll go."

"No, indeed; it's past ten, and dark as Egypt. I can't stop here, for the house is full; Sallie has some girls staying with her. I'll rest till Hannah comes, and then do the best I can."

---

8. Short for German cotillion, a kind of quadrille or square dance with a particularly elaborate series of steps.

"I'll ask Laurie; he will go," said Jo, looking relieved as the idea occurred to her.

"Mercy, no! don't ask or tell any one. Get me my rubbers, and put
these slippers with our things. I can't dance any more; but as soon as
supper is over, watch for Hannah, and tell me the minute she comes."

"They are going out to supper now. I'll stay with you; I'd rather."

"No, dear; run along, and bring me some coffee. I'm so tired, I can't
stir."

So Meg reclined, with the rubbers well hidden, and Jo went blundering away to the dining-room, which she found after going into a
china-closet and opening the door of a room where old Mr. Gardiner
was taking a little private refreshment. Making a dive at the table, she
secured the coffee, which she immediately spilt, thereby making the
front of her dress as bad as the back.

"Oh dear! what a blunderbuss I am!" exclaimed Jo, finishing Meg's
glove by scrubbing her gown with it.

"Can I help you?" said a friendly voice; and there was Laurie, with a
full cup in one hand and a plate of ice in the other.

"I was trying to get something for Meg, who is very tired, and some
one shook me, and here I am, in a nice state," answered Jo, glancing,
dismally, from the stained skirt to the coffee-colored glove.

"Too bad! I was looking for some one to give this to; may I take it to
your sister?"

"Oh, thank you; I'll show you where she is. I don't offer to take it
myself, for I should only get into another scrape if I did."

Jo led the way; and, as if used to waiting on ladies, Laurie drew up
a little table, brought a second instalment of coffee and ice for Jo, and
was so obliging that even particular Meg pronounced him a "nice boy."
They had a merry time over the bonbons and mottos,[9] and were in the
midst of a quiet game of "buzz"[1] with two or three other young people
who had strayed in, when Hannah appeared. Meg forgot her foot, and
rose so quickly that she was forced to catch hold of Jo, with an exclamation of pain.

"Hush! don't say anything," she whispered; adding aloud, "It's nothing; I turned my foot a little,—that's all," and limped up stairs to put
her things on.

Hannah scolded, Meg cried, and Jo was at her wits' end, till she decided to take things into her own hands. Slipping out, she ran down,
and finding a servant, asked if he could get her a carriage. It happened
to be a hired waiter, who knew nothing about the neighborhood; and
Jo was looking round for help, when Laurie, who had heard what she
said, came up and offered his grandfather's carriage, which had just
come for him, he said.

"It's so early,—you can't mean to go yet," began Jo, looking relieved,
but hesitating to accept the offer.

9. Inspirational or poetic sayings on small pieces of paper wrapped inside sweets or crackers, in
   the style of fortune cookies.
1. Game in which the players say numbers in numerical order except for the number seven and
   multiples of seven, where the word "buzz" is substituted.

"I always go early,—I do, truly. Please let me take you home; it's all on my way, you know, and it rains, they say."

That settled it; and telling him of Meg's mishap, Jo gratefully accepted, and rushed up to bring down the rest of the party. Hannah hated rain as much as a cat does; so she made no trouble, and they rolled away in the luxurious close carriage, feeling very festive and elegant. Laurie went on the box, so Meg could keep her foot up, and the girls talked over their party in freedom.

"I had a capital time; did you?" asked Jo, rumpling up her hair, and making herself comfortable.

"Yes, till I hurt myself. Sallie's friend, Annie Moffat, took a fancy to me, and asked me to come and spend a week with her when Sallie does. She is going in the spring, when the opera comes, and it will be perfectly splendid if mother only lets me go," answered Meg, cheering up at the thought.

"I saw you dancing with the red-headed man I ran away from; was he nice?"

"Oh, very! his hair is auburn, not red; and he was very polite, and I had a delicious redowa² with him!"

"He looked like a grasshopper in a fit, when he did the new step. Laurie and I couldn't help laughing; did you hear us?"

"No, but it was very rude. What *were* you about all that time, hidden away there?"

Jo told her adventures, and by the time she had finished they were at home. With many thanks, they said "Good-night," and crept in, hoping to disturb no one; but the instant their door creaked, two little night-caps bobbed up, and two sleepy but eager voices cried out,—

"Tell about the party! tell about the party!"

With what Meg called "a great want of manners," Jo had saved some bonbons for the little girls, and they soon subsided, after hearing the most thrilling events of the evening.

"I declare, it really seems like being a fine young lady, to come home from my party in my carriage, and sit in my dressing-gown with a maid to wait on me," said Meg, as Jo bound up her foot with arnica, and brushed her hair.

"I don't believe fine young ladies enjoy themselves a bit more than we do, in spite of our burnt hair, old gowns, one glove apiece, and tight slippers, that sprain our ankles when we are silly enough to wear them." And I think Jo was quite right.

CHAPTER IV.

BURDENS.

OH dear, how hard it does seem to take up our packs and go on," sighed Meg, the morning after the party; for now the holidays were

2. Lively Bohemian folk dance in a quick three-four time.

over, the week of merry-making did not fit her for going on easily with the task she never liked.

"I wish it was Christmas or New-Year all the time; wouldn't it be fun?" answered Jo, yawning dismally.

"We shouldn't enjoy ourselves half so much as we do now. But it does seem so nice to have little suppers and bouquets, and go to parties, and drive home in a carriage, and read and rest, and not grub. It's like other people, you know, and I always envy girls who do such things; I'm so fond of luxury," said Meg, trying to decide which of two shabby gowns was the least shabby.

"Well, we can't have it, so don't let's grumble, but shoulder our bundles and trudge along as cheerfully as Marmee does. I'm sure Aunt March is a regular Old Man of the Sea[3] to me, but I suppose when I've learned to carry her without complaining, she will tumble off, or get so light that I shan't mind her."

This idea tickled Jo's fancy, and put her in good spirits; but Meg didn't brighten, for her burden, consisting of four spoilt children, seemed heavier than ever. She hadn't heart enough even to make herself pretty, as usual, by putting on a blue neck-ribbon, and dressing her hair in the most becoming way.

"Where's the use of looking nice, when no one sees me but those cross midgets, and no one cares whether I'm pretty or not," she muttered, shutting her drawer with a jerk. "I shall have to toil and moil all my days, with only little bits of fun now and then, and get old and ugly and sour, because I'm poor, and can't enjoy my life as other girls do. It's a shame!"

So Meg went down, wearing an injured look, and wasn't at all agreeable at breakfast-time. Every one seemed rather out of sorts, and inclined to croak. Beth had a headache, and lay on the sofa trying to comfort herself with the cat and three kittens; Amy was fretting because her lessons were not learned, and she couldn't find her rubbers; Jo *would* whistle, and make a great racket getting ready; Mrs. March was very busy trying to finish a letter, which must go at once; and Hannah had the grumps, for being up late didn't suit her.

"There never *was* such a cross family!" cried Jo, losing her temper when she had upset an inkstand, broken both boot-lacings, and sat down upon her hat.

"You're the crossest person in it!" returned Amy, washing out the sum, that was all wrong, with the tears that had fallen on her slate.

"Beth, if you don't keep these horrid cats down cellar I'll have them drowned," exclaimed Meg, angrily, as she tried to get rid of the kitten, who had swarmed up her back, and stuck like a burr just out of reach.

Jo laughed, Meg scolded, Beth implored, and Amy wailed, because she couldn't remember how much nine times twelve was.

"Girls! girls! do be quiet one minute. I *must* get this off by the early

---

3. Burden from which it is difficult to free oneself. In "Sinbad the Sailor," one of the tales from *The Thousand and One Nights*, or *Arabian Nights*, the Old Man of the Sea clings to Sinbad's back and refuses to get down.

mail, and you drive me distracted with your worry," cried Mrs. March, crossing out the third spoilt sentence in her letter.

There was a momentary lull, broken by Hannah, who bounced in, laid two hot turn-overs on the table, and bounced out again. These turn-overs were an institution; and the girls called them "muffs," for they had no others, and found the hot pies very comforting to their hands on cold mornings. Hannah never forgot to make them, no matter how busy or grumpy she might be, for the walk was long and bleak; the poor things got no other lunch, and were seldom home before three.

"Cuddle your cats, and get over your headache, Bethy. Good-by, Marmee; we are a set of rascals this morning, but we'll come home regular angels. Now then, Meg," and Jo tramped away, feeling that the pilgrims were not setting out as they ought to do.

They always looked back before turning the corner, for their mother was always at the window, to nod, and smile, and wave her hand to them. Somehow it seemed as if they couldn't have got through the day without that, for whatever their mood might be, the last glimpse of that motherly face was sure to affect them like sunshine.

"If Marmee shook her fist instead of kissing her hand to us, it would serve us right, for more ungrateful minxes than we are were never seen," cried Jo, taking a remorseful satisfaction in the slushy road and bitter wind.

"Don't use such dreadful expressions," said Meg, from the depths of the veil in which she had shrouded herself like a nun sick of the world.

"I like good, strong words, that mean something," replied Jo, catching her hat as it took a leap off her head, preparatory to flying away altogether.

"Call yourself any names you like; but *I* am neither a rascal nor a minx, and I don't choose to be called so."

"You're a blighted being, and decidedly cross to-day, because you can't sit in the lap of luxury all the time. Poor dear! just wait till I make my fortune, and you shall revel in carriages, and ice-cream, and high-heeled slippers, and posies, and red-headed boys to dance with."

"How ridiculous you are, Jo!" but Meg laughed at the nonsense, and felt better in spite of herself.

"Lucky for you I am; for if I put on crushed airs, and tried to be dismal, as you do, we should be in a nice state. Thank goodness, I can always find something funny to keep me up. Don't croak any more, but come home jolly, there's a dear."

Jo gave her sister an encouraging pat on the shoulder as they parted for the day, each going a different way, each hugging her little warm turn-over, and each trying to be cheerful in spite of wintry weather, hard work, and the unsatisfied desires of pleasure-loving youth.

When Mr. March lost his property in trying to help an unfortunate friend, the two oldest girls begged to be allowed to do something toward their own support, at least. Believing that they could not begin too early to cultivate energy, industry, and independence, their parents consented, and both fell to work with the hearty good-will which, in spite of all obstacles, is sure to succeed at last. Margaret found a place as nursery governess, and felt rich with her small salary. As she said, she *was* "fond of luxury," and her chief trouble was poverty. She found it harder to bear than the others, because she could remember a time when home was beautiful, life full of ease and pleasure, and want of any kind unknown. She tried not to be envious or discontented, but it was very natural that the young girl should long for pretty things, gay friends, accomplishments, and a happy life. At the Kings she daily saw all she wanted, for the children's older sisters were just out,[4] and Meg caught frequent glimpses of dainty ball-dresses and bouquets, heard lively gossip about theatres, concerts, sleighing parties and merry-makings of all kinds, and saw money lavished on trifles which would have been so precious to her. Poor Meg seldom complained, but a sense of injustice made her feel bitter toward every one sometimes, for she had not yet learned to know how rich she was in the blessings which alone can make life happy.

Jo happened to suit Aunt March, who was lame, and needed an active person to wait upon her. The childless old lady had offered to adopt one of the girls when the troubles came, and was much offended because her offer was declined. Other friends told the Marches that they had lost all chance of being remembered in the rich old lady's will; but the unworldly Marches only said,—

"We can't give up our girls for a dozen fortunes. Rich or poor, we will keep together and be happy in one another."

The old lady wouldn't speak to them for a time, but, happening to meet Jo at a friend's, something in her comical face and blunt manners struck the old lady's fancy, and she proposed to take her for a companion. This did not suit Jo at all; but she accepted the place, since nothing better appeared, and, to every one's surprise, got on remarkably well with her irascible relative. There was an occasional tempest, and once Jo had marched home, declaring she couldn't bear it any longer; but Aunt March always cleared up quickly, and sent for her back again with such urgency that she could not refuse, for in her heart she rather liked the peppery old lady.

I suspect that the real attraction was a large library of fine books, which was left to dust and spiders since Uncle March died. Jo remembered the kind old gentleman who used to let her build railroads and bridges with his big dictionaries, tell her stories about the queer pictures in his Latin books, and buy her cards of gingerbread whenever he met her in the street. The dim, dusty room, with the busts staring down from the tall book-cases, the cosy chairs, the globes, and, best of all, the wilderness of books, in which she could wander where she liked, made the library a region of bliss to her. The moment Aunt March took her nap, or was busy with company, Jo hurried to this quiet place, and, curling herself up in the big chair, devoured poetry,

---

4. The young women have just entered society or come out into upper-class circles of socializing and courtship.

romance, history, travels, and pictures, like a regular bookworm. But, like all happiness, it did not last long; for as sure as she had just reached the heart of the story, the sweetest verse of the song, or the most perilous adventure of her traveller, a shrill voice called, "Josy-phine! Josy-phine!" and she had to leave her paradise to wind yarn, wash the poodle, or read Belsham's Essays,[5] by the hour together.

Jo's ambition was to do something very splendid; what it was she had no idea, but left it for time to tell her; and, meanwhile, found her greatest affliction in the fact that she couldn't read, run, and ride as much as she liked. A quick temper, sharp tongue, and restless spirit were always getting her into scrapes, and her life was a series of ups and downs, which were both comic and pathetic. But the training she received at Aunt March's was just what she needed; and the thought that she was doing something to support herself made her happy, in spite of the perpetual "Josy-phine!"

Beth was too bashful to go to school; it had been tried, but she suf-fered so much that it was given up, and she did her lessons at home, with her father. Even when he went away, and her mother was called to devote her skill and energy to Soldiers' Aid Societies, Beth went faithfully on by herself, and did the best she could. She was a house-wifely little creature, and helped Hannah keep home neat and com-fortable for the workers, never thinking of any reward but to be loved. Long, quiet days she spent, not lonely nor idle, for her little world was peopled with imaginary friends, and she was by nature a busy bee. There were six dolls to be taken up and dressed every morning, for Beth was a child still, and loved her pets as well as ever; not one whole or handsome one among them; all were outcasts till Beth took them in; for, when her sisters outgrew these idols, they passed to her, be-cause Amy would have nothing old or ugly. Beth cherished them all the more tenderly for that very reason, and set up a hospital for infirm dolls. No pins were ever stuck into their cotton vitals; no harsh words or blows were ever given them; no neglect ever saddened the heart of the most repulsive, but all were fed and clothed, nursed and caressed, with an affection which never failed. One forlorn fragment of *dollanity* had belonged to Jo; and, having led a tempestuous life, was left a wreck in the rag-bag, from which dreary poor-house it was rescued by Beth, and taken to her refuge. Having no top to its head, she tied on a neat little cap, and, as both arms and legs were gone, she hid these de-ficiencies by folding it in a blanket, and devoting her best bed to this chronic invalid. If any one had known the care lavished on that dolly, I think it would have touched their hearts, even while they laughed. She brought it bits of bouquets; she read to it, took it out to breathe the air, hidden under her coat; she sung it lullabys, and never went to bed without kissing its dirty face, and whispering tenderly, "I hope you'll have a good night, my poor dear."

Beth had her troubles as well as the others; and not being an angel,

---

5. William Belsham's *Essays, Philosophical, Historical, and Literary* (1789, 1791), a two-volume collection of thirty-five edifying essays, sharply contrasts with Jo's preference for fiction, ad-venture, and humor.

but a very human little girl, she often "wept a little weep," as Jo said, because she couldn't take music lessons and have a fine piano. She loved music so dearly, tried so hard to learn, and practised away so patiently at the jingling old instrument, that it did seem as if some one (not to hint Aunt March) ought to help her. Nobody did, however, and nobody saw Beth wipe the tears off the yellow keys, that wouldn't keep in tune when she was all alone. She sung like a little lark about her work, never was too tired to play for Marmee and the girls, and day after day said hopefully to herself, "I know I'll get my music some time, if I'm good."

There are many Beths in the world, shy and quiet, sitting in corners till needed, and living for others so cheerfully, that no one sees the sacrifices till the little cricket on the hearth stops chirping,[6] and the sweet, sunshiny presence vanishes, leaving silence and shadow behind.

If anybody had asked Amy what the greatest trial of her life was, she would have answered at once, "My nose." When she was a baby, Jo had accidentally dropped her into the coal-hod, and Amy insisted that the fall had ruined her nose forever. It was not big, nor red, like poor "Petrea's;"[7] it was only rather flat, and all the pinching in the world could not give it an aristocratic point. No one minded it but herself, and it was doing its best to grow, but Amy felt deeply the want of a Grecian nose, and drew whole sheets of handsome ones to console herself.

"Little Raphael,"[8] as her sisters called her, had a decided talent for drawing, and was never so happy as when copying flowers, designing fairies, or illustrating stories with queer specimens of art. Her teachers complained that instead of doing her sums, she covered her slate with animals; the blank pages of her atlas were used to copy maps on, and caricatures of the most ludicrous description came fluttering out of all her books at unlucky moments. She got through her lessons as well as she could, and managed to escape reprimands by being a model of deportment. She was a great favorite with her mates, being good-tempered, and possessing the happy art of pleasing without effort. Her little airs and graces were much admired, so were her accomplishments; for beside her drawing, she could play twelve tunes, crochet, and read French without mispronouncing more than two-thirds of the words. She had a plaintive way of saying, "When papa was rich we did so-and-so," which was very touching; and her long words were considered "perfectly elegant" by the girls.

Amy was in a fair way to be spoilt; for every one petted her, and her small vanities and selfishnesses were growing nicely. One thing, however, rather quenched the vanities; she had to wear her cousin's clothes. Now Florence's mamma hadn't a particle of taste, and Amy

6. Reference to Charles Dickens's *Cricket on the Hearth* (1845).
7. A sympathetic, large-nosed character from *The Home, or Family Cares and Family Joys* (1839, trans. 1843) by Swedish author Fredrika Bremer.
8. Reference to the great early modern Italian painter Raffaello Sanzio (1483–1520), or Raphael.

suffered deeply at having to wear a red instead of a blue bonnet, un-becoming gowns, and fussy aprons that did not fit. Everything was good, well made, and little worn; but Amy's artistic eyes were much af-flicted, especially this winter, when her school dress was a dull purple, with yellow dots, and no trimming.

"My only comfort," she said to Meg, with tears in her eyes, "is, that mother don't take tucks in my dresses whenever I'm naughty, as Maria Parks' mother does. My dear, it's really dreadful; for sometimes she is so bad, her frock is up to her knees, and she can't come to school. When I think of this *deggerredation*, I feel that I can bear even my flat nose and purple gown, with yellow sky-rockets on it."

Meg was Amy's confidant and monitor, and, by some strange attrac-tion of opposites, Jo was gentle Beth's. To Jo alone did the shy child tell her thoughts; and over her big, harum-scarum sister, Beth uncon-sciously exercised more influence than any one in the family. The two older girls were a great deal to each other, but both took one of the younger into their keeping, and watched over them in their own way; "playing mother" they called it, and put their sisters in the places of discarded dolls, with the maternal instinct of little women.

"Has anybody got anything to tell? It's been such a dismal day I'm really dying for some amusement," said Meg, as they sat sewing to-gether that evening.

"I had a queer time with aunt to-day, and, as I got the best of it, I'll tell you about it," began Jo, who dearly loved to tell stories. "I was reading that everlasting Belsham, and droning away as I always do, for aunt soon drops off, and then I take out some nice book, and read like fury, till she wakes up. I actually made myself sleepy; and, before she began to nod, I gave such a gape that she asked me what I meant by opening my mouth wide enough to take the whole book in at once.

" 'I wish I could, and be done with it,' " said I, trying not to be saucy.

"Then she gave me a long lecture on my sins, and told me to sit and think them over while she just 'lost' herself for a moment. She never finds herself very soon; so the minute her cap began to bob, like a top-heavy dahlia, I whipped the 'Vicar of Wakefield'[9] out of my pocket, and read away, with one eye on him, and one on aunt. I'd just got to where they all tumbled into the water, when I forgot, and laughed out loud. Aunt woke up; and, being more good-natured after her nap, told me to read a bit, and show what frivolous work I preferred to the worthy and instructive Belsham. I did my very best, and she liked it, though she only said,—

" 'I don't understand what it's all about; go back and begin it, child.'

"Back I went, and made the Primroses as interesting as ever I could. Once I was wicked enough to stop in a thrilling place, and say meekly, 'I'm afraid it tires you, ma'am; shan't I stop now?'

"She caught up her knitting which had dropped out of her hands, gave me a sharp look through her specs, and said, in her short way,—

---

9. Oliver Goldsmith's novel *The Vicar of Wakefield* (1766) tells the humorous, sentimental story of a country parson, Dr. Primrose, and his family. Like the Marches, the Primroses struggle against financial adversity.

" 'Finish the chapter, and don't be impertinent, miss.' "

"Did she own she liked it?" asked Meg.

"Oh, bless you, no! but she let old Belsham rest; and, when I ran back after my gloves this afternoon, there she was, so hard at the Vicar, that she didn't hear me laugh as I danced a jig in the hall, because of the good time coming. What a pleasant life she might have, if she only chose. I don't envy her much, in spite of her money, for after all rich people have about as many worries as poor ones, I guess," added Jo.

"That reminds me," said Meg, "that I've got something to tell. It isn't funny, like Jo's story, but I thought about it a good deal as I came home. At the Kings to-day I found everybody in a flurry, and one of the children said that her oldest brother had done something dreadful, and papa had sent him away. I heard Mrs. King crying, and Mr. King talking very loud, and Grace and Ellen turned away their faces when they passed me, so I shouldn't see how red their eyes were. I didn't ask any questions, of course; but I felt so sorry for them, and was rather glad I hadn't any wild brothers to do wicked things, and disgrace the family."

"I think being disgraced in school is a great deal try*inger* than anything bad boys can do," said Amy, shaking her head, as if her experience of life had been a deep one. "Susie Perkins came to school to-day with a lovely red carnelian ring; I wanted it dreadfully, and wished I was her with all my might. Well, she drew a picture of Mr. Davis, with a monstrous nose and a hump, and the words, 'Young ladies, my eye is upon you!' coming out of his mouth in a balloon thing. We were laughing over it, when all of a sudden his eye *was* on us, and he ordered Susie to bring up her slate. She was *parry*lized with fright, but she went, and oh, what *do* you think he did? He took her by the ear, the ear! just fancy how horrid! and led her to the recitation platform, and made her stand there half an hour, holding that slate so every one could see."

"Didn't the girls shout at the picture?" asked Jo, who relished the scrape.

"Laugh! not a one; they sat as still as mice, and Susie cried quarts, I know she did. I didn't envy her then, for I felt that millions of carnelian rings wouldn't have made me happy after that. I never, never should have got over such a agonizing mortification;" and Amy went on with her work, in the proud consciousness of virtue, and the successful utterance of two long words in a breath.

"I saw something that I liked this morning, and I meant to tell it at dinner, but I forgot," said Beth, putting Jo's topsy-turvy basket in order as she talked. "When I went to get some oysters for Hannah, Mr. Laurence was in the fish shop, but he didn't see me, for I kept behind a barrel, and he was busy with Mr. Cutter, the fish-man. A poor woman came in with a pail and a mop, and asked Mr. Cutter if he would let her do some scrubbing for a bit of fish, because she hadn't any dinner for her children, and had been disappointed of a day's work. Mr. Cutter was in a hurry, and said 'No,' rather crossly; so she was going away,

looking hungry and sorry, when Mr. Laurence hooked up a big fish
with the crooked end of his cane, and held it out to her. She was so
glad and surprised she took it right in her arms, and thanked him over
and over. He told her to 'go along and cook it,' and she hurried off, so
happy! wasn't it nice of him? Oh, she did look so funny, hugging the
big, slippery fish, and hoping Mr. Laurence's bed in heaven would be
'aisy.' "

When they had laughed at Beth's story, they asked their mother for
one; and, after a moment's thought, she said soberly,—

"As I sat cutting out blue flannel jackets to-day, at the rooms, I felt
very anxious about father, and thought how lonely and helpless we
should be if anything happened to him. It was not a wise thing to do,
but I kept on worrying, till an old man came in with an order for some
things. He sat down near me, and I began to talk to him, for he looked
poor, and tired, and anxious.

" 'Have you sons in the army?' I asked, for the note he brought was
not to me.

" 'Yes, ma'am; I had four, but two were killed; one is a prisoner, and
I'm going to the other, who is very sick in a Washington hospital,' he
answered, quietly.

" 'You have done a great deal for your country, sir,' I said, feeling respect now, instead of pity.

" 'Not a mite more than I ought, ma'am. I'd go myself, if I was any
use; as I ain't, I give my boys, and give 'em free.'

"He spoke so cheerfully, looked so sincere, and seemed so glad to
give his all, that I was ashamed of myself. I'd given one man, and
thought it too much, while he gave four, without grudging them; I had
all my girls to comfort me at home, and his last son was waiting, miles
away, to say 'good-by' to him, perhaps. I felt so rich, so happy, thinking
of my blessings, that I made him a nice bundle, gave him some money,
and thanked him heartily for the lesson he had taught me."

"Tell another story, mother; one with a moral to it, like this. I like to
think about them afterwards, if they are real, and not too preachy,"
said Jo, after a minute's silence.

Mrs. March smiled, and began at once; for she had told stories to
this little audience for many years, and knew how to please them.

"Once upon a time there were four girls, who had enough to eat,
and drink, and wear; a good many comforts and pleasures, kind
friends and parents, who loved them dearly, and yet they were not contented." (Here the listeners stole sly looks at one another, and began
to sew diligently.) "These girls were anxious to be good, and made
many excellent resolutions, but somehow they did not keep them very
well, and were constantly saying, 'If we only had this,' or 'if we could
only do that,' quite forgetting how much they already had, and how
many pleasant things they actually could do; so they asked an old
woman what spell they could use to make them happy, and she said,
'When you feel discontented, think over your blessings, and be grateful.' " (Here Jo looked up quickly, as if about to speak, but changed her
mind, seeing that the story was not done yet.)

"Being sensible girls, they decided to try her advice, and soon were surprised to see how well off they were. One discovered that money couldn't keep shame and sorrow out of rich people's houses; another that though she was poor, she was a great deal happier with her youth, health, and good spirits, than a certain fretful, feeble old lady, who couldn't enjoy her comforts; a third, that, disagreeable as it was to help get dinner, it was harder still to have to go begging for it; and the fourth, that even carnelian rings were not so valuable as good behavior. So they agreed to stop complaining, to enjoy the blessings already possessed, and try to deserve them, lest they should be taken away entirely, instead of increased; and I believe they were never disappointed, or sorry that they took the old woman's advice."

"Now, Marmee, that is very cunning of you to turn our own stories against us, and give us a sermon instead of a 'spin,' " cried Meg.

"I like that kind of sermon; it's the sort father used to tell us," said Beth, thoughtfully, putting the needles straight on Jo's cushion.

"I don't complain near as much as the others do, and I shall be more careful than ever now, for I've had warning from Susie's downfall," said Amy, morally.

"We needed that lesson, and we won't forget. If we do, you just say to us as Old Chloe did in Uncle Tom,[1]—'Tink ob yer marcies, chillen, tink ob yer marcies,' " added Jo, who could not for the life of her help getting a morsel of fun out of the little sermon, though she took it to heart as much as any of them.

CHAPTER V.

BEING NEIGHBORLY.

WHAT in the world are you going to do now, Jo?" asked Meg, one snowy afternoon, as her sister came clumping through the hall, in rubber boots, old sack and hood, with a broom in one hand and a shovel in the other.

"Going out for exercise," answered Jo, with a mischievous twinkle in her eyes.

"I should think two long walks, this morning, would have been enough. It's cold and dull out, and I advise you to stay, warm and dry, by the fire, as I do," said Meg, with a shiver.

"Never take advice; can't keep still all day, and not being a pussycat, I don't like to doze by the fire. I like adventures, and I'm going to find some."

Meg went back to toast her feet, and read "Ivanhoe,"[2] and Jo began to dig paths with great energy. The snow was light; and with her broom she soon swept a path all round the garden, for Beth to walk in when the sun came out; and the invalid dolls needed air. Now the gar-

---

1. The enslaved but patient and devout Uncle Tom and Aunt Chloe are a married couple from Harriet Beecher Stowe's *Uncle Tom's Cabin* (1852).
2. Historical romance (published in 1819) by Scottish author Sir Walter Scott.

den separated the Marches' house from that of Mr. Laurence; both stood in a suburb of the city, which was still country-like, with groves and lawns, large gardens, and quiet streets. A low hedge parted the two estates. On one side was an old brown house, looking rather bare and shabby, robbed of the vines that in summer covered its walls, and the flowers which then surrounded it. On the other side was a stately stone mansion, plainly betokening every sort of comfort and luxury, from the big coach-house and well-kept grounds to the conservatory, and the glimpses of lovely things one caught between the rich curtains. Yet it seemed a lonely, lifeless sort of house; for no children frolicked on the lawn, no motherly face ever smiled at the windows, and few people went in and out, except the old gentleman and his grandson.

To Jo's lively fancy this fine house seemed a kind of enchanted palace, full of splendors and delights, which no one enjoyed. She had long wanted to behold these hidden glories, and to know the "Laurence boy," who looked as if he would like to be known, if he only knew how to begin. Since the party she had been more eager than ever, and had planned many ways of making friends with him; but he had not been lately seen, and Jo began to think he had gone away, when she one day spied a brown face at an upper window, looking wistfully down into their garden, where Beth and Amy were snowballing one another.

"That boy is suffering for society and fun," she said to herself. "His grandpa don't know what's good for him, and keeps him shut up all alone. He needs a lot of jolly boys to play with, or somebody young and lively. I've a great mind to go over and tell the old gentleman so."

The idea amused Jo, who liked to do daring things, and was always scandalizing Meg by her queer performances. The plan of "going over" was not forgotten; and, when the snowy afternoon came, Jo resolved to try what could be done. She saw Mr. Laurence drive off, and then sallied out to dig her way down to the hedge, where she paused, and took a survey. All quiet; curtains down at the lower windows; servants out of sight, and nothing human visible but a curly black head leaning on a thin hand, at the upper window.

"There he is," thought Jo; "poor boy! all alone, and sick, this dismal day! It's a shame! I'll toss up a snow-ball, and make him look out, and then say a kind word to him."

Up went a handful of soft snow, and the head turned at once, showing a face which lost its listless look in a minute, as the big eyes brightened, and the mouth began to smile. Jo nodded, and laughed, and flourished her broom as she called out,—

"How do you do? Are you sick?"

Laurie opened the window and croaked out as hoarsely as a raven,—

"Better, thank you. I've had a horrid cold, and been shut up a week."

"I'm sorry. What do you amuse yourself with?"

"Nothing; it's as dull as tombs up here."

"Don't you read?"

"Not much; they won't let me."

"Can't somebody read to you?"

"Grandpa does, sometimes; but my books don't interest him, and I hate to ask Brooke all the time."

"Have some one come and see you, then."

"There isn't any one I'd like to see. Boys make such a row, and my head is weak."

"Isn't there some nice girl who'd read and amuse you? Girls are quiet, and like to play nurse."

"Don't know any."

"You know me," began Jo, then laughed, and stopped.

"So I do! Will you come, please?" cried Laurie.

"I'm not quiet and nice; but I'll come, if mother will let me. I'll go ask her. Shut that window, like a good boy, and wait till I come."

With that, Jo shouldered her broom and marched into the house, wondering what they would all say to her. Laurie was in a little flutter of excitement at the idea of having company, and flew about to get ready; for, as Mrs. March said, he was "a little gentleman," and did honor to the coming guest by brushing his curly pate, putting on a fresh collar, and trying to tidy up the room, which, in spite of half a dozen servants, was anything but neat. Presently, there came a loud ring, then a decided voice, asking for "Mr. Laurie," and a surprised-looking servant came running up to announce a young lady.

"All right, show her up, it's Miss Jo," said Laurie, going to the door of his little parlor to meet Jo, who appeared, looking rosy and kind, and quite at her ease, with a covered dish in one hand, and Beth's three kittens in the other.

"Here I am, bag and baggage," she said, briskly. "Mother sent her love, and was glad if I could do anything for you. Meg wanted me to bring some of her blanc-mange; she makes it very nice, and Beth thought her cats would be comforting. I knew you'd shout at them, but I couldn't refuse, she was so anxious to do something."

It so happened that Beth's funny loan was just the thing; for, in laughing over the kits, Laurie forgot his bashfulness, and grew sociable at once.

"That looks too pretty to eat," he said, smiling with pleasure, as Jo uncovered the dish, and showed the blanc-mange, surrounded by a garland of green leaves, and the scarlet flowers of Amy's pet geranium.

"It isn't anything, only they all felt kindly, and wanted to show it. Tell the girl to put it away for your tea; it's so simple, you can eat it; and, being soft, it will slip down without hurting your sore throat. What a cosy room this is."

"It might be, if it was kept nice; but the maids are lazy, and I don't know how to make them mind. It worries me, though."

"I'll right it up in two minutes; for it only needs to have the hearth brushed, so,—and the things stood straight on the mantel-piece, so,—and the books put here, and the bottles there, and your sofa turned from the light, and the pillows plumped up a bit. Now, then, you're fixed."

And so he was; for, as she laughed and talked, Jo had whisked things into place, and given quite a different air to the room. Laurie watched her in respectful silence; and, when she beckoned him to his sofa, he sat down with a sigh of satisfaction, saying, gratefully,—

"How kind you are! Yes, that's what it wanted. Now please take the big chair, and let me do something to amuse my company."

"No; I came to amuse you. Shall I read aloud?" and Jo looked affectionately toward some inviting books near by.

"Thank you; I've read all those, and if you don't mind, I'd rather talk," answered Laurie.

"Not a bit; I'll talk all day if you'll only set me going. Beth says I never know when to stop."

"Is Beth the rosy one, who stays at home a good deal, and sometimes goes out with a little basket?" asked Laurie, with interest.

"Yes, that's Beth; she's my girl, and a regular good one she is, too."

"The pretty one is Meg, and the curly-haired one is Amy, I believe?"

"How did you find that out?"

Laurie colored up, but answered, frankly, "Why, you see, I often hear you calling to one another, and when I'm alone up here, I can't help looking over at your house, you always seem to be having such good times. I beg your pardon for being so rude, but sometimes you forget to put down the curtain at the window where the flowers are; and, when the lamps are lighted, it's like looking at a picture to see the fire, and you all round the table with your mother; her face is right opposite, and it looks so sweet behind the flowers, I can't help watching it. I haven't got any mother, you know;" and Laurie poked the fire to hide a little twitching of the lips that he could not control.

The solitary, hungry look in his eyes went straight to Jo's warm heart. She had been so simply taught that there was no nonsense in her head, and at fifteen she was as innocent and frank as any child. Laurie was sick and lonely; and, feeling how rich she was in home-love and happiness, she gladly tried to share it with him. Her brown face was very friendly, and her sharp voice unusually gentle, as she said,—

"We'll never draw that curtain any more, and I give you leave to look as much as you like. I just wish, though, instead of peeping, you'd come over and see us. Mother is so splendid, she'd do you heaps of good, and Beth would sing to you if I begged her to, and Amy would dance; Meg and I would make you laugh over our funny stage properties, and we'd have jolly times. Wouldn't your grandpa let you?"

"I think he would, if your mother asked him. He's very kind, though he don't look it; and he lets me do what I like, pretty much, only he's afraid I might be a bother to strangers," began Laurie, brightening more and more.

"We ain't strangers, we are neighbors, and you needn't think you'd be a bother. We *want* to know you, and I've been trying to do it this ever so long. We haven't been here a great while, you know, but we have got acquainted with all our neighbors but you."

"You see grandpa lives among his books, and don't mind much what happens outside. Mr. Brooke, my tutor, don't stay here, you know, and I have no one to go round with me, so I just stop at home and get on as I can."

"That's bad; you ought to make a dive, and go visiting everywhere you are asked; then you'll have lots of friends, and pleasant places to go to. Never mind being bashful, it won't last long if you keep going."

Laurie turned red again, but wasn't offended at being accused of bashfulness; for there was so much good-will in Jo, it was impossible not to take her blunt speeches as kindly as they were meant.

"Do you like your school?" asked the boy, changing the subject, after a little pause, during which he stared at the fire, and Jo looked about her well pleased.

"Don't go to school; I'm a business man—girl, I mean. I go to wait on my aunt, and a dear, cross old soul she is, too," answered Jo.

Laurie opened his mouth to ask another question; but remembering just in time that it wasn't manners to make too many inquiries into people's affairs, he shut it again, and looked uncomfortable. Jo liked his good breeding, and didn't mind having a laugh at Aunt March, so she gave him a lively description of the fidgety old lady, her fat poodle, the parrot that talked Spanish, and the library where she revelled. Laurie enjoyed that immensely; and when she told about the prim old gentleman who came once to woo Aunt March, and, in the middle of a fine speech, how Poll had tweaked his wig off to his great dismay, the boy lay back and laughed till the tears ran down his cheeks, and a maid popped her head in to see what was the matter.

"Oh! that does me lots of good; tell on, please," he said, taking his face out of the sofa-cushion, red and shining with merriment.

Much elated with her success, Jo did "tell on," all about their plays and plans, their hopes and fears for father, and the most interesting events of the little world in which the sisters lived. Then they got to talking about books; and to Jo's delight she found that Laurie loved them as well as she did, and had read even more than herself.

"If you like them so much, come down and see ours. Grandpa is out, so you needn't be afraid," said Laurie, getting up.

"I'm not afraid of anything," returned Jo, with a toss of the head.

"I don't believe you are!" exclaimed the boy, looking at her with much admiration, though he privately thought she would have good reason to be a trifle afraid of the old gentleman, if she met him in some of his moods.

The atmosphere of the whole house being summer-like, Laurie led the way from room to room, letting Jo stop to examine whatever struck her fancy; and so at last they came to the library, where she clapped her hands, and pranced, as she always did when especially delighted. It was lined with books, and there were pictures and statues, and distracting little cabinets full of coins and curiosities, and Sleepy-Hollow chairs,[3] and queer tables, and bronzes; and, best of all, a great, open fireplace, with quaint tiles all round it.

---

3. Large and comfortable upholstered armchair with hollowed seat, high back, and low arms.

"What richness!" sighed Jo, sinking into the depths of a velvet chair, and gazing about her with an air of intense satisfaction. "Theodore Laurence, you ought to be the happiest boy in the world," she added, impressively.

"A fellow can't live on books," said Laurie, shaking his head, as he perched on a table opposite.

Before he could say more, a bell rung, and Jo flew up, exclaiming with alarm, "Mercy me! it's your grandpa!"

"Well, what if it is? You are not afraid of anything, you know," returned the boy, looking wicked.

"I think I am a little bit afraid of him, but I don't know why I should be. Marmee said I might come, and I don't think you're any the worse for it," said Jo, composing herself, though she kept her eyes on the door.

"I'm a great deal better for it, and ever so much obliged. I'm only afraid you are very tired talking to me; it was *so* pleasant, I couldn't bear to stop," said Laurie, gratefully.

"The doctor to see you, sir," and the maid beckoned as she spoke.

"Would you mind if I left you for a minute? I suppose I must see him," said Laurie.

"Don't mind me. I'm as happy as a cricket here," answered Jo.

Laurie went away, and his guest amused herself in her own way. She was standing before a fine portrait of the old gentleman, when the door opened again, and, without turning, she said decidedly, "I'm sure now that I shouldn't be afraid of him, for he's got kind eyes, though his mouth is grim, and he looks as if he had a tremendous will of his own. He isn't as handsome as *my* grandfather, but I like him."

"Thank you, ma'am," said a gruff voice behind her; and there, to her great dismay, stood old Mr. Laurence.

Poor Jo blushed till she couldn't blush any redder, and her heart began to beat uncomfortably fast as she thought what she had said. For a minute a wild desire to run away possessed her; but that was cowardly, and the girls would laugh at her; so she resolved to stay, and get out of the scrape as she could. A second look showed her that the living eyes, under the bushy gray eyebrows, were kinder even than the painted ones; and there was a sly twinkle in them, which lessened her fear a good deal. The gruff voice was gruffer than ever, as the old gentleman said abruptly, after that dreadful pause, "So, you're not afraid of me, hey?"

"Not much, sir."

"And you don't think me as handsome as your grandfather?"

"Not quite, sir."

"And I've got a tremendous will, have I?"

"I only said I thought so."

"But you like me, in spite of it?"

"Yes, I do, sir."

That answer pleased the old gentleman; he gave a short laugh, shook hands with her, and putting his finger under her chin, turned up her face, examined it gravely, and let it go, saying, with a nod,

"You've got your grandfather's spirit, if you haven't his face. He *was* a fine man, my dear; but, what is better, he was a brave and an honest one, and I was proud to be his friend."

"Thank you, sir;" and Jo was quite comfortable after that, for it suited her exactly.

"What have you been doing to this boy of mine, hey?" was the next question, sharply put.

"Only trying to be neighborly, sir;" and Jo told how her visit came about.

"You think he needs cheering up a bit, do you?"

"Yes, sir; he seems a little lonely, and young folks would do him good, perhaps. We are only girls, but we should be glad to help if we could, for we don't forget the splendid Christmas present you sent us," said Jo, eagerly.

"Tut, tut, tut; that was the boy's affair. How is the poor woman?"

"Doing nicely, sir;" and off went Jo, talking very fast, as she told all about the Hummels, in whom her mother had interested richer friends than they were.

"Just her father's way of doing good. I shall come and see your mother some fine day. Tell her so. There's the tea-bell; we have it early, on the boy's account. Come down, and go on being neighborly."

"If you'd like to have me, sir."

"Shouldn't ask you, if I didn't;" and Mr. Laurence offered her his arm with old-fashioned courtesy.

"What *would* Meg say to this?" thought Jo, as she was marched away, while her eyes danced with fun as she imagined herself telling the story at home.

"Hey! why what the dickens has come to the fellow?" said the old gentleman, as Laurie came running down stairs, and brought up with a start of surprise at the astonishing sight of Jo arm in arm with his redoubtable grandfather.

"I didn't know you'd come, sir," he began, as Jo gave him a triumphant little glance.

"That's evident, by the way you racket down stairs. Come to your tea, sir, and behave like a gentleman;" and having pulled the boy's hair by way of a caress, Mr. Laurence walked on, while Laurie went through a series of comic evolutions behind their backs, which nearly produced an explosion of laughter from Jo.

The old gentleman did not say much as he drank his four cups of tea, but he watched the young people, who soon chatted away like old friends, and the change in his grandson did not escape him. There was color, light and life in the boy's face now, vivacity in his manner, and genuine merriment in his laugh.

"She's right; the lad *is* lonely. I'll see what these little girls can do for him," thought Mr. Laurence, as he looked and listened. He liked Jo, for her odd, blunt ways suited him; and she seemed to understand the boy almost as well as if she had been one herself.

If the Laurences had been what Jo called "prim and poky," she would not have got on at all, for such people always made her shy and awkward; but finding them free and easy, she was so herself, and made a good impression. When they rose she proposed to go, but Laurie said he had something more to show her, and took her away to the conservatory, which had been lighted for her benefit. It seemed quite fairy-like to Jo, as she went up and down the walks, enjoying the blooming walls on either side,—the soft light, the damp, sweet air, and the wonderful vines and trees that hung above her,—while her new friend cut the finest flowers till his hands were full; then he tied them up, saying, with the happy look Jo liked to see, "Please give these to your mother, and tell her I like the medicine she sent me very much."

They found Mr. Laurence standing before the fire in the great drawing-room, but Jo's attention was entirely absorbed by a grand piano which stood open.

"Do you play?" she asked, turning to Laurie with a respectful expression.

"Sometimes," he answered, modestly.

"Please do now; I want to hear it, so I can tell Beth."

"Won't you first?"

"Don't know how; too stupid to learn, but I love music dearly."

So Laurie played, and Jo listened, with her nose luxuriously buried in heliotrope and tea roses. Her respect and regard for the "Laurence boy" increased very much, for he played remarkably well, and didn't put on any airs. She wished Beth could hear him, but she did not say so; only praised him till he was quite abashed, and his grandfather came to the rescue. "That will do, that will do, young lady; too many sugar-plums are not good for him. His music isn't bad, but I hope he will do as well in more important things. Going? Well, I'm much obliged to you, and I hope you'll come again. My respects to your mother; good-night, Doctor Jo."

He shook hands kindly, but looked as if something did not please him. When they got into the hall, Jo asked Laurie if she had said anything amiss; he shook his head.

"No, it was me; he don't like to hear me play."

"Why not?"

"I'll tell you some day. John is going home with you, as I can't."

"No need of that; I ain't a young lady, and it's only a step. Take care of yourself, won't you?"

"Yes, but you will come again, I hope?"

"If you promise to come and see us after you are well."

"I will."

"Good-night, Laurie."

"Good-night, Jo, good-night."

When all the afternoon's adventures had been told, the family felt inclined to go visiting in a body, for each found something very attractive in the big house on the other side of the hedge. Mrs. March wanted to talk of her father with the old man who had not forgotten him; Meg longed to walk in the conservatory; Beth sighed for the grand piano, and Amy was eager to see the fine pictures and statues.

"Mother, why didn't Mr. Laurence like to have Laurie play?" asked Jo, who was of an inquiring disposition.

"I am not sure, but I think it was because his son, Laurie's father, married an Italian lady, a musician, which displeased the old man, who is very proud. The lady was good and lovely and accomplished, but he did not like her, and never saw his son after he married. They both died when Laurie was a little child, and then his grandfather took him home. I fancy the boy, who was born in Italy, is not very strong, and the old man is afraid of losing him, which makes him so careful. Laurie comes naturally by his love of music, for he is like his mother, and I dare say his grandfather fears that he may want to be a musician; at any rate, his skill reminds him of the woman he did not like, and so he 'glowered,' as Jo said."

"Dear me, how romantic!" exclaimed Meg.

"How silly," said Jo; "let him be a musician, if he wants to, and not plague his life out sending him to college, when he hates to go."

"That's why he has such handsome black eyes and pretty manners, I suppose; Italians are always nice," said Meg, who was a little sentimental.

"What do you know about his eyes and his manners? you never spoke to him, hardly;" cried Jo, who was *not* sentimental.

"I saw him at the party, and what you tell shows that he knows how to behave. That was a nice little speech about the medicine mother sent him."

"He meant the blanc-mange, I suppose."

"How stupid you are, child; he meant you, of course."

"Did he?" and Jo opened her eyes as if it had never occurred to her before.

"I never saw such a girl! You don't know a compliment when you get it," said Meg, with the air of a young lady who knew all about the matter.

"I think they are great nonsense, and I'll thank you not to be silly, and spoil my fun. Laurie's a nice boy, and I like him, and I won't have any sentimental stuff about compliments and such rubbish. We'll all be good to him, because he hasn't got any mother, and he *may* come over and see us, mayn't he, Marmee?"

"Yes, Jo, your little friend is very welcome, and I hope Meg will remember that children should be children as long as they can."

"I don't call myself a child, and I'm not in my teens yet," observed Amy. "What do you say, Beth?"

"I was thinking about our 'Pilgrim's Progress,' " answered Beth, who had not heard a word. "How we got out of the Slough and through the Wicket Gate by resolving to be good, and up the steep hill, by trying; and that maybe the house over there, full of splendid things, is going to be our Palace Beautiful."[4]

"We have got to get by the lions, first," said Jo, as if she rather liked the prospect.

4. See p. 17, n. 1 (part 1, chap. 1).

CHAPTER VI.

BETH FINDS THE PALACE BEAUTIFUL.

THE big house did prove a Palace Beautiful, though it took some time for all to get in, and Beth found it very hard to pass the lions. Old Mr. Laurence was the biggest one; but, after he had called, said something funny or kind to each one of the girls, and talked over old times with their mother, nobody felt much afraid of him, except timid Beth. The other lion was the fact that they were poor and Laurie rich; for this made them shy of accepting favors which they could not return. But after a while they found that he considered them the benefactors, and could not do enough to show how grateful he was for Mrs. March's motherly welcome, their cheerful society, and the comfort he took in that humble home of theirs; so they soon forgot their pride, and interchanged kindnesses without stopping to think which was the greater.

All sorts of pleasant things happened about that time, for the new friendship flourished like grass in spring. Every one liked Laurie, and he privately informed his tutor that "the Marches were regularly splendid girls." With the delightful enthusiasm of youth, they took the solitary boy into their midst, and made much of him, and he found something very charming in the innocent companionship of these simple-hearted girls. Never having known mother or sisters, he was quick to feel the influences they brought about him; and their busy, lively ways made him ashamed of the indolent life he led. He was tired of books, and found people so interesting now, that Mr. Brooke was obliged to make very unsatisfactory reports; for Laurie was always playing truant, and running over to the Marches.

"Never mind, let him take a holiday, and make it up afterward," said the old gentleman. "The good lady next door says he is studying too hard, and needs young society, amusement, and exercise. I suspect she is right, and that I've been coddling the fellow as if I'd been his grandmother. Let him do what he likes, as long as he is happy; he can't get into mischief in that little nunnery over there, and Mrs. March is doing more for him than we can."

What good times they had, to be sure! Such plays and tableaux; such sleigh-rides and skating frolics; such pleasant evenings in the old parlor, and now and then such gay little parties at the great house. Meg could walk in the conservatory whenever she liked, and revel in bouquets; Jo browsed over the new library voraciously, and convulsed the old gentleman with her criticisms; Amy copied pictures and enjoyed beauty to her heart's content, and Laurie played lord of the manor in the most delightful style.

But Beth, though yearning for the grand piano, could not pluck up courage to go to the "mansion of bliss," as Meg called it. She went once with Jo, but the old gentleman, not being aware of her infirmity, stared at her so hard from under his heavy eyebrows, and said "hey!" so loud, that he frightened her so much her "feet chattered on the floor," she told her mother; and she ran away, declaring she would

never go there any more, not even for the dear piano. No persuasions
or enticements could overcome her fear, till the fact coming to Mr.
Laurence's ear in some mysterious way, he set about mending matters.
During one of the brief calls he made, he artfully led the conversation
to music, and talked away about great singers whom he had seen, fine
organs he had heard, and told such charming anecdotes, that Beth
found it impossible to stay in her distant corner, but crept nearer and
nearer, as if fascinated. At the back of his chair she stopped, and stood
listening with her great eyes wide open, and her cheeks red with the
excitement of this unusual performance. Taking no more notice of her
than if she had been a fly, Mr. Laurence talked on about Laurie's lessons and teachers; and presently, as if the idea had just occurred to
him, he said to Mrs. March,—

"The boy neglects his music now, and I'm glad of it, for he was getting too fond of it. But the piano suffers for want of use; wouldn't
some of your girls like to run over, and practise on it now and then,
just to keep it in tune, you know, ma'am?"

Beth took a step forward, and pressed her hands tightly together, to
keep from clapping them, for this was an irresistible temptation; and
the thought of practising on that splendid instrument quite took her
breath away. Before Mrs. March could reply, Mr. Laurence went on
with an odd little nod and smile,—

"They needn't see or speak to any one, but run in at any time, for
I'm shut up in my study at the other end of the house. Laurie is out a
great deal, and the servants are never near the drawing-room after
nine o'clock." Here he rose, as if going, and Beth made up her mind to
speak, for that last arrangement left nothing to be desired. "Please tell
the young ladies what I say, and if they don't care to come, why, never
mind;" here a little hand slipped into his, and Beth looked up at him
with a face full of gratitude, as she said, in her earnest, yet timid
way,—

"Oh, sir! they do care, very, very much!"

"Are you the musical girl?" he asked, without any startling "hey!" as
he looked down at her very kindly.

"I'm Beth; I love it dearly, and I'll come if you are quite sure nobody
will hear me—and be disturbed," she added, fearing to be rude, and
trembling at her own boldness as she spoke.

"Not a soul, my dear; the house is empty half the day, so come and
drum away as much as you like, and I shall be obliged to you."

"How kind you are, sir."

Beth blushed like a rose under the friendly look he wore, but she
was not frightened now, and gave the big hand a grateful squeeze, because she had no words to thank him for the precious gift he had
given her. The old gentleman softly stroked the hair off her forehead,
and, stooping down, he kissed her, saying in a tone few people ever
heard,—

"I had a little girl once with eyes like these; God bless you, my dear;
good-day, madam," and away he went, in a great hurry.

Beth had a rapture with her mother, and then rushed up to impart the glorious news to her family of invalids, as the girls were not at home. How blithely she sung that evening, and how they all laughed at her, because she woke Amy in the night, by playing the piano on her face in her sleep. Next day, having seen both the old and young gentleman out of the house, Beth, after two or three retreats, fairly got in at the side-door, and made her way as noiselessly as any mouse to the drawing-room, where her idol stood. Quite by accident, of course, some pretty, easy music lay on the piano; and, with trembling fingers, and frequent stops to listen and look about, Beth at last touched the great instrument, and straightway forgot her fear, herself, and everything else but the unspeakable delight which the music gave her, for it was like the voice of a beloved friend.

She stayed till Hannah came to take her home to dinner; but she had no appetite, and could only sit and smile upon every one in a general state of beatitude.

After that, the little brown hood slipped through the hedge nearly every day, and the great drawing-room was haunted by a tuneful spirit that came and went unseen. She never knew that Mr. Laurence often opened his study door to hear the old-fashioned airs he liked; she never saw Laurie mount guard in the hall, to warn the servants away; she never suspected that the exercise-books and new songs which she found in the rack were put there for her especial benefit; and when he talked to her about music at home, she only thought how kind he was to tell things that helped her so much. So she enjoyed herself heartily, and found, what isn't always the case, that her granted wish was all she had hoped. Perhaps it was because she was so grateful for this blessing that a greater was given her; at any rate, she deserved both.

"Mother, I'm going to work Mr. Laurence a pair of slippers. He is so kind to me I must thank him, and I don't know any other way. Can I do it?" asked Beth, a few weeks after that eventful call of his.

"Yes, dear; it will please him very much, and be a nice way of thanking him. The girls will help you about them, and I will pay for the making up," replied Mrs. March, who took peculiar pleasure in granting Beth's requests, because she so seldom asked anything for herself.

After many serious discussions with Meg and Jo, the pattern was chosen, the materials bought, and the slippers begun. A cluster of grave yet cheerful pansies, on a deeper purple ground, was pronounced very appropriate and pretty, and Beth worked away early and late, with occasional lifts over hard parts. She was a nimble little needle-woman, and they were finished before any one got tired of them. Then she wrote a very short, simple note, and, with Laurie's help, got them smuggled on to the study-table one morning before the old gentleman was up.

When this excitement was over, Beth waited to see what would happen. All that day passed, and a part of the next, before any acknowledgment arrived, and she was beginning to fear she had offended her crotchety friend. On the afternoon of the second day she went out to do an errand, and give poor Joanna, the invalid doll, her daily exercise. As she came up the street on her return she saw three—yes, four heads popping in and out of the parlor windows; and the moment they saw her several hands were waved, and several joyful voices screamed,—

"Here's a letter from the old gentleman; come quick, and read it!"

"Oh, Beth! he's sent you—" began Amy, gesticulating with unseemly energy; but she got no further, for Jo quenched her by slamming down the window.

Beth hurried on in a twitter of suspense; at the door her sisters seized and bore her to the parlor in a triumphal procession, all pointing, and all saying at once, "Look there! look there!" Beth did look, and turned pale with delight and surprise; for there stood a little cabinet piano, with a letter lying on the glossy lid, directed like a signboard, to "Miss Elizabeth March."

"For me?" gasped Beth, holding on to Jo, and feeling as if she should tumble down, it was such an overwhelming thing altogether.

"Yes; all for you, my precious! Isn't it splendid of him? Don't you think he's the dearest old man in the world? Here's the key in the letter; we didn't open it, but we are dying to know what he says," cried Jo, hugging her sister, and offering the note.

"You read it; I can't, I feel so queer. Oh, it is too lovely!" and Beth hid her face in Jo's apron, quite upset by her present.

Jo opened the paper, and began to laugh, for the first words she saw were:—

"MISS MARCH:
    "Dear Madam—"

"How nice it sounds! I wish some one would write to me so!" said Amy, who thought the old-fashioned address very elegant.

" 'I have had many pairs of slippers in my life, but I never had any that suited me so well as yours,' " continued Jo. " 'Heart's-ease[5] is my favorite flower, and these will always remind me of the gentle giver. I like to pay my debts, so I know you will allow "the old gentleman" to send you something which once belonged to the little granddaughter he lost. With hearty thanks, and best wishes, I remain,

    " 'Your grateful friend and humble servant,

    " 'JAMES LAURENCE.' "

"There, Beth, that's an honor to be proud of, I'm sure! Laurie told me how fond Mr. Laurence used to be of the child who died, and how he kept all her little things carefully. Just think; he's given you her piano! That comes of having big blue eyes and loving music," said Jo, trying to soothe Beth, who trembled, and looked more excited than she had ever been before.

"See the cunning brackets to hold candles, and the nice green silk, puckered up with a gold rose in the middle, and the pretty rack and stool, all complete," added Meg, opening the instrument, and displaying its beauties.

5. Pansy.

" 'Your humble servant, James Laurence;' only think of his writing that to you. I'll tell the girls; they'll think it's killing," said Amy, much impressed by the note.

"Try it, honey; let's hear the sound of the baby pianny," said Hannah, who always took a share in the family joys and sorrows.

So Beth tried it, and every one pronounced it the most remarkable piano ever heard. It had evidently been newly tuned, and put in apple-pie order; but, perfect as it was, I think the real charm of it lay in the happiest of all happy faces which leaned over it, as Beth lovingly touched the beautiful black and white keys, and pressed the shiny pedals.

"You'll have to go and thank him," said Jo, by way of a joke; for the idea of the child's really going, never entered her head.

"Yes, I mean to; I guess I'll go now, before I get frightened thinking about it;" and, to the utter amazement of the assembled family, Beth walked deliberately down the garden, through the hedge, and in at the Laurences' door.

"Well, I wish I may die, if it ain't the queerest thing I ever see! The pianny has turned her head; she'd never have gone, in her right mind," cried Hannah, staring after her, while the girls were rendered quite speechless by the miracle.

They would have been still more amazed, if they had seen what Beth did afterward. If you will believe me, she went and knocked at the study door, before she gave herself time to think; and when a gruff voice called out, "Come in!" she did go in, right up to Mr. Laurence, who looked quite taken aback, and held out her hand, saying, with only a small quaver in her voice, "I came to thank you, sir, for—" but she didn't finish, for he looked so friendly that she forgot her speech; and, only remembering that he had lost the little girl he loved, she put both arms around his neck, and kissed him.

If the roof of the house had suddenly flown off, the old gentleman wouldn't have been more astonished; but he liked it—oh dear, yes! he liked it amazingly; and was so touched and pleased by that confiding little kiss, that all his crustiness vanished; and he just set her on his knee, and laid his wrinkled cheek against her rosy one, feeling as if he had got his own little granddaughter back again. Beth ceased to fear him from that moment, and sat there talking to him as cosily as if she had known him all her life; for love casts out fear, and gratitude can conquer pride. When she went home, he walked with her to her own gate, shook hands cordially, and touched his hat as he marched back again, looking very stately and erect, like a handsome, soldierly old gentleman, as he was.

When the girls saw that performance, Jo began to dance a jig, by way of expressing her satisfaction; Amy nearly fell out of the window in her surprise, and Meg exclaimed, with uplifted hands, "Well, I do believe the world is coming to an end!"

CHAPTER VII.

AMY'S VALLEY OF HUMILIATION.

THAT boy is a perfect Cyclops, isn't he?" said Amy, one day, as Laurie clattered by on horseback, with a flourish of his whip as he passed.

"How dare you say so, when he's got both his eyes? and very handsome ones they are, too;" cried Jo, who resented any slighting remarks about her friend.

"I didn't say anything about his eyes, and I don't see why you need fire up when I admire his riding."

"Oh, my goodness! that little goose means a centaur, and she called him a Cyclops," exclaimed Jo, with a burst of laughter.

"You needn't be so rude, it's only a 'lapse of lingy,'[6] as Mr. Davis says," retorted Amy, finishing Jo with her Latin. "I just wish I had a little of the money Laurie spends on that horse," she added, as if to herself, yet hoping her sisters would hear.

"Why?" asked Meg, kindly, for Jo had gone off in another laugh at Amy's second blunder.

"I need it so much; I'm dreadfully in debt, and it won't be my turn to have the rag-money for a month."

"In debt, Amy; what do you mean?" and Meg looked sober.

"Why, I owe at least a dozen pickled limes, and I can't pay them, you know, till I have money, for Marmee forbid my having anything charged at the shop."

"Tell me all about it. Are limes the fashion now? It used to be pricking bits of rubber to make balls;" and Meg tried to keep her countenance, Amy looked so grave and important.

"Why, you see, the girls are always buying them, and unless you want to be thought mean, you must do it, too. It's nothing but limes now, for every one is sucking them in their desks in school-time, and trading them off for pencils, bead-rings, paper dolls, or something else, at recess. If one girl likes another, she gives her a lime; if she's mad with her, she eats one before her face, and don't offer even a suck. They treat by turns; and I've had ever so many, but haven't returned them, and I ought, for they are debts of honor, you know."

"How much will pay them off, and restore your credit?" asked Meg, taking out her purse.

"A quarter would more than do it, and leave a few cents over for a treat for you. Don't you like limes?"

"Not much; you may have my share. Here's the money,—make it last as long as you can, for it isn't very plenty, you know."

"Oh, thank you! it must be so nice to have pocket-money. I'll have a grand feast, for I haven't tasted a lime this week. I felt delicate about taking any, as I couldn't return them, and I'm actually suffering for one."

Next day Amy was rather late at school; but could not resist the

---

6. Amy means to say "lapsus linguae" (Latin for "slip of the tongue").

temptation of displaying, with pardonable pride, a moist brown paper parcel, before she consigned it to the inmost recesses of her desk. During the next few minutes the rumor that Amy March had got twenty-four delicious limes (she ate one on the way), and was going to treat, circulated through her "set," and the attentions of her friends became quite overwhelming. Katy Brown invited her to her next party on the spot; Mary Kingsley insisted on lending her her watch till recess, and Jenny Snow, a satirical young lady who had basely twitted Amy upon her limeless state, promptly buried the hatchet, and offered to furnish answers to certain appalling sums. But Amy had not forgotten Miss Snow's cutting remarks about "some persons whose noses were not too flat to smell other people's limes, and stuck-up people, who were not too proud to ask for them;" and she instantly crushed "that Snow girl's" hopes by the withering telegram, "You needn't be so polite all of a sudden, for you won't get any."

A distinguished personage happened to visit the school that morning, and Amy's beautifully drawn maps received praise, which honor to her foe rankled in the soul of Miss Snow, and caused Miss March to assume the airs of a studious young peacock. But, alas, alas! pride goes before a fall, and the revengeful Snow turned the tables with disastrous success. No sooner had the guest paid the usual stale compliments, and bowed himself out, than Jenny, under pretence of asking an important question, informed Mr. Davis, the teacher, that Amy March had pickled limes in her desk.

Now Mr. Davis had declared limes a contraband article, and solemnly vowed to publicly ferule the first person who was found breaking the law. This much-enduring man had succeeded in banishing gum after a long and stormy war, had made a bonfire of the confiscated novels and newspapers, had suppressed a private post-office, had forbidden distortions of the face, nicknames, and caricatures, and done all that one man could do to keep half a hundred rebellious girls in order. Boys are trying enough to human patience, goodness knows! but girls are infinitely more so, especially to nervous gentlemen with tyrannical tempers, and no more talent for teaching than "Dr. Blimber."[7] Mr. Davis knew any quantity of Greek, Latin, Algebra, and ologies of all sorts, so he was called a fine teacher; and manners, morals, feelings, and examples were not considered of any particular importance. It was a most unfortunate moment for denouncing Amy, and Jenny knew it. Mr. Davis had evidently taken his coffee too strong that morning; there was an east wind, which always affected his neuralgia, and his pupils had not done him the credit which he felt he deserved; therefore, to use the expressive, if not elegant, language of a schoolgirl, "he was as nervous as a witch and as cross as a bear." The word "limes" was like fire to powder; his yellow face flushed, and he rapped on his desk with an energy which made Jenny skip to her seat with unusual rapidity.

---

7. Headmaster with a coercive but ineffective pedagogy, from Charles Dickens's *Dombey and Son* (1847–48).

"Young ladies, attention, if you please!"

At the stern order the buzz ceased, and fifty pairs of blue, black, gray, and brown eyes were obediently fixed upon his awful countenance.

"Miss March, come to the desk."

Amy rose to comply, with outward composure, but a secret fear oppressed her, for the limes weighed upon her conscience.

"Bring with you the limes you have in your desk," was the unexpected command which arrested her before she got out of her seat.

"Don't take all," whispered her neighbor, a young lady of great presence of mind.

Amy hastily shook out half a dozen, and laid the rest down before Mr. Davis, feeling that any man possessing a human heart would relent when that delicious perfume met his nose. Unfortunately, Mr. Davis particularly detested the odor of the fashionable pickle, and disgust added to his wrath.

"Is that all?"

"Not quite," stammered Amy.

"Bring the rest, immediately."

With a despairing glance at her set she obeyed.

"You are sure there are no more?"

"I never lie, sir."

"So I see. Now take these disgusting things, two by two, and throw them out of the window."

There was a simultaneous sigh, which created quite a little gust as the last hope fled, and the treat was ravished from their longing lips. Scarlet with shame and anger, Amy went to and fro twelve mortal times; and as each doomed couple, looking, oh, so plump and juicy! fell from her reluctant hands, a shout from the street completed the anguish of the girls, for it told them that their feast was being exulted over by the little Irish children, who were their sworn foes. This—this was too much; all flashed indignant or appealing glances at the inexorable Davis, and one passionate lime-lover burst into tears.

As Amy returned from her last trip, Mr. Davis gave a portentous "hem," and said, in his most impressive manner,—

"Young ladies, you remember what I said to you a week ago. I am sorry this has happened; but I never allow my rules to be infringed, and I *never* break my word. Miss March, hold out your hand."

Amy started, and put both hands behind her, turning on him an imploring look, which pleaded for her better than the words she could not utter. She was rather a favorite with "old Davis," as, of course, he was called, and it's my private belief that he *would* have broken his word if the indignation of one irrepressible young lady had not found vent in a hiss. That hiss, faint as it was, irritated the irascible gentleman, and sealed the culprit's fate.

"Your hand, Miss March!" was the only answer her mute appeal received; and, too proud to cry or beseech, Amy set her teeth, threw back her head defiantly, and bore without flinching several tingling blows on her little palm. They were neither many nor heavy, but that

made no difference to her. For the first time in her life she had been
struck; and the disgrace, in her eyes, was as deep as if he had knocked
her down.

"You will now stand on the platform till recess," said Mr. Davis, resolved to do the thing thoroughly, since he had begun.

That was dreadful; it would have been bad enough to go to her seat
and see the pitying faces of her friends, or the satisfied ones of her few
enemies; but to face the whole school, with that shame fresh upon
her, seemed impossible, and for a second she felt as if she could only
drop down where she stood, and break her heart with crying. A bitter
sense of wrong, and the thought of Jenny Snow, helped her to bear it;
and, taking the ignominious place, she fixed her eyes on the stove-
funnel above what now seemed a sea of faces, and stood there so motionless and white, that the girls found it very hard to study, with that
pathetic little figure before them.

During the fifteen minutes that followed, the proud and sensitive
little girl suffered a shame and pain which she never forgot. To others
it might seem a ludicrous or trivial affair, but to her it was a hard experience; for during the twelve years of her life she had been governed
by love alone, and a blow of that sort had never touched her before.
The smart of her hand, and the ache of her heart, were forgotten in
the sting of the thought,—

"I shall have to tell at home, and they will be so disappointed in
me!"

The fifteen minutes seemed an hour; but they came to an end at last,
and the word "recess!" had never seemed so welcome to her before.

"You can go, Miss March," said Mr. Davis, looking, as he felt, uncomfortable.

He did not soon forget the reproachful look Amy gave him, as she
went, without a word to any one, straight into the anteroom, snatched
her things, and left the place "forever," as she passionately declared to
herself. She was in a sad state when she got home; and when the older
girls arrived, some time later, an indignation meeting was held at once.
Mrs. March did not say much, but looked disturbed, and comforted
her afflicted little daughter in her tenderest manner. Meg bathed the
insulted hand with glycerine and tears; Beth felt that even her beloved
kittens would fail as a balm for griefs like this, and Jo wrathfully proposed that Mr. Davis be arrested without delay, while Hannah shook
her fist at the "villain," and pounded potatoes for dinner as if she had
him under her pestle.

No notice was taken of Amy's flight, except by her mates; but the
sharp-eyed demoiselles discovered that Mr. Davis was quite benignant
in the afternoon, also unusually nervous. Just before school closed, Jo
appeared, wearing a grim expression, as she stalked up to the desk,
and delivered a letter from her mother; then collected Amy's property,
and departed, carefully scraping the mud from her boots on the door-
mat, as if she shook the dust of the place off her feet.[8]

8. Cf. Matthew 10.14, Mark 6.11, and Luke 9.5.

"Yes, you can have a vacation from school, but I want you to study a little every day, with Beth," said Mrs. March, that evening. "I don't approve of corporal punishment, especially for girls. I dislike Mr. Davis' manner of teaching, and don't think the girls you associate with are doing you any good, so I shall ask your father's advice before I send you anywhere else."

"That's good! I wish all the girls would leave, and spoil his old school. It's perfectly maddening to think of those lovely limes," sighed Amy, with the air of a martyr.

"I am not sorry you lost them, for you broke the rules, and deserved some punishment for disobedience," was the severe reply, which rather disappointed the young lady, who expected nothing but sympathy.

"Do you mean you are glad I was disgraced before the whole school?" cried Amy.

"I should not have chosen that way of mending a fault," replied her mother; "but I'm not sure that it won't do you more good than a milder method. You are getting to be altogether too conceited and important, my dear, and it is quite time you set about correcting it. You have a good many little gifts and virtues, but there is no need of parading them, for conceit spoils the finest genius. There is not much danger that real talent or goodness will be overlooked long; even if it is, the consciousness of possessing and using it well should satisfy one, and the great charm of all power is modesty."

"So it is," cried Laurie, who was playing chess in a corner with Jo. "I knew a girl, once, who had a really remarkable talent for music, and she didn't know it; never guessed what sweet little things she composed when she was alone, and wouldn't have believed it if any one had told her."

"I wish I'd known that nice girl, maybe she would have helped me, I'm so stupid," said Beth, who stood beside him, listening eagerly.

"You do know her, and she helps you better than any one else could," answered Laurie, looking at her with such mischievous meaning in his merry black eyes, that Beth suddenly turned very red, and hid her face in the sofa-cushion, quite overcome by such an unexpected discovery.

Jo let Laurie win the game, to pay for that praise of her Beth, who could not be prevailed upon to play for them after her compliment. So Laurie did his best, and sung delightfully, being in a particularly lively humor, for to the Marches he seldom showed the moody side of his character. When he was gone, Amy, who had been pensive all the evening, said, suddenly, as if busy over some new idea,—

"Is Laurie an accomplished boy?"

"Yes; he has had an excellent education, and has much talent; he will make a fine man, if not spoilt by petting," replied her mother.

"And he isn't conceited, is he?" asked Amy.

"Not in the least; that is why he is so charming, and we all like him so much."

"I see; it's nice to have accomplishments, and be elegant; but not to show off, or get perked up," said Amy, thoughtfully.

"These things are always seen and felt in a person's manner and conversation, if modestly used; but it is not necessary to display them," said Mrs. March.

"Any more than it's proper to wear all your bonnets, and gowns, and ribbons, at once, that folks may know you've got 'em," added Jo; and the lecture ended in a laugh.

CHAPTER VIII.

JO MEETS APOLLYON.[9]

GIRLS, where are you going?" asked Amy, coming into their room one Saturday afternoon, and finding them getting ready to go out, with an air of secrecy which excited her curiosity.

"Never mind; little girls shouldn't ask questions," returned Jo, sharply.

Now if there *is* anything mortifying to our feelings, when we are young, it is to be told that; and to be bidden to "run away, dear," is still more trying to us. Amy bridled up at this insult, and determined to find out the secret, if she teased for an hour. Turning to Meg, who never refused her anything very long, she said, coaxingly, "Do tell me! I should think you might let me go, too; for Beth is fussing over her dolls, and I haven't got anything to do, and am *so* lonely."

"I can't, dear, because you aren't invited," began Meg; but Jo broke in impatiently, "Now, Meg, be quiet, or you will spoil it all. You can't go, Amy; so don't be a baby, and whine about it."

"You are going somewhere with Laurie, I know you are; you were whispering and laughing together, on the sofa, last night, and you stopped when I came in. Aren't you going with him?"

"Yes, we are; now do be still, and stop bothering."

Amy held her tongue, but used her eyes, and saw Meg slip a fan into her pocket.

"I know! I know! you're going to the theatre to see the 'Seven Castles!' "[1] she cried; adding, resolutely, "and I *shall* go, for mother said I might see it; and I've got my rag-money, and it was mean not to tell me in time."

"Just listen to me a minute, and be a good child," said Meg, soothingly. "Mother doesn't wish you to go this week, because your eyes are not well enough yet to bear the light of this fairy piece. Next week you can go with Beth and Hannah, and have a nice time."

"I don't like that half as well as going with you and Laurie. Please let me; I've been sick with this cold so long, and shut up, I'm dying for some fun. Do, Meg! I'll be ever so good," pleaded Amy, looking as pathetic as she could.

9. See p. 17, n. 1 (part 1, chap. 1).
1. Although no play called *The Seven Castles of the Diamond Lake* appears to exist (see next page, where this full title is used), the title may allude to Edward Stirling's *The Seven Castles of the Passions: A Drama of Enchantment in Two Acts* (1844).

"Suppose we take her. I don't believe mother would mind, if we bundle her up well," began Meg.

"If *she* goes *I* shan't; and if I don't, Laurie won't like it; and it will be very rude, after he invited only us, to go and drag in Amy. I should think she'd hate to poke herself where she isn't wanted," said Jo, crossly, for she disliked the trouble of overseeing a fidgety child, when she wanted to enjoy herself.

Her tone and manner angered Amy, who began to put her boots on, saying, in her most aggravating way, "I *shall* go; Meg says I may; and if I pay for myself, Laurie hasn't anything to do with it."

"You can't sit with us, for our seats are reserved, and you mustn't sit alone; so Laurie will give you his place, and that will spoil our pleasure; or he'll get another seat for you, and that isn't proper, when you weren't asked. You shan't stir a step; so you may just stay where you are," scolded Jo, crosser than ever, having just pricked her finger in her hurry.

Sitting on the floor, with one boot on, Amy began to cry, and Meg to reason with her, when Laurie called from below, and the two girls hurried down, leaving their sister wailing; for now and then she forgot her grown-up ways, and acted like a spoilt child. Just as the party was setting out, Amy called over the banisters, in a threatening tone, "You'll be sorry for this, Jo March! see if you ain't."

"Fiddlesticks!" returned Jo, slamming the door.

They had a charming time, for "The Seven Castles of the Diamond Lake" were as brilliant and wonderful as heart could wish. But, in spite of the comical red imps, sparkling elves, and gorgeous princes and princesses, Jo's pleasure had a drop of bitterness in it; the fairy queen's yellow curls reminded her of Amy; and between the acts she amused herself with wondering what her sister would do to make her "sorry for it." She and Amy had had many lively skirmishes in the course of their lives, for both had quick tempers, and were apt to be violent when fairly roused. Amy teased Jo, and Jo irritated Amy, and semi-occasional explosions occurred, of which both were much ashamed afterward. Although the oldest, Jo had the least self-control, and had hard times trying to curb the fiery spirit which was continually getting her into trouble; her anger never lasted long, and, having humbly confessed her fault, she sincerely repented, and tried to do better. Her sisters used to say, that they rather liked to get Jo into a fury, because she was such an angel afterward. Poor Jo tried desperately to be good, but her bosom enemy was always ready to flame up and defeat her; and it took years of patient effort to subdue it.

When they got home, they found Amy reading in the parlor. She assumed an injured air as they came in; never lifted her eyes from her book, or asked a single question. Perhaps curiosity might have conquered resentment, if Beth had not been there to inquire, and receive a glowing description of the play. On going up to put away her best hat, Jo's first look was toward the bureau; for, in their last quarrel, Amy had soothed her feelings by turning Jo's top drawer upside down, on the floor. Everything was in its place, however; and after a hasty glance into her various closets, bags and boxes, Jo decided that Amy had forgiven and forgotten her wrongs.

There Jo was mistaken; for next day she made a discovery which produced a tempest. Meg, Beth and Amy were sitting together, late in the afternoon, when Jo burst into the room, looking excited, and demanding, breathlessly, "Has any one taken my story?"

Meg and Beth said "No," at once, and looked surprised; Amy poked the fire, and said nothing. Jo saw her color rise, and was down upon her in a minute.

"Amy, you've got it!"

"No, I haven't."

"You know where it is, then!"

"No, I don't."

"That's a fib!" cried Jo, taking her by the shoulders, and looking fierce enough to frighten a much braver child than Amy.

"It isn't. I haven't got it, don't know where it is now, and don't care."

"You know something about it, and you'd better tell at once, or I'll make you," and Jo gave her a slight shake.

"Scold as much as you like, you'll never get your silly old story again," cried Amy, getting excited in her turn.

"Why not?"

"I burnt it up."

"What! my little book I was so fond of, and worked over, and meant to finish before father got home? Have you really burnt it?" said Jo, turning very pale, while her eyes kindled and her hands clutched Amy nervously.

"Yes, I did! I told you I'd make you pay for being so cross yesterday, and I have, so—"

Amy got no farther, for Jo's hot temper mastered her, and she shook Amy till her teeth chattered in her head; crying, in a passion of grief and anger,—

"You wicked, wicked girl! I never can write it again, and I'll never forgive you as long as I live."

Meg flew to rescue Amy, and Beth to pacify Jo, but Jo was quite beside herself; and, with a parting box on her sister's ear, she rushed out of the room up to the old sofa in the garret, and finished her fight alone.

The storm cleared up below, for Mrs. March came home, and, having heard the story, soon brought Amy to a sense of the wrong she had done her sister. Jo's book was the pride of her heart, and was regarded by her family as a literary sprout of great promise. It was only half a dozen little fairy tales, but Jo had worked over them patiently, putting her whole heart into her work, hoping to make something good enough to print. She had just copied them with great care, and had destroyed the old manuscript, so that Amy's bonfire had consumed the loving work of several years. It seemed a small loss to others, but to Jo it was a dreadful calamity, and she felt that it never could be made up to her. Beth mourned as for a departed kitten, and Meg refused to defend her pet; Mrs. March looked grave and grieved, and Amy felt that no one would love her till she had asked pardon for the act which she now regretted more than any of them.

When the tea-bell rung, Jo appeared, looking so grim and unapproachable, that it took all Amy's courage to say, meekly,—

"Please forgive me, Jo; I'm very, very sorry."

"I never shall forgive you," was Jo's stern answer, and, from that moment, she ignored Amy entirely.

No one spoke of the great trouble,—not even Mrs. March,—for all had learned by experience that when Jo was in that mood words were wasted; and the wisest course was to wait till some little accident, or her own generous nature, softened Jo's resentment, and healed the breach. It was not a happy evening; for, though they sewed as usual, while their mother read aloud from Bremer, Scott, or Edgeworth,[2] something was wanting, and the sweet home-peace was disturbed. They felt this most when singing-time came; for Beth could only play, Jo stood dumb as a stone, and Amy broke down, so Meg and mother sung alone. But, in spite of their efforts to be as cheery as larks, the flute-like voices did not seem to chord as well as usual, and all felt out of tune.

As Jo received her good-night kiss, Mrs. March whispered, gently,—

"My dear, don't let the sun go down upon your anger; forgive each other, help each other, and begin again to-morrow."

Jo wanted to lay her head down on that motherly bosom, and cry her grief and anger all away; but tears were an unmanly weakness, and she felt so deeply injured that she really *couldn't* quite forgive yet. So she winked hard, shook her head, and said, gruffly, because Amy was listening,—

"It was an abominable thing, and she don't deserve to be forgiven."

With that she marched off to bed, and there was no merry or confidential gossip that night.

Amy was much offended that her overtures of peace had been repulsed, and began to wish she had not humbled herself, to feel more injured than ever, and to plume herself on her superior virtue in a way which was particularly exasperating. Jo still looked like a thundercloud, and nothing went well all day. It was bitter cold in the morning; she dropped her precious turn-over in the gutter, Aunt March had an attack of fidgets, Meg was pensive, Beth *would* look grieved and wistful when she got home, and Amy kept making remarks about people who were always talking about being good, and yet wouldn't try, when other people set them a virtuous example.

"Everybody is so hateful, I'll ask Laurie to go skating. He is always kind and jolly, and will put me to rights, I know," said Jo to herself, and off she went.

Amy heard the clash of skates, and looked out with an impatient exclamation,—

2. Three popular novelists from the first half of the nineteenth century. The Swedish author Fredrika Bremer (1801–1865) wrote domestic and feminist novels. Sir Walter Scott (1771–1832) is perhaps the most famous of all Scottish writers. A champion of education for women, Maria Edgeworth (1767–1849) was an Irish novelist who wrote didactic stories for children and tales of Irish life.

"There! she promised I should go next time, for this is the last ice we shall have. But it's no use to ask such a cross patch to take me."

"Don't say that; you *were* very naughty, and it *is* hard to forgive the loss of her precious little book; but I think she might do it now, and I guess she will, if you try her at the right minute," said Meg. "Go after them; don't say anything till Jo has got good-natured with Laurie, then take a quiet minute, and just kiss her, or do some kind thing, and I'm sure she'll be friends again, with all her heart."

"I'll try," said Amy, for the advice suited her; and, after a flurry to get ready, she ran after the friends, who were just disappearing over the hill.

It was not far to the river, but both were ready before Amy reached them. Jo saw her coming, and turned her back; Laurie did not see, for he was carefully skating along the shore, sounding the ice, for a warm spell had preceded the cold snap.

"I'll go on to the first bend, and see if it's all right, before we begin to race," Amy heard him say, as he shot away, looking like a young Russian, in his fur-trimmed coat and cap.

Jo heard Amy panting after her run, stamping her feet, and blowing her fingers, as she tried to put her skates on; but Jo never turned, and went slowly zigzagging down the river, taking a bitter, unhappy sort of satisfaction in her sister's troubles. She had cherished her anger till it grew strong, and took possession of her, as evil thoughts and feelings always do, unless cast out at once. As Laurie turned the bend, he shouted back,—

"Keep near the shore; it isn't safe in the middle."

Jo heard, but Amy was just struggling to her feet, and did not catch a word. Jo glanced over her shoulder, and the little demon she was harboring said in her ear,—

"No matter whether she heard or not, let her take care of herself."

Laurie had vanished round the bend; Jo was just at the turn, and Amy, far behind, striking out toward the smoother ice in the middle of the river. For a minute Jo stood still, with a strange feeling at her heart; then she resolved to go on, but something held and turned her round, just in time to see Amy throw up her hands and go down, with the sudden crash of rotten ice, the splash of water, and a cry that made Jo's heart stand still with fear. She tried to call Laurie, but her voice was gone; she tried to rush forward, but her feet seemed to have no strength in them; and, for a second, she could only stand motionless, staring, with a terror-stricken face, at the little blue hood above the black water. Something rushed swiftly by her, and Laurie's voice cried out,—

"Bring a rail; quick, quick!"

How she did it, she never knew; but for the next few minutes she worked as if possessed, blindly obeying Laurie, who was quite self-possessed; and, lying flat, held Amy up by his arm and hockey,[3] till Jo dragged a rail from the fence, and together they got the child out, more frightened than hurt.

3. Hockey stick.

"Keep near the shore; it isn't safe in the middle." Jo heard, but Amy was just struggling to her feet, and did not catch a word.—PAGE 66.

"Now then, we must walk her home as fast as we can; pile our things on her, while I get off these confounded skates," cried Laurie, wrapping his coat round Amy, and tugging away at the straps, which never seemed so intricate before.

Shivering, dripping, and crying, they got Amy home; and, after an exciting time of it, she fell asleep, rolled in blankets, before a hot fire. During the bustle Jo had scarcely spoken; but flown about, looking pale and wild, with her things half off, her dress torn, and her hands cut and bruised by ice and rails, and refractory buckles. When Amy was comfortably asleep, the house quiet, and Mrs. March sitting by the bed, she called Jo to her, and began to bind up the hurt hands.

"Are you sure she is safe?" whispered Jo, looking remorsefully at the golden head, which might have been swept away from her sight forever, under the treacherous ice.

"Quite safe, dear; she is not hurt, and won't even take cold, I think, you were so sensible in covering and getting her home quickly," replied her mother, cheerfully.

"Laurie did it all; I only let her go. Mother, if she *should* die, it would be my fault;" and Jo dropped down beside the bed, in a passion of penitent tears, telling all that had happened, bitterly condemning her hardness of heart, and sobbing out her gratitude for being spared the heavy punishment which might have come upon her.

"It's my dreadful temper! I try to cure it; I think I have, and then it breaks out worse than ever. Oh, mother! what shall I do! what shall I do?" cried poor Jo, in despair.

"Watch and pray, dear; never get tired of trying; and never think it is impossible to conquer your fault," said Mrs. March, drawing the blowzy head to her shoulder, and kissing the wet cheek so tenderly, that Jo cried harder than ever.

"You don't know; you can't guess how bad it is! It seems as if I could do anything when I'm in a passion; I get so savage, I could hurt any one, and enjoy it. I'm afraid I *shall* do something dreadful some day, and spoil my life, and make everybody hate me. Oh, mother! help me, do help me!"

"I will, my child; I will. Don't cry so bitterly, but remember this day, and resolve, with all your soul, that you will never know another like it. Jo, dear, we all have our temptations, some far greater than yours, and it often takes us all our lives to conquer them. You think your temper is the worst in the world; but mine used to be just like it."

"Yours, mother? Why, you are never angry!" and, for the moment, Jo forgot remorse in surprise.

"I've been trying to cure it for forty years, and have only succeeded in controlling it. I am angry nearly every day of my life, Jo; but I have learned not to show it; and I still hope to learn not to feel it, though it may take me another forty years to do so."

The patience and the humility of the face she loved so well, was a better lesson to Jo than the wisest lecture, the sharpest reproof. She felt comforted at once by the sympathy and confidence given her; the knowledge that her mother had a fault like hers, and tried to mend it, made her own easier to bear, and strengthened her resolution to cure it; though forty years seemed rather a long time to watch and pray, to a girl of fifteen.

"Mother, are you angry when you fold your lips tight together, and go out of the room sometimes, when Aunt March scolds, or people worry you?" asked Jo, feeling nearer and dearer to her mother than ever before.

"Yes, I've learned to check the hasty words that rise to my lips; and when I feel that they mean to break out against my will, I just go away a minute, and give myself a little shake, for being so weak and wicked," answered Mrs. March, with a sigh and a smile, as she smoothed and fastened up Jo's dishevelled hair.

"How did you learn to keep still? That is what troubles me—for the sharp words fly out before I know what I'm about; and the more I say the worse I get, till it's a pleasure to hurt people's feelings, and say dreadful things. Tell me how you do it, Marmee dear."

"My good mother used to help me—"

"As you do us—" interrupted Jo, with a grateful kiss.

"But I lost her when I was a little older than you are, and for years had to struggle on alone, for I was too proud to confess my weakness to any one else. I had a hard time, Jo, and shed a good many bitter tears over my failures; for, in spite of my efforts, I never seemed to get on. Then your father came, and I was so happy that I found it easy to be good. But by and by, when I had four little daughters round me, and we were poor, then the old trouble began again; for I am not patient by nature, and it tried me very much to see my children wanting anything."

"Poor mother! what helped you then?"

"Your father, Jo. He never loses patience,—never doubts or complains,—but always hopes, and works, and waits so cheerfully, that one is ashamed to do otherwise before him. He helped and comforted me, and showed me that I must try to practise all the virtues I would have my little girls possess, for I was their example. It was easier to try for your sakes than for my own; a startled or surprised look from one of you, when I spoke sharply, rebuked me more than any words could have done; and the love, respect, and confidence of my children was the sweetest reward I could receive for my efforts to be the woman I would have them copy."

"Oh, mother! if I'm ever half as good as you, I shall be satisfied," cried Jo, much touched.

"I hope you will be a great deal better, dear; but you must keep watch over your 'bosom enemy,' as father calls it, or it may sadden, if not spoil your life. You have had a warning; remember it, and try with heart and soul to master this quick temper, before it brings you greater sorrow and regret than you have known today."

"I will try, mother; I truly will. But you must help me, remind me, and keep me from flying out. I used to see father sometimes put his finger on his lips, and look at you with a very kind, but sober face; and you always folded your lips tight, or went away; was he reminding you then?" asked Jo, softly.

"Yes; I asked him to help me so, and he never forgot it, but saved me from many a sharp word by that little gesture and kind look."

Jo saw that her mother's eyes filled, and her lips trembled, as she spoke; and, fearing that she had said too much, she whispered anxiously, "Was it wrong to watch you, and to speak of it? I didn't mean to be rude, but it's so comfortable to say all I think to you, and feel so safe and happy here."

"My Jo, you may say anything to your mother, for it is my greatest happiness and pride to feel that my girls confide in me, and know how much I love them."

"I thought I'd grieved you."

"No, dear; but speaking of father reminded me how much I miss him, how much I owe him, and how faithfully I should watch and work to keep his little daughters safe and good for him."

"Yet you told him to go, mother, and didn't cry when he went, and never complain now, or seem as if you needed any help," said Jo, wondering.

"I gave my best to the country I love, and kept my tears till he was gone. Why should I complain, when we both have merely done our duty, and will surely be the happier for it in the end? If I don't seem to need help, it is because I have a better friend, even than father, to comfort and sustain me. My child, the troubles and temptations of your life are beginning, and may be many; but you can overcome and outlive them all, if you learn to feel the strength and tenderness of your Heavenly Father as you do that of your earthly one. The more you love and trust Him, the nearer you will feel to Him, and the less you will depend on human power and wisdom. His love and care never tire or change, can never be taken from you, but may become the source of life-long peace, happiness, and strength. Believe this heartily, and go to God with all your little cares, and hopes, and sins, and sorrows, as freely and confidingly as you come to your mother."

Jo's only answer was to hold her mother close, and, in the silence which followed, the sincerest prayer she had ever prayed left her heart, without words; for in that sad, yet happy hour, she had learned not only the bitterness of remorse and despair, but the sweetness of self-denial and self-control; and, led by her mother's hand, she had drawn nearer to the Friend who welcomes every child with a love stronger than that of any father, tenderer than that of any mother.

Amy stirred, and sighed in her sleep; and, as if eager to begin at once to mend her fault, Jo looked up with an expression on her face which it had never worn before.

"I let the sun go down on my anger; I wouldn't forgive her, and to-day, if it hadn't been for Laurie, it might have been too late! How could I be so wicked?" said Jo, half aloud, as she leaned over her sister, softly stroking the wet hair scattered on the pillow.

As if she heard, Amy opened her eyes, and held out her arms, with a smile that went straight to Jo's heart. Neither said a word, but they hugged one another close, in spite of the blankets, and everything was forgiven and forgotten in one hearty kiss.

CHAPTER IX.

MEG GOES TO VANITY FAIR.

I DO think it was the most fortunate thing in the world, that those children should have the measles just now," said Meg, one April day, as she stood packing the "go abroady" trunk in her room, surrounded by her sisters.

"And so nice of Annie Moffat, not to forget her promise. A whole fortnight of fun will be regularly splendid," replied Jo, looking like a windmill, as she folded skirts with her long arms.

"And such lovely weather; I'm so glad of that," added Beth, tidily sorting neck and hair ribbons in her best box, lent for the great occasion.

"I wish I was going to have a fine time, and wear all these nice things," said Amy, with her mouth full of pins, as she artistically replenished her sister's cushion.

"I wish you were all going; but, as you can't, I shall keep my adventures to tell you when I come back. I'm sure it's the least I can do, when you have been so kind, lending me things, and helping me get ready," said Meg, glancing round the room at the very simple outfit, which seemed nearly perfect in their eyes.

"What did mother give you out of the treasure-box?" asked Amy, who had not been present at the opening of a certain cedar chest, in which Mrs. March kept a few relics of past splendor, as gifts for her girls when the proper time came.

"A pair of silk stockings, that pretty carved fan, and a lovely blue sash. I wanted the violet silk; but there isn't time to make it over, so I must be contented with my old tarlatan."

"It will look nicely over my new muslin skirt, and the sash will set it off beautifully. I wish I hadn't smashed my coral bracelet, for you might have had it," said Jo, who loved to give and lend, but whose possessions were usually too dilapidated to be of much use.

"There is a lovely old-fashioned pearl set in the treasure-box; but mother said real flowers were the prettiest ornament for a young girl, and Laurie promised to send me all I want," replied Meg. "Now, let me see; there's my new gray walking-suit,—just curl up the feather in my hat, Beth,—then my poplin, for Sunday, and the small party,—it looks heavy for spring, don't it? the violet silk would be so nice; oh, dear!"

"Never mind; you've got the tarlatan for the big party, and you always look like an angel in white," said Amy, brooding over the little store of finery in which her soul delighted.

"It isn't low-necked, and it don't sweep enough, but it will have to do. My blue house-dress looks so well, turned and freshly trimmed,

that I feel as if I'd got a new one. My silk sacque isn't a bit the fashion
and my bonnet don't look like Sallie's; I didn't like to say anything, but
I was dreadfully disappointed in my umbrella. I told mother black,
with a white handle, but she forgot, and bought a green one, with an
ugly yellowish handle. It's strong and neat, so I ought not to complain,
but I know I shall feel ashamed of it beside Annie's silk one, with a
gold top," sighed Meg, surveying the little umbrella with great disfa-
vor.

"Change it," advised Jo.

"I won't be so silly, or hurt Marmee's feelings, when she took so
much pains to get my things. It's nonsensical notion of mine, and I'm
not going to give up to it. My silk stockings and two pairs of spandy
gloves are my comfort. You are a dear, to lend me yours, Jo; I feel so
rich, and sort of elegant, with two new pairs, and the old ones cleaned
up for common;" and Meg took a refreshing peep at her glove-box.

"Annie Moffat has blue and pink bows on her night-caps; would you
put some on mine?" she asked, as Beth brought up a pile of snowy
muslins, fresh from Hannah's hands.

"No, I wouldn't; for the smart caps won't match the plain gowns,
without any trimming on them. Poor folks shouldn't rig," said Jo, decidedly.

"I wonder if I shall *ever* be happy enough to have real lace on my
clothes, and bows on my caps?" said Meg, impatiently.

"You said the other day that you'd be perfectly happy if you could
only go to Annie Moffat's," observed Beth, in her quiet way.

"So I did! Well, I *am* happy, and I *won't* fret; but it does seem as if
the more one gets the more one wants, don't it? There, now, the trays
are ready, and everything in but my ball-dress, which I shall leave for
mother," said Meg, cheering up, as she glanced from the half-filled
trunk to the many-times pressed and mended white tarlatan, which
she called her "ball-dress," with an important air.

The next day was fine, and Meg departed, in style, for a fortnight of
novelty and pleasure. Mrs. March had consented to the visit rather reluctantly, fearing that Margaret would come back more discontented
than she went. But she had begged so hard, and Sallie had promised
to take good care of her, and a little pleasure seemed so delightful after a winter of hard work, that the mother yielded, and the daughter
went to take her first taste of fashionable life.

The Moffats *were* very fashionable, and simple Meg was rather
daunted, at first, by the splendor of the house, and the elegance of its
occupants. But they were kindly people, in spite of the frivolous life
they led, and soon put their guest at her ease. Perhaps Meg felt, without understanding why, that they were not particularly cultivated or
intelligent people, and that all their gilding could not quite conceal
the ordinary material of which they were made. It certainly was agreeable to fare sumptuously, drive in a fine carriage, wear her best frock
every day, and do nothing but enjoy herself. It suited her exactly; and
soon she began to imitate the manners and conversation of those
about her; to put on little airs and graces, use French phrases, crimp

her hair, take in her dresses, and talk about the fashions, as well as she could. The more she saw of Annie Moffat's pretty things, the more she envied her, and sighed to be rich. Home now looked bare and dismal as she thought of it, work grew harder than ever, and she felt that she was a very destitute and much injured girl, in spite of the new gloves and silk stockings.

She had not much time for repining, however, for the three young girls were busily employed in "having a good time." They shopped, walked, rode, and called all day; went to theatres and operas, or frolicked at home in the evening; for Annie had many friends, and knew how to entertain them. Her older sisters were very fine young ladies, and one was engaged, which was extremely interesting and romantic, Meg thought. Mr. Moffat was a fat, jolly old gentleman, who knew her father; and Mrs. Moffat, a fat, jolly old lady, who took as great a fancy to Meg as her daughter had done. Every one petted her; and "Daisy,"[4] as they called her, was in a fair way to have her head turned.

When the evening for the "small party" came, she found that the poplin wouldn't do at all, for the other girls were putting on thin dresses, and making themselves very fine indeed; so out came the tarlatan, looking older, limper, and shabbier than ever, beside Sallie's crisp new one. Meg saw the girls glance at it, and then at one another, and her cheeks began to burn; for, with all her gentleness, she was very proud. No one said a word about it, but Sallie offered to do her hair, and Annie to tie her sash, and Belle, the engaged sister, praised her white arms; but, in their kindness, Meg saw only pity for her poverty, and her heart felt very heavy as she stood by herself, while the others laughed and chattered, prinked, and flew about like gauzy butterflies. The hard, bitter feeling was getting pretty bad, when the maid brought in a box of flowers. Before she could speak, Annie had the cover off, and all were exclaiming at the lovely roses, heath, and ferns within.

"It's for Belle, of course; George always sends her some, but these are altogether ravishing," cried Annie, with a great sniff.

"They are for Miss March, the man said. And here's a note," put in the maid, holding it to Meg.

"What fun! Who are they from? Didn't know you had a lover," cried the girls, fluttering about Meg in a high state of curiosity and surprise.

"The note is from mother, and the flowers from Laurie," said Meg, simply, yet much gratified that he had not forgotten her.

"Oh, indeed!" said Annie, with a funny look, as Meg slipped the note into her pocket, as a sort of talisman against envy, vanity, and false pride; for the few loving words had done her good, and the flowers cheered her up by their beauty.

Feeling almost happy again, she laid by a few ferns and roses for herself, and quickly made up the rest in dainty bouquets for the breasts, hair, or skirts of her friends, offering them so prettily, that Clara, the elder sister, told her she was "the sweetest little thing she

4. Familiar form of the name Margaret.

ever saw;" and they looked quite charmed with her small attention. Somehow the kind act finished her despondency; and, when all the rest went to show themselves to Mrs. Moffat, she saw a happy, bright-eyed face in the mirror, as she laid her ferns against her rippling hair, and fastened the roses in the dress that didn't strike her as so *very* shabby now.

She enjoyed herself very much that evening, for she danced to her heart's content; every one was very kind, and she had three compli-ments. Annie made her sing, and some one said she had a remarkably fine voice; Major Lincoln asked who "the fresh little girl, with the beautiful eyes, was;" and Mr. Moffat insisted on dancing with her, be-cause she "didn't dawdle, but had some spring in her," as he gracefully expressed it. So, altogether, she had a very nice time, till she over-heard a bit of a conversation, which disturbed her extremely. She was sitting just inside the conservatory, waiting for her partner to bring her an ice, when she heard a voice ask, on the other side of the flowery wall,—

"How old is he?"

"Sixteen or seventeen, I should say," replied another voice.

"It would be a grand thing for one of those girls, wouldn't it? Sallie says they are very intimate now, and the old man quite dotes on them."

"Mrs. M. has laid her plans, I dare say, and will play her cards well, early as it is. The girl evidently doesn't think of it yet," said Mrs. Mof-fat.

"She told that fib about her mamma, as if she did know, and colored up when the flowers came, quite prettily. Poor thing! she'd be so nice if she was only got up in style. Do you think she'd be offended if we of-fered to lend her a dress for Thursday?" asked another voice.

"She's proud, but I don't believe she'd mind, for that dowdy tarlatan is all she has got. She may tear it to-night, and that will be a good ex-cuse for offering a decent one."

"We'll see; I shall ask that Laurence, as a compliment to her, and we'll have fun about it afterward."

Here Meg's partner appeared, to find her looking much flushed, and rather agitated. She was proud, and her pride was useful just then, for it helped her hide her mortification, anger, and disgust, at what she had just heard; for, innocent and unsuspicious as she was, she could not help understanding the gossip of her friends. She tried to forget it, but could not, and kept repeating to herself, "Mrs. M. has her plans," "that fib about her mamma," and "dowdy tarlatan," till she was ready to cry, and rush home to tell her troubles, and ask for advice. As that was impossible, she did her best to seem gay; and, being rather ex-cited, she succeeded so well, that no one dreamed what an effort she was making. She was very glad when it was all over, and she was quiet in her bed, where she could think and wonder and fume till her head ached, and her hot cheeks were cooled by a few natural tears. Those foolish, yet well-meant words, had opened a new world to Meg, and much disturbed the peace of the old one, in which, till now, she had lived as happily as a child. Her innocent friendship with Laurie was spoilt by the silly speeches she had overheard; her faith in her mother was a little shaken by the worldly plans attributed to her by Mrs. Moffat, who judged others by herself; and the sensible resolution to be contented with the simple wardrobe which suited a poor man's daughter was weakened by the unnecessary pity of girls, who thought a shabby dress one of the greatest calamities under heaven.

Poor Meg had a restless night, and got up heavy-eyed, unhappy, half resentful toward her friends, and half ashamed of herself for not speaking out frankly, and setting everything right. Everybody dawdled that morning, and it was noon before the girls found energy enough even to take up their worsted work. Something in the manner of her friends struck Meg at once; they treated her with more respect, she thought; took quite a tender interest in what she said, and looked at her with eyes that plainly betrayed curiosity. All this surprised and flattered her, though she did not understand it till Miss Belle looked up from her writing, and said, with a sentimental air,—

"Daisy, dear, I've sent an invitation to your friend, Mr. Laurence, for Thursday. We should like to know him, and it's only a proper compliment to you."

Meg colored, but a mischievous fancy to tease the girls made her reply, demurely,—

"You are very kind, but I'm afraid he won't come."

"Why not, cherie?" asked Miss Belle.

"He's too old."

"My child, what do you mean? What is his age, I beg to know!" cried Miss Clara.

"Nearly seventy, I believe," answered Meg, counting stitches, to hide the merriment in her eyes.

"You sly creature! of course, we meant the young man," exclaimed Miss Belle, laughing.

"There isn't any; Laurie is only a little boy," and Meg laughed also at the queer look which the sisters exchanged, as she thus described her supposed lover.

"About your age," Nan said.

"Nearer my sister Jo's; I am seventeen in August," returned Meg, tossing her head.

"It's very nice of him to send you flowers, isn't it?" said Annie, looking wise about nothing.

"Yes, he often does, to all of us; for their house is full, and we are so fond of them. My mother and old Mr. Laurence are friends, you know, so it is quite natural that we children should play together;" and Meg hoped they would say no more.

"It's evident Daisy isn't out yet," said Miss Clara to Belle, with a nod.

"Quite a pastoral state of innocence all round," returned Miss Belle, with a shrug.

"I'm going out to get some little matters for my girls; can I do anything for you, young ladies?" asked Mrs. Moffat, lumbering in, like an elephant, in silk and lace.

"No, thank you, ma'am," replied Sallie; "I've got my new pink silk for Thursday, and don't want a thing."

"Nor I—" began Meg, but stopped, because it occurred to her that she *did* want several things, and could not have them.

"What shall you wear?" asked Sallie.

"My old white one again, if I can mend it fit to be seen; it got sadly torn last night," said Meg, trying to speak quite easily, but feeling very uncomfortable.

"Why don't you send home for another?" said Sallie, who was not an observing young lady.

"I haven't got any other." It cost Meg an effort to say that, but Sallie did not see it, and exclaimed, in amiable surprise,—

"Only that? how funny—." She did not finish her speech, for Belle shook her head at her, and broke in, saying, kindly,—

"Not at all; where is the use of having a lot of dresses when she isn't out? There's no need of sending home, Daisy, even if you had a dozen, for I've got a sweet blue silk laid away, which I've outgrown, and you shall wear it, to please me; won't you, dear?"

"You are very kind, but I don't mind my old dress, if you don't; it does well enough for a little girl like me," said Meg.

"Now do let me please myself by dressing you up in style. I admire to do it, and you'd be a regular little beauty, with a touch here and there. I shan't let any one see you till you are done, and then we'll burst upon them like Cinderella and her godmother, going to the ball," said Belle, in her persuasive tone.

Meg couldn't refuse the offer so kindly made, for a desire to see if she would be "a little beauty" after touching up caused her to accept, and forget all her former uncomfortable feelings towards the Moffats.

On the Thursday evening, Belle shut herself up with her maid; and, between them, they turned Meg into a fine lady. They crimped and curled her hair, they polished her neck and arms with some fragrant powder, touched her lips with coralline salve, to make them redder, and Hortense would have added "a *soupçon* of rouge,"[5] if Meg had not rebelled. They laced her into a sky-blue dress, which was so tight she could hardly breathe, and so low in the neck that modest Meg blushed at herself in the mirror. A set of silver filagree was added, bracelets, necklace, brooch, and even ear-rings, for Hortense tied them on, with a bit of pink silk, which did not show. A cluster of tea rose-buds at the bosom, and a *ruche*, reconciled Meg to the display of her pretty white shoulders, and a pair of high-heeled blue silk boots satisfied the last wish of her heart. A laced handkerchief, a plumy fan, and a bouquet in a silver holder, finished her off; and Miss Belle surveyed her with the satisfaction of a little girl with a newly dressed doll.

"Mademoiselle is charmante, tres jolie,[6] is she not?" cried Hortense, clasping her hands in an affected rapture.

---

5. A touch or hint of rouge. Literally, *soupçon* is French for suspicion or inkling.
6. Lovely, very pretty (French).

"Come and show yourself," said Miss Belle, leading the way to the room where the others were waiting.

As Meg went rustling after, with her long skirts trailing, her earrings tinkling, her curls waving, and her heart beating, she felt as if her "fun" had really begun at last, for the mirror had plainly told her that she *was* "a little beauty." Her friends repeated the pleasing phrase enthusiastically; and, for several minutes, she stood, like the jackdaw in the fable, enjoying her borrowed plumes, while the rest chattered like a party of magpies.[7]

"While I dress, do you drill her, Nan, in the management of her skirt, and those French heels, or she will trip herself up. Put your silver butterfly in the middle of that white barbe,[8] and catch up that long curl on the left side of her head, Clara, and don't any of you disturb the charming work of my hands," said Belle, as she hurried away, looking well pleased with her success.

"I'm afraid to go down, I feel so queer and stiff, and half-dressed," said Meg to Sallie, as the bell rang, and Mrs. Moffat sent to ask the young ladies to appear at once.

"You don't look a bit like yourself, but you are very nice. I'm nowhere beside you, for Belle has heaps of taste, and you're quite French, I assure you. Let your flowers hang; don't be so careful of them, and be sure you don't trip," returned Sallie, trying not to care that Meg was prettier than herself.

Keeping that warning carefully in mind, Margaret got safely down stairs, and sailed into the drawing-rooms, where the Moffats and a few early guests were assembled. She very soon discovered that there is a charm about fine clothes which attracts a certain class of people, and secures their respect. Several young ladies, who had taken no notice of her before, were very affectionate all of a sudden; several young gentlemen, who had only stared at her at the other party, now not only stared, but asked to be introduced, and said all manner of foolish, but agreeable things to her; and several old ladies, who sat on sofas, and criticised the rest of the party, inquired who she was, with an air of interest. She heard Mrs. Moffat reply to one of them,—

"Daisy March—father a colonel in the army—one of our first families, but reverses of fortune, you know; intimate friends of the Laurences; sweet creature, I assure you; my Ned is quite wild about her."

"Dear me!" said the old lady, putting up her glass for another observation of Meg, who tried to look as if she had not heard, and been rather shocked at Mrs. Moffat's fibs.

The "queer feeling" did not pass away, but she imagined herself acting the new part of fine lady, and so got on pretty well, though the tight dress gave her a side-ache, the train kept getting under her feet, and she was in constant fear lest her ear-rings should fly off, and get

7. This tale, attributed to Aesop, tells the story of a jackdaw (a small and ordinary black-and-gray bird) who dresses himself in flashy feathers from other birds in an attempt to be selected king of the birds. As he is about to be made king, the other birds strip the jackdaw of his borrowed feathers and expose him as a fraud.
8. Pleated strip of fabric on a headdress or bonnet.

For several minutes, she stood like the jackdaw in the fable, enjoying her borrowed plumes.—PAGE 77.

lost or broken. She was flirting her fan, and laughing at the feeble jokes of a young gentleman who tried to be witty, when she suddenly stopped laughing, and looked confused; for, just opposite, she saw Laurie. He was staring at her with undisguised surprise, and disapproval also, she thought; for, though he bowed and smiled, yet something in his honest eyes made her blush, and wish she had her old dress on. To complete her confusion, she saw Belle nudge Annie, and both glance from her to Laurie, who, she was happy to see, looked unusually boyish and shy.

"Silly creatures, to put such thoughts into my head! I won't care for it, or let it change me a bit," thought Meg, and rustled across the room to shake hands with her friend.

"I'm glad you came, for I was afraid you wouldn't," she said, with her most grown-up air.

"Jo wanted me to come, and tell her how you looked, so I did;" answered Laurie, without turning his eyes upon her, though he half smiled at her maternal tone.

"What shall you tell her?" asked Meg, full of curiosity to know his opinion of her, yet feeling ill at ease with him, for the first time.

"I shall say I didn't know you; for you look so grown-up, and unlike yourself, I'm quite afraid of you," he said, fumbling at his glove-button.

"How absurd of you! the girls dressed me up for fun, and I rather like it. Wouldn't Jo stare if she saw me?" said Meg, bent on making him say whether he thought her improved or not.

"Yes, I think she would," returned Laurie, gravely.

"Don't you like me so?" asked Meg.

"No, I don't," was the blunt reply.

"Why not?" in an anxious tone.

He glanced at her frizzled head, bare shoulders, and fantastically trimmed dress, with an expression that abashed her more than his answer, which had not a particle of his usual politeness about it.

"I don't like fuss and feathers."

That was altogether too much from a lad younger than herself; and Meg walked away, saying, petulantly,—

"You are the rudest boy I ever saw."

Feeling very much ruffled, she went and stood at a quiet window, to cool her cheeks, for the tight dress gave her an uncomfortably brilliant color. As she stood there, Major Lincoln passed by; and, a minute after, she heard him saying to his mother,—

"They are making a fool of that little girl; I wanted you to see her, but they have spoilt her entirely; she's nothing but a doll, to-night."

"Oh, dear!" sighed Meg; "I wish I'd been sensible, and worn my own things; then I should not have disgusted other people, or felt so uncomfortable and ashamed myself."

She leaned her forehead on the cool pane, and stood half hidden by the curtains, never minding that her favorite waltz had begun, till some one touched her; and, turning, she saw Laurie looking penitent, as he said, with his very best bow, and his hand out,—

And turning, she saw Laurie looking penitent, as he said, with his very best bow, and his hand out.—PAGE 79.

"Please forgive my rudeness, and come and dance with me."

"I'm afraid it will be too disagreeable to you," said Meg, trying to look offended, and failing entirely.

"Not a bit of it; I'm dying to do it. Come, I'll be good; I don't like your gown, but I do think you are—just splendid;" and he waved his hands, as if words failed to express his admiration.

Meg smiled, and relented, and whispered, as they stood waiting to catch the time,—

"Take care my skirt don't trip you up; it's the plague of my life, and I was a goose to wear it."

"Pin it round your neck, and then it will be useful," said Laurie, looking down at the little blue boots, which he evidently approved of.

Away they went, fleetly and gracefully; for, having practised at home, they were well matched, and the blithe young couple were a pleasant sight to see, as they twirled merrily round and round, feeling more friendly than ever after their small tiff.

"Laurie, I want you to do me a favor; will you?" said Meg, as he stood fanning her, when her breath gave out, which it did, very soon, though she would not own why.

"Won't I!" said Laurie, with alacrity.

"Please don't tell them at home about my dress to-night. They won't understand the joke, and it will worry mother."

"Then why did you do it?" said Laurie's eyes, so plainly, that Meg hastily added,—

"I shall tell them, myself, all about it, and ' 'fess' to mother how silly I've been. But I'd rather do it myself; so you'll not tell, will you?"

"I give you my word I won't; only what shall I say when they ask me?"

"Just say I looked nice, and was having a good time."

"I'll say the first, with all my heart; but how about the other? You don't look as if you were having a good time; are you?" and Laurie looked at her with an expression which made her answer, in a whisper,—

"No; not just now. Don't think I'm horrid; I only wanted a little fun, but this sort don't pay, I find, and I'm getting tired of it."

"Here comes Ned Moffat; what does he want?" said Laurie, knitting his black brows, as if he did not regard his young host in the light of a pleasant addition to the party.

"He put his name down for three dances, and I suppose he's coming for them; what a bore!" said Meg, assuming a languid air, which amused Laurie immensely.

He did not speak to her again till supper-time, when he saw her drinking champagne with Ned, and his friend Fisher, who were behaving "like a pair of fools," as Laurie said to himself, for he felt a brotherly sort of right to watch over the Marches, and fight their battles, whenever a defender was needed.

"You'll have a splitting headache to-morrow, if you drink much of that. I wouldn't, Meg; your mother don't like it, you know," he whispered, leaning over her chair, as Ned turned to refill her glass, and Fisher stooped to pick up her fan.

"I'm not Meg, to-night; I'm 'a doll,' who does all sorts of crazy things. To-morrow I shall put away my 'fuss and feathers,' and be desperately good again," she answered, with an affected little laugh.

"Wish to-morrow was here, then," muttered Laurie, walking off, ill-pleased at the change he saw in her.

Meg danced and flirted, chattered and giggled, as the other girls did; after supper she undertook the German,[9] and blundered through it, nearly upsetting her partner with her long skirt, and romping in a way that scandalized Laurie, who looked on and meditated a lecture. But he got no chance to deliver it, for Meg kept away from him till he came to say good-night.

"Remember!" she said, trying to smile, for the splitting headache had already begun.

"Silence à la mort,"[1] replied Laurie, with a melodramatic flourish, as he went away.

This little bit of by-play excited Annie's curiosity; but Meg was too tired for gossip, and went to bed, feeling as if she had been to a masquerade, and hadn't enjoyed herself as much as she expected. She was sick all the next day, and on Saturday went home, quite used up with her fortnight's fun, and feeling that she had sat in the lap of luxury long enough.

"It does seem pleasant to be quiet, and not have company manners on all the time. Home *is* a nice place, though it isn't splendid," said Meg, looking about her with a restful expression, as she sat with her mother and Jo on the Sunday evening.

"I'm glad to hear you say so, dear, for I was afraid home would seem dull and poor to you, after your fine quarters," replied her mother, who had given her many anxious looks that day; for motherly eyes are quick to see any change in children's faces.

Meg had told her adventures gayly, and said over and over what a charming time she had had; but something still seemed to weigh upon her spirits, and, when the younger girls were gone to bed, she sat thoughtfully staring at the fire, saying little, and looking worried. As the clock struck nine, and Jo proposed bed, Meg suddenly left her chair, and, taking Beth's stool, leaned her elbows on her mother's knee, saying, bravely,—

"Marmee, I want to ' 'fess.' "

"I thought so; what is it, dear?"

"Shall I go away?" asked Jo, discreetly.

"Of course not; don't I always tell you everything? I was ashamed to speak of it before the children, but I want you to know all the dreadful things I did at the Moffats."

"We are prepared," said Mrs. March, smiling, but looking a little anxious.

"I told you they rigged me up, but I didn't tell you that they powdered, and squeezed, and frizzled, and made me look like a fashion-

9. See p. 32, n. 8 (part 1, chap. 3).
1. Literally, silence unto death (French), a promise to keep the secret.

plate. Laurie thought I wasn't proper; I know he did, though he didn't say so, and one man called me 'a doll.' I knew it was silly, but they flattered me, and said I was a beauty, and quantities of nonsense, so I let them make a fool of me."

"Is that all?" asked Jo, as Mrs. March looked silently at the downcast face of her pretty daughter, and could not find it in her heart to blame her little follies.

"No; I drank champagne, and romped, and tried to flirt, and was, altogether, abominable," said Meg, self-reproachfully.

"There is something more, I think;" and Mrs. March smoothed the soft cheek, which suddenly grew rosy, as Meg answered, slowly,—

"Yes; it's very silly, but I want to tell it, because I hate to have people say and think such things about us and Laurie."

Then she told the various bits of gossip she had heard at the Moffats; and, as she spoke, Jo saw her mother fold her lips tightly, as if ill pleased that such ideas should be put into Meg's innocent mind.

"Well, if that isn't the greatest rubbish I ever heard," cried Jo, indignantly. "Why didn't you pop out and tell them so, on the spot?"

"I couldn't, it was so embarrassing for me. I couldn't help hearing, at first, and then I was so angry and ashamed, I didn't remember that I ought to go away."

"Just wait till *I* see Annie Moffat, and I'll show you how to settle such ridiculous stuff. The idea of having 'plans,' and being kind to Laurie, because he's rich, and may marry us by and by! Won't he shout, when I tell him what those silly things say about us poor children?" and Jo laughed, as if, on second thoughts, the thing struck her as a good joke.

"If you tell Laurie, I'll never forgive you! She mustn't, must she, mother?" said Meg, looking distressed.

"No; never repeat that foolish gossip, and forget it as soon as you can," said Mrs. March, gravely. "I was very unwise to let you go among people of whom I know so little; kind, I dare say, but worldly, ill-bred, and full of these vulgar ideas about young people. I am more sorry than I can express, for the mischief this visit may have done you, Meg."

"Don't be sorry, I won't let it hurt me; I'll forget all the bad, and remember only the good; for I did enjoy a great deal, and thank you very much for letting me go. I'll not be sentimental or dissatisfied, mother; I know I'm a silly little girl, and I'll stay with you till I'm fit to take care of myself. But it *is* nice to be praised and admired, and I can't help saying I like it," said Meg, looking half ashamed of the confession.

"That is perfectly natural, and quite harmless, if the liking does not become a passion, and lead one to do foolish or unmaidenly things. Learn to know and value the praise which is worth having, and to excite the admiration of excellent people, by being modest as well as pretty, Meg."

Margaret sat thinking a moment, while Jo stood with her hands behind her, looking both interested and a little perplexed; for it was a new thing to see Meg blushing and talking about admiration, lovers, and things of that sort, and Jo felt as if during that fortnight her sister had grown up amazingly, and was drifting away from her into a world where she could not follow.

"Mother, do you have 'plans,' as Mrs. Moffat said?" asked Meg, bashfully.

"Yes, my dear, I have a great many; all mothers do, but mine differ somewhat from Mrs. Moffat's, I suspect. I will tell you some of them, for the time has come when a word may set this romantic little head and heart of yours right, on a very serious subject. You are young, Meg; but not too young to understand me, and mothers' lips are the fittest to speak of such things to girls like you. Jo, your turn will come in time, perhaps, so listen to my 'plans,' and help me carry them out, if they are good."

Jo went and sat on one arm of the chair, looking as if she thought they were about to join in some very solemn affair. Holding a hand of each, and watching the two young faces wistfully, Mrs. March said, in her serious yet cheery way,—

"I want my daughters to be beautiful, accomplished, and good; to be admired, loved, and respected, to have a happy youth, to be well and wisely married, and to lead useful, pleasant lives, with as little care and sorrow to try them as God sees fit to send. To be loved and chosen by a good man is the best and sweetest thing which can happen to a woman; and I sincerely hope my girls may know this beautiful experience. It is natural to think of it, Meg; right to hope and wait for it, and wise to prepare for it; so that, when the happy time comes, you may feel ready for the duties, and worthy of the joy. My dear girls, I *am* ambitious for you, but not to have you make a dash in the world,—marry rich men merely because they are rich, or have splendid houses, which are not homes, because love is wanting. Money is a needful and precious thing,—and, when well used, a noble thing,—but I never want you to think it is the first or only prize to strive for. I'd rather see you poor men's wives, if you were happy, beloved, contented, than queens on thrones, without self-respect and peace."

"Poor girls don't stand any chance, Belle says, unless they put themselves forward," sighed Meg.

"Then we'll be old maids," said Jo, stoutly.

"Right, Jo; better be happy old maids than unhappy wives, or unmaidenly girls, running about to find husbands," said Mrs. March, decidedly. "Don't be troubled, Meg; poverty seldom daunts a sincere lover. Some of the best and most honored women I know were poor girls, but so love-worthy that they were not allowed to be old maids. Leave these things to time; make this home happy, so that you may be fit for homes of your own, if they are offered you, and contented here if they are not. One thing remember, my girls, mother is always ready to be your confidant, father to be your friend; and both of us trust and hope that our daughters, whether married or single, will be the pride and comfort of our lives."

"We will, Marmee, we will!" cried both, with all their hearts, as she bade them good-night.

CHAPTER X.

THE P. C. AND P. O.

As spring came on, a new set of amusements became the fashion, and the lengthening days gave long afternoons for work and play of all sorts. The garden had to be put in order, and each sister had a quarter of the little plot to do what she liked with. Hannah used to say, "I'd know which each of them gardings belonged to, ef I see 'em in Chiny;" and so she might, for the girls' tastes differed as much as their characters. Meg's had roses and heliotrope, myrtle, and a little orange-tree in it. Jo's bed was never alike two seasons, for she was always trying experiments; this year it was to be a plantation of sun-flowers, the seeds of which cheerful and aspiring plant were to feed "Aunt Cockle-top" and her family of chicks. Beth had old-fashioned, fragrant flowers in her garden; sweet peas and mignonette, larkspur, pinks, pansies, and southernwood, with chickweed for the bird and catnip for the pussies. Amy had a bower in hers,—rather small and earwiggy, but very pretty to look at,—with honeysuckles and morning-glories hanging their colored horns and bells in graceful wreaths all over it; tall white lilies, delicate ferns, and as many brilliant, picturesque plants as would consent to blossom there.

Gardening, walks, rows on the river, and flower-hunts employed the fine days; and for rainy ones, they had house diversions,—some old, some new,—all more or less original. One of these was the "P. C."; for, as secret societies were the fashion, it was thought proper to have one; and, as all of the girls admired Dickens, they called themselves the Pickwick Club.[2] With a few interruptions, they had kept this up for a year, and met every Saturday evening in the big garret, on which occasions the ceremonies were as follows: Three chairs were arranged in a row before a table, on which was a lamp, also four white badges, with a big "P. C." in different colors on each, and the weekly newspaper, called "The Pickwick Portfolio," to which all contributed something; while Jo, who revelled in pens and ink, was the editor. At seven o'clock, the four members ascended to the club-room, tied their badges round their heads, and took their seats with great solemnity. Meg, as the eldest, was Samuel Pickwick; Jo, being of a literary turn, Augustus Snodgrass; Beth, because she was round and rosy, Tracy Tupman; and Amy, who was always trying to do what she couldn't, was Nathaniel Winkle. Pickwick, the President, read the paper, which was filled with original tales, poetry, local news, funny advertisements, and hints, in which they good-naturedly reminded each other of their faults and short-comings. On one occasion, Mr. Pickwick put on a pair of spectacles without any glasses, rapped upon the table,

2. In Charles Dickens's *Pickwick Papers* (1836–37), the Pickwick Club forms a four-person committee to travel around the country and report back its findings and misadventures. A good-hearted bachelor and retired businessman, Samuel Pickwick, the founder of the club, leads the corresponding society. The other three traveling Pickwickians include Augustus Snodgrass, a poet; Tracy Tupman, an enthusiastic admirer of "the fair sex"; and Nathaniel Winkle, an amusing but rarely competent sportsman.

hemmed, and, having stared hard at Mr. Snodgrass, who was tilting back in his chair, till he arranged himself properly, began to read,—

"The Pickwick Portfolio."

MAY 20, 18-.

Poet's Corner.

ANNIVERSARY ODE.

Again we meet to celebrate
　With badge and solemn rite,
Our fifty-second anniversary,
　In Pickwick Hall, to-night.

We all are here in perfect health,
　None gone from our small band;
Again we see each well-known face,
　And press each friendly hand.

Our Pickwick, always at his post,
　With reverence we greet,
As, spectacles on nose, he reads
　Our well-filled weekly sheet.

Although he suffers from a cold,
　We joy to hear him speak,
For words of wisdom from him fall,
　In spite of croak or squeak.

Old six-foot Snodgrass looms on high,
　With elephantine grace,
And beams upon the company,
　With brown and jovial face.

Poetic fire lights up his eye,
　He struggles 'gainst his lot;
Behold ambition on his brow,
　And on his nose a blot!

Next our peaceful Tupman comes,
　So rosy, plump and sweet,
Who chokes with laughter at the
　　puns,
　And tumbles off his seat.

Prim little Winkle too is here,
　With every hair in place,
A model of propriety,
　Though he hates to wash his face.

The year is gone, we still unite
　To joke and laugh and read,
And tread the path of literature
　That doth to glory lead.

Long may our paper prosper well,
　Our club unbroken be,
And coming years their blessings
　　pour
　On the useful, gay "P. C."
　　　　　　　　　　A. SNODGRASS.

THE MASKED MARRIAGE.[3]
A TALE OF VENICE.

Gondola after gondola swept up to the marble steps, and left its lovely load to swell the brilliant throng that filled the stately halls of Count de Adelon. Knights and ladies, elves and pages, monks and flower-girls, all mingled gaily in the dance. Sweet voices and rich melody filled the air; and so with mirth and music the masquerade went on.

"Has your Highness seen the Lady Viola to-night?" asked a gallant troubadour of the fairy queen who floated down the hall upon his arm.

"Yes; is she not lovely, though so sad! Her dress is well chosen, too, for in a week she weds Count An-

---

3. Meg's romance is an excerpt from a story of the same title that Alcott published in *Dodge's Literary Museum* (18 December 1852). For the full text, see p. 496 of this Norton Critical Edition.

tonio, whom she passionately hates."

"By my faith I envy him. Yonder he comes, arrayed like a bridegroom, except the black mask. When that is off we shall see how he regards the fair maid whose heart he cannot win, though her stern father bestows her hand," returned the troubadour.

" 'Tis whispered that she loves the young English artist who haunts her steps, and is spurned by the old count," said the lady, as they joined the dance.

The revel was at its height when a priest appeared, and, withdrawing the young pair to an alcove hung with purple velvet, he motioned them to kneel. Instant silence fell upon the gay throng; and not a sound, but the dash of fountains or the rustle of orange groves sleeping in the moonlight, broke the hush, as Count de Adelon spoke thus:—

"My lords and ladies; pardon the ruse by which I have gathered you here to witness the marriage of my daughter. Father, we wait your services."

All eyes turned toward the bridal party, and a low murmur of amazement went through the throng, for neither bride nor groom removed their masks. Curiosity and wonder possessed all hearts, but respect restrained all tongues till the holy rite was over. Then the eager spectators gathered round the count, demanding an explanation.

"Gladly would I give it if I could; but I only know that it was the whim of my timid Viola, and I yielded to it. Now, my children, let the play end. Unmask, and receive my blessing."

But neither bent the knee; for the young bridegroom replied, in a tone that startled all listeners, as the mask fell, disclosing the noble face of Ferdinand Devereux, the artist lover, and, leaning on the breast where now flashed the star of an English earl, was the lovely Viola, radiant with joy and beauty.

"My lord, you scornfully bade me claim your daughter when I could boast as high a name and vast a fortune as the Count Antonio. I can do more; for even your ambitious soul cannot refuse the Earl of Devereux and De Vere, when he gives his ancient name and boundless wealth in return for the beloved hand of this fair lady, now my wife."

The count stood like one changed to stone; and, turning to the bewildered crowd, Ferdinand added, with a gay smile of triumph, "To you, my gallant friends, I can only wish that your wooing may prosper as mine has done; and that you may all win as fair a bride as I have, by this masked marriage."

S. PICKWICK.

Why is the P. C. like the Tower of Babel? It is full of unruly members.

THE HISTORY OF A SQUASH.

Once upon a time a farmer planted a little seed in his garden, and after a while it sprouted and became a vine, and bore many squashes. One day in October, when they were ripe, he picked one and took it to market. A grocer man bought and put it in his shop. That same morning, a little girl, in a brown hat and blue dress, with a round face and snubby nose, went and bought it for her mother. She lugged it home, cut it up, and boiled it in the big pot; mashed some of it, with salt and butter, for dinner; and to the rest she added a pint of milk, two eggs, four spoons of sugar, nutmeg, and some crackers; put it in a deep dish, and baked it till it was brown and nice; and next day it was eaten by a family named March.

T. TUPMAN.

MR. PICKWICK, Sir:—

I address you upon the subject of sin the sinner I mean is a man named Winkle who makes trouble in his club by laughing and sometimes won't write his piece in this fine paper I hope you will pardon his badness and let him send a French fable because he can't write out of his head as he has so many lessons to do and no brains in future I will try to take time by the fetlock and prepare some work which will be all *commy la fo*[4] that means all right I am in haste as it is nearly school time

Yours respectably　　　N. WINKLE.

[The above is a manly and handsome acknowledgment of past misdemeanors. If our young friend studied punctuation, it would be well.]

A SAD ACCIDENT.

On Friday last, we were startled by a violent shock in our basement, followed by cries of distress. On rushing, in a body, to the cellar, we discovered our beloved President prostrate upon the floor, having tripped and fallen while getting wood for domestic purposes. A perfect scene of ruin met our eyes; for in his fall Mr. Pickwick had plunged his head and shoulders into a tub of water, upset a keg of soft soap upon his manly form, and torn his garments badly. On being removed from this perilous situation, it was discovered that he had suffered no injury but several bruises; and, we are happy to add, is now doing well.

ED.

THE PUBLIC BEREAVEMENT.

It is our painful duty to record the sudden and mysterious disappearance of our cherished friend, Mrs. Snowball Pat Paw. This lovely and beloved cat was the pet of a large circle of warm and admiring friends; for her beauty attracted all eyes, her graces and virtues endeared her to all hearts, and her loss is deeply felt by the whole community.

When last seen, she was sitting at the gate, watching the butcher's cart; and it is feared that some villain, tempted by her charms, basely stole her. Weeks have passed, but no trace of her has been discovered; and we relinquish all hope, tie a black ribbon to her basket, set aside her dish, and weep for her as one lost to us forever.

A sympathizing friend sends the following gem:—

A LAMENT
FOR S. B. PAT PAW.

We mourn the loss of our little pet,
　And sigh o'er her hapless fate,
For never more by the fire she'll sit,
　Nor play by the old green gate.

The little grave where her infant
　　sleeps,
　Is 'neath the chestnut tree;
But o'er *her* grave we may not weep,
　We know not where it may be.

Her empty bed, her idle ball,
　Will never see her more;
No gentle tap, no loving purr
　Is heard at the parlor door.

Another cat comes after her mice,
　A cat with a dirty face;
But she does not hunt as our darling
　　did,
　Nor play with her airy grace.

Her stealthy paws tread the very hall
　Where Snowball used to play,
But she only spits at the dogs our pet
　So gallantly drove away.

She is useful and mild, and does her
　　best,
But she is not fair to see;

---

4. Amy means to say *comme il faut*, a French phrase meaning "as is respectable." She also misquotes "Take Time by the forelock" (act quickly), a maxim attributed to the Greek philosopher Thales of Miletus (c.636–c.546 B.C.E.), thereby suggesting that Time should be grasped not by its hair but by its ankle as if it were a horse (since a fetlock is the tuft of hair above the hoof on the back of the leg of a horse).

And we cannot give her your place,
dear,
Nor worship her as we worship
thee.

A. S.

ADVERTISEMENTS.

MISS ORANTHY BLUGGAGE, the accomplished Strong-Minded Lecturer, will deliver her famous Lecture on "WOMAN AND HER POSITION," at Pickwick Hall, next Saturday Evening, after the usual performances.[5]

A WEEKLY MEETING will be held at Kitchen Place, to teach young ladies how to cook. Hannah Brown will preside; and all are invited to attend.

THE DUSTPAN SOCIETY will meet on Wednesday next, and parade in the upper story of the Club House. All members to appear in uniform and shoulder their brooms at nine precisely.

MRS. BETH BOUNCER will open her new assortment of Doll's Millinery next week. The latest Paris Fashions have arrived, and orders are respectfully solicited.

A NEW PLAY will appear at the Barnville Theatre, in the course of a few weeks, which will surpass anything ever seen on the American stage. "THE GREEK SLAVE,[6] or Constantine the Avenger," is the name of this thrilling drama!!!

HINTS.

If S. P. didn't use so much soap on his hands, he wouldn't always be late at breakfast. A. S. is requested not to whistle in the street. T. T., please don't forget Amy's napkin. N. W. must not fret because his dress has not nine tucks.

WEEKLY REPORT.

Meg—Good.
Jo—Bad.
Beth—Very good.
Amy—Middling.

As the President finished reading the paper (which I beg leave to assure my readers is a *bona fide* copy of one written by *bona fide* girls once upon a time),[7] a round of applause followed, and then Mr. Snodgrass rose to make a proposition.

"Mr. President and gentlemen," he began, assuming a parliamentary attitude and tone, "I wish to propose the admission of a new member; one who highly deserves the honor, would be deeply grateful for it, and would add immensely to the spirit of the club, the literary value of the paper, and be no end jolly and nice. I propose Mr. Theodore Laurence as an honorary member of the P. C. Come now, do have him."

Jo's sudden change of tone made the girls laugh; but all looked rather anxious, and no one said a word, as Snodgrass took his seat.

5. "Woman, and Her Position; by Oronthy Bluggage" is the title of a comic monologue written and performed by Alcott during the mid-1850s. See *Journals*, 74.
6. Title of an Alcott girls' play, collected in *Comic Tragedies* (1893).
7. Harvard's Houghton Library holds the extant copies of the Alcott family newspapers. Transcribed selections appear in *Journals*, 338–41.

"We'll put it to vote," said the President. "All in favor of this motion please to manifest it by saying 'Aye.'"

A loud response from Snodgrass, followed, to everybody's surprise, by a timid one from Beth.

"Contrary minded say 'No.'"

Meg and Amy were contrary minded; and Mr. Winkle rose to say, with great elegance, "We don't wish any boys; they only joke and bounce about. This is a ladies' club, and we wish to be private and proper."

"I'm afraid he'll laugh at our paper, and make fun of us afterward," observed Pickwick, pulling the little curl on her forehead, as she always did when doubtful.

Up bounced Snodgrass, very much in earnest. "Sir! I give you my word as a gentleman, Laurie won't do anything of the sort. He likes to write, and he'll give a tone to our contributions, and keep us from being sentimental, don't you see? We can do so little for him, and he does so much for us, I think the least we can do is to offer him a place here, and make him welcome, if he comes."

This artful allusion to benefits conferred, brought Tupman to his feet, looking as if he had quite made up his mind.

"Yes; we ought to do it, even if we *are* afraid. I say he *may* come, and his grandpa too, if he likes."

This spirited burst from Beth electrified the club, and Jo left her seat to shake hands approvingly. "Now then, vote again. Everybody remember it's our Laurie, and say 'Aye!'" cried Snodgrass, excitedly.

"Aye! aye! aye!" replied three voices at once.

"Good! bless you! now, as there's nothing like 'taking time by the *fetlock*,' as Winkle characteristically observes, allow me to present the new member;" and, to the dismay of the rest of the club, Jo threw open the door of the closet, and displayed Laurie sitting on a rag-bag, flushed and twinkling with suppressed laughter.

"You rogue! you traitor! Jo, how could you?" cried the three girls, as Snodgrass led her friend triumphantly forth; and, producing both a chair and a badge, installed him in a jiffy.

"The coolness of you two rascals is amazing," began Mr. Pickwick, trying to get up an awful frown, and only succeeding in producing an amiable smile. But the new member was equal to the occasion; and, rising with a grateful salutation to the Chair, said, in the most engaging manner,—"Mr. President and ladies,—I beg pardon, gentlemen,— allow me to introduce myself as Sam Weller,[8] the very humble servant of the club."

"Good, good!" cried Jo, pounding with the handle of the old warming-pan on which she leaned.

"My faithful friend and noble patron," continued Laurie, with a wave of the hand, "who has so flatteringly presented me, is not to be blamed for the base stratagem of to-night. I planned it, and she only gave in after lots of teasing."

---

8. Pickwick's witty and clever cockney servant, who pronounces *v* as *w*.

"Come now, don't lay it all on yourself; you know I proposed the cupboard," broke in Snodgrass, who was enjoying the joke amazingly.

"Never you mind what she says. I'm the wretch that did it, sir," said the new member, with a Welleresque nod to Mr. Pickwick. "But on my honor, I never will do so again, and henceforth *dewote* myself to the interest of this immortal club."

"Hear! hear!" cried Jo, clashing the lid of the warming-pan like a cymbal.

"Go on, go on!" added Winkle and Tupman, while the President bowed benignly.

"I merely wish to say, that as a slight token of my gratitude for the honor done me, and as a means of promoting friendly relations between adjoining nations, I have set up a post-office in the hedge in the lower corner of the garden; a fine, spacious building, with padlocks on the doors, and every convenience for the mails,—also the females, if I may be allowed the expression. It's the old martin-house; but I've stopped up the door, and made the roof open, so it will hold all sorts of things, and save our valuable time. Letters, manuscripts, books and bundles can be passed in there; and, as each nation has a key, it will be uncommonly nice, I fancy. Allow me to present the club key; and, with many thanks for your favor, take my seat."

Great applause as Mr. Weller deposited a little key on the table, and subsided; the warming-pan clashed and waved wildly, and it was some time before order could be restored. A long discussion followed, and every one came out surprising, for every one did her best; so it was an unusually lively meeting, and did not adjourn till a late hour, when it broke up with three shrill cheers for the new member.

No one ever regretted the admittance of Sam Weller, for a more devoted, well-behaved, and jovial member no club could have. He certainly did add "spirit" to the meetings, and "a tone" to the paper; for his orations convulsed his hearers, and his contributions were excellent, being patriotic, classical, comical, or dramatic, but never sentimental. Jo regarded them as worthy of Bacon, Milton, or Shakespeare; and remodelled her own works with good effect, she thought.

The P.O. was a capital little institution, and flourished wonderfully, for nearly as many queer things passed through it as through the real office. Tragedies and cravats, poetry and pickles, garden seeds and long letters, music and gingerbread, rubbers, invitations, scoldings and puppies. The old gentleman liked the fun, and amused himself by sending odd bundles, mysterious messages, and funny telegrams; and his gardener, who was smitten with Hannah's charms, actually sent a love-letter to Jo's care. How they laughed when the secret came out, never dreaming how many love-letters that little post-office would hold in the years to come!

CHAPTER XI.

EXPERIMENTS.

THE first of June; the Kings are off to the seashore to-morrow, and I'm free! Three months' vacation! how I shall enjoy it!" exclaimed Meg, coming home one warm day to find Jo laid upon the sofa in an unusual state of exhaustion, while Beth took off her dusty boots, and Amy made lemonade for the refreshment of the whole party.

"Aunt March went to-day, for which, oh be joyful!" said Jo. "I was mortally afraid she'd ask me to go with her; if she had, I should have felt as if I ought to do it; but Plumfield is about as festive as a church-yard, you know, and I'd rather be excused. We had a flurry getting the old lady off, and I had a scare every time she spoke to me, for I was in such a hurry to be through that I was uncommonly helpful and sweet, and feared she'd find it impossible to part from me. I quaked till she was fairly in the carriage, and had a final fright, for, as it drove off, she popped out her head, saying, 'Josy-phine, won't you—?' I didn't hear any more, for I basely turned and fled; I did actually run, and whisked round the corner, where I felt safe."

"Poor old Jo! she came in looking as if bears were after her," said Beth, as she cuddled her sister's feet with a motherly air.

"Aunt March is a regular samphire,[9] is she not?" observed Amy, tasting her mixture critically.

"She means *vampire*, not sea-weed; but it don't matter; it's too warm to be particular about one's parts of speech," murmured Jo.

"What shall you do all your vacation?" asked Amy, changing the subject, with tact.

"I shall lie abed late, and do nothing," replied Meg, from the depths of the rocking-chair. "I've been routed up early all winter, and had to spend my days working for other people; so now I'm going to rest and revel to my heart's content."

"Hum!" said Jo; "that dozy way wouldn't suit me. I've laid in a heap of books, and I'm going to improve my shining hours reading on my perch in the old apple-tree, when I'm not having l—"

"Don't say 'larks!' " implored Amy, as a return snub for the "samphire" correction.

"I'll say 'nightingales,' then, with Laurie; that's proper and appropriate, since he's a warbler."

"Don't let us do any lessons, Beth, for a while, but play all the time, and rest, as the girls mean to," proposed Amy.

"Well, I will, if mother don't mind. I want to learn some new songs, and my children need fixing up for the summer; they are dreadfully out of order, and really suffering for clothes."

"May we, mother?" asked Meg, turning to Mrs. March, who sat sewing, in what they called "Marmee's corner."

"You may try your experiment for a week, and see how you like it. I

---

9. Glasswort, a fleshy plant that grows in salt marshes and along sea beaches.

think by Saturday night you will find that all play, and no work, is as bad as all work, and no play."

"Oh, dear, no! it will be delicious, I'm sure," said Meg, complacently.

"I now propose a toast, as my 'friend and pardner, Sairy Gamp,'[1] says. Fun forever, and no grubbage," cried Jo, rising, glass in hand, as the lemonade went round.

They all drank it merrily, and began the experiment by lounging for the rest of the day. Next morning, Meg did not appear till ten o'clock; her solitary breakfast did not taste good, and the room seemed lonely and untidy, for Jo had not filled the vases, Beth had not dusted, and Amy's books lay scattered about. Nothing was neat and pleasant but "Marmee's corner," which looked as usual; and there she sat, to "rest and read," which meant yawn, and imagine what pretty summer dresses she would get with her salary. Jo spent the morning on the river, with Laurie, and the afternoon reading and crying over "The Wide, Wide World,"[2] up in the apple-tree. Beth began by rummaging everything out of the big closet, where her family resided; but, getting tired before half done, she left her establishment topsy-turvy, and went to her music, rejoicing that she had no dishes to wash. Amy arranged her bower, put on her best white frock, smoothed her curls, and sat down to draw, under the honeysuckles, hoping some one would see and inquire who the young artist was. As no one appeared but an inquisitive daddy-long-legs, who examined her work with interest, she went to walk, got caught in a shower, and came home dripping.

At tea-time they compared notes, and all agreed that it had been a delightful, though unusually long day. Meg, who went shopping in the afternoon, and got a "sweet blue muslin," had discovered, after she had cut the breadths[3] off, that it wouldn't wash, which mishap made her slightly cross. Jo had burnt the skin off her nose boating, and got a raging headache by reading too long. Beth was worried by the confusion of her closet, and the difficulty of learning three or four songs at once; and Amy deeply regretted the damage done her frock, for Katy Brown's party was to be the next day; and now, like Flora McFlimsy, she had "nothing to wear."[4] But these were mere trifles; and they assured their mother that the experiment was working finely. She smiled, said nothing, and, with Hannah's help, did their neglected work, keeping home pleasant, and the domestic machinery running smoothly. It was astonishing what a peculiar and uncomfortable state of things was produced by the "resting and revelling" process. The days kept getting longer and longer; the weather was unusually vari-

---

1. Sairey Gamp is the red-nosed, cockney nurse in Charles Dickens's *Life and Adventures of Martin Chuzzlewit* (1843–44). A memorable comic character, she mispronounces words, drinks alcoholic spirits, and enjoys toasts.
2. Susan Warner's enormously popular sentimental novel published in 1850 under the pseudonym Elizabeth Wetherell.
3. Selvage, or edges, on either side of a woven fabric, usually treated or finished to prevent raveling and meant to be cut off and discarded.
4. In William Allen Butler's popular poem "Nothing to Wear" (first published in *Harper's Weekly* in 1857), Miss Flora McFlimsey agonizes about finding a suitable gown for an upcoming social event, despite her already large and expensive wardrobe.

able, and so were tempers; an unsettled feeling possessed every one, and Satan found plenty of mischief for the idle hands to do. As the height of luxury, Meg put out some of her sewing, and then found time hang so heavily, that she fell to snipping and spoiling her clothes, in her attempts to furbish them up, à la Moffat. Jo read till her eyes gave out, and she was sick of books; got so fidgety that even good-natured Laurie had a quarrel with her, and so reduced in spirits that she desperately wished she had gone with Aunt March. Beth got on pretty well, for she was constantly forgetting that it was to be *all play, and no work*, and fell back into her old ways, now and then; but something in the air affected her, and, more than once, her tranquillity was much disturbed; so much so, that, on one occasion, she actually shook poor dear Joanna, and told her she was "a fright." Amy fared worst of all, for her resources were small; and, when her sisters left her to amuse and care for herself, she soon found that accomplished and important little self a great burden. She didn't like dolls; fairy tales were childish, and one couldn't draw all the time. Tea-parties didn't amount to much, neither did picnics, unless very well conducted. "If one could have a fine house, full of nice girls, or go travelling, the summer would be delightful; but to stay at home with three selfish sisters, and a grown-up boy, was enough to try the patience of a Boaz," complained Miss Malaprop,[5] after several days devoted to pleasure, fretting, and *ennui*.

No one would own that they were tired of the experiment; but, by Friday night, each acknowledged to herself that they were glad the week was nearly done. Hoping to impress the lesson more deeply, Mrs. March, who had a good deal of humor, resolved to finish off the trial in an appropriate manner; so she gave Hannah a holiday, and let the girls enjoy the full effect of the play system.

When they got up on Saturday morning, there was no fire in the kitchen, no breakfast in the dining-room, and no mother anywhere to be seen.

"Mercy on us! what *has* happened?" cried Jo, staring about her in dismay.

Meg ran up stairs, and soon came back again, looking relieved, but rather bewildered, and a little ashamed.

"Mother isn't sick, only very tired, and she says she is going to stay quietly in her room all day, and let us do the best we can. It's a very queer thing for her to do, she don't act a bit like herself; but she says it *has* been a hard week for her, so we mustn't grumble, but take care of ourselves."

"That's easy enough, and I like the idea; I'm aching for something to do—that is, some new amusement, you know," added Jo, quickly.

In fact it *was* an immense relief to them all to have a little work, and they took hold with a will, but soon realized the truth of Hannah's saying, "Housekeeping ain't no joke." There was plenty of food in the

---

5. Amy means the patience of Job, the long-suffering Old Testament figure, not Boaz, Ruth's husband, in the Bible. In Richard Brinsley Sheridan's comedy *The Rivals* (1775), Mrs. Mala-prop distorts or misuses words in unintentionally amusing ways.

larder, and, while Beth and Amy set the table, Meg and Jo got breakfast; wondering, as they did so, why servants ever talked about hard
work.

"I shall take some up to mother, though she said we were not to
think of her, for she'd take care of herself," said Meg, who presided,
and felt quite matronly behind the teapot.

So a tray was fitted out before any one began, and taken up, with
the cook's compliments. The boiled tea was very bitter, the omelette
scorched, and the biscuits speckled with saleratus; but Mrs. March
received her repast with thanks, and laughed heartily over it after Jo
was gone.

"Poor little souls, they will have a hard time, I'm afraid; but they
won't suffer, and it will do them good," she said, producing the more
palatable viands with which she had provided herself, and disposing of
the bad breakfast, so that their feelings might not be hurt;—a motherly little deception, for which they were grateful.

Many were the complaints below, and great the chagrin of the head
cook, at her failures. "Never mind, I'll get the dinner, and be servant;
you be missis, keep your hands nice, see company, and give orders,"
said Jo, who knew still less than Meg about culinary affairs.

This obliging offer was gladly accepted; and Margaret retired to the
parlor, which she hastily put in order by whisking the litter under the
sofa, and shutting the blinds, to save the trouble of dusting. Jo, with
perfect faith in her own powers, and a friendly desire to make up the
quarrel, immediately put a note in the office, inviting Laurie to dinner.

"You'd better see what you have got before you think of having company," said Meg, when informed of the hospitable, but rash act.

"Oh, there's corned beef, and plenty of potatoes; and I shall get
some asparagus, and a lobster, 'for a relish,' as Hannah says. We'll
have lettuce, and make a salad; I don't know how, but the book tells.
I'll have blanc-mange and strawberries for dessert; and coffee, too, if
you want to be elegant."

"Don't try too many messes, Jo, for you can't make anything but
gingerbread and molasses candy, fit to eat. I wash my hands of the dinner-party; and, since you have asked Laurie on your own responsibility, you may just take care of him."

"I don't want you to do anything but be clever to him, and help to
the pudding. You'll give me your advice if I get stuck, won't you?"
asked Jo, rather hurt.

"Yes; but I don't know much, except about bread, and a few trifles.
You had better ask mother's leave, before you order anything," returned Meg, prudently.

"Of course I shall; I ain't a fool," and Jo went off in a huff at the
doubts expressed of her powers.

"Get what you like, and don't disturb me; I'm going out to dinner,
and can't worry about things at home," said Mrs. March, when Jo
spoke to her. "I never enjoyed housekeeping, and I'm going to take a
vacation today, and read, write, go visiting and amuse myself."

The unusual spectacle of her busy mother rocking comfortably, and

reading early in the morning, made Jo feel as if some natural phenomenon had occurred; for an eclipse, an earthquake, or a volcanic erup-
tion would hardly have seemed stranger.

"Everything is out of sorts, somehow," she said to herself, going
down stairs. "There's Beth crying; that's a sure sign that something is
wrong with this family. If Amy is bothering, I'll shake her."

Feeling very much out of sorts herself, Jo hurried into the parlor to
find Beth sobbing over Pip, the canary, who lay dead in the cage, with
his little claws pathetically extended, as if imploring the food, for want
of which he had died.

"It's all my fault—I forgot him—there isn't a seed or drop left—oh,
Pip! oh, Pip! how could I be so cruel to you?" cried Beth, taking the
poor thing in her hands, and trying to restore him.

Jo peeped into his half-open eye, felt his little heart, and finding
him stiff and cold, shook her head, and offered her domino-box for a
coffin.

"Put him in the oven, and maybe he will get warm, and revive," said
Amy, hopefully.

"He's been starved, and he shan't be baked, now he's dead. I'll make
him a shroud, and he shall be buried in the grave; and I'll never have
another bird, never, my Pip! for I am too bad to own one," murmured
Beth, sitting on the floor with her pet folded in her hands.

"The funeral shall be this afternoon, and we will all go. Now, don't
cry, Bethy; it's a pity, but nothing goes right this week, and Pip has had
the worst of the experiment. Make the shroud, and lay him in my box;
and, after the dinner-party, we'll have a nice little funeral," said Jo, beginning to feel as if she had undertaken a good deal.

Leaving the others to console Beth, she departed to the kitchen,
which was in a most discouraging state of confusion. Putting on a big
apron, she fell to work, and got the dishes piled up ready for washing,
when she discovered that the fire was out.

"Here's a sweet prospect!" muttered Jo, slamming the stove door
open, and poking vigorously among the cinders.

Having rekindled it, she thought she would go to market while the
water heated. The walk revived her spirits; and, flattering herself that
she had made good bargains, she trudged home again, after buying a
very young lobster, some very old asparagus, and two boxes of acid
strawberries. By the time she got cleared up, the dinner arrived, and
the stove was red-hot. Hannah had left a pan of bread to rise, Meg had
worked it up early, set it on the hearth for a second rising, and forgotten it. Meg was entertaining Sallie Gardiner, in the parlor, when the
door flew open, and a floury, crocky,[6] flushed and dishevelled figure
appeared, demanding, tartly,—

"I say, isn't bread 'riz' enough when it runs over the pans?"

Sallie began to laugh; but Meg nodded, and lifted her eyebrows as high
as they would go, which caused the apparition to vanish, and put the
sour bread into the oven without further delay. Mrs. March went out, af-

6. Broken-down.

ter peeping here and there to see how matters went, also saying a word of comfort to Beth, who sat making a winding-sheet, while the dear departed lay in state in the domino-box. A strange sense of helplessness fell upon the girls as the gray bonnet vanished round the corner; and despair seized them, when, a few minutes later, Miss Crocker appeared, and said she'd come to dinner. Now this lady was a thin, yellow spinster, with a sharp nose, and inquisitive eyes, who saw everything, and gossiped about all she saw. They disliked her, but had been taught to be kind to her, simply because she was old and poor, and had few friends. So Meg gave her the easy-chair, and tried to entertain her, while she asked questions, criticised everything, and told stories of the people whom she knew.

Language cannot describe the anxieties, experiences, and exertions which Jo underwent that morning; and the dinner she served up became a standing joke. Fearing to ask any more advice, she did her best alone, and discovered that something more than energy and good-will is necessary to make a cook. She boiled the asparagus hard for an hour, and was grieved to find the heads cooked off, and the stalks harder than ever. The bread burnt black; for the salad dressing so aggravated her, that she let everything else go, till she had convinced herself that she could not make it fit to eat. The lobster was a scarlet mystery to her, but she hammered and poked, till it was unshelled, and its meagre proportions concealed in a grove of lettuce-leaves. The potatoes had to be hurried, not to keep the asparagus waiting, and were not done at last. The blanc-mange was lumpy, and the strawberries not as ripe as they looked, having been skilfully "deaconed."[7]

"Well, they can eat beef, and bread and butter, if they are hungry; only it's mortifying to have to spend your whole morning for nothing," thought Jo, as she rang the bell half an hour later than usual, and stood hot, tired, and dispirited, surveying the feast spread for Laurie, accustomed to all sorts of elegance, and Miss Crocker, whose curious eyes would mark all failures, and whose tattling tongue would report them far and wide.

Poor Jo would gladly have gone under the table, as one thing after another was tasted and left; while Amy giggled, Meg looked distressed, Miss Crocker pursed up her lips, and Laurie talked and laughed with all his might, to give a cheerful tone to the festive scene. Jo's one strong point was the fruit, for she had sugared it well, and had a pitcher of rich cream to eat with it. Her hot cheeks cooled a trifle, and she drew a long breath, as the pretty glass plates went round, and every one looked graciously at the little rosy islands floating in a sea of cream. Miss Crocker tasted first, made a wry face, and drank some water hastily. Jo, who had refused, thinking there might not be enough, for they dwindled sadly after the picking over, glanced at Laurie, but he was eating away manfully, though there was a slight pucker about his mouth, and he kept his eye fixed on his plate. Amy, who was fond of delicate fare, took a heaping spoonful, choked, hid her face in her napkin, and left the table precipitately.

7. Deceptively arranged or packed so as to put the finest fruit on top.

"Oh, what is it?" exclaimed Jo, trembling.

"Salt instead of sugar, and the cream is sour," replied Meg, with a tragic gesture.

Jo uttered a groan, and fell back in her chair; remembering that she had given a last hasty powdering to the berries out of one of the two boxes on the kitchen table, and had neglected to put the milk in the refrigerator. She turned scarlet, and was on the verge of crying, when she met Laurie's eyes, which *would* look merry in spite of his heroic efforts; the comical side of the affair suddenly struck her, and she laughed till the tears ran down her cheeks. So did every one else, even "Croaker," as the girls called the old lady; and the unfortunate dinner ended gaily, with bread and butter, olives and fun.

"I haven't strength of mind enough to clear up now, so we will sober ourselves with a funeral," said Jo, as they rose; and Miss Crocker made ready to go, being eager to tell the new story at another friend's dinner-table.

They did sober themselves, for Beth's sake; Laurie dug a grave under the ferns in the grove, little Pip was laid in, with many tears, by his tender-hearted mistress, and covered with moss, while a wreath of violets and chickweed was hung on the stone which bore his epitaph, composed by Jo, while she struggled with the dinner:—

> "Here lies Pip March,
> 　Who died the 7th of June;
> Loved and lamented sore,
> 　And not forgotten soon."

At the conclusion of the ceremonies, Beth retired to her room, overcome with emotion and lobster; but there was no place of repose, for the beds were not made, and she found her grief much assuaged by beating up pillows and putting things in order. Meg helped Jo clear away the remains of the feast, which took half the afternoon, and left them so tired that they agreed to be contented with tea and toast for supper. Laurie took Amy to drive, which was a deed of charity, for the sour cream seemed to have had a bad effect upon her temper. Mrs. March came home to find the three older girls hard at work in the middle of the afternoon; and a glance at the closet gave her an idea of the success of one part of the experiment.

Before the housewives could rest, several people called, and there was a scramble to get ready to see them; then tea must be got, errands done; and one or two bits of sewing were necessary, but neglected till the last minute. As twilight fell, dewy and still, one by one they gathered in the porch where the June roses were budding beautifully, and each groaned or sighed as she sat down, as if tired or troubled.

"What a dreadful day this has been!" begun Jo, usually the first to speak.

"It has seemed shorter than usual, but *so* uncomfortable," said Meg.

"Not a bit like home," added Amy.

"It can't seem so without Marmee and little Pip," sighed Beth, glancing, with full eyes, at the empty cage above her head.

"Here's mother, dear, and you shall have another bird to-morrow, if you want it."

As she spoke, Mrs. March came and took her place among them, looking as if her holiday had not been much pleasanter than theirs.

"Are you satisfied with your experiment, girls, or do you want another week of it?" she asked, as Beth nestled up to her, and the rest turned toward her with brightening faces, as flowers turn toward the sun.

"I don't!" cried Jo, decidedly.

"Nor I," echoed the others.

"You think, then, that it is better to have a few duties, and live a little for others, do you?"

"Lounging and larking don't pay," observed Jo, shaking her head. "I'm tired of it, and mean to go to work at something right off."

"Suppose you learn plain cooking; that's a useful accomplishment, which no woman should be without," said Mrs. March, laughing audibly at the recollection of Jo's dinner-party; for she had met Miss Crocker, and heard her account of it.

"Mother! did you go away and let everything be, just to see how we'd get on?" cried Meg, who had had suspicions all day.

"Yes; I wanted you to see how the comfort of all depends on each doing her share faithfully. While Hannah and I did your work, you got on pretty well, though I don't think you were very happy or amiable; so I thought, as a little lesson, I would show you what happens when every one thinks only of herself. Don't you feel that it is pleasanter to help one another, to have daily duties which make leisure sweet when it comes, and to bear or forbear, that home may be comfortable and lovely to us all?"

"We do, mother, we do!" cried the girls.

"Then let me advise you to take up your little burdens again; for though they seem heavy sometimes, they are good for us, and lighten as we learn to carry them. Work is wholesome, and there is plenty for every one; it keeps us from *ennui* and mischief; is good for health and spirits, and gives us a sense of power and independence better than money or fashion."

"We'll work like bees, and love it too; see if we don't!" said Jo. "I'll learn plain cooking for my holiday task; and the next dinner-party I have shall be a success."

"I'll make the set of shirts for father, instead of letting you do it, Marmee. I can and I will, though I'm not fond of sewing; that will be better than fussing over my own things, which are plenty nice enough as they are," said Meg.

"I'll do my lessons every day, and not spend so much time with my music and dolls. I am a stupid thing, and ought to be studying, not playing," was Beth's resolution; while Amy followed their example, by heroically declaring, "I shall learn to make button-holes, and attend to my parts of speech."

"Very good! then I am quite satisfied with the experiment, and fancy that we shall not have to repeat it; only don't go to the other extreme, and delve like slaves. Have regular hours for work and play; make each day both useful and pleasant, and prove that you understand the worth of time by employing it well. Then youth will be delightful, old age will bring few regrets, and life become a beautiful success, in spite of poverty."

"We'll remember, mother!" and they did.

CHAPTER XII.

CAMP LAURENCE.

BETH was post-mistress, for, being most at home, she could attend to it regularly, and dearly liked the daily task of unlocking the little door and distributing the mail. One July day she came in with her hands full, and went about the house leaving letters and parcels, like the penny post.

"Here's your posy, mother! Laurie never forgets that," she said, putting the fresh nosegay in the vase that stood in "Marmee's corner," and was kept supplied by the affectionate boy.

"Miss Meg March, one letter, and a glove," continued Beth, delivering the articles to her sister, who sat near her mother, stitching wristbands.

"Why, I left a pair over there, and here is only one," said Meg, looking at the gray cotton glove.

"Didn't you drop the other in the garden?"

"No, I'm sure I didn't; for there was only one in the office."

"I hate to have odd gloves! Never mind, the other may be found. My letter is only a translation of the German song I wanted; I guess Mr. Brooke did it, for this isn't Laurie's writing."

Mrs. March glanced at Meg, who was looking very pretty in her gingham morning-gown, with the little curls blowing about her forehead, and very womanly, as she sat sewing at her little work-table, full of tidy white rolls; so, unconscious of the thought in her mother's mind, she sewed and sung while her fingers flew, and her mind was busied with girlish fancies as innocent and fresh as the pansies in her belt, that Mrs. March smiled, and was satisfied.

"Two letters for Doctor Jo, a book, and a funny old hat, which covered the whole post-office, stuck outside," said Beth, laughing, as she went into the study, where Jo sat writing.

"What a sly fellow Laurie is! I said I wished bigger hats were the fashion, because I burn my face every hot day. He said, 'Why mind the fashion? wear a big hat, and be comfortable!' I said I would, if I had one, and he has sent me this, to try me; I'll wear it, for fun, and show him I *don't* care for the fashion;" and, hanging the antique broad-brim on a bust of Plato, Jo read her letters.

One from her mother made her cheeks glow, and her eyes fill, for it said to her,—

"MY DEAR:

"I write a little word to tell you with how much satisfaction I watch your efforts to control your temper. You say nothing about your trials, failures, or successes, and think, perhaps, that no one sees them but the Friend whose help you daily ask, if I may trust the well-worn cover of your guide-book. *I*, too, have seen them all, and heartily believe in the sincerity of your resolution, since it begins to bear fruit. Go on, dear, patiently and bravely, and always believe that no one sympathizes more tenderly with you than your loving   MOTHER."

"That does me good! that's worth millions of money, and pecks of praise. Oh, Marmee, I do try! I will keep on trying, and not get tired, since I have you to help me."

Laying her head on her arms, Jo wet her little romance with a few happy tears, for she *had* thought that no one saw and appreciated her efforts to be good, and this assurance was doubly precious, doubly encouraging, because unexpected, and from the person whose commendation she most valued. Feeling stronger than ever to meet and subdue her Apollyon,[8] she pinned the note inside her frock, as a shield and a reminder, lest she be taken unaware, and proceeded to open her other letter, quite ready for either good or bad news. In a big, dashing hand, Laurie wrote,—

"DEAR JO,
What ho!

Some English girls and boys are coming to see me to-morrow, and I want to have a jolly time. If it's fine, I'm going to pitch my tent in Longmeadow, and row up the whole crew to lunch and croquet;—have a fire, make messes, gypsy fashion, and all sorts of larks. They are nice people, and like such things. Brooke will go, to keep us boys steady, and Kate Vaughn will play propriety[9] for the girls. I want you all to come; can't let Beth off, at any price, and nobody shall worry her. Don't bother about rations,—I'll see to that, and everything else,—only do come, there's a good fellow!

"In a tearing hurry,
Yours ever, LAURIE."

"Here's richness!" cried Jo, flying in to tell the news to Meg. "Of course we can go, mother! it will be such a help to Laurie, for I can row, and Meg see to the lunch, and the children be useful some way."

"I hope the Vaughn's are not fine, grown-up people. Do you know anything about them, Jo?" asked Meg.

"Only that there are four of them. Kate is older than you, Fred and Frank (twins) about my age, and a little girl (Grace), who is nine or

8. See p. 17, n. 1 (part 1, chap. 1).
9. Serve as chaperon.

ten. Laurie knew them abroad, and liked the boys; I fancied, from the way he primmed up his mouth in speaking of her, that he didn't admire Kate much."

"I'm so glad my French print is clean, it's just the thing, and so becoming!" observed Meg, complacently. "Have you anything decent, Jo?"

"Scarlet and gray boating suit, good enough for me; I shall row and tramp about, so I don't want any starch to think of. You'll come, Betty?"

"If you won't let any of the boys talk to me."

"Not a boy!"

"I like to please Laurie; and I'm not afraid of Mr. Brooke, he is so kind; but I don't want to play, or sing, or say anything. I'll work hard, and not trouble any one; and you'll take care of me, Jo, so I'll go."

"That's my good girl; you do try to fight off your shyness, and I love you for it; fighting faults isn't easy, as I know; and a cheery word kind of gives a lift. Thank you, mother," and Jo gave the thin cheek a grateful kiss, more precious to Mrs. March than if it had given her back the rosy roundness of her youth.

"I had a box of chocolate drops, and the picture I wanted to copy," said Amy, showing her mail.

"And I got a note from Mr. Laurence, asking me to come over and play to him to-night, before the lamps are lighted, and I shall go," added Beth, whose friendship with the old gentleman prospered finely.

"Now let's fly round, and do double duty today, so that we can play to-morrow with free minds," said Jo, preparing to replace her pen with a broom.

When the sun peeped into the girls' room early next morning, to promise them a fine day, he saw a comical sight. Each had made such preparation for the fête as seemed necessary and proper. Meg had an extra row of little curl papers across her forehead, Jo had copiously anointed her afflicted face with cold cream, Beth had taken Joanna to bed with her to atone for the approaching separation, and Amy had capped the climax by putting a clothes-pin on her nose, to uplift the offending feature. It was one of the kind artists use to hold the paper on their drawing-boards; therefore, quite appropriate and effective for the purpose to which it was now put. This funny spectacle appeared to amuse the sun, for he burst out with such radiance that Jo woke up, and roused all her sisters by a hearty laugh at Amy's ornament.

Sunshine and laughter were good omens for a pleasure party, and soon a lively bustle began in both houses. Beth, who was ready first, kept reporting what went on next door, and enlivened her sisters' toilets by frequent telegrams from the window.

"There goes the man with the tent! I see Mrs. Barker doing up the lunch, in a hamper, and a great basket. Now Mr. Laurence is looking up at the sky, and the weathercock; I wish he would go, too! There's Laurie looking like a sailor,—nice boy! Oh, mercy me! here's a carriage full of people—a tall lady, a little girl, and two dreadful boys. One is lame; poor thing, he's got a crutch! Laurie didn't tell us that. Be quick, girls! it's getting late. Why, there is Ned Moffat, I do declare. Look, Meg! isn't that the man who bowed to you one day, when we were shopping?"

"So it is; how queer that he should come! I thought he was at the Mountains. There is Sallie; I'm glad she got back in time. Am I all right, Jo?" cried Meg, in a flutter.

"A regular daisy; hold up your dress, and put your hat straight; it looks sentimental tipped that way, and will fly off at the first puff. Now, then, come on!"

"Oh, oh, Jo! you ain't going to wear that awful hat? It's too absurd! You shall *not* make a guy of yourself," remonstrated Meg, as Jo tied down, with a red ribbon, the broad-brimmed, old-fashioned Leghorn Laurie had sent for a joke.

"I just will, though! it's capital; so shady, light, and big. It will make fun; and I don't mind being a guy, if I'm comfortable." With that Jo marched straight away, and the rest followed; a bright little band of sisters, all looking their best, in summer suits, with happy faces, under the jaunty hat-brims.

Laurie ran to meet, and present them to his friends, in the most cordial manner. The lawn was the reception room, and for several minutes a lively scene was enacted there. Meg was grateful to see that Miss Kate, though twenty, was dressed with a simplicity which American girls would do well to imitate; and she was much flattered by Mr. Ned's assurances that he came especially to see her. Jo understood why Laurie "primmed up his mouth" when speaking of Kate, for that young lady had a stand-off-don't-touch-me air, which contrasted strongly with the free and easy demeanor of the other girls. Beth took an observation of the new boys, and decided that the lame one was not "dreadful," but gentle and feeble, and she would be kind to him, on that account. Amy found Grace a well-mannered, merry little person; and, after staring dumbly at one another for a few minutes, they suddenly became very good friends.

Tents, lunch, and croquet utensils having been sent on beforehand, the party was soon embarked, and the two boats pushed off together, leaving Mr. Laurence waving his hat on the shore. Laurie and Jo rowed one boat; Mr. Brooke and Ned the other; while Fred Vaughn, the riotous twin, did his best to upset both, by paddling about in a wherry, like a disturbed water-bug. Jo's funny hat deserved a vote of thanks, for it was of general utility; it broke the ice in the beginning, by producing a laugh; it created quite a refreshing breeze, flapping to and fro, as she rowed, and would make an excellent umbrella for the whole party, if a shower came up, she said. Kate looked rather amazed at Jo's proceedings, especially as she exclaimed "Christopher Columbus!" when she lost her oar; and Laurie said, "My dear fellow, did I hurt you?" when he tripped over her feet in taking his place. But after putting up her glass to examine the queer girl several times, Miss Kate decided that she was "odd, but rather clever," and smiled upon her from afar.

Meg, in the other boat, was delightfully situated, face to face with the rowers, who both admired the prospect, and feathered their oars with uncommon "skill and dexterity." Mr. Brooke was a grave, silent young man, with handsome brown eyes, and a pleasant voice. Meg liked his quiet manners, and considered him a walking encyclopædia of useful knowledge. He never talked to her much; but he looked at her a good deal, and she felt sure that he did not regard her with aversion. Ned being in college, of course put on all the airs which Freshmen think it their bounden duty to assume; he was not very wise, but very good-natured and merry, and, altogether, an excellent person to carry on a picnic. Sallie Gardiner was absorbed in keeping her white piquè dress clean, and chattering with the ubiquitous Fred, who kept Beth in constant terror by his pranks.

It was not far to Longmeadow; but the tent was pitched, and the wickets down, by the time they arrived. A pleasant green field, with three wide-spreading oaks in the middle, and a smooth strip of turf for croquet.

"Welcome to Camp Laurence!" said the young host, as they landed, with exclamations of delight. "Brooke is commander-in-chief; I am commissary-general; the other fellows are staff-officers; and you, ladies, are company. The tent is for your especial benefit, and that oak is your drawing-room; this is the mess-room, and the third is the camp kitchen. Now let's have a game before it gets hot, and then we'll see about dinner."

Frank, Beth, Amy, and Grace, sat down to watch the game played by the other eight. Mr. Brooke chose Meg, Kate, and Fred; Laurie took Sallie, Jo, and Ned. The Englishers played well; but the Americans played better, and contested every inch of the ground as strongly as if the spirit of '76[1] inspired them. Jo and Fred had several skirmishes, and once narrowly escaped high words. Jo was through the last wicket, and had missed the stroke, which failure ruffled her a good deal. Fred was close behind her, and his turn came before hers; he gave a stroke, his ball hit the wicket, and stopped an inch on the wrong side. No one was very near; and, running up to examine, he gave it a sly nudge with his toe, which put it just an inch on the right side.

"I'm through! now, Miss Jo, I'll settle you, and get in first," cried the young gentleman, swinging his mallet for another blow.

"You pushed it; I saw you; it's my turn now," said Jo, sharply.

"Upon my word I didn't move it! it rolled a bit, perhaps, but that is allowed; so stand off, please, and let me have a go at the stake."

"We don't cheat in America; but *you* can, if you choose," said Jo, angrily.

"Yankees are a deal the most tricky, everybody knows. There you go," returned Fred, croqueting her ball far away.

Jo opened her lips to say something rude; but checked herself in time, colored up to her forehead, and stood a minute, hammering down a wicket with all her might, while Fred hit the stake, and de-

1. The enthusiastic loyalty that inspired American support for the Declaration of Independence (1776) and the Revolutionary War against British rule (1775–83).

clared himself out, with much exultation. She went off to get her ball, and was a long time finding it, among the bushes; but she came back, looking cool and quiet, and waited her turn patiently. It took several strokes to regain the place she had lost; and, when she got there, the other side had nearly won, for Kate's ball was the last but one, and lay near the stake.

"By George, it's all up with us! Good-by, Kate; Miss Jo owes me one, so you are finished," cried Fred, excitedly, as they all drew near to see the finish.

"Yankees have a trick of being generous to their enemies," said Jo, with a look that made the lad redden, "especially when they beat them," she added, as, leaving Kate's ball untouched, she won the game by a clever stroke.

Laurie threw up his hat; then remembered that it wouldn't do to exult over the defeat of his guests, and stopped in the middle of a cheer to whisper to his friend,—

"Good for you, Jo! he did cheat, I saw him; we can't tell him so, but he won't do it again, take my word for it."

Meg drew her aside, under pretence of pinning up a loose braid, and said, approvingly,—

"It was dreadfully provoking; but you kept your temper, and I'm so glad, Jo."

"Don't praise me, Meg, for I could box his ears this minute. I should certainly have boiled over, if I hadn't stayed among the nettles till I got my rage under enough to hold my tongue. It's simmering now, so I hope he'll keep out of my way," returned Jo, biting her lips, as she glowered at Fred from under her big hat.

"Time for lunch," said Mr. Brooke, looking at his watch. "Commissary-general, will you make the fire, and get water, while Miss March, Miss Sallie, and I spread the table. Who can make good coffee?"

"Jo can," said Meg, glad to recommend her sister. So Jo, feeling that her late lessons in cookery were to do her honor, went to preside over the coffee-pot, while the children collected dry sticks, and the boys made a fire, and got water from a spring near by. Miss Kate sketched, and Frank talked to Beth, who was making little mats of braided rushes, to serve as plates.

The commander-in-chief and his aids soon spread the table-cloth with an inviting array of eatables and drinkables, prettily decorated with green leaves. Jo announced that the coffee was ready, and every one settled themselves to a hearty meal; for youth is seldom dyspeptic, and exercise develops wholesome appetites. A very merry lunch it was; for everything seemed fresh and funny, and frequent peals of laughter startled a venerable horse, who fed near by. There was a pleasing inequality in the table, which produced many mishaps to cups and plates; acorns dropped into the milk, little black ants partook of the refreshments without being invited, and fuzzy caterpillars swung down from the tree, to see what was going on. Three white-headed children peeped over the fence, and an objectionable dog barked at them from the other side of the river, with all his might and main.

"There's salt, here, if you prefer it," said Laurie, as he handed Jo a saucer of berries.

"Thank you; I prefer spiders," she replied, fishing up two unwary little ones, who had gone to a creamy death. "How dare you remind me of that horrid dinner-party, when yours is so nice in every way?" added Jo, as they both laughed, and ate out of one plate, the china having run short.

"I had an uncommonly good time that day, and haven't got over it yet. This is no credit to me, you know; I don't do anything; it's you, and Meg, and Brooke, who make it go, and I'm no end obliged to you. What shall we do when we can't eat any more?" asked Laurie, feeling that his trump card had been played when lunch was over.

"Have games, till it's cooler. I brought 'Authors,'[2] and I dare say Miss Kate knows something new and nice. Go and ask her; she's company, and you ought to stay with her more."

"Aren't you company, too? I thought she'd suit Brooke; but he keeps talking to Meg, and Kate just stares at them through that ridiculous glass of hers. I'm going, so you needn't try to preach propriety, for you can't do it, Jo."

Miss Kate did know several new games; and as the girls would not, and the boys could not, eat any more, they all adjourned to the drawing-room, to play "Rigmarole."

"One person begins a story, any nonsense you like, and tells as long as they please, only taking care to stop short at some exciting point, when the next takes it up, and does the same. It's very funny, when well done, and makes a perfect jumble of tragical comical stuff to laugh over. Please start it, Mr. Brooke," said Kate, with a commanding gesture, which surprised Meg, who treated the tutor with as much respect as any other gentleman.

Lying on the grass, at the feet of the two young ladies, Mr. Brooke obediently began the story, with the handsome brown eyes steadily fixed upon the sunshiny river.

"Once on a time, a knight went out into the world to seek his fortune, for he had nothing but his sword and his shield. He travelled a long while, nearly eight-and-twenty years, and had a hard time of it, till he came to the palace of a good old king, who had offered a reward to any one who would tame and train a fine, but unbroken colt, of which he was very fond. The knight agreed to try, and got on slowly, but surely; for the colt was a gallant fellow, and soon learned to love his new master, though he was freakish and wild. Every day, when he gave his lessons to this pet of the king's, the knight rode him through the city; and, as he rode, he looked everywhere for a certain beautiful face, which he had seen many times in his dreams, but never found. One day, as he went prancing down a quiet street, he saw at the window of a ruinous castle the lovely face. He was delighted, inquired who lived in this old castle, and was told that several captive princesses were kept there by a spell, and spun all day to lay up money

---

2. A card game.

to buy their liberty. The knight wished intensely that he could free them; but he was poor, and could only go by each day, watching for the sweet face, and longing to see it out in the sunshine. At last, he resolved to get into the castle, and ask how he could help them. He went and knocked; the great door flew open, and he beheld—"

"A ravishingly lovely lady, who exclaimed, with a cry of rapture, 'At last! at last!'" continued Kate, who had read French novels, and admired the style. "' 'Tis she!' cried Count Gustave, and fell at her feet in an ecstasy of joy. 'Oh, rise!' she said, extending a hand of marble fairness. 'Never! till you tell me how I may rescue you,' swore the knight, still kneeling. 'Alas, my cruel fate condemns me to remain here till my tyrant is destroyed.' 'Where is the villain?' 'In the mauve salon; go, brave heart, and save me from despair.' 'I obey, and return victorious or dead!' With these thrilling words he rushed away, and, flinging open the door of the mauve salon, was about to enter, when he received—"

"A stunning blow from the big Greek lexicon, which an old fellow in a black gown fired at him," said Ned. "Instantly Sir What's-his-name recovered himself, pitched the tyrant out of the window, and turned to join the lady, victorious, but with a bump on his brow; found the door locked, tore up the curtains, made a rope ladder, got half-way down when ladder broke, and he went head first into the moat, sixty feet below. Could swim like a duck, paddled round the castle till he came to a little door guarded by two stout fellows; knocked their heads together till they cracked like a couple of nuts, then, by a trifling exertion of his prodigious strength, he smashed in the door, went up a pair of stone steps covered with dust a foot thick, toads as big as your fist, and spiders that would frighten you into hysterics, Miss March. At the top of these steps he came plump upon a sight that took his breath away and chilled his blood—"

"A tall figure, all in white, with a veil over its face, and a lamp in its wasted hand," went on Meg. "It beckoned, gliding noiselessly before him down a corridor as dark and cold as any tomb. Shadowy effigies in armor stood on either side, a dead silence reigned, the lamp burned blue, and the ghostly figure ever and anon turned its face toward him, showing the glitter of awful eyes through its white veil. They reached a curtained door, behind which sounded lovely music; he sprang forward to enter, but the spectre plucked him back, and waved, threateningly, before him a—"

"Snuff-box," said Jo, in a sepulchral tone, which convulsed the audience. "'Thankee,' said the knight, politely, as he took a pinch, and sneezed seven times so violently that his head fell off. 'Ha! ha!' laughed the ghost; and, having peeped through the keyhole at the princesses spinning away for dear life, the evil spirit picked up her victim and put him in a large tin box, where there were eleven other knights packed together without their heads, like sardines, who all rose and began to—"

"Dance a hornpipe," cut in Fred, as Jo paused for breath; "and, as they danced, the rubbishy old castle turned to a man-of-war in full sail. 'Up with the jib, reef the tops'l halliards, helm hard a lee, and man the guns,' roared the captain, as a Portuguese pirate hove in sight, with a flag black as ink flying from her foremast. 'Go in and win my hearties,' says the captain; and a tremendous fight begun. Of course the British beat—they always do; and, having taken the pirate captain prisoner, sailed slap over the schooner, whose decks were piled with dead, and whose lee-scuppers ran blood, for the order had been 'Cutlasses, and die hard.' 'Bosen's mate,[3] take a bight of the flying jib sheet, and start this villain if he don't confess his sins double quick,' said the British captain. The Portuguese held his tongue like a brick, and walked the plank, while the jolly tars cheered like mad. But the sly dog dived, came up under the man-of-war, scuttled her, and down she went, with all sail set, 'To the bottom of the sea, sea, sea,'[4] where—"

"Oh, gracious! what *shall* I say?" cried Sallie, as Fred ended his rig-marole, in which he had jumbled together, pell-mell, nautical phrases and facts, out of one of his favorite books. "Well, they went to the bot-tom, and a nice mermaid welcomed them, but was much grieved on finding the box of headless knights, and kindly pickled them in brine, hoping to discover the mystery about them; for, being a woman, she was curious. By and by a diver came down, and the mermaid said, 'I'll give you this box of pearls if you can take it up;' for she wanted to re-store the poor things to life, and couldn't raise the heavy load herself. So the diver hoisted it up, and was much disappointed, on opening it, to find no pearls. He left it in a great lonely field, where it was found by a—"

"Little goose-girl, who kept a hundred fat geese in the field," said Amy, when Sallie's invention gave out. "The little girl was sorry for them, and asked an old woman what she should do to help them. 'Your geese will tell you, they know everything,' said the old woman. So she asked what she should use for new heads, since the old ones were lost, and all the geese opened their hundred mouths, and screamed—"

" 'Cabbages!' continued Laurie, promptly. 'Just the thing,' said the girl, and ran to get twelve fine ones from her garden. She put them on, the knights revived at once, thanked her, and went on their way re-joicing, never knowing the difference, for there were so many other heads like them in the world, that no one thought anything of it. The knight in whom I'm interested went back to find the pretty face, and learned that the princesses had spun themselves free, and all gone to be married, but one. He was in a great state of mind at that; and, mounting the colt, who stood by him through thick and thin, rushed to the castle to see which was left. Peeping over the hedge, he saw the queen of his affections picking flowers in her garden. 'Will you give me a rose?' said he. 'You must come and get it; I can't come to you; it isn't proper,' said she, as sweet as honey. He tried to climb over the hedge, but it seemed to grow higher and higher; then he tried to push through, but it grew thicker and thicker, and he was in despair. So he

---

3. Shortening of "boatswain's mate," i.e., the assistant to the boatswain, the officer in charge of the sails, rigging, etc.
4. Line from a jump-rope song that begins "Columbus went to sea, sea, sea."

patiently broke twig after twig, till he had made a little hole, through which he peeped, saying, imploringly, 'Let me in! let me in!' But the pretty princess did not seem to understand, for she picked her roses quietly, and left him to fight his way in. Whether he did or not, Frank will tell you."

"I can't; I'm not playing, I never do," said Frank, dismayed at the sentimental predicament out of which he was to rescue the absurd couple. Beth had disappeared behind Jo, and Grace was asleep.

"So the poor knight is to be left sticking in the hedge, is he?" asked Mr. Brooke, still watching the river, and playing with the wild rose in his button-hole.

"I guess the princess gave him a posy, and opened the gate, after awhile," said Laurie, smiling to himself, as he threw acorns at his tutor.

"What a piece of nonsense we have made! With practice we might do something quite clever. Do you know 'Truth?'" asked Sallie, after they had laughed over their story.

"I hope so," said Meg, soberly.

"The game, I mean?"

"What is it?" said Fred.

"Why, you pile up your hands, choose a number, and draw out in turn, and the person who draws at the number has to answer truly any questions put by the rest. It's great fun."

"Let's try it," said Jo, who liked new experiments.

Miss Kate and Mr. Brooke, Meg and Ned, declined; but Fred, Sallie, Jo and Laurie piled and drew; and the lot fell to Laurie.

"Who are your heroes?" asked Jo.

"Grandfather and Napoleon."

"What lady do you think prettiest?" said Sallie.

"Margaret."

"Which do you like best?" from Fred.

"Jo, of course."

"What silly questions you ask!" and Jo gave a disdainful shrug as the rest laughed at Laurie's matter-of-fact tone.

"Try again; Truth isn't a bad game," said Fred.

"It's a very good one for you," retorted Jo, in a low voice. Her turn came next.

"What is your greatest fault?" asked Fred, by way of testing in her the virtue he lacked himself.

"A quick temper."

"What do you most wish for?" said Laurie.

"A pair of boot-lacings," returned Jo, guessing and defeating his purpose.

"Not a true answer; you must say what you really do want most."

"Genius; don't you wish you could give it to me, Laurie?" and she slyly smiled in his disappointed face.

"What virtues do you most admire in a man?" asked Sallie.

"Courage and honesty."

"Now my turn," said Fred, as his hand came last.

"Let's give it to him," whispered Laurie to Jo, who nodded, and asked at once,—

"Didn't you cheat at croquet?"

"Well, yes, a little bit."

"Good! Didn't you take your story out of 'The Sea Lion?'"[5] said Laurie.

"Rather."

"Don't you think the English nation perfect in every respect?" asked Sallie.

"I should be ashamed of myself if I didn't."

"He's a true John Bull. Now, Miss Sallie, you shall have a chance without waiting to draw. I'll harrow up your feelings first by asking if you don't think you are something of a flirt," said Laurie, as Jo nodded to Fred, as a sign that peace was declared.

"You impertinent boy! of course I'm not," exclaimed Sallie, with an air that proved the contrary.

"What do you hate most?" asked Fred.

"Spiders and rice pudding."

"What do you like best?" asked Jo.

"Dancing and French gloves."

"Well, I think Truth is a very silly play; let's have a sensible game of Authors, to refresh our minds," proposed Jo.

Ned, Frank, and the little girls joined in this, and, while it went on, the three elders sat apart, talking. Miss Kate took out her sketch again, and Margaret watched her, while Mr. Brooke lay on the grass, with a book, which he did not read.

"How beautifully you do it; I wish I could draw," said Meg, with mingled admiration and regret in her voice.

"Why don't you learn? I should think you had taste and talent for it," replied Miss Kate, graciously.

"I haven't time."

"Your mamma prefers other accomplishments, I fancy. So did mine; but I proved to her that I had talent, by taking a few lessons privately, and then she was quite willing I should go on. Can't you do the same with your governess?"

"I have none."

"I forgot; young ladies in America go to school more than with us. Very fine schools they are, too, papa says. You go to a private one, I suppose?"

"I don't go at all; I am a governess myself."

"Oh, indeed!" said Miss Kate; but she might as well have said, "Dear me, how dreadful!" for her tone implied it, and something in her face made Meg color, and wish she had not been so frank.

Mr. Brooke looked up, and said, quickly, "Young ladies in America love independence as much as their ancestors did, and are admired and respected for supporting themselves."

5. Sylvanus Cobb's *The Sea Lion; or, The Privateer of the Penobscot: A Story of Ocean Life and the Heart's Love* (1853).

"Oh, yes; of course! it's very nice and proper in them to do so. We have many most respectable and worthy young women, who do the same; and are employed by the nobility, because, being the daughters of gentlemen, they are both well-bred and accomplished, you know," said Miss Kate, in a patronizing tone, that hurt Meg's pride, and made her work seem not only more distasteful, but degrading.

"Did the German song suit, Miss March?" inquired Mr. Brooke, breaking an awkward pause.

"Oh, yes! it was very sweet, and I'm much obliged to whoever translated it for me;" and Meg's downcast face brightened as she spoke.

"Don't you read German?" asked Miss Kate, with a look of surprise.

"Not very well. My father, who taught me, is away, and I don't get on very fast alone, for I've no one to correct my pronunciation."

"Try a little now; here is Schiller's 'Mary Stuart,'[6] and a tutor who loves to teach," and Mr. Brooke laid his book on her lap, with an inviting smile.

"It's so hard, I'm afraid to try," said Meg, grateful, but bashful in the presence of the accomplished young lady beside her.

"I'll read a bit, to encourage you;" and Miss Kate read one of the most beautiful passages, in a perfectly correct, but perfectly expressionless, manner.

Mr. Brooke made no comment, as she returned the book to Meg, who said, innocently,—

"I thought it was poetry."

"Some of it is; try this passage."

There was a queer smile about Mr. Brooke's mouth, as he opened at poor Mary's lament.

Meg, obediently following the long grass-blade which her new tutor used to point with, read, slowly and timidly, unconsciously making poetry of the hard words, by the soft intonation of her musical voice. Down the page went the green guide, and presently, forgetting her listener in the beauty of the sad scene, Meg read as if alone, giving a little touch of tragedy to the words of the unhappy queen. If she had seen the brown eyes then, she would have stopped short; but she never looked up, and the lesson was not spoilt for her.

"Very well, indeed!" said Mr. Brooke, as she paused, quite ignoring her many mistakes, and looking as if he did, indeed, "love to teach."

Miss Kate put up her glass, and, having taken a survey of the little tableau before her, shut her sketch-book, saying, with condescension,—

"You've a nice accent, and, in time, will be a clever reader. I advise you to learn, for German is a valuable accomplishment to teachers. I must look after Grace, she is romping;" and Miss Kate strolled away, adding to herself, with a shrug, "I didn't come to chaperone a gov-

6. The German poet and playwright Friedrich von Schiller's blank-verse tragedy *Mary Stuart* (1800) explores the sixteenth-century struggle between Elizabeth I, the powerful queen of England, and a young, sensual, and tragic Mary Stuart, the deposed and ultimately executed queen of Scotland.

erness, though she *is* young and pretty. What odd people these Yankees are! I'm afraid Laurie will be quite spoilt among them."

"I forgot that English people rather turn up their noses at governesses, and don't treat them as we do," said Meg, looking after the retreating figure with an annoyed expression.

"Tutors, also, have rather a hard time of it there, as I know to my sorrow. There's no place like America for us workers, Miss Margaret," and Mr. Brooke looked so contented and cheerful, that Meg was ashamed to lament her hard lot.

"I'm glad I live in it, then. I don't like my work, but I get a good deal of satisfaction out of it, after all, so I won't complain; I only wish I liked teaching as you do."

"I think you would, if you had Laurie for a pupil. I shall be very sorry to lose him next year," said Mr. Brooke, busily punching holes in the turf.

"Going to college, I suppose?" Meg's lips asked that question, but her eyes added, "And what becomes of you?"

"Yes; it's high time he went, for he is nearly ready, and as soon as he is off I shall turn soldier."

"I'm glad of that!" exclaimed Meg; "I should think every young man would want to go; though it is hard for the mothers and sisters, who stay at home," she added, sorrowfully.

"I have neither, and very few friends, to care whether I live or die," said Mr. Brooke, rather bitterly, as he absently put the dead rose in the hole he had made, and covered it up, like a little grave.

"Laurie and his grandfather would care a great deal, and we should all be very sorry to have any harm happen to you," said Meg, heartily.

"Thank you; that sounds pleasant," began Mr. Brooke, looking cheerful again; but, before he could finish his speech, Ned, mounted on the old horse, came lumbering up, to display his equestrian skill before the young ladies, and there was no more quiet that day.

"Don't you love to ride?" asked Grace of Amy, as they stood resting, after a race round the field with the others, led by Ned.

"I dote upon it; my sister Meg used to ride, when papa was rich, but we don't keep any horses now, except Ellen Tree," added Amy, laughing.

"Tell me about Ellen Tree; is it a donkey?" asked Grace, curiously.

"Why, you see, Jo is crazy about horses, and so am I, but we've only got an old side-saddle, and no horse. Out in our garden is an apple-tree, that has a nice low branch; so I put the saddle on it, fixed some reins on the part that turns up, and we bounce away on Ellen Tree whenever we like."

"How funny!" laughed Grace. "I have a pony at home, and ride nearly every day in the park, with Fred and Kate; it's very nice, for my friends go too, and the Row[7] is full of ladies and gentlemen."

"Dear, how charming! I hope I shall go abroad, some day; but I'd rather go to Rome than the Row," said Amy, who had not the remotest idea what the Row was, and wouldn't have asked for the world.

---

7. Rotten Row, a famous horseback riding trail in London's Hyde Park.

Frank, sitting just behind the little girls, heard what they were say-ing, and pushed his crutch away from him with an impatient gesture, as he watched the active lads going through all sorts of comical gym-nastics. Beth, who was collecting the scattered Author-cards, looked up, and said, in her shy yet friendly way,—

"I'm afraid you are tired; can I do anything for you?"

"Talk to me, please; it's dull, sitting by myself," answered Frank, who had evidently been used to being made much of at home.

If he had asked her to deliver a Latin oration, it would not have seemed a more impossible task to bashful Beth; but there was no place to run to, no Jo to hide behind now, and the poor boy looked so wistfully at her, that she bravely resolved to try.

"What do you like to talk about?" she asked, fumbling over the cards, and dropping half as she tried to tie them up.

"Well, I like to hear about cricket, and boating, and hunting," said Frank, who had not yet learned to suit his amusements to his strength.

"My heart! whatever shall I do! I don't know anything about them," thought Beth; and, forgetting the boy's misfortune in her flurry, she said, hoping to make him talk, "I never saw any hunting, but I suppose you know all about it."

"I did once; but I'll never hunt again, for I got hurt leaping a con-founded five-barred gate; so there's no more horses and hounds for me," said Frank, with a sigh that made Beth hate herself for her inno-cent blunder.

"Your deer are much prettier than our ugly buffaloes," she said, turning to the prairies for help, and feeling glad that she had read one of the boys' books in which Jo delighted.

Buffaloes proved soothing and satisfactory; and, in her eagerness to amuse another, Beth forgot herself, and was quite unconscious of her sis-ter's surprise and delight at the unusual spectacle of Beth talking away to one of the dreadful boys, against whom she had begged protection.

"Bless her heart! She pities him, so she is good to him," said Jo, beaming at her from the croquet-ground.

"I always said she was a little saint," added Meg, as if there could be no further doubt of it.

"I haven't heard Frank laugh so much for ever so long," said Grace to Amy, as they sat discussing dolls, and making tea-sets out of the acorn-cups.

"My sister Beth is a very fastidious girl, when she likes to be," said Amy, well pleased at Beth's success. She meant "fascinating," but, as Grace didn't know the exact meaning of either word, "fastidious" sounded well, and made a good impression.

An impromptu circus, fox and geese,[8] and an amicable game of cro-quet, finished the afternoon. At sunset the tent was struck, hampers packed, wickets pulled up, boats loaded, and the whole party floated down the river, singing at the tops of their voices. Ned, getting senti-mental, warbled a serenade with the pensive refrain,—

8. A game, a version of tag similar to Red Rover.

> "Alone, alone, ah! woe, alone,"

and at the lines—

> "We each are young, we each have a heart,
> Oh, why should we stand thus coldly apart?"[9]

he looked at Meg with such a lackadaisical expression, that she laughed outright, and spoilt his song.

"How can you be so cruel to me?" he whispered, under cover of a lively chorus; "you've kept close to that starched-up English woman all day, and now you snub me."

"I didn't mean to; but you looked so funny I really couldn't help it," replied Meg, passing over the first part of his reproach; for it was quite true that she *had* shunned him, remembering the Moffat party and the talk after it.

Ned was offended, and turned to Sallie for consolation, saying to her, rather pettishly, "There isn't a bit of flirt in that girl, is there?"

"Not a particle; but she's a dear," returned Sallie, defending her friend even while confessing her short-comings.

"She's not a stricken deer, any-way," said Ned, trying to be witty, and succeeding as well as very young gentlemen usually do.

On the lawn where it had gathered, the little party separated with cordial good-nights and good-byes, for the Vaughns were going to Canada. As the four sisters went home through the garden, Miss Kate looked after them, saying, without the patronizing tone in her voice, "In spite of their demonstrative manners, American girls are very nice when one knows them."

"I quite agree with you," said Mr. Brooke.

CHAPTER XIII.

CASTLES IN THE AIR.

LAURIE lay luxuriously swinging to and fro in his hammock, one warm September afternoon, wondering what his neighbors were about, but too lazy to go and find out. He was in one of his moods; for the day had been both unprofitable and unsatisfactory, and he was wishing he could live it over again. The hot weather made him indolent; and he had shirked his studies, tried Mr. Brooke's patience to the utmost, displeased his grandfather by practising half the afternoon, frightened the maid-servants half out of their wits, by mischievously hinting that one of his dogs was going mad, and, after high words with the stableman about some fancied neglect of his horse, he had flung himself into his hammock, to fume over the stupidity of the world in general,

---

9. The words are from the American poet James Russell Lowell's poem "The Serenade" (1840). The refrain is "Alone, alone, ah woe! alone," and lines 21–22 read: "We each are young, we each have a heart, / Why stand we ever coldly apart?" By the mid-1860s his poem had become the lyrics to a popular song known as the "Alone! Alone! Serenade," with music by George Boweryem.

till the peace of the lovely day quieted him in spite of himself. Staring up into the green gloom of the horse-chestnut trees above him, he dreamed dreams of all sorts, and was just imagining himself tossing on the ocean, in a voyage round the world, when the sound of voices brought him ashore in a flash. Peeping through the meshes of the hammock, he saw the Marches coming out, as if bound on some expedition.

"What in the world are those girls about now?" thought Laurie, opening his sleepy eyes to take a good look, for there was something rather peculiar in the appearance of his neighbors. Each wore a large, flapping hat, a brown linen pouch slung over one shoulder, and carried a long staff; Meg had a cushion, Jo a book, Beth a dipper, and Amy a portfolio. All walked quietly through the garden, out at the little back gate, and began to climb the hill that lay between the house and river.

"Well, that's cool!" said Laurie to himself, "to have a picnic and never ask me. They can't be going in the boat, for they haven't got the key. Perhaps they forgot it; I'll take it to them, and see what's going on."

Though possessed of half a dozen hats, it took him some time to find one; then there was a hunt for the key, which was at last discovered in his pocket, so that the girls were quite out of sight when he leaped the fence and ran after them. Taking the shortest way to the boat-house, he waited for them to appear; but no one came, and he went up the hill to take an observation. A grove of pines covered one part of it, and from the heart of this green spot came a clearer sound than the soft sigh of the pines, or the drowsy chirp of the crickets.

"Here's a landscape!" thought Laurie, peeping through the bushes, and looking wide awake and good-natured already.

It *was* rather a pretty little picture; for the sisters sat together in the shady nook, with sun and shadow flickering over them,—the aromatic wind lifting their hair and cooling their hot cheeks,—and all the little wood-people going on with their affairs as if these were no strangers, but old friends. Meg sat upon her cushion, sewing daintily with her white hands, and looking as fresh and sweet as a rose, in her pink dress, among the green. Beth was sorting the cones that lay thick under the hemlock near by, for she made pretty things of them. Amy was sketching a group of ferns, and Jo was knitting as she read aloud. A shadow passed over the boy's face as he watched them, feeling that he ought to go, because uninvited; yet lingering, because home seemed very lonely, and this quiet party in the woods most attractive to his restless spirit. He stood so still, that a squirrel, busy with its harvesting, ran down a pine close beside him, saw him suddenly, and skipped back, scolding so shrilly that Beth looked up, espied the wistful face behind the birches, and beckoned with a reassuring smile.

"May I come in, please? or shall I be a bother?" he asked, advancing slowly.

Meg lifted her eyebrows, but Jo scowled at her defiantly, and said, at once, "Of course you may. We should have asked you before, only we thought you wouldn't care for such a girl's game as this."

"I always like your games; but if Meg don't want me, I'll go away."

"I've no objection, if you do something; it's against the rule to be idle here," replied Meg, gravely, but graciously.

"Much obliged; I'll do anything if you'll let me stop a bit, for it's as dull as the desert of Sahara down there. Shall I sew, read, cone, draw, or do all at once? Bring on your bears;[1] I'm ready," and Laurie sat down with a submissive expression delightful to behold.

"Finish this story while I set my heel," said Jo, handing him the book.

"Yes'm," was the meek answer, as he began, doing his best to prove his gratitude for the favor of an admission into the "Busy Bee Society."

The story was not a long one, and, when it was finished, he ventured to ask a few questions as a reward of merit.

"Please, mum, could I inquire if this highly instructive and charming institution is a new one?"

"Would you tell him?" asked Meg of her sisters.

"He'll laugh," said Amy, warningly.

"Who cares?" said Jo.

"I guess he'll like it," added Beth.

"Of course I shall! I give you my word I won't laugh. Tell away, Jo, and don't be afraid."

"The idea of being afraid of you! Well, you see we used to play 'Pilgrim's Progress,'[2] and we have been going on with it in earnest, all winter and summer."

"Yes, I know," said Laurie, nodding wisely.

"Who told you?" demanded Jo.

"Spirits."

"No, it was me; I wanted to amuse him one night when you were all away, and he was rather dismal. He did like it, so don't scold, Jo," said Beth, meekly.

"You can't keep a secret. Never mind; it saves trouble now."

"Go on, please," said Laurie, as Jo became absorbed in her work, looking a trifle displeased.

"Oh, didn't she tell you about this new plan of ours? Well, we have tried not to waste our holiday, but each has had a task, and worked at it with a will. The vacation is nearly over, the stints are all done, and we are ever so glad that we didn't dawdle."

"Yes, I should think so;" and Laurie thought regretfully of his own idle days.

"Mother likes to have us out of doors as much as possible; so we bring our work here, and have nice times. For the fun of it we bring our things in these bags, wear the old hats, use poles to climb the hill,

---

1. Colloquial, irreverent declaration of one's readiness to face any obstacle or challenge. The origins of the phrase are difficult to trace, but they may be related to a nineteenth-century joke: "the case of the youth who was told the story of the two-and-forty children who were torn by the bears for mocking the prophet. Instead of heeding the moral, he went right out and saluted the first baldheaded individual with 'Go up, baldhead! Now bring on your bears!' " See S. S. Cox, "American Humor. Part II," *Harper's,* May 1875, 847–60, quote from 851.

2. See p. 17, n. 1 (part 1, chap. 1). The Delectable Mountain and the Celestial City mentioned below are also references to Bunyan's allegory.

and play pilgrims, as we used to do years ago. We call this hill the 'Delectable Mountain,' for we can look far away and see the country where we hope to live some time."

Jo pointed, and Laurie sat up to examine; for through an opening in the wood one could look across the wide, blue river,—the meadows on the other side,—far over the outskirts of the great city,[3] to the green hills that rose to meet the sky. The sun was low, and the heavens glowed with the splendor of an autumn sunset. Gold and purple clouds lay on the hill-tops; and rising high into the ruddy light were silvery white peaks, that shone like the airy spires of some Celestial City.

"How beautiful that is!" said Laurie, softly, for he was quick to see and feel beauty of any kind.

"It's often so; and we like to watch it, for it is never the same, but always splendid," replied Amy, wishing she could paint it.

"Jo talks about the country where we hope to live some time; the real country, she means, with pigs and chickens, and haymaking. It would be nice, but I wish the beautiful country up there was real, and we could ever go to it," said Beth, musingly.

"There is a lovelier country even than that, where we *shall* go, by and by, when we are good enough," answered Meg, with her sweet voice.

"It seems so long to wait, so hard to do; I want to fly away at once, as those swallows fly, and go in at that splendid gate."

"You'll get there, Beth, sooner or later; no fear of that," said Jo; "I'm the one that will have to fight and work, and climb and wait, and maybe never get in after all."

"You'll have me for company, if that's any comfort. I shall have to do a deal of travelling before I come in sight of your Celestial City. If I arrive late, you'll say a good word for me, won't you, Beth?"

Something in the boy's face troubled his little friend; but she said cheerfully, with her quiet eyes on the changing clouds, "If people really want to go, and really try all their lives, I think they will get in; for I don't believe there are any locks on that door, or any guards at the gate. I always imagine it is as it is in the picture, where the shining ones stretch out their hands to welcome poor Christian as he comes up from the river."

"Wouldn't it be fun if all the castles in the air which we make could come true, and we could live in them?" said Jo, after a little pause.

"I've made such quantities it would be hard to choose which I'd have," said Laurie, lying flat, and throwing cones at the squirrel who had betrayed him.

"You'd have to take your favorite one. What is it?" asked Meg.

"If I tell mine, will you tell yours?"

"Yes, if the girls will too."

"We will. Now, Laurie!"

"After I'd seen as much of the world as I want to, I'd like to settle in

3. Boston.

Germany, and have just as much music as I choose. I'm to be a famous musician myself, and all creation is to rush to hear me; and I'm never to be bothered about money or business, but just enjoy myself, and live for what I like. That's my favorite castle. What's yours, Meg?"

Margaret seemed to find it a little hard to tell hers, and moved a brake before her face, as if to disperse imaginary gnats, while she said, slowly, "I should like a lovely house, full of all sorts of luxurious things; nice food, pretty clothes, handsome furniture, pleasant people, and heaps of money. I am to be mistress of it, and manage it as I like, with plenty of servants, so I never need work a bit. How I should enjoy it! for I wouldn't be idle, but do good, and make every one love me dearly."

"Wouldn't you have a master for your castle in the air?" asked Laurie, slyly.

"I said 'pleasant people,' you know;" and Meg carefully tied up her shoe as she spoke, so that no one saw her face.

"Why don't you say you'd have a splendid, wise, good husband, and some angelic little children? you know your castle wouldn't be perfect without," said blunt Jo, who had no tender fancies yet, and rather scorned romance, except in books.

"You'd have nothing but horses, inkstands, and novels in yours," answered Meg, petulantly.

"Wouldn't I, though! I'd have a stable full of Arabian steeds, rooms piled with books, and I'd write out of a magic inkstand, so that my works should be as famous as Laurie's music. I want to do something splendid before I go into my castle,—something heroic, or wonderful,—that won't be forgotten after I'm dead. I don't know what, but I'm on the watch for it, and mean to astonish you all, some day. I think I shall write books, and get rich and famous; that would suit me, so that is *my* favorite dream."

"Mine is to stay at home safe with father and mother, and help take care of the family," said Beth, contentedly.

"Don't you wish for anything else?" asked Laurie.

"Since I had my little piano I am perfectly satisfied. I only wish we may all keep well, and be together; nothing else."

"I have lots of wishes; but the pet one is to be an artist, and go to Rome, and do fine pictures, and be the best artist in the whole world," was Amy's modest desire.

"We're an ambitious set, aren't we? Every one of us, but Beth, wants to be rich and famous, and gorgeous in every respect. I do wonder if any of us will ever get our wishes," said Laurie, chewing grass, like a meditative calf.

"I've got the key to my castle in the air; but whether I can unlock the door, remains to be seen," observed Jo, mysteriously.

"I've got the key to mine, but I'm not allowed to try it. Hang college!" muttered Laurie, with an impatient sigh.

"Here's mine!" and Amy waved her pencil.

"I haven't got any," said Meg, forlornly.

"Yes you have," said Laurie, at once.

"Where?"

"In your face."

"Nonsense; that's of no use."

"Wait and see if it doesn't bring you something worth having," replied the boy, laughing at the thought of a charming little secret which he fancied he knew.

Meg colored behind the brake, but asked no questions, and looked across the river with the same expectant expression which Mr. Brooke had worn when he told the story of the knight.

"If we are all alive ten years hence, let's meet, and see how many of us have got our wishes, or how much nearer we are them than now," said Jo, always ready with a plan.

"Bless me! how old I shall be,—twenty-seven!" exclaimed Meg, who felt grown up already, having just reached seventeen.

"You and I shall be twenty-six, Teddy; Beth twenty-four, and Amy twenty-two; what a venerable party!" said Jo.

"I hope I shall have done something to be proud of by that time; but I'm such a lazy dog, I'm afraid I shall 'dawdle,' Jo."

"You need a motive, mother says; and when you get it, she is sure you'll work splendidly."

"Is she? By Jupiter I will, if I only get the chance!" cried Laurie, sitting up with sudden energy. "I ought to be satisfied to please grandfather, and I do try, but it's working against the grain, you see, and comes hard. He wants me to be an India merchant, as he was, and I'd rather be shot; I hate tea, and silk, and spices, and every sort of rubbish his old ships bring, and I don't care how soon they go to the bottom when I own them. Going to college ought to satisfy him, for if I give him four years he ought to let me off from the business; but he's set, and I've got to do just as he did, unless I break away and please myself, as my father did. If there was any one left to stay with the old gentleman, I'd do it to-morrow."

Laurie spoke excitedly, and looked ready to carry his threat into execution on the slightest provocation; for he was growing up very fast, and, in spite of his indolent ways, had a young man's hatred of subjection,—a young man's restless longing to try the world for himself.

"I advise you to sail away in one of your ships, and never come home again till you have tried your own way," said Jo, whose imagination was fired by the thought of such a daring exploit, and whose sympathy was excited by what she called "Teddy's wrongs."

"That's not right, Jo; you mustn't talk in that way, and Laurie mustn't take your bad advice. You should do just what your grandfather wishes, my dear boy," said Meg, in her most maternal tone. "Do your best at college, and, when he sees that you try to please him, I'm sure he won't be hard or unjust to you. As you say, there is no one else to stay with and love him, and you'd never forgive yourself if you left him without his permission. Don't be dismal, or fret, but do your duty; and you'll get your reward, as good Mr. Brooke has, by being respected and loved."

"What do you know about him?" asked Laurie, grateful for the good advice, but objecting to the lecture, and glad to turn the conversation from himself, after his unusual outbreak.

"Only what your grandpa told mother about him; how he took good care of his own mother till she died, and wouldn't go abroad as tutor to some nice person, because he wouldn't leave her; and how he provides now for an old woman who nursed his mother; and never tells any one, but is just as generous, and patient, and good as he can be."

"So he is, dear old fellow!" said Laurie, heartily, as Meg paused, looking flushed and earnest, with her story. "It's like grandpa to find out all about him, without letting him know, and to tell all his goodness to others, so that they might like him. Brooke couldn't understand why your mother was so kind to him, asking him over with me, and treating him in her beautiful, friendly way. He thought she was just perfect, and talked about it for days and days, and went on about you all, in flaming style. If ever I do get my wish, you see what I'll do for Brooke."

"Begin to do something now, by not plaguing his life out," said Meg, sharply.

"How do you know I do, miss?"

"I can always tell by his face, when he goes away. If you have been good, he looks satisfied, and walks briskly; if you have plagued him, he's sober, and walks slowly, as if he wanted to go back and do his work better."

"Well, I like that! So you keep an account of my good and bad marks in Brooke's face, do you? I see him bow and smile as he passes your window, but I didn't know you'd got up a telegraph."

"We haven't; don't be angry, and oh, don't tell him I said anything! It was only to show that I cared how you get on, and what is said here is said in confidence, you know," cried Meg, much alarmed at the thought of what might follow from her careless speech.

"*I* don't tell tales," replied Laurie, with his "high and mighty" air, as Jo called a certain expression which he occasionally wore. "Only if Brooke is going to be a thermometer, I must mind and have fair weather for him to report."

"Please don't be offended; I didn't mean to preach or tell tales, or be silly; I only thought Jo was encouraging you in a feeling which you'd be sorry for, by and by. You are so kind to us, we feel as if you were our brother, and say just what we think; forgive me, I meant it kindly!" and Meg offered her hand with a gesture both affectionate and timid.

Ashamed of his momentary pique, Laurie squeezed the kind little hand, and said, frankly, "I'm the one to be forgiven; I'm cross, and have been out of sorts all day. I like to have you tell me my faults, and be sisterly; so don't mind if I am grumpy sometimes; I thank you all the same."

Bent on showing that he was not offended, he made himself as agreeable as possible; wound cotton for Meg, recited poetry to please Jo, shook down cones for Beth, and helped Amy with her ferns, proving himself a fit person to belong to the "Busy Bee Society." In the midst of an animated discussion on the domestic habits of turtles (one

of which amiable creatures having strolled up from the river), the faint
sound of a bell warned them that Hannah had put the tea "to draw,"
and they would just have time to get home to supper.

"May I come again?" asked Laurie.

"Yes, if you are good, and love your book, as the boys in the primer
are told to do,"[4] said Meg, smiling.

"I'll try."

"Then you may come, and I'll teach you to knit as the Scotchmen
do; there's a demand for socks just now,"[5] added Jo, waving hers, like a
big blue worsted banner, as they parted at the gate.

That night, when Beth played to Mr. Laurence in the twilight, Laurie, standing in the shadow of the curtain, listened to the little David,[6]
whose simple music always quieted his moody spirit, and watched the
old man, who sat with his gray head on his hand, thinking tender
thoughts of the dead child he had loved so much. Remembering the
conversation of the afternoon, the boy said to himself, with the resolve
to make the sacrifice cheerfully, "I'll let my castle go, and stay with the
dear old gentleman while he needs me, for I am all he has."

CHAPTER XIV.

SECRETS.

JO was very busy up in the garret, for the October days began to grow
chilly, and the afternoons were short. For two or three hours the sun
lay warmly in at the high window, showing Jo seated on the old sofa
writing busily, with her papers spread out upon a trunk before her,
while Scrabble, the pet rat, promenaded the beams overhead, accompanied by his oldest son, a fine young fellow, who was evidently very
proud of his whiskers. Quite absorbed in her work, Jo scribbled away
till the last page was filled, when she signed her name with a flourish,
and threw down her pen, exclaiming,—

"There, I've done my best! If this don't suit I shall have to wait till I
can do better."

Lying back on the sofa, she read the manuscript carefully through,
making dashes here and there, and putting in many exclamation
points, which looked like little balloons; then she tied it up with a
smart red ribbon, and sat a minute looking at it with a sober, wistful
expression, which plainly showed how earnest her work had been. Jo's

4. Although Meg seems to refer to a specific tale, it is difficult to establish exactly which one
   she means because so many American primers, from the seventeenth-century *New-England
   Primer* ("My *Book* and *Heart* / Shall never part") to Samuel G. Goodrich's numerous nineteenth-
   century readers and primers (e.g., the Peter Parley tales), tell stories that encourage young
   readers to love their books.
5. Reference to Scotland's long and famous tradition of knitting (see Helen M. Bennett, *Scottish Knitting* [Aylesburg: Shire Publications, 1986]). During the Civil War, civilians in the
   North volunteering for humanitarian agencies, such as the Sanitary Commission or the
   Christian Commission, often made small articles of clothing, especially socks, to provide to
   the characteristically blue-clad Union soldiers.
6. Reference to David, who played his lyre to soothe a distressed Saul. See 1 Samuel
   16.14–23.

desk up here was an old tin kitchen,[7] which hung against the wall. In it she kept her papers, and a few books, safely shut away from Scrabble, who, being likewise of a literary turn, was fond of making a circulating library of such books as were left in his way, by eating the leaves. From this tin receptacle Jo produced another manuscript; and, putting both in her pocket, crept quietly down stairs, leaving her friends to nibble her pens and taste her ink.

She put on her hat and jacket as noiselessly as possible, and, going to the back entry window, got out upon the roof of a low porch, swung herself down to the grassy bank, and took a roundabout way to the road. Once there she composed herself, hailed a passing omnibus, and rolled away to town, looking very merry and mysterious.

If any one had been watching her, he would have thought her movements decidedly peculiar; for, on alighting, she went off at a great pace till she reached a certain number in a certain busy street; having found the place with some difficulty, she went into the doorway, looked up the dirty stairs, and, after standing stock still a minute, suddenly dived into the street, and walked away as rapidly as she came. This manœuvre she repeated several times, to the great amusement of a black-eyed young gentleman lounging in the window of a building opposite. On returning for the third time, Jo gave herself a shake, pulled her hat over her eyes, and walked up the stairs, looking as if she was going to have all her teeth out.

There was a dentist's sign, among others, which adorned the entrance, and, after staring a moment at the pair of artificial jaws which slowly opened and shut to draw attention to a fine set of teeth, the young gentleman put on his coat, took his hat, and went down to post himself in the opposite door-way, saying, with a smile and a shiver,—

"It's like her to come alone, but if she has a bad time she'll need some one to help her home."

In ten minutes Jo came running down stairs with a very red face, and the general appearance of a person who had just passed through a trying ordeal of some sort. When she saw the young gentleman she looked anything but pleased, and passed him with a nod; but he followed, asking with an air of sympathy,—

"Did you have a bad time?"

"Not very."

"You got through quick."

"Yes, thank goodness!"

"Why did you go alone?"

"Didn't want any one to know."

"You're the oddest fellow I ever saw. How many did you have out?"

Jo looked at her friend as if she did not understand him; then began to laugh, as if mightily amused at something.

"There are two which I want to have come out, but I must wait a week."

7. An early American cooking appliance, a reflector oven used for roasting meat before a fire.

"What are you laughing at? You are up to some mischief, Jo," said Laurie, looking mystified.

"So are you. What were you doing, sir, up in that billiard saloon?"

"Begging your pardon, ma'am, it wasn't a billiard saloon, but a gymnasium, and I was taking a lesson in fencing."

"I'm glad of that!"

"Why?"

"You can teach me; and then, when we play Hamlet, you can be Laertes, and we'll make a fine thing of the fencing scene."[8]

Laurie burst out with a hearty boy's laugh, which made several passers-by smile in spite of themselves.

"I'll teach you, whether we play Hamlet or not; it's grand fun, and will straighten you up capitally. But I don't believe that was your only reason for saying 'I'm glad,' in that decided way; was it, now?"

"No, I was glad you were not in the saloon, because I hope you never go to such places. Do you?"

"Not often."

"I wish you wouldn't."

"It's no harm, Jo, I have billiards at home, but it's no fun unless you have good players; so, as I'm fond of it, I come sometimes and have a game with Ned Moffat or some of the other fellows."

"Oh dear, I'm so sorry, for you'll get to liking it better and better, and will waste time and money, and grow like those dreadful boys. I did hope you'd stay respectable, and be a satisfaction to your friends," said Jo, shaking her head.

"Can't a fellow take a little innocent amusement now and then without losing his respectability?" asked Laurie, looking nettled.

"That depends upon how and where he takes it. I don't like Ned and his set, and wish you'd keep out of it. Mother won't let us have him at our house, though he wants to come, and if you grow like him she won't be willing to have us frolic together as we do now."

"Won't she?" asked Laurie, anxiously.

"No, she can't bear fashionable young men, and she'd shut us all up in bandboxes rather than have us associate with them."

"Well, she needn't get out her bandboxes yet; I'm not a fashionable party, and don't mean to be; but I do like harmless larks now and then, don't you?"

"Yes, nobody minds them, so lark away, but don't get wild, will you? or there will be an end of all our good times."

"I'll be a double distilled saint."

"I can't bear saints; just be a simple, honest, respectable boy, and we'll never desert you. I don't know what I *should* do if you acted like Mr. King's son; he had plenty of money, but didn't know how to spend it, and got tipsy, and gambled, and ran away, and forged his father's name, I believe, and was altogether horrid."

"You think I'm likely to do the same? Much obliged."

8. Shakespeare's *Hamlet* (1603) ends with an exciting but tragic fencing battle between Hamlet and Laertes.

"No I don't—oh, *dear*, no!—but I hear people talking about money being such a temptation, and I sometimes wish you were poor; I shouldn't worry then."

"Do you worry about me, Jo?"

"A little, when you look moody or discontented, as you sometimes do, for you've got such a strong will if you once get started wrong, I'm afraid it would be hard to stop you."

Laurie walked in silence a few minutes, and Jo watched him, wishing she had held her tongue, for his eyes looked angry, though his lips still smiled as if at her warnings.

"Are you going to deliver lectures all the way home?" he asked, presently.

"Of course not; why?"

"Because if you are, I'll take a 'bus; if you are not, I'd like to walk with you, and tell you something very interesting."

"I won't preach any more, and I'd like to hear the news immensely."

"Very well, then; come on. It's a secret, and if I tell you, you must tell me yours."

"I haven't got any," began Jo, but stopped suddenly, remembering that she had.

"You know you have; you can't hide anything, so up and 'fess, or I won't tell," cried Laurie.

"Is your secret a nice one?"

"Oh, isn't it! all about people you know, and such fun! You ought to hear it, and I've been aching to tell this long time. Come! you begin."

"You'll not say anything about it at home, will you?"

"Not a word."

"And you won't tease me in private?"

"I never tease."

"Yes, you do; you get everything you want out of people. I don't know how you do it, but you are a born wheedler."

"Thank you; fire away!"

"Well, I've left two stories with a newspaper man, and he's to give his answer next week," whispered Jo, in her confidant's ear.

"Hurrah for Miss March, the celebrated American authoress!" cried Laurie, throwing up his hat and catching it again, to the great delight of two ducks, four cats, five hens, and half a dozen Irish children; for they were out of the city now.

"Hush! it won't come to anything, I dare say; but I couldn't rest till I had tried, and I said nothing about it, because I didn't want any one else to be disappointed."

"It won't fail! Why, Jo, your stories are works of Shakespeare compared to half the rubbish that's published every day. Won't it be fun to see them in print; and shan't we feel proud of our authoress?"

Jo's eyes sparkled, for it's always pleasant to be believed in; and a friend's praise is always sweeter than a dozen newspaper puffs.

"Where's *your* secret? Play fair, Teddy, or I'll never believe you again," she said, trying to extinguish the brilliant hopes that blazed up at a word of encouragement.

"I may get into a scrape for telling; but I didn't promise not to, so I will, for I never feel easy in my mind till I've told you any plummy bit of news I get. I know where Meg's glove is."

"Is that all?" said Jo, looking disappointed, as Laurie nodded and twinkled, with a face full of mysterious intelligence.

"It's quite enough for the present, as you'll agree when I tell you where it is."

"Tell, then."

Laurie bent and whispered three words in Jo's ear, which produced a comical change. She stood and stared at him for a minute, looking both surprised and displeased, then walked on, saying sharply, "How do you know?"

"Saw it."

"Where?"

"Pocket."

"All this time?"

"Yes; isn't that romantic?"

"No, it's horrid."

"Don't you like it?"

"Of course I don't; it's ridiculous; it won't be allowed. My patience! what would Meg say?"

"You are not to tell any one; mind that."

"I didn't promise."

"That was understood, and I trusted you."

"Well, I won't for the present, any way; but I'm disgusted, and wish you hadn't told me."

"I thought you'd be pleased."

"At the idea of anybody coming to take Meg away? No, thank you."

"You'll feel better about it when somebody comes to take you away."

"I'd like to see any one try it," cried Jo, fiercely.

"So should I!" and Laurie chuckled at the idea.

"I don't think secrets agree with me; I feel rumpled up in my mind since you told me that," said Jo, rather ungratefully.

"Race down this hill with me, and you'll be all right," suggested Laurie.

No one was in sight; the smooth road sloped invitingly before her, and, finding the temptation irresistible, Jo darted away, soon leaving hat and comb behind her, and scattering hair-pins as she ran. Laurie reached the goal first, and was quite satisfied with the success of his treatment; for his Atlanta came panting up with flying hair, bright eyes, ruddy cheeks, and no signs of dissatisfaction in her face.[9]

"I wish I was a horse; then I could run for miles in this splendid air, and not lose my breath. It was capital; but see what a guy it's made me. Go, pick up my things, like a cherub as you are," said Jo, dropping

9. In classical mythology, Atalanta (a devoted follower of the virgin goddess Artemis) possesses great speed along with famous hunting and wrestling skills, and she refuses to marry anyone who cannot outrace her. She is defeated only when Melanion (in some versions, Hippomenes) obtains from Aphrodite, the goddess of love, golden apples, which he drops to distract Atalanta. As she pauses to collect them, he races ahead to win and become her husband.

down under a maple tree, which was carpeting the bank with crimson leaves.

Laurie leisurely departed to recover the lost property, and Jo bundled up her braids, hoping no one would pass by till she was tidy again. But some one did pass, and who should it be but Meg, looking particularly lady-like in her state and festival suit,[1] for she had been making calls.

"What in the world are you doing here?" she asked, regarding her dishevelled sister with well-bred surprise.

"Getting leaves," meekly answered Jo, sorting the rosy handful she had just swept up.

"And hair-pins," added Laurie, throwing half a dozen into Jo's lap. "They grow on this road, Meg; so do combs and brown straw hats."

"You have been running, Jo; how could you? When *will* you stop such romping ways?" said Meg, reprovingly, as she settled her cuffs and smoothed her hair, with which the wind had taken liberties.

"Never till I'm stiff and old, and have to use a crutch. Don't try to make me grow up before my time, Meg; it's hard enough to have you change all of a sudden; let me be a little girl as long as I can."

As she spoke, Jo bent over her work to hide the trembling of her lips; for lately she had felt that Margaret was fast getting to be a woman, and Laurie's secret made her dread the separation which must surely come some time, and now seemed very near. He saw the trouble in her face, and drew Meg's attention from it by asking, quickly, "Where have you been calling, all so fine?"

"At the Gardiners; and Sallie has been telling me all about Belle Moffat's wedding. It was very splendid, and they have gone to spend the winter in Paris; just think how delightful that must be!"

"Do you envy her, Meg?" said Laurie.

"I'm afraid I do."

"I'm glad of it!" muttered Jo, tying on her hat with a jerk.

"Why?" asked Meg, looking surprised.

"Because, if you care much about riches, you will never go and marry a poor man," said Jo, frowning at Laurie, who was mutely warning her to mind what she said.

"I shall never 'go and marry' any one," observed Meg, walking on with great dignity, while the others followed, laughing, whispering, skipping stones, and "behaving like children," as Meg said to herself, though she might have been tempted to join them if she had not had her best dress on.

For a week or two Jo behaved so queerly, that her sisters got quite bewildered. She rushed to the door when the postman rang; was rude to Mr. Brooke whenever they met; would sit looking at Meg with a woe-begone face, occasionally jumping up to shake, and then to kiss her, in a very mysterious manner; Laurie and she were always making signs to one another, and talking about "Spread Eagles," till the girls declared they had both lost their wits. On the second Saturday after Jo

---

1. A coordinated outfit of clothing for formal, public, and social occasions.

got out of the window, Meg, as she sat sewing at her window, was scandalized by the sight of Laurie chasing Jo all over the garden, and finally capturing her in Amy's bower. What went on there, Meg could not see, but shrieks of laughter were heard, followed by the murmur of voices, and a great flapping of newspapers.

"What shall we do with that girl? She never *will* behave like a young lady," sighed Meg, as she watched the race with a disapproving face.

"I hope she won't; she is so funny and dear as she is," said Beth, who had never betrayed that she was a little hurt at Jo's having secrets with any one but her.

"It's very trying, but we never can make her *comme la fo*,"[2] added Amy, who sat making some new frills for herself, with her curls tied up in a very becoming way,—two agreeable things, which made her feel unusually elegant and lady-like.

In a few minutes Jo bounced in, laid herself on the sofa, and affected to read.

"Have you anything interesting there?" asked Meg, with condescension.

"Nothing but a story; don't amount to much, I guess," returned Jo, carefully keeping the name of the paper out of sight.

"You'd better read it loud; that will amuse us, and keep you out of mischief," said Amy, in her most grown-up tone.

"What's the name?" asked Beth, wondering why Jo kept her face behind the sheet.

"The Rival Painters."[3]

"That sounds well; read it," said Meg.

With a loud "hem!" and a long breath, Jo began to read very fast. The girls listened with interest, for the tale was romantic, and somewhat pathetic, as most of the characters died in the end.

"I like that about the splendid picture," was Amy's approving remark, as Jo paused.

"I prefer the lovering part. Viola and Angelo are two of our favorite names; isn't that queer?" said Meg, wiping her eyes, for the "lovering part" was tragical.

"Who wrote it?" asked Beth, who had caught a glimpse of Jo's face.

The reader suddenly sat up, cast away the paper, displaying a flushed countenance, and, with a funny mixture of solemnity and excitement, replied in a loud voice, "Your sister!"

"You?" cried Meg, dropping her work.

"It's very good," said Amy, critically.

"I knew it! I knew it! oh, my Jo, I *am* so proud!" and Beth ran to hug her sister and exult over this splendid success.

Dear me, how delighted they all were, to be sure; how Meg wouldn't believe it till she saw the words, "Miss Josephine March," actually printed in the paper; how graciously Amy criticised the artistic

---

2. See p. 88, n. 4 (part 1, chap. 10).
3. See Louisa May Alcott, "The Rival Painters: A Tale of Rome" (1852), Alcott's first published short story, which appeared anonymously in the *Olive Branch*, a Boston paper. The lovers in Alcott's story are named Madeline and Guido, not Viola and Angelo.

parts of the story, and offered hints for a sequel, which unfortunately couldn't be carried out, as the hero and heroine were dead; how Beth got excited, and skipped and sung with joy; how Hannah came in to exclaim, "Sakes alive, well I never!" in great astonishment at "that Jo's doins;" how proud Mrs. March was when she knew it; how Jo laughed, with tears in her eyes, as she declared she might as well be a peacock and done with it; and how the "Spread Eagle" might be said to flap his wings triumphantly over the house of March, as the paper passed from hand to hand.

"Tell us about it." "When did it come?" "How much did you get for it?" "What *will* father say?" "Won't Laurie laugh?" cried the family, all in one breath, as they clustered about Jo; for these foolish, affectionate people made a jubilee of every little household joy.

"Stop jabbering, girls, and I'll tell you everything," said Jo, wondering if Miss Burney felt any grander over her "Evelina,"[4] than she did over her "Rival Painters." Having told how she disposed of her tales, Jo added,—"And when I went to get my answer the man said he liked them both, but didn't pay beginners, only let them print in his paper, and noticed the stories. It was good practice, he said; and, when the beginners improved, any one would pay. So I let him have the two stories, and today this was sent to me, and Laurie caught me with it, and insisted on seeing it, so I let him; and he said it was good, and I shall write more, and he's going to get the next paid for, and oh—I *am* so happy, for in time I may be able to support myself and help the girls."

Jo's breath gave out here; and, wrapping her head in the paper, she bedewed her little story with a few natural tears; for to be independent, and earn the praise of those she loved, were the dearest wishes of her heart, and this seemed to be the first step toward that happy end.

CHAPTER XV.

A TELEGRAM.

NOVEMBER is the most disagreeable month in the whole year," said Margaret, standing at the window one dull afternoon, looking out at the frost-bitten garden.

"That's the reason I was born in it," observed Jo, pensively, quite unconscious of the blot on her nose.

"If something very pleasant should happen now, we should think it a delightful month," said Beth, who took a hopeful view of everything, even November.

"I dare say; but nothing pleasant ever *does* happen in this family," said Meg, who was out of sorts. "We go grubbing along day after day,

---

4. In 1778, Fanny Burney secretly published *Evelina*, her first published novel, not revealing its authorship to her father, Dr. Charles Burney, a famous musicologist, who had discouraged her literary ambitions. Following the novel's wide acclaim, she let him know of her authorship. He responded with great pride and introduced her as the author of the novel to Samuel Johnson, who had praised it.

without a bit of change, and very little fun. We might as well be in a tread-mill."

"My patience, how blue we are!" cried Jo. "I don't much wonder, poor dear, for you see other girls having splendid times, while you grind, grind, year in and year out. Oh, don't I wish I could fix things for you as I do for my heroines! you're pretty enough and good enough already, so I'd have some rich relation leave you a fortune unexpectedly; then you'd dash out as an heiress, scorn every one who has slighted you, go abroad, and come home my Lady Something, in a blaze of splendor and elegance."

"People don't have fortunes left them in that style nowadays; men have to work, and women to marry for money. It's a dreadfully unjust world," said Meg, bitterly.

"Jo and I are going to make fortunes for you all; just wait ten years, and see if we don't," said Amy, who sat in a corner making "mud pies," as Hannah called her little clay models of birds, fruit and faces.

"Can't wait, and I'm afraid I haven't much faith in ink and dirt, though I'm grateful for your good intentions."

Meg sighed, and turned to the frost-bitten garden again; Jo groaned, and leaned both elbows on the table in a despondent attitude, but Amy spatted away energetically; and Beth, who sat at the other window, said, smiling, "Two pleasant things are going to happen right away; Marmee is coming down the street, and Laurie is tramping through the garden as if he had something nice to tell."

In they both came, Mrs. March with her usual question, "Any letter from father, girls?" and Laurie to say, in his persuasive way, "Won't some of you come for a drive? I've been pegging away at mathematics till my head is in a muddle, and I'm going to freshen my wits by a brisk turn. It's a dull day, but the air isn't bad, and I'm going to take Brooke home, so it will be gay inside, if it isn't out. Come, Jo, you and Beth will go, won't you?"

"Of course we will."

"Much obliged, but I'm busy;" and Meg whisked out her work-basket, for she had agreed with her mother that it was best, for her at least, not to drive often with the young gentleman.

"We three will be ready in a minute," cried Amy, running away to wash her hands.

"Can I do anything for you, Madam Mother?" asked Laurie, leaning over Mrs. March's chair, with the affectionate look and tone he always gave her.

"No, thank you, except call at the office, if you'll be so kind, dear. It's our day for a letter, and the penny postman hasn't been. Father is as regular as the sun, but there's some delay on the way, perhaps."

A sharp ring interrupted her, and a minute after Hannah came in with a letter.

"It's one of them horrid telegraph things, mum," she said, handing it as if she was afraid it would explode, and do some damage.

At the word "telegraph," Mrs. March snatched it, read the two lines it contained, and dropped back into her chair as white as if the little

paper had sent a bullet to her heart. Laurie dashed down stairs for water, while Meg and Hannah supported her, and Jo read aloud, in a
frightened voice,—

"MRS. MARCH:
    "Your husband is very ill. Come at once.
                                                            "S. HALE,
                                        "Blank Hospital, Washington."

How still the room was as they listened breathlessly! how strangely
the day darkened outside! and how suddenly the whole world seemed
to change, as the girls gathered about their mother, feeling as if all the
happiness and support of their lives was about to be taken from them.
Mrs. March was herself again directly; read the message over, and
stretched out her arms to her daughters, saying, in a tone they never
forgot, "I shall go at once, but it may be too late; oh, children, children! help me to bear it!"

For several minutes there was nothing but the sound of sobbing in
the room, mingled with broken words of comfort, tender assurances of
help, and hopeful whispers, that died away in tears. Poor Hannah was
the first to recover, and with unconscious wisdom she set all the rest a
good example; for, with her, work was the panacea for most afflictions.

"The Lord keep the dear man! I won't waste no time a cryin', but git
your things ready right away, mum," she said, heartily, as she wiped her
face on her apron, gave her mistress a warm shake of the hand with her
own hard one, and went away to work, like three women in one.

"She's right; there's no time for tears now. Be calm, girls, and let me
think."

They tried to be calm, poor things, as their mother sat up, looking
pale, but steady, and put away her grief to think and plan for them.

"Where's Laurie?" she asked presently, when she had collected her
thoughts, and decided on the first duties to be done.

"Here, ma'am; oh, let me do something!" cried the boy, hurrying
from the next room, whither he had withdrawn, feeling that their first
sorrow was too sacred for even his friendly eyes to see.

"Send a telegram saying I will come at once. The next train goes
early in the morning; I'll take that."

"What else? The horses are ready; I can go anywhere,—do anything," he said, looking ready to fly to the ends of the earth.

"Leave a note at Aunt March's. Jo, give me that pen and paper."

Tearing off the blank side of one of her newly-copied pages, Jo drew
the table before her mother, well knowing that money for the long, sad
journey, must be borrowed, and feeling as if she could do anything to
add a little to the sum for her father.

"Now go, dear; but don't kill yourself driving at a desperate pace;
there is no need of that."

Mrs. March's warning was evidently thrown away; for five minutes
later Laurie tore by the window, on his own fleet horse, riding as if for
his life.

"Jo, run to the rooms, and tell Mrs. King that I can't come. On the way get these things. I'll put them down; they'll be needed, and I must go prepared for nursing. Hospital stores are not always good. Beth, go and ask Mr. Laurence for a couple of bottles of old wine; I'm not too proud to beg for father; he shall have the best of everything. Amy, tell Hannah to get down the black trunk; and Meg, come and help me find my things, for I'm half bewildered."

Writing, thinking, and directing all at once, might well bewilder the poor lady, and Meg begged her to sit quietly in her room for a little while, and let them work. Every one scattered, like leaves before a gust of wind; and the quiet, happy household was broken up as suddenly as if the paper had been an evil spell.

Mr. Laurence came hurrying back with Beth, bringing every comfort the kind old gentleman could think of for the invalid, and friendliest promises of protection for the girls, during the mother's absence, which comforted her very much. There was nothing he didn't offer, from his own dressing-gown to himself as escort. But that last was impossible. Mrs. March would not hear of the old gentleman's undertaking the long journey; yet an expression of relief was visible when he spoke of it, for anxiety ill fits one for travelling. He saw the look, knit his heavy eyebrows, rubbed his hands, and marched abruptly away, saying he'd be back directly. No one had time to think of him again till, as Meg ran through the entry, with a pair of rubbers in one hand and a cup of tea in the other, she came suddenly upon Mr. Brooke.

"I'm very sorry to hear of this, Miss March," he said, in the kind, quiet tone which sounded very pleasantly to her perturbed spirit. "I came to offer myself as escort to your mother. Mr. Laurence has commissions for me in Washington, and it will give me real satisfaction to be of service to her there."

Down dropped the rubbers, and the tea was very near following, as Meg put out her hand, with a face so full of gratitude, that Mr. Brooke would have felt repaid for a much greater sacrifice than the trifling one of time and comfort, which he was about to make.

"How kind you all are! Mother will accept, I'm sure; and it will be such a relief to know that she has some one to take care of her. Thank you very, very much!"

Meg spoke earnestly, and forgot herself entirely till something in the brown eyes looking down at her made her remember the cooling tea, and lead the way into the parlor, saying she would call her mother.

Everything was arranged by the time Laurie returned with a note from Aunt March, enclosing the desired sum, and a few lines repeating what she had often said before, that she had always told them it was absurd for March to go into the army, always predicted that no good would come of it, and she hoped they would take her advice next time. Mrs. March put the note in the fire, the money in her purse, and went on with her preparations, with her lips folded tightly, in a way which Jo would have understood if she had been there.

The short afternoon wore away; all the other errands were done, and Meg and her mother busy at some necessary needle-work, while

Beth and Amy got tea, and Hannah finished her ironing with what she called a "slap and a bang," but still Jo did not come. They began to get anxious; and Laurie went off to find her, for no one ever knew what freak Jo might take into her head. He missed her, however, and she came walking in with a very queer expression of countenance, for there was a mixture of fun and fear, satisfaction and regret in it, which puzzled the family as much as did the roll of bills she laid before her mother, saying, with a little choke in her voice, "That's my contribution towards making father comfortable, and bringing him home!"

"My dear, where did you get it! Twenty-five dollars! Jo, I hope you haven't done anything rash?"

"No, it's mine honestly; I didn't beg, borrow, nor steal it. I earned it; and I don't think you'll blame me, for I only sold what was my own."

As she spoke, Jo took off her bonnet, and a general outcry arose, for all her abundant hair was cut short.

"Your hair! Your beautiful hair!" "Oh, Jo, how could you? Your one beauty." "My dear girl, there was no need of this." "She don't look like my Jo any more, but I love her dearly for it!"

As every one exclaimed, and Beth hugged the cropped head tenderly, Jo assumed an indifferent air, which did not deceive any one a particle, and said, rumpling up the brown bush, and trying to look as if she liked it, "It doesn't affect the fate of the nation, so don't wail, Beth. It will be good for my vanity; I was getting too proud of my wig. It will do my brains good to have that mop taken off; my head feels deliciously light and cool, and the barber said I could soon have a curly crop, which will be boyish, becoming, and easy to keep in order. I'm satisfied; so please take the money, and let's have supper."

"Tell me all about it, Jo; *I* am not quite satisfied, but I can't blame you, for I know how willingly you sacrificed your vanity, as you call it, to your love. But, my dear, it was not necessary, and I'm afraid you will regret it, one of these days," said Mrs. March.

"No I won't!" returned Jo, stoutly, feeling much relieved that her prank was not entirely condemned.

"What made you do it?" asked Amy, who would as soon have thought of cutting off her head as her pretty hair.

"Well, I was wild to do something for father," replied Jo, as they gathered about the table, for healthy young people can eat even in the midst of trouble. "I hate to borrow as much as mother does, and I knew Aunt March would croak; she always does, if you ask for a ninepence.[5] Meg gave all her quarterly salary toward the rent, and I only got some clothes with mine, so I felt wicked, and was bound to have some money, if I sold the nose off my face to get it."

"You needn't feel wicked, my child, you had no winter things, and got the simplest, with your own hard earnings," said Mrs. March, with a look that warmed Jo's heart.

"I hadn't the least idea of selling my hair at first, but as I went along I

5. A Spanish real, a coin once used in the United States and worth twelve and a half cents (New England colloquialism).

kept thinking *what* I could do, and feeling as if I'd like to dive into some of the rich stores and help myself. In a barber's window I saw tails of hair with the prices marked; and one black tail, longer, but not so thick as mine, was forty dollars. It came over me all of a sudden that I had one thing to make money out of, and, without stopping to think, I walked in, asked if they bought hair, and what they would give for mine."

"I don't see how you dared to do it," said Beth, in a tone of awe.

"Oh, he was a little man who looked as if he merely lived to oil his hair. He rather stared, at first, as if he wasn't used to having girls bounce into his shop and ask him to buy their hair. He said he didn't care about mine, it wasn't the fashionable color, and he never paid much for it in the first place; the work put into it made it dear, and so on. It was getting late, and I was afraid, if it wasn't done right away, that I shouldn't have it done at all, and you know, when I start to do a thing, I hate to give it up; so I begged him to take it, and told him why I was in such a hurry. It was silly, I dare say, but it changed his mind, for I got rather excited, and told the story in my topsy-turvy way, and his wife heard, and said so kindly,"—

"'Take it, Thomas, and oblige the young lady; I'd do as much for our Jimmy any day if I had a spire of hair worth selling.'"

"Who was Jimmy?" asked Amy, who liked to have things explained as they went along.

"Her son, she said, who is in the army. How friendly such things make strangers feel, don't they? She talked away all the time the man clipped, and diverted my mind nicely."

"Didn't you feel dreadfully when the first cut came?" asked Meg, with a shiver.

"I took a last look at my hair while the man got his things, and that was the end of it. I never snivel over trifles like that; I will confess, though, I felt queer when I saw the dear old hair laid out on the table, and felt only the short, rough ends on my head. It almost seemed as if I'd an arm or a leg off. The woman saw me look at it, and picked out a long lock for me to keep. I'll give it to you, Marmee, just to remember past glories by; for a crop is so comfortable I don't think I shall ever have a mane again."

Mrs. March folded the wavy, chestnut lock, and laid it away with a short gray one in her desk. She only said "Thank you, deary," but something in her face made the girls change the subject, and talk as cheerfully as they could about Mr. Brooke's kindness, the prospect of a fine day to-morrow, and the happy times they would have when father came home to be nursed.

No one wanted to go to bed, when, at ten o'clock, Mrs. March put by the last finished job, and said, "Come, girls." Beth went to the piano and played the father's favorite hymn; all began bravely, but broke down one by one till Beth was left alone, singing with all her heart, for to her music was always a sweet consoler.

"Go to bed, and don't talk, for we must be up early, and shall need all the sleep we can get. Good-night, my darlings," said Mrs. March, as the hymn ended, for no one cared to try another.

They kissed her quietly, and went to bed as silently as if the dear invalid lay in the next room. Beth and Amy soon fell asleep in spite of
the great trouble, but Meg lay awake thinking the most serious
thoughts she had ever known in her short life. Jo lay motionless, and
her sister fancied that she was asleep, till a stifled sob made her exclaim, as she touched a wet cheek,—

"Jo, dear, what is it? Are you crying about father?"

"No, not now."

"What then?"

"My—my hair," burst out poor Jo, trying vainly to smother her emotion in the pillow.

It did not sound at all comical to Meg, who kissed and caressed the
afflicted heroine in the tenderest manner.

"I'm not sorry," protested Jo, with a choke. "I'd do it again to-
morrow, if I could. It's only the vain, selfish part of me that goes and
cries in this silly way. Don't tell any one, it's all over now. I thought
you were asleep, so I just made a little private moan for my one
beauty. How came you to be awake?"

"I can't sleep, I'm so anxious," said Meg.

"Think about something pleasant, and you'll soon drop off."

"I tried it, but felt wider awake than ever."

"What did you think of?"

"Handsome faces; eyes particularly," answered Meg smilingly, to
herself, in the dark.

"What color do you like best?"

"Brown—that is sometimes—blue are lovely."

Jo laughed, and Meg sharply ordered her not to talk, then amiably
promised to make her hair curl, and fell asleep to dream of living in
her castle in the air.

The clocks were striking midnight, and the rooms were very still, as
a figure glided quietly from bed to bed, smoothing a coverlid[6] here,
setting a pillow there, and pausing to look long and tenderly at each
unconscious face, to kiss each with lips that mutely blessed, and to
pray the fervent prayers which only mothers utter. As she lifted the
curtain to look out into the dreary night, the moon broke suddenly
from behind the clouds, and shone upon her like a bright benignant
face, which seemed to whisper in the silence, "Be comforted, dear
heart! there is always light behind the clouds."

CHAPTER XVI.

LETTERS.

In the cold gray dawn the sisters lit their lamp, and read their chapter
with an earnestness never felt before, for now the shadow of a real
trouble had come, showing them how rich in sunshine their lives had
been. The little books were full of help and comfort; and, as they

6. Bedspread.

dressed, they agreed to say good-by cheerfully, hopefully, and send their mother on her anxious journey unsaddened by tears or complaints from them. Everything seemed very strange when they went down; so dim and still outside, so full of light and bustle within. Breakfast at that early hour seemed odd, and even Hannah's familiar face looked unnatural as she flew about her kitchen with her night cap on. The big trunk stood ready in the hall, mother's cloak and bonnet lay on the sofa, and mother herself sat trying to eat, but looking so pale and worn with sleeplessness and anxiety, that the girls found it very hard to keep their resolution. Meg's eyes kept filling in spite of herself; Jo was obliged to hide her face in the kitchen roller[7] more than once, and the little girls' young faces wore a grave, troubled expression, as if sorrow was a new experience to them.

Nobody talked much, but, as the time drew very near, and they sat waiting for the carriage, Mrs. March said to the girls, who were all busied about her, one folding her shawl, another smoothing out the strings of her bonnet, a third putting on her overshoes, and a fourth fastening up her travelling bag,—

"Children, I leave you to Hannah's care, and Mr. Laurence's protection; Hannah is faithfulness itself, and our good neighbor will guard you as if you were his own. I have no fears for you, yet I am anxious that you should take this trouble rightly. Don't grieve and fret when I am gone, or think that you can comfort yourselves by being idle, and trying to forget. Go on with your work as usual, for work is a blessed solace. Hope, and keep busy;[8] and, whatever happens, remember that you never can be fatherless."

"Yes, mother."

"Meg, dear, be prudent, watch over your sisters, consult Hannah, and, in any perplexity, go to Mr. Laurence. Be patient, Jo, don't get despondent, or do rash things; write to me often, and be my brave girl, ready to help and cheer us all. Beth, comfort yourself with your music, and be faithful to the little home duties; and you, Amy, help all you can, be obedient, and keep happy safe at home."

"We will, mother! we will!"

The rattle of an approaching carriage made them all start and listen. That was the hard minute, but the girls stood it well; no one cried, no one ran away, or uttered a lamentation, though their hearts were very heavy as they sent loving messages to father, remembering, as they spoke, that it might be too late to deliver them. They kissed their mother quietly, clung about her tenderly, and tried to wave their hands cheerfully, when she drove away.

Laurie and his grandfather came over to see her off, and Mr. Brooke looked so strong, and sensible, and kind, that the girls christened him "Mr. Greatheart,"[9] on the spot.

---

7. Roller towel.
8. Favorite motto of Abba Alcott, Louisa May Alcott's mother and the model for Marmee. See *Journals*, 55.
9. See p. 17, n. 1 (part 1, chap. 1). Part 2 of *The Pilgrim's Progress* depicts Great-heart, Interpreter's servant, as strong but also caring, kind, and helpful.

"Good-by, my darlings! God bless and keep us all," whispered Mrs. March, as she kissed one dear little face after the other, and hurried into the carriage.

As she rolled away, the sun came out, and, looking back, she saw it shining on the group at the gate, like a good omen. They saw it also, and smiled and waved their hands; and the last thing she beheld, as she turned the corner, was the four bright faces, and behind them, like a body-guard, old Mr. Laurence, faithful Hannah, and devoted Laurie.

"How kind every one is to us," she said, turning to find fresh proof of it in the respectful sympathy of the young man's face.

"I don't see how they can help it," returned Mr. Brooke, laughing so infectiously that Mrs. March could not help smiling; and so the long journey began with the good omens of sunshine, smiles, and cheerful words.

"I feel as if there had been an earthquake," said Jo, as their neighbors went home to breakfast, leaving them to rest and refresh themselves.

"It seems as if half the house was gone," added Meg, forlornly.

Beth opened her lips to say something, but could only point to the pile of nicely-mended hose which lay on mother's table, showing that even in her last hurried moments she had thought and worked for them. It was a little thing, but it went straight to their hearts; and, in spite of their brave resolutions, they all broke down, and cried bitterly.

Hannah wisely allowed them to relieve their feelings; and, when the shower showed signs of clearing up, she came to the rescue, armed with a coffee-pot.

"Now, my dear young ladies, remember what your ma said, and don't fret; come and have a cup of coffee all round, and then let's fall to work, and be a credit to the family."

Coffee was a treat, and Hannah showed great tact in making it that morning. No one could resist her persuasive nods, or the fragrant invitation issuing from the nose of the coffee-pot. They drew up to the table, exchanged their handkerchiefs for napkins, and, in ten minutes, were all right again.

"'Hope and keep busy,' that's the motto for us, so let's see who will remember it best. I shall go to Aunt March, as usual; oh, won't she lecture, though!" said Jo, as she sipped, with returning spirit.

"I shall go to my Kings, though I'd much rather stay at home and attend to things here," said Meg, wishing she hadn't made her eyes so red.

"No need of that; Beth and I can keep house perfectly well," put in Amy, with an important air.

"Hannah will tell us what to do; and we'll have everything nice when you come home," added Beth, getting out her mop and dish-tub without delay.

"I think anxiety is very interesting," observed Amy, eating sugar, pensively.

The girls couldn't help laughing, and felt better for it, though Meg shook her head at the young lady who could find consolation in a sugar-bowl.

The sight of the turn-overs made Jo sober again; and, when the two went out to their daily tasks, they looked sorrowfully back at the window where they were accustomed to see their mother's face. It was gone; but Beth had remembered the little household ceremony, and there she was, nodding away at them like a rosy-faced mandarin.

"That's so like my Beth!" said Jo, waving her hat, with a grateful face. "Good-by, Meggy; I hope the Kings won't train[1] to-day. Don't fret about father, dear," she added, as they parted.

"And I hope Aunt March won't croak. Your hair *is* becoming, and it looks very boyish and nice," returned Meg, trying not to smile at the curly head, which looked comically small on her tall sister's shoulders.

"That's my only comfort;" and, touching her hat à la Laurie, away went Jo, feeling like a shorn sheep on a wintry day.

News from their father comforted the girls very much; for, though dangerously ill, the presence of the best and tenderest of nurses had already done him good. Mr. Brooke sent a bulletin every day, and, as the head of the family, Meg insisted on reading the despatches, which grew more and more cheering as the week passed. At first, every one was eager to write, and plump envelopes were carefully poked into the letter-box, by one or other of the sisters, who felt rather important with their Washington correspondence. As one of these packets contained characteristic notes from the party, we will rob an imaginary mail, and read them:—

"MY DEAREST MOTHER,—

"It is impossible to tell you how happy your last letter made us, for the news was so good we couldn't help laughing and crying over it. How very kind Mr. Brooke is, and how fortunate that Mr. Laurence's business detains him near you so long, since he is so useful to you and father. The girls are all as good as gold. Jo helps me with the sewing, and insists on doing all sorts of hard jobs. I should be afraid she might overdo, if I didn't know that her 'moral fit' wouldn't last long. Beth is as regular about her tasks as a clock, and never forgets what you told her. She grieves about father, and looks sober, except when she is at her little piano. Amy minds me nicely, and I take great care of her. She does her own hair, and I am teaching her to make button-holes, and mend her stockings. She tries very hard, and I know you will be pleased with her improvement when you come. Mr. Laurence watches over us like a motherly old hen, as Jo says; and Laurie is very kind and neighborly. He and Jo keep us merry, for we get pretty blue sometimes, and feel like orphans, with you so far away. Hannah is a perfect saint; she does not scold at all, and always calls me 'Miss Margaret,' which is quite proper, you know, and treats me with respect. We are all well and busy; but we long, day and night, to have you back. Give my dearest love to father, and believe me, ever your own   MEG."

1. Romp about or carry on (New England colloquialism).

This note, prettily written on scented paper, was a great contrast to the next, which was scribbled on a big sheet of thin, foreign paper, ornamented with blots, and all manner of flourishes and curly-tailed letters:—

"MY PRECIOUS MARMEE,—

"Three cheers for dear old father! Brooke was a trump to telegraph right off, and let us know the minute he was better. I rushed up garret when the letter came, and tried to thank God for being so good to us; but I could only cry, and say, 'I'm glad! I'm glad!' Didn't that do as well as a regular prayer? for I felt a great many in my heart. We have such funny times; and now I can enjoy 'em, for every one is so desperately good, it's like living in a nest of turtle-doves. You'd laugh to see Meg head the table, and try to be motherish. She gets prettier every day, and I'm in love with her sometimes. The children are regular archangels, and I—well, I'm Jo, and never shall be anything else. Oh, I must tell you that I came near having a quarrel with Laurie. I freed my mind about a silly little thing, and he was offended. I was right, but didn't speak as I ought, and he marched home, saying he wouldn't come again till I begged pardon. I declared I wouldn't, and got mad. It lasted all day; I felt bad, and wanted you very much. Laurie and I are both so proud, it's hard to beg pardon; but I thought he'd come to it, for I *was* in the right. He didn't come; and just at night I remembered what you said when Amy fell into the river. I read my little book, felt better, resolved not to let the sun set on *my* anger, and ran over to tell Laurie I was sorry. I met him at the gate, coming for the same thing. We both laughed, begged each other's pardon, and felt all good and comfortable again.

"I made a 'pome' yesterday, when I was helping Hannah wash; and, as father likes my silly little things, I put it in to amuse him. Give him the lovingest hug that ever was, and kiss yourself a dozen times, for your

                                                          "TOPSY-TURVY JO.

"A SONG FROM THE SUDS.

"Queen of my tub, I merrily sing,
    While the white foam rises high;
And sturdily wash, and rinse, and wring,
    And fasten the clothes to dry;
Then out in the free fresh air they swing,
    Under the sunny sky.

"I wish we could wash from our hearts and souls
    The stains of the week away,
And let water and air by their magic make
    Ourselves as pure as they;
Then on the earth there would be indeed
    A glorious washing-day!

"Along the path of a useful life,
    Will heart's-ease ever bloom;
The busy mind has no time to think
    Of sorrow, or care, or gloom;
And anxious thoughts may be swept away,
    As we busily wield a broom.

"I am glad a task to me is given,
    To labor at day by day;
For it brings me health, and strength, and hope,
    And I cheerfully learn to say,—
'Head you may think, Heart you may feel,
    But Hand you shall work alway!'"

"DEAR MOTHER:

"There is only room for me to send my love, and some pressed pansies from the root I have been keeping safe in the house, for father to see. I read every morning, try to be good all day, and sing myself to sleep with father's tune. I can't sing 'Land of the Leal'[2] now; it makes me cry. Every one is very kind, and we are as happy as we can be without you. Amy wants the rest of the page, so I must stop. I didn't forget to cover the holders, and I wind the clock and air the rooms every day.

"Kiss dear father on the cheek he calls mine. Oh, do come soon to your loving

"LITTLE BETH."

"MA CHERE MAMMA:

"We are all well I do my lessons always and never corroberate the girls—Meg says I mean contradick so I put in both words and you can take the properest. Meg is a great comfort to me and lets me have jelly every night at tea its so good for me Jo says because it keeps me sweet tempered. Laurie is not as respeckful as he ought to be now I am almost in my teens, he calls me Chick and hurts my feelings by talking French to me very fast when I say Merci or Bon jour as Hattie King does. The sleeves of my blue dress were all worn out and Meg put in new ones but the full front came wrong and they are more blue than the dress. I felt bad but did not fret I bear my troubles well but I do wish Hannah would put more starch in my aprons and have buck wheats every day. Can't she? Didn't I make that interrigation point nice. Meg says my punchtuation and spelling are disgraceful and I am mortyfied but dear me I have so many things to do I can't stop. Adieu, I send heaps of love to Papa.

"Your affectionate daughter,

"AMY CURTIS MARCH."

---

2. The Scottish lyricist Carolina Oliphant (later Baroness Nairne) wrote "Land o' the Leal" (1798) for a friend whose child had died. Based on a traditional tune, this popular song promises a better life in the land of the leal (that is, the land of the faithful, or heaven).

"DEAR MIS MARCH:

"I jes drop a line to say we git on fust rate. The girls is clever and fly round right smart. Miss Meg is goin to make a proper good house-keeper; she hes the liking for it, and gits the hang of things surprisin quick. Jo doos beat all for goin ahead, but she don't stop to cal'k'late fust, and you never know where she's like to bring up. She done out a tub of clothes on Monday, but she starched em afore they was wrenched, and blued a pink calico dress till I thought I should a died a laughin. Beth is the best of little creeters, and a sight of help to me, bein so forehanded and dependable. She tries to learn everything, and really goes to market beyond her years; likewise keeps accounts, with my help, quite wonderful. We have got on very economical so fur; I don't let the girls hev coffee only once a week, accordin to your wish, and keep em on plain wholesome vittles. Amy does well about frettin, wearin her best clothes and eatin sweet stuff. Mr. Laurie is as full of didoes as usual, and turns the house upside down frequent; but he heartens up the girls, and so I let em hev full swing. The old man sends heaps of things, and is rather wearin, but means wal, and it aint my place to say nothin. My bread is riz, so no more at this time. I send my duty to Mr. March, and hope he's seen the last of his Pewmonia.

"Yours respectful,

"HANNAH MULLET."

"HEAD NURSE OF WARD II.:

"All serene on the Rappahannock,[3] troops in fine condition, com-missary department well conducted, the Home Guard under Colonel Teddy always on duty, Commander-in-chief General Laurence reviews the army daily, Quartermaster Mullett keeps order in camp, and Major Lion does picket duty at night. A salute of twenty-four guns was fired on receipt of good news from Washington, and a dress parade took place at head-quarters. Commander-in-chief sends best wishes, in which he is heartily joined by

COLONEL TEDDY."

"DEAR MADAM:

"The little girls are all well; Beth and my boy report daily; Hannah is a model servant, guards pretty Meg like a dragon. Glad the fine weather holds; pray make Brooke useful, and draw on me for funds if expenses exceed your estimate. Don't let your husband want anything. Thank God he is mending.

"Your sincere friend and servant,

"JAMES LAURENCE."

3. River in northern Virginia along which several Civil War battles and skirmishes were fought in 1862–63.

CHAPTER XVII.

LITTLE FAITHFUL.

FOR a week the amount of virtue in the old house would have supplied the neighborhood. It was really amazing, for every one seemed in a heavenly frame of mind, and self-denial was all the fashion. Relieved of their first anxiety about their father, the girls insensibly relaxed their praiseworthy efforts a little, and began to fall back into the old ways. They did not forget their motto, but hoping and keeping busy seemed to grow easier; and, after such tremendous exertions, they felt that Endeavor deserved a holiday, and gave it a good many.

Jo caught a bad cold through neglecting to cover the shorn head enough, and was ordered to stay at home till she was better, for Aunt March didn't like to hear people read with colds in their heads. Jo liked this, and after an energetic rummage from garret to cellar, subsided on to the sofa to nurse her cold with arsenicum[4] and books. Amy found that house-work and art did not go well together, and returned to her mud pies. Meg went daily to her kingdom, and sewed, or thought she did, at home, but much time was spent in writing long letters to her mother, or reading the Washington despatches over and over. Beth kept on with only slight relapses into idleness or grieving. All the little duties were faithfully done each day, and many of her sisters' also, for they were forgetful, and the house seemed like a clock, whose pendulum was gone a-visiting. When her heart got heavy with longings for mother, or fears for father, she went away into a certain closet, hid her face in the folds of a certain dear old gown, and made her little moan, and prayed her little prayer quietly by herself. Nobody knew what cheered her up after a sober fit, but every one felt how sweet and helpful Beth was, and fell into a way of going to her for comfort or advice in their small affairs.

All were unconscious that this experience was a test of character; and, when the first excitement was over, felt that they had done well, and deserved praise. So they did; but their mistake was in ceasing to do well, and they learned this lesson through much anxiety and regret.

"Meg, I wish you'd go and see the Hummels; you know mother told us not to forget them," said Beth, ten days after Mrs. March's departure.

"I'm too tired to go this afternoon," replied Meg, rocking comfortably, as she sewed.

"Can't you, Jo?" asked Beth.

"Too stormy for me, with my cold."

"I thought it was most well."

"It's well enough for me to go out with Laurie, but not well enough to go to the Hummels," said Jo, laughing, but looking a little ashamed of her inconsistency.

"Why don't you go yourself?" asked Meg.

---

4. Arsenicum album, or arsenic oxide, used in diluted forms as a homeopathic treatment.

"I *have* been every day, but the baby is sick, and I don't know what to do for it. Mrs. Hummel goes away to work, and Lottchen takes care of it; but it gets sicker and sicker, and I think you or Hannah ought to go."

Beth spoke earnestly, and Meg promised she would go to-morrow.

"Ask Hannah for some nice little mess, and take it round, Beth, the air will do you good;" said Jo, adding apologetically, "I'd go, but I want to finish my story."

"My head aches, and I'm tired, so I thought maybe some of you would go," said Beth.

"Amy will be in presently, and she will run down for us," suggested Meg.

"Well, I'll rest a little, and wait for her."

So Beth lay down on the sofa, the others returned to their work, and the Hummels were forgotten. An hour passed, Amy did not come; Meg went to her room to try on a new dress; Jo was absorbed in her story, and Hannah was sound asleep before the kitchen fire, when Beth quietly put on her hood, filled her basket with odds and ends for the poor children, and went out into the chilly air with a heavy head, and a grieved look in her patient eyes. It was late when she came back, and no one saw her creep upstairs and shut herself into her mother's room. Half an hour after Jo went to "mother's closet" for something, and there found Beth sitting on the medicine chest, looking very grave, with red eyes, and a camphor bottle in her hand.

"Christopher Columbus! what's the matter?" cried Jo, as Beth put out her hand as if to warn her off, and asked quickly,—

"You've had scarlet fever, haven't you?"

"Years ago, when Meg did. Why?"

"Then I'll tell you—oh, Jo, the baby's dead!"

"What baby?"

"Mrs. Hummel's; it died in my lap before she got home," cried Beth, with a sob.

"My poor dear, how dreadful for you! I ought to have gone," said Jo, taking her sister in her lap as she sat down in her mother's big chair, with a remorseful face.

"It wasn't dreadful, Jo, only so sad! I saw in a minute that it was sicker, but Lottchen said her mother had gone for a doctor, so I took baby and let Lotty rest. It seemed asleep, but all of a sudden it gave a little cry, and trembled, and then lay very still. I tried to warm its feet, and Lotty gave it some milk, but it didn't stir, and I knew it was dead."

"Don't cry, dear! what did you do?"

"I just sat and held it softly till Mrs. Hummel came with the doctor. He said it was dead, and looked at Heinrich and Minna, who have got sore throats. 'Scarlet fever, ma'am; ought to have called me before,' he said, crossly. Mrs. Hummel told him she was poor, and had tried to cure baby herself, but now it was too late, and she could only ask him to help the others, and trust to charity for his pay. He smiled then, and was kinder, but it was very sad, and I cried with them till he turned round all of a sudden, and told me to go home and take belladonna right away, or I'd have the fever."

"No you won't!" cried Jo, hugging her close, with a frightened look. "Oh, Beth, if you should be sick I never could forgive myself! What *shall* we do?"

"Don't be frightened, I guess I shan't have it badly; I looked in mother's book, and saw that it begins with headache, sore throat, and queer feelings like mine, so I did take some belladonna, and I feel better," said Beth, laying her cold hands on her hot forehead, and trying to look well.

"If mother was only at home!" exclaimed Jo, seizing the book, and feeling that Washington was an immense way off. She read a page, looked at Beth, felt her head, peeped into her throat, and then said, gravely, "You've been over the baby every day for more than a week, and among the others who are going to have it, so I'm afraid you're going to have it, Beth. I'll call Hannah; she knows all about sickness."

"Don't let Amy come; she never had it, and I should hate to give it to her. Can't you and Meg have it over again?" asked Beth, anxiously.

"I guess not; don't care if I do; serve me right, selfish pig, to let you go, and stay writing rubbish myself!" muttered Jo, as she went to consult Hannah.

The good soul was wide awake in a minute, and took the lead at once, assuring Jo that there was no need to worry; every one had scarlet fever, and, if rightly treated, nobody died; all of which Jo believed, and felt much relieved as they went up to call Meg.

"Now I'll tell you what we'll do," said Hannah, when she had examined and questioned Beth; "we will have Dr. Bangs, just to take a look at you, dear, and see that we start right; then we'll send Amy off to Aunt March's, for a spell, to keep her out of harm's way, and one of you girls can stay at home and amuse Beth for a day or two."

"I shall stay, of course, I'm oldest;" began Meg, looking anxious and self-reproachful.

"*I* shall, because it's my fault she is sick; I told mother I'd do the errands, and I haven't," said Jo, decidedly.

"Which will you have, Beth? there ain't no need of but one," said Hannah.

"Jo, please;" and Beth leaned her head against her sister, with a contented look, which effectually settled that point.

"I'll go and tell Amy," said Meg, feeling a little hurt, yet rather relieved, on the whole, for she did not like nursing, and Jo did.

Amy rebelled outright, and passionately declared that she had rather have the fever than go to Aunt March. Meg reasoned, pleaded, and commanded, all in vain. Amy protested that she would *not* go; and Meg left her in despair, to ask Hannah what should be done. Before she came back, Laurie walked into the parlor to find Amy sobbing, with her head in the sofa cushions. She told her story, expecting to be consoled; but Laurie only put his hands in his pockets and walked about the room, whistling softly, as he knit his brows in deep thought. Presently he sat down beside her, and said, in his most wheedlesome tone, "Now be a sensible little woman, and do as they say. No, don't cry, but hear what a jolly plan I've got. You go to Aunt March's, and I'll come and take you out every day, driving or walking, and we'll have capital times. Won't that be better than moping here?"

"I don't wish to be sent off as if I was in the way," began Amy, in an injured voice.

"Bless your heart, child! it's to keep you well. You don't want to be sick, do you?"

"No, I'm sure I don't; but I dare say I shall be, for I've been with Beth all this time."

"That's the very reason you ought to go away at once, so that you may escape it. Change of air and care will keep you well, I dare say; or, if it don't entirely, you will have the fever more lightly. I advise you to be off as soon as you can, for scarlet fever is no joke, miss."

"But it's dull at Aunt March's, and she is so cross," said Amy, looking rather frightened.

"It won't be dull with me popping in every day to tell you how Beth is, and take you out gallivanting. The old lady likes me, and I'll be as clever as possible to her, so she won't peck at us, whatever we do."

"Will you take me out in the trotting wagon with Puck?"

"On my honor as a gentleman."

"And come every single day?"

"See if I don't."

"And bring me back the minute Beth is well?"

"The identical minute."

"And go to the theatre, truly?"

"A dozen theatres, if we may."

"Well—I guess—I will," said Amy, slowly.

"Good girl! Sing out for Meg, and tell her you'll give in," said Laurie, with an approving pat, which annoyed Amy more than the "giving in."

Meg and Jo came running down to behold the miracle which had been wrought; and Amy, feeling very precious and self-sacrificing, promised to go, if the doctor said Beth was going to be ill.

"How is the little dear?" asked Laurie; for Beth was his especial pet, and he felt more anxious about her than he liked to show.

"She is lying down on mother's bed, and feels better. The baby's death troubled her, but I dare say she has only got cold. Hannah *says* she thinks so; but she *looks* worried, and that makes me fidgety," answered Meg.

"What a trying world it is!" said Jo, rumpling up her hair in a fretful sort of way. "No sooner do we get out of one trouble than down comes another. There don't seem to be anything to hold on to when mother's gone; so I'm all at sea."

"Well, don't make a porcupine of yourself, it isn't becoming. Settle your wig, Jo, and tell me if I shall telegraph to your mother, or do anything?" asked Laurie, who never had been reconciled to the loss of his friend's one beauty.

"That is what troubles me," said Meg. "I think we ought to tell her if Beth is really ill, but Hannah says we mustn't, for mother can't leave father, and it will only make them anxious. Beth won't be sick long, and Hannah knows just what to do, and mother said we were to mind her, so I suppose we must, but it don't seem quite right to me."

"Hum, well, I can't say; suppose you ask grandfather, after the doctor has been."

"We will; Jo, go and get Dr. Bangs at once," commanded Meg; "we can't decide anything till he has been."

"Stay where you are, Jo; I'm errand boy to this establishment," said Laurie, taking up his cap.

"I'm afraid you are busy," began Meg.

"No, I've done my lessons for the day."

"Do you study in vacation time?" asked Jo.

"I follow the good example my neighbors set me," was Laurie's answer, as he swung himself out of the room.

"I have great hopes of my boy," observed Jo, watching him fly over the fence with an approving smile.

"He does very well—for a boy," was Meg's somewhat ungracious answer, for the subject did not interest her.

Dr. Bangs came, said Beth had symptoms of the fever, but thought she would have it lightly, though he looked sober over the Hummel story. Amy was ordered off at once, and provided with something to ward off danger; she departed in great state, with Jo and Laurie as escort.

Aunt March received them with her usual hospitality.

"What do you want now?" she asked, looking sharply over her spectacles, while the parrot, sitting on the back of her chair, called out,—

"Go away; no boys allowed here."

Laurie retired to the window, and Jo told her story.

"No more than I expected, if you are allowed to go poking about among poor folks. Amy can stay and make herself useful if she isn't sick, which I've no doubt she will be,—looks like it now. Don't cry, child, it worries me to hear people sniff."

Amy *was* on the point of crying, but Laurie slyly pulled the parrot's tail, which caused Polly to utter an astonished croak, and call out,—

"Bless my boots!" in such a funny way, that she laughed instead.

"What do you hear from your mother?" asked the old lady, gruffly.

"Father is much better," replied Jo, trying to keep sober.

"Oh, is he? Well, that won't last long, I fancy, March never had any stamina," was the cheerful reply.

"Ha, ha! never say die, take a pinch of snuff, good-by, good-by!" squalled Polly, dancing on her perch, and clawing at the old lady's cap as Laurie tweaked him in the rear.

"Hold your tongue, you disrespectful old bird! and, Jo, you'd better go at once; it isn't proper to be gadding about so late with a rattle-pated boy like—"

"Hold your tongue, you disrespectful old bird!" cried Polly, tumbling off the chair with a bounce and running to peck the "rattle-pated" boy, who was shaking with laughter at the last speech.

"I don't think I *can* bear it, but I'll try," thought Amy, as she was left alone with Aunt March.

"Get along, you're a fright!" screamed Polly, and at that rude speech Amy could not restrain a sniff.

CHAPTER XVIII.

DARK DAYS.

BETH did have the fever, and was much sicker than any one but Hannah and the doctor suspected. The girls knew nothing about illness, and Mr. Laurence was not allowed to see her, so Hannah had everything all her own way, and busy Dr. Bangs did his best, but left a good deal to the excellent nurse. Meg stayed at home, lest she should infect the Kings, and kept house, feeling very anxious, and a little guilty, when she wrote letters in which no mention was made of Beth's illness. She could not think it right to deceive her mother, but she had been bidden to mind Hannah, and Hannah wouldn't hear of "Mrs. March bein' told, and worried just for sech a trifle." Jo devoted herself to Beth day and night; not a hard task, for Beth was very patient, and bore her pain uncomplainingly as long as she could control herself. But there came a time when during the fever fits she began to talk in a hoarse, broken voice, to play on the coverlet, as if on her beloved little piano, and try to sing with a throat so swollen, that there was no music left; a time when she did not know the familiar faces round her, but addressed them by wrong names, and called imploringly for her mother. Then Jo grew frightened, Meg begged to be allowed to write the truth, and even Hannah said she "would think of it, though there was no danger *yet*." A letter from Washington added to their trouble, for Mr. March had had a relapse, and could not think of coming home for a long while.

How dark the days seemed now, how sad and lonely the house, and how heavy were the hearts of the sisters as they worked and waited, while the shadow of death hovered over the once happy home! Then it was that Margaret, sitting alone with tears dropping often on her work, felt how rich she had been in things more precious than any luxuries money could buy; in love, protection, peace and health, the real blessings of life. Then it was that Jo, living in the darkened room with that suffering little sister always before her eyes, and that pathetic voice sounding in her ears, learned to see the beauty and the sweetness of Beth's nature, to feel how deep and tender a place she filled in all hearts, and to acknowledge the worth of Beth's unselfish ambition, to live for others, and make home happy by the exercise of those simple virtues which all may possess, and which all should love and value more than talent, wealth or beauty. And Amy, in her exile, longed eagerly to be at home, that she might work for Beth, feeling now that no service would be hard or irksome, and remembering, with regretful grief, how many neglected tasks those willing hands had done for her. Laurie haunted the house like a restless ghost, and Mr. Laurence locked the grand piano, because he could not bear to be reminded of the young neighbor who used to make the twilight pleasant for him. Every one missed Beth. The milk-man, baker, grocer and butcher inquired how she did; poor Mrs. Hummel came to beg pardon for her thoughtlessness, and to get a shroud for Minna; the neighbors sent all sorts of comforts and good wishes, and even those who knew her best, were surprised to find how many friends shy little Beth had made.

Meanwhile she lay on her bed with old Joanna at her side, for even in her wanderings she did not forget her forlorn *protégé*. She longed for her cats, but would not have them brought, lest they should get sick; and, in her quiet hours, she was full of anxiety about Jo. She sent loving messages to Amy, bade them tell her mother that she would write soon; and often begged for pencil and paper to try to say a word, that father might not think she had neglected him. But soon even these intervals of consciousness ended, and she lay hour after hour tossing to and fro with incoherent words on her lips, or sank into a heavy sleep which brought her no refreshment. Dr. Bangs came twice a day, Hannah sat up at night, Meg kept a telegram in her desk all ready to send off at any minute, and Jo never stirred from Beth's side.

The first of December was a wintry day indeed to them, for a bitter wind blew, snow fell fast, and the year seemed getting ready for its death. When Dr. Bangs came that morning, he looked long at Beth, held the hot hand in both his own a minute, and laid it gently down, saying, in a low tone, to Hannah,—

"If Mrs. March *can* leave her husband, she'd better be sent for."

Hannah nodded without speaking, for her lips twitched nervously; Meg dropped down into a chair as the strength seemed to go out of her limbs at the sound of those words, and Jo, after standing with a pale face for a minute, ran to the parlor, snatched up the telegram, and, throwing on her things, rushed out into the storm. She was soon back, and, while noiselessly taking off her cloak, Laurie came in with a letter, saying that Mr. March was mending again. Jo read it thankfully, but the heavy weight did not seem lifted off her heart, and her face was so full of misery that Laurie asked, quickly,—

"What is it? is Beth worse?"

"I've sent for mother," said Jo, tugging at her rubber boots with a tragical expression.

"Good for you, Jo! Did you do it on your own responsibility?" asked Laurie, as he seated her in the hall chair, and took off the rebellious boots, seeing how her hands shook.

"No, the doctor told us to."

"Oh, Jo, it's not so bad as that?" cried Laurie, with a startled face.

"Yes, it is; she don't know us, she don't even talk about the flocks of green doves, as she calls the vine leaves on the wall; she don't look like my Beth, and there's nobody to help us bear it; mother and father both gone, and God seems so far away I can't find Him."

As the tears streamed fast down poor Jo's cheeks, she stretched out her hand in a helpless sort of way, as if groping in the dark, and Laurie took it in his, whispering, as well as he could, with a lump in his throat,—

"I'm here, hold on to me, Jo, dear!"

She could not speak, but she did "hold on," and the warm grasp of the friendly human hand comforted her sore heart, and seemed to lead her nearer to the Divine arm which alone could uphold her in her trouble. Laurie longed to say something tender and comfortable, but no fitting words came to him, so he stood silent, gently stroking her bent head as her mother used to do. It was the best thing he could have done; far more soothing than the most eloquent words, for Jo felt the unspoken sympathy, and, in the silence, learned the sweet solace which affection administers to sorrow. Soon she dried the tears which had relieved her, and looked up with a grateful face.

"Thank you, Teddy, I'm better now; I don't feel so forlorn, and will try to bear it if it comes."

"Keep hoping for the best; that will help you lots, Jo. Soon your mother will be here, and then everything will be right."

"I'm so glad father is better; now she won't feel bad about leaving him. Oh, me! it does seem as if all the troubles came in a heap, and I got the heaviest part on my shoulders," sighed Jo, spreading her wet handkerchief over her knees, to dry.

"Don't Meg pull fair?"[5] asked Laurie, looking indignant.

"Oh, yes; she tries to, but she don't love Bethy as I do; and she won't miss her as I shall. Beth is my conscience, and I *can't* give her up; I can't! I can't!"

Down went Jo's face into the wet handkerchief, and she cried despairingly; for she had kept up bravely till now, and never shed a tear. Laurie drew his hand across his eyes, but could not speak till he had subdued the choky feeling in his throat, and steadied his lips. It might be unmanly, but he couldn't help it, and I am glad of it. Presently, as Jo's sobs quieted, he said, hopefully, "I don't think she will die; she's so good, and we all love her so much, I don't believe God will take her away yet."

"The good and dear people always do die," groaned Jo, but she stopped crying, for her friend's words cheered her up, in spite of her own doubts and fears.

"Poor girl! you're worn out. It isn't like you to be forlorn. Stop a bit; I'll hearten you up in a jiffy."

Laurie went off two stairs at a time, and Jo laid her wearied head down on Beth's little brown hood, which no one had thought of moving from the table where she left it. It must have possessed some magic, for the submissive spirit of its gentle owner seemed to enter into Jo; and, when Laurie came running down with a glass of wine, she took it with a smile, and said, bravely, "I drink—Health to my Beth! You are a good doctor, Teddy, and *such* a comfortable friend; how can I ever pay you?" she added, as the wine refreshed her body, as the kind words had done her troubled mind.

"I'll send in my bill, by and by; and to-night I'll give you something that will warm the cockles of your heart better than quarts of wine," said Laurie, beaming at her with a face of suppressed satisfaction at something.

"What is it?" cried Jo, forgetting her woes for a minute, in her wonder.

5. Carry out (her) duties, perform (her) commitments.

"I telegraphed to your mother yesterday, and Brooke answered she'd come at once, and she'll be here to-night, and everything will be all right. Aren't you glad I did it?"

Laurie spoke very fast, and turned red and excited all in a minute, for he had kept his plot a secret, for fear of disappointing the girls or harming Beth. Jo grew quite white, flew out of her chair, and the moment he stopped speaking she electrified him by throwing her arms round his neck, and crying out, with a joyful cry, "Oh, Laurie! oh, mother! I *am* so glad!" She did not weep again, but laughed hysterically, and trembled and clung to her friend as if she was a little bewildered by the sudden news. Laurie, though decidedly amazed, behaved with great presence of mind; he patted her back soothingly, and, finding that she was recovering, followed it up by a bashful kiss or two, which brought Jo round at once. Holding on to the banisters, she put him gently away, saying, breathlessly, "Oh, don't! I didn't mean to; it was dreadful of me; but you were such a dear to go and do it in spite of Hannah, that I couldn't help flying at you. Tell me all about it, and don't give me wine again; it makes me act so."

"I don't mind!" laughed Laurie, as he settled his tie. "Why, you see I got fidgety, and so did grandpa. We thought Hannah was overdoing the authority business, and your mother ought to know. She'd never forgive us if Beth,—well, if anything happened, you know. So I got grandpa to say it was high time we did something, and off I pelted to the office yesterday, for the doctor looked sober, and Hannah most took my head off when I proposed a telegram. I never *can* bear to be 'marmed over';[6] so that settled my mind, and I did it. Your mother will come, I know, and the late train is in at two, A.M. I shall go for her; and you've only got to bottle up your rapture, and keep Beth quiet, till that blessed lady gets here."

"Laurie, you're an angel! How shall I ever thank you?"

"Fly at me again; I rather like it," said Laurie, looking mischievous,—a thing he had not done for a fortnight.

"No, thank you. I'll do it by proxy, when your grandpa comes. Don't tease, but go home and rest, for you'll be up half the night. Bless you, Teddy; bless you!"

Jo had backed into a corner; and, as she finished her speech, she vanished precipitately into the kitchen, where she sat down upon a dresser, and told the assembled cats that she was "happy, oh, *so* happy!" while Laurie departed, feeling that he had made rather a neat thing of it.

"That's the interferingest chap I ever see; but I forgive him, and do hope Mrs. March is coming on right away," said Hannah, with an air of relief, when Jo told the good news.

Meg had a quiet rapture, and then brooded over the letter, while Jo set the sick-room in order, and Hannah "knocked up a couple of pies in case of company unexpected." A breath of fresh air seemed to blow

6. To be taken care of, instructed, or ordered about by a woman with authority, from "marm," which is like "ma'am" a vocal version of "madam." The so-called regular edition of *Little Women* prints "lorded over" (see Textual Variants, p. 396).

through the house, and something better than sunshine brightened the quiet rooms; everything appeared to feel the hopeful change; Beth's bird began to chirp again, and a half-blown rose was discovered on Amy's bush in the window; the fires seemed to burn with unusual cheeriness, and every time the girls met their pale faces broke into smiles as they hugged one another, whispering, encouragingly, "Mother's coming, dear! mother's coming!" Every one rejoiced but Beth; she lay in that heavy stupor, alike unconscious of hope and joy, doubt and danger. It was a piteous sight,—the once rosy face so changed and vacant,—the once busy hands so weak and wasted,—the once smiling lips quite dumb,—and the once pretty, well-kept hair scattered rough and tangled on the pillow. All day she lay so, only rousing now and then to mutter, "Water!" with lips so parched they could hardly shape the word; all day Jo and Meg hovered over her, watching, waiting, hoping, and trusting in God and mother; and all day the snow fell, the bitter wind raged, and the hours dragged slowly by. But night came at last; and every time the clock struck the sisters, still sitting on either side the bed, looked at each other with brightening eyes, for each hour brought help nearer. The doctor had been in to say that some change for better or worse would probably take place about midnight, at which time he would return.

Hannah, quite worn out, lay down on the sofa at the bed's foot, and fell fast asleep; Mr. Laurence marched to and fro in the parlor, feeling that he would rather face a rebel battery than Mrs. March's anxious countenance as she entered; Laurie lay on the rug, pretending to rest, but staring into the fire with the thoughtful look which made his black eyes beautifully soft and clear.

The girls never forgot that night, for no sleep came to them as they kept their watch, with that dreadful sense of powerlessness which comes to us in hours like those.

"If God spares Beth I never will complain again," whispered Meg, earnestly.

"If God spares Beth I'll try to love and serve Him all my life," answered Jo, with equal fervor.

"I wish I had no heart, it aches so," sighed Meg, after a pause.

"If life is often as hard as this, I don't see how we ever shall get through it," added her sister, despondently.

Here the clock struck twelve, and both forgot themselves in watching Beth, for they fancied a change passed over her wan face. The house was still as death, and nothing but the wailing of the wind broke the deep hush. Weary Hannah slept on, and no one but the sisters saw the pale shadow which seemed to fall upon the little bed. An hour went by, and nothing happened except Laurie's quiet departure for the station. Another hour,—still no one came; and anxious fears of delay in the storm, or accidents by the way, or, worst of all, a great grief at Washington, haunted the poor girls.

It was past two, when Jo, who stood at the window thinking how dreary the world looked in its winding-sheet of snow, heard a movement by the bed, and, turning quickly, saw Meg kneeling before their mother's easy-chair, with her face hidden. A dreadful fear passed coldly over Jo, as she thought, "Beth is dead, and Meg is afraid to tell me."

She was back at her post in an instant, and to her excited eyes a great change seemed to have taken place. The fever flush, and the look of pain, were gone, and the beloved little face looked so pale and peaceful in its utter repose, that Jo felt no desire to weep or to lament. Leaning low over this dearest of her sisters, she kissed the damp forehead with her heart on her lips, and softly whispered, "Good-by, my Beth; good-by!"

As if waked by the stir, Hannah started out of her sleep, hurried to the bed, looked at Beth, felt her hands, listened at her lips, and then, throwing her apron over her head, sat down to rock to and fro, exclaiming, under her breath, "The fever's turned; she's sleepin nat'ral; her skin's damp, and she breathes easy. Praise be given! Oh, my goodness me!"

Before the girls could believe the happy truth, the doctor came to confirm it. He was a homely man, but they thought his face quite heavenly when he smiled, and said, with a fatherly look at them, "Yes, my dears; I think the little girl will pull through this time. Keep the house quiet; let her sleep, and when she wakes, give her—"

What they were to give, neither heard; for both crept into the dark hall, and, sitting on the stairs, held each other close, rejoicing with hearts too full for words. When they went back to be kissed and cuddled by faithful Hannah, they found Beth lying, as she used to do, with her cheek pillowed on her hand, the dreadful pallor gone, and breathing quietly, as if just fallen asleep.

"If mother would only come now!" said Jo, as the winter night began to wane.

"See," said Meg, coming up with a white, half-opened rose, "I thought this would hardly be ready to lay in Beth's hand to-morrow if she—went away from us. But it has blossomed in the night, and now I mean to put it in my vase here, so that when the darling wakes, the first thing she sees will be the little rose, and mother's face."

Never had the sun risen so beautifully, and never had the world seemed so lovely, as it did to the heavy eyes of Meg and Jo, as they looked out in the early morning, when their long, sad vigil was done.

"It looks like a fairy world," said Meg, smiling to herself, as she stood behind the curtain watching the dazzling sight.

"Hark!" cried Jo, starting to her feet.

Yes, there was a sound of bells at the door below, a cry from Hannah, and then Laurie's voice, saying, in a joyful whisper, "Girls! she's come! she's come!"

CHAPTER XIX.

AMY'S WILL.

WHILE these things were happening at home, Amy was having hard times at Aunt March's. She felt her exile deeply, and, for the first time in her life, realized how much she was beloved and petted at home. Aunt March never petted any one; she did not approve of it; but she meant to be kind, for the well-behaved little girl pleased her very much, and Aunt March had a soft place in her old heart for her nephew's children, though she didn't think proper to confess it. She really did her best to make Amy happy, but, dear me, what mistakes she made! Some old people keep young at heart in spite of wrinkles and gray hairs, can sympathize with children's little cares and joys, make them feel at home, and can hide wise lessons under pleasant plays, giving and receiving friendship in the sweetest way. But Aunt March had not this gift, and she worried Amy most to death with her rules and orders, her prim ways, and long, prosy talks. Finding the child more docile and amiable than her sister, the old lady felt it her duty to try and counteract, as far as possible, the bad effects of home freedom and indulgence. So she took Amy in hand, and taught her as she herself had been taught sixty years ago; a process which carried dismay to Amy's soul, and made her feel like a fly in the web of a very strict spider.

She had to wash the cups every morning, and polish up the old-fashioned spoons, the fat silver teapot, and the glasses, till they shone. Then she must dust the room, and what a trying job that was! Not a speck escaped Aunt March's eye, and all the furniture had claw legs, and much carving, which was never dusted to suit. Then Polly must be fed, the lap-dog combed, and a dozen trips upstairs and down, to get things or deliver orders, for the old lady was very lame, and seldom left her big chair. After these tiresome labors she must do her lessons, which was a daily trial of every virtue she possessed. Then she was allowed one hour for exercise or play, and didn't she enjoy it? Laurie came every day, and wheedled Aunt March till Amy was allowed to go out with him, when they walked and rode, and had capital times. After dinner she had to read aloud, and sit still while the old lady slept, which she usually did for an hour, as she dropped off over the first page. Then patch-work or towels appeared, and Amy sewed with outward meekness and inward rebellion till dusk, when she was allowed to amuse herself as she liked, till tea-time. The evenings were the worst of all, for Aunt March fell to telling long stories about her youth, which were so unutterably dull, that Amy was always ready to go to bed, intending to cry over her hard fate, but usually going to sleep before she had squeezed out more than a tear or two.

If it had not been for Laurie and old Esther, the maid, she felt that she never could have got through that dreadful time. The parrot alone was enough to drive her distracted, for he soon felt that she did not admire him, and revenged himself by being as mischievous as possible.

He pulled her hair whenever she came near him, upset his bread and milk to plague her when she had newly cleaned his cage, made Mop bark by pecking at him while Madame dozed; called her names before company, and behaved in all respects like a reprehensible old bird. Then she could not endure the dog, a fat, cross beast, who snarled and yelped at her when she made his toilet, and who laid on his back with all his legs in the air, and a most idiotic expression of countenance, when he wanted something to eat, which was about a dozen times a day. The cook was bad-tempered, the old coachman deaf, and Esther the only one who ever took any notice of the young lady.

Esther was a French woman, who had lived with "Madame," as she called her mistress, for many years, and who rather tyrannized over the old lady, who could not get along without her. Her real name was Estelle; but Aunt March ordered her to change it, and she obeyed, on condition that she was never asked to change her religion. She took a fancy to Mademoiselle, and amused her very much, with odd stories of her life in France, when Amy sat with her while she got up Madame's laces. She also allowed her to roam about the great house, and examine the curious and pretty things stored away in the big wardrobes and the ancient chests; for Aunt March hoarded like a magpie. Amy's chief delight was an Indian cabinet full of queer drawers, little pigeon-holes, and secret places in which were kept all sorts of ornaments, some precious, some merely curious, all more or less antique. To examine and arrange these things gave Amy great satisfaction, especially the jewel cases; in which, on velvet cushions, reposed the ornaments which had adorned a belle forty years ago. There was the garnet set which Aunt March wore when she came out, the pearls her father gave her on her wedding day, her lover's diamonds, the jet mourning rings and pins, the queer lockets, with portraits of dead friends, and weeping willows made of hair inside, the baby bracelets her one little daughter had worn; Uncle March's big watch, with the red seal so many childish hands had played with, and in a box, all by itself, lay Aunt March's wedding ring, too small now for her fat finger, but put carefully away, like the most precious jewel of them all.

"Which would Mademoiselle choose if she had her will?" asked Esther, who always sat near to watch over and lock up the valuables.

"I like the diamonds best, but there is no necklace among them, and I'm fond of necklaces, they are so becoming. I should choose this if I might," replied Amy, looking with great admiration at a string of gold and ebony beads, from which hung a heavy cross of the same.

"I, too, covet that, but not as a necklace; ah, no! to me it is a rosary, and as such I should use it like a good Catholic," said Esther, eyeing the handsome thing wistfully.

"Is it meant to use as you use the string of good-smelling wooden beads hanging over your glass?" asked Amy.

"Truly, yes, to pray with. It would be pleasing to the saints if one used so fine a rosary as this, instead of wearing it as a vain bijou."

"You seem to take a deal of comfort in your prayers, Esther, and always come down looking quiet and satisfied. I wish I could."

"If Mademoiselle was a Catholic, she would find true comfort; but as that is not to be, it would be well if you went apart each day to meditate, and pray, as did the good mistress whom I served before Madame. She had a little chapel, and in it found solacement for much trouble."

"Would it be right for me to do so too?" asked Amy, who, in her loneliness, felt the need of help of some sort, and found that she was apt to forget her little book, now that Beth was not there to remind her of it.

"It would be excellent and charming; and I shall gladly arrange the little dressing-room for you, if you like it. Say nothing to Madame, but when she sleeps go you and sit alone a while to think good thoughts, and ask the dear God to preserve your sister."

Esther was truly pious, and quite sincere in her advice; for she had an affectionate heart, and felt much for the sisters in their anxiety. Amy liked the idea, and gave her leave to arrange the light closet next her room, hoping it would do her good.

"I wish I knew where all these pretty things would go when Aunt March dies," she said, as she slowly replaced the shining rosary, and shut the jewel cases one by one.

"To you and your sisters. I know it; Madame confides in me; I witnessed her will, and it is to be so," whispered Esther, smiling.

"How nice! but I wish she'd let us have them now. Pro-cras-ti-nation is not agreeable," observed Amy, taking a last look at the diamonds.

"It is too soon yet for the young ladies to wear these things. The first one who is affianced will have the pearls—Madame has said it; and I have a fancy that the little turquoise ring will be given to you when you go, for Madame approves your good behavior and charming manners."

"Do you think so? Oh, I'll be a lamb, if I can only have that lovely ring! It's ever so much prettier than Kitty Bryant's. I do like Aunt March, after all;" and Amy tried on the blue ring with a delighted face, and a firm resolve to earn it.

From that day she was a model of obedience, and the old lady complacently admired the success of her training. Esther fitted up the closet with a little table, placed a footstool before it, and over it a picture, taken from one of the shut-up rooms. She thought it was of no great value, but, being appropriate, she borrowed it, well knowing that Madame would never know it, nor care if she did. It was, however, a very valuable copy of one of the famous pictures of the world, and Amy's beauty-loving eyes were never tired of looking up at the sweet face of the divine mother, while tender thoughts of her own were busy at her heart. On the table she laid her little Testament and hymn-book, kept a vase always full of the best flowers Laurie brought her, and came every day to "sit alone, thinking good thoughts, and praying the dear God to preserve her sister." Esther had given her a rosary of black beads, with a silver cross, but Amy hung it up, and did not use it, feeling doubtful as to its fitness for Protestant prayers.

The little girl was very sincere in all this, for, being left alone outside the safe home-nest, she felt the need of some kind hand to hold by so sorely, that she instinctively turned to the strong and tender Friend, whose fatherly love most closely surrounds His little children. She missed her mother's help to understand and rule herself, but having been taught where to look, she did her best to find the way, and walk in it confidingly. But Amy was a young pilgrim, and just now her burden seemed very heavy. She tried to forget herself, to keep cheerful, and be satisfied with doing right, though no one saw or praised her for it. In her first effort at being very, very good, she decided to make her will, as Aunt March had done; so that if she *did* fall ill and die, her possessions might be justly and generously divided. It cost her a pang even to think of giving up the little treasures which in her eyes were as precious as the old lady's jewels.

During one of her play hours she wrote out the important document as well as she could, with some help from Esther as to certain legal terms; and, when the good-natured French woman had signed her name, Amy felt relieved, and laid it by to show Laurie, whom she wanted as a second witness. As it was a rainy day, she went up stairs to amuse herself in one of the large chambers, and took Polly with her for company. In this room there was a wardrobe full of old-fashioned costumes, with which Esther allowed her to play, and it was her favorite amusement to array herself in the faded brocades, and parade up and down before the long mirror, making stately courtesies, and sweeping her train about, with a rustle which delighted her ears. So busy was she on this day, that she did not hear Laurie's ring, nor see his face peeping in at her, as she gravely promenaded to and fro, flirting her fan and tossing her head, on which she wore a great pink turban, contrasting oddly with her blue brocade dress and yellow quilted petticoat. She was obliged to walk carefully, for she had on high-heeled shoes, and, as Laurie told Jo afterward, it was a comical sight to see her mince along in her gay suit, with Polly sidling and bridling just behind her, imitating her as well as he could, and occasionally stopping to laugh or exclaim, "Ain't we fine? Get along you fright! Hold your tongue! Kiss me, dear; ha! ha!"

Having with difficulty restrained an explosion of merriment, lest it should offend her majesty, Laurie tapped, and was graciously received.

"Sit down and rest while I put these things away; then I want to consult you about a very serious matter," said Amy, when she had shown her splendor, and driven Polly into a corner. "That bird is the trial of my life," she continued, removing the pink mountain from her head, while Laurie seated himself astride of a chair. "Yesterday, when aunt was asleep, and I was trying to be as still as a mouse, Polly began to squall and flap about in his cage; so I went to let him out, and found a big spider there. I poked it out, and it ran under the bookcase; Polly marched straight after it, stooped down and peeped under the book-case, saying, in his funny way, with a cock of his eye, 'Come out and take a walk, my dear.' I *couldn't* help laughing, which made Poll swear, and aunt woke up and scolded us both."

"Did the spider accept the old fellow's invitation?" asked Laurie, yawning.

"Yes; out it came, and away ran Polly, frightened to death, and scrambled up on aunt's chair, calling out, 'Catch her! catch her! catch her!' as I chased the spider."

"That's a lie! Oh lor!" cried the parrot, pecking at Laurie's toes.

"I'd wring your neck if you were mine, you old torment," cried Laurie, shaking his fist at the bird, who put his head on one side, and gravely croaked, "Allyluyer! bless your buttons, dear!"

"Now I'm ready," said Amy, shutting the wardrobe, and taking a paper out of her pocket. "I want you to read that, please, and tell me if it is legal and right. I felt that I ought to do it, for life is uncertain, and I don't want any ill-feeling over my tomb."

Laurie bit his lips, and turning a little from the pensive speaker, read the following document, with praiseworthy gravity, considering the spelling:—

"MY LAST WILL AND TESTIMENT.

"I, Amy Curtis March, being in my sane mind, do give and bequeethe all my earthly property—viz. to wit:—namely

"To my father, my best pictures, sketches, maps, and works of art, including frames. Also my $100, to do what he likes with.

"To my mother, all my clothes, except the blue apron with pockets,—also my likeness, and my medal, with much love.

"To my dear sister Margaret, I give my turkquoise ring (if I get it), also my green box with the doves on it, also my piece of real lace for her neck, and my sketch of her as a memorial of her 'little girl.'

"To Jo I leave my breast-pin, the one mended with sealing wax, also my bronze inkstand—she lost the cover,—and my most precious plaster rabbit, because I am sorry I burnt up her story.

"To Beth (if she lives after me) I give my dolls and the little bureau, my fan, my linen collars and my new slippers if she can wear them being thin when she gets well. And I herewith also leave her my regret that I ever made fun of old Joanna.

"To my friend and neighbor Theodore Laurence I bequeethe my paper marshay portfolio, my clay model of a horse though he did say it hadn't any neck. Also in return for his great kindness in the hour of affliction any one of my artistic works he likes, Noter Dame is the best.

"To our venerable benefactor Mr. Laurence I leave my purple box with a looking glass in the cover which will be nice for his pens and remind him of the departed girl who thanks him for his favors to her family, specially Beth.

"I wish my favorite playmate Kitty Bryant to have the blue silk apron and my gold-bead ring with a kiss.

"To Hannah I give the band-box she wanted and all the patch work I leave hoping she 'will remember me, when it you see.'[7]

7. Conventional inscription, found on grave markers and in books, asking the living to remember the dead. It typically reads, "When this you see, remember me."

"And now having disposed of my most valuable property I hope all will be satisfied and not blame the dead. I forgive every one, and trust we may all meet when the trump shall sound. Amen.

"To this will and testament I set my hand and seal on this 20th day of Nov. Anni Domino 1861.[8]

"AMY CURTIS MARCH.

"*Witnesses:* { ESTELLE VALNOR, THEODORE LAURENCE."

The last name was written in pencil, and Amy explained that he was to rewrite it in ink, and seal it up for her properly.

"What put it into your head? Did any one tell you about Beth's giving away her things?" asked Laurie, soberly, as Amy laid a bit of red tape, with sealing-wax, a taper, and a standish[9] before him.

She explained; and then asked, anxiously, "What about Beth?"

"I'm sorry I spoke; but as I did, I'll tell you. She felt so ill one day, that she told Jo she wanted to give her piano to Meg, her bird to you, and the poor old doll to Jo, who would love it for her sake. She was sorry she had so little to give, and left locks of hair to the rest of us, and her best love to grandpa. *She* never thought of a will."

Laurie was signing and sealing as he spoke, and did not look up till a great tear dropped on the paper. Amy's face was full of trouble; but she only said, "Don't people put sort of postscrips to their wills, sometimes?"

"Yes; 'codicils,' they call them."

"Put one in mine then—that I wish *all* my curls cut off, and given round to my friends. I forgot it; but I want it done, though it will spoil my looks."

Laurie added it, smiling at Amy's last and greatest sacrifice. Then he amused her for an hour, and was much interested in all her trials. But when he came to go, Amy held him back to whisper, with trembling lips, "Is there really any danger about Beth?"

"I'm afraid there is; but we must hope for the best, so don't cry, dear;" and Laurie put his arm about her with a brotherly gesture, which was very comforting.

When he had gone, she went to her little chapel, and, sitting in the twilight, prayed for Beth with streaming tears and an aching heart, feeling that a million turquoise rings would not console her for the loss of her gentle little sister.

8. Amy means "anno Domini," the year of the Lord. Because the book opens in December 1861, the first Christmas season during the Civil War, the correct year here should be 1862. Although the mistake could be Alcott's own, it might also be attributable to error-prone Amy.
9. Inkstand or holder for writing implements.

CHAPTER XX.

CONFIDENTIAL.

I DON'T think I have any words in which to tell the meeting of the mother and daughters; such hours are beautiful to live, but very hard to describe, so I will leave it to the imagination of my readers; merely saying that the house was full of genuine happiness, and that Meg's tender hope was realized; for when Beth woke from that long, healing sleep, the first objects on which her eyes fell *were* the little rose and mother's face. Too weak to wonder at anything, she only smiled, and nestled close into the loving arms about her, feeling that the hungry longing was satisfied at last. Then she slept again, and the girls waited upon their mother, for she would not unclasp the thin hand which clung to hers, even in sleep. Hannah had "dished up" an astonishing breakfast for the traveller, finding it impossible to vent her excitement in any other way; and Meg and Jo fed their mother like dutiful young storks, while they listened to her whispered account of father's state, Mr. Brooke's promise to stay and nurse him, the delays which the storm occasioned on the homeward journey, and the unspeakable comfort Laurie's hopeful face had given her when she arrived, worn out with fatigue, anxiety and cold.

What a strange, yet pleasant day that was! so brilliant and gay without, for all the world seemed abroad to welcome the first snow; so quiet and reposeful within, for every one slept, spent with watching, and a Sabbath stillness reigned through the house, while nodding Hannah mounted guard at the door. With a blissful sense of burdens lifted off, Meg and Jo closed their weary eyes, and lay at rest like storm-beaten boats, safe at anchor in a quiet harbor. Mrs. March would not leave Beth's side, but rested in the big chair, waking often to look at, touch, and brood over her child, like a miser over some recovered treasure.

Laurie, meanwhile, posted off to comfort Amy, and told his story so well that Aunt March actually "sniffed" herself, and never once said, "I told you so." Amy came out so strong on this occasion, that I think the good thoughts in the little chapel really began to bear fruit. She dried her tears quickly, restrained her impatience to see her mother, and never even thought of the turquoise ring, when the old lady heartily agreed in Laurie's opinion, that she behaved "like a capital little woman." Even Polly seemed impressed, for he called her "good girl," blessed her buttons, and begged her to "come and take a walk, dear," in his most affable tone. She would very gladly have gone out to enjoy the bright wintry weather; but, discovering that Laurie was dropping with sleep in spite of manful efforts to conceal the fact, she persuaded him to rest on the sofa, while she wrote a note to her mother. She was a long time about it; and, when returned, he was stretched out with both arms under his head, sound asleep, while Aunt March had pulled down the curtains, and sat doing nothing in an unusual fit of benignity.

After a while, they began to think he was not going to wake till night, and I'm not sure that he would, had he not been effectually roused by Amy's cry of joy at sight of her mother. There probably were a good many happy little girls in and about the city that day, but it is my private opinion that Amy was the happiest of all, when she sat in her mother's lap and told her trials, receiving consolation and compensation in the shape of approving smiles and fond caresses. They were alone together in the chapel, to which her mother did not object when its purpose was explained to her.

"On the contrary, I like it very much, dear," she said, looking from the dusty rosary to the well-worn little book, and the lovely picture with its garland of evergreen. "It is an excellent plan to have some place where we can go to be quiet, when things vex or grieve us. There are a good many hard times in this life of ours, but we can always bear them if we ask help in the right way. I think my little girl is learning this?"

"Yes, mother; and when I go home I mean to have a corner in the big closet to put my books, and the copy of that picture which I've tried to make. The woman's face is not good, it's too beautiful for me to draw, but the baby is done better, and I love it very much. I like to think He was a little child once, for then I don't seem so far away, and that helps me."

As Amy pointed to the smiling Christ-child on his mother's knee, Mrs. March saw something on the lifted hand that made her smile. She said nothing, but Amy understood the look, and, after a minute's pause, she added, gravely,—

"I wanted to speak to you about this, but I forgot it. Aunt gave me the ring today; she called me to her and kissed me, and put it on my finger, and said I was a credit to her, and she'd like to keep me always. She gave that funny guard to keep the turquoise on, as it's too big. I'd like to wear them, mother; can I?"

"They are very pretty, but I think you're rather too young for such ornaments, Amy," said Mrs. March, looking at the plump little hand, with the band of sky-blue stones on the forefinger, and the quaint guard, formed of two tiny, golden hands clasped together.

"I'll try not to be vain," said Amy; "I don't think I like it, only because it's so pretty; but I want to wear it as the girl in the story wore her bracelet, to remind me of something."

"Do you mean Aunt March?" asked her mother, laughing.

"No, to remind me not to be selfish." Amy looked so earnest and sincere about it, that her mother stopped laughing, and listened respectfully to the little plan.

"I've thought a great deal lately about 'my bundle of naughties,' and being selfish is the largest one in it; so I'm going to try hard to cure it, if I can. Beth isn't selfish, and that's the reason every one loves her, and feels so bad at the thoughts of losing her. People wouldn't feel half so bad about me if I was sick, and I don't deserve to have them; but I'd like to be loved and missed by a great many friends, so I'm going to try and be like Beth all I can. I'm apt to forget my resolutions; but, if I had something always about me to remind me, I guess I should do better. May I try this way?"

"Yes; but I have more faith in the corner of the big closet. Wear your ring, dear, and do your best; I think you will prosper, for the sincere wish to be good is half the battle. Now, I must go back to Beth. Keep up your heart, little daughter, and we will soon have you home again."

That evening, while Meg was writing to her father, to report the traveller's safe arrival, Jo slipped upstairs into Beth's room, and, finding her mother in her usual place, stood a minute twisting her fingers in her hair, with a worried gesture and an undecided look.

"What is it, deary?" asked Mrs. March, holding out her hand with a face which invited confidence.

"I want to tell you something, mother."

"About Meg?"

"How quick you guessed! Yes, it's about her, and though it's a little thing, it fidgets me."

"Beth is asleep; speak low, and tell me all about it. That Moffat hasn't been here, I hope?" asked Mrs. March, rather sharply.

"No; I should have shut the door in his face if he had," said Jo, settling herself on the floor at her mother's feet. "Last summer Meg left a pair of gloves over at the Laurences, and only one was returned. We forgot all about it, till Teddy told me that Mr. Brooke had it. He kept it in his waistcoat pocket, and once it fell out, and Teddy joked him about it, and Mr. Brooke owned that he liked Meg, but didn't dare say so, she was so young and he so poor. Now isn't it a *dread*ful state of things?"

"Do you think Meg cares for him?" asked Mrs. March, with an anxious look.

"Mercy me! I don't know anything about love, and such nonsense!" cried Jo, with a funny mixture of interest and contempt. "In novels, the girls show it by starting and blushing, fainting away, growing thin, and acting like fools. Now Meg don't do anything of the sort; she eats and drinks, and sleeps, like a sensible creature; she looks straight in my face when I talk about that man, and only blushes a little bit when Teddy jokes about lovers. I forbid him to do it, but he don't mind me as he ought."

"Then you fancy that Meg is *not* interested in John?"

"Who?" cried Jo, staring.

"Mr. Brooke; I call him 'John' now; we fell into the way of doing so at the hospital, and he likes it."

"Oh, dear! I know you'll take his part; he's been good to father, and you won't send him away, but let Meg marry him, if she wants to. Mean thing! to go petting pa and truckling to you, just to wheedle you into liking him;" and Jo pulled her hair again with a wrathful tweak.

"My dear, don't get angry about it, and I will tell you how it happened. John went with me at Mr. Laurence's request, and was so devoted to poor father, that we couldn't help getting fond of him. He was perfectly open and honorable about Meg, for he told us he loved her; but would earn a comfortable home before he asked her to marry him.

He only wanted our leave to love her and work for her, and the right to make her love him if he could. He is a truly excellent young man, and we could not refuse to listen to him; but I will not consent to Meg's engaging herself so young."

"Of course not; it would be idiotic! I knew there was mischief brewing; I felt it; and now it's worse than I imagined. I just wish I could marry Meg myself, and keep her safe in the family."

This odd arrangement made Mrs. March smile; but she said, gravely, "Jo, I confide in you, and don't wish you to say anything to Meg yet. When John comes back, and I see them together, I can judge better of her feelings toward him."

"She'll see his in those handsome eyes that she talks about, and then it will be all up with her. She's got such a soft heart, it will melt like butter in the sun if any one looks sentimentally at her. She read the short reports he sent more than she did your letters, and pinched me when I spoke of it, and likes brown eyes, and don't think John an ugly name, and she'll go and fall in love, and there's an end of peace and fun, and cosy times, together. I see it all! they'll go lovering round the house, and we shall have to dodge; Meg will be absorbed, and no good to me any more; Brooke will scratch up a fortune somehow,— carry her off and make a hole in the family; and I shall break my heart, and everything will be abominably uncomfortable. Oh, deary me! why weren't we all boys? then there wouldn't be any bother!"

Jo leaned her chin on her knees, in a disconsolate attitude, and shook her fist at the reprehensible John. Mrs. March sighed, and Jo looked up with an air of relief.

"You don't like it, mother? I'm glad of it; let's send him about his business, and not tell Meg a word of it, but all be jolly together as we always have been."

"I did wrong to sigh, Jo. It is natural and right you should all go to homes of your own, in time; but I do want to keep my girls as long as I can; and I am sorry that this happened so soon, for Meg is only seventeen, and it will be some years before John can make a home for her. Your father and I have agreed that she shall not bind herself in any way, nor be married, before twenty. If she and John love one another, they can wait, and test the love by doing so. She is conscientious, and I have no fear of her treating him unkindly. My pretty, tender-hearted girl! I hope things will go happily with her."

"Hadn't you rather have her marry a rich man?" asked Jo, as her mother's voice faltered a little over the last words.

"Money is a good and useful thing, Jo; and I hope my girls will never feel the need of it too bitterly, nor be tempted by too much. I should like to know that John was firmly established in some good business, which gave him an income large enough to keep free from debt, and make Meg comfortable. I'm not ambitious for a splendid fortune, a fashionable position, or a great name for my girls. If rank and money come with love and virtue, also, I should accept them gratefully, and enjoy your good fortune; but I know, by experience, how much genuine happiness can be had in a plain little house, where the daily

bread is earned, and some privations give sweetness to the few pleasures; I am content to see Meg begin humbly, for, if I am not mistaken, she will be rich in the possession of a good man's heart, and
that is better than a fortune."

"I understand, mother, and quite agree; but I'm disappointed about
Meg, for I'd planned to have her marry Teddy by and by, and sit in the
lap of luxury all her days. Wouldn't it be nice?" asked Jo, looking up
with a brighter face.

"He is younger than she, you know," began Mrs. March; but Jo
broke in,—

"Oh, that don't matter; he's old for his age, and tall; and can be
quite grown-up in his manners, if he likes. Then he's rich, and generous, and good, and loves us all; and *I* say it's a pity my plan is spoilt."

"I'm afraid Laurie is hardly grown-up enough for Meg, and altogether too much of a weathercock, just now, for any one to depend on.
Don't make plans, Jo; but let time and their own hearts mate your
friends. We can't meddle safely in such matters, and had better not get
'romantic rubbish,' as you call it, into our heads, lest it spoil our
friendship."

"Well, I won't; but I hate to see things going all criss-cross, and getting snarled up, when a pull here, and a snip there, would straighten it
out. I wish wearing flat-irons on our heads would keep us from growing up. But buds will be roses, and kittens, cats,—more's the pity!"

"What's that about flat-irons and cats?" asked Meg, as she crept into
the room, with the finished letter in her hand.

"Only one of my stupid speeches. I'm going to bed; come on, Peggy,"
said Jo, unfolding herself, like an animated puzzle.

"Quite right, and beautifully written. Please add that I send my love
to John," said Mrs. March, as she glanced over the letter, and gave it
back.

"Do you call him 'John'?" asked Meg, smiling, with her innocent
eyes looking down into her mother's.

"Yes; he has been like a son to us, and we are very fond of him,"
replied Mrs. March, returning the look with a keen one.

"I'm glad of that; he is so lonely. Good-night, mother, dear. It is so
inexpressibly comfortable to have you here," was Meg's quiet answer.

The kiss her mother gave her was a very tender one; and, as she
went away, Mrs. March said, with a mixture of satisfaction and regret,
"She does not love John yet, but will soon learn to."

CHAPTER XXI.

LAURIE MAKES MISCHIEF, AND JO MAKES PEACE.

JO'S face was a study next day, for the secret rather weighed upon her,
and she found it hard not to look mysterious and important. Meg observed it, but did not trouble herself to make inquiries, for she had
learned that the best way to manage Jo was by the law of contraries, so

she felt sure of being told everything if she did not ask. She was rather surprised, therefore, when the silence remained unbroken, and Jo assumed a patronizing air, which decidedly aggravated Meg, who in her turn assumed an air of dignified reserve, and devoted herself to her mother. This left Jo to her own devices; for Mrs. March had taken her place as nurse, and bid her rest, exercise, and amuse herself after her long confinement. Amy being gone, Laurie was her only refuge; and, much as she enjoyed his society, she rather dreaded him just then, for he was an incorrigible tease, and she feared he would coax her secret from her.

She was quite right; for the mischief-loving lad no sooner suspected a mystery, than he set himself to finding it out, and led Jo a trying life of it. He wheedled, bribed, ridiculed, threatened and scolded; affected indifference, that he might surprise the truth from her; declared he knew, then that he didn't care; and, at last, by dint of perseverance, he satisfied himself that it concerned Meg and Mr. Brooke. Feeling indignant that he was not taken into his tutor's confidence, he set his wits to work to devise some proper retaliation for the slight.

Meg meanwhile had apparently forgotten the matter, and was absorbed in preparations for her father's return; but all of a sudden a change seemed to come over her, and, for a day or two, she was quite unlike herself. She started when spoken to, blushed when looked at, was very quiet, and sat over her sewing with a timid, troubled look on her face. To her mother's inquiries she answered that she was quite well, and Jo's she silenced by begging to be let alone.

"She feels it in the air—love, I mean—and she's going very fast. She's got most of the symptoms, is twittery and cross, don't eat, lies awake, and mopes in corners. I caught her singing that song about 'the silver-voiced brook,' and once she said 'John,' as you do, and then turned as red as a poppy. Whatever shall we do?" said Jo, looking ready for any measures, however violent.

"Nothing but wait. Let her alone, be kind and patient, and father's coming will settle everything," replied her mother.

"Here's a note to you, Meg, all sealed up. How odd! Teddy never seals mine," said Jo, next day, as she distributed the contents of the little post-office.

Mrs. March and Jo were deep in their own affairs, when a sound from Meg made them look up to see her staring at her note, with a frightened face.

"My child, what is it?" cried her mother, running to her, while Jo tried to take the paper which had done the mischief.

"It's all a mistake—he didn't send it—oh, Jo, how could you do it?" and Meg hid her face in her hands, crying as if her heart was quite broken.

"Me! I've done nothing! What's she talking about?" cried Jo, bewildered.

Meg's mild eyes kindled with anger as she pulled a crumpled note from her pocket, and threw it at Jo, saying, reproachfully,—

"You wrote it, and that bad boy helped you. How could you be so rude, so mean, and cruel to us both?"

Jo hardly heard her, for she and her mother were reading the note, which was written in a peculiar hand.

"MY DEAREST MARGARET,—

"I can no longer restrain my passion, and must know my fate before I return. I dare not tell your parents yet, but I think they would consent if they knew that we adored one another. Mr. Laurence will help me to some good place, and then, my sweet girl, you will make me happy. I implore you to say nothing to your family yet, but to send one word of hope through Laurie to

"Your devoted

"JOHN."

"Oh, the little villain! that's the way he meant to pay me for keeping my word to mother. I'll give him a hearty scolding, and bring him over to beg pardon," cried Jo, burning to execute immediate justice. But her mother held her back, saying, with a look she seldom wore,—

"Stop, Jo, you must clear yourself first. You have played so many pranks, that I am afraid you have had a hand in this."

"On my word, mother, I haven't! I never saw that note before, and don't know anything about it, as true as I live!" said Jo, so earnestly, that they believed her. "If I *had* taken a part in it I'd have done it better than this, and have written a sensible note. I should think you'd have known Mr. Brooke wouldn't write such stuff as that," she added, scornfully tossing down the paper.

"It's like his writing," faltered Meg, comparing it with the note in her hand.

"Oh, Meg, you didn't answer it?" cried Mrs. March, quickly.

"Yes, I did!" and Meg hid her face again, overcome with shame.

"Here's a scrape! *Do* let me bring that wicked boy over to explain, and be lectured. I can't rest till I get hold of him;" and Jo made for the door again.

"Hush! let me manage this, for it is worse than I thought. Margaret, tell me the whole story," commanded Mrs. March, sitting down by Meg, yet keeping hold of Jo, lest she should fly off.

"I received the first letter from Laurie, who didn't look as if he knew anything about it," began Meg, without looking up. "I was worried at first, and meant to tell you; then I remembered how you liked Mr. Brooke, so I thought you wouldn't mind if I kept my little secret for a few days. I'm so silly that I liked to think no one knew; and, while I was deciding what to say, I felt like the girls in books, who have such things to do. Forgive me, mother, I'm paid for my silliness now; I never can look him in the face again."

"What did you say to him?" asked Mrs. March.

"I only said I was too young to do anything about it yet; that I didn't wish to have secrets from you, and he must speak to father. I was very grateful for his kindness, and would be his friend, but nothing more, for a long while."

Mrs. March smiled, as if well pleased, and Jo clapped her hands, exclaiming, with a laugh,—

"You are almost equal to Caroline Percy,[1] who was a pattern of prudence! Tell on, Meg. What did he say to that?"

"He writes in a different way entirely; telling me that he never sent any love-letter at all, and is very sorry that my roguish sister, Jo, should take such liberties with our names. It's very kind and respectful, but think how dreadful for me!"

Meg leaned against her mother, looking the image of despair, and Jo tramped about the room, calling Laurie names. All of a sudden she stopped, caught up the two notes, and, after looking at them closely, said, decidedly, "I don't believe Brooke ever saw either of these letters. Teddy wrote both, and keeps yours to crow over me with, because I wouldn't tell him my secret."

"Don't have any secrets, Jo; tell it to mother, and keep out of trouble, as I should have done," said Meg, warningly.

"Bless you, child! mother told me."

"That will do, Jo. I'll comfort Meg while you go and get Laurie. I shall sift the matter to the bottom, and put a stop to such pranks at once."

Away ran Jo, and Mrs. March gently told Meg Mr. Brooke's real feelings. "Now, dear, what are your own? Do you love him enough to wait till he can make a home for you, or will you keep yourself quite free for the present?"

"I've been so scared and worried, I don't want to have anything to do with lovers for a long while,—perhaps never," answered Meg, petulantly. "If John *doesn't* know anything about this nonsense, don't tell him, and make Jo and Laurie hold their tongues. I won't be deceived and plagued, and made a fool of,—it's a shame!"

Seeing that Meg's usually gentle temper was roused, and her pride hurt by this mischievous joke, Mrs. March soothed her by promises of entire silence, and great discretion for the future. The instant Laurie's step was heard in the hall, Meg fled into the study, and Mrs. March received the culprit alone. Jo had not told him why he was wanted, fearing he wouldn't come; but he knew the minute he saw Mrs. March's face, and stood twirling his hat with a guilty air, which convicted him at once. Jo was dismissed, but chose to march up and down the hall like a sentinel, having some fear that the prisoner might bolt. The sound of voices in the parlor rose and fell for half an hour; but what happened during that interview the girls never knew.

When they were called in, Laurie was standing by their mother with such a penitent face, that Jo forgave him on the spot, but did not think it wise to betray the fact. Meg received his humble apology, and was much comforted by the assurance that Brooke knew nothing of the joke.

"I'll never tell him to my dying day,—wild horses shan't drag it out of

---

1. In Irish novelist Maria Edgeworth's *Patronage* (1814), the unaffected, independent, and practical Miss Caroline Percy embodies prudence in all matters touching on courtship and engagement.

me; so you'll forgive me, Meg, and I'll do anything to show how out-
and-out sorry I am," he added, looking very much ashamed of himself.

"I'll try; but it was a very ungentlemanly thing to do. I didn't think
you could be so sly and malicious, Laurie," replied Meg, trying to hide
her maidenly confusion under a gravely reproachful air.

"It was altogether abominable, and I don't deserve to be spoken to
for a month; but you will, though, won't you?" and Laurie folded his
hands together, with such an imploring gesture, and rolled up his eyes
in such a meekly repentant way, as he spoke in his irresistibly persuasive tone, that it was impossible to frown upon him, in spite of his
scandalous behavior. Meg pardoned him, and Mrs. March's grave face
relaxed, in spite of her efforts to keep sober, when she heard him declare that he would atone for his sins by all sorts of penances, and
abase himself like a worm before the injured damsel.

Jo stood aloof, meanwhile, trying to harden her heart against him,
and succeeding only in primming up her face into an expression of entire disapprobation. Laurie looked at her once or twice, but, as she
showed no sign of relenting, he felt injured, and turned his back on
her till the others were done with him, when he made her a low bow,
and walked off without a word.

As soon as he had gone, she wished she had been more forgiving;
and, when Meg and her mother went up stairs, she felt lonely, and
longed for Teddy. After resisting for some time, she yielded to the impulse, and, armed with a book to return, went over to the big house.

"Is Mr. Laurence in?" asked Jo, of a housemaid, who was coming
down stairs.

"Yes, miss; but I don't believe he's seeable just yet."

"Why not; is he ill?"

"La, no, miss! but he's had a scene with Mr. Laurie, who is in one of
his tantrums about something, which vexes the old gentleman, so I
dursn't go nigh him."

"Where is Laurie?"

"Shut up in his room, and he won't answer, though I've been
a-tapping. I don't know what's to become of the dinner, for it's ready,
and there's no one to eat it."

"I'll go and see what the matter is. I'm not afraid of either of them."

Up went Jo, and knocked smartly on the door of Laurie's little study.

"Stop that, or I'll open the door and make you!" called out the young
gentleman, in a threatening tone.

Jo immediately pounded again; the door flew open, and in she
bounced, before Laurie could recover from his surprise. Seeing that
he really *was* out of temper, Jo, who knew how to manage him, assumed a contrite expression, and, going artistically down upon her
knees, said, meekly, "Please forgive me for being so cross. I came to
make it up, and can't go away till I have."

"It's all right; get up, and don't be a goose, Jo," was the cavalier reply to her petition.

"Thank you; I will. Could I ask what's the matter? You don't look exactly easy in your mind."

"I've been shaken, and I won't bear it!" growled Laurie, indignantly.

"Who did it?" demanded Jo.

"Grandfather; if it had been any one else I'd have—" and the injured youth finished his sentence by an energetic gesture of the right arm.

"That's nothing; I often shake you, and you don't mind," said Jo, soothingly.

"Pooh! you're a girl, and it's fun; but I'll allow no man to shake *me*."

"I don't think any one would care to try it, if you looked as much like a thunder-cloud as you do now. Why were you treated so?"

"Just because I wouldn't say what your mother wanted me for. I'd promised not to tell, and of course I wasn't going to break my word."

"Couldn't you satisfy your grandpa in any other way?"

"No; he *would* have the truth, the whole truth, and nothing but the truth. I'd have told my part of the scrape, if I could, without bringing Meg in. As I couldn't, I held my tongue, and bore the scolding till the old gentleman collared me. Then I got angry, and bolted, for fear I should forget myself."

"It wasn't nice, but he's sorry, I know; so go down and make up. I'll help you."

"Hanged if I do! I'm not going to be lectured and pummelled by every one, just for a bit of a frolic. I *was* sorry about Meg, and begged pardon like a man; but I won't do it again, when I wasn't in the wrong."

"He didn't know that."

"He ought to trust me, and not act as if I was a baby. It's no use, Jo; he's got to learn that I'm able to take care of myself, and don't need any one's apron-string to hold on by."

"What pepper-pots you are!" sighed Jo. "How do you mean to settle this affair?"

"Well, he ought to beg pardon, and believe me when I say I can't tell him what the row's about."

"Bless you! he won't do that."

"I won't go down till he does."

"Now, Teddy, be sensible; let it pass, and I'll explain what I can. You can't stay here, so what's the use of being melodramatic?"

"I don't intend to stay here long, any-way. I'll slip off and take a journey somewhere, and when grandpa misses me he'll come round fast enough."

"I dare say; but you ought not to go and worry him."

"Don't preach. I'll go to Washington and see Brooke; it's gay there, and I'll enjoy myself after the troubles."

"What fun you'd have! I wish I could run off too!" said Jo, forgetting her part of Mentor[2] in lively visions of martial life at the capital.

"Come on, then! Why not? You go and surprise your father, and I'll stir up old Brooke. It would be a glorious joke; let's do it, Jo! We'll leave a letter saying we are all right, and trot off at once. I've got

2. Telemachus's tutor and Odysseus's friend in Homer's *Odyssey*. The name is synonymous with wise counsel.

money enough; it will do you good, and be no harm, as you go to your father."

For a moment Jo looked as if she would agree; for, wild as the plan was, it just suited her. She was tired of care and confinement, longed for change, and thoughts of her father blended temptingly with the novel charms of camps and hospitals, liberty and fun. Her eyes kindled as they turned wistfully toward the window, but they fell on the old house opposite, and she shook her head with sorrowful decision.

"If I was a boy, we'd run away together, and have a capital time; but as I'm a miserable girl, I must be proper, and stop at home. Don't tempt me, Teddy, it's a crazy plan."

"That's the fun of it!" began Laurie, who had got a wilful fit on him, and was possessed to break out of bounds in some way.

"Hold your tongue!" cried Jo, covering her ears. " 'Prunes and prisms'[3] are my doom, and I may as well make up my mind to it. I came here to moralize, not to hear about things that make me skip to think of."

"I knew Meg would wet-blanket such a proposal, but I thought you had more spirit," began Laurie, insinuatingly.

"Bad boy, be quiet. Sit down and think of your own sins, don't go making me add to mine. If I get your grandpa to apologize for the shaking, will you give up running away?" asked Jo, seriously.

"Yes, but you won't do it," answered Laurie, who wished to "make up," but felt that his outraged dignity must be appeased first.

"If I can manage the young one I can the old one," muttered Jo, as she walked away, leaving Laurie bent over a railroad map, with his head propped up on both hands.

"Come in!" and Mr. Laurence's gruff voice sounded gruffer than ever, as Jo tapped at his door.

"It's only me, sir, come to return a book," she said, blandly, as she entered.

"Want any more?" asked the old gentleman, looking grim and vexed, but trying not to show it.

"Yes, please, I like old Sam[4] so well, I think I'll try the second volume," returned Jo, hoping to propitiate him by accepting a second dose of "Boswell's Johnson," as he had recommended that lively work.

The shaggy eyebrows unbent a little, as he rolled the steps toward the shelf where the Johnsonian literature was placed. Jo skipped up, and, sitting on the top step, affected to be searching for her book, but was really wondering how best to introduce the dangerous object of her visit. Mr. Laurence seemed to suspect that something was brewing in her mind; for, after taking several brisk turns about the room, he

3. Colloquialism for propriety, for words that are proper for a young woman to utter.
4. Samuel Johnson (1709–1784), English writer and editor, one of the central figures in eighteenth-century British literary history. His Scottish friend James Boswell (1740–1795) wrote a dazzling and entertaining biography, *The Life of Samuel Johnson, LL.D.* (1791). Known for his dictionary and his wisdom literature, Johnson produced a regular series of essays in the periodical the *Rambler* from 1750 to 1752. He also authored the allegorical, philosophical *The Prince of Abissinia: A Tale* (1759), retitled *The History of Rasselas, Prince of Abissinia* in 1768.

faced round on her, speaking so abruptly, that "Rasselas" tumbled face downward on the floor.

"What has that boy been about? Don't try to shield him, now! I know he has been in mischief, by the way he acted when he came home. I can't get a word from him; and, when I threatened to shake the truth out of him, he bolted up stairs, and locked himself into his room."

"He did do wrong, but we forgave him, and all promised not to say a word to any one," began Jo, reluctantly.

"That won't do; he shall not shelter himself behind a promise from you soft-hearted girls. If he's done anything amiss, he shall confess, beg pardon, and be punished. Out with it, Jo! I won't be kept in the dark."

Mr. Laurence looked so alarming, and spoke so sharply, that Jo would have gladly run away, if she could, but she was perched aloft on the steps, and he stood at the foot, a lion in the path, so she had to stay and brave it out.

"Indeed, sir, I cannot tell, mother forbid it. Laurie has confessed, asked pardon, and been punished quite enough. We don't keep silence to shield him, but some one else, and it will make more trouble if you interfere. Please don't; it was partly my fault, but it's all right now, so let's forget it, and talk about the 'Rambler,' or something pleasant."

"Hang the 'Rambler!' come down and give me your word that this harum-scarum boy of mine hasn't done anything ungrateful or impertinent. If he has, after all your kindness to him, I'll thrash him with my own hands."

The threat sounded awful, but did not alarm Jo, for she knew the irascible old man would never lift a finger against his grandson, whatever he might say to the contrary. She obediently descended, and made as light of the prank as she could without betraying Meg, or forgetting the truth.

"Hum! ha! well, if the boy held his tongue because he'd promised, and not from obstinacy, I'll forgive him. He's a stubborn fellow, and hard to manage," said Mr. Laurence, rubbing up his hair till it looked as if he'd been out in a gale, and smoothing the frown from his brow with an air of relief.

"So am I; but a kind word will govern me when all the king's horses and all the king's men couldn't,"[5] said Jo, trying to say a kind word for her friend, who seemed to get out of one scrape only to fall into another.

"You think I'm not kind to him, hey?" was the sharp answer.

"Oh, dear, no, sir; you are rather too kind sometimes, and then just a trifle hasty when he tries your patience. Don't you think you are?"

Jo was determined to have it out now, and tried to look quite placid, though she quaked a little after her bold speech. To her great relief

---

5. Allusion to the traditional children's rhyme "Humpty Dumpty." The version with the lines that Jo quotes first appeared as a manuscript addition to an edition of *Mother Goose's Melody* published around 1803. The first printed version is in *Gammer Gurton's Garland* (1810 edition).

and surprise, the old gentleman only threw his spectacles on to the table with a rattle, and exclaimed, frankly,—

"You're right, girl, I am! I love the boy, but he tries my patience past bearing, and I don't know how it will end, if we go on so."

"I'll tell you,—he'll run away." Jo was sorry for that speech the minute it was made; she meant to warn him that Laurie would not bear much restraint, and hoped he would be more forbearing with the lad.

Mr. Laurence's ruddy face changed suddenly, and he sat down with a troubled glance at the picture of a handsome man, which hung over his table. It was Laurie's father, who *had* run away in his youth, and married against the imperious old man's will. Jo fancied he remembered and regretted the past, and she wished she had held her tongue.

"He won't do it, unless he is very much worried, and only threatens it sometimes, when he gets tired of studying. I often think I should like to, especially since my hair was cut; so, if you ever miss us, you may advertise for two boys, and look among the ships bound for India."

She laughed as she spoke, and Mr. Laurence looked relieved, evidently taking the whole as a joke.

"You hussy, how dare you talk in that way? where's your respect for me, and your proper bringing up? Bless the boys and girls! what torments they are; yet we can't do without them," he said, pinching her cheeks good-humoredly.

"Go and bring that boy down to his dinner, tell him it's all right, and advise him not to put on tragedy airs with his grandfather; I won't bear it."

"He won't come, sir; he feels badly because you didn't believe him when he said he couldn't tell. I think the shaking hurt his feelings very much."

Jo tried to look pathetic, but must have failed, for Mr. Laurence began to laugh, and she knew the day was won.

"I'm sorry for that, and ought to thank him for not shaking *me*, I suppose. What the dickens does the fellow expect?" and the old gentleman looked a trifle ashamed of his own testiness.

"If I was you, I'd write him an apology, sir. He says he won't come down till he has one; and talks about Washington, and goes on in an absurd way. A formal apology will make him see how foolish he is, and bring him down quite amiable. Try it; he likes fun, and this way is better than talking. I'll carry it up, and teach him his duty."

Mr. Laurence gave her a sharp look, and put on his spectacles, saying, slowly, "You're a sly puss! but I don't mind being managed by you and Beth. Here, give me a bit of paper, and let us have done with this nonsense."

The note was written in the terms which one gentleman would use to another after offering some deep insult. Jo dropped a kiss on the top of Mr. Laurence's bald head, and ran up to slip the apology under Laurie's door, advising him, through the keyhole, to be submissive, decorous, and a few other agreeable impossibilities. Finding the door locked again, she left the note to do its work, and was going quietly away, when the young gentleman slid down the banisters, and waited for her at the bottom, saying, with his most virtuous expression of countenance, "What a good fellow you are, Jo! Did you get blown up?" he added, laughing.

"No; he was pretty clever,[6] on the whole."

"Ah! I got it all round! even you cast me off over there, and I felt just ready to go to the deuce," he began, apologetically.

"Don't talk in that way; turn over a new leaf and begin again, Teddy, my son."

"I keep turning over new leaves, and spoiling them, as I used to spoil my copy-books; and I make so many beginnings there never will be an end," he said, dolefully.

"Go and eat your dinner; you'll feel better after it. Men always croak when they are hungry," and Jo whisked out at the front door after that.

"That's a 'label' on my 'sect,' " answered Laurie, quoting Amy, as he went to partake of humble-pie dutifully with his grandfather, who was quite saintly in temper, and overwhelmingly respectful in manner, all the rest of the day.

Every one thought the matter ended, and the little cloud blown over; but the mischief was done, for, though others forgot it, Meg remembered. She never alluded to a certain person, but she thought of him a good deal, dreamed dreams more than ever; and, once, Jo, rummaging her sister's desk for stamps, found a bit of paper scribbled over with the words, "Mrs. John Brooke;" whereat she groaned tragically, and cast it into the fire, feeling that Laurie's prank had hastened the evil day for her.

CHAPTER XXII.

PLEASANT MEADOWS.

LIKE sunshine after storm were the peaceful weeks which followed. The invalids improved rapidly, and Mr. March began to talk of returning early in the new year. Beth was soon able to lie on the study sofa all day, amusing herself with the well-beloved cats, at first, and, in time, with doll's sewing, which had fallen sadly behindhand. Her once active limbs were so stiff and feeble that Jo took her a daily airing about the house, in her strong arms. Meg cheerfully blackened and burnt her white hands cooking delicate messes for "the dear;" while Amy, a loyal slave of the ring, celebrated her return by giving away as many of her treasures as she could prevail on her sisters to accept.

As Christmas approached, the usual mysteries began to haunt the house, and Jo frequently convulsed the family by proposing utterly impossible, or magnificently absurd ceremonies, in honor of this unusu-

6. Nice, good-natured, amiable (colloquialism).

ally merry Christmas. Laurie was equally impracticable, and would have had bonfires, sky-rockets, and triumphal arches, if he had had his own way. After many skirmishes and snubbings, the ambitious pair were considered effectually quenched, and went about with forlorn faces, which were rather belied by explosions of laughter when the two got together.

Several days of unusually mild weather fitly ushered in a splendid Christmas-day. Hannah "felt in her bones that it was going to be an uncommonly plummy day," and she proved herself a true prophetess, for everybody and everything seemed bound to produce a grand success. To begin with: Mr. March wrote that he should soon be with them; then Beth felt uncommonly well that morning, and, being dressed in her mother's gift,—a soft crimson merino wrapper,—was borne in triumph to the window, to behold the offering of Jo and Laurie. The Unquenchables had done their best to be worthy of the name, for, like elves, they had worked by night, and conjured up a comical surprise. Out in the garden stood a stately snow-maiden, crowned with holly, bearing a basket of fruit and flowers in one hand, a great roll of new music in the other, a perfect rainbow of an Afghan round her chilly shoulders, and a Christmas carol issuing from her lips, on a pink paper streamer:—

"THE JUNGFRAU TO BETH.[7]

"God bless you, dear Queen Bess!
   May nothing you dismay;
But health, and peace, and happiness,
   Be yours, this Christmas-day.

"Here's fruit to feed our busy bee,
   And flowers for her nose;
Here's music for her pianee,—
   An Afghan for her toes.

"A portrait of Joanna, see,
   By Raphael No. 2,
Who labored with great industry,
   To make it fair and true.

"Accept a ribbon red I beg,
   For Madam Purrer's tail;
And ice cream made by lovely Peg,—
   A Mont Blanc in a pail.

"Their dearest love my makers laid
   Within my breast of snow,
Accept it, and the Alpine maid,
   From Laurie and from Jo."

7. Allusion to and partial adaptation of the traditional Christmas carol "God Rest Ye Merry Gentlemen." *Jungfrau* is German for virgin or maiden.

How Beth laughed when she saw it! how Laurie ran up and down to bring in the gifts, and what ridiculous speeches Jo made as she presented them!

"I'm so full of happiness, that, if father was only here, I couldn't hold one drop more," said Beth, quite sighing with contentment as Jo carried her off to the study to rest after the excitement, and to refresh herself with some of the delicious grapes the "Jungfrau" had sent her.

"So am I," added Jo, slapping the pocket wherein reposed the long-desired Undine and Sintram.

"I'm sure I am," echoed Amy, poring over the engraved copy of the Madonna and Child, which her mother had given her, in a pretty frame.

"Of course I am," cried Meg, smoothing the silvery folds of her first silk dress; for Mr. Laurence had insisted on giving it.

"How can *I* be otherwise!" said Mrs. March, gratefully, as her eyes went from her husband's letter to Beth's smiling face, and her hand caressed the brooch made of gray and golden, chestnut and dark brown hair, which the girls had just fastened on her breast.

Now and then, in this work-a-day world, things do happen in the delightful story-book fashion, and what a comfort that is. Half an hour after every one had said they were so happy they could only hold one drop more, the drop came. Laurie opened the parlor door, and popped his head in very quietly. He might just as well have turned a somersault, and uttered an Indian war-whoop; for his face was so full of suppressed excitement, and his voice so treacherously joyful, that every one jumped up, though he only said, in a queer, breathless voice, "Here's another Christmas present for the March family."

Before the words were well out of his mouth, he was whisked away somehow, and in his place appeared a tall man, muffled up to the eyes, leaning on the arm of another tall man, who tried to say something and couldn't. Of course there was a general stampede; and for several minutes everybody seemed to lose their wits, for the strangest things were done, and no one said a word. Mr. March became invisible in the embrace of four pairs of loving arms; Jo disgraced herself by nearly fainting away, and had to be doctored by Laurie in the china closet; Mr. Brooke kissed Meg entirely by mistake, as he somewhat incoherently explained; and Amy, the dignified, tumbled over a stool, and, never stopping to get up, hugged and cried over her father's boots in the most touching manner. Mrs. March was the first to recover herself, and held up her hand with a warning, "Hush! remember Beth!"

But it was too late; the study door flew open,—the little red wrapper appeared on the threshold,—joy put strength into the feeble limbs,—and Beth ran straight into her father's arms. Never mind what happened just after that; for the full hearts overflowed, washing away the bitterness of the past, and leaving only the sweetness of the present.

It was not at all romantic, but a hearty laugh set everybody straight again,—for Hannah was discovered behind the door, sobbing over the fat turkey, which she had forgotten to put down when she rushed up from the kitchen. As the laugh subsided, Mrs. March began to thank

But it was too late; the study-door flew open, and Beth ran straight into her father's arms.—Page 173.

Mr. Brooke for his faithful care of her husband, at which Mr. Brooke suddenly remembered that Mr. March needed rest, and, seizing Laurie, he precipitately retired. Then the two invalids were ordered to repose, which they did, by both sitting in one big chair, and talking hard.

Mr. March told how he had longed to surprise them, and how, when the fine weather came, he had been allowed by his doctor to take advantage of it; how devoted Brooke had been, and how he was altogether a most estimable and upright young man. Why Mr. March paused a minute just there, and, after a glance at Meg, who was violently poking the fire, looked at his wife with an inquiring lift of the eyebrows, I leave you to imagine; also why Mrs. March gently nodded her head, and asked, rather abruptly, if he wouldn't have something to eat. Jo saw and understood the look; and she stalked grimly away, to get wine and beef tea, muttering to herself, as she slammed the door, "I hate estimable young men with brown eyes!"

There never *was* such a Christmas dinner as they had that day. The fat turkey was a sight to behold, when Hannah sent him up, stuffed, browned and decorated. So was the plum-pudding, which quite melted in one's mouth; likewise the jellies, in which Amy revelled like a fly in a honey-pot. Everything turned out well; which was a mercy, Hannah said, "For my mind was that flustered, mum, that it's a merrycle I didn't roast the pudding and stuff the turkey with raisins, let alone bilin' of it in a cloth."

Mr. Laurence and his grandson dined with them; also Mr. Brooke,—at whom Jo glowered darkly, to Laurie's infinite amusement. Two easy-chairs stood side by side at the head of the table, in which sat Beth and her father, feasting, modestly, on chicken and a little fruit. They drank healths, told stories, sung songs, "reminisced," as the old folks say, and had a thoroughly good time. A sleigh-ride had been planned, but the girls would not leave their father; so the guests departed early, and, as twilight gathered, the happy family sat together round the fire.

"Just a year ago we were groaning over the dismal Christmas we expected to have. Do you remember?" asked Jo, breaking a short pause, which had followed a long conversation about many things.

"Rather a pleasant year on the whole!" said Meg, smiling at the fire, and congratulating herself on having treated Mr. Brooke with dignity.

"I think it's been a pretty hard one," observed Amy, watching the light shine on her ring, with thoughtful eyes.

"I'm glad it's over, because we've got you back," whispered Beth, who sat on her father's knee.

"Rather a rough road for you to travel, my little pilgrims, especially the latter part of it. But you have got on bravely; and I think the burdens are in a fair way to tumble off very soon," said Mr. March, looking, with fatherly satisfaction, at the four young faces gathered round him.

"How do you know? Did mother tell you?" asked Jo.

"Not much; straws show which way the wind blows; and I've made several discoveries today."

"Oh, tell us what they are!" cried Meg, who sat beside him.

"Here is one!" and, taking up the hand which lay on the arm of his chair, he pointed to the roughened forefinger, a burn on the back, and two or three little hard spots on the palm. "I remember a time when this hand was white and smooth, and your first care was to keep it so. It was very pretty then, but to me it is much prettier now,—for in these seeming blemishes I read a little history. A burnt offering has been made of vanity; this hardened palm has earned something better than blisters, and I'm sure the sewing done by these pricked fingers will last a long time, so much good-will went into the stitches. Meg, my dear, I value the womanly skill which keeps home happy, more than white hands or fashionable accomplishments; I'm proud to shake this good, industrious little hand, and hope I shall not soon be asked to give it away."

If Meg had wanted a reward for hours of patient labor, she received it in the hearty pressure of her father's hand, and the approving smile he gave her.

"What about Jo? Please say something nice; for she has tried so hard, and been so very, very good to me," said Beth, in her father's ear.

He laughed, and looked across at the tall girl who sat opposite, with an unusually mild expression in her brown face.

"In spite of the curly crop, I don't see the 'son Jo' whom I left a year ago," said Mr. March. "I see a young lady who pins her collar straight, laces her boots neatly, and neither whistles, talks slang, nor lies on the rug, as she used to do. Her face is rather thin and pale, just now, with watching and anxiety; but I like to look at it, for it has grown gentler, and her voice is lower; she doesn't bounce, but moves quietly, and takes care of a certain little person in a motherly way, which delights me. I rather miss my wild girl; but if I get a strong, helpful, tender-hearted woman in her place, I shall feel quite satisfied. I don't know whether the shearing sobered our black sheep, but I do know that in all Washington I couldn't find anything beautiful enough to be bought with the five-and-twenty dollars which my good girl sent me."

Jo's keen eyes were rather dim for a minute, and her thin face grew rosy in the firelight, as she received her father's praise, feeling that she did deserve a portion of it.

"Now Beth;" said Amy, longing for her turn, but ready to wait.

"There's so little of her I'm afraid to say much, for fear she will slip away altogether, though she is not so shy as she used to be," began their father, cheerfully; but, recollecting how nearly he *had* lost her, he held her close, saying, tenderly, with her cheek against his own, "I've got you safe, my Beth, and I'll keep you so, please God."

After a minute's silence, he looked down at Amy, who sat on the cricket at his feet, and said, with a caress of the shining hair,—

"I observed that Amy took drumsticks at dinner, ran errands for her mother all the afternoon, gave Meg her place to-night, and has waited on every one with patience and good-humor. I also observe that she does not fret much, nor prink at the glass, and has not even mentioned a very pretty ring which she wears; so I conclude that she has learned to think of other people more, and of herself less, and has decided to try and mould her character as carefully as she moulds her little clay figures. I am glad of this; for though I should be very proud of a graceful statue made by her, I shall be infinitely prouder of a lovable daughter, with a talent for making life beautiful to herself and others."

"What are you thinking of, Beth?" asked Jo, when Amy had thanked her father, and told about her ring.

"I read in 'Pilgrim's Progress' today, how, after many troubles, Christian and Hopeful came to a pleasant green meadow, where lilies bloomed all the year round, and there they rested happily, as we do now, before they went on to their journey's end,"[8] answered Beth; adding, as she slipped out of her father's arms, and went slowly to the instrument, "It's singing time now, and I want to be in my old place. I'll try to sing the song of the shepherd boy which the Pilgrims heard. I made the music for father, because he likes the verses."

So, sitting at the dear little piano, Beth softly touched the keys, and, in the sweet voice they had never thought to hear again, sung, to her own accompaniment, the quaint hymn, which was a singularly fitting song for her:—

> "He that is down need fear no fall;
>   He that is low no pride;
> He that is humble ever shall
>   Have God to be his guide.

> "I am content with what I have,
>   Little be it or much;
> And, Lord! contentment still I crave,
>   Because Thou savest such.

> "Fulness to them a burden is,
>   That go on Pilgrimage;
> Here little, and hereafter bliss,
>   Is best from age to age!"[9]

CHAPTER XXIII.

AUNT MARCH SETTLES THE QUESTION.

LIKE bees swarming after their queen, mother and daughters hovered about Mr. March the next day, neglecting everything to look at, wait upon, and listen to, the new invalid, who was in a fair way to be killed by kindness. As he sat propped up in the big chair by Beth's sofa, with the other three close by, and Hannah popping in her head now and then, "to peek at the dear man," nothing seemed needed to complete

---

8. Near the end of part 1 of *The Pilgrim's Progress*, the pilgrims enter "the Country of *Beulah*, whose Air was very sweet and pleasant."
9. This hymn's words are by John Bunyan, from the shepherd's boy's song in part 2 of *The Pilgrim's Progress*.

their happiness. But something *was* needed, and the elder ones felt it, though none confessed the fact. Mr. and Mrs. March looked at one another with an anxious expression, as their eyes followed Meg. Jo had sudden fits of sobriety, and was seen to shake her fist at Mr. Brooke's umbrella, which had been left in the hall; Meg was absent-minded, shy and silent, started when the bell rang, and colored when John's name was mentioned; Amy said "Every one seemed waiting for something, and couldn't settle down, which was queer, since father was safe at home," and Beth innocently wondered why their neighbors didn't run over as usual.

Laurie went by in the afternoon, and, seeing Meg at the window, seemed suddenly possessed with a melodramatic fit, for he fell down upon one knee in the snow, beat his breast, tore his hair, and clasped his hands imploringly, as if begging some boon; and when Meg told him to behave himself, and go away, he wrung imaginary tears out of his handkerchief, and staggered round the corner as if in utter despair.

"What does the goose mean?" said Meg, laughing, and trying to look unconscious.

"He's showing you how your John will go on by and by. Touching, isn't it?" answered Jo, scornfully.

"Don't say *my John*, it isn't proper or true;" but Meg's voice lingered over the words as if they sounded pleasant to her. "Please don't plague me, Jo; I've told you I don't care *much* about him, and there isn't to be anything said, but we are all to be friendly, and go on as before."

"We can't, for something *has* been said, and Laurie's mischief has spoilt you for me. I see it, and so does mother; you are not like your old self a bit, and seem ever so far away from me. I don't mean to plague you, and will bear it like a man, but I do wish it was all settled. I hate to wait; so if you mean ever to do it, make haste, and have it over quick," said Jo, pettishly.

"*I* can't say or do anything till he speaks, and he won't, because father said I was too young," began Meg, bending over her work with a queer little smile, which suggested that she did not quite agree with her father on that point.

"If he did speak, you wouldn't know what to say, but would cry or blush, or let him have his own way, instead of giving a good, decided, No."

"I'm not so silly and weak as you think. I know just what I should say, for I've planned it all, so I needn't be taken unawares; there's no knowing what may happen, and I wished to be prepared."

Jo couldn't help smiling at the important air which Meg had unconsciously assumed, and which was as becoming as the pretty color varying in her checks.

"Would you mind telling me what you'd say?" asked Jo, more respectfully.

"Not at all; you are sixteen now, quite old enough to be my confidant, and my experience will be useful to you by and by, perhaps, in your own affairs of this sort."

"Don't mean to have any; it's fun to watch other people philander, but I should feel like a fool doing it myself," said Jo, looking alarmed at the thought.

"I guess not, if you liked any one very much, and he liked you." Meg spoke as if to herself, and glanced out at the lane where she had often seen lovers walking together in the summer twilight.

"I thought you were going to tell your speech to that man," said Jo, rudely shortening her sister's little revery.

"Oh, I should merely say, quite calmly and decidedly, 'Thank you, Mr. Brooke, you are very kind, but I agree with father, that I am too young to enter into any engagement at present; so please say no more, but let us be friends as we were.' "

"Hum! that's stiff and cool enough. I don't believe you'll ever say it, and I know he won't be satisfied if you do. If he goes on like the rejected lovers in books, you'll give in, rather than hurt his feelings."

"No I won't! I shall tell him I've made up my mind, and shall walk out of the room with dignity."

Meg rose as she spoke, and was just going to rehearse the dignified exit, when a step in the hall made her fly into her seat, and begin to sew as if her life depended on finishing that particular seam in a given time. Jo smothered a laugh at the sudden change, and, when some one gave a modest tap, opened the door with a grim aspect, which was anything but hospitable.

"Good afternoon, I came to get my umbrella,—that is, to see how your father finds himself today," said Mr. Brooke, getting a trifle confused, as his eye went from one tell-tale face to the other.

"It's very well, he's in the rack, I'll get him, and tell it you are here," and having jumbled her father and the umbrella well together in her reply, Jo slipped out of the room to give Meg a chance to make her speech, and air her dignity. But the instant she vanished, Meg began to sidle toward the door, murmuring,—

"Mother will like to see you, pray sit down, I'll call her."

"Don't go; are you afraid of me, Margaret?" and Mr. Brooke looked so hurt, that Meg thought she must have done something very rude. She blushed up to the little curls on her forehead, for he had never called her Margaret before, and she was surprised to find how natural and sweet it seemed to hear him say it. Anxious to appear friendly and at her ease, she put out her hand with a confiding gesture, and said, gratefully,—

"How can I be afraid when you have been so kind to father? I only wish I could thank you for it."

"Shall I tell you how?" asked Mr. Brooke, holding the small hand fast in both his big ones, and looking down at Meg with so much love in the brown eyes, that her heart began to flutter, and she both longed to run away and to stop and listen.

"Oh no, please don't—I'd rather not," she said, trying to withdraw her hand, and looking frightened in spite of her denial.

"I won't trouble you, I only want to know if you care for me a little, Meg, I love you so much, dear," added Mr. Brooke, tenderly.

This was the moment for the calm, proper speech, but Meg didn't make it, she forgot every word of it, hung her head, and answered, "I don't know," so softly, that John had to stoop down to catch the foolish little reply.

He seemed to think it was worth the trouble, for he smiled to himself as if quite satisfied, pressed the plump hand gratefully, and said, in his most persuasive tone, "Will you try and find out? I want to know *so* much; for I can't go to work with any heart until I learn whether I am to have my reward in the end or not."

"I'm too young," faltered Meg, wondering why she was so fluttered, yet rather enjoying it.

"I'll wait; and, in the mean time, you could be learning to like me. Would it be a very hard lesson, dear?"

"Not if I chose to learn it, but—"

"Please choose to learn, Meg. I love to teach, and this is easier than German," broke in John, getting possession of the other hand, so that she had no way of hiding her face, as he bent to look into it.

His tone was properly beseeching; but, stealing a shy look at him, Meg saw that his eyes were merry as well as tender, and that he wore the satisfied smile of one who had no doubt of his success. This nettled her; Annie Moffat's foolish lessons in coquetry came into her mind, and the love of power, which sleeps in the bosoms of the best of little women, woke up all of a sudden, and took possession of her. She felt excited and strange, and, not knowing what else to do, followed a capricious impulse, and, withdrawing her hands, said, petulantly, "I *don't* choose; please go away, and let me be!"

Poor Mr. Brooke looked as if his lovely castle in the air was tumbling about his ears, for he had never seen Meg in such a mood before, and it rather bewildered him.

"Do you really mean that?" he asked, anxiously, following her as she walked away.

"Yes, I do; I don't want to be worried about such things. Father says I needn't; it's too soon, and I'd rather not."

"Mayn't I hope you'll change your mind by and by? I'll wait, and say nothing till you have had more time. Don't play with me, Meg. I didn't think that of you."

"Don't think of me at all. I'd rather you wouldn't," said Meg, taking a naughty satisfaction in trying her lover's patience and her own power.

He was grave and pale now, and looked decidedly more like the novel heroes whom she admired; but he neither slapped his forehead nor tramped about the room, as they did; he just stood looking at her so wistfully, so tenderly, that she found her heart relenting in spite of her. What would have happened next I cannot say, if Aunt March had not come hobbling in at this interesting minute.

The old lady couldn't resist her longing to see her nephew; for she had met Laurie as she took her airing, and, hearing of Mr. March's arrival, drove straight out to see him. The family were all busy in the back part of the house, and she had made her way quietly in, hoping to surprise them. She did surprise two of them so much, that Meg started as if she had seen a ghost, and Mr. Brooke vanished into the study.

"Bless me! what's all this?" cried the old lady, with a rap of her cane, as she glanced from the pale young gentleman to the scarlet young lady.

"It's father's friend. I'm *so* surprised to see you!" stammered Meg, feeling that she was in for a lecture now.

"That's evident," returned Aunt March, sitting down. "But what is father's friend saying, to make you look like a peony? There's mischief going on, and I insist upon knowing what it is!" with another rap.

"We were merely talking. Mr. Brooke came for his umbrella," began Meg, wishing that Mr. Brooke and the umbrella were safely out of the house.

"Brooke? That boy's tutor? Ah! I understand now. I know all about it. Jo blundered into a wrong message in one of your pa's letters, and I made her tell me. You haven't gone and accepted him, child?" cried Aunt March, looking scandalized.

"Hush! he'll hear! Shan't I call mother?" said Meg, much troubled.

"Not yet. I've something to say to you, and I must free my mind at once. Tell me, do you mean to marry this Cook? If you do, not one penny of my money ever goes to you. Remember that, and be a sensible girl," said the old lady, impressively.

Now Aunt March possessed, in perfection, the art of rousing the spirit of opposition in the gentlest people, and enjoyed doing it. The best of us have a spice of perversity in us, especially when we are young, and in love. If Aunt March had begged Meg to accept John Brooke, she would probably have declared she couldn't think of it; but, as she was peremptorily ordered *not* to like him, she immediately made up her mind that she would. Inclination as well as perversity made the decision easy, and, being already much excited, Meg opposed the old lady with unusual spirit.

"I shall marry whom I please, Aunt March, and you can leave your money to any one you like," she said, nodding her head with a resolute air.

"Highty tighty! Is that the way you take my advice, miss? You'll be sorry for it, by and by, when you've tried love in a cottage, and found it a failure."

"It can't be a worse one than some people find in big houses," retorted Meg.

Aunt March put on her glasses and took a look at the girl,—for she did not know her in this new mood. Meg hardly knew herself, she felt so brave and independent,—so glad to defend John, and assert her right to love him, if she liked. Aunt March saw that she had begun wrong, and, after a little pause, made a fresh start, saying, as mildly as she could, "Now, Meg, my dear, be reasonable, and take my advice. I mean it kindly, and don't want you to spoil your whole life by making a mistake at the beginning. You ought to marry well, and help your family; it's your duty to make a rich match, and it ought to be impressed upon you."

"Father and mother don't think so; they like John, though he *is* poor."

"Your pa and ma, my dear, have no more worldly wisdom than two babies."

"I'm glad of it," cried Meg, stoutly.

Aunt March took no notice, but went on with her lecture. "This Rook is poor, and hasn't got any rich relations, has he?"

"No; but he has many warm friends."

"You can't live on friends; try it, and see how cool they'll grow. He hasn't any business, has he?"

"Not yet; Mr. Laurence is going to help him."

"That won't last long. James Laurence is a crotchety old fellow, and not to be depended on. So you intend to marry a man without money, position, or business, and go on working harder than you do now, when you might be comfortable all your days by minding me, and doing better? I thought you had more sense, Meg."

"I couldn't do better if I waited half my life! John is good and wise; he's got heaps of talent; he's willing to work, and sure to get on, he's so energetic and brave. Every one likes and respects him, and I'm proud to think he cares for me, though I'm so poor, and young, and silly," said Meg, looking prettier than ever in her earnestness.

"He knows *you* have got rich relations, child; that's the secret of his liking, I suspect."

"Aunt March, how dare you say such a thing? John is above such meanness, and I won't listen to you a minute if you talk so," cried Meg, indignantly, forgetting everything but the injustice of the old lady's suspicions. "My John wouldn't marry for money, any more than I would. We are willing to work, and we mean to wait. I'm not afraid of being poor, for I've been happy so far, and I know I shall be with him, because he loves me, and I—"

Meg stopped there, remembering, all of a sudden, that she hadn't made up her mind; that she had told "her John" to go away, and that he might be overhearing her inconsistent remarks.

Aunt March was very angry, for she had set her heart on having her pretty niece make a fine match, and something in the girl's happy young face made the lonely old woman feel both sad and sour.

"Well; I wash my hands of the whole affair! You are a wilful child, and you've lost more than you know by this piece of folly. No, I won't stop; I'm disappointed in you, and haven't spirits to see your pa now. Don't expect anything from me when you are married; your Mr. Book's friends must take care of you. I'm done with you forever."

And, slamming the door in Meg's face, Aunt March drove off in high dudgeon. She seemed to take all the girl's courage with her; for, when left alone, Meg stood a moment undecided whether to laugh or cry. Before she could make up her mind, she was taken possession of by Mr. Brooke, who said, all in one breath, "I couldn't help hearing, Meg. Thank you for defending me, and Aunt March for proving that you *do* care for me a little bit."

"I didn't know how much, till she abused you," began Meg.

"And I needn't go away, but may stay and be happy—may I, dear?"

Here was another fine chance to make the crushing speech and the stately exit, but Meg never thought of doing either, and disgraced herself forever in Jo's eyes, by meekly whispering, "Yes, John," and hiding her face on Mr. Brooke's waistcoat.

Fifteen minutes after Aunt March's departure, Jo came softly down stairs, paused an instant at the parlor door, and, hearing no sound within, nodded and smiled, with a satisfied expression, saying to herself, "She has sent him away as we planned, and that affair is settled. I'll go and hear the fun, and have a good laugh over it."

But poor Jo never got her laugh, for she was transfixed upon the threshold by a spectacle which held her there, staring with her mouth nearly as wide open as her eyes. Going in to exult over a fallen enemy, and to praise a strong-minded sister for the banishment of an objectionable lover, it certainly *was* a shock to behold the aforesaid enemy serenely sitting on the sofa, with the strong-minded sister enthroned upon his knee, and wearing an expression of the most abject submission. Jo gave a sort of gasp, as if a cold shower-bath had suddenly fallen upon her,—for such an unexpected turning of the tables actually took her breath away. At the odd sound, the lovers turned and saw her. Meg jumped up, looking both proud and shy; but "that man," as Jo called him, actually laughed, and said, coolly, as he kissed the astonished new comer, "Sister Jo, congratulate us!"

That was adding insult to injury! it was altogether too much! and, making some wild demonstration with her hands, Jo vanished without a word. Rushing up stairs, she startled the invalids by exclaiming, tragically, as she burst into the room, "Oh, *do* somebody go down quick! John Brooke is acting dreadfully, and Meg likes it!"

Mr. and Mrs. March left the room with speed; and, casting herself upon the bed, Jo cried and scolded tempestuously as she told the awful news to Beth and Amy. The little girls, however, considered it a most agreeable and interesting event, and Jo got little comfort from them; so she went up to her refuge in the garret, and confided her troubles to the rats.

Nobody ever knew what went on in the parlor that afternoon; but a great deal of talking was done, and quiet Mr. Brooke astonished his friends by the eloquence and spirit with which he pleaded his suit, told his plans, and persuaded them to arrange everything just as he wanted it.

The tea-bell rang before he had finished describing the paradise which he meant to earn for Meg, and he proudly took her in to supper, both looking so happy, that Jo hadn't the heart to be jealous or dismal. Amy was very much impressed by John's devotion and Meg's dignity. Beth beamed at them from a distance, while Mr. and Mrs. March surveyed the young couple with such tender satisfaction, that it was perfectly evident Aunt March was right in calling them as "unworldly as a pair of babies." No one ate much, but every one looked very happy, and the old room seemed to brighten up amazingly when the first romance of the family began there.

"You can't say 'nothing pleasant ever happens now,' can you, Meg?" said Amy, trying to decide how she would group the lovers in the sketch she was planning to take.

"No, I'm sure I can't. How much has happened since I said that! It seems a year ago," answered Meg, who was in a blissful dream, lifted far above such common things as bread and butter.

"The joys come close upon the sorrows this time, and I rather think the changes have begun," said Mrs. March. "In most families there comes, now and then, a year full of events; this has been such an one, but it ends well, after all."

"Hope the next will end better," muttered Jo, who found it very hard to see Meg absorbed in a stranger before her face; for Jo loved a few persons very dearly, and dreaded to have their affection lost or lessened in any way.

"I hope the third year from this *will* end better; I mean it shall, if I live to work out my plans," said Mr. Brooke, smiling at Meg, as if everything had become possible to him now.

"Doesn't it seem very long to wait?" asked Amy, who was in a hurry for the wedding.

"I've got so much to learn before I shall be ready, it seems a short time to me," answered Meg, with a sweet gravity in her face, never seen there before.

"You have only to wait. *I* am to do the work," said John, beginning his labors by picking up Meg's napkin, with an expression which caused Jo to shake her head, and then say to herself, with an air of relief, as the front door banged, "Here comes Laurie; now we shall have a little sensible conversation."

But Jo was mistaken; for Laurie came prancing in, overflowing with spirits, bearing a great bridal-looking bouquet for "Mrs. John Brooke," and evidently laboring under the delusion that the whole affair had been brought about by his excellent management.

"I knew Brooke would have it all his own way,—he always does; for when he makes up his mind to accomplish anything, it's done, though the sky falls," said Laurie, when he had presented his offering and his congratulations.

"Much obliged for that recommendation. I take it as a good omen for the future, and invite you to my wedding on the spot," answered Mr. Brooke, who felt at peace with all mankind, even his mischievous pupil.

"I'll come if I'm at the ends of the earth; for the sight of Jo's face alone, on that occasion, would be worth a long journey. You don't look festive, ma'am; what's the matter?" asked Laurie, following her into a corner of the parlor, whither all had adjourned to greet Mr. Laurence.

"I don't approve of the match, but I've made up my mind to bear it, and shall not say a word against it," said Jo, solemnly. "You can't know how hard it is for me to give up Meg," she continued, with a little quiver in her voice.

"You don't give her up. You only go halves," said Laurie, consolingly.

"It never can be the same again. I've lost my dearest friend," sighed Jo.

"You've got me, anyhow. I'm not good for much, I know; but I'll stand by you, Jo, all the days of my life; upon my word I will!" and Laurie meant what he said.

"I know you will, and I'm ever so much obliged; you are always a great comfort to me, Teddy," returned Jo, gratefully shaking hands.

"Well, now, don't be dismal, there's a good fellow. It's all right, you see. Meg is happy; Brooke will fly round and get settled immediately; grandpa will attend to him, and it will be very jolly to see Meg in her own little house. We'll have capital times after she is gone, for I shall be through college before long, and then we'll go abroad, or some nice trip or other. Wouldn't that console you?"

"I rather think it would; but there's no knowing what may happen in three years," said Jo, thoughtfully.

"That's true! Don't you wish you could take a look forward, and see where we shall all be then? I do," returned Laurie.

"I think not, for I might see something sad; and every one looks so happy now, I don't believe they could be much improved," and Jo's eyes went slowly round the room, brightening as they looked, for the prospect was a pleasant one.

Father and mother sat together quietly re-living the first chapter of the romance which for them began some twenty years ago. Amy was drawing the lovers, who sat apart in a beautiful world of their own, the light of which touched their faces with a grace the little artist could not copy. Beth lay on her sofa talking cheerily with her old friend, who held her little hand as if he felt that it possessed the power to lead him along the peaceful ways she walked. Jo lounged in her favorite low seat, with the grave, quiet look which best became her; and Laurie, leaning on the back of her chair, his chin on a level with her curly head, smiled with his friendliest aspect, and nodded at her in the long glass which reflected them both.

So grouped the curtain falls upon Meg, Jo, Beth and Amy. Whether it ever rises again, depends upon the reception given to the first act of the domestic drama, called "Little Women."

END OF PART FIRST.

AMY AND LAURIE.

"I'm all ready for the secrets," said Laurie, looking up with a decided expression of interest in his eyes.—PAGE 317.

Little Women

OR

MEG, JO, BETH AND AMY

PART SECOND

BY LOUISA M. ALCOTT

WITH ILLUSTRATIONS

BOSTON
ROBERTS BROTHERS
1869

CONTENTS.

CHAPTER I.

GOSSIP.

IN order that we may start afresh and go to Meg's wedding with free minds, it will be well to begin with a little gossip about the Marches. And here let me premise, that if any of the elders think there is too much "lovering" in the story, as I fear they may (I'm not afraid the young folks will make that objection), I can only say with Mrs. March, "What *can* you expect when I have four gay girls in the house, and a dashing young neighbor over the way?"

The three years that have passed have brought but few changes to the quiet family. The war is over, and Mr. March safely at home, busy with his books and the small parish which found in him a minister by nature as by grace. A quiet, studious man, rich in the wisdom that is better than learning, the charity which calls all mankind "brother," the piety that blossoms into character, making it august and lovely.

These attributes, in spite of poverty and the strict integrity which shut him out from the more worldly successes, attracted to him many admirable persons, as naturally as sweet herbs draw bees, and as naturally he gave them the honey into which fifty years of hard experience had distilled no bitter drop. Earnest young men found the gray-headed scholar as earnest and as young at heart as they; thoughtful or troubled women instinctively brought their doubts and sorrows to him, sure of finding the gentlest sympathy, the wisest counsel; sinners told their sins to the pure-hearted old man, and were both rebuked and saved; gifted men found a companion in him; ambitious men caught glimpses of nobler ambitions than their own; and even worldlings confessed that his beliefs were beautiful and true, although "they wouldn't pay."

To outsiders, the five energetic women seemed to rule the house, and so they did in many things; but the quiet man sitting among his books was still the head of the family, the household conscience, anchor and comforter; for to him the busy, anxious women always turned in troublous times, finding him, in the truest sense of those sacred words, husband and father.

The girls gave their hearts into their mother's keeping—their souls into their father's; and to both parents, who lived and labored so faithfully for them, they gave a love that grew with their growth, and bound them tenderly together by the sweetest tie which blesses life and outlives death.

Mrs. March is as brisk and cheery, though rather grayer than when we saw her last, and just now so absorbed in Meg's affairs, that the hospitals and homes, still full of wounded "boys" and soldiers' widows, decidedly miss the motherly missionary's visits.

John Brooke did his duty manfully for a year, got wounded, was sent home, and not allowed to return. He received no stars or bars, but he deserved them, for he cheerfully risked all he had; and life and love are very precious when both are in full bloom. Perfectly resigned to his discharge, he devoted himself to getting well, preparing for business, and earning a home for Meg. With the good sense and sturdy independence that characterized him, he refused Mr. Laurence's more generous offers, and accepted the place of under book-keeper, feeling better satisfied to begin with an honestly-earned salary, than by running any risks with borrowed money.

Meg had spent the time in working as well as waiting, growing womanly in character, wise in housewifery arts, and prettier than ever; for love is a great beautifier. She had her girlish ambitions and hopes, and felt some disappointment at the humble way in which the new life must begin. Ned Moffat had just married Sallie Gardiner, and Meg couldn't help contrasting their fine house and carriage, many gifts, and splendid outfit, with her own, and secretly wishing she could have the same. But somehow envy and discontent soon vanished when she thought of all the patient love and labor John had put into the little home awaiting her; and when they sat together in the twilight, talking over their small plans, the future always grew so beautiful and bright, that she forgot Sallie's splendor, and felt herself the richest, happiest girl in Christendom.

Jo never went back to Aunt March, for the old lady took such a fancy to Amy, that she bribed her with the offer of drawing lessons from one of the best teachers going; and for the sake of this advantage, Amy would have served a far harder mistress. So she gave her mornings to duty, her afternoons to pleasure, and prospered finely. Jo, meantime, devoted herself to literature and Beth, who remained delicate long after the fever was a thing of the past. Not an invalid exactly, but never again the rosy, healthy creature she had been; yet always hopeful, happy, and serene, busy with the quiet duties she loved, every one's friend, and an angel in the house, long before those who loved her most had learned to know it.

As long as "The Spread Eagle" paid her a dollar a column for her "rubbish," as she called it, Jo felt herself a woman of means, and spun her little romances diligently. But great plans fermented in her busy brain and ambitious mind, and the old tin kitchen in the garret held a slowly increasing pile of blotted manuscript, which was one day to place the name of March upon the roll of fame.

Laurie, having dutifully gone to college to please his grandfather, was now getting through it in the easiest possible manner to please himself. A universal favorite, thanks to money, manners, much talent, and the kindest heart that ever got its owner into scrapes by trying to get other people out of them, he stood in great danger of being spoilt, and probably would have been, like many another promising boy, if he had not possessed a talisman against evil in the memory of the kind old man who was bound up in his success, the motherly friend who watched over him as if he were her son, and last, but not least by any means, the knowledge that four innocent girls loved, admired, and believed in him with all their hearts.

Being only "a glorious human boy," of course he frolicked and flirted, grew dandified, aquatic, sentimental or gymnastic, as college fashions ordained; hazed and was hazed, talked slang, and more than once came perilously near suspension and expulsion. But as high spirits and the love of fun were the causes of these pranks, he always managed to save himself by frank confession, honorable atonement, or the irresistible power of persuasion which he possessed in perfection. In fact, he rather prided himself on his narrow escapes, and liked to thrill the girls with graphic accounts of his triumphs over wrathful tutors, dignified professors, and vanquished enemies. The "men of my class" were heroes in the eyes of the girls, who never wearied of the exploits of "our fellows," and were frequently allowed to bask in the smiles of these great creatures, when Laurie brought them home with him.

Amy especially enjoyed this high honor, and became quite a belle among them; for her ladyship early felt and learned to use the gift of fascination with which she was endowed. Meg was too much absorbed in her private and particular John to care for any other lords of creation, and Beth too shy to do more than peep at them, and wonder how Amy dared to order them about so; but Jo felt quite in her element, and found it very difficult to refrain from imitating the gentlemanly attitudes, phrases, and feats which seemed more natural to her than the decorums prescribed for young ladies. They all liked Jo immensely, but never fell in love with her, though very few escaped without paying the tribute of a sentimental sigh or two at Amy's shrine. And speaking of sentiment brings us very naturally to the "Dove-cote."

That was the name of the little brown house which Mr. Brooke had prepared for Meg's first home. Laurie had christened it, saying it was highly appropriate to the gentle lovers, who "went on together like a pair of turtle-doves, with first a bill and then a coo." It was a tiny house, with a little garden behind, and a lawn about as big as a pocket-handkerchief in front. Here Meg meant to have a fountain, shrubbery, and a profusion of lovely flowers; though just at present the fountain was represented by a weather-beaten urn, very like a dilapidated slop-bowl; the shrubbery consisted of several young larches, who looked undecided whether to live or die, and the profusion of flowers was merely hinted by regiments of sticks, to show where seeds were planted. But inside, it was altogether charming, and the happy bride saw no fault from garret to cellar. To be sure, the hall was so narrow, it was fortunate that they had no piano, for one never could have been got in whole. The dining-room was so small, that six people were a tight fit, and the kitchen stairs seemed built for the express purpose of precipitating both servants and china pell-mell into the coal-bin. But once get used to these slight blemishes, and nothing could be more complete, for good sense and good taste had presided over the furnishing, and the result was highly satisfactory. There were no marble-topped tables, long mirrors, or lace curtains in the little parlor, but simple furniture, plenty of books, a fine picture or two, a stand of flowers in the bay-window, and, scattered all about, the pretty gifts which came from friendly hands, and were the fairer for the loving messages they brought.

I don't think the Parian Psyche[1] Laurie gave, lost any of its beauty because Brooke put up the bracket it stood upon; that any upholsterer could have draped the plain muslin curtains more gracefully than Amy's artistic hand; or that any store-room was ever better provided with good wishes, merry words, and happy hopes, than that in which Jo and her mother put away Meg's few boxes, barrels, and bundles; and I am morally certain that the spandy-new kitchen never *could* have looked so cosy and neat, if Hannah had not arranged every pot and pan a dozen times over, and laid the fire all ready for lighting, the minute "Mis. Brooke came home." I also doubt if any young matron ever began life with so rich a supply of dusters, holders, and piece-bags,—for Beth made enough to last till the silver wedding came round, and invented three different kinds of dishcloths for the express service of the bridal china.

People who hire all these things done for them, never know what they lose; for the homeliest tasks get beautified if loving hands do them, and Meg found so many proofs of this, that everything in her small nest, from the kitchen roller to the silver vase on her parlor table, was eloquent of home love and tender forethought.

What happy times they had planning together; what solemn shopping excursions, what funny mistakes they made, and what shouts of laughter arose over Laurie's ridiculous bargains! In his love of jokes, this young gentleman, though nearly through college, was as much of a boy as ever. His last whim had been to bring with him, on his weekly visits, some new, useful, and ingenious article for the young housekeeper. Now a bag of remarkable clothes-pins; next a wonderful nutmeg grater, which fell to pieces at the first trial; a knife-cleaner that spoilt all the knives; or a sweeper that picked the nap neatly off the carpet, and left the dirt; labor-saving soap that took the skin off one's hands; infallible cements which stuck firmly to nothing but the fingers of the deluded buyer; and every kind of tin-ware, from a toy savings-bank for odd pennies, to a wonderful boiler which would wash articles in its own steam, with every prospect of exploding in the process.

In vain Meg begged him to stop. John laughed at him, and Jo called him "Mr. Toodles."[2] He was possessed with a mania for patronizing Yankee ingenuity, and seeing his friends fitly furnished forth. So each week beheld some fresh absurdity.

Everything was done at last, even to Amy's arranging different colored soaps to match the different colored rooms, and Beth's setting the table for the first meal.

"Are you satisfied? Does it seem like home, and do you feel as if you should be happy here?" asked Mrs. March, as she and her daughter

---

1. Parian is a marblelike porcelain invented in the 1840s and popular among the middle classes. Psyche, Cupid's lover in Greek mythology, often symbolizes enduring love and devotion.
2. In Richard John Raymond's *The Farmer's Daughter of the Severn Side* (first published 1856, first performed 1847), it is actually Mrs. Toodles who loves to buy things at auctions.

went through the new kingdom, arm-in-arm—for just then they seemed to cling together more tenderly than ever.

"Yes, mother, perfectly satisfied, thanks to you all, and *so* happy that I can't talk about it," answered Meg, with a look that was better than words.

"If she only had a servant or two it would be all right," said Amy, coming out of the parlor, where she had been trying to decide whether the bronze Mercury looked best on the whatnot or the mantle-piece.

"Mother and I have talked that over, and I have made up my mind to try her way first. There will be so little to do, that, with Lotty to run my errands and help me here and there, I shall only have enough work to keep me from getting lazy or homesick," answered Meg, tranquilly.

"Sallie Moffat has four," began Amy.

"If Meg had four the house wouldn't hold them, and master and missis would have to camp in the garden," broke in Jo, who, enveloped in a big blue pinafore, was giving a last polish to the door-handles.

"Sallie isn't a poor man's wife, and many maids are in keeping with her fine establishment. Meg and John begin humbly, but I have a feeling that there will be quite as much happiness in the little house as in the big one. It's a great mistake for young girls like Meg to leave themselves nothing to do but dress, give orders, and gossip. When I was first married I used to long for my new clothes to wear out, or get torn, so that I might have the pleasure of mending them; for I got heartily sick of doing fancy work and tending my pocket handkerchief."

"Why didn't you go into the kitchen and make messes, as Sallie says she does, to amuse herself, though they never turn out well, and the servants laugh at her," said Meg.

"I did, after a while; not to 'mess,' but to learn of Hannah how things should be done, that my servants need *not* laugh at me. It was play then; but there came a time when I was truly grateful that I not only possessed the will, but the power to cook wholesome food for my little girls, and help myself when I could no longer afford to hire help. You begin at the other end, Meg, dear, but the lessons you learn now will be of use to you by and by, when John is a richer man, for the mistress of a house, however splendid, should know how work *ought* to be done, if she wishes to be well and honestly served."

"Yes, mother, I'm sure of that," said Meg, listening respectfully to the little lecture; for the best of women will hold forth upon the all-absorbing subject of housekeeping. "Do you know I like this room best of all in my baby-house," added Meg, a minute after, as they went upstairs, and she looked into her well-stored linen closet.

Beth was there, laying the snowy piles smoothly on the shelves, and exulting over the goodly array. All three laughed as Meg spoke; for that linen closet was a joke. You see, having said that if Meg married "that Brooke" she shouldn't have a cent of her money, Aunt March was rather in a quandary, when time had appeased her wrath, and made her repent her vow. She never broke her word, and was much exercised in her mind how to get round it, and at last devised a plan whereby she could satisfy herself. Mrs. Carrol, Florence's mamma, was ordered to buy, have made and marked a generous supply of house and table linen, and send it as *her* present. All of which was faithfully done, but the secret leaked out, and was greatly enjoyed by the family; for Aunt March tried to look utterly unconscious, and insisted that she could give nothing but the old-fashioned pearls, long promised to the first bride.

"That's a housewifely taste, which I am glad to see. I had a young friend who set up housekeeping with six sheets, but she had finger bowls for company, and that satisfied her," said Mrs. March, patting the damask table-cloths with a truly feminine appreciation of their fineness.

"I haven't a single finger bowl, but this is a 'set out' that will last me all my days, Hannah says;" and Meg looked quite contented, as well she might.

"Toodles is coming," cried Jo from below, and they all went down to meet Laurie, whose weekly visit was an important event in their quiet lives.

A tall, broad-shouldered young fellow, with a cropped head, a felt-basin of a hat, and a fly-away coat, came tramping down the road at a great pace, walked over the low fence, without stopping to open the gate, straight up to Mrs. March, with both hands out, and a hearty—

"Here I am, mother! Yes, it's all right."

The last words were in answer to the look the elder lady gave him; a kindly, questioning look, which the handsome eyes met so frankly that the little ceremony closed as usual, with a motherly kiss.

"For Mrs. John Brooke, with the maker's congratulations and compliments. Bless you, Beth! What a refreshing spectacle you are, Jo! Amy, you are getting altogether too handsome for a single lady."

As Laurie spoke, he delivered a brown paper parcel to Meg, pulled Beth's hair ribbon, stared at Jo's big pinafore, and fell into an attitude of mock rapture before Amy, then shook hands all round, and every one began to talk.

"Where is John?" asked Meg, anxiously.

"Stopped to get the license for to-morrow, ma'am."

"Which side won the last match, Teddy?" inquired Jo, who persisted in feeling an interest in manly sports, despite her nineteen years.

"Ours, of course. Wish you'd been there to see."

"How is the lovely Miss Randal?" asked Amy, with a significant smile.

"More cruel than ever; don't you see how I'm pining away?" and Laurie gave his broad chest a sounding slap, and heaved a melodramatic sigh.

"What's the last joke? Undo the bundle and see, Meg," said Beth, eyeing the knobby parcel with curiosity.

"It's a useful thing to have in the house in case of fire or thieves," observed Laurie, as a small watchman's rattle appeared amid the laughter of the girls.

"Any time when John is away, and you get frightened, Mrs. Meg, just swing that out of the front window, and it will rouse the neighborhood in a jiffy. Nice thing, isn't it?" and Laurie gave them a sample of its powers that made them cover up their ears.

"There's gratitude for you! and, speaking of gratitude, reminds me to mention that you may thank Hannah for saving your wedding-cake from destruction. I saw it going into your house as I came by, and if she hadn't defended it manfully I'd have had a pick at it, for it looked like a remarkably plummy one."

"I wonder if you will ever grow up, Laurie," said Meg, in a matronly tone.

"I'm doing my best, ma'am, but can't get much higher, I'm afraid, as six feet is about all men can do in these degenerate days," responded the young gentleman, whose head was about level with the little chandelier. "I suppose it would be profanation to eat anything in this bran-new bower, so, as I'm tremendously hungry, I propose an adjournment," he added, presently.

"Mother and I are going to wait for John. There are some last things to settle," said Meg, bustling away.

"Beth and I are going over to Kitty Bryant's to get more flowers for to-morrow," added Amy, tying a picturesque hat over her picturesque curls, and enjoying the effect as much as anybody.

"Come, Jo, don't desert a fellow. I'm in such a state of exhaustion I can't get home without help. Don't take off your apron, whatever you do; it's peculiarly becoming," said Laurie, as Jo bestowed his especial aversion in her capacious pocket, and offered him her arm to support his feeble steps.

"Now, Teddy, I want to talk seriously to you about to-morrow," began Jo, as they strolled away together. "You *must* promise to behave well, and not cut up any pranks, and spoil our plans."

"Not a prank."

"And don't say funny things when we ought to be sober."

"I never do; you are the one for that."

"And I implore you not to look at me during the ceremony; I shall certainly laugh if you do."

"You won't see me; you'll be crying so hard that the thick fog round you will obscure the prospect."

"I never cry unless for some great affliction."

"Such as old fellows going to college, hey?" cut in Laurie, with a suggestive laugh.

"Don't be a peacock. I only moaned a trifle to keep the girls company."

"Exactly. I say, Jo, how is grandpa this week; pretty amiable?"

"Very; why, have you got into a scrape, and want to know how he'll take it?" asked Jo, rather sharply.

"Now Jo, do you think I'd look your mother in the face, and say 'All right,' if it wasn't?"—and Laurie stopped short, with an injured air.

"No, I don't."

"Then don't go and be suspicious; I only want some money," said Laurie, walking on again, appeased by her hearty tone.

"You spend a great deal, Teddy."

"Bless you, *I* don't spend it; it spends itself, somehow, and is gone before I know it."

"You are so generous and kind-hearted, that you let people borrow, and can't say 'No' to any one. We heard about Henshaw, and all you did for him. If you always spent money in that way, no one would blame you," said Jo, warmly.

"Oh, he made a mountain out of a mole-hill. You wouldn't have me let that fine fellow work himself to death, just for the want of a little help, when he is worth a dozen of us lazy chaps, would you?"

"Of course not; but I don't see the use of your having seventeen waistcoats, endless neckties, and a new hat every time you come home. I thought you'd got over the dandy period; but every now and then it breaks out in a new spot. Just now it's the fashion to be hideous; to make your head look like a scrubbing brush, wear a strait-jacket, orange gloves, and clumping, square-toed boots. If it was cheap ugliness, I'd say nothing; but it costs as much as the other, and I don't get any satisfaction out of it."

Laurie threw back his head, and laughed so heartily at this attack, that the felt-basin fell off, and Jo trampled on it, which insult only afforded him an opportunity for expatiating on the advantages of a rough-and-ready costume, as he folded up the maltreated hat, and stuffed it into his pocket.

"Don't lecture any more, there's a good soul; I have enough all through the week, and like to enjoy myself when I come home. I'll get myself up regardless of expense, to-morrow, and be a satisfaction to my friends."

"I'll leave you in peace if you'll *only* let your hair grow. I'm not aristocratic, but I do object to being seen with a person who looks like a young prizefighter," observed Jo, severely.

"This unassuming style promotes study; that's why we adopt it," returned Laurie, who certainly could not be accused of vanity, having voluntarily sacrificed a handsome, curly crop, to the demand for quarter of an inch long stubble.

"By the way, Jo, I think that little Parker is really getting desperate about Amy. He talks of her constantly, writes poetry, and moons about in a most suspicious manner. He'd better nip his little passion in the bud, hadn't he?" added Laurie, in a confidential, elder-brotherly tone, after a minute's silence.

"Of course he had; we don't want any more marrying in this family for years to come. Mercy on us, what *are* the children thinking of!" and Jo looked as much scandalized as if Amy and little Parker were not yet in their teens.

"It's a fast age, and I don't know what we are coming to, ma'am. You are a mere infant, but you'll go next, Jo, and we'll be left lamenting," said Laurie, shaking his head over the degeneracy of the times.

"Me! don't be alarmed; I'm not one of the agreeable sort. Nobody will want me, and it's a mercy, for there should always be one old maid in a family."

"You won't give any one a chance," said Laurie, with a sidelong glance, and a little more color than before in his sunburnt face. "You won't show the soft side of your character; and if a fellow gets a look at it by accident, and can't help showing that he likes it, you treat him as Mrs. Gummidge did her sweetheart; throw cold water over him, and get so thorny no one dares touch or look at you."[3]

"I don't like that sort of thing; I'm too busy to be worried with non-sense, and I think it's dreadful to break up families so. Now don't say any more about it; Meg's wedding has turned all our heads, and we talk of nothing but lovers and such absurdities. I don't wish to get raspy, so let's change the subject;" and Jo looked quite ready to fling cold water on the slightest provocation.

Whatever his feelings might have been, Laurie found a vent for them in a long low whistle, and the fearful prediction, as they parted at the gate,—"Mark my words, Jo, you'll go next."

CHAPTER II.

THE FIRST WEDDING.

THE June roses over the porch were awake bright and early on that morning, rejoicing with all their hearts in the cloudless sunshine, like friendly little neighbors, as they were. Quite flushed with excitement were their ruddy faces, as they swung in the wind, whispering to one another what they had seen; for some peeped in at the dining-room windows, where the feast was spread, some climbed up to nod and smile at the sisters, as they dressed the bride, others waved a welcome to those who came and went on various errands in garden, porch and hall, and all, from the rosiest full-blown flower to the palest baby-bud, offered their tribute of beauty and fragrance to the gentle mistress who had loved and tended them so long.

Meg looked very like a rose herself; for all that was best and sweet-est in heart and soul, seemed to bloom into her face that day, making it fair and tender, with a charm more beautiful than beauty. Neither silk, lace, nor orange flowers would she have.[4] "I don't want to look strange or fixed up, to-day," she said; "I don't want a fashionable wed-ding, but only those about me whom I love, and to them I wish to look and be my familiar self."

So she made her wedding gown herself, sewing into it the tender hopes and innocent romances of a girlish heart. Her sisters braided up her pretty hair, and the only ornaments she wore were the lilies of the valley, which "her John" liked best of all the flowers that grew.

"You *do* look just like our own dear Meg, only so very sweet and lovely, that I should hug you if it wouldn't crumple your dress," cried Amy, surveying her with delight, when all was done.

---

3. In Dickens's *David Copperfield* (1849–50), the elderly widow Mrs. Gummidge responds to a ship's cook's proposal by hitting him over the head with a bucket. "Sweetheart" is a humor-ous exaggeration; the cook barely knows Mrs. Gummidge when he proposes.
4. Meg's refusal to wear orange flowers (used to adorn brides since the Crusades) signifies her desire to have a simple rather than a "fashionable" wedding.

"Then I am satisfied. But please hug and kiss me, every one, and don't mind my dress; I want a great many crumples of this sort put into it to-day;" and Meg opened her arms to her sisters, who clung about her with April faces, for a minute, feeling that the new love had not changed the old.

"Now I'm going to tie John's cravat for him, and then to stay a few minutes with father, quietly in the study;" and Meg ran down to perform these little ceremonies, and then to follow her mother wherever she went, conscious that in spite of the smiles on the motherly face, there was a secret sorrow hidden in the motherly heart, at the flight of the first bird from the nest.

As the younger girls stand together, giving the last touches to their simple toilet, it may be a good time to tell of a few changes which three years have wrought in their appearance; for all are looking their best, just now.

Jo's angles are much softened; she has learned to carry herself with ease, if not grace. The curly crop has been lengthened into a thick coil, more becoming to the small head atop of the tall figure. There is a fresh color in her brown cheeks, a soft shine in her eyes; only gentle words fall from her sharp tongue to-day.

Beth has grown slender, pale, and more quiet than ever; the beautiful, kind eyes, are larger, and in them lies an expression that saddens one, although it is not sad itself. It is the shadow of pain which touches the young face with such pathetic patience; but Beth seldom complains, and always speaks hopefully of "being better soon."

Amy is with truth considered "the flower of the family"; for at sixteen she has the air and bearing of a full-grown woman—not beautiful, but possessed of that indescribable charm called grace. One saw it in the lines of her figure, the make and motion of her hands, the flow of her dress, the droop of her hair—unconscious, yet harmonious, and as attractive to many as beauty itself. Amy's nose still afflicted her, for it never *would* grow Grecian; so did her mouth, being too wide, and having a decided underlip. These offending features gave character to her whole face, but she never could see it, and consoled herself with her wonderfully fair complexion, keen blue eyes, and curls, more golden and abundant than ever.

All three wore suits of thin, silvery gray (their best gowns for the summer), with blush roses in hair and bosom; and all three looked just what they were—fresh-faced, happy-hearted girls, pausing a moment in their busy lives to read with wistful eyes the sweetest chapter in the romance of womanhood.

There were to be no ceremonious performances; everything was to be as natural and homelike as possible; so when Aunt March arrived, she was scandalized to see the bride come running to welcome and lead her in, to find the bridegroom fastening up a garland that had fallen down, and to catch a glimpse of the paternal minister marching upstairs with a grave countenance, and a wine bottle under each arm.

"Upon my word, here's a state of things!" cried the old lady, taking the seat of honor prepared for her, and settling the folds of her lavender *moire* with a great rustle. "You oughtn't to be seen till the last minute, child."

"I'm not a show, aunty, and no one is coming to stare at me, to criticise my dress, or count the cost of my luncheon. I'm too happy to care what any one says or thinks, and I'm going to have my little wedding just as I like it. John, dear, here's your hammer," and away went Meg to help "that man" in his highly improper employment.

Mr. Brooke didn't even say "Thank you," but as he stooped for the unromantic tool, he kissed his little bride behind the folding-door, with a look that made Aunt March whisk out her pocket-handkerchief, with a sudden dew in her sharp old eyes.

A crash, a cry, and a laugh from Laurie, accompanied by the indecorous exclamation, "Jupiter Ammon![5] Jo's upset the cake again!" caused a momentary flurry, which was hardly over, when a flock of cousins arrived, and "the party came in," as Beth used to say when a child.

"Don't let that young giant come near me; he worries me worse than mosquitoes," whispered the old lady to Amy, as the rooms filled, and Laurie's black head towered above the rest.

"He has promised to be very good to-day, and he *can* be perfectly elegant if he likes," returned Amy, gliding away to warn Hercules to beware of the dragon, which warning caused him to haunt the old lady with a devotion that nearly distracted her.

There was no bridal procession, but a sudden silence fell upon the room as Mr. March and the young pair took their places under the green arch. Mother and sisters gathered close, as if loath to give Meg up; the fatherly voice broke more than once, which only seemed to make the service more beautiful and solemn; the bridegroom's hand trembled visibly, and no one heard his replies; but Meg looked straight up in her husband's eyes, and said, "I will!" with such tender trust in her own face and voice, that her mother's heart rejoiced, and Aunt March sniffed audibly.

Jo did *not* cry, though she was very near it once, and was only saved from a demonstration by the consciousness that Laurie was staring fixedly at her, with a comical mixture of merriment and emotion in his wicked black eyes. Beth kept her face hidden on her mother's shoulder, but Amy stood like a graceful statue, with a most becoming ray of sunshine touching her white forehead and the flower in her hair.

It wasn't at all the thing, I'm afraid, but the minute she was fairly married, Meg cried, "The first kiss for Marmee!" and, turning, gave it with her heart on her lips. During the next fifteen minutes she looked more like a rose than ever, for every one availed themselves of their privileges to the fullest extent, from Mr. Laurence to old Hannah, who, adorned with a head-dress fearfully and wonderfully made, fell upon her in the hall, crying, with a sob and a chuckle, "Bless you, deary, a hundred times! The cake ain't hurt a mite, and everything looks lovely."

---

5. Laurie's slang reference to the supreme Egyptian deity (in its Roman version) reflects his classical education.

Everybody cleared up after that, and said something brilliant, or tried to, which did just as well, for laughter is ready when hearts are light. There was no display of gifts, for they were already in the little house, nor was there an elaborate breakfast, but a plentiful lunch of cake and fruit, dressed with flowers. Mr. Laurence and Aunt March shrugged and smiled at one another when water, lemonade, and coffee were found to be the only sorts of nectar which the three Hebes[6] carried round. No one said anything, however, till Laurie, who insisted on serving the bride, appeared before her with a loaded salver in his hand, and a puzzled expression on his face.

"Has Jo smashed all the bottles by accident?" he whispered, "or am I merely laboring under a delusion that I saw some lying about loose this morning?"

"No; your grandfather kindly offered us his best, and Aunt March actually sent some, but father put away a little for Beth, and despatched the rest to the Soldier's Home. You know he thinks that wine should only be used in illness, and mother says that neither she nor her daughters will ever offer it to any young man under her roof."

Meg spoke seriously, and expected to see Laurie frown or laugh; but he did neither,—for after a quick look at her, he said, in his impetuous way, "I like that, for I've seen enough harm done to wish other women would think as you do!"

"You are not made wise by experience, I hope?" and there was an anxious accent in Meg's voice.

"No; I give you my word for it. Don't think too well of me, either; this is not one of my temptations. Being brought up where wine is as common as water, and almost as harmless, I don't care for it; but when a pretty girl offers it, one don't like to refuse, you see."

"But you will, for the sake of others, if not for your own. Come, Laurie, promise, and give me one more reason to call this the happiest day of my life."

A demand so sudden and so serious, made the young man hesitate a moment, for ridicule is often harder to bear than self-denial. Meg knew that if he gave the promise he would keep it at all costs; and, feeling her power, used it as a woman may for her friend's good. She did not speak, but she looked up at him with a face made very eloquent by happiness, and a smile which said, "No one can refuse me anything to-day." Laurie, certainly, could not; and, with an answering smile, he gave her his hand, saying, heartily, "I promise, Mrs. Brooke!"

"I thank you, very, very much."

"And I drink 'Long life to your resolution,' Teddy," cried Jo, baptizing him with a splash of lemonade, as she waved her glass, and beamed approvingly upon him.

So the toast was drunk, the pledge made,[7] and loyally kept, in spite of many temptations; for, with instinctive wisdom, the girls had seized

6. In Greek mythology, Hebe was the goddess of youth. The daughter of Zeus and Hera, she poured the nectar of the gods.
7. The "temperance pledge," a personal promise not to drink alcohol.

a happy moment to do their friend a service, for which he thanked them all his life.

After lunch, people strolled about, by twos and threes, through house and garden, enjoying the sunshine without and within. Meg and John happened to be standing together in the middle of the grass-plot, when Laurie was seized with an inspiration which put the finishing touch to this unfashionable wedding.

"All the married people take hands and dance round the new-made husband and wife, as the Germans do, while we bachelors and spinsters prance in couples outside!" cried Laurie, galloping down the path with Amy, with such infectious spirit and skill that every one else followed their example without a murmur. Mr. and Mrs. March, Aunt and Uncle Carrol, began it; others rapidly joined in; even Sallie Moffat, after a moment's hesitation, threw her train over her arm, and whisked Ned into the ring. But the crowning joke was Mr. Laurence and Aunt March; for when the stately old gentleman *chasséd* solemnly up to the old lady, she just tucked her cane under her arm, and hopped briskly away to join hands with the rest, and dance about the bridal pair, while the young folks pervaded the garden, like butterflies on a midsummer day.

Want of breath brought the impromptu ball to a close, and then people began to go.

"I wish you well, my dear; I heartily wish you well; but I think you'll be sorry for it," said Aunt March to Meg, adding to the bridegroom, as he led her to the carriage, "You've got a treasure, young man,—see that you deserve it."

"That is the prettiest wedding I've been to for an age, Ned, and I don't see why, for there wasn't a bit of style about it," observed Mrs. Moffat to her husband, as they drove away.

"Laurie, my lad, if you ever want to indulge in this sort of thing, get one of those little girls to help you, and I shall be perfectly satisfied," said Mr. Laurence, settling himself in his easy-chair to rest, after the excitement of the morning.

"I'll do my best to gratify you, sir," was Laurie's unusually dutiful reply, as he carefully unpinned the posy Jo had put in his button-hole.

The little house was not far away, and the only bridal journey Meg had was the quiet walk with John, from the old home to the new. When she came down, looking like a pretty Quakeress, in her dove-colored suit and straw bonnet tied with white, they all gathered about her to say "good-by," as tenderly as if she had been going to make the grand tour.[8]

"Don't feel that I am separated from you, Marmee dear, or that I love you any the less for loving John so much," she said, clinging to her mother, with full eyes, for a moment. "I shall come every day, father, and expect to keep my old place in all your hearts, though I *am* married. Beth is going to be with me a great deal, and the other girls

8. This term originally referred to an individual's educational experience among the remains of classical cultures, but it also came to represent the extended European honeymoon taken by many upper-class Americans.

will drop in now and then to laugh at my housekeeping struggles. Thank you all for my happy wedding-day. Good-by, good-by!"

They stood watching her with faces full of love, and hope, and tender pride, as she walked away, leaning on her husband's arm, with her hands full of flowers, and the June sunshine brightening her happy face,—and so Meg's married life began.

CHAPTER III.

ARTISTIC ATTEMPTS.

IT takes people a long time to learn the difference between talent and genius, especially ambitious young men and women. Amy was learning this distinction through much tribulation; for, mistaking enthusiasm for inspiration, she attempted every branch of art with youthful audacity. For a long time there was a lull in the "mud-pie" business, and she devoted herself to the finest pen-and-ink drawing, in which she showed such taste and skill, that her graceful handiwork proved both pleasant and profitable. But overstrained eyes soon caused pen and ink to be laid aside for a bold attempt at poker-sketching. While this attack lasted, the family lived in constant fear of a conflagration, for the odor of burning wood pervaded the house at all hours; smoke issued from attic and shed with alarming frequency, red-hot pokers lay about promiscuously, and Hannah never went to bed without a pail of water and the dinner-bell at her door, in case of fire. Raphael's face was found boldly executed on the under side of the moulding board,[9] and Bacchus[1] on the head of a beer barrel; a chanting cherub adorned the cover of the sugar bucket, and attempts to portray "Garrick buying gloves of the grisette,"[2] supplied kindlings for some time.

From fire to oil was a natural transition for burnt fingers, and Amy fell to painting with undiminished ardor. An artist friend fitted her out with his cast-off palettes, brushes, and colors, and she daubed away, producing pastoral and marine views, such as were never seen on land or sea. Her monstrosities in the way of cattle would have taken prizes at an agricultural fair; and the perilous pitching of her vessels would have produced sea-sickness in the most nautical observer, if the utter disregard to all known rules of ship building and rigging had not convulsed him with laughter at the first glance. Swarthy boys and dark-eyed Madonnas staring at you from one corner of the studio, did *not* suggest Murillo;[3] oily brown shadows of faces, with a lurid streak in the wrong place, meant Rembrandt; buxom ladies and dropsical in-

---

9. Bread board.
1. The Roman version of Dionysus, the Greek god of wine.
2. David Garrick (1717–1779) was a well-known English actor, producer, dramatist, poet, and comanager of the Drury Lane Theater. A grisette is a working-class French girl or young woman employed as a seamstress or shop assistant. This somewhat obscure reference may allude to an illustration or painting that has not been identified.
3. Bartolomé Esteban Murillo (1617–1682), Spanish painter whose works emphasized the serenity of spiritual life. His works are noted for their color, sharp contrasts, light, and naturalness.

fants, Rubens; and Turner[4] appeared in tempests of blue thunder, orange lightning, brown rain, and purple clouds, with a tomato-colored splash in the middle, which might be the sun or a buoy, a sailor's shirt or a king's robe, as the spectator pleased.

Charcoal portraits came next; and the entire family hung in a row, looking as wild and crocky as if just evoked from a coal-bin. Softened into crayon sketches, they did better; for the likenesses were good, and Amy's hair, Jo's nose, Meg's mouth, and Laurie's eyes were pronounced "wonderfully fine." A return to clay and plaster followed, and ghostly casts of her acquaintances haunted corners of the house, or tumbled off closet shelves on to people's heads. Children were enticed in as models, till their incoherent accounts of her mysterious doings caused Miss Amy to be regarded in the light of a young ogress. Her efforts in this line, however, were brought to an abrupt close by an untoward accident, which quenched her ardor. Other models failing her for a time, she undertook to cast her own pretty foot, and the family were one day alarmed by an unearthly bumping and screaming; and, running to the rescue, found the young enthusiast hopping wildly about the shed, with her foot held fast in a pan-full of plaster, which had hardened with unexpected rapidity. With much difficulty and some danger, she was dug out; for Jo was so overcome with laughter while she excavated, that her knife went too far, cut the poor foot, and left a lasting memorial of one artistic attempt, at least.

After this Amy subsided, till a mania for sketching from nature set her to haunting river, field, and wood, for picturesque studies, and sighing for ruins to copy. She caught endless colds sitting on damp grass to book "a delicious bit," composed of a stone, a stump, one mushroom, and a broken mullein stalk, or "a heavenly mass of clouds," that looked like a choice display of feather-beds when done. She sacrificed her complexion floating on the river in the midsummer sun, to study light and shade, and got a wrinkle over her nose, trying after "points of sight,"[5] or whatever the squint-and-string performance is called.

If "genius is eternal patience," as Michael Angelo affirms, Amy certainly had some claim to the divine attribute, for she persevered in spite of all obstacles, failures, and discouragements, firmly believing that in time she should do something worthy to be called "high art."

She was learning, doing, and enjoying other things, meanwhile, for she had resolved to be an attractive and accomplished woman, even if she never became a great artist. Here she succeeded better; for she was one of those happily created beings who please without effort, make friends everywhere, and take life so gracefully and easily, that less fortunate souls are tempted to believe that such are born under a lucky star. Everybody liked her, for among her good gifts was tact. She

---

4. Rembrandt van Rijn (1606–1669), Dutch painter, draftsman, and etcher; Peter Paul Rubens (1577–1640), Flemish painter noted for colorful, sensuous depictions of women and children; J. M. W. Turner (1775–1851), English Romantic landscape painter.
5. The position in a painting or an observation exactly opposite the position of the observer or the painter. Also known as sight point.

had an instinctive sense of what was pleasing and proper, always said the right thing to the right person, did just what suited the time and place, and was so self-possessed that her sisters used to say, "If Amy went to court without any rehearsal beforehand, she'd know exactly what to do."

One of her weaknesses was a desire to move in "our best society," without being quite sure what the *best* really was. Money, position, fashionable accomplishments, and elegant manners, were most desirable things in her eyes, and she liked to associate with those who possessed them; often mistaking the false for the true, and admiring what was not admirable. Never forgetting that by birth she was a gentlewoman, she cultivated her aristocratic tastes and feelings, so that when the opportunity came, she might be ready to take the place from which poverty now excluded her.

"My lady," as her friends called her, sincerely desired to be a genuine lady, and was so, at heart, but had yet to learn that money cannot buy refinement of nature, that rank does not always confer nobility, and that true breeding makes itself felt in spite of external drawbacks.

"I want to ask a favor of you, mamma," Amy said, coming in with an important air, one day.

"Well, little girl, what is it?" replied her mother, in whose eyes the stately young lady still remained "the baby."

"Our drawing class breaks up next week, and before the girls separate for the summer, I want to ask them out here for a day. They are wild to see the river, sketch the broken bridge, and copy some of the things they admire in my book. They have been very kind to me in many ways, and I am grateful; for they are all rich, and know I am poor, yet they never made any difference."

"Why should they!" and Mrs. March put the question with what the girls called her "Maria Theresa air."[6]

"You know as well as I that it *does* make a difference with nearly every one, so don't ruffle up like a dear, motherly hen, when your chickens get pecked by smarter birds; the ugly duckling turned out a swan you know;" and Amy smiled without bitterness, for she possessed a happy temper and hopeful spirit.

Mrs. March laughed, and smoothed down her maternal pride, as she asked,—

"Well, my swan, what is your plan?"

"I should like to ask the girls out to lunch next week, to take them a drive to the places they want to see,—a row on the river, perhaps,—and make a little artistic fête for them."

"That looks feasible. What do you want for lunch? Cake, sandwiches, fruit and coffee, will be all that is necessary, I suppose?"

"Oh dear, no! we must have cold tongue and chicken, French chocolate and ice-cream besides. The girls are used to such things,

6. Maria Theresa (1717–1780), queen of Hungary and Bohemia, archduchess of Austria, and Roman-German empress, noted for her imperial dignity. An intelligent, strong-willed woman, she led her people to war in order to preserve her empire.

and I want my lunch to be proper and elegant, though I *do* work for my living."

"How many young ladies are there?" asked her mother, beginning to look sober.

"Twelve or fourteen in the class, but I dare say they won't all come."

"Bless me, child, you will have to charter an omnibus to carry them about."

"Why, mother, how *can* you think of such a thing; not more than six or eight will probably come, so I shall hire a beach-wagon and borrow Mr. Laurence's cherry-bounce." (Hannah's pronunciation of *char-a-banc*.)[7]

"All this will be expensive, Amy."

"Not very; I've calculated the cost, and I'll pay for it myself."

"Don't you think, dear, that as these girls are used to such things, and the best we can do will be nothing new, that some simpler plan would be pleasanter to them, as a change, if nothing more, and much better for us than buying or borrowing what we don't need, and attempting a style not in keeping with our circumstances?"

"If I can't have it as I like I don't care to have it at all. I know that I can carry it out perfectly well, if you and the girls will help a little; and I don't see why I can't, if I'm willing to pay for it," said Amy, with the decision which opposition was apt to change into obstinacy.

Mrs. March knew that experience was an excellent teacher, and, when it was possible, she left her children to learn alone the lessons which she would gladly have made easier, if they had not objected to taking advice as much as they did salts and senna.

"Very well, Amy; if your heart is set upon it, and you see your way through without too great an outlay of money, time, and temper, I'll say no more. Talk it over with the girls, and whichever way you decide, I'll do my best to help you."

"Thanks, mother; you are always *so* kind," and away went Amy to lay her plan before her sisters.

Meg agreed at once, and promised her aid,—gladly offering anything she possessed, from her little house itself to her very best salt-spoons. But Jo frowned upon the whole project, and would have nothing to do with it at first.

"Why in the world should you spend your money, worry your family, and turn the house upside down for a parcel of girls who don't care a sixpence for you? I thought you had too much pride and sense to truckle to any mortal woman just because she wears French boots and rides in a *coupé*," said Jo, who, being called from the tragical climax of her novel, was not in the best mood for social enterprises.

"I *don't* truckle, and I hate being patronized as much as you do!" returned Amy, indignantly, for the two still jangled when such questions arose. "The girls do care for me, and I for them, and there's a great deal of kindness, and sense, and talent among them, in spite of what you call fashionable nonsense. You don't care to make people like you,

7. A long, light wagon with benches facing forward.

to go into good society, and cultivate your manners and tastes. I do, and I mean to make the most of every chance that comes. *You* can go through the world with your elbows out and your nose in the air, and call it independence, if you like. That's not my way."

When Amy whetted her tongue and freed her mind she usually got the best of it, for she seldom failed to have common sense on her side, while Jo carried her love of liberty and hate of conventionalities to such an unlimited extent, that she naturally found herself worsted in an argument. Amy's definition of Jo's idea of independence was such a good hit, that both burst out laughing, and the discussion took a more amiable turn. Much against her will, Jo at length consented to sacrifice a day to Mrs. Grundy,[8] and help her sister through what she regarded as "a nonsensical business."

The invitations were sent, most all accepted, and the following Monday was set apart for the grand event. Hannah was out of humor because her week's work was deranged, and prophesied that "ef the washin' and ironin' warn't done reg'lar nothin' would go well anywheres." This hitch in the main-spring of the domestic machinery had a bad effect upon the whole concern; but Amy's motto was *"Nil desperandum,"*[9] and having made up her mind what to do, she proceeded to do it in spite of all obstacles. To begin with: Hannah's cooking didn't turn out well; the chicken was tough, the tongue too salt, and the chocolate wouldn't froth properly. Then the cake and ice cost more than Amy expected, so did the wagon; and various other expenses, which seemed trifling at the outset, counted up rather alarmingly afterward. Beth got cold and took to her bed; Meg had an unusual number of callers to keep her at home, and Jo was in such a divided state of mind that her breakages, accidents, and mistakes were uncommonly numerous, serious, and trying.

"If it hadn't been for mother I never should have got through," as Amy declared afterward, and gratefully remembered, when "the best joke of the season" was entirely forgotten by everybody else.

If it was not fair on Monday, the young ladies were to come on Tuesday, an arrangement which aggravated Jo and Hannah to the last degree. On Monday morning the weather was in that undecided state which is more exasperating than a steady pour. It drizzled a little, shone a little, blew a little, and didn't make up its mind till it was too late for any one else to make up theirs. Amy was up at dawn, hustling people out of their beds and through their breakfasts, that the house might be got in order. The parlor struck her as looking uncommonly shabby, but without stopping to sigh for what she had not, she skilfully made the best of what she had, arranging chairs over the worn places in the carpet, covering stains on the walls with pictures framed in ivy, and filling up empty corners with home-made statuary, which gave an artistic air to the room, as did the lovely vases of flowers Jo scattered about.

---

8. A character referred to in Thomas Morton's play *Speed the Plough* (prod. 1798), Mrs. Grundy is supposed to be the standard of propriety: her neighbor Dame Ashfield continually wonders, "What would Mrs. Grundy think?"
9. Keep hoping; do not despair (Latin).

The lunch looked charmingly; and, as she surveyed it, she sincerely hoped it would taste good, and that the borrowed glass, china, and silver would get safely home again. The carriages were promised, Meg and mother were all ready to do the honors, Beth was able to help Hannah behind the scenes, Jo had engaged to be as lively and amiable as an absent mind, an aching head, and a very decided disapproval of everybody and everything would allow, and, as she wearily dressed, Amy cheered herself with anticipations of the happy moment when, lunch safely over, she should drive away with her friends for an afternoon of artistic delights; for the "cherry-bounce" and the broken bridge were her strong points.

Then came two hours of suspense, during which she vibrated from parlor to porch, while public opinion varied like the weathercock. A smart shower, at eleven, had evidently quenched the enthusiasm of the young ladies who were to arrive at twelve, for nobody came; and, at two, the exhausted family sat down in a blaze of sunshine to consume the perishable portions of the feast, that nothing might be lost.

"No doubt about the weather to-day; they will certainly come, so we must fly round and be ready for them," said Amy, as the sun woke her next morning. She spoke briskly, but in her secret soul she wished she had said nothing about Tuesday, for her interest, like her cake, was getting a little stale.

"I can't get any lobsters, so you will have to do without salad to-day," said Mr. March, coming in half an hour later, with an expression of placid despair.

"Use the chicken then, the toughness won't matter in a salad," advised his wife.

"Hannah left it on the kitchen table a minute, and the kittens got at it. I'm very sorry, Amy," added Beth, who was still a patroness of cats.

Then, I *must* have a lobster, for tongue alone won't do," said Amy, decidedly.

"Shall I rush into town and demand one?" asked Jo, with the magnanimity of a martyr.

"You'd come bringing it home under your arm, without any paper, just to try me. I'll go myself," answered Amy, whose temper was beginning to fail.

Shrouded in a thick veil, and armed with a genteel travelling-basket, she departed, feeling that a cool drive would soothe her ruffled spirit, and fit her for the labors of the day. After some delay, the object of her desire was procured, likewise a bottle of dressing, to prevent further loss of time at home, and off she drove again, well pleased with her own forethought.

As the omnibus contained only one other passenger, a sleepy old lady, Amy pocketed her veil, and beguiled the tedium of the way by trying to find out where all her money had gone to. So busy was she with her card full of refractory figures that she did not observe a newcomer, who entered without stopping the vehicle, till a masculine voice said, "Good morning, Miss March," and looking up she beheld one of Laurie's most elegant college friends. Fervently hoping that he would get out before she did, Amy utterly ignored the basket at her feet, and congratulating herself that she had on her new travelling dress, returned the young man's greeting with her usual suavity and spirit.

They got on excellently; for Amy's chief care was soon set at rest, by learning that the gentleman would leave first, and she was chatting away in a peculiarly lofty strain, when the old lady got out. In stumbling to the door, she upset the basket, and oh, horror! the lobster, in all its vulgar size and brilliancy, was revealed to the high-born eyes of a Tudor!

"By Jove, she's forgot her dinner!" cried the unconscious youth, poking the scarlet monster into its place with his cane, and preparing to hand out the basket after the old lady.

"Please don't—it's—it's mine," murmured Amy, with a face nearly as red as her fish.

"Oh, really, I beg pardon; it's an uncommonly fine one, isn't it?" said Tudor, with great presence of mind, and an air of sober interest that did credit to his breeding.

Amy recovered herself in a breath, set her basket boldly on the seat, and said, laughing,—

"Don't you wish you were to have some of the salad he's to make, and to see the charming young ladies who are to eat it?"

Now that was tact, for two of the ruling foibles of the masculine mind were touched; the lobster was instantly surrounded by a halo of pleasing reminiscences, and curiosity about "the charming young ladies" diverted his mind from the comical mishap.

"I suppose he'll laugh and joke over it with Laurie, but I shan't see them; that's a comfort," thought Amy, as Tudor bowed and departed.

She did not mention this meeting at home (though she discovered that, thanks to the upset, her new dress was much damaged by the rivulets of dressing that meandered down the skirt), but went through with the preparations which now seemed more irksome than before; and at twelve o'clock all was ready again. Feeling that the neighbors were interested in her movements, she wished to efface the memory of yesterday's failure by a grand success to-day; so she ordered the "cherry-bounce," and drove away in state to meet and escort her guests to the banquet.

"There's the rumble, they're coming! I'll go into the porch to meet them; it looks hospitable, and I want the poor child to have a good time after all her trouble," said Mrs. March, suiting the action to the word. But after one glance, she retired with an indescribable expression, for, looking quite lost in the big carriage, sat Amy and one young lady.

"Run, Beth, and help Hannah clear half the things off the table; it will be too absurd to put a luncheon for twelve before a single girl," cried Jo, hurrying away to the lower regions, too excited to stop even for a laugh.

In came Amy, quite calm, and delightfully cordial to the one guest who had kept her promise; the rest of the family, being of a dramatic turn, played their parts equally well, and Miss Eliott found them a most hilarious set; for it was impossible to entirely control the merriment which possessed them. The remodelled lunch being gaily partaken of, the studio and garden visited, and art discussed with enthusiasm, Amy ordered a buggy (alas for the elegant cherrybounce!) and drove her friend quietly about the neighborhood till sunset, when "the party went out."

As she came walking in, looking very tired, but as composed as ever, she observed that every vestige of the unfortunate fête had disappeared, except a suspicious pucker about the corners of Jo's mouth.

"You've had a lovely afternoon for your drive, dear," said her mother, as respectfully as if the whole twelve had come.

"Miss Eliott is a very sweet girl, and seemed to enjoy herself, I thought," observed Beth, with unusual warmth.

"Could you spare me some of your cake? I really need some, I have so much company, and I can't make such delicious stuff as yours," asked Meg, soberly.

"Take it all; I'm the only one here who likes sweet things, and it will mould before I can dispose of it," answered Amy, thinking with a sigh of the generous store she had laid in for such an end as this!

"It's a pity Laurie isn't here to help us," began Jo, as they sat down to ice-cream and salad for the fourth time in two days.

A warning look from her mother checked any further remarks, and the whole family ate in heroic silence, till Mr. March mildly observed, "Salad was one of the favorite dishes of the ancients, and Evelyn"— here a general explosion of laughter cut short the "history of sallets," to the great surprise of the learned gentleman.[1]

"Bundle everything into a basket, and send it to the Hummels— Germans like messes. I'm sick of the sight of this; and there's no reason you should all die of a surfeit because I've been a fool," cried Amy, wiping her eyes.

"I thought I *should* have died when I saw you two girls rattling about in the what-you-call-it, like two little kernels in a very big nutshell, and mother waiting in state to receive the throng," sighed Jo, quite spent with laughter.

"I'm very sorry you were disappointed, dear, but we all did our best to satisfy you," said Mrs. March, in a tone full of motherly regret.

"I *am* satisfied; I've done what I undertook, and it's not my fault that it failed; I comfort myself with that," said Amy, with a little quiver in her voice. "I thank you all very much for helping me, and I'll thank you still more, if you won't allude to it for a month, at least."

No one did for several months; but the word "fête" always produced a general smile, and Laurie's birthday gift to Amy was a tiny coral lobster in the shape of a charm for her watch-guard.

---

1. English diarist John Evelyn wrote *Acetaria, A Discourse of Sallets* (1699), in which he describes seventy-three different kinds of salad herbs and recommends uses for each.

CHAPTER IV.

LITERARY LESSONS.

FORTUNE suddenly smiled upon Jo, and dropped a good-luck penny in her path. Not a golden penny, exactly, but I doubt if half a million would have given more real happiness than did the little sum that came to her in this wise.

Every few weeks she would shut herself up in her room, put on her scribbling suit, and "fall into a vortex," as she expressed it, writing away at her novel with all her heart and soul, for till that was finished she could find no peace. Her "scribbling suit" consisted of a black pinafore on which she could wipe her pen at will, and a cap of the same material, adorned with a cheerful red bow, into which she bundled her hair when the decks were cleared for action. This cap was a beacon to the inquiring eyes of her family, who, during these periods, kept their distance, merely popping in their heads semi-occasionally, to ask, with interest, "Does genius burn, Jo?" They did not always venture even to ask this question, but took an observation of the cap, and judged accordingly. If this expressive article of dress was drawn low upon the forehead, it was a sign that hard work was going on; in exciting moments it was pushed rakishly askew, and when despair seized the author it was plucked wholly off, and cast upon the floor. At such times the intruder silently withdrew; and not until the red bow was seen gaily erect upon the gifted brow, did any one dare address Jo.

She did not think herself a genius by any means; but when the writing fit came on, she gave herself up to it with entire abandon, and led a blissful life, unconscious of want, care, or bad weather, while she sat safe and happy in an imaginary world, full of friends almost as real and dear to her as any in the flesh. Sleep forsook her eyes, meals stood untasted, day and night were all too short to enjoy the happiness which blessed her only at such times, and made these hours worth living, even if they bore no other fruit. The divine afflatus usually lasted a week or two, and then she emerged from her "vortex" hungry, sleepy, cross, or despondent.

She was just recovering from one of these attacks when she was prevailed upon to escort Miss Crocker to a lecture, and in return for her virtue was rewarded with a new idea. It was a People's Course,[2]— the lecture on the Pyramids,—and Jo rather wondered at the choice of such a subject for such an audience, but took it for granted that some great social evil would be remedied, or some great want supplied by unfolding the glories of the Pharaohs, to an audience whose thoughts were busy with the price of coal and flour, and whose lives were spent in trying to solve harder riddles than that of the Sphinx.

They were early; and while Miss Crocker set the heel of her stocking, Jo amused herself by examining the faces of the people who occupied the seat with them. On her left were two matrons with massive

---

2. Free public lectures on diverse subjects designed to further the education of the citizens of Boston.

JO IN A VORTEX.

Every few weeks she would shut herself up in her room, put on her scribbling suit,
and "fall into a vortex," as she expressed it.—PAGE 211.

foreheads, and bonnets to match, discussing Woman's Rights and making tatting. Beyond sat a pair of humble lovers artlessly holding each other by the hand, a sombre spinster eating peppermints out of a paper bag, and an old gentleman taking his preparatory nap behind a yellow bandanna. On her right, her only neighbor was a studious-looking lad absorbed in a newspaper.

It was a pictorial sheet, and Jo examined the work of art nearest her, idly wondering what unfortuitous concatenation of circumstances needed the melodramatic illustration of an Indian in full war costume, tumbling over a precipice with a wolf at his throat, while two infuriated young gentlemen, with unnaturally small feet and big eyes, were stabbing each other close by, and a dishevelled female was flying away in the background, with her mouth wide open. Pausing to turn a page, the lad saw her looking, and, with boyish good-nature, offered half his paper, saying, bluntly, "Want to read it? That's a first-rate story."

Jo accepted it with a smile, for she had never outgrown her liking for lads, and soon found herself involved in the usual labyrinth of love, mystery, and murder, for the story belonged to that class of light literature in which the passions have a holiday, and when the author's invention fails, a grand catastrophe clears the stage of one-half the *dramatis personæ*, leaving the other half to exult over their downfall.

"Prime, isn't it?" asked the boy, as her eye went down the last paragraph of her portion.

"I guess you and I could do most as well as that if we tried," returned Jo, amused at his admiration of the trash.

"I should think I was a pretty lucky chap if I could. She makes a good living out of such stories, they say;" and he pointed to the name of Mrs. S. L. A. N. G. Northbury,[3] under the title of the tale.

"Do you know her?" asked Jo, with sudden interest.

"No; but I read all her pieces, and I know a fellow that works in the office where this paper is printed."

"Do you say she makes a good living out of stories like this?" and Jo looked more respectfully at the agitated group and thickly-sprinkled exclamation points that adorned the page.

"Guess she does! she knows just what folks like, and gets paid well for writing it."

Here the lecture began, but Jo heard very little of it, for while Professor Sands was prosing away about Belzoni, Cheops, scarabei,[4] and hieroglyphics, she was covertly taking down the address of the paper, and boldly resolving to try for the hundred dollar prize offered in its columns for a sensational story. By the time the lecture ended, and the audience awoke, she had built up a splendid fortune for herself (not

3. A parody of the name of the popular and highly paid mid-nineteenth-century American sensational writer Mrs. E. D. E. N. Southworth, whose works included *The Hidden Hand*, originally serialized in the *Ledger* in 1859.

4. Giovanni Battista Belzoni (1778–1823), an engineer, explorer, and amateur archaeologist whose discoveries laid a foundation for the study of Egyptology. Cheops is the largest and the oldest of the pyramids of Giza, thought to have been built between 2589 and 2566 B.C.E.; Cheops (or Khufu) also refers to the king of ancient Egypt who built this great pyramid. Used by the Egyptians as official seals, amulets, and decorative objects, scarabei are images of beetles made from many different substances, including precious gems.

the first founded upon paper), and was already deep in the concoction
of her story, being unable to decide whether the duel should come before the elopement or after the murder.

She said nothing of her plan at home, but fell to work next day,
much to the disquiet of her mother, who always looked a little anxious
when "genius took to burning." Jo had never tried this style before,
contenting herself with very mild romances for the "Spread Eagle."
Her theatrical experience and miscellaneous reading were of service
now, for they gave her some idea of dramatic effect, and supplied plot,
language, and costumes. Her story was as full of desperation and despair as her limited acquaintance with those uncomfortable emotions
enabled her to make it, and, having located it in Lisbon, she wound up
with an earthquake, as a striking and appropriate *denouement*.[5] The
manuscript was privately despatched, accompanied by a note, modestly saying that if the tale didn't get the prize, which the writer hardly
dared expect, she would be very glad to receive any sum it might be
considered worth.

Six weeks is a long time to wait, and a still longer time for a girl to
keep a secret; but Jo did both, and was just beginning to give up all
hope of ever seeing her manuscript again, when a letter arrived which
almost took her breath away; for, on opening it, a check for a hundred
dollars fell into her lap. For a minute she stared at it as if it had been
a snake, then she read her letter, and began to cry. If the amiable gentleman who wrote that kindly note could have known what intense happiness he was giving a fellow creature, I think he would devote his
leisure hours, if he has any, to that amusement; for Jo valued the letter more than the money, because it was encouraging; and after years
of effort it was *so* pleasant to find that she had learned to do *something*, though it was only to write a sensation story.

A prouder young woman was seldom seen than she, when, having
composed herself, she electrified the family by appearing before them
with the letter in one hand, the check in the other, announcing that
she had won the prize! Of course there was a great jubilee, and when
the story came every one read and praised it; though after her father
had told her that the language was good, the romance fresh and
hearty, and the tragedy quite thrilling, he shook his head, and said in
his unworldly way,—

"You can do better than this, Jo. Aim at the highest, and never mind
the money."

"I think the money is the best part of it. What *will* you do with such
a fortune?" asked Amy, regarding the magic slip of paper with a rever-
ential eye.

"Send Beth and mother to the sea-side for a month or two," answered Jo promptly.

"Oh, how splendid! No, I can't do it, dear, it would be so selfish,"

---

5. On 1 November 1755, Lisbon, the capital of Portugal, was struck by a violent earthquake.
An ensuing tidal wave and fire destroyed most of the city; within the city limits alone, over
sixty thousand people died. At the time, many commentators considered the destruction a
symbol of God's displeasure with the sinners of Lisbon.

cried Beth, who had clapped her thin hands, and taken a long breath, as if pining for fresh ocean breezes; then stopped herself, and motioned away the check which her sister waved before her.

"Ah, but you shall go, I've set my heart on it; that's what I tried for, and that's why I succeeded. I never get on when I think of myself alone, so it will help me to work for you, don't you see. Besides, Marmee needs the change, and she won't leave you, so you *must* go. Won't it be fun to see you come home plump and rosy again? Hurrah for Dr. Jo, who always cures her patients!"

To the sea-side they went, after much discussion; and though Beth didn't come home as plump and rosy as could be desired, she was much better, while Mrs. March declared she felt ten years younger; so Jo was satisfied with the investment of her prize-money, and fell to work with a cheery spirit, bent on earning more of those delightful checks. She did earn several that year, and began to feel herself a power in the house; for by the magic of a pen, her "rubbish" turned into comforts for them all. "The Duke's Daughter" paid the butcher's bill, "A Phantom Hand" put down a new carpet, and "The Curse of the Coventrys" proved the blessing of the Marches in the way of groceries and gowns.

Wealth is certainly a most desirable thing, but poverty has its sunny side, and one of the sweet uses of adversity, is the genuine satisfaction which comes from hearty work of head or hand; and to the inspiration of necessity, we owe half the wise, beautiful, and useful blessings of the world. Jo enjoyed a taste of this satisfaction, and ceased to envy richer girls, taking great comfort in the knowledge that she could supply her own wants, and need ask no one for a penny.

Little notice was taken of her stories, but they found a market; and, encouraged by this fact, she resolved to make a bold stroke for fame and fortune. Having copied her novel for the fourth time, read it to all her confidential friends, and submitted it with fear and trembling to three publishers, she at last disposed of it, on condition that she would cut it down one-third, and omit all the parts which she particularly admired.

"Now I must either bundle it back into my tin-kitchen, to mould, pay for printing it myself, or chop it up to suit purchasers, and get what I can for it. Fame is a very good thing to have in the house, but cash is more convenient; so I wish to take the sense of the meeting on this important subject," said Jo, calling a family council.

"Don't spoil your book, my girl, for there is more in it than you know, and the idea is well worked out. Let it wait and ripen," was her father's advice; and he practised as he preached, having waited patiently thirty years for fruit of his own to ripen, and being in no haste to gather it, even now, when it was sweet and mellow.

"It seems to me that Jo will profit more by making the trial than by waiting," said Mrs. March. "Criticism is the best test of such work, for it will show her both unsuspected merits and faults, and help her to do better next time. We are too partial; but the praise and blame of outsiders will prove useful, even if she gets but little money."

"Yes," said Jo, knitting her brows, "that's just it; I've been fussing over the thing so long, I really don't know whether it's good, bad, or indifferent. It will be a great help to have cool, impartial persons take a look at it, and tell me what they think of it."

"I wouldn't leave out a word of it; you'll spoil it if you do, for the interest of the story is more in the minds than in the actions of the people, and it will be all a muddle if you don't explain as you go on," said Meg, who firmly believed that this book was the most remarkable novel ever written.

"But Mr. Allen says, 'Leave out the explanations, make it brief and dramatic, and let the characters tell the story,' " interrupted Jo, turning to the publisher's note.

"Do as he tells you; he knows what will sell, and we don't. Make a good, popular book, and get as much money as you can. By and by, when you've got a name, you can afford to digress, and have philosophical and metaphysical people in your novels," said Amy, who took a strictly practical view of the subject.

"Well," said Jo, laughing, "if my people *are* 'philosophical and metaphysical,' it isn't my fault, for I know nothing about such things, except what I hear father say, sometimes. If I've got some of his wise ideas jumbled up with my romance, so much the better for me. Now, Beth, what do you say?"

"I should so like to see it printed *soon*," was all Beth said, and smiled in saying it; but there was an unconscious emphasis on the last word, and a wistful look in the eyes that never lost their child-like candor, which chilled Jo's heart, for a minute, with a foreboding fear, and decided her to make her little venture "soon."

So, with Spartan firmness, the young authoress laid her first-born on her table, and chopped it up as ruthlessly as any ogre. In the hope of pleasing every one, she took every one's advice; and, like the old man and his donkey in the fable, suited nobody.[6]

Her father liked the metaphysical streak which had unconsciously got into it, so that was allowed to remain, though she had her doubts about it. Her mother thought that there *was* a trifle too much description; out, therefore, it nearly all came, and with it many necessary links in the story. Meg admired the tragedy; so Jo piled up the agony to suit her, while Amy objected to the fun, and, with the best intentions in life, Jo quenched the sprightly scenes which relieved the sombre character of the story. Then, to complete the ruin, she cut it down one-third, and confidingly sent the poor little romance, like a picked robin, out into the big, busy world, to try its fate.

Well, it was printed, and she got three hundred dollars for it; likewise plenty of praise and blame, both so much greater than she ex-

6. A fable attributed to Aesop in which an old man, his son, and their donkey travel to town. When the son rides the donkey, passersby criticize him for letting his father walk while he travels in comfort. When the man rides, passersby criticize him for letting his son walk. When both ride, they are accused of abusing the donkey. Finally, generating even more public derision, they carry the donkey. An accident occurs and the donkey is drowned. In trying to please everyone, they ultimately please no one.

pected, that she was thrown into a state of bewilderment, from which it took her some time to recover.

"You said, mother, that criticism would help me; but how can it, when it's so contradictory that I don't know whether I have written a promising book, or broken all the ten commandments," cried poor Jo, turning over a heap of notices, the perusal of which filled her with pride and joy one minute—wrath and dire dismay the next. "This man says 'An exquisite book, full of truth, beauty, and earnestness; all is sweet, pure, and healthy,' " continued the perplexed authoress. "The next, 'The theory of the book is bad,—full of morbid fancies, spiritualistic ideas, and unnatural characters.' Now, as I had no theory of any kind, don't believe in spiritualism, and copied my characters from life, I don't see how this critic *can* be right. Another says, 'It's one of the best American novels which has appeared for years' (I know better than that); and the next asserts that 'though it is original, and written with great force and feeling, it is a dangerous book.' 'Tisn't! Some make fun of it, some over-praise, and nearly all insist that I had a deep theory to expound, when I only wrote it for the pleasure and the money. I wish I'd printed it whole, or not at all, for I do hate to be so horridly misjudged."

Her family and friends administered comfort and commendation liberally; yet it was a hard time for sensitive, high-spirited Jo, who meant so well, and had apparently done so ill. But it did her good, for those whose opinion had real value, gave her the criticism which is an author's best education; and when the first soreness was over, she could laugh at her poor little book, yet believe in it still, and feel herself the wiser and stronger for the buffeting she had received.

"Not being a genius, like Keats, it won't kill me," she said stoutly;[7] "and I've got the joke on my side, after all; for the parts that were taken straight out of real life, are denounced as impossible and absurd, and the scenes that I made up out of my own silly head, are pronounced 'charmingly natural, tender, and true.' So I'll comfort myself with that; and, when I'm ready, I'll up again and take another."

CHAPTER V.

DOMESTIC EXPERIENCES.

LIKE most other young matrons, Meg began her married life with the determination to be a model housekeeper. John should find home a paradise; he should always see a smiling face, should fare sumptuously every day, and never know the loss of a button. She brought so much love, energy, and cheerfulness to the work, that she could not but suc-

---

7. John Keats (1795–1821), one of the greatest English Romantic poets, died at twenty-five. His friend Shelley suggested in the preface to *Adonais, An Elegy on the Death of John Keats* (1821) that the critics' attacks on Keats's poem *Endymion* were responsible for the health problems that led to Keats's early death.

ceed, in spite of some obstacles. Her paradise was not a tranquil one; for the little woman fussed, was over-anxious to please, and bustled about like a true Martha,[8] cumbered with many cares. She was too tired, sometimes, even to smile; John grew dyspeptic after a course of dainty dishes, and ungratefully demanded plain fare. As for buttons, she soon learned to wonder where they went, to shake her head over the carelessness of men, and to threaten to make him sew them on himself, and then see if *his* work would stand impatient tugs and clumsy fingers any better than hers.

They were very happy, even after they discovered that they couldn't live on love alone. John did not find Meg's beauty diminished, though she beamed at him from behind the family coffee-pot; nor did Meg miss any of the romance from the daily parting, when her husband followed up his kiss with the tender inquiry, "Shall I send home veal or mutton for dinner, darling?" The little house ceased to be a glorified bower, but it became a home, and the young couple soon felt that it was a change for the better. At first they played keep-house, and frolicked over it like children; then John took steadily to business, feeling the cares of the head of a family upon his shoulders; and Meg laid by her cambric wrappers, put on a big apron, and fell to work, as before said, with more energy than discretion.

While the cooking mania lasted she went through Mrs. Cornelius's Receipt Book[9] as if it was a mathematical exercise, working out the problems with patience and care. Sometimes her family were invited in to help eat up a too bounteous feast of successes, or Lotty would be privately despatched with a batch of failures which were to be concealed from all eyes, in the convenient stomachs of the little Hummels. An evening with John over the account books usually produced a temporary lull in the culinary enthusiasm, and a frugal fit would ensue, during which the poor man was put through a course of bread pudding, hash, and warmed-over coffee, which tried his soul, although he bore it with praiseworthy fortitude. Before the golden mean was found, however, Meg added to her domestic possessions what young couples seldom get on long without—a family jar.

Fired with a housewifely wish to see her store-room stocked with home-made preserves, she undertook to put up her own currant jelly. John was requested to order home a dozen or so of little pots, and an extra quantity of sugar, for their own currants were ripe, and were to be attended to at once. As John firmly believed that "my wife" was equal to anything, and took a natural pride in her skill, he resolved that she should be gratified, and their only crop of fruit laid by in a most pleasing form for winter use. Home came four dozen delightful little pots, half a barrel of sugar, and a small boy to pick the currants for her. With her pretty hair tucked into a little cap, arms bared to the

---

8. Martha and Mary are the sisters of Lazarus, whom Jesus raised from the dead. When Jesus comes to their home, according to the Gospel of Luke (10.38–42), Mary sits at his feet to listen while Martha is preoccupied with household duties.
9. Mary Hooker Cornelius, *The Young Housekeeper's Friend; or, A Guide to Domestic Economy and Comfort* (Boston: Tappan, Whittemore, & Mason, c. 1845).

elbow, and a checked apron which had a coquettish look in spite of the bib, the young housewife fell to work, feeling no doubts about her success; for hadn't she seen Hannah do it hundreds of times? The array of pots rather amazed her at first, but John was so fond of jelly, and the nice little jars would look so well on the top shelf, that Meg resolved to fill them all, and spent a long day picking, boiling, straining, and fussing over her jelly. She did her best; she asked advice of Mrs. Cornelius; she racked her brain to remember what Hannah did that she had left undone; she reboiled, resugared, and restrained, but that dreadful stuff wouldn't "*jell*."

She longed to run home, bib and all, and ask mother to lend a hand, but John and she had agreed that they would never annoy any one with their private worries, experiments, or quarrels. They had laughed over that last word as if the idea it suggested was a most preposterous one; but they had held to their resolve, and whenever they could get on without help they did so, and no one interfered,—for Mrs. March had advised the plan. So Meg wrestled alone with the refractory sweetmeats all that hot summer day, and at five o'clock sat down in her topsy-turvy kitchen, wrung her bedaubed hands, lifted up her voice, and wept.

Now in the first flush of the new life, she had often said,—

"My husband shall always feel free to bring a friend home whenever he likes. I shall always be prepared; there shall be no flurry, no scolding, no discomfort, but a neat house, a cheerful wife, and a good dinner. John, dear, never stop to ask my leave, invite whom you please, and be sure of a welcome from me."

How charming that was, to be sure! John quite glowed with pride to hear her say it, and felt what a blessed thing it was to have a superior wife. But, although they had had company from time to time, it never happened to be unexpected, and Meg had never had an opportunity to distinguish herself, till now. It always happens so in this vale of tears; there is an inevitability about such things which we can only wonder at, deplore, and bear as we best can.

If John had not forgotten all about the jelly, it really would have been unpardonable in him to choose that day, of all the days in the year, to bring a friend home to dinner unexpectedly. Congratulating himself that a handsome repast had been ordered that morning, feeling sure that it would be ready to the minute, and indulging in pleasant anticipations of the charming effect it would produce, when his pretty wife came running out to meet him, he escorted his friend to his mansion, with the irrepressible satisfaction of a young host and husband.

It is a world of disappointments, as John discovered when he reached the Dove-cote. The front door usually stood hospitably open; now it was not only shut, but locked, and yesterday's mud still adorned the steps. The parlor windows were closed and curtained, no picture of the pretty wife sewing on the piazza, in white, with a distracting little bow in her hair, or a bright-eyed hostess, smiling a shy welcome as she greeted her guest. Nothing of the sort—for not a soul appeared, but a sanguinary-looking boy asleep under the currant bushes.

"I'm afraid something has happened; step into the garden, Scott, while I look up Mrs. Brooke," said John, alarmed at the silence and solitude.

Round the house he hurried, led by a pungent smell of burnt sugar, and Mr. Scott strolled after him, with a queer look on his face. He paused discreetly at a distance when Brooke disappeared; but he could both see and hear, and, being a bachelor, enjoyed the prospect mightily.

In the kitchen reigned confusion and despair; one edition of jelly was trickled from pot to pot, another lay upon the floor, and a third was burning gaily on the stove. Lotty, with Teutonic phlegm, was calmly eating bread and currant wine, for the jelly was still in a hopelessly liquid state, while Mrs. Brooke, with her apron over her head, sat sobbing dismally.

"My dearest girl, what is the matter?" cried John, rushing in with awful visions of scalded hands, sudden news of affliction, and secret consternation at the thought of the guest in the garden.

"Oh, John, I *am* so tired, and hot, and cross, and worried! I've been at it till I'm all worn out. Do come and help me, or I *shall* die;" and the exhausted housewife cast herself upon his breast, giving him a sweet welcome in every sense of the word, for her pinafore had been baptized at the same time as the floor.

"What worries you, dear? Has anything dreadful happened?" asked the anxious John, tenderly kissing the crown of the little cap, which was all askew.

"Yes," sobbed Meg, despairingly.

"Tell me quick, then; don't cry, I can bear anything better than that. Out with it, love."

"The—the jelly won't jell—and I don't know what to do!"

John Brooke laughed then as he never dared to laugh afterward; and the derisive Scott smiled involuntarily as he heard the hearty peal, which put the finishing stroke to poor Meg's woe.

"Is that all? Fling it out of window, and don't bother any more about it. I'll buy you quarts if you want it; but for heaven's sake don't have hysterics, for I've brought Jack Scott home to dinner, and—"

John got no further, for Meg cast him off, and clasped her hands with a tragic gesture as she fell into a chair, exclaiming in a tone of mingled indignation, reproach, and dismay,—

"A man to dinner, and everything in a mess! John Brooke, how *could* you do such a thing?"

"Hush, he's in the garden; I forgot the confounded jelly, but it can't be helped now," said John, surveying the prospect with an anxious eye.

"You ought to have sent word, or told me this morning, and you ought to have remembered how busy I was," continued Meg, petulantly; for even turtle-doves will peck when ruffled.

"I didn't know it this morning, and there was no time to send word, for I met him on the way out. I never thought of asking leave, when you have always told me to do as I liked. I never tried it before, and hang me if I ever do again!" added John, with an aggrieved air.

"I should hope not! Take him away at once; I can't see him, and there isn't any dinner."

"Well, I like that! Where's the beef and vegetables I sent home, and the pudding you promised?" cried John, rushing to the larder.

"I hadn't time to cook anything; I meant to dine at mother's. I'm sorry, but I was *so* busy,"—and Meg's tears began again.

John was a mild man, but he was human; and after a long day's work, to come home tired, hungry and hopeful, to find a chaotic house, an empty table, and a cross wife, was not exactly conducive to repose of mind or manner. He restrained himself, however, and the little squall would have blown over but for one unlucky word.

"It's a scrape, I acknowledge; but if you will lend a hand, we'll pull through, and have a good time yet. Don't cry, dear, but just exert yourself a bit, and knock us up something to eat. We're both as hungry as hunters, so we shan't mind what it is. Give us the cold meat, and bread and cheese; we won't ask for jelly."

He meant it for a good-natured joke; but that one word sealed his fate. Meg thought it was *too* cruel to hint about her sad failure, and the last atom of patience vanished as he spoke.

"You must get yourself out of the scrape as you can; I'm too used up to 'exert' myself for any one. It's like a man, to propose a bone and vulgar bread and cheese for company. I won't have anything of the sort in my house. Take that Scott up to mother's, and tell him I'm away—sick, dead, anything. I won't see him, and you two can laugh at me and my jelly as much as you like; you won't have anything else here;" and having delivered her defiance all in one breath, Meg cast away her pinafore, and precipitately left the field to bemoan herself in her own room.

What those two creatures did in her absence, she never knew; but Mr. Scott was not taken "up to mother's," and when Meg descended, after they had strolled away together, she found traces of a promiscuous lunch which filled her with horror. Lotty reported that they had eaten "a much, and greatly laughed; and the master bid her throw away all the sweet stuff, and hide the pots."

Meg longed to go and tell mother; but a sense of shame at her own short-comings, of loyalty to John, "who might be cruel, but nobody should know it," restrained her; and after a summary clearing up, she dressed herself prettily, and sat down to wait for John to come and be forgiven.

Unfortunately, John didn't come, not seeing the matter in that light. He had carried it off as a good joke with Scott, excused his little wife as well as he could, and played the host so hospitably, that his friend enjoyed the impromptu dinner, and promised to come again. But John was angry, though he did not show it; he felt that Meg had got him into a scrape, and then deserted him in his hour of need. "It wasn't fair to tell a man to bring folks home any time, with perfect freedom, and when he took you at your word, to flare up and blame him, and leave him in the lurch, to be laughed at or pitied. No, by George, it wasn't! and Meg must know it." He had fumed inwardly during the feast, but when the flurry was over, and he strolled home, after seeing Scott off, a milder mood came over him. "Poor little thing! it was hard upon her when she tried so heartily to please me. She was wrong, of course, but then she was young. I must be patient, and teach her." He hoped she had not gone home—he hated gossip and interference. For a minute he was ruffled again at the mere thought of it; and then the fear that Meg would cry herself sick, softened his heart, and sent him on at a quicker pace, resolving to be calm and kind, but firm, quite firm, and show her where she had failed in her duty to her spouse.

Meg likewise resolved to be "calm and kind, but firm," and show *him* his duty. She longed to run to meet him, and beg pardon, and be kissed and comforted, as she was sure of being; but, of course, she did nothing of the sort; and when she saw John coming, began to hum quite naturally, as she rocked and sewed like a lady of leisure in her best parlor.

John was a little disappointed not to find a tender Niobe;[1] but, feeling that his dignity demanded the first apology, he made none: only came leisurely in, and laid himself upon the sofa, with the singularly relevant remark,—

"We are going to have a new moon, my dear."

"I've no objection," was Meg's equally soothing remark.

A few other topics of general interest were introduced by Mr. Brooke, and wet-blanketed by Mrs. Brooke, and conversation languished. John went to one window, unfolded his paper, and wrapt himself in it, figuratively speaking. Meg went to the other window, and sewed as if new rosettes for her slippers were among the necessaries of life. Neither spoke—both looked quite "calm and firm," and both felt desperately uncomfortable.

"Oh, dear," thought Meg, "married life is very trying, and does need infinite patience, as well as love, as mother says." The word "mother" suggested other maternal counsels given long ago, and received with unbelieving protests.

"John is a good man, but he has his faults, and you must learn to see and bear with them, remembering your own. He is very decided, but never will be obstinate, if you reason kindly, not oppose impatiently. He is very accurate, and particular about the truth—a good trait, though you call him 'fussy.' Never deceive him by look or word, Meg, and he will give you the confidence you deserve, the support you need. He has a temper, not like ours,—one flash, and then all over— but the white, still anger that is seldom stirred, but once kindled, is hard to quench. Be careful, very careful, not to wake this anger against yourself, for peace and happiness depend on keeping his respect. Watch yourself, be the first to ask pardon if you both err, and guard against the little piques, misunderstandings, and hasty words that often pave the way for bitter sorrow and regret."

These words came back to Meg, as she sat sewing in the sunset,—

---

1. In Greek mythology, Niobe, the queen of Thebes, boasts of her fruitfulness (having borne, in some versions, six sons and six daughters). Apollo and Artemis punish Niobe by slaying her children, and Zeus turns her into a stone image that weeps perpetually.

especially the last. This was the first serious disagreement; her own hasty speeches sounded both silly and unkind, as she recalled them, her own anger looked childish now, and thoughts of poor John coming home to such a scene quite melted her heart. She glanced at him with tears in her eyes, but he did not see them; she put down her work and got up, thinking, "I *will* be the first to say, 'forgive me,'" but he did not seem to hear her; she went very slowly across the room, for pride was hard to swallow, and stood by him, but he did not turn his head. For a minute, she felt as if she really couldn't do it; then came the thought, "This is the beginning, I'll do my part, and have nothing to reproach myself with," and stooping down she softly kissed her husband on the forehead. Of course that settled it; the penitent kiss was better than a world of words, and John had her on his knee in a minute, saying tenderly,—

"It was too bad to laugh at the poor little jelly-pots; forgive me, dear, I never will again!"

But he did, oh, bless you, yes, hundreds of times, and so did Meg, both declaring that it was the sweetest jelly they ever made; for family peace was preserved in that little family jar.

After this, Meg had Mr. Scott to dinner by special invitation, and served him up a pleasant feast without a cooked wife for the first course; on which occasion she was so gay and gracious, and made everything go off so charmingly, that Mr. Scott told John he was a happy fellow, and shook his head over the hardships of bachelor-hood all the way home.

In the autumn, new trials and experiences came to Meg. Sallie Moffat renewed her friendship, was always running out for a dish of gossip at the little house, or inviting "that poor dear" to come in and spend the day at the big house. It was pleasant, for in dull weather Meg often felt lonely;—all were busy at home, John absent till night, and nothing to do but sew, or read, or potter about. So it naturally fell out that Meg got into the way of gadding and gossiping with her friend. Seeing Sallie's pretty things made her long for such, and pity herself because she had not got them. Sallie was very kind, and often offered her the coveted trifles; but Meg declined them, knowing that John wouldn't like it; and then this foolish little woman went and did what John disliked infinitely worse.

She knew her husband's income, and she loved to feel that he trusted her, not only with his happiness, but what some men seem to value more, his money. She knew where it was, was free to take what she liked, and all he asked was that she should keep account of every penny, pay bills once a month, and remember that she was a poor man's wife. Till now she had done well, been prudent and exact, kept her little account-books neatly, and showed them to him monthly, without fear. But that autumn the serpent got into Meg's paradise, and tempted her, like many a modern Eve, not with apples, but with dress. Meg didn't like to be pitied and made to feel poor; it irritated her; but she was ashamed to confess it, and now and then she tried to console herself by buying something pretty, so that Sallie needn't think she had to scrimp. She always felt wicked after it, for the pretty things were seldom necessaries; but then they cost so little, it wasn't worth worrying about; so the trifles increased unconsciously, and in the shopping excursions she was no longer a passive looker-on.

But the trifles cost more than one would imagine; and when she cast up her accounts at the end of the month, the sum total rather scared her. John was busy that month, and left the bills to her; the next month he was absent; but the third he had a grand quarterly settling up, and Meg never forgot it. A few days before she had done a dreadful thing, and it weighed upon her conscience. Sallie had been buying silks, and Meg ached for a new one—just a handsome light one for parties—her black silk was so common, and thin things for evening wear were only proper for girls. Aunt March usually gave the sisters a present of twenty-five dollars apiece, at New-Year; that was only a month to wait, and here was a lovely violet silk going at a bargain, and she had the money, if she only dared to take it. John always said what was his was hers; but would he think it right to spend not only the prospective five-and-twenty, but another five-and-twenty out of the household fund? That was the question. Sallie had urged her to do it, had offered to loan the money, and with the best intentions in life, had tempted Meg beyond her strength. In an evil moment the shopman held up the lovely, shimmering folds, and said, "A bargain, I assure you, ma'am." She answered, "I'll take it"; and it was cut off and paid for, and Sallie had exulted, and she had laughed as if it was a thing of no consequence, and driven away feeling as if she had stolen something, and the police were after her.

When she got home, she tried to assuage the pangs of remorse by spreading forth the lovely silk; but it looked less silvery now, didn't become her, after all, and the words "fifty dollars" seemed stamped like a pattern down each breadth. She put it away; but it haunted her, not delightfully, as a new dress should, but dreadfully, like the ghost of a folly that was not easily laid. When John got out his books that night, Meg's heart sank; and, for the first time in her married life, she was afraid of her husband. The kind, brown eyes looked as if they could be stern; and though he was unusually merry, she fancied he had found her out, but didn't mean to let her know it. The house bills were all paid, the books all in order. John had praised her, and was undoing the old pocket-book which they called the "bank," when Meg, knowing that it was quite empty, stopped his hand, saying nervously,—

"You haven't seen my private expense book, yet."

John never asked to see it; but she always insisted on his doing so, and used to enjoy his masculine amazement at the queer things women wanted, and make him guess what "piping" was, demand fiercely the meaning of a "hug-me-tight," or wonder how a little thing composed of three rosebuds, a bit of velvet and a pair of strings, could possibly be a bonnet, and cost five or six dollars. That night he looked as if he would like the fun of quizzing her figures, and pretending to be horrified at her extravagance, as he often did, being particularly proud of his prudent wife.

The little book was brought slowly out, and laid down before him. Meg got behind his chair, under pretence of smoothing the wrinkles out of his tired forehead, and standing there, she said, with her panic increasing with every word,—

"John, dear, I'm ashamed to show you my book, for I've really been dreadfully extravagant lately. I go about so much I must have things, you know, and Sallie advised my getting it, so I did; and my New-Year's money will partly pay for it; but I was sorry after I'd done it, for I knew you'd think it wrong in me."

John laughed, and drew her round beside him, saying good-humoredly, "Don't go and hide, I won't beat you if you *have* got a pair of killing boots; I'm rather proud of my wife's feet, and don't mind if she does pay eight or nine dollars for her boots, if they are good ones."

That had been one of her last "trifles," and John's eye had fallen on it as he spoke. "Oh, what *will* he say when he comes to that awful fifty dollars!" thought Meg, with a shiver.

"It's worse than boots, it's a silk dress," she said, with the calmness of desperation, for she wanted the worst over.

"Well, dear, what is 'the dem'd total?' as Mr. Mantalini says."[2]

That didn't sound like John, and she knew he was looking up at her with the straightforward look that she had always been ready to meet and answer with one as frank, till now. She turned the page and her head at the same time, pointing to the sum which would have been bad enough without the fifty, but which was appalling to her with that added. For a minute the room was very still; then John said, slowly— but she could feel it cost him an effort to express no displeasure,—

"Well, I don't know that fifty is much for a dress, with all the furbe-lows and quinny-dingles you have to have to finish it off these days."[3]

"It isn't made or trimmed," sighed Meg faintly, for a sudden recol-lection of the cost still to be incurred quite overwhelmed her.

"Twenty yards of silk seems a good deal to cover one small woman, but I've no doubt my wife will look as fine as Ned Moffat's when she gets it on," said John dryly.

"I know you are angry, John, but I can't help it; I don't mean to waste your money, and I didn't think those little things would count up so. I can't resist them when I see Sallie buying all she wants, and pity-ing me because I don't; I try to be contented, but it is hard, and I'm tired of being poor."

The last words were spoken so low she thought he did not hear them, but he did, and they wounded him deeply, for he had denied himself many pleasures for Meg's sake. She could have bitten her tongue out the minute she had said it, for John pushed the books away and got up, saying, with a little quiver in his voice, "I was afraid of this; I do my best, Meg." If he had scolded her, or even shaken her, it

2. In Dickens's *Nicholas Nickleby* (1838–39), Mr. Mantalini is a character who injects "damned," in some form, into almost every sentence he utters. An extravagant man, he ruins his wife's business and embezzles from her, finally ending up in debtor's prison.
3. A furbelow is a woman's flounce or ruffle or superfluous decoration. The expression "quinny-dingle" might be equivalent to "thingamajig" or "whatsit."

would not have broken her heart like those few words. She ran to him and held him close, crying, with repentant tears, "Oh, John! my dear, kind, hard-working boy, I didn't mean it! It was so wicked, so untrue and ungrateful, how could I say it! Oh, how could I say it!"

He was very kind, forgave her readily, and did not utter one reproach; but Meg knew that she had done and said a thing which would not be forgotten soon, although he might never allude to it again. She had promised to love him for better for worse; and then she, his wife, had reproached him with his poverty, after spending his earnings recklessly. It was dreadful; and the worst of it was John went on so quietly afterward, just as if nothing had happened, except that he stayed in town later, and worked at night when she had gone to cry herself to sleep. A week of remorse nearly made Meg sick; and the discovery that John had countermanded the order for his new great-coat, reduced her to a state of despair which was pathetic to behold. He had simply said, in answer to her surprised inquiries as to the change, "I can't afford it, my dear."

Meg said no more, but a few minutes after he found her in the hall with her face buried in the old great-coat, crying as if her heart would break.

They had a long talk that night, and Meg learned to love her husband better for his poverty, because it seemed to have made a man of him—giving him the strength and courage to fight his own way—and taught him a tender patience with which to bear and comfort the natural longings and failures of those he loved.

Next day she put her pride in her pocket, went to Sallie, told the truth, and asked her to buy the silk as a favor. The good-natured Mrs. Moffat willingly did so, and had the delicacy not to make her a present of it immediately afterward. Then Meg ordered home the great-coat, and, when John arrived, she put it on, and asked him how he liked her new silk gown. One can imagine what answer he made, how he received his present, and what a blissful state of things ensued. John came home early, Meg gadded no more; and that great-coat was put on in the morning by a very happy husband, and taken off at night by a most devoted little wife. So the year rolled round, and at midsummer there came to Meg a new experience,—the deepest and tenderest of a woman's life.

Laurie came creeping into the kitchen of the Dove-cote one Saturday, with an excited face, and was received with the clash of cymbals; for Hannah clapped her hands with a saucepan in one, and the cover in the other.

"How's the little Ma? Where is everybody? Why didn't you tell me before I came home?" began Laurie, in a loud whisper.

"Happy as a queen, the dear! Every soul of 'em is upstairs a worshipin'; we didn't want no hurrycanes round. Now you go into the parlor, and I'll send 'em down to you," with which somewhat involved reply Hannah vanished, chuckling ecstatically.

Presently Jo appeared, proudly bearing a small flannel bundle laid forth upon a large pillow. Jo's face was very sober, but her eyes twinkled, and there was an odd sound in her voice of repressed emotion of some sort.

"Shut your eyes and hold out your arms," she said invitingly.

Laurie backed precipitately into a corner, and put his hands behind him with an imploring gesture,—"No, thank you; I'd rather not. I shall drop it, or smash it, as sure as fate."

"Then you shan't see your nevvy," said Jo, decidedly, turning as if to go.

"I will, I will! only you must be responsible for damages;" and, obeying orders, Laurie heroically shut his eyes while something was put into his arms. A peal of laughter from Jo, Amy, Mrs. March, Hannah and John, caused him to open them the next minute, to find himself invested with two babies instead of one.

No wonder they laughed, for the expression of his face was droll enough to convulse a Quaker, as he stood and stared wildly from the unconscious innocents to the hilarious spectators, with such dismay that Jo sat down on the floor and screamed.

"Twins, by Jupiter!" was all he said for a minute; then turning to the women with an appealing look that was comically piteous, he added, "Take 'em quick, somebody! I'm going to laugh, and I shall drop 'em."

John rescued his babies, and marched up and down, with one on each arm, as if already initiated into the mysteries of baby-tending, while Laurie laughed till the tears ran down his cheeks.

"It's the best joke of the season, isn't it? I wouldn't have you told, for I set my heart on surprising you, and I flatter myself I've done it," said Jo, when she got her breath.

"I never was more staggered in my life. Isn't it fun? Are they boys? What are you going to name them? Let's have another look. Hold me up, Jo; for upon my life it's one too many for me," returned Laurie, regarding the infants with the air of a big, benevolent Newfoundland looking at a pair of infantile kittens.

"Boy and girl. Aren't they beauties?" said the proud papa, beaming upon the little, red squirmers as if they were unfledged angels.

"Most remarkable children I ever saw. Which is which?" and Laurie bent like a well-sweep to examine the prodigies.

"Amy put a blue ribbon on the boy and a pink on the girl, French fashion, so you can always tell. Besides, one has blue eyes and one brown. Kiss them, Uncle Teddy," said wicked Jo.

"I'm afraid they mightn't like it," began Laurie, with unusual timidity in such matters.

"Of course they will; they are used to it now; do it this minute, sir," commanded Jo, fearing he might propose a proxy.

Laurie screwed up his face, and obeyed with a gingerly peck at each little cheek that produced another laugh, and made the babies squeal.

"There, I knew they didn't like it! That's the boy; see him kick! he hits out with his fists like a good one. Now then, young Brooke, pitch into a man of your own size, will you?" cried Laurie, delighted with a poke in the face from a tiny fist, flapping aimlessly about.

"He's to be named John Laurence, and the girl Margaret, after mother and grandmother. We shall call her Daisy, so as not to have two Megs, and I suppose the mannie will be Jack, unless we find a better name," said Amy, with aunt-like interest.

"Name him Demijohn, and call him 'Demi' for short," said Laurie.

"Daisy and Demi,—just the thing! I *knew* Teddy would do it," cried Jo, clapping her hands.

Teddy certainly had done it that time, for the babies were "Daisy" and "Demi" to the end of the chapter.

CHAPTER VI.

CALLS.

COME, Jo, it's time."

"For what?"

"You don't mean to say you have forgotten that you promised to make half a dozen calls with me to-day?"

"I've done a good many rash and foolish things in my life, but I don't think I ever was mad enough to say I'd make six calls in one day, when a single one upsets me for a week."

"Yes you did; it was a bargain between us. I was to finish the crayon of Beth for you, and you were to go properly with me, and return our neighbors' visits."

"If it was fair—that was in the bond; and I stand to the letter of my bond, Shylock.[4] There is a pile of clouds in the east; it's *not* fair, and I don't go."

"Now that's shirking. It's a lovely day, no prospect of rain, and you pride yourself on keeping promises; so be honorable; come and do your duty, and then be at peace for another six months."

At that minute Jo was particularly absorbed in dressmaking; for she was mantua-maker general to the family, and took especial credit to herself because she could use a needle as well as a pen. It was very provoking to be arrested in the act of a first trying-on, and ordered out to make calls in her best array, on a warm July day. She hated calls of the formal sort, and never made any till Amy cornered her with a bargain, bribe, or promise. In the present instance, there was no escape; and having clashed her scissors rebelliously, while protesting that she smelt thunder, she gave in, put away her work, and taking up her hat and gloves with an air of resignation, told Amy the victim was ready.

"Jo March, you are perverse enough to provoke a saint! You don't intend to make calls in that state, I hope," cried Amy, surveying her with amazement.

"Why not? I'm neat, and cool, and comfortable; quite proper for a

---

4. Shylock, a Jewish merchant in Shakespeare's *Merchant of Venice* (c. 1596), is noted for his adherence to the letter rather than the spirit of the law. Antonio has borrowed money from Shylock; when his ships are lost, Shylock demands that Antonio repay him with a pound of flesh. Shylock cries, "I'll have my bond. Speak not against my bond. I have sworn an oath that I will have my bond" (3.3.4–5).

dusty walk on a warm day. If people care more for my clothes than they do for me, I don't wish to see them. You can dress for both, and be as elegant as you please; it pays for you to be fine; it doesn't for me, and furbelows only worry me."

"Oh dear!" sighed Amy; "now she's in a contrary fit, and will drive me distracted before I can get her properly ready. I'm sure it's no pleasure to me to go to-day, but it's a debt we owe society, and there's no one to pay it but you and me. I'll do anything for you, Jo, if you'll only dress yourself nicely, and come and help me do the civil. You can talk so well, look so aristocratic in your best things, and behave so beautifully, if you try, that I'm proud of you. I'm afraid to go alone; do come and take care of me."

"You're an artful little puss to flatter and wheedle your cross old sister in that way. The idea of my being aristocratic and well-bred, and your being afraid to go anywhere alone! I don't know which is the most absurd. Well, I'll go if I must, and do my best; you shall be commander of the expedition, and I'll obey blindly; will that satisfy you?" said Jo, with a sudden change from perversity to lamb-like submission.

"You're a perfect cherub! Now put on all your best things, and I'll tell you how to behave at each place, so that you will make a good impression. I want people to like you, and they would if you'd only try to be a little more agreeable. Do your hair the pretty way, and put the pink rose in your bonnet; it's becoming, and you look too sober in your plain suit. Take your light kids and the embroidered handkerchief. We'll stop at Meg's, and borrow her white sun-shade, and then you can have my dove-colored one."

While Amy dressed, she issued her orders, and Jo obeyed them; not without entering her protest, however, for she sighed as she rustled into her new organdie, frowned darkly at herself as she tied her bonnet strings in an irreproachable bow, wrestled viciously with pins as she put on her collar, wrinkled up her features generally as she shook out the handkerchief, whose embroidery was as irritating to her nose as the present mission was to her feelings; and when she had squeezed her hands into tight gloves with two buttons and a tassel, as the last touch of elegance, she turned to Amy with an imbecile expression of countenance, saying meekly,—

"I'm perfectly miserable; but if you consider me presentable, I die happy."

"You are highly satisfactory; turn slowly round, and let me get a careful view." Jo revolved, and Amy gave a touch here and there, then fell back with her head on one side, observing graciously, "Yes, you'll do, your head is all I could ask, for that white bonnet *with* the rose is quite ravishing. Hold back your shoulders, and carry your hands easily, no matter if your gloves do pinch. There's one thing you can do well, Jo, that is, wear a shawl—I can't; but it's very nice to see you, and I'm so glad Aunt March gave you that lovely one; it's simple, but handsome, and those folds over the arm are really artistic. Is the point of my mantle in the middle, and have I looped my dress evenly? I like to show my boots, for my feet *are* pretty, though my nose isn't."

"You are a thing of beauty, and a joy forever,"[5] said Jo, looking through her hand with the air of a connoisseur at the blue feather against the gold hair. "Am I to drag my best dress through the dust, or loop it up, please ma'am?"

"Hold it up when you walk, but drop it in the house; the sweeping style suits you best, and you must learn to trail your skirts gracefully. You haven't half buttoned one cuff; do it at once. You'll never look finished if you are not careful about the little details, for they make up the pleasing whole."

Jo sighed, and proceeded to burst the buttons off her glove, in doing up her cuff; but at last both were ready, and sailed away, looking as "pretty as picters," Hannah said, as she hung out of the upper window to watch them.

"Now, Jo dear, the Chesters are very elegant people, so I want you to put on your best deportment. Don't make any of your abrupt remarks, or do anything odd, will you? Just be calm, cool and quiet,—that's safe and lady-like; and you can easily do it for fifteen minutes," said Amy, as they approached the first place, having borrowed the white parasol and been inspected by Meg, with a baby on each arm.

"Let me see; 'Calm, cool and quiet'! yes, I think I can promise that. I've played the part of a prim young lady on the stage, and I'll try it off. My powers are great, as you shall see; so be easy in your mind, my child."

Amy looked relieved, but naughty Jo took her at her word; for, during the first call, she sat with every limb gracefully composed, every fold correctly draped, calm as a summer sea, cool as a snow-bank, and as silent as a sphinx. In vain Mrs. Chester alluded to her "charming novel," and the Misses Chester introduced parties, picnics, the Opera and the fashions; each and all were answered by a smile, a bow, and a demure "Yes" or "No," with the chill on. In vain Amy telegraphed the word "Talk," tried to draw her out, and administered covert pokes with her foot; Jo sat as if blandly unconscious of it all, with deportment like "Maud's" face, "Icily regular, splendidly null."[6]

"What a haughty, uninteresting creature that oldest Miss March is!" was the unfortunately audible remark of one of the ladies, as the door closed upon their guests. Jo laughed noiselessly all through the hall, but Amy looked disgusted at the failure of her instructions, and very naturally laid the blame upon Jo.

"How could you mistake me so? I merely meant you to be properly dignified and composed, and you made yourself a perfect stock and stone. Try to be sociable at the Lambs; gossip as other girls do, and be interested in dress, and flirtations, and whatever nonsense comes up. They move in the best society, are valuable persons for us to know, and I wouldn't fail to make a good impression there for anything."

5. Cf. Keats's *Endymion* (1818), line 1.
6. See Alfred Lord Tennyson, "Maud," (1855), lines 78–83: "she has neither savour nor salt, / But a cold and clear-cut face, as I found when her carriage past, / Perfectly beautiful: let it be granted her: where is the fault? / All that I saw (for her eyes were downcast, not to be seen) / Faultily faultless, icily regular, splendidly null, / Dead perfection, no more . . ."

"I'll be agreeable; I'll gossip and giggle, and have horrors and raptures over any trifle you like. I rather enjoy this, and now I'll imitate what is called 'a charming girl'; I can do it, for I have May Chester as a model, and I'll improve upon her. See if the Lambs don't say, 'What a lively, nice creature that Jo March is!'"

Amy felt anxious, as well she might, for when Jo turned freakish there was no knowing where she would stop. Amy's face was a study when she saw her sister skim into the next drawing-room, kiss all the young ladies with effusion, beam graciously upon the young gentlemen, and join in the chat with a spirit which amazed the beholder. Amy was taken possession of by Mrs. Lamb, with whom she was a favorite, and forced to hear a long account of Lucretia's last attack, while three delightful young gentlemen hovered near, waiting for a pause when they might rush in and rescue her. So situated she was powerless to check Jo, who seemed possessed by a spirit of mischief, and talked away as volubly as the old lady. A knot of heads gathered about her, and Amy strained her ears to hear what was going on; for broken sentences filled her with alarm, round eyes and uplifted hands tormented her with curiosity, and frequent peals of laughter made her wild to share the fun. One may imagine her suffering on overhearing fragments of this sort of conversation:—

"She rides splendidly,—who taught her?"

"No one; she used to practise mounting, holding the reins, and sitting straight on an old saddle in a tree. Now she rides anything, for she don't know what fear is, and the stable-man lets her have horses cheap, because she trains them to carry ladies so well. She has such a passion for it, I often tell her if everything else fails she can be a pretty horse-breaker, and get her living so."

At this awful speech Amy contained herself with difficulty, for the impression was being given that she was rather a fast young lady, which was her especial aversion. But what could she do? for the old lady was in the middle of her story, and long before it was done Jo was off again, making more droll revelations, and committing still more fearful blunders.

"Yes, Amy was in despair that day, for all the good beasts were gone, and of three left, one was lame, one blind, and the other so balky that you had to put dirt in his mouth before he would start. Nice animal for a pleasure party, wasn't it?"

"Which did she choose?" asked one of the laughing gentlemen, who enjoyed the subject.

"None of them; she heard of a young horse at the farm-house over the river, and, though a lady had never ridden him, she resolved to try, because he was handsome and spirited. Her struggles were really pathetic; there was no one to bring the horse to the saddle, so she took the saddle to the horse. My dear creature, she actually rowed it over the river, put it on her head, and marched up to the barn, to the utter amazement of the old man!"

"Did she ride the horse?"

"Of course she did, and had a capital time. I expected to see her brought home in fragments, but she managed him perfectly, and was the life of the party."

"Well, I call that plucky!" and young Mr. Lamb turned an approving glance upon Amy, wondering what his mother could be saying to make the girl look so red and uncomfortable.

She was still redder and more uncomfortable a moment after, when a sudden turn in the conversation introduced the subject of dress. One of the young ladies asked Jo where she got the pretty drab hat she wore to the picnic; and stupid Jo, instead of mentioning the place where it was bought two years ago, must needs answer, with unnecessary frankness, "Oh, Amy painted it; you can't buy those soft shades, so we paint ours any color we like. It's a great comfort to have an artistic sister."

"Isn't that an original idea?" cried Miss Lamb, who found Jo great fun.

"That's nothing compared to some of her brilliant performances. There's nothing the child can't do. Why, she wanted a pair of blue boots for Sallie's party, so she just painted her soiled white ones the loveliest shade of sky-blue you ever saw, and they looked exactly like satin," added Jo, with an air of pride in her sister's accomplishments that exasperated Amy till she felt that it would be a relief to throw her card-case at her.

"We read a story of yours the other day, and enjoyed it very much," observed the elder Miss Lamb, wishing to compliment the literary lady, who did not look the character just then, it must be confessed. Any mention of her "works" always had a bad effect upon Jo, who either grew rigid and looked offended, or changed the subject with a *brusque* remark, as now. "Sorry you could find nothing better to read. I write that rubbish because it sells, and ordinary people like it. Are you going to New York this winter?"

As Miss Lamb had "enjoyed" the story, this speech was not exactly grateful or complimentary. The minute it was made Jo saw her mistake; but, fearing to make the matter worse, suddenly remembered that it was for her to make the first move toward departure, and did so with an abruptness that left three people with half-finished sentences in their mouths.

"Amy, we *must* go. *Good*-by, dear; *do* come and see us; we are *pining* for a visit. I don't dare to ask *you*, Mr. Lamb; but if you *should* come, I don't think I shall have the heart to send you away."

Jo said this with such a droll imitation of May Chester's gushing style, that Amy got out of the room as rapidly as possible, feeling a strong desire to laugh and cry at the same time.

"Didn't I do that well?" asked Jo, with a satisfied air, as they walked away.

"Nothing could have been worse," was Amy's crushing reply. "What possessed you to tell those stories about my saddle, and the hats and boots, and all the rest of it?"

"Why, it's funny, and amuses people. They know we are poor, so it's no use pretending that we have grooms, buy three or four hats a season, and have things as easy and fine as they do."

"You needn't go and tell them all our little shifts, and expose our poverty in that perfectly unnecessary way. You haven't a bit of proper pride, and never will learn when to hold your tongue, and when to speak," said Amy despairingly.

Poor Jo looked abashed, and silently chafed the end of her nose with the stiff handkerchief, as if performing a penance for her misdemeanors.

"How shall I behave here?" she asked, as they approached the third mansion.

"Just as you please; I wash my hands of you," was Amy's short answer.

"Then I'll enjoy myself. The boys are at home, and we'll have a comfortable time. Goodness knows I need a little change, for elegance has a bad effect upon my constitution," returned Jo, gruffly, being disturbed by her failures to suit.

An enthusiastic welcome from three big boys and several pretty children, speedily soothed her ruffled feelings; and, leaving Amy to entertain the hostess and Mr. Tudor, who happened to be calling likewise, Jo devoted herself to the young folks, and found the change refreshing. She listened to college stories with deep interest, caressed pointers and poodles without a murmur, agreed heartily that "Tom Brown was a brick,"[7] regardless of the improper form of praise; and when one lad proposed a visit to his turtle-tank, she went with an alacrity which caused mamma to smile upon her, as that motherly lady settled the cap, which was left in a ruinous condition by filial hugs,—bear-like but affectionate,—and dearer to her than the most faultless *coiffure* from the hands of an inspired Frenchwoman.

Leaving her sister to her own devices, Amy proceeded to enjoy herself to her heart's content. Mr. Tudor's uncle had married an English lady who was third cousin to a living lord, and Amy regarded the whole family with great respect. For, in spite of her American birth and breeding, she possessed that reverence for titles which haunts the best of us,—that unacknowledged loyalty to the early faith in kings which set the most democratic nation under the sun in a ferment at the coming of a royal yellow-haired laddie, some years ago,[8] and which still has something to do with the love the young country bears the old,— like that of a big son for an imperious little mother, who held him while she could, and let him go with a farewell scolding when he rebelled. But even the satisfaction of talking with a distant connection of the British nobility did not render Amy forgetful of time; and, when the proper number of minutes had passed, she reluctantly tore herself from this aristocratic society, and looked about for Jo,—fervently hoping that her incorrigible sister would not be found in any position which should bring disgrace upon the name of March.

7. The hero of Thomas Hughes's *Tom Brown's School Days* (1857), which depicts Tom's adventures at Rugby, a boys' boarding school.
8. In the fall of 1860, nineteen-year-old Edward, the eldest son of Queen Victoria and Prince Albert, and the prince of Wales, became the first member of the British royal family to tour Canada and the United States. Alcott saw him in Boston. See *Journals*, 100.

It might have been worse; but Amy considered it bad, for Jo sat on the grass with an encampment of boys about her, and a dirty-footed dog reposing on the skirt of her state and festival dress, as she related one of Laurie's pranks to her admiring audience. One small child was poking turtles with Amy's cherished parasol, a second was eating ginger-bread over Jo's best bonnet, and a third playing ball with her gloves. But all were enjoying themselves; and when Jo collected her damaged property to go, her escort accompanied her, begging her to come again, "it was such fun to hear about Laurie's larks."

"Capital boys, aren't they? I feel quite young and brisk again after that," said Jo, strolling along with her hands behind her, partly from habit, partly to conceal the bespattered parasol.

"Why do you always avoid Mr. Tudor?" asked Amy, wisely refraining from any comment upon Jo's dilapidated appearance.

"Don't like him; he puts on airs, snubs his sisters, worries his father, and don't speak respectfully of his mother. Laurie says he is fast, and I don't consider him a desirable acquaintance; so I let him alone."

"You might treat him civilly, at least. You gave him a cool nod; and just now you bowed and smiled in the politest way to Tommy Chamberlain, whose father keeps a grocery store. If you had just reversed the nod and the bow, it would have been right," said Amy, reprovingly.

"No it wouldn't," returned perverse Jo; "I neither like, respect, nor admire Tudor, though his grandfather's uncle's nephew's niece *was* third cousin to a lord. Tommy is poor, and bashful, and good, and very clever; I think well of him, and like to show that I do, for he *is* a gentleman in spite of the brown paper parcels."

"It's no use trying to argue with you," began Amy.

"Not the least, my dear," cut in Jo; "so let us look amiable, and drop a card here, as the Kings are evidently out, for which I'm deeply grateful."

The family card-case having done its duty, the girls walked on, and Jo uttered another thanksgiving on reaching the fifth house, and being told that the young ladies were engaged.

"Now let us go home, and never mind Aunt March to-day. We can run down there any time, and it's really a pity to trail through the dust in our best bibs and tuckers, when we are tired and cross."

"Speak for yourself, if you please; aunt likes to have us pay her the compliment of coming in style, and making a formal call; it's a little thing to do, but it gives her pleasure, and I don't believe it will hurt your things half so much as letting dirty dogs and clumping boys spoil them. Stoop down, and let me take the crumbs off of your bonnet."

"What a good girl you are, Amy," said Jo, with a repentant glance from her own damaged costume to that of her sister, which was fresh and spotless still. "I wish it was as easy for me to do little things to please people, as it is for you. I think of them, but it takes too much time to do them; so I wait for a chance to confer a big favor, and let the small ones slip; but they tell best in the end, I guess."

Amy smiled, and was mollified at once, saying with a maternal air,—

"Women should learn to be agreeable, particularly poor ones; for they have no other way of repaying the kindnesses they receive. If you'd remember that, and practise it, you'd be better liked than I am, because there is more of you."

"I'm a crotchety old thing, and always shall be; but I'm willing to own that you are right; only it's easier for me to risk my life for a person than to be pleasant to them when I don't feel like it. It's a great misfortune to have such strong likes and dislikes, isn't it?"

"It's a greater not to be able to hide them. I don't mind saying that I don't approve of Tudor any more than you do; but I'm not called upon to tell him so; neither are you, and there is no use in making yourself disagreeable because he is."

"But I think girls ought to show when they disapprove of young men; and how can they do it except by their manners? Preaching don't do any good, as I know to my sorrow, since I've had Teddy to manage; but there are many little ways in which I can influence him without a word, and I say we *ought* to do it to others if we can."

"Teddy is a remarkable boy, and can't be taken as a sample of other boys," said Amy, in a tone of solemn conviction, which would have convulsed the "remarkable boy," if he had heard it. "If we were belles, or women of wealth and position, we might do something, perhaps; but for us to frown at one set of young gentlemen, because we don't approve of them, and smile upon another set, because we do, wouldn't have a particle of effect, and we should only be considered odd and Puritanical."

"So we are to countenance things and people which we detest, merely because we are not belles and millionaires, are we? That's a nice sort of morality."

"I can't argue about it, I only know that it's the way of the world; and people who set themselves against it, only get laughed at for their pains. I don't like reformers, and I hope you will never try to be one."

"I do like them, and I shall be one if I can; for in spite of the laughing, the world would never get on without them. We can't agree about that, for you belong to the old set, and I to the new; you will get on the best, but I shall have the liveliest time of it. I should rather enjoy the brickbats and hooting, I think."

"Well, compose yourself now, and don't worry aunt with your new ideas."

"I'll try not to, but I'm always possessed to burst out with some particularly blunt speech or revolutionary sentiment before her; it's my doom, and I can't help it."

They found Aunt Carrol with the old lady, both absorbed in some very interesting subject; but they dropped it as the girls came in, with a conscious look which betrayed that they had been talking about their nieces. Jo was not in a good humor, and the perverse fit returned; but Amy, who had virtuously done her duty, kept her temper, and pleased everybody, was in a most angelic frame of mind. This amiable spirit was felt at once, and both the aunts "my dear'd" her affectionately, looking what they afterwards said emphatically,—"That child improves every day."

"Are you going to help about the fair, dear?" asked Mrs. Carrol, as Amy sat down beside her with the confiding air elderly people like so well in the young.

"Yes, aunt, Mrs. Chester asked me if I would, and I offered to tend a table, as I have nothing but my time to give."

"I'm not," put in Jo, decidedly; "I hate to be patronized, and the Chesters think it's a great favor to allow us to help with their highly connected fair. I wonder you consented, Amy—they only want you to work."

"I am willing to work,—it's for the Freedmen[9] as well as the Chesters, and I think it very kind of them to let me share the labor and the fun. Patronage don't trouble me when it is well meant."

"Quite right and proper; I like your grateful spirit, my dear; it's a pleasure to help people who appreciate our efforts; some don't, and that is trying," observed Aunt March, looking over her spectacles at Jo, who sat apart rocking herself with a somewhat morose expression.

If Jo had only known what a great happiness was wavering in the balance for one of them, she would have turned dove-like in a minute; but, unfortunately, we don't have windows in our breasts, and cannot see what goes on in the minds of our friends; better for us that we cannot as a general thing, but now and then it would be such a comfort—such a saving of time and temper. By her next speech, Jo deprived herself of several years of pleasure, and received a timely lesson in the art of holding her tongue.

"I don't like favors; they oppress and make me feel like a slave; I'd rather do everything for myself, and be perfectly independent."

"Ahem!" coughed Aunt Carrol, softly, with a look at Aunt March.

"I told you so," said Aunt March, with a decided nod to Aunt Carrol.

Mercifully unconscious of what she had done, Jo sat with her nose in the air, and a revolutionary aspect, which was anything but inviting.

"Do you speak French, dear?" asked Mrs. Carrol, laying her hand on Amy's.

"Pretty well, thanks to Aunt March, who lets Esther talk to me as often as I like," replied Amy, with a grateful look, which caused the old lady to smile affably.

"How are you about languages?" asked Mrs. Carrol of Jo.

"Don't know a word; I'm very stupid about studying anything; can't bear French, it's such a slippery, silly sort of language," was the *brusque* reply.

Another look passed between the ladies, and Aunt March said to Amy, "You are quite strong and well, now dear, I believe? Eyes don't trouble you any more, do they?"

"Not at all, thank you, ma'am; I'm very well, and mean to do great things next winter, so that I may be ready for Rome, whenever that joyful time arrives."

"Good girl! you deserve to go, and I'm sure you will some day," said

9. The formerly enslaved African Americans emancipated by President Lincoln and the events of the Civil War.

Aunt March, with an approving pat on the head, as Amy picked up her ball for her.

> "Cross patch, draw the latch,
> Sit by the fire and spin,"[1]

squalled Polly, bending down from his perch on the back of her chair, to peep into Jo's face, with such a comical air of impertinent inquiry, that it was impossible to help laughing.

"Most observing bird," said the old lady.

"Come and take a walk, my dear?" cried Polly, hopping toward the china-closet, with a look suggestive of lump-sugar.

"Thank you, I will—come Amy," and Jo brought the visit to an end, feeling, more strongly than ever, that calls did have a bad effect upon her constitution. She shook hands in a gentlemanly manner, but Amy kissed both the aunts, and the girls departed, leaving behind them the impression of shadow and sunshine; which impression caused Aunt March to say, as they vanished,—

"You'd better do it, Mary; I'll supply the money," and Aunt Carrol to reply decidedly, "I certainly will, if her father and mother consent."

CHAPTER VII.

CONSEQUENCES.

MRS. CHESTER'S fair was so very elegant and select, that it was considered a great honor by the young ladies of the neighborhood to be invited to take a table, and every one was much interested in the matter. Amy was asked, but Jo was not, which was fortunate for all parties, as her elbows were decidedly akimbo at this period of her life, and it took a good many hard knocks to teach her how to get on easily. The "haughty, uninteresting creature" was let severely alone; but Amy's talent and taste were duly complimented by the offer of the Art table, and she exerted herself to prepare and secure appropriate and valuable contributions to it.

Everything went on smoothly till the day before the fair opened; then there occurred one of the little skirmishes which it is almost impossible to avoid, when some five-and-twenty women, old and young, with all their private piques and prejudices, try to work together.

May Chester was rather jealous of Amy because the latter was a greater favorite than herself; and, just at this time, several trifling circumstances occurred to increase the feeling. Amy's dainty pen-and-ink work entirely eclipsed May's painted vases; that was one thorn; then the all-conquering Tudor had danced four times with Amy, at a late party, and only once with May; that was thorn number two; but the chief grievance that rankled in her soul, and gave her an excuse for

---

1. This nursery rhyme about a cranky person originally appeared in *Mother Goose's Melody; or, Sonnets for the Cradle* (c. 1760).

her unfriendly conduct, was a rumor which some obliging gossip had whispered to her, that the March girls had made fun of her at the Lambs. All the blame of this should have fallen upon Jo, for her naughty imitation had been too lifelike to escape detection, and the frolicsome Lambs had permitted the joke to escape. No hint of this had reached the culprits, however, and Amy's dismay can be imagined, when, the very evening before the fair, as she was putting her last touches to her pretty table, Mrs. Chester, who, of course, resented the supposed ridicule of her daughter, said in a bland tone, but with a cold look,—

"I find, dear, that there is some feeling among the young ladies about my giving this table to any one but my girls. As this is the most prominent, and some say the most attractive table of all—and they are the chief getters-up of the fair—it is thought best for them to take this place. I'm sorry, but I know you are too sincerely interested in the cause to mind a little personal disappointment, and you shall have another table if you like."

Mrs. Chester had fancied beforehand that it would be easy to deliver this little speech; but when the time came, she found it rather difficult to utter it naturally, with Amy's unsuspicious eyes looking straight at her, full of surprise and trouble.

Amy felt that there was something behind this, but could not guess what, and said quietly—feeling hurt, and showing that she did,—

"Perhaps you had rather I took no table at all?"

"Now, my dear, don't have any ill feeling, I beg; it's merely a matter of expediency, you see; my girls will naturally take the lead, and this table is considered their proper place. I think it very appropriate to you, and feel very grateful for your efforts to make it so pretty; but we must give up our private wishes, of course, and I will see that you have a good place elsewhere. Wouldn't you like the flower-table? The little girls undertook it, but they are discouraged. You could make a charming thing of it, and the flower-table is always attractive, you know."

"Especially to gentlemen," added May, with a look which enlightened Amy as to one cause of her sudden fall from favor. She colored angrily, but took no other notice of that girlish sarcasm, and answered with unexpected amiability,—

"It shall be as you please, Mrs. Chester; I'll give up my place here at once, and attend to the flowers, if you like."

"You can put your own things on your own table, if you prefer," began May, feeling a little conscience-stricken, as she looked at the pretty racks, the painted shells, and quaint illuminations Amy had so carefully made and so gracefully arranged. She meant it kindly, but Amy mistook her meaning, and said quickly,—

"Oh, certainly, if they are in your way;" and sweeping her contributions into her apron, pell-mell, she walked off, feeling that herself and her works of art had been insulted past forgiveness.

"Now she's mad; Oh dear, I wish I hadn't asked you to speak, mamma," said May, looking disconsolately at the empty spaces on her table.

"Girls' quarrels are soon over," returned her mother, feeling a trifle ashamed of her own part in this one, as well she might.

The little girls hailed Amy and her treasures with delight, which cordial reception somewhat soothed her perturbed spirit, and she fell to work, determined to succeed florally, if she could not artistically. But everything seemed against her; it was late, and she was tired; every one was too busy with their own affairs to help her, and the little girls were only hindrances, for the dears fussed and chattered like so many magpies, making a great deal of confusion in their artless efforts to preserve the most perfect order. The evergreen arch wouldn't stay firm after she got it up, but wiggled and threatened to tumble down on her head when the hanging baskets were filled; her best tile got a splash of water, which left a sepia tear on the cupid's cheek; she bruised her hands with hammering, and got cold working in a draught, which last affliction filled her with apprehensions for the morrow. Any girl-reader who has suffered like afflictions, will sympathize with poor Amy, and wish her well through with her task.

There was great indignation at home when she told her story that evening. Her mother said it was a shame, but told her she had done right. Beth declared she wouldn't go to the old fair at all, and Jo demanded why she didn't take all her pretty things and leave those mean people to get on without her.

"Because they are mean is no reason why I should be. I hate such things; and though I think I've a right to be hurt, I don't intend to show it. They will feel that more than angry speeches or huffy actions, won't they, Marmee?"

"That's the right spirit, my dear; a kiss for a blow is always best, though it's not very easy to give it, sometimes," said her mother, with the air of one who had learned the difference between preaching and practising.

In spite of various very natural temptations to resent and retaliate, Amy adhered to her resolution all the next day, bent on conquering her enemy by kindness. She began well, thanks to a silent reminder that came to her unexpectedly, but most opportunely. As she arranged her table that morning, while the little girls were in an ante-room filling the baskets; she took up her pet production, a little book, the antique cover of which her father had found among his treasures, and in which, on leaves of vellum, she had beautifully illuminated different texts. As she turned the pages, rich in dainty devices, with very pardonable pride, her eye fell upon one verse that made her stop and think. Framed in a brilliant scroll-work of scarlet, blue and gold, with little spirits of good-will helping one another up and down among the thorns and flowers, were the words, "Thou shalt love thy neighbor as thyself."[2]

"I ought, but I don't," thought Amy, as her eye went from the bright page to May's discontented face behind the big vases, that could not hide the vacancies her pretty work had once filled. Amy stood a

2. Cf. Leviticus 19.18.

minute, turning the leaves in her hand, reading on each some sweet rebuke for all heart-burnings and uncharitableness of spirit. Many wise and true sermons are preached us every day by unconscious ministers in street, school, office, or home; even a fair-table may become a pulpit, if it can offer the good and helpful words which are never out of season. Amy's conscience preached her a little sermon from that text, then and there; and she did what many of us don't always do— took the sermon to heart, and straightway put it in practice.

A group of girls were standing about May's table, admiring the pretty things, and talking over the change of saleswomen. They dropped their voices, but Amy knew they were speaking of her, hearing one side of the story, and judging accordingly. It was not pleasant, but a better spirit had come over her, and, presently, a chance offered for proving it. She heard May say, sorrowfully,—

"It's too bad, for there is no time to make other things, and I don't want to fill up with odds and ends. The table was just complete then— now it's spoilt."

"I dare say she'd put them back if you asked her," suggested some one.

"How could I, after all the fuss;" began May, but she did not finish, for Amy's voice came across the hall, saying pleasantly,—

"You may have them, and welcome, without asking, if you want them. I was just thinking I'd offer to put them back, for they belong to your table rather than mine. Here they are; please take them, and forgive me if I was hasty in carrying them away last night."

As she spoke, Amy returned her contribution with a nod and a smile, and hurried away again, feeling that it was easier to do a friendly thing than it was to stay and be thanked for it.

"Now I call that lovely of her, don't you?" cried one girl.

May's answer was inaudible; but another young lady, whose temper was evidently a little soured by making lemonade, added, with a disagreeable laugh, "Very lovely; for she knew she wouldn't sell them at her own table."

Now that was hard; when we make little sacrifices we like to have them appreciated, at least; and for a minute Amy was sorry she had done it, feeling that virtue was not always its own reward. But it is,— as she presently discovered; for her spirits began to rise, and her table to blossom under her skilful hands; the girls were very kind, and that one little act seemed to have cleared the atmosphere amazingly.

It was a very long day, and a hard one to Amy, as she sat behind her table often quite alone, for the little girls deserted very soon; few cared to buy flowers in summer, and her bouquets began to droop long before night.

The Art table *was* the most attractive in the room; there was a crowd about it all day long, and the tenders were constantly flying to and fro with important faces and rattling money-boxes. Amy often looked wistfully across, longing to be there, where she felt at home and happy, instead of in a corner with nothing to do. It might seem no hardship to some of us; but to a pretty, blithe young girl, it was not only tedious, but very trying; and the thought of being found there in the evening by her family, and Laurie and his friends, made it a real martyrdom.

She did not go home till night, and then she looked so pale and quiet that they knew the day had been a hard one, though she made no complaint, and did not even tell what she had done. Her mother gave her an extra cordial cup of tea, Beth helped her dress, and made a charming little wreath for her hair, while Jo astonished her family by getting herself up with unusual care, and hinting, darkly, that the tables were about to be turned.

"Don't do anything rude, pray, Jo; I won't have any fuss made, so let it all pass, and behave yourself," begged Amy, as she departed early, hoping to find a reinforcement of flowers to refresh her poor little table.

"I merely intend to make myself entrancingly agreeable to every one I know, and to keep them in your corner as long as possible. Teddy and his boys will lend a hand, and we'll have a good time yet," returned Jo, leaning over the gate to watch for Laurie. Presently the familiar tramp was heard in the dusk, and she ran out to meet him.

"Is that my boy?"

"As sure as this is my girl!" and Laurie tucked her hand under his arm with the air of a man whose every wish was gratified.

"Oh, Teddy, such doings!" and Jo told Amy's wrongs with sisterly zeal.

"A flock of our fellows are going to drive over by and by, and I'll be hanged if I don't make them buy every flower she's got, and camp down before her table afterward," said Laurie, espousing her cause with warmth.

"The flowers are not at all nice, Amy says, and the fresh ones may not arrive in time. I don't wish to be unjust or suspicious, but I shouldn't wonder if they never came at all. When people do one mean thing they are very likely to do another," observed Jo, in a disgusted tone.

"Didn't Hayes give you the best out of our gardens? I told him to."

"I didn't know that; he forgot, I suppose; and, as your grandpa was poorly, I didn't like to worry him by asking, though I did want some."

"Now, Jo, how could you think there was any need of asking? They are just as much yours as mine; don't we always go halves in everything?" began Laurie, in the tone that always made Jo turn thorny.

"Gracious! I hope not! half of some of your things wouldn't suit me at all. But we mustn't stand philandering here; I've got to help Amy, so you go and make yourself splendid; and if you'll be so very kind as to let Hayes take a few nice flowers up to the Hall, I'll bless you forever."

"Couldn't you do it now?" asked Laurie, so suggestively that Jo shut the gate in his face with inhospitable haste, and called through the bars, "Go away, Teddy; I'm busy."

Thanks to the conspirators, the tables *were* turned that night, for Hayes sent up a wilderness of flowers, with a lovely basket arranged in his best manner for a centre-piece; then the March family turned out *en masse*, and Jo exerted herself to some purpose, for people not only came, but stayed, laughing at her nonsense, admiring Amy's taste, and apparently enjoying themselves very much. Laurie and his friends gallantly threw themselves into the breach, bought up the bouquets, encamped before the table, and made that corner the liveliest spot in the room. Amy was in her element now, and, out of gratitude, if nothing more, was as sprightly and gracious as possible,—coming to the conclusion, about that time, that virtue *was* its own reward, after all.

Jo behaved herself with exemplary propriety; and when Amy was happily surrounded by her guard of honor, Jo circulated about the hall, picking up various bits of gossip, which enlightened her upon the subject of the Chester change of base. She reproached herself for her share of the ill-feeling, and resolved to exonerate Amy as soon as possible; she also discovered what Amy had done about the things in the morning, and considered her a model of magnanimity. As she passed the Art table, she glanced over it for her sister's things, but saw no signs of them. "Tucked away out of sight, I dare say," thought Jo, who could forgive her own wrongs, but hotly resented any insult offered to her family.

"Good evening, Miss Jo; how does Amy get on?" asked May, with a conciliatory air,—for she wanted to show that she also could be generous.

"She has sold everything she had that was worth selling, and now she is enjoying herself. The flower table is always attractive, you know, 'especially to gentlemen.'"

Jo *couldn't* resist giving that little slap, but May took it so meekly she regretted it a minute after, and fell to praising the great vases, which still remained unsold.

"Is Amy's illumination anywhere about? I took a fancy to buy that for father;" said Jo, very anxious to learn the fate of her sister's work.

"Everything of Amy's sold long ago; I took care that the right people saw them, and they made a nice little sum of money for us," returned May, who had overcome sundry small temptations as well as Amy that day.

Much gratified, Jo rushed back to tell the good news; and Amy looked both touched and surprised by the report of May's words and manner.

"Now, gentlemen, I want you to go and do your duty by the other tables as generously as you have by mine—especially the Art-table," she said, ordering out "Teddy's Own," as the girls called the college friends.

" 'Charge, Chester, charge!' is the motto for that table; but do your duty like men, and you'll get your money's worth of *art* in every sense of the word," said the irrepressible Jo, as the devoted phalanx prepared to take the field.

"To hear is to obey, but March is fairer far than May," said little Parker, making a frantic effort to be both witty and tender, and getting promptly quenched by Laurie, who said: "Very well, my son, for a small boy!" and walked him off with a paternal pat on the head.

"Buy the vases," whispered Amy to Laurie, as a final heaping of coals of fire on her enemy's head.

To May's great delight, Mr. Laurence not only bought the vases, but pervaded the hall with one under each arm. The other gentlemen speculated with equal rashness in all sorts of frail trifles, and wandered helplessly about afterward, burdened with wax flowers, painted fans, filagree portfolios, and other useful and appropriate purchases.

Aunt Carrol was there, heard the story, looked pleased, and said something to Mrs. March in a corner, which made the latter lady beam with satisfaction, and watch Amy with a face full of mingled pride and anxiety, though she did not betray the cause of her pleasure till several days later.

The fair was pronounced a success; and when May bid Amy "goodnight," she did not "gush," as usual, but gave her an affectionate kiss, and a look which said, "Forgive and forget." That satisfied Amy; and when she got home she found the vases paraded on the parlor chimney-piece, with a great bouquet in each. "The reward of merit for a magnanimous March," as Laurie announced with a flourish.

"You've a deal more principle, and generosity, and nobleness of character than I ever gave you credit for, Amy. You've behaved sweetly, and I respect you with all my heart," said Jo, warmly, as they brushed their hair together late that night.

"Yes, we all do, and love her for being so ready to forgive. It must have been dreadfully hard, after working so long, and setting your heart on selling your own pretty things. I don't believe I could have done it as kindly as you did," added Beth, from her pillow.

"Why, girls, you needn't praise me so; I only did as I'd be done by. You laugh at me when I say I want to be a lady, but I mean a true gentlewoman in mind and manners, and I try to do it as far as I know how. I can't explain exactly, but I want to be above the little meannesses, and follies, and faults that spoil so many women. I'm far from it now, but I do my best, and hope in time to be what mother is."

Amy spoke earnestly, and Jo said, with a cordial hug,—

"I understand now what you mean, and I'll never laugh at you again. You are getting on faster than you think, and I'll take lessons of you in true politeness, for you've learned the secret, I believe. Try away, deary, you'll get your reward some day, and no one will be more delighted than I shall."

A week later Amy did get her reward, and poor Jo found it hard to be delighted. A letter came from Aunt Carrol, and Mrs. March's face was illuminated to such a degree when she read it, that Jo and Beth, who were with her, demanded what the glad tidings were.

"Aunt Carrol is going abroad next month, and wants—"

"Me to go with her!" burst in Jo, flying out of her chair in an uncontrollable rapture.

"No, dear, not you, it's Amy."

"Oh, mother! she's too young; it's my turn first; I've wanted it so long—it would do me so much good, and be so altogether splendid—I *must* go."

"I'm afraid it's impossible, Jo; aunt says Amy, decidedly, and it is not for us to dictate when she offers such a favor."

"It's always so; Amy has all the fun, and I have all the work. It isn't fair, oh, it isn't fair!" cried Jo, passionately.

"I'm afraid it is partly your own fault, dear. When aunt spoke to me the other day, she regretted your blunt manners and too independent spirit; and here she writes as if quoting something you had said,—'I planned at first to ask Jo; but as "favors burden her," and she "hates French," I think I won't venture to invite her. Amy is more docile, will make a good companion for Flo, and receive gratefully any help the trip may give her.'"

"Oh, my tongue, my abominable tongue! why can't I learn to keep it quiet?" groaned Jo, remembering words which had been her undoing. When she had heard the explanation of the quoted phrases, Mrs. March said, sorrowfully,—

"I wish you could have gone, but there is no hope of it this time; so try to bear it cheerfully, and don't sadden Amy's pleasure by reproaches or regrets."

"I'll try," said Jo, winking hard, as she knelt down to pick up the basket she had joyfully upset. "I'll take a leaf out of her book, and try not only to seem glad, but to be so, and not grudge her one minute of happiness; but it won't be easy, for it is a dreadful disappointment;" and poor Jo bedewed the little fat pincushion she held, with several very bitter tears.

"Jo, dear, I'm very selfish, but I couldn't spare you, and I'm glad you ain't going quite yet," whispered Beth, embracing her, basket and all, with such a clinging touch and loving face, that Jo felt comforted in spite of the sharp regret that made her want to box her own ears, and humbly beg Aunt Carrol to burden her with this favor, and see how gratefully she would bear it.

By the time Amy came in, Jo was able to take her part in the family jubilation; not quite as heartily as usual, perhaps, but without repinings at Amy's good fortune. The young lady herself received the news as tidings of great joy,[3] went about in a solemn sort of rapture, and began to sort her colors and pack her pencils that evening, leaving such trifles as clothes, money, and passports, to those less absorbed in visions of art than herself.

"It isn't a mere pleasure trip to me, girls," she said impressively, as she scraped her best palette. "It will decide my career; for if I have any genius, I shall find it out in Rome, and will do something to prove it."

"Suppose you haven't?" said Jo, sewing away, with red eyes, at the new collars which were to be handed over to Amy.

"Then I shall come home and teach drawing for my living," replied the aspirant for fame, with philosophic composure; but she made a wry face at the prospect, and scratched away at her palette as if bent on vigorous measures before she gave up her hopes.

"No you won't; you hate hard work, and you'll marry some rich man, and come home to sit in the lap of luxury all your days," said Jo.

"Your predictions sometimes come to pass, but I don't believe that

3. Cf. Luke 2.10.

one will. I'm sure I wish it would, for if I can't be an artist myself, I should like to be able to help those who are," said Amy, smiling, as if the part of Lady Bountiful[4] would suit her better than that of a poor drawing teacher.

"Hum!" said Jo, with a sigh; "if you wish it you'll have it, for your wishes are always granted—mine never."

"Would you like to go?" asked Amy, thoughtfully flattening her nose with her knife.

"Rather!"

"Well, in a year or two I'll send for you, and we'll dig in the Forum for relics,[5] and carry out all the plans we've made so many times."

"Thank you; I'll remind you of your promise when that joyful day comes, if it ever does," returned Jo, accepting the vague but magnificent offer as gratefully as she could.

There was not much time for preparation, and the house was in a ferment till Amy was off. Jo bore up very well till the last flutter of blue ribbon vanished, when she retired to her refuge, the garret, and cried till she couldn't cry any more. Amy likewise bore up stoutly till the steamer sailed; then, just as the gangway was about to be withdrawn, it suddenly came over her, that a whole ocean was soon to roll between her and those who loved her best, and she clung to Laurie, the last lingerer, saying with a sob,—

"Oh, take care of them for me; and if anything should happen—"

"I will, dear, I will; and if anything happens, I'll come and comfort you," whispered Laurie, little dreaming how soon he would be called upon to keep his word.

So Amy sailed away to find the old world, which is always new and beautiful to young eyes, while her father and friend watched her from the shore, fervently hoping that none but gentle fortunes would befall the happy-hearted girl, who waved her hand to them till they could see nothing but the summer sunshine dazzling on the sea.

CHAPTER VIII.

OUR FOREIGN CORRESPONDENT.

"LONDON.

DEAREST PEOPLE:

"Here I really sit at a front window of the Bath Hotel, Piccadilly. It's not a fashionable place, but uncle stopped here years ago, and won't go anywhere else; however, we don't mean to stay long, so it's no great matter. Oh, I can't begin to tell you how I enjoy it all! I never can, so I'll only give you bits out of my note-book, for I've done nothing but sketch and scribble since I started.

---

4. The benevolent lady of a village in *The Beaux' Stratagem* (1707), a comedy by George Farquhar.
5. Erected around 600 B.C.E., the Roman Forum ("Forum Romanum") was a marketplace and activity center of the Roman Empire. Its ruins continue to attract tourists.

"I sent a line from Halifax when I felt pretty miserable, but after that I got on delightfully, seldom ill, on deck all day, with plenty of pleasant people to amuse me. Every one was very kind to me, especially the officers. Don't laugh, Jo, gentlemen really are very necessary aboard ship, to hold on to, or to wait upon one; and as they have nothing to do, it's a mercy to make them useful, otherwise they would smoke themselves to death, I'm afraid.

"Aunt and Flo were poorly all the way, and liked to be let alone, so when I had done what I could for them, I went and enjoyed myself. Such walks on deck, such sunsets, such splendid air and waves! It was almost as exciting as riding a fast horse, when we went rushing on so grandly. I wish Beth could have come, it would have done her so much good; as for Jo, she would have gone up and sat on the main-top jib, or whatever the high thing is called, made friends with the engineers, and tooted on the Captain's speaking trumpet, she'd have been in such a state of rapture.

"It was all heavenly, but I was glad to see the Irish coast, and found it very lovely, so green and sunny, with brown cabins here and there, ruins on some of the hills, and gentlemen's country-seats in the valleys, with deer feeding in the parks. It was early in the morning, but I didn't regret getting up to see it, for the bay was full of little boats, the shore *so* picturesque, and a rosy sky over head; I never shall forget it.

"At Queenstown one of my new acquaintances left us,—Mr. Lennox,—and when I said something about the Lakes of Killarney,[6] he sighed, and sung, with a look at me,—

> 'Oh, have you e'er heard of Kate Kearney,
> She lives on the banks of Killarney;
> From the glance of her eye,
> Shun danger and fly,
> For fatal's the glance of Kate Kearney.'

Wasn't that nonsensical?

"We only stopped at Liverpool a few hours. It's a dirty, noisy place, and I was glad to leave it. Uncle rushed out and bought a pair of dog-skin gloves, some ugly, thick shoes, and an umbrella, and got shaved *à la* mutton-chop, the first thing. Then he flattered himself that he looked like a true Briton; but the first time he had the mud cleaned off his shoes, the little boot-black knew that an American stood in them, and said, with a grin, 'There yer har, sir, I've give 'em the latest Yankee shine.' It amused uncle immensely. Oh, I *must* tell you what that absurd Lennox did! He got his friend Ward, who came on with us, to order a bouquet for me, and the first thing I saw in my room, was a lovely one, with 'Robert Lennox's compliments,' on the card. Wasn't that fun, girls? I like travelling.

"I never *shall* get to London if I don't hurry. The trip was like riding through a long picture-gallery, full of lovely landscapes. The farm-

---

6. The three lakes of Killarney—Lough Leane, Middle Lake, and Upper Lake—are among Ireland's most popular tourist attractions.

houses were my delight; with thatched roofs, ivy up to the eaves, lat-
ticed windows, and stout women with rosy children at the doors. The
very cattle looked more tranquil than ours, as they stood knee-deep in
clover, and the hens had a contented cluck, as if they never got nervous, like Yankee biddies. Such perfect color I never saw—the grass so
green, sky so blue, grain so yellow, woods so dark—I was in a rapture
all the way. So was Flo; and we kept bouncing from one side to the
other, trying to see everything while we were whisking along at the
rate of sixty miles an hour. Aunt was tired, and went to sleep, but uncle read his guide-book, and wouldn't be astonished at anything. This
is the way we went on: Amy flying up,—'Oh, that must be Kenilworth,[7]
that gray place among the trees!' Flo darting to my window,—'How
sweet; we must go there some time, won't we, pa?' Uncle calmly admiring his boots,—'No my dear, not unless you want beer; that's a
brewery.'

"A pause,—then Flo cried out, 'Bless me, there's a gallows and a
man going up.' 'Where, where!' shrieks Amy, staring out at two tall
posts with a cross-beam, and some dangling chains. 'A colliery,' remarks uncle, with a twinkle of the eye. 'Here's a lovely flock of lambs
all lying down,' says Amy. 'See, pa, aren't they pretty!' added Flo, sentimentally. 'Geese, young ladies,' returns uncle, in a tone that keeps
us quiet till Flo settles down to enjoy 'The Flirtations of Capt.
Cavendish,'[8] and I have the scenery all to myself.

"Of course it rained when we got to London, and there was nothing
to be seen but fog and umbrellas. We rested, unpacked, and shopped
a little between the showers. Aunt Mary got me some new things, for I
came off in such a hurry I wasn't half ready. A sweet white hat and
blue feather, a distracting muslin to match, and the loveliest mantle
you ever saw. Shopping in Regent Street[9] is perfectly splendid; things
seem so cheap—nice ribbons only sixpence a yard. I laid in a stock,
but shall get my gloves in Paris. Don't that sound sort of elegant and
rich?

"Flo and I, for the fun of it, ordered a Hansom cab, while aunt and
uncle were out, and went for a drive, though we learned afterward
that it wasn't the thing for young ladies to ride in them alone. It was so
droll! for when we were shut in by the wooden apron, the man drove
so fast that Flo was frightened, and told me to stop him. But he was
up outside behind somewhere, and I couldn't get at him. He didn't
hear me call, nor see me flap my parasol in front, and there we were,
quite helpless, rattling away, and whirling round corners, at a break-
neck pace. At last, in my despair, I saw a little door in the roof, and on
poking it open, a red eye appeared, and a beery voice said,—

" 'Now then, mum?'

"I gave my order as soberly as I could, and slamming down the door,

7. Kenilworth Castle was built in about 1122 in the Forest of Arden in Warwickshire. King
John, John of Gaunt, and Henry V all lived there at different times.
8. Captain Cavendish (1560–1592) was an English explorer; he was the subject of several
popular tales published throughout the nineteenth century.
9. Planned by architect John Nash in 1811 and finished in 1825, Regent Street is the center of
London's social and commercial activity.

with a 'Aye, aye, mum,' the old thing made his horse walk, as if going to a funeral. I poked again, and said, 'A little faster;' then off he went, helter-skelter, as before, and we resigned ourselves to our fate.

"To-day was fair, and we went to Hyde Park,[1] close by, for we are more aristocratic than we look. The Duke of Devonshire lives near. I often see his footmen lounging at the back gate; and the Duke of Wellington's house is not far off. Such sights as I saw, my dear! It was as good as Punch,[2] for there were fat dowagers, rolling about in their red and yellow coaches, with gorgeous Jeameses[3] in silk stockings and velvet coats, up behind, and powdered coachmen in front. Smart maids, with the rosiest children I ever saw; handsome girls, looking half asleep; dandies, in queer English hats and lavender kids, lounging about, and tall soldiers, in short red jackets and muffin caps stuck on one side, looking so funny, I longed to sketch them.

"Rotten Row[4] means '*Route de Roi*,' or the king's way; but now it's more like a riding-school than anything else. The horses are splendid, and the men, especially the grooms, ride well, but the women are stiff, and bounce, which isn't according to our rules. I longed to show them a tearing American gallop, for they trotted solemnly up and down in their scant habits and high hats, looking like the women in a toy Noah's Ark. Every one rides—old men, stout ladies, little children, and the young folks do a deal of flirting here; I saw a pair exchange rose-buds, for it's the thing to wear one in the button-hole, and I thought it rather a nice little idea.

"In the P.M. to Westminster Abbey;[5] but don't expect me to describe it, that's impossible—so I'll only say it was sublime! This evening we are going to see Fechter,[6] which will be an appropriate end to the happiest day of my life.

"*Midnight.*

"It's very late, but I can't let my letter go in the morning without telling you what happened last evening. Who do you think came in, as we were at tea? Laurie's English friends, Fred and Frank Vaughn! I was *so* surprised, for I shouldn't have known them, but for the cards. Both are tall fellows, with whiskers; Fred handsome in the English style, and Frank much better, for he only limps slightly, and uses no crutches. They had heard from Laurie where we were to be, and came to ask us to their house, but uncle won't go, so we shall return the call, and see them as we can. They went to the theatre with us, and we did have *such* a good time, for Frank devoted himself to Flo, and Fred and I talked over past, present and future fun as if we had known each

---

1. A royal park since 1536, Hyde Park has for centuries attracted the social and fashionable elite, who promenade through the park.
2. An English illustrated magazine that was popular in the nineteenth century and noted for its political and humorous cartoons.
3. Footmen or flunkeys.
4. See p. 112, n. 7 (part 1, chap. 12).
5. Consecrated in 1065, Westminster Abbey is one of England's most significant historical and architectural attractions. Since 1066, every English monarch has been crowned there; it also contains Poet's Corner, where many of Britain's most famous poets and writers are buried.
6. Charles Albert Fechter (1824–1879), actor who played roles in both French and English; between 1860 and 1869, he was one of London's leading performers.

other all our days. Tell Beth Frank asked for her, and was sorry to hear of her ill health. Fred laughed when I spoke of Jo, and sent his 'respectful compliments to the big hat.' Neither of them had forgotten Camp Laurence, or the fun we had there. What ages ago it seems, don't it?

"Aunt is tapping on the wall for the third time, so I *must* stop. I really feel like a dissipated London fine lady, writing here so late, with my room full of pretty things, and my head a jumble of parks, theatres, new gowns and gallant creatures, who say 'Ah,' and twirl their blond mustaches, with the true English lordliness. I long to see you all, and in spite of my nonsense am, as ever, your loving   AMY."

                                                                    "PARIS.

"DEAR GIRLS:

"In my last I told you about our London visit,—how kind the Vaughns were, and what pleasant parties they made for us. I enjoyed the trips to Hampton Court and the Kensington Museum, more than anything else,—for at Hampton I saw Raphael's Cartoons,[7] and, at the Museum, rooms full of pictures by Turner, Lawrence, Reynolds, Hogarth, and the other great creatures. The day in Richmond Park[8] was charming,—for we had a regular English picnic,—and I had more splendid oaks and groups of deer than I could copy; also heard a nightingale, and saw larks go up. We 'did' London to our hearts' content,—thanks to Fred and Frank,—and were sorry to go away; for, though English people are slow to take you in, when they once make up their minds to do it they cannot be outdone in hospitality, I think. The Vaughns hope to meet us in Rome next winter, and I shall be dreadfully disappointed if they don't, for Grace and I are great friends, and the boys very nice fellows,—especially Fred.

"Well, we were hardly settled here when he turned up again, saying he had come for a holiday, and was going to Switzerland. Aunt looked sober at first, but he was so cool about it she couldn't say a word; and now we get on nicely, and are very glad he came, for he speaks French like a native, and I don't know what we should do without him. Uncle don't know ten words, and insists on talking English very loud, as if that would make people understand him. Aunt's pronunciation is old-fashioned, and Flo and I, though we flattered ourselves that we knew a good deal, find we don't, and are very grateful to have Fred do the *'parley-vooing,'* as uncle calls it.

"Such delightful times as we are having! sight-seeing from morning till night! stopping for nice lunches in the gay *cafés,* and meeting with all sorts of droll adventures. Rainy days I spend in the Louvre,[9] revel-

---

7. Raphael was commissioned by Pope Leo X to draft sketches for the completion of Michaelangelo's iconography in the Sistine Chapel. The tapestries based on his sketches were hung in the chapel in 1519, and the seven surviving sketches were purchased by the future Charles in 1623. Beginning in 1838, they were on display at Hampton Court.
8. Established by Charles in 1637, Richmond Park includes more than twenty-five hundred acres and lies on both sides of the river Thames. Hampton Court is included within Richmond Park.
9. One of Europe's most distinguished museums, established in Paris in 1793.

ling in pictures. Jo would turn up her naughty nose at some of the finest, because she has no soul for art; but *I* have, and I'm cultivating eye and taste as fast as I can. She would like the relics of great people better, for I've seen her Napoleon's cocked hat and gray coat, his baby's cradle and his old toothbrush; also Marie Antoinette's little shoe, the ring of Saint Denis, Charlemagne's sword, and many other interesting things.[1] I'll talk for hours about them when I come, but haven't time to write.

"The Palais Royale[2] is a heavenly place,—so full of *bijouterie* and lovely things that I'm nearly distracted because I can't buy them. Fred wanted to get me some, but of course I didn't allow it. Then the Bois and the Champs Elysées[3] are *tres magnifique*. I've seen the imperial family several times,—the Emperor an ugly, hard-looking man, the Empress pale and pretty, but dressed in horrid taste, *I* thought,—purple dress, green hat, and yellow gloves. Little Nap. is a handsome boy, who sits chatting to his tutor, and kisses his hand to the people as he passes in his four-horse barouche, with postilions in red satin jackets, and a mounted guard before and behind.[4]

"We often walk in the Tuileries gardens, for they are lovely, though the antique Luxembourg gardens suit me better. Pere la Chaise[5] is very curious,—for many of the tombs are like small rooms, and, looking in, one sees a table, with images or pictures of the dead, and chairs for the mourners to sit in when they come to lament. That is so Frenchy,—*n'est ce pas?*[6]

"Our rooms are on the Rue de Rivoli,[7] and, sitting in the balcony, we look up and down the long, brilliant street. It is so pleasant that we spend our evenings talking there,—when too tired with our day's work to go out. Fred is very entertaining, and is altogether the most agreeable young man I ever knew,—except Laurie,—whose manners are more charming. I wish Fred was dark, for I don't fancy light men; however, the Vaughns are very rich, and come of an excellent family, so I won't find fault with their yellow hair, as my own is yellower.

"Next week we are off to Germany and Switzerland; and, as we shall travel fast, I shall only be able to give you hasty letters. I keep my diary, and try to 'remember correctly and describe clearly all that I see and admire,' as father advised. It is good practice for me, and, with my

1. Napoleon (1769–1821) led France from 1799 and proclaimed himself emperor in 1804. Marie Antoinette (1755–1793) was queen of France from 1774 until her death by guillotine in 1793. First bishop of Paris, Denis was martyred c. 275. Charlemagne (742–814) was the king of the Franks.
2. Location of the famous shopping arcades built in the first part of the nineteenth century in central Paris.
3. The Bois de Boulogne is a large and beautiful wooded park on the western edge of Paris; the Champs-Elysées is the busy, wide, and well-known Parisian avenue that ends at the Arc de Triomphe.
4. Napoleon III (1808–1873) was emperor from 1852 to 1870. His wife was Eugénie Marie de Montijo de Guzmán (1826–1920), and their only son was Eugène-Louis-Jean-Joseph Napoleon (1856–1879).
5. A beautifully landscaped cemetery in Paris.
6. Isn't it? (French).
7. An important Parisian street that features a number of famous landmarks, such as the Louvre and the Tuileries Gardens.

sketch-book, will give you a better idea of my tour than these scribbles.

"Adieu; I embrace you tenderly.

"Votre Amie."

"HEIDELBERG.

"MY DEAR MAMMA:

"Having a quiet hour before we leave for Berne, I'll try to tell you what has happened, for some of it is very important, as you will see.

"The sail up the Rhine was perfect, and I just sat and enjoyed it with all my might. Get father's old guide-books, and read about it; I haven't words beautiful enough to describe it. At Coblentz we had a lovely time, for some students from Bonn, with whom Fred got acquainted on the boat, gave us a serenade. It was a moonlight night, and, about one o'clock, Flo and I were waked by the most delicious music under our windows. We flew up, and hid behind the curtains; but sly peeps showed us Fred and the students singing away down below. It was the most romantic thing I ever saw; the river, the bridge of boats, the great fortress opposite, moonlight everywhere, and music fit to melt a heart of stone.

"When they were done we threw down some flowers, and saw them scramble for them, kiss their hands to the invisible ladies, and go laughing away,—to smoke, and drink beer, I suppose. Next morning Fred showed me one of the crumpled flowers in his vest pocket, and looked very sentimental. I laughed at him, and said I didn't throw it, but Flo,—which seemed to disgust him, for he tossed it out of the window, and turned sensible again. I'm afraid I'm going to have trouble with that boy,—it begins to look like it.

"The baths at Nassau were very gay, so was Baden-Baden, where Fred lost some money, and I scolded him. He needs some one to look after him when Frank is not with him. Kate said once she hoped he'd marry soon, and I quite agree with her that it would be well for him. Frankfort was delightful; I saw Goethe's house, Schiller's statue, and Dannecker's famous 'Ariadne.'[8] It was very lovely, but I should have enjoyed it more if I had known the story better. I didn't like to ask, as every one knew it, or pretended they did. I wish Jo would tell me all about it; I ought to have read more, for I find I don't know anything, and it mortifies me.

"Now comes the serious part,—for it happened here, and Fred is just gone. He has been so kind and jolly that we all got quite fond of him; I never thought of anything but a travelling friendship, till the serenade night. Since then I've begun to feel that the moonlight walks, balcony talks, and daily adventures were something more to him than fun. I haven't flirted, mother, truly,—but remembered what you said to

---

8. Johann Wolfgang von Goethe (1749–1832), prominent German Romantic author and poet; Friedrich von Schiller (1759–1805), German dramatist, poet, and literary theorist; Johann Heinrich von Dannecker (1758–1841), German sculptor, whose famous work "Ariadne on a Panther" (1806) was inspired by the mythological story that after Theseus abandoned Ariadne, she had children with Dionysus, who loved panthers because they were the most excitable of animals.

me, and have done my very best. I can't help it if people like me; I don't try to make them, and it worries me if I don't care for them, though Jo says I haven't got any heart. Now I know mother will shake her head, and the girls say, 'Oh, the mercenary little wretch!' but I've made up my mind, and, if Fred asks me, I shall accept him, though I'm not madly in love. I like him, and we get on comfortably together. He is handsome, young, clever enough, and very rich,—ever so much richer than the Laurences. I don't think his family would object, and I should be very happy, for they are all kind, well-bred, generous people, and they like me. Fred, as the eldest twin, will have the estate, I suppose,—and such a splendid one as it is! A city house, in a fashionable street,—not so showy as our big houses, but twice as comfortable, and full of solid luxury, such as English people believe in. I like it, for it's genuine; I've seen the plate, the family jewels, the old servants, and pictures of the country place with its park, great house, lovely grounds, and fine horses. Oh, it would be all I should ask! and I'd rather have it than any title such as girls snap up so readily, and find nothing behind. I may be mercenary, but I hate poverty, and don't mean to bear it a minute longer than I can help. One of us *must* marry well; Meg didn't, Jo won't, Beth can't, yet,—so I shall, and make everything cosy all round. I wouldn't marry a man I hated or despised. You may be sure of that; and, though Fred is not my model hero, he does very well, and, in time, I should get fond enough of him if he was very fond of me, and let me do just as I liked. So I've been turning the matter over in my mind the last week,—for it was impossible to help seeing that Fred liked me. He said nothing, but little things showed it; he never goes with Flo, always gets on my side of the carriage, table, or promenade, looks sentimental when we are alone, and frowns at any one else who ventures to speak to me. Yesterday, at dinner, when an Austrian officer stared at us, and then said something to his friend,— a rakish-looking Baron,—about '*ein wonderschönes Blöndchen*,' Fred looked as fierce as a lion, and cut his meat so savagely, it nearly flew off his plate. He isn't one of the cool, stiff Englishmen, but is rather peppery, for he has Scotch blood in him, as one might guess from his bonnie blue eyes.

"Well, last evening we went up to the castle[9] about sunset,—at least all of us but Fred, who was to meet us there after going to the Poste Restante for letters. We had a charming time poking about the ruins, the vaults where the monster tun is, and the beautiful gardens made by the Elector, long ago, for his English wife.[1] I liked the great terrace best, for the view was divine; so, while the rest went to see the rooms inside, I sat there trying to sketch the gray-stone lion's head on the wall, with scarlet woodbine sprays hanging round it. I felt as if I'd got into a romance, sitting there watching the Neckar rolling through the

---

9. Heidelberg Castle is one of the most famous ruins in Europe. Destroyed for the last time in 1693, the castle was maintained as a tourist attraction beginning in 1810.
1. Friedrich V, elector of the Holy Roman Empire (1610–32), known as the "Winter King," had the gardens at Heidelberg Castle built in honor of his wife, Elisabeth Stuart, the daughter of James I of England.

valley, listening to the music of the Austrian band below, and waiting for my lover,—like a real story-book girl. I had a feeling that something was going to happen, and I was ready for it. I didn't feel blushy or quakey, but quite cool, and only a little excited.

"By and by I heard Fred's voice, and then he came hurrying through the great arch to find me. He looked so troubled that I forgot all about myself, and asked what the matter was. He said he'd just got a letter begging him to come home, for Frank was very ill; so he was going at once, in the night train, and only had time to say 'good-by.' I was very sorry for him, and disappointed for myself,—but only for a minute,— because he said, as he shook hands,—and said it in a way that I could not mistake,—'I shall soon come back,—you won't forget me, Amy?'

"I didn't promise, but I looked at him and he seemed satisfied,—and there was no time for anything but messages and good-byes, for he was off in an hour, and we all miss him very much. I know he wanted to speak, but I think, from something he once hinted, that he had promised his father not to do anything of the sort yet awhile,—for he is a rash boy, and the old gentleman dreads a foreign daughter-in-law. We shall soon meet in Rome; and then, if I don't change my mind, I'll say 'Yes, thank you,' when he says, 'Will you, please?'

"Of course this is all *very private*, but I wished you to know what was going on. Don't be anxious about me; remember I am your 'prudent Amy,' and be sure I will do nothing rashly. Send me as much advice as you like; I'll use it if I can. I wish I could see you for a good talk, Marmee. Love and trust me.

Ever your   AMY."

CHAPTER IX.

TENDER TROUBLES.

Jo, I'm anxious about Beth."

"Why, mother, she has seemed unusually well since the babies came."

"It's not her health that troubles me now; it's her spirits. I'm sure there is something on her mind, and I want you to discover what it is."

"What makes you think so, mother?"

"She sits alone a good deal, and doesn't talk to her father as much as she used. I found her crying over the babies the other day. When she sings, the songs are always sad ones, and now and then I see a look in her face that I don't understand. This isn't like Beth, and it worries me."

"Have you asked her about it?"

"I have tried once or twice; but she either evaded my questions, or looked so distressed, that I stopped. I never force my children's confidence, and I seldom have to wait for it long."

Mrs. March glanced at Jo as she spoke, but the face opposite seemed quite unconscious of any secret disquietude but Beth's; and, after sewing thoughtfully for a minute, Jo said,—

"I think she is growing up, and so begins to dream dreams, and have hopes, and fears, and fidgets, without knowing why, or being able to explain them. Why, mother, Beth's eighteen; but we don't realize it, and treat her like a child, forgetting she's a woman."

"So she is; dear heart, how fast you do grow up," returned her mother, with a sigh and a smile.

"Can't be helped, Marmee; so you must resign yourself to all sorts of worries, and let your birds hop out of the nest, one by one. I promise never to hop very far, if that is any comfort to you."

"It is a great comfort, Jo; I always feel strong when you are at home, now Meg is gone. Beth is too feeble, and Amy too young to depend upon; but when the tug comes, you are always ready."

"Why, you know I don't mind hard jobs much, and there must always be one scrub in a family. Amy is splendid in fine works, and I'm not; but I feel in my element when all the carpets are to be taken up, or half the family fall sick at once. Amy is distinguishing herself abroad; but if anything is amiss at home, I'm your man."

"I leave Beth to your hands then, for she will open her tender little heart to her Jo sooner than to any one else. Be very kind, and don't let her think any one watches or talks about her. If she only would get quite strong and cheerful again, I shouldn't have a wish in the world."

"Happy woman! I've got heaps."

"My dear, what are they?"

"I'll settle Bethy's troubles, and then I'll tell you mine. They are not very wearing, so they'll keep;" and Jo stitched away with a wise nod, which set her mother's heart at rest about her, for the present at least.

While apparently absorbed in her own affairs, Jo watched Beth; and, after many conflicting conjectures, finally settled upon one which seemed to explain the change in her. A slight incident gave Jo the clue to the mystery, she thought, and lively fancy, loving heart did the rest. She was affecting to write busily one Saturday afternoon, when she and Beth were alone together; yet, as she scribbled, she kept her eye on her sister, who seemed unusually quiet. Sitting at the window, Beth's work often dropped into her lap, and she leaned her head upon her hand, in a dejected attitude, while her eyes rested on the dull, autumnal landscape. Suddenly some one passed below, whistling like an operatic black-bird, and a voice called out,—

"All serene! Coming in to-night."

Beth started, leaned forward, smiled and nodded, watched the passer-by till his quick tramp died away, then said softly, as if to herself,—

"How strong, and well, and happy that dear boy looks."

"Hum!" said Jo, still intent upon her sister's face; for the bright color faded as quickly as it came, the smile vanished, and presently a tear lay shining on the window-ledge. Beth whisked it off, and glanced apprehensively at Jo; but she was scratching away at a tremendous rate, apparently engrossed in "Olympia's Oath." The instant Beth turned, Jo began her watch again, saw Beth's hand go quietly to her eyes more than once, and, in her half-averted face, read a tender sorrow that made her own eyes fill. Fearing to betray herself, she slipped away, murmuring something about needing more paper.

"Mercy on me, Beth loves Laurie!" she said, sitting down in her own room, pale with the shock of the discovery which she believed she had just made. "I never dreamt of such a thing! What *will* mother say? I wonder if he—" there Jo stopped, and turned scarlet with a sudden thought. "If he shouldn't love back again, how dreadful it would be. He must; I'll make him!" and she shook her head threateningly at the picture of the mischievous looking boy laughing at her from the wall. "Oh dear, we *are* growing up with a vengeance. Here's Meg married, and a ma, Amy flourishing away at Paris, and Beth in love. I'm the only one that has sense enough to keep out of mischief." Jo thought intently for a minute, with her eyes fixed on the picture; then she smoothed out her wrinkled forehead, and said, with a decided nod at the face opposite,—"No, thank you sir! you're very charming, but you've no more stability than a weathercock; so you needn't write touching notes, and smile in that insinuating way, for it won't do a bit of good, and I won't have it."

Then she sighed, and fell into a reverie, from which she did not wake till the early twilight sent her down to take new observations, which only confirmed her suspicion. Though Laurie flirted with Amy, and joked with Jo, his manner to Beth had always been peculiarly kind and gentle, but so was everybody's; therefore, no one thought of imagining that he cared more for her than for the others. Indeed, a general impression had prevailed in the family, of late, that "our boy" was getting fonder than ever of Jo, who, however, wouldn't hear a word upon the subject, and scolded violently if any one dared to suggest it. If they had known the various tender passages of the past year, or rather attempts at tender passages, which had been nipped in the bud, they would have had the immense satisfaction of saying, "I told you so." But Jo hated "philandering," and wouldn't allow it, always having a joke or a frown ready at the least sign of impending danger.

When Laurie first went to college, he fell in love about once a month; but these small flames were as brief as ardent, did no damage, and much amused Jo, who took great interest in the alternations of hope, despair, and resignation, which were confided to her in their weekly conferences. But there came a time when Laurie ceased to worship at many shrines, hinted darkly at one all-absorbing passion, and indulged occasionally in Byronic fits of gloom. Then he avoided the tender subject altogether, wrote philosophical notes to Jo, turned studious, and gave out that he was going to "dig," intending to graduate in a blaze of glory. This suited the young lady better than twilight confidences, tender pressures of the hand, and eloquent glances of the eye; for with Jo, brain developed earlier than heart, and she preferred imaginary heroes to real ones, because, when tired of them, the former could be shut up in the tin-kitchen till called for, and the latter were less manageable.

Things were in this state when the grand discovery was made, and Jo watched Laurie that night as she had never done before. If she had not got the new idea into her head, she would have seen nothing unusual in the fact, that Beth was very quiet, and Laurie very kind to her. But having given the rein to her lively fancy, it galloped away with her at a great pace; and common sense, being rather weakened by a long course of romance writing, did not come to the rescue. As usual, Beth lay on the sofa, and Laurie sat in a low chair close by, amusing her with all sorts of gossip; for she depended on her weekly "spin," and he never disappointed her. But that evening, Jo fancied that Beth's eyes rested on the lively, dark face beside her with peculiar pleasure, and that she listened with intense interest to an account of some exciting cricket match, though the phrases, "caught off a tice," "stumped off his ground," and "the leg hit for three," were as intelligible to her as Sanscrit. She also fancied, having set her heart upon seeing it, that she saw a certain increase of gentleness in Laurie's manner, that he dropped his voice now and then, laughed less than usual, was a little absent-minded, and settled the afghan over Beth's feet with an assiduity that was really almost tender.

"Who knows? stranger things have happened," thought Jo, as she fussed about the room. "She will make quite an angel of him, and he will make life delightfully easy and pleasant for the dear, if they only love each other. I don't see how he can help it; and I do believe he would if the rest of us were out of the way."

As every one *was* out of the way but herself, Jo began to feel that she ought to dispose of herself with all speed. But where should she go? and burning to lay herself upon the shrine of sisterly devotion, she sat down to settle that point.

Now the old sofa was a regular patriarch of a sofa—long, broad, well-cushioned and low. A trifle shabby, as well it might be, for the girls had slept and sprawled on it as babies, fished over the back, rode on the arms, and had menageries under it as children, and rested tired heads, dreamed dreams, and listened to tender talk on it as young women. They all loved it, for it was a family refuge, and one corner had always been Jo's favorite lounging place. Among the many pillows that adorned the venerable couch was one, hard, round, covered with prickly horse-hair, and furnished with a knobby button at each end; this repulsive pillow was her especial property, being used as a weapon of defence, a barricade, or a stern preventive of too much slumber.

Laurie knew this pillow well, and had cause to regard it with deep aversion; having been unmercifully pummelled with it in former days, when romping was allowed, and now frequently debarred by it from taking the seat he most coveted, next to Jo in the sofa corner. If "the sausage," as they called it, stood on end, it was a sign that he might approach and repose; but if it laid flat across the sofa, woe to the man, woman or child who dared disturb it. That evening Jo forgot to barricade her corner, and had not been in her seat five minutes, before a massive form appeared beside her, and with both arms spread over the sofa-back, both long legs stretched out before him, Laurie exclaimed with a sigh of satisfaction,—

"Now *this* is filling at the price!"

"No slang," snapped Jo, slamming down the pillow. But it was too late—there was no room for it; and coasting on to the floor, it disappeared in a most mysterious manner.

"Come, Jo, don't be thorny. After studying himself to a skeleton all the week, a fellow deserves petting, and ought to get it."

"Beth will pet you, I'm busy."

"No, she's not to be bothered with me; but you like that sort of thing, unless you've suddenly lost your taste for it. Have you? Do you hate your boy, and want to fire pillows at him?"

Anything more wheedlesome than that touching appeal was seldom seen, but Jo quenched "her boy" by turning on him with the stern query,—

"How many bouquets have you sent Miss Randal this week?"

"Not one, upon my word! She's engaged. Now then."

"I'm glad of it; that's one of your foolish extravagances, sending flowers and things to girls, for whom you don't care two pins," continued Jo, reprovingly.

"Sensible girls, for whom I do care whole papers of pins, won't let me send them 'flowers and things,' so what can I do? my feelings must have a *went*."

"Mother doesn't approve of flirting, even in fun; and you do flirt desperately, Teddy."

"I'd give anything if I could answer, 'So do you.' As I can't, I'll merely say that I don't see any harm in that pleasant little game, if all parties understand that it's only play."

"Well, it does look pleasant, but I can't learn how it's done. I've tried, because one feels awkward in company, not to do as everybody else is doing; but I don't seem to get on," said Jo, forgetting to play Mentor.

"Take lessons of Amy; she has a regular talent for it."

"Yes, she does it very prettily, and never seems to go too far. I suppose it's natural to some people to please without trying, and others to always say and do the wrong thing in the wrong place."

"I'm glad you can't flirt; it's really refreshing to see a sensible, straightforward girl, who can be jolly and kind without making a fool of herself. Between ourselves, Jo, some of the girls I know really do go on at such a rate I'm ashamed of them. They don't mean any harm, I'm sure; but if they knew how we fellows talked about them afterward, they'd mend their ways, I fancy."

"They do the same; and, as their tongues are the sharpest, you fellows get the worst of it, for you are as silly as they, every bit. If you behaved properly, they would; but, knowing you like their nonsense, they keep it up, and then you blame them."

"Much you know about it, ma'am!" said Laurie, in a superior tone. "We don't like romps and flirts, though we may act as if we did some-

times. The pretty, modest girls are never talked about, except respectfully, among gentlemen. Bless your innocent soul, if you could be in
my place for a month you'd see things that would astonish you a trifle.
Upon my word, when I see one of those harem-scarem girls, I always
want to say with our friend Cock Robin,—

> "'Out upon you, fie upon you,
> Bold-faced jig!'"[2]

It was impossible to help laughing at the funny conflict between
Laurie's chivalrous reluctance to speak ill of womankind, and his very
natural dislike of the unfeminine folly of which fashionable society
showed him many samples. Jo knew that "young Laurence" was regarded as a most eligible *parti* by worldly mammas, was much smiled
upon by their daughters, and flattered enough by ladies of all ages to
make a cockscomb of him; so she watched him rather jealously, fearing he would be spoilt, and rejoiced more than she confessed to find
that he still believed in modest girls. Returning suddenly to her ad-
monitory tone, she said, dropping her voice, "If you *must* have a 'went,'
Teddy, go and devote yourself to one of the 'pretty modest girls' whom
you do respect, and not waste your time with the silly ones."

"You really advise it?" and Laurie looked at her with an odd mixture
of anxiety and merriment in his face.

"Yes, I do; but you'd better wait till you are through college, on
the whole, and be fitting yourself for the place meantime. You're not
half good enough for—well, whoever the modest girl may be;" and Jo
looked a little queer likewise, for a name had almost escaped her.

"That I'm not!" acquiesced Laurie, with an expression of humility
quite new to him, as he dropped his eyes, and absently wound Jo's
apron tassel round his finger.

"Mercy on us, this will never do," thought Jo; adding aloud, "Go and
sing to me. I'm dying for some music, and always like yours."

"I'd rather stay here, thank you."

"Well, you can't; there isn't room. Go and make yourself useful,
since you are too big to be ornamental. I thought you hated to be
tied to a woman's apron-string," retorted Jo, quoting certain rebellious
words of his own.

"Ah, that depends on who wears the apron!" and Laurie gave an audacious tweak at the tassel.

"Are you going?" demanded Jo, diving for the pillow.

He fled at once, and the minute it was well "Up with the bonnets of
bonnie Dundee,"[3] she slipped away, to return no more till the young
gentleman had departed in high dudgeon.

2. In the nursery rhyme "Little Jenny Wren," Robin Redbreast (not Cock Robin) brings Jenny
   Wren cake and wine when she is ill; at the time she agrees to marry him. When she is well,
   she spurns his advances, prompting Robin to scold her, "Out upon you! Fie upon you! /
   Bold-faced jig!"
3. Folk song, written by Sir Walter Scott (1771–1832) for his melodrama *The Doom of Devor-
   goil* (1830), based on the exploits of John Graham ("Bonnie Dundee"), a Highlander and Ja-
   cobite who with his men outfought thousands of English soldiers. The phrase "up with the
   bonnets of bonnie Dundee" appears at the end of the song.

Jo lay long awake that night, and was just dropping off when the sound of a stifled sob made her fly to Beth's bedside, with the anxious inquiry, "What is it, dear?"

"I thought you were asleep," sobbed Beth.

"Is it the old pain, my precious?"

"No; it's a new one; but I can bear it," and Beth tried to check her tears.

"Tell me all about it, and let me cure it as I often did the other."

"You can't; there is no cure." There Beth's voice gave way, and, clinging to her sister, she cried so despairingly that Jo was frightened.

"Where is it? Shall I call mother?"

Beth did not answer the first question; but in the dark one hand went involuntarily to her heart, as if the pain were there; with the other she held Jo fast, whispering eagerly, "No, no, don't call her; don't tell her! I shall be better soon. Lie down here and 'poor' my head. I'll be quiet, and go to sleep; indeed I will."

Jo obeyed; but as her hand went softly to and fro across Beth's hot forehead and wet eyelids, her heart was very full, and she longed to speak. But young as she was Jo had learned that hearts, like flowers, cannot be rudely handled, but must open naturally; so, though she believed she knew the cause of Beth's new pain, she only said, in her tenderest tone, "Does anything trouble you, deary?"

"Yes, Jo!" after a long pause.

"Wouldn't it comfort you to tell me what it is?"

"Not now, not yet."

"Then I won't ask; but remember, Bethy, that mother and Jo are always glad to hear and help you, if they can."

"I know it. I'll tell you by and by."

"Is the pain better now?"

"Oh, yes, much better; you are so comfortable, Jo!"

"Go to sleep, dear; I'll stay with you."

So cheek to cheek they fell asleep, and on the morrow Beth seemed quite herself again; for, at eighteen, neither heads nor hearts ache long, and a loving word can medicine most ills.

But Jo had made up her mind, and, after pondering over a project for some days, she confided it to her mother.

"You asked me the other day what my wishes were. I'll tell you one of them, Marmee," she began, as they sat alone together. "I want to go away somewhere this winter for a change."

"Why, Jo?" and her mother looked up quickly, as if the words suggested a double meaning.

With her eyes on her work, Jo answered soberly, "I want something new; I feel restless, and anxious to be seeing, doing, and learning more than I am. I brood too much over my own small affairs and need stirring up, so, as I can be spared this winter I'd like to hop a little way and try my wings."

"Where will you hop?"

"To New York. I had a bright idea yesterday, and this is it. You know Mrs. Kirke wrote to you for some respectable young person to teach her children and sew. It's rather hard to find just the thing, but I think I should suit if I tried."

"My dear, go out to service in that great boarding-house!" and Mrs. March looked surprised, but not displeased.

"It's not exactly going out to service; for Mrs. Kirke is your friend,—the kindest soul that ever lived,—and would make things pleasant for me, I know. Her family is separate from the rest, and no one knows me there. Don't care if they do; it's honest work, and I'm not ashamed of it."

"Nor I; but your writing?"

"All the better for the change. I shall see and hear new things, get new ideas, and, even if I haven't much time there, I shall bring home quantities of material for my rubbish."

"I have no doubt of it; but are these your only reasons for this sudden fancy?"

"No, mother."

"May I know the others?"

Jo looked up and Jo looked down, then said slowly, with sudden color in her cheeks, "It may be vain and wrong to say it, but—I'm afraid—Laurie is getting too fond of me."

"Then you don't care for him in the way it is evident he begins to care for you?" and Mrs. March looked anxious as she put the question.

"Mercy, no! I love the dear boy as I always have, and am immensely proud of him; but as for anything more, it's out of the question."

"I'm glad of that, Jo!"

"Why, please?"

"Because, dear, I don't think you suited to one another. As friends, you are very happy, and your frequent quarrels soon blow over; but I fear you would both rebel if you were mated for life. You are too much alike, and too fond of freedom, not to mention hot tempers and strong wills, to get on happily together, in a relation which needs infinite patience and forbearance, as well as love."

"That's just the feeling I had, though I couldn't express it. I'm glad you think he is only beginning to care for me. It would trouble me sadly to make him unhappy; for I couldn't fall in love with the dear old fellow merely out of gratitude, could I?"

"You are sure of his feeling for you?"

The color deepened in Jo's cheeks, as she answered with the look of mingled pleasure, pride, and pain which young girls wear when speaking of first lovers,—

"I'm afraid it is so, mother; he hasn't said anything, but he looks a great deal. I think I had better go away before it comes to anything."

"I agree with you, and if it can be managed you shall go."

Jo looked relieved, and, after a pause, said,—smiling,—

"How Mrs. Moffat would wonder at your want of management, if she knew; and how she will rejoice that Annie still may hope."

"Ah, Jo, mothers may differ in their management, but the hope is the same in all—the desire to see their children happy. Meg is so, and I am content with her success. You I leave to enjoy your liberty till you tire of it; for only then will you find that there is something sweeter. Amy is my chief care now, but her good sense will help her. For Beth, I indulge no hopes except that she may be well. By the way, she seems brighter this last day or two. Have you spoken to her?"

"Yes; she owned she had a trouble, and promised to tell me by and by. I said no more, for I think I know it;" and Jo told her little story.

Mrs. March shook her head, and did not take so romantic a view of the case, but looked grave, and repeated her opinion that, for Laurie's sake, Jo should go away for a time.

"Let us say nothing about it to him till the plan is settled; then I'll run away before he can collect his wits and be tragical. Beth must think I'm going to please myself, as I am, for I can't talk about Laurie to her; but she can pet and comfort him after I'm gone, and so cure him of this romantic notion. He's been through so many little trials of the sort, he's used to it, and will soon get over his love-lornity."

Jo spoke hopefully, but could not rid herself of the foreboding fear that this "little trial" would be harder than the others, and that Laurie would not get over his "love-lornity" as easily as heretofore.

The plan was talked over in a family council, and agreed upon; for Mrs. Kirke gladly accepted Jo, and promised to make a pleasant home for her. The teaching would render her independent; and such leisure as she got might be made profitable by writing, while the new scenes and society would be both useful and agreeable. Jo liked the prospect, and was eager to be gone, for the home-nest was growing too narrow for her restless nature and adventurous spirit. When all was settled, with fear and trembling she told Laurie; but, to her surprise, he took it very quietly. He had been graver than usual of late, but very pleasant; and, when jokingly accused of turning over a new leaf, he answered, soberly, "So I am; and I mean this one shall stay turned."

Jo was very much relieved that one of his virtuous fits should come on just then, and made her preparations with a lightened heart,—for Beth seemed more cheerful,—and hoped she was doing the best for all.

"One thing I leave to your especial care," she said, the night before she left.

"You mean your papers?" asked Beth.

"No—my boy; be very good to him, won't you?"

"Of course I will; but I can't fill your place, and he'll miss you sadly."

"It won't hurt him; so remember, I leave him in your charge, to plague, pet, and keep in order."

"I'll do my best, for your sake," promised Beth, wondering why Jo looked at her so queerly.

When Laurie said "Good-by," he whispered, significantly, "It won't do a bit of good, Jo. My eye is on you; so mind what you do, or I'll come and bring you home."

CHAPTER X.

JO'S JOURNAL.

"NEW YORK, NOV.

DEAR MARMEE AND BETH:

I'm going to write you a regular volume, for I've got lots to tell, though I'm not a fine young lady travelling on the continent. When I lost sight of father's dear old face, I felt a trifle blue, and might have shed a briny drop or two, if an Irish lady with four small children, all crying more or less, hadn't diverted my mind; for I amused myself by dropping gingerbread nuts over the seat every time they opened their mouths to roar.

"Soon the sun came out; and taking it as a good omen, I cleared up likewise, and enjoyed my journey with all my heart.

"Mrs. Kirke welcomed me so kindly I felt at home at once, even in that big house full of strangers. She gave me a funny little sky-parlor— all she had; but there is a stove in it, and a nice table in a sunny window, so I can sit here and write whenever I like. A fine view, and a church tower opposite, atone for the many stairs, and I took a fancy to my den on the spot. The nursery, where I am to teach and sew, is a pleasant room next Mrs. Kirke's private parlor, and the two little girls are pretty children—rather spoilt, I guess, but they took to me after telling them 'The Seven Bad Pigs'; and I've no doubt I shall make a model governess.

"I am to have my meals with the children, if I prefer it to the great table, and for the present I do, for I *am* bashful, though no one will believe it.

" 'Now my dear, make yourself at home,' said Mrs. K. in her motherly way; 'I'm on the drive from morning to night, as you may suppose, with such a family; but a great anxiety will be off my mind if I know the children are safe with you. My rooms are always open to you, and your own shall be as comfortable as I can make it. There are some pleasant people in the house, if you feel sociable, and your evenings are always free. Come to me if anything goes wrong, and be as happy as you can. There's the tea-bell; I must run and change my cap'; and off she bustled, leaving me to settle myself in my new nest.

"As I went down stairs, soon after, I saw something I liked. The flights are very long in this tall house, and as I stood waiting at the head of the third one for a little servant girl to lumber up, I saw a queer-looking man come along behind her, take the heavy hod of coal out of her hand, carry it all the way up, put it down at a door near by, and walk away, saying, with a kind nod and a foreign accent,—

" 'It goes better so. The little back is too young to haf such heaviness.'

"Wasn't it good of him? I like such things; for, as father says, trifles show character. When I mentioned it to Mrs. K., that evening, she laughed, and said,—

" 'That must have been Professor Bhaer; he's always doing things of that sort.'

"Mrs. K. told me he was from Berlin; very learned and good, but poor as a church mouse, and gives lessons to support himself and two little orphan nephews whom he is educating here, according to the wishes of his sister, who married an American. Not a very romantic story, but it interested me; and I was glad to hear that Mrs. K. lends him her parlor for some of his scholars. There is a glass door between it and the nursery, and I mean to peep at him, and then I'll tell you how he looks. He's most forty, so it's no harm, Marmee.

"After tea and a go-to-bed romp with the little girls, I attacked the big work-basket, and had a quiet evening chatting with my new friend. I shall keep a journal-letter, and send it once a week; so good-night, and more to-morrow."

"Tuesday Eve.

"Had a lively time in my seminary, this morning, for the children acted like Sancho;[4] and at one time I really thought I should shake them all round. Some good angel inspired me to try gymnastics, and I kept it up till they were glad to sit down and keep still. After luncheon, the girl took them out for a walk, and I went to my needle-work, like little Mabel, 'with a willing mind.'[5] I was thanking my stars that I'd learned to make nice button-holes, when the parlor door opened and shut, and some one began to hum,—

'Kennst du das land,'[6]

like a big bumble-bee. It was dreadfully improper, I know, but I couldn't resist the temptation; and lifting one end of the curtain before the glass door, I peeped in. Professor Bhaer was there; and while he arranged his books, I took a good look at him. A regular German— rather stout, with brown hair tumbled all over his head, a bushy beard, droll nose, the kindest eyes I ever saw, and a splendid big voice that does one's ears good, after our sharp or slipshod American gabble. His clothes were rusty, his hands were large, and he hadn't a handsome feature in his face, except his beautiful teeth; yet I liked him, for he had a fine head; his linen was spandy nice, and he looked like a gentleman, though two buttons were off his coat, and there was a patch on one shoe. He looked sober in spite of his humming, till he went to the window to turn the hyacinth bulbs toward the sun, and stroke the cat, who received him like an old friend. Then he smiled; and when a tap came at the door, called out in a loud, brisk tone,—

"'Herein!'

"I was just going to run, when I caught sight of a morsel of a child carrying a big book, and stopped to see what was going on.

---

4. See p. 22, n. 4 (part 1, chap. 2).
5. See Mary Botham Howitt, "Mabel on Midsummer Day: A Story of the Olden Time," in *Marien's Pilgrimage; A Fire-Side Story, and Other Poems* (1859). The final stanza reads, " 'Tis good to make all duty sweet, / To be alert and kind; / 'Tis good, like little Mabel, / To have a willing mind!"
6. Opening line of Mignon's song from book 3, chap. 1 of *Wilhelm Meister's Apprenticeship* (1796) by Goethe. For the text of the song, see p. 466 of this Norton Critical Edition.

THE PROFESSOR AND TINA.

"Come then, my Tina, and haf a goot hug from thy Bhaer."—PAGE 265.

"'Me wants my Bhaer,' said the mite, slamming down her book, and running to meet him.

"'Thou shalt haf thy Bhaer; come, then, and take a goot hug from him, my Tina,' said the Professor, catching her up, with a laugh, and holding her so high over his head that she had to stoop her little face to kiss him.

"'Now me mus tuddy my lessin,' went on the funny little thing; so he put her up at the table, opened the great dictionary she had brought, and gave her a paper and pencil, and she scribbled away, turning a leaf now and then, and passing her little fat finger down the page, as if finding a word, so soberly, that I nearly betrayed myself by a laugh, while Mr. Bhaer stood stroking her pretty hair, with a fatherly look, that made me think she must be his own, though she looked more French than German.

"Another knock, and the appearance of two young ladies sent me back to my work, and there I virtuously remained through all the noise and gabbling that went on next door. One of the girls kept laughing affectedly, and saying 'Now Professor,' in a coquettish tone, and the other pronounced her German with an accent that must have made it hard for him to keep sober.

"Both seemed to try his patience sorely; for more than once I heard him say, emphatically, 'No, no, it is *not* so; you haf not attend to what I say'; and once there was a loud rap, as if he struck the table with his book, followed by the despairing exclamation, 'Prut![7] it all goes bad this day.'

"Poor man, I pitied him; and when the girls were gone, took just one more peep, to see if he survived it. He seemed to have thrown himself back in his chair, tired out, and sat there with his eyes shut, till the clock struck two, when he jumped up, put his books in his pocket, as if ready for another lesson, and, taking little Tina, who had fallen asleep on the sofa, in his arms, he carried her quietly away. I guess he has a hard life of it.

"Mrs. Kirke asked me if I wouldn't go down to the five-o'clock dinner; and, feeling a little bit homesick, I thought I would, just to see what sort of people are under the same roof with me. So I made myself respectable, and tried to slip in behind Mrs. Kirke; but as she is short, and I'm tall, my efforts at concealment were rather a failure. She gave me a seat by her, and after my face cooled off, I plucked up courage, and looked about me. The long table was full, and every one intent on getting their dinner—the gentlemen especially, who seemed to be eating on time, for they *bolted* in every sense of the word, vanishing as soon as they were done. There was the usual assortment of young men, absorbed in themselves; young couples absorbed in each other; married ladies in their babies, and old gentlemen in politics. I don't think I shall care to have much to do with any of them, except one sweet-faced maiden lady, who looks as if she had something in her.

7. Germanic interjection denoting frustration or negation.

"Cast away at the very bottom of the table was the Professor, shouting answers to the questions of a very inquisitive, deaf old gentleman on one side, and talking philosophy with a Frenchman on the other. If Amy had been here, she'd have turned her back on him forever, because, sad to relate, he had a great appetite, and shovelled in his dinner in a manner which would have horrified 'her ladyship.' I didn't mind, for I like 'to see folks eat with a relish,' as Hannah says, and the poor man must have needed a deal of food, after teaching idiots all day.

"As I went upstairs after dinner, two of the young men were settling their beavers before the hall mirror, and I heard one say low to the other, 'Who's the new party?'

"'Governess, or something of that sort.'

"'What the deuce is she at our table for?'

"'Friend of the old lady's.'

"'Handsome head, but no style.'

"'Not a bit of it. Give us a light and come on.'

"I felt angry at first, and then I didn't care, for a governess is as good as a clerk, and I've got sense, if I haven't style, which is more than some people have, judging from the remarks of the elegant beings who clattered away, smoking like bad chimneys. I hate ordinary people!"

"Thursday.

"Yesterday was a quiet day, spent in teaching, sewing, and writing in my little room,—which is very cosy, with a light and fire. I picked up a few bits of news, and was introduced to the Professor. It seems that Tina is the child of the Frenchwoman who does the fine ironing in the laundry here. The little thing has lost her heart to Mr. Bhaer, and follows him about the house like a dog whenever he is at home, which delights him,—as he is very fond of children, though a 'bacheldore.' Kitty and Minnie Kirke likewise regard him with affection, and tell all sorts of stories about the plays he invents, the presents he brings, and the splendid tales he tells. The young men quiz him, it seems, call him Old Fritz, Lager Beer, Ursa Major, and make all manner of jokes on his name. But he enjoys it like a boy, Mrs. K. says, and takes it so good-naturedly that they all like him, in spite of his odd ways.

"The maiden lady is a Miss Norton,—rich, cultivated, and kind. She spoke to me at dinner to-day (for I went to table again, it's such fun to watch people), and asked me to come and see her at her room. She has fine books and pictures, knows interesting persons, and seems friendly; so I shall make myself agreeable, for I *do* want to get into good society, only it isn't the same sort that Amy likes.

"I was in our parlor last evening, when Mr. Bhaer came in with some newspapers for Mrs. Kirke. She wasn't there, but Minnie, who is a little old woman, introduced me very prettily: 'This is mamma's friend, Miss March.'

"'Yes; and she's jolly, and we like her lots,' added Kitty, who is an *'enfant terrible.'*

"We both bowed, and then we laughed, for the prim introduction and the blunt addition were rather a comical contrast.

" 'Ah, yes; I hear these naughty ones go to vex you, Mees Marsch. If so again, call at me and I come,' he said, with a threatening frown that delighted the little wretches.

"I promised I would, and he departed; but it seems as if I was doomed to see a good deal of him, for to-day, as I passed his door on my way out, by accident I knocked against it with my umbrella. It flew open, and there he stood in his dressing-gown, with a big blue sock on one hand and a darning needle in the other; he didn't seem at all ashamed of it, for when I explained and hurried on, he waved his hand, sock and all, saying, in his loud, cheerful way,—

" 'You haf a fine day to make your walk. *Bon voyage, mademoiselle.*'

"I laughed all the way down stairs; but it was a little pathetic, also, to think of the poor man having to mend his own clothes. The German gentlemen embroider, I know,—but darning hose is another thing, and not so pretty."

"Saturday.

"Nothing has happened to write about, except a call on Miss Norton, who has a room full of lovely things, and who was very charming, for she showed me all her treasures, and asked me if I would sometimes go with her to lectures and concerts, as her escort,—if I enjoyed them. She put it as a favor; but I'm sure Mrs. Kirke has told her about us, and she does it out of kindness to me. I'm as proud as Lucifer, but such favors from such people don't burden me, and I accepted gratefully.

"When I got back to the nursery there was such an uproar in the parlor that I looked in, and there was Mr. Bhaer down on his hands and knees, with Tina on his back, Kitty leading him with a jump-rope, and Minnie feeding two small boys with seed-cakes, as they roared and ramped in cages built of chairs.

" 'We are playing *nargerie*,' explained Kitty.

" 'Dis is mine effalunt!' added Tina, holding on by the Professor's hair.

" 'Mamma always allows us to do what we like Saturday afternoon, when Franz and Emil come, don't she, Mr. Bhaer?' said Minnie.

"The 'effalunt' sat up, looking as much in earnest as any of them, and said, soberly, to me,—

" 'I gif you my wort it is so. If we make too large a noise you shall say "hush!" to us, and we go more softly.'

"I promised to do so, but left the door open, and enjoyed the fun as much as they did,—for a more glorious frolic I never witnessed. They played tag, and soldiers, danced and sung, and when it began to grow dark they all piled on to the sofa about the Professor, while he told charming fairy stories of the storks on the chimney-tops, and the little 'Kobolds,'[8] who ride the snow-flakes as they fall. I wish Americans were as simple and natural as Germans, don't you?

8. Germanic gnomes that inhabit caves and mines. They are tricksters but not evil.

"I'm so fond of writing, I should go spinning on forever if motives of economy didn't stop me; for though I've used thin paper, and written fine, I tremble to think of the stamps this long letter will need. Pray forward Amy's as soon as you can spare them. My small news will sound very flat after her splendors, but you will like them, I know. Is Teddy studying so hard that he can't find time to write to his friends? Take good care of him for me, Beth, and tell me all about the babies, and give heaps of love to every one.

    "From your faithful   Jo.

"P. S. On reading over my letter, it strikes me as rather Bhaery; but I'm always interested in odd people, and I really had nothing else to write about. Bless you."

                                  "Dec.

"My Precious Betsey:
"As this is to be a scribble-scrabble letter, I direct it to you, for it may amuse you, and give you some idea of my goings on; for, though quiet, they are rather amusing, for which, oh, be joyful! After what Amy would call Herculaneum efforts, in the way of mental and moral agriculture, my young ideas begin to shoot, and my little twigs to bend, as I could wish. They are not so interesting to me as Tina and the boys, but I do my duty by them, and they are fond of me. Franz and Emil are jolly little lads, quite after my own heart, for the mixture of German and American spirit in them produces a constant state of effervescence. Saturday afternoons are riotous times, whether spent in the house or out; for on pleasant days they all go to walk, like a seminary, with the Professor and myself to keep order; and then such fun!

"We are very good friends now, and I've begun to take lessons. I really couldn't help it, and it all came about in such a funny way, that I must tell you. To begin at the beginning. Mrs. Kirke called to me, one day, as I passed Mr. Bhaer's room, where she was rummaging.

"'Did you ever see such a den, my dear? Just come and help me put these books to rights, for I've turned everything upside down, trying to discover what he has done with the six new handkerchiefs I gave him, not long ago.'

"I went in, and while we worked I looked about me, for it was 'a den,' to be sure. Books and papers, everywhere; a broken meerschaum, and an old flute over the mantle-piece, as if done with; a ragged bird, without any tail, chirped on one window-seat, and a box of white mice adorned the other; half-finished boats, and bits of string, lay among the manuscripts; dirty little boots stood drying before the fire, and traces of the dearly beloved boys, for whom he makes a slave of himself, were to be seen all over the room. After a grand rummage three of the missing articles were found,—one over the bird-cage, one covered with ink, and a third burnt brown, having been used as a holder.

"'Such a man!' laughed good-natured Mrs. K., as she put the relics in the rag-bag. 'I suppose the others are torn up to rig ships, bandage cut fingers, or make kite tails. It's dreadful, but I can't scold him; he's so absent-minded and good-natured, he lets those boys ride over him rough-shod. I agreed to do his washing and mending, but he forgets to give out his things, and I forget to look them over, so he comes to a sad pass sometimes.'

"'Let me mend them,' said I; 'I don't mind it, and he needn't know. I'd like to,—he's so kind to me about bringing my letters, and lending books.'

"So I have got his things in order, and knit heels into two pairs of the socks,—for they were boggled out of shape with his queer darns. Nothing was said, and I hoped he wouldn't find it out,—but one day last week he caught me at it. Hearing the lessons he gives to others has interested and amused me so much, that I took a fancy to learn; for Tina runs in and out, leaving the door open, and I can hear. I had been sitting near this door, finishing off the last sock, and trying to understand what he said to a new scholar, who is as stupid as I am; the girl had gone, and I thought he had also, it was so still, and I was busily gabbling over a verb, and rocking to and fro in a most absurd way, when a little crow made me look up, and there was Mr. Bhaer looking and laughing quietly, when he made signs to Tina not to betray him.

"'So,' he said, as I stopped and stared like a goose, 'you peep at me, I peep at you, and that is not bad; but see, I am not pleasanting when I say, haf you a wish for German?'

"'Yes; but you are too busy; I am too stupid to learn,' I blundered out, as red as a beet.

"'Prut! we will make the time, and we fail not to find the sense. At efening I shall gif a little lesson with much gladness; for, look you, Mees Marsch, I haf this debt to pay,' and he pointed to my work. 'Yes! they say to one another, these so kind ladies, "he is a stupid old fellow; he will see not what we do; he will never opserve that his sock-heels go not in holes any more; he will think his buttons grow out new when they fall, and believe that strings make theirselves." Ah! but I haf an eye, and I see much. I haf a heart and I feel the thanks for this. Come,—a little lesson then and now, or—no more good fairy works for me and mine.'

"Of course I couldn't say anything after that, and as it really is a splendid opportunity, I made the bargain, and we began. I took four lessons, and then I stuck fast in a grammatical bog. The Professor was very patient with me, but it must have been torment to him, and now and then he'd look at me with such an expression of mild despair, that it was a toss up with me whether to laugh or cry. I tried both ways; and when it came to a sniff of utter mortification and woe, he just threw the grammar on to the floor, and marched out of the room. I felt myself disgraced and deserted forever, but didn't blame him a particle, and was scrambling my papers together, meaning to rush upstairs and shake myself hard, when in he came, as brisk and beaming as if I'd covered my name with glory:—

"'Now we shall try a new way. You and I will read these pleasant little Märchen together, and dig no more in that dry book, that goes in the corner for making us trouble.'

"He spoke so kindly, and opened Hans Andersen's[9] fairy tales so invitingly before me, that I was more ashamed than ever, and went at my lesson in a neck-or-nothing style that seemed to amuse him immensely. I forgot my bashfulness, and pegged away (no other word will express it) with all my might, tumbling over long words, pronouncing according to the inspiration of the minute, and doing my very best. When I finished reading my first page, and stopped for breath, he clapped his hands and cried out, in his hearty way, 'Das ist gute! Now we go well! My turn. I do him in German; gif me your ear.' And away he went, rumbling out the words with his strong voice, and a relish which was good to see as well as hear. Fortunately, the story was the 'Constant Tin Soldier,' which is droll, you know, so I could laugh,— and I did,—though I didn't understand half he read,—for I couldn't help it, he was so earnest, I so excited, and the whole thing so comical.

"After that we got on better, and now I read my lessons pretty well; for this way of studying suits me, and I can see that the grammar gets tucked into the tales and poetry, as one gives pills in jelly. I like it very much, and he don't seem tired of it yet,—which is very good of him, isn't it? I mean to give him something on Christmas, for I don't dare offer money. Tell me something nice, Marmee.

"I'm glad Laurie seems so happy and busy,—that he has given up smoking, and lets his hair grow. You see Beth manages him better than I did. I'm not jealous, dear; do your best, only don't make a saint of him. I'm afraid I couldn't like him without a spice of human naughtiness. Read him bits of my letters. I haven't time to write much, and that will do just as well. Thank heaven Beth continues so comfortable."

"*Jan.*

"A happy New-Year to you all, my dearest family, which of course includes Mr. L. and a young man by the name of Teddy. I can't tell you how much I enjoyed your Christmas bundle, for I didn't get it till night, and had given up hoping. Your letter came in the morning, but you said nothing about a parcel, meaning it for a surprise; so I was disappointed, for I'd had a 'kind of a feeling' that you wouldn't forget me. I felt a little low in my mind, as I sat up in my room, after tea; and when the big, muddy, battered-looking bundle was brought to me, I just hugged it, and pranced. It was so *homey* and refreshing, that I sat down on the floor, and read, and looked, and eat, and laughed and cried, in my usual absurd way. The things were just what I wanted, and all the better for being made instead of bought. Beth's new 'ink-bib' was capital; and Hannah's box of hard gingerbread will be a treasure. I'll be sure and wear the nice flannels you sent, Marmee, and read carefully the books father has marked. Thank you all, heaps and heaps!

9. Hans Christian Andersen (1805–1875), Danish author of over 150 fairy tales.

"Speaking of books, reminds me that I'm getting rich in that line; for, on New-Year's day, Mr. Bhaer gave me a fine Shakespeare. It is one he values much, and I've often admired it, set up in the place of honor, with his German Bible, Plato, Homer, and Milton; so you may imagine how I felt when he brought it down, without its cover, and showed me my name in it, 'from my friend Friedrich Bhaer.'

"'You say often you wish a library; here I gif you one; for between these two lids (he meant covers) is many books in one. Read him well, and he will help you much; for the study of character in this book will help you to read it in the world, and paint it with your pen.'

"I thanked him as well as I could, and talk now about 'my library,' as if I had a hundred books. I never knew how much there was in Shakespeare before; but then I never had a Bhaer to explain it to me. Now, *don't* laugh at his horrid name; it isn't pronounced either Bear or Beer, as people *will* say it, but something between the two, as only Germans can do it. I'm glad you both like what I tell you about him, and hope you will know him some day. Mother would admire his warm heart, father his wise head. I admire both, and feel rich in my new 'friend Friedrich Bhaer.'

"Not having much money, or knowing what he'd like, I got several little things, and put them about the room, where he would find them unexpectedly. They were useful, pretty, or funny—a new stand-dish[1] on his table, a little vase for his flower—he always has one—or a bit of green in a glass, to keep him fresh, he says; and a holder for his blower, so that he needn't burn up what Amy calls 'mouchoirs.'[2] I made it like those Beth invented—a big butterfly with a fat body, and black and yellow wings, worsted feelers, and bead eyes. It took his fancy immensely, and he put it on his mantle-piece as an article of *virtu*; so it was rather a failure after all. Poor as he is, he didn't forget a servant or a child in the house; and not a soul here, from the French laundry-woman to Miss Norton, forgot him. I was so glad of that.

"They got up a masquerade, and had a gay time, New-Year's eve. I didn't mean to go down, having no dress; but, at the last minute, Mrs. Kirke remembered some old brocades, and Miss Norton lent me lace and feathers; so I rigged up as Mrs. Malaprop, and sailed in with a mask on. No one knew me, for I disguised my voice, and no one dreamed of the silent, haughty Miss March (for they think I am very stiff and cool, most of them; and so I am to whipper-snappers) could dance, and dress, and burst out into a 'nice derangement of epitaphs, like an allegory on the banks of the Nile.'[3] I enjoyed it very much; and when we unmasked, it was fun to see them stare at me. I heard one of the young men tell another that he knew I'd been an actress; in fact, he thought he remembered seeing me at one of the minor theatres. Meg will relish that joke. Mr. Bhaer was Nick Bottom, and Tina was

1. Alternate spelling for standish. See p. 157, n. 9 (part 1, chap. 19).
2. Handkerchiefs.
3. Phrases uttered separately by Mrs. Malaprop in Sheridan's *Rivals* 3.3. See p. 94, n. 5 (part 1, chap. 11).

Titania[4]—a perfect little fairy in his arms. To see them dance was 'quite a landscape,' to use a Teddyism.

"I had a very happy New-Year, after all; and when I thought it over in my room, I felt as if I was getting on a little in spite of my many failures; for I'm cheerful all the time now, work with a will, and take more interest in other people than I used to, which is satisfactory. Bless you all. Ever your loving   Jo."

CHAPTER XI.

A FRIEND.

THOUGH very happy in the social atmosphere about her, and very busy with the daily work that earned her bread, and made it sweeter for the effort, Jo still found time for literary labors. The purpose which now took possession of her was a natural one to a poor and ambitious girl; but the means she took to gain her end were not the best. She saw that money conferred power; money and power, therefore, she resolved to have; not to be used for herself alone, but for those whom she loved more than self. The dream of filling home with comforts, giving Beth everything she wanted, from strawberries in winter to an organ in her bedroom; going abroad herself, and always having *more* than enough, so that she might indulge in the luxury of charity, had been for years Jo's most cherished castle in the air.

The prize-story experience had seemed to open a way which might, after long travelling, and much up-hill work, lead to this delightful *chateau en Espagne*. But the novel disaster quenched her courage for a time, for public opinion is a giant which has frightened stouter-hearted Jacks on bigger beanstalks than hers. Like that immortal hero, she reposed a while after the first attempt, which resulted in a tumble, and the least lovely of the giant's treasures, if I remember rightly. But the "up again and take another" spirit was as strong in Jo as in Jack; so she scrambled up on the shady side, this time, and got more booty, but nearly left behind her what was far more precious than the money-bags.

She took to writing sensation stories—for in those dark ages, even all-perfect America read rubbish. She told no one, but concocted a "thrilling tale," and boldly carried it herself to Mr. Dashwood, editor of the "Weekly Volcano." She had never read Sartor Resartus,[5] but she had a womanly instinct that clothes possess an influence more powerful over many than the worth of character or the magic of manners. So she dressed herself in her best, and, trying to persuade herself that she was neither excited nor nervous, bravely climbed two pairs of dark and dirty

---

4. Bottom is a weaver and Titania is the queen of the fairies in Shakespeare's *A Midsummer Night's Dream* (c. 1595).
5. Thomas Carlyle's *Sartor Resartus* (1833–34) is both an autobiographical romance and a depiction of the main character's "philosophy of clothes."

stairs to find herself in a disorderly room, a cloud of cigar smoke, and the presence of three gentlemen sitting with their heels rather higher than their hats, which articles of dress none of them took the trouble to remove on her appearance. Somewhat daunted by this reception, Jo hesitated on the threshold, murmuring in much embarrassment,—

"Excuse me; I was looking for the 'Weekly Volcano' office; I wished to see Mr. Dashwood."

Down went the highest pair of heels, up rose the smokiest gentleman, and, carefully cherishing his cigar between his fingers, he advanced with a nod, and a countenance expressive of nothing but sleep. Feeling that she must get through with the matter somehow, Jo produced her manuscript, and, blushing redder and redder with each sentence, blundered out fragments of the little speech carefully prepared for the occasion.

"A friend of mine desired me to offer—a story—just as an experiment—would like your opinion—be glad to write more if this suits."

While she blushed and blundered, Mr. Dashwood had taken the manuscript, and was turning over the leaves with a pair of rather dirty fingers, and casting critical glances up and down the neat pages.

"Not a first attempt, I take it?" observing that the pages were numbered, covered only on one side, and *not* tied up with a ribbon—sure sign of a novice.

"No sir; she has had some experience, and got a prize for a tale in the 'Blarneystone Banner.'"

"Oh, did she?" and Mr. Dashwood gave Jo a quick look, which seemed to take note of everything she had on, from the bow in her bonnet to the buttons on her boots. "Well, you can leave it, if you like; we've more of this sort of thing on hand than we know what to do with, at present; but I'll run my eye over it, and give you an answer next week."

Now Jo did *not* like to leave it, for Mr. Dashwood didn't suit her at all; but, under the circumstances, there was nothing for her to do but bow and walk away, looking particularly tall and dignified, as she was apt to do, when nettled or abashed. Just then she was both; for it was perfectly evident from the knowing glances exchanged among the gentlemen, that her little fiction of "my friend" was considered a good joke; and a laugh produced by some inaudible remark of the editor, as he closed the door, completed her discomfiture. Half resolving never to return, she went home, and worked off her irritation by stitching pinafores vigorously; and in an hour or two was cool enough to laugh over the scene, and long for next week.

When she went again, Mr. Dashwood was alone, whereat she rejoiced. Mr. Dashwood was much wider awake than before,—which was agreeable,—and Mr. Dashwood was not too deeply absorbed in a cigar to remember his manners,—so the second interview was much more comfortable than the first.

"We'll take this" (editors never say "I"), "if you don't object to a few alterations. It's too long,—but omitting the passages I've marked will make it just the right length," he said, in a business-like tone.

Jo hardly knew her own MS. again, so crumpled and underscored were its pages and paragraphs; but, feeling as a tender parent might on being asked to cut off her baby's legs in order that it might fit into a new cradle, she looked at the marked passages, and was surprised to find that all the moral reflections,—which she had carefully put in as ballast for much romance,—had all been stricken out.

"But, sir, I thought every story should have some sort of a moral, so I took care to have a few of my sinners repent."

Mr. Dashwood's editorial gravity relaxed into a smile, for Jo had forgotten her "friend," and spoken as only an author could.

"People want to be amused, not preached at, you know. Morals don't sell nowadays;" which was not quite a correct statement, by the way.

"You think it would do with these alterations, then?"

"Yes; it's a new plot, and pretty well worked up—language good, and so on," was Mr. Dashwood's affable reply.

"What do you—that is, what compensation—" began Jo, not exactly knowing how to express herself.

"Oh, yes,—well, we give from twenty-five to thirty for things of this sort. Pay when it comes out," returned Mr. Dashwood, as if that point had escaped him; such trifles often do escape the editorial mind, it is said.

"Very well; you can have it," said Jo, handing back the story, with a satisfied air; for, after the dollar-a-column work, even twenty-five seemed good pay.

"Shall I tell my friend you will take another if she has one better than this?" asked Jo, unconscious of her little slip of the tongue, and emboldened by her success.

"Well, we'll look at it; can't promise to take it; tell her to make it short and spicy, and never mind the moral. What name would your friend like to put to it?" in a careless tone.

"None at all, if you please; she doesn't wish her name to appear, and has no *nom de plume*," said Jo, blushing in spite of herself.

"Just as she likes, of course. The tale will be out next week; will you call for the money, or shall I send it?" asked Mr. Dashwood, who felt a natural desire to know who his new contributor might be.

"I'll call; good morning, sir."

As she departed, Mr. Dashwood put up his feet, with the graceful remark, "Poor and proud, as usual, but she'll do."

Following Mr. Dashwood's directions, and making Mrs. Northbury her model, Jo rashly took a plunge into the frothy sea of sensational literature; but, thanks to the life-preserver thrown her by a friend, she came up again, not much the worse for her ducking.

Like most young scribblers, she went abroad for her characters and scenery, and banditti, counts, gypsies, nuns, and duchesses appeared upon her stage, and played their parts with as much accuracy and spirit as could be expected. Her readers were not particular about such trifles as grammar, punctuation, and probability, and Mr. Dashwood graciously permitted her to fill his columns at the lowest prices, not thinking it necessary to tell her that the real cause of his hospitality was the fact that one of his hacks, on being offered higher wages, had basely left him in the lurch.

She soon became interested in her work,—for her emaciated purse grew stout, and the little hoard she was making to take Beth to the mountains next summer, grew slowly but surely, as the weeks passed. One thing disturbed her satisfaction, and that was that she did not tell them at home. She had a feeling that father and mother would not approve,—and preferred to have her own way first, and beg pardon afterward. It was easy to keep her secret, for no name appeared with her stories; Mr. Dashwood had, of course, found it out very soon, but promised to be dumb; and, for a wonder, kept his word.

She thought it would do her no harm, for she sincerely meant to write nothing of which she should be ashamed, and quieted all pricks of conscience by anticipations of the happy minute when she should show her earnings and laugh over her well-kept secret.

But Mr. Dashwood rejected any but thrilling tales; and, as thrills could not be produced except by harrowing up the souls of the readers, history and romance, land and sea, science and art, police records and lunatic asylums, had to be ransacked for the purpose. Jo soon found that her innocent experience had given her but few glimpses of the tragic world which underlies society; so, regarding it in a business light, she set about supplying her deficiencies with characteristic energy. Eager to find material for stories, and bent on making them original in plot, if not masterly in execution, she searched newspapers for accidents, incidents, and crimes; she excited the suspicions of public librarians by asking for works on poisons; she studied faces in the street,—and characters good, bad, and indifferent, all about her; she delved in the dust of ancient times, for facts or fictions so old that they were as good as new, and introduced herself to folly, sin, and misery, as well as her limited opportunities allowed. She thought she was prospering finely; but, unconsciously, she was beginning to desecrate some of the womanliest attributes of a woman's character. She was living in bad society; and, imaginary though it was, its influence affected her, for she was feeding heart and fancy on dangerous and unsubstantial food, and was fast brushing the innocent bloom from her nature by a premature acquaintance with the darker side of life, which comes soon enough to all of us.

She was beginning to feel rather than see this, for much describing of other people's passions and feelings set her to studying and speculating about her own,—a morbid amusement, in which healthy young minds do not voluntarily indulge. Wrong-doing always brings its own punishment; and, when Jo most needed hers, she got it.

I don't know whether the study of Shakespeare helped her to read character, or the natural instinct of a woman for what was honest, brave and strong; but while endowing her imaginary heroes with every perfection under the sun, Jo was discovering a live hero, who interested her in spite of many human imperfections. Mr. Bhaer, in one of their conversations, had advised her to study simple, true, and lovely characters, wherever she found them, as good training for a writer; Jo took him at his word,—for she coolly turned round and studied him,— a proceeding which would have much surprised him, had he known it,—for the worthy Professor was very humble in his own conceit.

Why everybody liked him was what puzzled Jo, at first. He was neither rich nor great, young nor handsome,—in no respect what is called fascinating, imposing, or brilliant; and yet he was as attractive as a genial fire, and people seemed to gather about him as naturally as about a warm hearth. He was poor, yet always appeared to be giving something away,—a stranger, yet every one was his friend; no longer young,—but as happy-hearted as a boy; plain and odd,—yet his face looked beautiful to many, and his oddities were freely forgiven for his sake. Jo often watched him, trying to discover the charm, and, at last, decided that it was benevolence which worked the miracle. If he had any sorrow "it sat with its head under its wing,"[6] and he turned only his sunny side to the world. There were lines upon his forehead, but Time seemed to have touched him gently, remembering how kind he was to others. The pleasant curves about his mouth were the memorials of many friendly words and cheery laughs; his eyes were never cold or hard, and his big hand had a warm, strong grasp that was more expressive than words.

His very clothes seemed to partake of the hospitable nature of the wearer. They looked as if they were at ease, and liked to make him comfortable; his capacious waistcoat was suggestive of a large heart underneath; his rusty coat had a social air, and the baggy pockets plainly proved that little hands often went in empty and came out full; his very boots were benevolent, and his collars never stiff and raspy like other people's.

"That's it!" said Jo to herself, when she at length discovered that genuine good-will toward one's fellow-men could beautify and dignify even a stout German teacher, who shovelled in his dinner, darned his own socks, and was burdened with the name of Bhaer.

Jo valued goodness highly, but she also possessed a most feminine respect for intellect, and a little discovery which she made about the Professor added much to her regard for him. He never spoke of himself, and no one ever knew that in his native city he had been a man much honored and esteemed for learning and integrity, till a countryman came to see him, and, in a conversation with Miss Norton, divulged the pleasing fact. From her Jo learned it,—and liked it all the better because Mr. Bhaer had never told it. She felt proud to know that he was an honored Professor in Berlin, though only a poor language-master in America, and his homely, hard-working life, was much beautified by the spice of romance which this discovery gave it.

Another and a better gift than intellect was shown her in a most unexpected manner. Miss Norton had the *entrée* into literary society, which Jo would have had no chance of seeing but for her. The solitary woman felt an interest in the ambitious girl, and kindly conferred

6. Cf. Joseph Mather's "Song 45: Bang Beggar," in *The Songs* (1862), line 7.

many favors of this sort both on Jo and the Professor. She took them with her, one night, to a select symposium, held in honor of several celebrities.

Jo went prepared to bow down and adore the mighty ones whom she had worshipped with youthful enthusiasm afar off. But her reverence for genius received a severe shock that night, and it took her some time to recover from the discovery that the great creatures were only men and women, after all. Imagine her dismay, on stealing a glance of timid admiration at the poet whose lines suggested an ethereal being fed on "spirit, fire, and dew,"[7] to behold him devouring his supper with an ardor which flushed his intellectual countenance. Turning as from a fallen idol, she made other discoveries which rapidly dispelled her romantic illusions. The great novelist vibrated between two decanters with the regularity of a pendulum; the famous divine flirted openly with one of the Madame de Staëls[8] of the age, who looked daggers at another Corinne, who was amiably satirizing her, after outmanœuvreing her in efforts to absorb the profound philosopher, who imbibed tea Johnsonianly[9] and appeared to slumber,—the loquacity of the lady rendering speech impossible. The scientific celebrities, forgetting their mollusks and Glacial Periods,[1] gossiped about art, while devoting themselves to oysters and ices with characteristic energy; the young musician, who was charming the city like a second Orpheus,[2] talked horses; and the specimen of the British nobility present happened to be the most ordinary man of the party.

Before the evening was half over, Jo felt so completely désillusionée, that she sat down in a corner, to recover herself. Mr. Bhaer soon joined her, looking rather out of his element, and presently several of the philosophers, each mounted on his hobby,[3] came ambling up to hold an intellectual tournament in the recess. The conversation was miles beyond Jo's comprehension, but she enjoyed it, though Kant and Hegel[4] were unknown gods, the Subjective and Objective unintelligible terms; and the only thing "evolved from her inner consciousness," was a bad headache after it was all over. It dawned upon her gradually, that the world was being picked to pieces, and put together on new, and, according to the talkers, on infinitely better principles than before; that religion was in a fair way to be reasoned into nothingness,

7. Robert Browning, "Evelyn Hope," in *Men and Women* (1855), line 20.
8. Anne-Louise-Germaine Necker, Madame de Staël-Holstein (1766–1817), French author of *Corinne* (1807), a novel about a celebrated woman poet and her love affairs.
9. See p. 168, n. 4 (book 1, chap. 21). In his *Life of Johnson*, Boswell describes Johnson's vast consumption and appreciation for tea.
1. Reference to Swiss-American naturalist Louis Agassiz (1807–1873) and his followers.
2. In Greek mythology, Orpheus is taught by Apollo to play the lyre and becomes renowned for the beauty of his music. He goes to the underworld to rescue his dead wife, Eurydice, and his music charms even Hades, the king of the underworld, who permits him to lead his wife back to the world of the living on the condition that he not look back at her until they are clear of the underworld regions; he loses her when he looks back too soon, just as they reach the portal of the underworld.
3. Subject to which one repeatedly returns, short for "hobbyhorse."
4. The New England thinkers and writers associated with transcendentalism greatly admired the German idealist philosophers Immanuel Kant (1724–1804) and Georg Wilhelm Friedrich Hegel (1770–1831); yet many nineteenth-century Americans found German idealism profoundly abstract, its psychology and worldview anticommonsensical, and its theology diffuse and perhaps skeptical.

and intellect was to be the only God. Jo knew nothing about philosophy or metaphysics of any sort, but a curious excitement, half pleasurable, half painful, came over her, as she listened with a sense of being turned adrift into time and space, like a young balloon out on a holiday.

She looked round to see how the Professor liked it and found him looking at her with the grimmest expression she had ever seen him wear. He shook his head, and beckoned her to come away, but she was fascinated, just then, by the freedom of Speculative Philosophy, and kept her seat, trying to find out what the wise gentlemen intended to rely upon after they annihilated all the old beliefs.

Now Mr. Bhaer was a diffident man, and slow to offer his own opinions, not because they were unsettled, but too sincere and earnest to be lightly spoken. As he glanced from Jo to several other young people attracted by the brilliancy of the philosophic pyrotechnics, he knit his brows, and longed to speak, fearing that some inflammable young soul would be led astray by the rockets, to find, when the display was over, that they had only an empty stick, or a scorched hand.

He bore it as long as he could; but when he was appealed to for an opinion, he blazed up with honest indignation, and defended religion with all the eloquence of truth—an eloquence which made his broken English musical, and his plain face beautiful. He had a hard fight, for the wise men argued well; but he didn't know when he was beaten, and stood to his colors like a man. Somehow, as he talked, the world got right again to Jo; the old beliefs that had lasted so long, seemed better than the new. God was not a blind force, and immortality was not a pretty fable, but a blessed fact. She felt as if she had solid ground under her feet again; and when Mr. Bhaer paused, out-talked, but not one whit convinced, Jo wanted to clap her hands and thank him.

She did neither; but she remembered this scene, and gave the Professor her heartiest respect, for she knew it cost him an effort to speak out then and there, because his conscience would not let him be silent. She began to see that character is a better possession than money, rank, intellect, or beauty; and to feel that if greatness is what a wise man has defined it to be,—"truth, reverence, and good-will,"[5]—then her friend Friedrich Bhaer was not only good, but great.

This belief strengthened daily. She valued his esteem, she coveted his respect, she wanted to be worthy of his friendship; and, just when the wish was sincerest, she came near losing everything. It all grew out of a cocked-hat; for one evening the Professor came in to give Jo her lesson, with a paper soldier-cap on his head, which Tina had put there, and he had forgotten to take off.

"It's evident he doesn't prink at his glass before coming down," thought Jo, with a smile, as he said "Goot efening," and sat soberly

5. See Ralph Waldo Emerson, "Greatness," in *Letters and Social Aims* (1876), delivered as a lecture by the author in Boston and elsewhere in New England during 1868–69.

down, quite unconscious of the ludicrous contrast between his subject and his head-gear, for he was going to read her the "Death of Wallenstein."[6]

She said nothing at first, for she liked to hear him laugh out his big, hearty laugh, when anything funny happened, so she left him to discover it for himself, and presently forgot all about it; for to hear a German read Schiller is rather an absorbing occupation. After the reading came the lesson, which was a lively one, for Jo was in a gay mood that night, and the cocked-hat kept her eyes dancing with merriment. The Professor didn't know what to make of her, and stopped, at last, to ask with an air of mild surprise that was irresistible,—

"Mees Marsch, for what do you laugh in your master's face? Haf you no respect for me, that you go on so bad?"

"How can I be respectful, sir, when you forget to take your hat off?" said Jo.

Lifting his hand to his head, the absent-minded Professor gravely felt and removed the little cocked-hat, looked at it a minute, and then threw back his head, and laughed like a merry bass-viol.

"Ah! I see him now; it is that imp Tina who makes me a fool with my cap. Well, it is nothing; but see you, if this lesson goes not well, you too shall wear him."

But the lesson did not go at all, for a few minutes, because Mr. Bhaer caught sight of a picture on the hat; and, unfolding it, said with an air of great disgust,—

"I wish these papers did not come in the house; they are not for children to see, nor young people to read. It is not well; and I haf no patience with those who make this harm."

Jo glanced at the sheet, and saw a pleasing illustration composed of a lunatic, a corpse, a villain, and a viper. She did not like it; but the impulse that made her turn it over was not one of displeasure, but fear, because, for a minute, she fancied the paper was the "Volcano." It was not, however, and her panic subsided as she remembered that, even if it had been, and one of her own tales in it, there would have been no name to betray her. She had betrayed herself, however, by a look and a blush; for, though an absent man, the Professor saw a good deal more than people fancied. He knew that Jo wrote, and had met her down among the newspaper offices more than once; but as she never spoke of it, he asked no questions, in spite of a strong desire to see her work. Now it occurred to him that she was doing what she was ashamed to own, and it troubled him. He did not say to himself, "It is none of my business; I've no right to say anything," as many people would have done; he only remembered that she was young and poor, a girl far away from mother's love and father's care; and he was moved to help her with an impulse as quick and natural as that which would prompt him to put out his hand to save a baby from a puddle. All this

6. *The Death of Wallenstein* (1799) is part of Schiller's dramatic trilogy about the Thirty Years War.

flashed through his mind in a minute, but not a trace of it appeared in his face; and by the time the paper was turned, and Jo's needle threaded, he was ready to say quite naturally, but very gravely,—

"Yes, you are right to put it from you. I do not like to think that good young girls should see such things. They are made pleasant to some, but I would more rather give my boys gunpowder to play with than this bad trash."

"All may not be bad—only silly, you know; and if there is a demand for it, I don't see any harm in supplying it. Many very respectable people make an honest living out of what are called sensation stories," said Jo, scratching gathers so energetically that a row of little slits followed her pin.

"There is a demand for whiskey, but I think you and I do not care to sell it. If the respectable people knew what harm they did, they would not feel that the living *was* honest. They haf no right to put poison in the sugar-plum, and let the small ones eat it. No; they should think a little, and sweep mud in the street before they do this thing!"

Mr. Bhaer spoke warmly, and walked to the fire, crumpling the paper in his hands. Jo sat still, looking as if the fire had come to her; for her cheeks burned long after the cocked-hat had turned to smoke, and gone harmlessly up the chimney.

"I should like much to send all the rest after him," muttered the Professor, coming back with a relieved air.

Jo thought what a blaze her pile of papers, upstairs, would make, and her hard-earned money lay rather heavily on her conscience at that minute. Then she thought consolingly to herself, "Mine are not like that; they are only silly, never bad; so I won't be worried;" and, taking up her book, she said, with a studious face,—

"Shall we go on, sir? I'll be very good and proper now."

"I shall hope so," was all he said, but he meant more than she imagined; and the grave, kind look he gave her, made her feel as if the words "Weekly Volcano" were printed in large type, on her forehead.

As soon as she went to her room, she got out her papers, and carefully re-read every one of her stories. Being a little short-sighted, Mr. Bhaer sometimes used eye-glasses, and Jo had tried them once, smiling to see how they magnified the fine print of her book; now she seemed to have got on the Professor's mental or moral spectacles also, for the faults of these poor stories glared at her dreadfully, and filled her with dismay.

"They *are* trash, and will soon be worse than trash if I go on; for each is more sensational than the last. I've gone blindly on, hurting myself and other people, for the sake of money;—I know it's so—for I can't read this stuff in sober earnest without being horribly ashamed of it; and *what should* I do if they were seen at home, or Mr. Bhaer got hold of them?"

Jo turned hot at the bare idea, and stuffed the whole bundle into her stove, nearly setting the chimney afire with the blaze.

"Yes, that's the best place for such inflammable nonsense; I'd better burn the house down, I suppose, than let other people blow themselves up with my gunpowder," she thought, as she watched the "Demon of the Jura" whisk away, a little black cinder with fiery eyes.

But when nothing remained of all her three months' work, except a heap of ashes, and the money in her lap, Jo looked sober, as she sat on the floor, wondering what she ought to do about her wages.

"I think I haven't done much harm *yet*, and may keep this to pay for my time," she said, after a long meditation, adding, impatiently, "I almost wish I hadn't any conscience, it's so inconvenient. If I didn't care about doing right, and didn't feel uncomfortable when doing wrong, I should get on capitally. I can't help wishing, sometimes, that father and mother hadn't been so dreadfully particular about such things."

Ah, Jo, instead of wishing that, thank God that "father and mother *were* particular," and pity from your heart those who have no such guardians to hedge them round with principles which may seem like prison walls to impatient youth, but which will prove sure foundations to build character upon in womanhood.

Jo wrote no more sensational stories, deciding that the money did not pay for her share of the sensation; but, going to the other extreme, as is the way with people of her stamp, she took a course of Mrs. Sherwood, Miss Edgeworth, and Hannah More;[7] and then produced a tale which might have been more properly called an essay or a sermon, so intensely moral was it. She had her doubts about it from the beginning; for her lively fancy and girlish romance felt as ill at ease in the new style as she would have done masquerading in the stiff and cumbrous costume of the last century. She sent this didactic gem to several markets, but it found no purchaser; and she was inclined to agree with Mr. Dashwood, that morals didn't sell.

Then she tried a child's story, which she could easily have disposed of if she had not been mercenary enough to demand filthy lucre for it. The only person who offered enough to make it worth her while to try juvenile literature, was a worthy gentleman who felt it his mission to convert all the world to his particular belief. But much as she liked to write for children, Jo could not consent to depict all her naughty boys as being eaten by bears, or tossed by mad bulls, because they did not go to a particular Sabbath-school, nor all the good infants who did go, of course, as rewarded by every kind of bliss, from gilded gingerbread to escorts of angels, when they departed this life, with psalms or sermons on their lisping tongues. So nothing came of these trials; and Jo corked up her inkstand, and said, in a fit of very wholesome humility,—

"I don't know anything; I'll wait till I do before I try again, and, meantime, 'sweep mud in the street,' if I can't do better—that's honest, any way;" which decision proved that her second tumble down the bean-stalk had done her some good.

While these internal revolutions were going on, her external life had been as busy and uneventful as usual; and if she sometimes looked se-

7. Like Edgeworth (see p. 65, n. 2 [part 1, chap. 8]), Mary Martha Sherwood (1775–1851) and Hannah More (1745–1833), both English, were writers of didactic, religious, and moral works for children.

rious, or a little sad, no one observed it but Professor Bhaer. He did it so quietly, that Jo never knew he was watching to see if she would accept and profit by his reproof; but she stood the test, and he was satisfied; for, though no words passed between them, he knew that she had given up writing. Not only did he guess it by the fact that the second finger of her right hand was no longer inky, but she spent her evenings down stairs, now, was met no more among newspaper offices, and studied with a dogged patience, which assured him that she was bent on occupying her mind with something useful, if not pleasant.

He helped her in many ways, proving himself a true friend, and Jo was happy; for while her pen lay idle, she was learning other lessons beside German, and laying a foundation for the sensation story of her own life.

It was a pleasant winter and a long one, for she did not leave Mrs. Kirke till June. Every one seemed sorry when the time came; the children were inconsolable, and Mr. Bhaer's hair stuck straight up all over his head—for he always rumpled it wildly when disturbed in mind.

"Going home! Ah, you are happy that you haf a home to go in," he said, when she told him, and sat silently pulling his beard, in the corner, while she held a little levee on that last evening.

She was going early, so she bade them all good-by over night; and when his turn came, she said, warmly,—

"Now, sir, you won't forget to come and see us, if you ever travel our way, will you? I'll never forgive you, if you do, for I want them all to know my friend."

"Do you? Shall I come?" he asked, looking down at her with an eager expression, which she did not see.

"Yes, come next month; Laurie graduates then, and you'd enjoy Commencement as something new."

"That is your best friend, of whom you speak?" he said, in an altered tone.

"Yes, my boy Teddy; I'm very proud of him, and should like you to see him."

Jo looked up, then, quite unconscious of anything but her own pleasure, in the prospect of showing them to one another. Something in Mr. Bhaer's face suddenly recalled the fact that she might find Laurie more than a best friend, and simply because she particularly wished not to look as if anything was the matter, she involuntarily began to blush; and the more she tried not to, the redder she grew. If it had not been for Tina on her knee, she didn't know what would have become of her. Fortunately, the child was moved to hug her; so she managed to hide her face an instant, hoping the Professor did not see it. But he did, and his own changed again from that momentary anxiety to its usual expression, as he said, cordially,—

"I fear I shall not make the time for that, but I wish the friend much success, and you all happiness; Gott bless you!" and with that, he shook hands warmly, shouldered Tina, and went away.

But after the boys were abed, he sat long before his fire, with the tired look on his face, and the "*heimweh*," or homesickness lying heavy at his heart. Once when he remembered Jo, as she sat with the little child in her lap, and that new softness in her face, he leaned his head on his hands a minute, and then roamed about the room, as if in search of something that he could not find.

"It is not for me; I must not hope it now," he said to himself, with a sigh that was almost a groan; then, as if reproaching himself for the longing that he could not repress, he went and kissed the two towzled heads upon the pillow, took down his seldom-used meerschaum, and opened his Plato.

He did his best, and did it manfully; but I don't think he found that a pair of rampant boys, a pipe, or even the divine Plato, were very satisfactory substitutes for wife and child, and home.

Early as it was, he was at the station, next morning, to see Jo off; and, thanks to him, she began her solitary journey with the pleasant memory of a familiar face smiling its farewell, a bunch of violets to keep her company, and, best of all, the happy thought,—

"Well, the winter's gone, and I've written no books—earned no fortune; but I've made a friend worth having, and I'll try to keep him all my life."

CHAPTER XII.

HEARTACHE.

WHATEVER his motive might have been, Laurie "dug" to some purpose that year, for he graduated with honor, and gave the Latin Oration with the grace of a Phillips, and the eloquence of a Demosthenes,[8]— so his friends said. They were all there—his grandfather, oh, so proud! Mr. and Mrs. March, John and Meg, Jo and Beth, and all exulted over him with the sincere admiration which boys make light of at the time, but fail to win from the world by any after-triumphs.

"I've got to stay for this confounded supper,—but I shall be home early to-morrow; you'll come and meet me as usual, girls?" Laurie said, as he put the sisters into the carriage after the joys of the day were over. He said "girls," but he meant Jo,—for she was the only one who kept up the old custom; she had not the heart to refuse her splendid, successful boy anything, and answered, warmly,—

"I'll come, Teddy, rain or shine, and march before you, playing 'Hail the conquering hero comes,'[9] on a jews-harp."

Laurie thanked her with a look that made her think, in a sudden panic, "Oh, deary me! I know he'll say something, and then what shall I do?"

---

8. Wendell Phillips (1811–1884) was an American antislavery and women's rights activist who was noted for his simple diction and powerful delivery. Demosthenes (384?–322 B.C.E.) was one of the greatest Greek orators, famous for his passionate and articulate speeches.
9. Actually "See the conqu'ring hero comes"; it was composed by George Frideric Handel for his oratorio *Joshua* (1748). In 1750 he inserted it into his oratorio *Judas Maccabaeus* (composed 1745–46; premiere 1747). *Judas Maccabaeus* was dedicated to the duke of Cumberland on his return to England after defeating the Scottish Jacobins at the battle of Culloden in April 1746.

Evening meditation and morning work somewhat allayed her fears, and, having decided that she wouldn't be vain enough to think people were going to propose when she had given them every reason to know what her answer would be, she set forth at the appointed time, hoping Teddy wouldn't go and make her hurt his poor little feelings. A call at Meg's, and a refreshing sniff and sip at the Daisy and Demijohn, still further fortified her for the *tête-a-tête*, but when she saw a stalwart figure looming in the distance, she had a strong desire to turn about and run away.

"Where's the jews-harp, Jo?" cried Laurie, as soon as he was within speaking distance.

"I forgot it"; and Jo took heart again, for that salutation could not be called lover-like.

She always used to take his arm on these occasions, now she did not, and he made no complaint,—which was a bad sign,—but talked on rapidly about all sorts of far-away subjects, till they turned from the road into the little path that led homeward through the grove. Then he walked more slowly, suddenly lost his fine flow of language, and, now and then, a dreadful pause occurred. To rescue the conversation from one of the wells of silence into which it kept falling, Jo said, hastily,—

"Now you must have a good, long holiday!"

"I intend to."

Something in his resolute tone made Jo look up quickly, to find him looking down at her with an expression that assured her the dreaded moment had come, and made her put out her hand with an imploring,—

"No, Teddy,—please don't!"

"I will; and you *must* hear me. It's no use, Jo; we've got to have it out, and the sooner the better for both of us," he answered, getting flushed and excited all at once.

"Say what you like, then; I'll listen," said Jo, with a desperate sort of patience.

Laurie was a young lover, but he was in earnest, and meant to "have it out," if he died in the attempt; so he plunged into the subject with characteristic impetuosity, saying, in a voice that *would* get choky now and then, in spite of manful efforts to keep it steady,—

"I've loved you ever since I've known you, Jo,—couldn't help it, you've been so good to me,—I've tried to show it, but you wouldn't let me; now I'm going to make you hear, and give me an answer, for I *can't* go on so any longer."

"I wanted to save you this; I thought you'd understand—" began Jo, finding it a great deal harder than she expected.

"I know you did; but girls are so queer you never know what they mean. They say No, when they mean Yes; and drive a man out of his wits just for the fun of it," returned Laurie, entrenching himself behind an undeniable fact.

"*I* don't. I never wanted to make you care for me so, and I went away to keep you from it if I could."

"I thought so; it was like you, but it was no use. I only loved you all the more, and I worked hard to please you, and I gave up billiards and everything you didn't like, and waited and never complained, for I hoped you'd love me, though I'm not half good enough—" here there was a choke that couldn't be controlled, so he decapitated butter-cups while he cleared his "confounded throat."

"Yes, you are; you're a great deal too good for me, and I'm so grateful to you, and so proud and fond of you, I don't see why I can't love you as you want me to. I've tried, but I can't change the feeling, and it would be a lie to say I do when I don't."

"Really, truly, Jo?"

He stopped short, and caught both her hands as he put his question with a look that she did not soon forget.

"Really, truly, dear!"

They were in the grove now,—close by the stile; and when the last words fell reluctantly from Jo's lips, Laurie dropped her hands and turned as if to go on, but for once in his life that fence was too much for him; so he just laid his head down on the mossy post, and stood so still that Jo was frightened.

"Oh, Teddy, I'm so sorry, so desperately sorry, I could kill myself if it would do any good! I wish you wouldn't take it so hard; I can't help it; you know it's impossible for people to make themselves love other people if they don't," cried Jo, inelegantly but remorsefully, as she softly patted his shoulder, remembering the time when he had comforted her so long ago.

"They do sometimes," said a muffled voice from the post.

"I don't believe it's the right sort of love, and I'd rather not try it," was the decided answer.

There was a long pause, while a blackbird sung blithely on the willow by the river, and the tall grass rustled in the wind. Presently Jo said, very soberly, as she sat down on the step of the stile,—

"Laurie, I want to tell you something."

He started as if he had been shot, threw up his head, and cried out, in a fierce tone,—

"*Don't* tell me that, Jo; I can't bear it now!"

"Tell what?" she asked, wondering at his violence.

"That you love that old man."

"What old man?" demanded Jo, thinking he must mean his grandfather.

"That devilish Professor you were always writing about. If you say you love him I know I shall do something desperate"—and he looked as if he would keep his word, as he clenched his hands with a wrathful spark in his eyes.

Jo wanted to laugh, but restrained herself, and said, warmly, for she, too, was getting excited with all this,—

"Don't swear, Teddy! He isn't old, nor anything bad, but good and kind, and the best friend I've got—next to you. Pray don't fly into a passion; I want to be kind, but I know I shall get angry if you abuse my Professor. I haven't the least idea of loving him, or anybody else."

"But you will after a while, and then what will become of me?"

"You'll love some one else, too, like a sensible boy, and forget all this trouble."

"I *can't* love any one else; and I'll never forget you, Jo, never! never!" with a stamp to emphasize his passionate words.

"What *shall* I do with him?" sighed Jo, finding that emotions were more unmanageable than she expected. "You haven't heard what I wanted to tell you. Sit down and listen; for indeed I want to do right, and make you happy," she said, hoping to soothe him with a little reason,—which proved that she knew nothing about love.

Seeing a ray of hope in that last speech, Laurie threw himself down on the grass at her feet, leaned his arm on the lower step of the stile, and looked up at her with an expectant face. Now that arrangement was not conducive to calm speech or clear thought on Jo's part; for how *could* she say hard things to her boy while he watched her with eyes full of love and longing, and lashes still wet with the bitter drop or two her hardness of heart had wrung from him? She gently turned his head away, saying, as she stroked the wavy hair which had been allowed to grow for her sake,—how touching that was to be sure!—

"I agree with mother, that you and I are not suited to each other, because our quick tempers and strong wills would probably make us very miserable, if we were so foolish as to—" Jo paused a little over the last word, but Laurie uttered it with a rapturous expression,—

"Marry,—no we shouldn't! If you loved me, Jo, I should be a perfect saint,—for you can make me anything you like!"

"No I can't. I've tried it and failed, and I won't risk our happiness by such a serious experiment. We don't agree, and we never shall; so we'll be good friends all our lives, but we won't go and do anything rash."

"Yes, we will if we get the chance," muttered Laurie, rebelliously.

"Now do be reasonable, and take a sensible view of the case," implored Jo, almost at her wit's end.

"I won't be reasonable; I don't want to take what you call 'a sensible view'; it won't help me, and it only makes you harder. I don't believe you've got any heart."

"I wish I hadn't!"

There was a little quiver in Jo's voice, and, thinking it a good omen, Laurie turned round, bringing all his persuasive powers to bear as he said, in the wheedlesome tone that had never been so dangerously wheedlesome before,—

"Don't disappoint us, dear! every one expects it. Grandpa has set his heart upon it,—your people like it,—and I can't get on without you. Say you will, and let's be happy! do, do!"

Not until months afterward did Jo understand how she had the strength of mind to hold fast to the resolution she had made when she decided that she did not love her boy, and never could. It was very hard to do, but she did it, knowing that delay was both useless and cruel.

"I can't say 'Yes' truly, so I won't say it at all. You'll see that I'm right, by and by, and thank me for it"—she began, solemnly.

"I'll be hanged if I do!" and Laurie bounced up off the grass, burning with indignation at the bare idea.

"Yes you will!" persisted Jo; "you'll get over this after a while, and find some lovely, accomplished girl, who will adore you, and make a fine mistress for your fine house. I shouldn't. I'm homely, and awkward, and odd, and old, and you'd be ashamed of me, and we should quarrel,—we can't help it even now, you see,—and I shouldn't like elegant society and you would, and you'd hate my scribbling, and I couldn't get on without it, and we should be unhappy, and wish we hadn't done it,—and everything would be horrid!"

"Anything more?" asked Laurie, finding it hard to listen patiently to this prophetic burst.

"Nothing more,—except that I don't believe I shall ever marry; I'm happy as I am, and love my liberty too well to be in any hurry to give it up for any mortal man."

"I know better!" broke in Laurie, "you think so now; but there'll come a time when you *will* care for somebody, and you'll love him tremendously, and live and die for him. I know you will,—it's your way,—and I shall have to stand by and see it"—and the despairing lover cast his hat upon the ground with a gesture that would have seemed comical, if his face had not been so tragical.

"Yes, I *will* live and die for him, if he ever comes and makes me love him in spite of myself, and you must do the best you can," cried Jo, losing patience with poor Teddy. "I've done my best, but you *won't* be reasonable, and it's selfish of you to keep teasing for what I can't give. I shall always be fond of you,—very fond indeed, as a friend,—but I'll never marry you; and the sooner you believe it the better for both of us,—so now."

That speech was like fire to gunpowder. Laurie looked at her a minute, as if he did not quite know what to do with himself, then turned sharply away, saying, in a desperate sort of tone,—

"You'll be sorry some day, Jo."

"Oh, where are you going?" she cried, for his face frightened her.

"To the devil!" was the consoling answer.

For a minute Jo's heart stood still, as he swung himself down the bank, toward the river; but it takes much folly, sin, or misery to send a young man to a violent death, and Laurie was not one of the weak sort, who are conquered by a single failure. He had no thought of a melodramatic plunge, but some blind instinct led him to fling hat and coat into his boat, and row away with all his might, making better time up the river than he had done in many a race. Jo drew a long breath, and unclasped her hands as she watched the poor fellow trying to outstrip the trouble which he carried in his heart.

"That will do him good, and he'll come home in such a tender, penitent state of mind, that I shan't dare to see him," she said; adding, as she went slowly home, feeling as if she had murdered some innocent thing, and buried it under the leaves,—

"Now I must go and prepare Mr. Laurence to be very kind to my poor boy. I wish he'd love Beth; perhaps he may, in time, but I begin to think I was mistaken about her. Oh dear! how can girls like to have lovers, and refuse them. I think it's dreadful."

Being sure that no one could do it so well as herself, she went straight to Mr. Laurence, told the hard story bravely through, and then broke down, crying so dismally over her own insensibility, that the kind old gentleman, though sorely disappointed, did not utter a reproach. He found it difficult to understand how any girl could help loving Laurie, and hoped she would change her mind, but he knew even better than Jo, that love cannot be forced, so he shook his head sadly, and resolved to carry his boy out of harm's way; for Young Impetuosity's parting words to Jo disturbed him more than he would confess.

When Laurie came home, dead tired, but quite composed, his grandfather met him as if he knew nothing, and kept up the delusion very successfully, for an hour or two. But when they sat together in the twilight, the time they used to enjoy so much, it was hard work for the old man to ramble on as usual, and harder still for the young one to listen to praises of the last year's success, which to him now seemed love's labor lost. He bore it as long as he could, then went to his piano, and began to play. The windows were open; and Jo, walking in the garden with Beth, for once understood music better than her sister, for he played the "Sonata Pathetique,"[1] and played it as he never did before.

"That's very fine, I dare say, but it's sad enough to make one cry; give us something gayer, lad," said Mr. Laurence, whose kind old heart was full of sympathy, which he longed to show, but knew not how.

Laurie dashed into a livelier strain, played stormily for several minutes, and would have got through bravely, if, in a momentary lull, Mrs. March's voice had not been heard calling,—

"Jo, dear, come in; I want you."

Just what Laurie longed to say, with a different meaning! As he listened, he lost his place; the music ended with a broken chord, and the musician sat silent in the dark.

"I can't stand this," muttered the old gentleman—up he got, groped his way to the piano, laid a kind hand on either of the broad shoulders, and said, as gently as a woman,—

"I know, my boy, I know."

No answer for an instant; then Laurie asked, sharply,—

"Who told you?"

"Jo herself."

"Then there's an end of it!" and he shook off his grandfather's hands with an impatient motion; for, though grateful for the sympathy, his man's pride could not bear a man's pity.

"Not quite; I want to say one thing, and then there shall be an end of it," returned Mr. Laurence, with unusual mildness. "You won't care to stay at home, just now, perhaps?"

---

1. Ludwig van Beethoven's moody, urgent, and emotionally intense *Sonata Pathétique*, Piano Sonata no. 8 in C Minor, Op. 13 (1797–98).

"I don't intend to run away from a girl. Jo can't prevent my seeing her, and I shall stay and do it as long as I like," interrupted Laurie, in a defiant tone.

"Not if you are the gentleman I think you. I'm disappointed, but the girl can't help it; and the only thing left for you to do, is to go away for a time. Where will you go?"

"Anywhere; I don't care what becomes of me;" and Laurie got up, with a reckless laugh, that grated on his grandfather's ear.

"Take it like a man, and don't do anything rash, for God's sake. Why not go abroad, as you planned, and forget it?"

"I can't."

"But you've been wild to go, and I promised you should, when you got through college."

"Ah, but I didn't mean to go alone!" and Laurie walked fast through the room, with an expression which it was well his grandfather did not see.

"I don't ask you to go alone; there's some one ready and glad to go with you, anywhere in the world."

"Who, sir?" stopping to listen.

"Myself."

Laurie came back as quickly as he went, and put out his hand, saying huskily,—

"I'm a selfish brute; but—you know—grandfather—"

"Lord help me, yes, I do know, for I've been through it all before, once in my own young days, and then with your father. Now, my dear boy, just sit quietly down, and hear my plan. It's all settled, and can be carried out at once," said Mr. Laurence, keeping hold of the young man, as if fearful that he would break away, as his father had done before him.

"Well, sir, what is it?" and Laurie sat down without a sign of interest in face or voice.

"There is business in London that needs looking after; I meant you should attend to it; but I can do it better myself, and things here will get on very well with Brooke to manage them. My partners do almost everything; I'm merely holding on till you take my place, and can be off at any time."

"But you hate travelling, sir; I can't ask it of you at your age," began Laurie, who was grateful for the sacrifice, but much preferred to go alone, if he went at all.

The old gentleman knew that perfectly well, and particularly desired to prevent it; for the mood in which he found his grandson, assured him that it would not be wise to leave him to his own devices. So, stifling a natural regret at the thought of the home comforts he would leave behind him, he said, stoutly,—

"Bless your soul, I'm not superannuated yet. I quite enjoy the idea; it will do me good, and my old bones won't suffer, for travelling nowadays is almost as easy as sitting in a chair."

A restless movement from Laurie suggested that *his* chair was not easy, or that he did not like the plan, and made the old man add, hastily,—

"I don't mean to be a marplot or a burden; I go because I think you'd feel happier than if I were left behind. I don't intend to gad about with you, but leave you free to go where you like, while I amuse myself in my own way. I've friends in London and Paris, and should like to visit them; meantime, you can go to Italy, Germany, Switzerland, where you will, and enjoy pictures, music, scenery and adventures, to your heart's content."

Now, Laurie felt just then that his heart was entirely broken, and the world a howling wilderness; but, at the sound of certain words which the old gentleman artfully introduced into his closing sentence, the broken heart gave an unexpected leap, and a green oasis or two suddenly appeared in the howling wilderness. He sighed, and then said, in a spiritless tone,—

"Just as you like, sir; it doesn't matter where I go, or what I do."

"It does to me—remember that, my lad; I give you entire liberty, but I trust you to make an honest use of it. Promise me that, Laurie."

"Anything you like, sir."

"Good!" thought the old gentleman; "you don't care now, but there'll come a time when that promise will keep you out of mischief, or I'm much mistaken."

Being an energetic individual, Mr. Laurence struck while the iron was hot; and before the blighted being recovered spirit enough to rebel, they were off. During the time necessary for preparation, Laurie bore himself as young gentlemen usually do in such cases. He was moody, irritable, and pensive by turns; lost his appetite, neglected his dress, and devoted much time to playing tempestously on his piano; avoided Jo, but consoled himself by staring at her from his window, with a tragical face that haunted her dreams by night, and oppressed her with a heavy sense of guilt by day. Unlike some sufferers, he never spoke of his unrequited passion, and would allow no one, not even Mrs. March, to attempt consolation, or offer sympathy. On some accounts, this was a relief to his friends; but the weeks before his departure were very uncomfortable, and every one rejoiced that the "poor, dear fellow was going away to forget his trouble, and come home happy." Of course he smiled darkly at their delusion, but passed it by, with the sad superiority of one who knew that his fidelity, like his love, was unalterable.

When the parting came he affected high spirits to conceal certain inconvenient emotions which seemed inclined to assert themselves. This gayety did not impose upon anybody, but they tried to look as if it did, for his sake, and he got on very well till Mrs. March kissed him, with a whisper full of motherly solicitude; then, feeling that he was going very fast, he hastily embraced them all round, not forgetting the afflicted Hannah, and ran down stairs as if for his life. Jo followed a minute after to wave her hand to him if he looked round. He did look round, came back, put his arms about her, as she stood on the step above him, and looked up at her with a face that made his short appeal both eloquent and pathetic.

"Oh, Jo, can't you?"

"Teddy, dear, I wish I could!"

That was all, except a little pause; then Laurie straightened himself up, said "It's all right, never mind," and went away without another word. Ah, but it wasn't all right, and Jo *did* mind; for while the curly head lay on her arm a minute after her hard answer, she felt as if she had stabbed her dearest friend; and when he left her, without a look behind him, she knew that the boy Laurie never would come again.

CHAPTER XIII.

BETH'S SECRET.

WHEN Jo came home that spring, she had been struck with the change in Beth. No one spoke of it, or seemed aware of it, for it had come too gradually to startle those who saw her daily; but to eyes sharpened by absence it was very plain, and a heavy weight fell on Jo's heart as she saw her sister's face. It was no paler, and but little thinner than in the autumn; yet there was a strange, transparent look about it, as if the mortal was being slowly refined away, and the immortal shining through the frail flesh with an indescribably pathetic beauty. Jo saw and felt it, but said nothing at the time, and soon the first impression lost much of its power, for Beth seemed happy,—no one appeared to doubt that she was better; and, presently, in other cares, Jo for a time forgot her fear.

But when Laurie was gone, and peace prevailed again, the vague anxiety returned and haunted her. She had confessed her sins and been forgiven; but when she showed her savings and proposed the mountain trip, Beth had thanked her heartily, but begged not to go so far away from home. Another little visit to the seashore would suit her better, and, as grandma could not be prevailed upon to leave the babies, Jo took Beth down to the quiet place, where she could live much in the open air, and let the fresh sea-breezes blow a little color into her pale cheeks.

It was not a fashionable place, but, even among the pleasant people there, the girls made few friends, preferring to live for one another. Beth was too shy to enjoy society, and Jo too wrapt up in her to care for any one else; so they were all in all to each other, and came and went, quite unconscious of the interest they excited in those about them,—who watched with sympathetic eyes the strong sister and the feeble one, always together, as if they felt instinctively that a long separation was not far away.

They did feel it, yet neither spoke of it; for often between ourselves and those nearest and dearest to us there exists a reserve which it is very hard to overcome. Jo felt as if a veil had fallen between her heart and Beth's; but when she put out her hand to lift it up there seemed something sacred in the silence, and she waited for Beth to speak. She wondered, and was thankful also, that her parents did not seem to see what she saw; and, during the quiet weeks, when the shadow grew so

JO AND BETH.

With her head in Jo's lap, while the winds blew healthfully over her and the sea
made music at her feet.—PAGE 293.

plain to her, she said nothing of it to those at home, believing that it would tell itself when Beth came back no better. She wondered still more if her sister really guessed the hard truth, and what thoughts were passing through her mind during the long hours when she lay on the warm rocks with her head in Jo's lap, while the winds blew health-fully over her, and the sea made music at her feet.

One day Beth told her. Jo thought she was asleep, she lay so still; and, putting down her book, sat looking at her with wistful eyes,—try-ing to see signs of hope in the faint color on Beth's cheeks. But she could not find enough to satisfy her,—for the cheeks were very thin, and the hands seemed too feeble to hold even the rosy little shells they had been gathering. It came to her then more bitterly than ever that Beth was slowly drifting away from her, and her arms instinctively tightened their hold upon the dearest treasure she possessed. For a minute her eyes were too dim for seeing, and, when they cleared, Beth was looking up at her so tenderly, that there was hardly any need for her to say,—

"Jo, dear, I'm glad you know it. I've tried to tell you, but I couldn't."

There was no answer except her sister's cheek against her own,—not even tears,—for when most deeply moved Jo did not cry. She was the weaker then, and Beth tried to comfort and sustain her with her arms about her, and the soothing words she whispered in her ear.

"I've known it for a good while, dear, and now I'm used to it, it isn't hard to think of or to bear. Try to see it so, and don't be troubled about me, because it's best; indeed it is."

"Is this what made you so unhappy in the autumn, Beth? You did not feel it then, and keep it to yourself so long, did you?" asked Jo, re-fusing to see or say that it *was* best, but glad to know that Laurie had no part in Beth's trouble.

"Yes; I gave up hoping then, but I didn't like to own it; I tried to think it was a sick fancy, and would not let it trouble any one. But when I saw you all so well, and strong, and full of happy plans, it was hard to feel that I could never be like you,—and then I was miserable, Jo."

"Oh, Beth, and you didn't tell me,—didn't let me comfort and help you! How could you shut me out, and bear it all alone?"

Jo's voice was full of tender reproach, and her heart ached to think of the solitary struggle that must have gone on while Beth learned to say good-by to health, love, and life, and take up her cross so cheer-fully.

"Perhaps it was wrong, but I tried to do right; I wasn't sure, no one said anything, and I hoped I was mistaken. It would have been selfish to frighten you all when Marmee was so anxious about Meg, and Amy away, and you so happy with Laurie,—at least I thought so then."

"And I thought that you loved him, Beth, and I went away because I couldn't," cried Jo,—glad to say all the truth.

Beth looked so amazed at the idea, that Jo smiled in spite of her pain, and added, softly,—

"Then you didn't, deary? I was afraid it was so, and imagined your poor little heart full of love-lornity all that while."

"Why, Jo! how could I, when he was so fond of you?" asked Beth, as innocently as a child. "I do love him dearly; he is so good to me, how can I help it? But he never could be anything to me but my brother. I hope he truly will be, some time."

"Not through me," said Jo, decidedly. "Amy is left for him, and they would suit excellently,—but I have no heart for such things now. I don't care what becomes of anybody but you, Beth. You *must* get well."

"I want to,—oh, so much! I try, but every day I lose a little, and feel more sure that I shall never gain it back. It's like the tide, Jo, when it turns,—it goes slowly, but it can't be stopped."

"It *shall* be stopped,—your tide must not turn so soon,—nineteen is too young. Beth, I can't let you go. I'll work, and pray, and fight against it. I'll keep you in spite of everything; there must be ways,—it can't be too late. God won't be so cruel as to take you from me," cried poor Jo, rebelliously,—for her spirit was far less piously submissive than Beth's.

Simple, sincere people seldom speak much of their piety; it shows itself in acts, rather than in words, and has more influence than homilies or protestations. Beth could not reason upon or explain the faith that gave her courage and patience to give up life, and cheerfully wait for death. Like a confiding child, she asked no questions, but left everything to God and nature, Father and mother of us all, feeling sure that they, and they only, could teach and strengthen heart and spirit for this life and the life to come. She did not rebuke Jo with saintly speeches, only loved her better for her passionate affection, and clung more closely to the dear human love, from which our Father never means us to be weaned, but through which He draws us closer to Himself. She could not say, "I'm glad to go," for life was very sweet to her; she could only sob out, "I'll try to be willing," while she held fast to Jo, as the first bitter wave of this great sorrow broke over them together.

By and by Beth said, with recovered serenity,—

"You'll tell them this, when we go home?"

"I think they will see it without words," sighed Jo; for now it seemed to her that Beth changed every day.

"Perhaps not; I've heard that the people who love best are often blindest to such things. If they don't see it, you will tell them for me. I don't want any secrets, and it's kinder to prepare them. Meg has John and the babies to comfort her, but you must stand by father and mother, won't you, Jo?"

"If I can, but, Beth, I don't give up yet; I'm going to believe that it *is* a sick fancy, and not let you think it's true," said Jo, trying to speak cheerfully.

Beth lay a minute thinking, and then said in her quiet way,—

"I don't know how to express myself, and shouldn't try to any one but you, because I can't speak out, except to my old Jo. I only mean to say, that I have a feeling that it never was intended I should live long. I'm not like the rest of you; I never made any plans about what I'd do when I grew up; I never thought of being married, as you all did. I couldn't seem to imagine myself anything but stupid little Beth, trotting about at home, of no use anywhere but there. I never wanted to go away, and the hard part now is the leaving you all. I'm not afraid, but it seems as if I should be homesick for you even in heaven."

Jo could not speak; and for several minutes there was no sound but the sigh of the wind, and the lapping of the tide. A white-winged gull flew by, with the flash of sunshine on its silvery breast; Beth watched it till it vanished, and her eyes were full of sadness. A little gray-coated sand-bird came tripping over the beach, "peeping" softly to itself, as if enjoying the sun and sea; it came quite close to Beth, looked at her with a friendly eye, and sat upon a warm stone dressing its wet feathers, quite at home. Beth smiled, and felt comforted, for the tiny thing seemed to offer its small friendship, and remind her that a pleasant world was still to be enjoyed.

"Dear little bird! See, Jo, how tame it is. I like peeps better than the gulls, they are not so wild and handsome, but they seem happy, confiding little things. I used to call them my birds, last summer; and mother said they reminded her of me—busy, quaker-colored creatures, always near the shore, and always chirping that contented little song of theirs. You are the gull, Jo, strong and wild, fond of the storm and the wind, flying far out to sea, and happy all alone. Meg is the turtle-dove, and Amy is like the lark she writes about, trying to get up among the clouds, but always dropping down into its nest again. Dear little girl! she's so ambitious, but her heart is good and tender, and no matter how high she flies, she never will forget home. I hope I shall see her again, but she seems *so* far away."

"She is coming in the spring, and I mean that you shall be all ready to see and enjoy her. I'm going to have you well and rosy, by that time," began Jo, feeling that of all the changes in Beth, the talking change was the greatest, for it seemed to cost no effort now, and she thought aloud in a way quite unlike bashful Beth.

"Jo, dear, don't hope any more; it won't do any good, I'm sure of that. We won't be miserable, but enjoy being together while we wait. We'll have happy times, for I don't suffer much, and I think the tide will go out easily, if you help me."

Jo leaned down to kiss the tranquil face; and with that silent kiss, she dedicated herself soul and body to Beth.

She was right—there was no need of any words when they got home, for father and mother saw plainly, now, what they had prayed to be saved from seeing. Tired with her short journey, Beth went at once to bed, saying how glad she was to be at home; and when Jo went down, she found that she would be spared the hard task of telling Beth's secret. Her father stood leaning his head on the mantle-piece, and did not turn as she came in; but her mother stretched out her arms as if for help, and Jo went to comfort her without a word.

CHAPTER XIV.

NEW IMPRESSIONS.

AT three o'clock in the afternoon, all the fashionable world at Nice may be seen on the Promenade des Anglais[2]—a charming place; for the wide walk, bordered with palms, flowers, and tropical shrubs, is bounded on one side by the sea, on the other by the grand drive, lined with hotels and villas, while beyond lie orange orchards and the hills. Many nations are represented, many languages spoken, many costumes worn; and, on a sunny day, the spectacle is as gay and brilliant as a carnival. Haughty English, lively French, sober Germans, handsome Spaniards, ugly Russians, meek Jews, free-and-easy Americans,—all drive, sit, or saunter here, chatting over the news, and criticising the latest celebrity who has arrived—Ristori or Dickens, Victor Emanuel or the Queen of the Sandwich Islands.[3] The equipages are as varied as the company, and attract as much attention, especially the low basket barouches in which ladies drive themselves, with a pair of dashing ponies, gay nets to keep their voluminous flounces from overflowing the diminutive vehicles, and little grooms on the perch behind.

Along this walk, on Christmas day, a tall young man walked slowly, with his hands behind him, and a somewhat absent expression of countenance. He looked like an Italian, was dressed like an Englishman, and had the independent air of an American—a combination which caused sundry pairs of feminine eyes to look approvingly after him, and sundry dandies in black velvet suits, with rose-colored neckties, buff gloves, and orange flowers in their button-holes, to shrug their shoulders, and then envy him his inches. There were plenty of pretty faces to admire, but the young man took little notice of them, except to glance now and then at some blonde girl or lady in blue. Presently he strolled out of the promenade, and stood a moment at the crossing, as if undecided whether to go and listen to the band in the Jardin Publique, or to wander along the beach toward Castle Hill. The quick trot of ponies' feet made him look up, as one of the little carriages, containing a single lady, came rapidly down the street. The lady was young, blonde, and dressed in blue. He stared a minute, then his whole face woke up, and, waving his hat like a boy, he hurried forward to meet her.

"Oh Laurie! is it really you? I thought you'd never come!" cried Amy, dropping the reins, and holding out both hands, to the great scandal-

---

2. A wide path along the shore built in 1821–22 through the efforts of the English church as one of Nice's attractions for tourists. Its name became official in 1846.
3. Adelaide Ristori (1822–1906) was an Italian actress renowned throughout Europe and America for her portrayals of Mary Stuart, Elizabeth, and Lady Macbeth, among other roles. See Alcott's evaluation of her performances, *Journals*, 150–51. Victor Emmanuel II (1820–1878) was the king of Sardinia (1849–61) and then became the first king of united Italy (1861–78). Lydia Liliuokalani (1838–1917) traveled through Europe as a member of the royal family of Hawaii, although she did not become queen until 1891. The Hawaiian Islands were once known as the Sandwich Islands, a name given them by Captain James Cook, the British explorer, in honor of his patron, John Montagu, the fourth earl of Sandwich.

ization of a French mamma, who hastened her daughter's steps, lest she should be demoralized by beholding the free manners of these "mad English."[4]

"I was detained by the way, but I promised to spend Christmas with you, and here I am."

"How is your grandfather? When did you come? Where are you staying?"

"Very well—last night—at the Chauvain. I called at your hotel, but you were all out."

"Mon Dieu! I have so much to say, and don't know where to begin. Get in, and we can talk at our ease; I was going for a drive, and longing for company. Flo's saving up for to-night."

"What happens, then—a ball?"

"A Christmas party at our hotel. There are many Americans there, and they give it in honor of the day. You'll go with us, of course? aunt will be charmed."

"Thank you! where now?" asked Laurie, leaning back and folding his arms, a proceeding which suited Amy, who preferred to drive; for her parasol-whip and blue reins, over the white ponies' backs, afforded her infinite satisfaction.

"I'm going to the banker's first, for letters, and then to Castle Hill;[5] the view is so lovely, and I like to feed the peacocks. Have you ever been there?"

"Often, years ago; but I don't mind having a look at it."

"Now tell me all about yourself. The last I heard of you, your grandfather wrote that he expected you from Berlin."

"Yes, I spent a month there, and then joined him in Paris, where he has settled for the winter. He has friends there, and finds plenty to amuse him; so I go and come, and we get on capitally."

"That's a sociable arrangement," said Amy, missing something in Laurie's manner, though she couldn't tell what.

"Why, you see he hates to travel, and I hate to keep still; so we each suit ourselves, and there is no trouble. I am often with him, and he enjoys my adventures, while I like to feel that some one is glad to see me when I get back from my wanderings. Dirty old hole, isn't it?" he added, with a sniff of disgust, as they drove along the boulevard to the Place Napoleon,[6] in the old city.

"The dirt is picturesque, so I don't mind. The river and the hills are delicious, and these glimpses of the narrow cross streets are my delight. Now we shall have to wait for that procession to pass; it's going to the Church of St. John."

While Laurie listlessly watched the procession of priests under their canopies, white-veiled nuns bearing lighted tapers, and some brotherhood in blue, chanting as they walked, Amy watched him, and felt a

4. A common phrase inspired perhaps by the "mad" English king George III (r. 1760–1820), who suffered from porphyria, an inherited disease that commonly affects the skin and the nervous system.
5. An enormous hillside park overlooking the French Riviera.
6. Designed by Antonio Spinelli, this central town square in Nice is also known as the Place Garibaldi.

new sort of shyness steal over her, for he was changed, and she couldn't find the merry-faced boy she left, in the moody-looking man beside her. He was handsomer than ever, and greatly improved, she thought; but now that the flush of pleasure at meeting her was over, he looked tired and spiritless—not sick, nor exactly unhappy, but older and graver than a year or two of prosperous life should have made him. She couldn't understand it, and did not venture to ask questions; so she shook her head, and touched up her ponies, as the procession wound away across the arches of the Paglioni bridge, and vanished in the church.

"*Que pensez vous?*"[7] she said, airing her French, which had improved in quantity, if not in quality, since she came abroad.

"That mademoiselle has made good use of her time, and the result is charming," replied Laurie, bowing, with his hand on his heart, and an admiring look.

She blushed with pleasure, but, somehow, the compliment did not satisfy her like the blunt praises he used to give her at home, when he promenaded round her on festival occasions, and told her she was "altogether jolly," with a hearty smile and an approving pat on the head. She didn't like the new tone; for though not *blasé*, it sounded indifferent in spite of the look.

"If that's the way he's going to grow up, I wish he'd stay a boy," she thought, with a curious sense of disappointment and discomfort; trying, meantime, to seem quite easy and gay.

At Avigdor's[8] she found the precious home-letters, and, giving the reins to Laurie, read them luxuriously as they wound up the shady road between green hedges, where tea-roses bloomed as freshly as in June.

"Beth is very poorly, mother says. I often think I ought to go home, but they all say 'stay'; so I do, for I shall never have another chance like this," said Amy, looking sober over one page.

"I think you are right, there; you could do nothing at home, and it is a great comfort to them to know that you are well and happy, and enjoying so much, my dear."

He drew a little nearer, and looked more like his old self, as he said that; and the fear that sometimes weighed on Amy's heart was lightened,—for the look, the act, the brotherly "my dear," seemed to assure her that if any trouble did come, she would not be alone in a strange land. Presently she laughed, and showed him a small sketch of Jo in her scribbling suit, with the bow rampantly erect upon her cap, and issuing from her mouth the words, "Genius burns!"

Laurie smiled, took it, put it in his vest pocket "to keep it from blowing away," and listened with interest to the lively letter Amy read him.

"This will be a regularly merry Christmas to me, with presents in the morning, you and letters in the afternoon, and a party at night," said Amy, as they alighted among the ruins of the old fort, and a flock of splendid peacocks came trooping about them, tamely waiting to be

---

7. What do you think? (French).
8. Although this establishment is unidentified, Avigdor has been a familiar proper name throughout Nice's history.

fed. While Amy stood laughing on the bank above him as she scattered crumbs to the brilliant birds, Laurie looked at her as she had looked at him, with a natural curiosity to see what changes time and absence had wrought. He found nothing to perplex or disappoint, much to admire and approve; for, overlooking a few little affectations of speech and manner, she was as sprightly and graceful as ever, with the addition of that indescribable something in dress and bearing which we call elegance. Always mature for her age, she had gained a certain *aplomb* in both carriage and conversation, which made her seem more of a woman of the world than she was; but her old petulance now and then showed itself, her strong will still held its own, and her native frankness was unspoiled by foreign polish.

Laurie did not read all this while he watched her feed the peacocks, but he saw enough to satisfy and interest him, and carried away a pretty little picture of a bright-faced girl standing in the sunshine, which brought out the soft hue of her dress, the fresh color of her cheeks, the golden gloss of her hair, and made her a prominent figure in the pleasant scene.

As they came up on to the stone plateau that crowns the hill, Amy waved her hand as if welcoming him to her favorite haunt, and said, pointing here and there,—

"Do you remember the Cathedral and the Corso, the fishermen dragging their nets in the bay, and the lovely road to Villa Franca, Schubert's Tower, just below, and, best of all, that speck far out to sea which they say is Corsica?"[9]

"I remember; it's not much changed," he answered, without enthusiasm.

"What Jo would give for a sight of that famous speck!" said Amy, feeling in good spirits, and anxious to see him so also.

"Yes," was all he said, but he turned and strained his eyes to see the island which a greater usurper than even Napoleon now made interesting in his sight.

"Take a good look at it for her sake, and then come and tell me what you have been doing with yourself all this while," said Amy, seating herself, ready for a good talk.

But she did not get it; for, though he joined her, and answered all her questions freely, she could only learn that he had roved about the continent and been to Greece. So, after idling away an hour, they drove home again; and, having paid his respects to Mrs. Carrol, Laurie left them, promising to return in the evening.

It must be recorded of Amy, that she deliberately "prinked" that night. Time and absence had done its work on both the young people; she had seen her old friend in a new light,—not as "our boy," but as a handsome and agreeable man, and she was conscious of a very natural desire to find favor in his sight. Amy knew her good points, and made the most of them, with the taste and skill which is a fortune to a poor and pretty woman.

9. Reference to tourist sights in and around Nice.

Tarlatan and tulle were cheap at Nice, so she enveloped herself in them on such occasions, and, following the sensible English fashion of simple dress for young girls, got up charming little toilettes with fresh flowers, a few trinkets, and all manner of dainty devices, which were both inexpensive and effective. It must be confessed that the artist sometimes got possession of the woman, and indulged in antique *coiffures*, statuesque attitudes, and classic draperies. But, dear heart, we all have our little weaknesses, and find it easy to pardon such in the young, who satisfy our eyes with their comeliness, and keep our hearts merry with their artless vanities.

"I do want him to think I look well, and tell them so at home," said Amy to herself, as she put on Flo's old white silk ball dress, and covered it with a cloud of fresh illusion, out of which her white shoulders and golden head emerged with a most artistic effect. Her hair she had the sense to let alone, after gathering up the thick waves and curls into a Hebe-like knot at the back of her head.

"It's not the fashion, but it's becoming, and I can't afford to make a fright of myself," she used to say, when advised to frizzle, puff, or braid as the latest style commanded.

Having no ornaments fine enough for this important occasion, Amy looped her fleecy skirts with rosy clusters of azalea, and framed the white shoulders in delicate green vines. Remembering the painted boots, she surveyed her white satin slippers with girlish satisfaction, and *chasséd* down the room, admiring her aristocratic feet all by herself.

"My new fan just matches my flowers, my gloves fit to a charm, and the real lace on aunt's *mouchoir* gives an air to my whole dress. If I only had a classical nose and mouth I should be perfectly happy," she said, surveying herself with a critical eye, and a candle in each hand.

In spite of this affliction, she looked unusually gay and graceful as she glided away; she seldom ran,—it did not suit her style, she thought,—for, being tall, the stately and Junoesque was more appropriate than the sportive or piquante. She walked up and down the long saloon while waiting for Laurie, and once arranged herself under the chandelier, which had a good effect upon her hair; then she thought better of it, and went away to the other end of the room,—as if ashamed of the girlish desire to have the first view a propitious one. It so happened that she could not have done a better thing, for Laurie came in so quietly she did not hear him; and, as she stood at the distant window with her head half turned, and one hand gathering up her dress, the slender, white figure against the red curtains was as effective as a well-placed statue.

"Good evening, Diana!"[1] said Laurie, with the look of satisfaction she liked to see in his eyes when they rested on her.

"Good evening, Apollo!"[2] she answered, smiling back at him,—for

---

1. Diana (in Greek mythology known as Artemis) is the goddess of wilderness, the hunt, and fertility. Daughter of Zeus and Leto, she is the twin sister of Apollo.
2. The twin brother of Artemis and leader of the Muses, Apollo is associated with music and the arts; he epitomizes male attractiveness.

he, too, looked unusually *débonnaire*,—and the thought of entering the ball-room on the arm of such a personable man, caused Amy to pity the four plain Misses Davis from the bottom of her heart.

"Here are your flowers! I arranged them myself, remembering that you didn't like what Hannah calls a 'sot-bookay,' " said Laurie, handing her a delicate nosegay, in a holder that she had long coveted as she daily passed it in Cardiglia's window.

"How kind you are!" she exclaimed, gratefully; "if I'd known you were coming I'd have had something ready for you to-day,—though not as pretty as this, I'm afraid."

"Thank you; it isn't what it should be, but you have improved it," he added, as she snapped the silver bracelet on her wrist.

"Please don't!"

"I thought you liked that sort of thing!"

"Not from you; it doesn't sound natural, and I like your old bluntness better."

"I'm glad of it!" he answered, with a look of relief; then buttoned her gloves for her, and asked if his tie was straight, just as he used to do when they went to parties together, at home.

The company assembled in the long *salle a manger*,[3] that evening, was such as one sees nowhere but on the continent. The hospitable Americans had invited every acquaintance they had in Nice, and, having no prejudice against titles, secured a few to add lustre to their Christmas ball.

A Russian prince condescended to sit in a corner for an hour, and talk with a massive lady, dressed like Hamlet's mother, in black velvet, with a pearl bridle under her chin.[4] A Polish count, aged eighteen, devoted himself to the ladies, who pronounced him "a fascinating dear," and a German Serene Something, having come for the supper alone, roamed vaguely about, seeking what he might devour. Baron Rothschild's private secretary, a large-nosed Jew, in tight boots, affably beamed upon the world, as if his master's name crowned him with a golden halo; a stout Frenchman, who knew the Emperor, came to indulge his mania for dancing, and Lady de Jones, a British matron, adorned the scene with her little family of eight. Of course, there were many light-footed, shrill-voiced American girls, handsome, lifeless looking English ditto, and a few plain but piquante French demoiselles. Likewise the usual set of travelling young gentlemen, who disported themselves gaily, while mammas of all nations lined the walls, and smiled upon them benignly when they danced with their daughters.

Any young girl can imagine Amy's state of mind when she "took the stage" that night, leaning on Laurie's arm. She knew she looked well, she loved to dance, she felt that her foot was on her native heath in a

---

3. Dining room.
4. Although Shakespeare does not specify this attire in the stage directions for *Hamlet*, Gertrude may have been costumed in this fashion in some nineteenth-century productions of the tragedy.

ball-room, and enjoyed the delightful sense of power which comes when young girls first discover the new and lovely kingdom they are born to rule by virtue of beauty, youth, and womanhood. She did pity the Davis girls, who were awkward, plain, and destitute of escort—except a grim papa and three grimmer maiden aunts—and she bowed to them in her friendliest manner, as she passed; which was good of her, as it permitted them to see her dress, and burn with curiosity to know who her distinguished-looking friend might be. With the first burst of the band, Amy's color rose, her eyes began to sparkle, and her feet to tap the floor impatiently; for she danced well, and wanted Laurie to know it; therefore, the shock she received can better be imagined than described, when he said, in a perfectly tranquil tone,—

"Do you care to dance?"

"One usually does at a ball!"

Her amazed look and quick answer caused Laurie to repair his error as fast as possible.

"I meant the first dance. May I have the honor?"

"I can give you one if I put off the Count. He dances divinely; but he will excuse me, as you are an old friend," said Amy, hoping that the name would have a good effect, and show Laurie that she was not to be trifled with.

"Nice little boy, but rather a short Pole to support the steps of

> 'A daughter of the gods
> Divinely tall, and most divinely fair,' "[5]

was all the satisfaction she got, however.

The set in which they found themselves was composed of English, and Amy was compelled to walk decorously through a cotillion, feeling all the while as if she could dance the Tarantula[6] with a relish. Laurie resigned her to the "nice little boy," and went to do his duty to Flo, without securing Amy for the joys to come, which reprehensible want of forethought was properly punished, for she immediately engaged herself till supper, meaning to relent if he then gave any sign of penitence. She showed him her ball-book with demure satisfaction when he strolled, instead of rushing, up to claim her for the next, a glorious polka-redowa; but his polite regrets didn't impose upon her, and when she gallopaded away with the Count, she saw Laurie sit down by her aunt, with an actual expression of relief.

That was unpardonable; and Amy took no more notice of him for a long while, except a word now and then, when she came to her chaperon, between the dances, for a necessary pin or a moment's rest. Her anger had a good effect, however, for she hid it under a smiling face, and seemed unusually blithe and brilliant. Laurie's eyes followed her with pleasure, for she neither romped nor sauntered, but danced with spirit and grace, making the delightsome pastime what it should be. He very naturally fell to studying her from this new point of view; and

---

5. See Tennyson, *A Dream of Fair Women* (1833), lines 87–88.
6. "Tarantula" (a large, hairy spider) is substituted for "tarantella," a whirling peasant dance. At one time, dancing the tarantella was believed to be a remedy for being bit by a tarantula.

before the evening was half over, had decided that "little Amy was going to make a very charming woman."

It was a lively scene, for soon the spirit of the social season took
possession of every one, and Christmas merriment made all faces
shine, hearts happy, and heels light. The musicians fiddled, tooted,
and banged as if they enjoyed it; everybody danced who could, and
those who couldn't admired their neighbors with uncommon warmth.
The air was dark with Davises, and many Joneses gambolled like a
flock of young giraffes. The golden secretary darted through the room
like a meteor, with a dashing Frenchwoman, who carpeted the floor
with her pink satin train. The Serene Teuton found the supper-table,
and was happy, eating steadily through the bill of fare, and dismaying
the garçons by the ravages he committed. But the Emperor's friend
covered himself with glory, for he danced *everything*, whether he knew
it or not, and introduced impromptu pirouettes when the figures bewildered him. The boyish abandon of that stout man was charming to
behold; for, though he "carried weight," he danced like an india-
rubber ball. He ran, he flew, he pranced; his face glowed, his bald
head shone, his coat tails waved wildly, his pumps actually twinkled in
the air, and when the music stopped, he wiped the drops from his
brow, and beamed upon his fellow-men like a French Pickwick without glasses.

Amy and her Pole distinguished themselves by equal enthusiasm,
but more graceful agility; and Laurie found himself involuntarily keeping time to the rhythmic rise and fall of the white slippers, as they flew
by, as indefatigably as if winged. When little Vladimir finally relinquished her, with assurances that he was "desolated to leave so early,"
she was ready to rest, and see how her recreant knight had borne his
punishment.

It had been successful; for, at three-and-twenty, blighted affections
find a balm in friendly society, and young nerves will thrill, young
blood dance, and healthy young spirits rise, when subjected to the enchantment of beauty, light, music, and motion. Laurie had a waked-up
look as he rose to give her his seat; and when he hurried away to bring
her some supper, she said to herself, with a satisfied smile,—

"Ah, I thought that would do him good!"

"You look like Balzac's 'Femme piente par elle même,' "[7] he said, as
he fanned her with one hand, and held her coffee-cup in the other.

"My rouge won't come off;" and Amy rubbed her brilliant cheek,
and showed him her white glove, with a sober simplicity that made
him laugh outright.

"What do you call this stuff?" he asked, touching a fold of her dress
that had blown over his knee.

"Illusion."

7. A reference to Honoré de Balzac's story "La Femme comme il faut" (The proper woman),
first published in a multiauthored collection titled *Les Français peints par eux-mêmes* (1839).
Balzac expanded and revised this story into "Autre étude de femme" (Another study of
woman) in *La Comédie humaine* (The human comedy) (1842). Alcott's French spelling errors ("Femme piente par elle même") are corrected in the regular edition ("Femme peinte
par elle-même").

"Good name for it; it's very pretty—new thing, isn't it?"

"It's as old as the hills; you have seen it on dozens of girls, and you never found out that it was pretty till now—*stupide!*"

"I never saw it on you, before, which accounts for the mistake, you see."

"None of that, it is forbidden; I'd rather take coffee than compliments, just now. No, don't lounge, it makes me nervous."

Laurie sat bolt upright, and meekly took her empty plate, feeling an odd sort of pleasure in having "little Amy" order him about; for she had lost her shyness now, and felt an irresistible desire to trample on him, as girls have a delightful way of doing when lords of creation show any signs of subjection.

"Where did you learn all this sort of thing?" he asked, with a quizzical look.

"As 'this sort of thing' is rather a vague expression, would you kindly explain?" returned Amy, knowing perfectly well what he meant, but wickedly leaving him to describe what is indescribable.

"Well—the general air, the style, the self-possession, the—the—illusion—you know," laughed Laurie, breaking down, and helping himself out of his quandary with the new word.

Amy was gratified, but, of course, didn't show it, and demurely answered,—

"Foreign life polishes one in spite of one's self; I study as well as play; and as for this"—with a little gesture toward her dress—"why, tulle is cheap, posies to be had for nothing, and I am used to making the most of my poor little things."

Amy rather regretted that last sentence, fearing it wasn't in good taste; but Laurie liked her the better for it, and found himself both admiring and respecting the brave patience that made the most of opportunity, and the cheerful spirit that covered poverty with flowers. Amy did not know why he looked at her so kindly, nor why he filled up her book with his own name, and devoted himself to her for the rest of the evening, in the most delightful manner; but the impulse that wrought this agreeable change was the result of one of the new impressions which both of them were unconsciously giving and receiving.

CHAPTER XV.

ON THE SHELF.

IN France the young girls have a dull time of it till they are married, when "*Vive la liberté*" becomes their motto. In America, as every one knows, girls early sign a declaration of independence, and enjoy their freedom with republican zest; but the young matrons usually abdicate with the first heir to the throne, and go into a seclusion almost as close as a French nunnery, though by no means as quiet. Whether they like it or not, they are virtually put upon the shelf as soon as the wedding excitement is over, and most of them might exclaim, as did a very pretty woman the other day, "I'm as handsome as ever, but no one takes any notice of me because I'm married."

Not being a belle, or even a fashionable lady, Meg did not experience this affliction till her babies were a year old,—for in her little world primitive customs prevailed, and she found herself more admired and beloved than ever.

As she was a womanly little woman, the maternal instinct was very strong, and she was entirely absorbed in her children, to the utter exclusion of everything and everybody else. Day and night she brooded over them with tireless devotion and anxiety, leaving John to the tender mercies of the help,—for an Irish lady now presided over the kitchen department. Being a domestic man, John decidedly missed the wifely attentions he had been accustomed to receive; but, as he adored his babies, he cheerfully relinquished his comfort for a time, supposing, with masculine ignorance, that peace would soon be restored. But three months passed, and there was no return of repose; Meg looked worn and nervous,—the babies absorbed every minute of her time,— the house was neglected,—and Kitty, the cook, who took life "aisy," kept him on short commons. When he went out in the morning he was bewildered by small commissions for the captive mamma; if he came gaily in at night, eager to embrace his family, he was quenched by a "Hush! they are just asleep after worrying all day." If he proposed a little amusement at home, "No, it would disturb the babies." If he hinted at a lecture or concert, he was answered with a reproachful look, and a decided—"Leave my children for pleasure, never!" His sleep was broken by infant wails and visions of a phantom figure pacing noiselessly to and fro, in the watches of the night; his meals were interrupted by the frequent flight of the presiding genius, who deserted him, half-helped, if a muffled chirp sounded from the nest above; and, when he read his paper of an evening, Demi's colic got into the shipping-list, and Daisy's fall affected the price of stocks,—for Mrs. Brooke was only interested in domestic news.

The poor man was very uncomfortable, for the children had bereft him of his wife; home was merely a nursery, and the perpetual "hushing" made him feel like a brutal intruder whenever he entered the sacred precincts of Babydom. He bore it very patiently for six months, and, when no signs of amendment appeared, he did what other paternal exiles do,—tried to get a little comfort elsewhere. Scott had married and gone to housekeeping not far off, and John fell into the way of running over for an hour or two of an evening, when his own parlor was empty, and his own wife singing lullabies that seemed to have no end. Mrs. Scott was a lively, pretty girl, with nothing to do but be agreeable,—and she performed her mission most successfully. The parlor was always bright and attractive, the chess-board ready, the piano in tune, plenty of gay gossip, and a nice little supper set forth in tempting style.

John would have preferred his own fireside if it had not been so lonely; but as it was, he gratefully took the next best thing, and enjoyed his neighbor's society.

Meg rather approved of the new arrangement at first, and found it a relief to know that John was having a good time instead of dozing in the parlor, or tramping about the house and waking the children. But by and by, when the teething worry was over, and the idols went to sleep at proper hours, leaving mamma time to rest, she began to miss John, and find her work-basket dull company, when he was not sitting opposite in his old dressing-gown, comfortably scorching his slippers on the fender. She would not ask him to stay at home, but felt injured because he did not know that she wanted him without being told,—entirely forgetting the many evenings he had waited for her in vain. She was nervous and worn out with watching and worry, and in that unreasonable frame of mind which the best of mothers occasionally experience when domestic cares oppress them, want of exercise robs them of cheerfulness, and too much devotion to that idol of American women,—the teapot,—makes them feel as if they were all nerve and no muscle.

"Yes," she would say, looking in the glass, "I'm getting old and ugly; John don't find me interesting any longer, so he leaves his faded wife and goes to see his pretty neighbor, who has no incumbrances. Well, the babies love me; they don't care if I am thin and pale, and haven't time to crimp my hair; they are my comfort, and some day John will see what I've gladly sacrificed for them,—won't he, my precious?"

To which pathetic appeal Daisy would answer with a coo, or Demi with a crow, and Meg would put by her lamentations for a maternal revel, which soothed her solitude for the time being. But the pain increased as politics absorbed John, who was always running over to discuss interesting points with Scott, quite unconscious that Meg missed him. Not a word did she say, however, till her mother found her in tears one day, and insisted on knowing what the matter was,—for Meg's drooping spirits had not escaped her observation.

"I wouldn't tell any one except you, mother; but I really do need advice, for, if John goes on so much longer I might as well be a widow," replied Mrs. Brooke, drying her tears on Daisy's bib, with an injured air.

"Goes on how, my dear?" asked her mother, anxiously.

"He's away all day, and at night, when I want to see him, he is continually going over to the Scotts'. It isn't fair that I should have the hardest work, and never any amusement. Men are very selfish, even the best of them."

"So are women; don't blame John till you see where you are wrong yourself."

"But it can't be right for him to neglect me."

"Don't you neglect him?"

"Why, mother; I thought you'd take my part!"

"So I do as far as sympathizing goes; but I think the fault is yours, Meg."

"I don't see how."

"Let me show you. Did John ever neglect you, as you call it, while you made it a point to give him your society of an evening,—his only leisure time?"

"No; but I can't do it now, with two babies to tend."

"I think you could, dear; and I think you ought. May I speak quite freely, and will you remember that it's mother who blames as well as mother who sympathizes?"

"Indeed I will! speak to me as if I was little Meg again. I often feel as if I needed teaching more than ever, since these babies look to me for everything."

Meg drew her low chair beside her mother's, and, with a little interruption in either lap, the two women rocked and talked lovingly together, feeling that the tie of motherhood made them more one than ever.

"You have only made the mistake that most young wives make,—forgotten your duty to your husband in your love for your children. A very natural and forgivable mistake, Meg, but one that had better be remedied before you take to different ways; for children should draw you nearer than ever, not separate you,—as if they were all yours, and John had nothing to do but support them. I've seen it for some weeks, but have not spoken, feeling sure it would come right, in time."

"I'm afraid it won't. If I ask him to stay he'll think I'm jealous; and I wouldn't insult him by such an idea. He don't see that I want him, and I don't know how to tell him without words."

"Make it so pleasant he won't want to go away. My dear, he's longing for his little home; but it isn't home without you, and you are always in the nursery."

"Oughtn't I to be there?"

"Not all the time; too much confinement makes you nervous, and then you are unfitted for everything. Besides, you owe something to John as well as to the babies; don't neglect husband for children,— don't shut him out of the nursery, but teach him how to help in it. His place is there as well as yours, and the children need him; let him feel that he has his part to do, and he will do it gladly and faithfully, and it will be better for you all."

"You really think so, mother?"

"I know it, Meg, for I've tried it; and I seldom give advice unless I've proved its practicability. When you and Jo were little, I went on just as you do, feeling as if I didn't do my duty unless I devoted myself wholly to you. Poor father took to his books, after I had refused all offers of help, and left me to try my experiment alone. I struggled along as well as I could, but Jo was too much for me. I nearly spoilt her by indulgence. You were poorly, and I worried about you till I fell sick myself. Then father came to the rescue, quietly managed everything, and made himself so helpful that I saw my mistake, and never have been able to get on without him since. That is the secret of our home happiness; he does not let business wean him from the little cares and duties that affect us all, and I try not to let domestic worries destroy my interest in his pursuits. Each do our part alone in many things, but at home we work together, always."

"It is so, mother; and my great wish is to be to my husband and children what you have been to yours. Show me how; I'll do anything you say."

"You always were my docile daughter. Well, dear, if I were you I'd let John have more to do with the management of Demi,—for the boy needs training, and it's none too soon to begin. Then I'd do what I have often proposed,—let Hannah come and help you; she is a capital nurse, and you may trust the precious babies to her while you do more housework. You need the exercise, Hannah would enjoy the rest, and John would find his wife again. Go out more; keep cheerful as well as busy,— for you are the sunshine-maker of the family, and if you get dismal there is no fair weather. Then I'd try to take an interest in whatever John likes, talk with him, let him read to you, exchange ideas, and help each other in that way. Don't shut yourself up in a bandbox because you are a woman, but understand what is going on, and educate yourself to take your part in the world's work, for it all affects you and yours."

"John is so sensible, I'm afraid he will think I'm stupid if I ask questions about politics and things."

"I don't believe he would; love covers a multitude of sins, and of whom could you ask more freely than of him? Try it, and see if he doesn't find your society far more agreeable than Mrs. Scott's suppers."

"I will. Poor John! I'm afraid I *have* neglected him sadly, but I thought I was right, and he never said anything."

"He tried not to be selfish, but he *has* felt rather forlorn, I fancy. This is just the time, Meg, when young married people are apt to grow apart, and the very time when they ought to be most together; for the first tenderness soon wears off, unless care is taken to preserve it; and no time is so beautiful and precious to parents, as the first years of the little lives given them to train. Don't let John be a stranger to the babies, for they will do more to keep him safe and happy in this world of trial and temptation, than anything else, and through them you will learn to know and love one another as you should. Now, dear, good-by; think over mother's preachment, act upon it if it seems good, and God bless you all!"

Meg did think it over, found it good, and acted upon it, though the first attempt was not made exactly as she planned to have it. Of course, the children tyrannized over her, and ruled the house as soon as they found out that kicking and squalling brought them whatever they wanted. Mamma was an abject slave to their caprices, but papa was not so easily subjugated, and occasionally afflicted his tender spouse, by an attempt at paternal discipline with his obstreperous son. For Demi inherited a trifle of his sire's firmness of character—we won't call it obstinacy—and when he made up his little mind to have or to do anything, all the king's horses, and all the king's men could not change that pertinacious little mind.[8] Mamma thought the dear too young to be taught to conquer his prejudices, but papa believed

8. See p. 169, n. 5 (part 1, chap. 21).

that it never was too soon to learn obedience; so Master Demi early discovered, that when he undertook to "wrastle" with "parpar," he always got the worst of it; yet, like the Englishman, Baby respected the man who conquered him, and loved the father, whose grave, "No, no" was more impressive than all the mother's love pats.

A few days after the talk with her mother, Meg resolved to try a social evening with John; so she ordered a nice supper, set the parlor in order, dressed herself prettily, and put the children to bed early, that nothing should interfere with her experiment. But, unfortunately, Demi's most unconquerable prejudice was against going to bed, and that night he decided to go on a rampage; so poor Meg sung and rocked, told stories, and tried every sleep-provoking wile she could devise, but all in vain—the big eyes wouldn't shut; and long after Daisy had gone to byelow,[9] like the chubby little bunch of good nature she was, naughty Demi lay staring at the light, with the most discouragingly wide-awake expression of countenance.

"Will Demi lie still, like a good boy, while mamma runs down and gives poor papa his tea?" asked Meg, as the hall door softly closed, and the well-known step went tip-toeing into the dining-room.

"Me has tea!" said Demi, preparing to join in the revel.

"No; but I'll save you some little cakies for breakfast, if you'll go bye-bye, like Daisy. Will you, lovey?"

"Iss!" and Demi shut his eyes tight, as if to catch sleep, and hurry the desired day.

Taking advantage of the propitious moment, Meg slipped away, and ran down to greet her husband with a smiling face, and the little blue bow in her hair, which was his especial admiration. He saw it at once, and said, with pleased surprise,—

"Why, little mother, how gay we are to-night. Do you expect company?"

"Only you, dear."

"Is it a birthday, anniversary, or anything?"

"No; I'm tired of being a dowdy, so I dressed up as a change. You always make yourself nice for table, no matter how tired you are; so, why shouldn't I, when I have the time?"

"I do it out of respect to you, my dear," said old-fashioned John.

"Ditto, ditto, Mr. Brooke," laughed Meg, looking young and pretty again, as she nodded to him over the teapot.

"Well, it's altogether delightful, and like old times. This tastes right; I drink your health, dear!" and John sipped his tea with an air of reposeful rapture, which was of very short duration, however; for, as he put down his cup, the door-handle rattled mysteriously, and a little voice was heard, saying, impatiently,—

"Opy doy; me's tummin!"

"It's that naughty boy; I told him to go to sleep alone, and here he is, down stairs, getting his death a-cold pattering over that canvas," said Meg, answering the call.

9. A way of saying good-bye.

"Mornin' now," announced Demi, in a joyful tone, as he entered, with his long night-gown gracefully festooned over his arm, and every curl bobbing gaily, as he pranced about the table, eyeing the "cakies" with loving glances.

"No, it isn't morning yet; you must go to bed, and not trouble poor mamma; then you can have the little cake with sugar on it."

"Me loves parpar," said the artful one, preparing to climb the paternal knee, and revel in forbidden joys. But John shook his head, and said to Meg,—

"If you told him to stay up there, and go to sleep alone, make him do it, or he will never learn to mind you."

"Yes, of course; come, Demi!" and Meg led her son away, feeling a strong desire to spank the little marplot who hopped beside her, laboring under the delusion that the bribe was to be administered as soon as they reached the nursery.

Nor was he disappointed; for that short-sighted woman actually gave him a lump of sugar, tucked him into his bed, and forbade any more promenades till morning.

"Iss!" said Demi the perjured, blissfully sucking his sugar, and regarding his first attempt as eminently successful.

Meg returned to her place, and supper was progressing pleasantly, when the little ghost walked again, and exposed the maternal delinquencies, by boldly demanding,—

"More sudar, marmar."

"Now this won't do," said John, hardening his heart against the engaging little sinner. "We shall never know any peace till that child learns to go to bed properly. You have made a slave of yourself long enough; give him one lesson, and then there will be an end of it. Put him in his bed, and leave him, Meg."

"He won't stay there; he never does, unless I sit by him."

"I'll manage him. Demi, go upstairs, and get into your bed, as mamma bids you."

"S'ant!" replied the young rebel, helping himself to the coveted "cakie," and beginning to eat the same with calm audacity.

"You must never say that to papa; I shall carry you if you don't go yourself."

"Go 'way; me don't love parpar;" and Demi retired to his mother's skirts for protection.

But even that refuge proved unavailing, for he was delivered over to the enemy, with a "Be gentle with him, John," which struck the culprit with dismay; for when mamma deserted him, then the judgment-day was at hand. Bereft of his cake, defrauded of his frolic, and borne away by a strong hand to that detested bed, poor Demi could not restrain his wrath, but openly defied papa, and kicked and screamed lustily all the way upstairs. The minute he was put into bed on one side, he rolled out at the other, and made for the door, only to be ignominiously caught up by the tail of his little toga, and put back again, which lively performance was kept up till the young man's strength gave out, when he devoted himself to roaring at the top of his voice.

This vocal exercise usually conquered Meg; but John sat as unmoved as the post, which is popularly believed to be deaf. No coaxing, no sugar, no lullaby, no story—even the light was put out, and only the red glow of the fire enlivened the "big dark" which Demi regarded with curiosity rather than fear. This new order of things disgusted him, and he howled dismally for "marmar," as his angry passions subsided, and recollections of his tender bond-woman returned to the captive autocrat. The plaintive wail which succeeded the passionate roar went to Meg's heart, and she ran up to say, beseechingly,—

"Let me stay with him; he'll be good, now, John."

"No, my dear, I've told him he must go to sleep, as you bid him; and he must, if I stay here all night."

"But he'll cry himself sick," pleaded Meg, reproaching herself for deserting her boy.

"No he won't, he's so tired he will soon drop off, and then the matter is settled; for he will understand that he has got to mind. Don't interfere; I'll manage him."

"He's my child, and I can't have his spirit broken by harshness."

"He's my child, and I won't have his temper spoilt by indulgence. Go down, my dear, and leave the boy to me."

When John spoke in that masterful tone, Meg always obeyed, and never regretted her docility.

"Please let me kiss him once, John?"

"Certainly; Demi, say 'good-night' to mamma, and let her go and rest, for she is very tired with taking care of you all day."

Meg always insisted upon it, that the kiss won the victory; for, after it was given, Demi sobbed more quietly, and lay quite still at the bottom of the bed, whither he had wriggled in his anguish of mind.

"Poor little man! he's worn out with sleep and crying; I'll cover him up, and then go and set Meg's heart at rest," thought John, creeping to the bedside, hoping to find his rebellious heir asleep.

But he wasn't; for the moment his father peeped at him, Demi's eyes opened, his little chin began to quiver, and he put up his arms, saying, with a penitent hiccough, "Me's dood, now."

Sitting on the stairs, outside, Meg wondered at the long silence which followed the uproar; and, after imagining all sorts of impossible accidents, she slipped into the room, to set her fears at rest. Demi lay fast asleep; not in his usual spread-eagle attitude, but in a subdued bunch, cuddled close in the circle of his father's arm, and holding his father's finger, as if he felt that justice was tempered with mercy, and had gone to sleep a sadder and a wiser baby. So held, John had waited with womanly patience till the little hand relaxed its hold; and, while waiting, had fallen asleep, more tired by that tussle with his little son than with his whole day's work.

As Meg stood watching the two faces on the pillow, she smiled to herself, and then slipped away again, saying, in a satisfied tone,—

"I never need fear that John will be too harsh with my babies, he *does* know how to manage them, and will be a great help, for Demi *is* getting too much for me."

When John came down at last, expecting to find a pensive or re-proachful wife, he was agreeably surprised to find Meg placidly trim-ming a bonnet, and to be greeted with the request to read something about the election, if he was not too tired. John saw in a minute that a revolution of some kind was going on, but wisely asked no questions, knowing that Meg was such a transparent little person, she couldn't keep a secret to save her life, and therefore the clue would soon ap-pear. He read a long debate with the most amiable readiness, and then explained it in his most lucid manner, while Meg tried to look deeply interested, to ask intelligent questions, and keep her thoughts from wandering from the state of the nation to the state of her bonnet. In her secret soul, however, she decided that politics were as bad as mathematics, and that the mission of politicians seemed to be calling each other names; but she kept these feminine ideas to herself, and when John paused, shook her head, and said with what she thought diplomatic ambiguity,—

"Well, I really don't see what we are coming to."

John laughed, and watched her for a minute, as she poised a pretty little preparation of tulle and flowers on her hand, and regarded it with the genuine interest which his harangue had failed to waken.

"She is trying to like politics for my sake, so I'll try and like millinery for hers—that's only fair," thought John the just, adding aloud,—

"That's very pretty; is it what you call a breakfast cap?"

"My dear man, it's a bonnet—my very best go-to-concert and the-atre bonnet!"

"I beg your pardon; it was so very small, I naturally mistook it for one of the fly-away things you sometimes wear. How do you keep it on?"

"These bits of lace are fastened under the chin, with a rose-bud, so"—and Meg illustrated by putting on the bonnet, and regarding him with an air of calm satisfaction, that was irresistible.

"It's a love of a bonnet, but I prefer the face inside, for it looks young and happy again," and John kissed the smiling face, to the great detriment of the rose-bud under the chin.

"I'm glad you like it, for I want you to take me to one of the new concerts some night; I really need some music to put me in tune. Will you, please?"

"Of course I will, with all my heart, or anywhere else you like. You have been shut up so long, it will do you no end of good, and I shall enjoy it, of all things. What put it into your head, little mother?"

"Well, I had a talk with Marmee the other day, and told her how nervous, and cross, and out of sorts I felt, and she said I needed change, and less care; so Hannah is to help me with the children, and I'm to see to things about the house more, and now and then have a little fun, just to keep me from getting to be a fidgety, broken-down old woman before my time. It's only an experiment, John, and I want to try it for your sake, as much as for mine, because I've neglected you shamefully lately, and I'm going to make home what it used to be, if I can. You don't object, I hope?"

Never mind what John said, or what a very narrow escape the little bonnet had from utter ruin; all that we have any business to know, is that John did *not* appear to object, judging from the changes which gradually took place in the house and its inmates. It was not all Paradise by any means, but every one was better for the division of labor system; the children throve under the paternal rule, for accurate, steadfast John brought order and obedience into Babydom, while Meg recovered her spirits, and composed her nerves, by plenty of wholesome exercise, a little pleasure, and much confidential conversation with her sensible husband. Home grew home-like again, and John had no wish to leave it, unless he took Meg with him. The Scotts came to the Brookes now, and every one found the little house a cheerful place, full of happiness, content, and family love; even gay Sallie Moffat liked to go there. "It is always so quiet and pleasant here; it does me good, Meg," she used to say, looking about her with wistful eyes, as if trying to discover the charm, that she might use it in her great house, full of splendid loneliness, for there were no riotous, sunny-faced babies there, and Ned lived in a world of his own, where there was no place for her.

This household happiness did not come all at once, but John and Meg had found the key to it, and each year of married life taught them how to use it, unlocking the treasuries of real home-love and mutual helpfulness, which the poorest may possess, and the richest cannot buy. This is the sort of shelf on which young wives and mothers may consent to be laid, safe from the restless fret and fever of the world, finding loyal lovers in the little sons and daughters who cling to them, undaunted by sorrow, poverty, or age; walking side by side, through fair and stormy weather, with a faithful friend, who is, in the true sense of the good old Saxon word, the "house-band,"[1] and learning, as Meg learned, that a woman's happiest kingdom is home, her highest honor the art of ruling it—not as a queen, but a wise wife and mother.

CHAPTER XVI.

LAZY LAURENCE.

LAURIE went to Nice intending to stay a week, and remained a month. He was tired of wandering about alone, and Amy's familiar presence seemed to give a home-like charm to the foreign scenes in which she bore a part. He rather missed the "munching"[2] he used to receive, and enjoyed a taste of it again,—for no attentions, however flattering, from strangers, were half so pleasant as the sisterly adoration of the girls at home. Amy never would pet him like the others, but she was very glad to see him now, and quite clung to him,—feeling that he was the rep-

---

1. From "húsbonda" (Old English), the master of a house.
2. A shortening of the phrase "Making much of"—as in, Laurie enjoyed being made much of.

resentative of the dear family for whom she longed more than she would confess. They naturally took comfort in each other's society, and were much together,—riding, walking, dancing, or dawdling,—for, at Nice, no one can be very industrious during the gay season. But, while apparently amusing themselves in the most careless fashion, they were half-consciously making discoveries and forming opinions about each other. Amy rose daily in the estimation of her friend, but he sunk in hers, and each felt the truth before a word was spoken. Amy tried to please, and succeeded,—for she was grateful for the many pleasures he gave her, and repaid him with the little services to which womanly women know how to lend an indescribable charm. Laurie made no effort of any kind, but just let himself drift along as comfortably as possible, trying to forget, and feeling that all women owed him a kind word because one had been cold to him. It cost him no effort to be generous, and he would have given Amy all the trinkets in Nice if she would have taken them,—but, at the same time, he felt that he could not change the opinion she was forming of him, and he rather dreaded the keen blue eyes that seemed to watch him with such half-sorrowful, half-scornful surprise.

"All the rest have gone to Monaco for the day; I preferred to stay at home and write letters. They are done now, and I am going to Valrosa[3] to sketch; will you come?" said Amy, as she joined Laurie one lovely day when he lounged in as usual, about noon.

"Well, yes; but isn't it rather warm for such a long walk?" he answered slowly,—for the shaded *salon* looked inviting, after the glare without.

"I'm going to have the little carriage, and Baptiste can drive,—so you'll have nothing to do but hold your umbrella and keep your gloves nice," returned Amy, with a sarcastic glance at the immaculate kids, which were a weak point with Laurie.

"Then I'll go with pleasure," and he put out his hand for her sketchbook. But she tucked it under her arm with a sharp—

"Don't trouble yourself; it's no exertion to me, but *you* don't look equal to it."

Laurie lifted his eyebrows, and followed at a leisurely pace as she ran down stairs; but when they got into the carriage he took the reins himself, and left little Baptiste nothing to do but fold his arms and fall asleep on his perch.

The two never quarrelled; Amy was too well-bred, and just now Laurie was too lazy; so, in a minute he peeped under her hat-brim with an inquiring air; she answered with a smile, and they went on together in the most amicable manner.

It was a lovely drive, along winding roads rich in the picturesque scenes that delight beauty-loving eyes. Here an ancient monastery, whence the solemn chanting of the monks came down to them. There a bare-legged shepherd, in wooden shoes, pointed hat, and rough jacket over one shoulder, sat piping on a stone, while his goats skipped

---

3. Valrosa was an estate outside of Nice. See *Journals*, 150.

among the rocks or lay at his feet. Meek, mouse-colored donkeys, laden with panniers of freshly-cut grass, passed by, with a pretty girl in a *capaline*[4] sitting between the green piles, or an old woman spinning with a distaff as she went. Brown, soft-eyed children ran out from the quaint stone hovels to offer nosegays, or bunches of oranges still on the bough. Gnarled olive-trees covered the hills with their dusky foliage, fruit hung golden in the orchard, and great scarlet anemones fringed the roadside; while beyond green slopes and craggy heights, the Maritime Alps rose sharp and white against the blue Italian sky.

Valrosa well deserved its name,—for in that climate of perpetual summer roses blossomed everywhere. They overhung the archway, thrust themselves between the bars of the great gate with a sweet welcome to passers-by, and lined the avenue, winding through lemon-trees and feathery palms up to the villa on the hill. Every shadowy nook, where seats invited one to stop and rest, was a mass of bloom; every cool grotto had its marble nymph smiling from a veil of flowers; and every fountain reflected crimson, white, or pale pink roses, leaning down to smile at their own beauty. Roses covered the walls of the house, draped the cornices, climbed the pillars, and ran riot over the balustrade of the wide terrace, whence one looked down on the sunny Mediterranean and the white-walled city on its shore.

"This is a regular honey-moon Paradise, isn't it? Did you ever see such roses?" asked Amy, pausing on the terrace to enjoy the view, and a luxurious whiff of perfume that came wandering by.

"No, nor felt such thorns," returned Laurie, with his thumb in his mouth, after a vain attempt to capture a solitary scarlet flower that grew just beyond his reach.

"Try lower down, and pick those that have no thorns," said Amy, deftly gathering three of the tiny cream-colored ones that starred the wall behind her. She put them in his button-hole, as a peace-offering, and he stood a minute looking down at them with a curious expression, for in the Italian part of his nature there was a touch of superstition, and he was just then in that state of half-sweet, half-bitter melancholy, when imaginative young men find significance in trifles, and food for romance everywhere. He had thought of Jo in reaching after the thorny red rose,—for vivid flowers became her,—and she had often worn ones like that, from the green-house at home. The pale roses Amy gave him were the sort that the Italians lay in dead hands,—never in bridal wreaths,—and, for a moment, he wondered if the omen was for Jo or for himself. But the next instant his American common-sense got the better sentimentality, and he laughed a heartier laugh than Amy had heard since he came.

"It's good advice,—you'd better take it and save your fingers," she said, thinking her speech amused him.

"Thank you, I will!" he answered in jest,—and a few months later he did it in earnest.

---

4. Probably *capelina* or *capellina* (Spanish), the first a rustic, wide-brimmed straw hat worn by women, and the second a large scarf or cape worn by women over the head as a hood or bonnet.

"Laurie, when are you going to your grandfather?" she asked, presently, as she settled herself on a rustic seat.

"Very soon."

"You have said that a dozen times within the last three weeks."

"I dare say; short answers save trouble."

"He expects you, and you really ought to go."

"Hospitable creature! I know it."

"Then why don't you do it?"

"Natural depravity, I suppose."

"Natural indolence, you mean. It's really dreadful!" and Amy looked severe.

"Not so bad as it seems, for I should only plague him if I went, so I might as well stay, and plague you a little longer—you can bear it better; in fact, I think it agrees with you excellently!" and Laurie composed himself for a lounge on the broad ledge of the balustrade.

Amy shook her head, and opened her sketch-book with an air of resignation, but she had made up her mind to lecture "that boy," and in a minute she began again.

"What are you doing just now?"

"Watching lizards."

"No, no! I mean what do you intend, and wish to do?"

"Smoke a cigarette, if you'll allow me."

"How provoking you are! I don't approve of cigars, and I will only allow it on condition that you let me put you into my sketch; I need a figure."

"With all the pleasure in life. How will you have me? full-length, or three-quarters; on my head or my heels? I should respectfully suggest a recumbent posture, then put yourself in also, and call it, 'Dolce far niente.' "[5]

"Stay as you are, and go to sleep if you like. I intend to work hard," said Amy, in her most energetic tone.

"What delightful enthusiasm!" and he leaned against a tall urn, with an air of entire satisfaction.

"What would Jo say if she saw you now?" asked Amy impatiently, hoping to stir him up by the mention of her still more energetic sister's name.

"As usual: 'Go away, Teddy, I'm busy'!" He laughed as he spoke, but the laugh was not natural, and a shade passed over his face, for the utterance of the familiar name touched the wound that was not healed yet. Both tone and shadow struck Amy, for she had seen and heard them before, and now she looked up in time to catch a new expression on Laurie's face—a hard, bitter look, full of pain, dissatisfaction and regret. It was gone before she could study it, and the listless expression back again. She watched him for a moment with artistic pleasure, thinking how like an Italian he looked, as he lay basking in the sun, with uncovered head, and eyes full of Southern dreaminess; for he seemed to have forgotten her, and fallen into a reverie.

5. Delightful idleness (Italian).

"You look like the effigy of a young knight asleep on his tomb," she said, carefully tracing the well-cut profile defined against the dark stone.

"Wish I was!"

"That's a foolish wish, unless you have spoilt your life. You are so changed I sometimes think—" there Amy stopped with a half-timid, half-wistful look, more significant than her unfinished speech.

Laurie saw and understood the affectionate anxiety which she hesitated to express, and looking straight into her eyes, said, just as he used to say it to her mother,—

"It's all right, ma'am!"

That satisfied her, and set at rest the doubts that had began to worry her lately. It also touched her, and she showed that it did, by the cordial tone in which she said,—

"I'm glad of that! I didn't think you'd been a very bad boy, but I fancied you might have wasted money at that wicked Baden-Baden, lost your heart to some charming Frenchwoman with a husband, or got into some of the scrapes that young men seem to consider a necessary part of a foreign tour. Don't stay out there in the sun, come and lie on the grass here, and 'let us be friendly,' as Jo used to say when we got in the sofa-corner and told secrets."

Laurie obediently threw himself down on the turf, and began to amuse himself by sticking daisies into the ribbons of Amy's hat, that lay there.

"I'm all ready for the secrets," and he glanced up with a decided expression of interest in his eyes.

"I've none to tell; you may begin."

"Haven't one to bless myself with. I thought perhaps you'd had some news from home."

"You have heard all that has come lately. Don't you hear often? I fancied Jo would send you volumes."

"She's very busy; I'm roving about so, it's impossible to be regular, you know. When do you begin your great work of art, Raphaella?" he asked, changing the subject abruptly after another pause, in which he had been wondering if Amy knew his secret, and wanted to talk about it.

"Never!" she answered, with a despondent, but decided air. "Rome took all the vanity out of me, for after seeing the wonders there, I felt too insignificant to live, and gave up all my foolish hopes in despair."

"Why should you, with so much energy and talent?"

"That's just why, because talent isn't genius, and no amount of energy can make it so. I want to be great, or nothing. I won't be a common-place dauber, so I don't intend to try any more."

"And what are you going to do with yourself now, if I may ask?"

"Polish up my other talents, and be an ornament to society, if I get the chance."

It was a characteristic speech, and sounded daring; but audacity becomes young people, and Amy's ambition had a good foundation. Laurie smiled, but he liked the spirit with which she took up a new purpose, when a long cherished one died, and spent no time lamenting.

"Good! and here is where Fred Vaughn comes in, I fancy."

Amy preserved a discreet silence, but there was a conscious look in her downcast face, that made Laurie sit up and say gravely,—

"Now I'm going to play brother, and ask questions. May I?"

"I don't promise to answer."

"Your face will, if your tongue don't. You aren't woman of the world enough yet to hide your feelings, my dear. I've heard rumors about Fred and you last year, and it's my private opinion, that if he had not been called home so suddenly, and detained so long, that something would have come of it—hey?"

"That's not for me to say," was Amy's prim reply; but her lips would smile, and there was a traitorous sparkle of the eye, which betrayed that she knew her power and enjoyed the knowledge.

"You are not engaged, I hope?" and Laurie looked very elder-brotherly and grave all of a sudden.

"No."

"But you will be, if he comes back and goes properly down upon his knees, won't you?"

"Very likely."

"Then you are fond of old Fred?"

"I could be if I tried."

"But you don't intend to try till the proper moment? Bless my soul, what unearthly prudence! He's a good fellow, Amy, but not the man I fancied you'd like."

"He is rich, a gentleman, and has delightful manners,"—began Amy, trying to be quite cool and dignified, but feeling a little ashamed of herself, in spite of the sincerity of her intentions.

"I understand—queens of society can't get on without money, so you mean to make a good match and start in that way? Quite right and proper as the world goes, but it sounds odd from the lips of one of your mother's girls."

"True, nevertheless!"

A short speech, but the quiet decision with which it was uttered, contrasted curiously with the young speaker. Laurie felt this instinctively, and laid himself down again, with a sense of disappointment which he could not explain. His look and silence, as well as a certain inward self-disapproval, ruffled Amy—and made her resolve to deliver her lecture without delay.

"I wish you'd do me the favor to rouse yourself a little," she said sharply.

"Do it for me, there's a dear girl!"

"I could if I tried," and she looked as if she would like doing it in the most summary style.

"Try then, I give you leave," returned Laurie, who enjoyed having some one to tease, after his long abstinence from his favorite pastime.

"You'd be angry in five minutes."

"I'm never angry with you. It takes two flints to make a fire; you are as cool and soft as snow."

"You don't know what I can do—snow produces a glow and a tingle, if applied rightly. Your indifference is half affectation, and a good stirring up would prove it."

"Stir away, it won't hurt me, and it may amuse you, as the big man said when his little wife beat him. Regard me in the light of a husband or a carpet, and beat till you are tired, if that sort of exercise agrees with you."

Being decidedly nettled herself, and longing to see him shake off the apathy that so altered him, Amy sharpened both tongue and pencil, and began,—

"Flo and I have got a new name for you; it's 'Lazy Laurence';[6] how do you like it?"

She thought it would annoy him, but he only folded his arms under his head, with an imperturbable—"That's not bad! thank you, ladies."

"Do you want to know what I honestly think of you?"

"Pining to be told."

"Well, I despise you."

If she had even said "I hate you," in a petulant or coquettish tone, he would have laughed, and rather liked it; but the grave, almost sad accent of her voice, made him open his eyes, and ask quickly,—

"Why, if you please?"

"Because with every chance for being good, useful and happy, you are faulty, lazy and miserable."

"Strong language, mademoiselle."

"If you like it, I'll go on."

"Pray do, it's quite interesting."

"I thought you'd find it so; selfish people always like to talk about themselves."

"Am *I* selfish?" the question slipped out involuntarily, and in a tone of surprise, for the one virtue on which he prided himself was generosity.

"Yes, very selfish," continued Amy, in a calm, cool voice, twice as effective, just then, as an angry one. "I'll show you how, for I've studied you while we have been frolicking, and I'm not at all satisfied with you. Here you have been abroad nearly six months, and done nothing but waste time and money, and disappoint your friends."

"Isn't a fellow to have any pleasure after a four-years' grind?"

"You don't look as if you'd had much; at any rate you are none the better for it, as far as I can see. I said when we first met, that you had improved; now I take it all back, for I don't think you half so nice as when I left you at home. You have grown abominably lazy, you like gossip, and waste time on frivolous things; you are contented to be petted and admired by silly people, instead of being loved and respected by wise ones. With money, talent, position, health, and beauty,—ah, you

6. Short story by Edgeworth published in *The Parent's Assistant* (1800).

like that, old vanity! but it's the truth, so I can't help saying it,—with all these splendid things to use and enjoy, you can find nothing to do but dawdle, and instead of being the man you might and ought to be, you are only—" there she stopped, with a look that had both pain and pity in it.

"Saint Laurence on a gridiron,"[7] added Laurie, blandly finishing the sentence. But the lecture began to take effect, for there was a wide-awake sparkle in his eyes now, and a half-angry, half-injured expression replaced the former indifference.

"I supposed you'd take it so. You men tell us we are angels, and say we can make you what we will; but the instant we honestly try to do you good, you laugh at us, and won't listen, which proves how much your flattery is worth." Amy spoke bitterly, and turned her back on the exasperating martyr at her feet.

In a minute a hand came down over the page, so that she could not draw, and Laurie's voice said, with a droll imitation of a penitent child,—

"I will be good! oh, I will be good!"

But Amy did not laugh, for she was in earnest; and, tapping on the outspread hand with her pencil, said soberly,—

"Aren't you ashamed of a hand like that? It's as soft and white as a woman's, and looks as if it never did anything but wear Jouvin's best gloves,[8] and pick flowers for ladies. You are not a dandy, thank heaven! so I'm glad to see there are no diamonds or big seal rings on it, only the little old one Jo gave you so long ago. Dear soul! I wish she was here to help me."

"So do I!"

The hand vanished as suddenly as it came, and there was energy enough in the echo of her wish to suit even Amy. She glanced down at him with a new thought in her mind,—but he was lying with his hat half over his face, as if for shade, and his mustache hid his mouth. She only saw his chest rise and fall, with a long breath that might have been a sigh, and the hand that wore the ring nestle down into the grass, as if to hide something too precious or too tender to be spoken of. All in a minute various hints and trifles assumed shape and significance in Amy's mind, and told her what her sister never had confided to her. She remembered that Laurie never spoke voluntarily of Jo; she recalled the shadow on his face just now, the change in his character, and the wearing of the little old ring, which was no ornament to a handsome hand. Girls are quick to read such signs, and feel their eloquence; Amy had fancied that perhaps a love-trouble was at the bottom of the alteration, and now she was sure of it; her keen eyes filled, and, when she spoke again, it was in a voice that could be beautifully soft and kind when she chose to make it so.

"I know I have no right to talk so to you, Laurie; and if you weren't

---

7. Saint Lawrence was martyred in Rome on 10 August 258, according to oral tradition, by burning on an iron gridwork.
8. Xavier Jouvin (1800–1844), a French master glover who in 1834 originated a new way of cutting and sizing gloves in order to produce a closer fit.

the sweetest-tempered fellow in the world, you'd be very angry with me. But we are all so fond and proud of you, I couldn't bear to think they should be disappointed in you at home as I have been,—though perhaps they would understand the change better than I do."

"I think they would," came from under the hat, in a grim tone, quite as touching as a broken one.

"They ought to have told me, and not let me go blundering and scolding, when I should have been more kind and patient than ever. I never did like that Miss Randal, and now I hate her!" said artful Amy,—wishing to be sure of her facts this time.

"Hang Miss Randal!" and Laurie knocked the hat off his face with a look that left no doubt of his sentiments toward that young lady.

"I beg pardon; I thought—" and there she paused diplomatically.

"No, you didn't; you knew perfectly well I never cared for any one but Jo." Laurie said that in his old, impetuous tone, and turned his face away as he spoke.

"I did think so; but as they never said anything about it, and you came away, I supposed I was mistaken. And Jo wouldn't be kind to you? Why, I was sure she loved you dearly."

"She *was* kind, but not in the right way; and it's lucky for her she didn't love me, if I'm the good-for-nothing fellow you think me. It's her fault, though, and you may tell her so."

The hard, bitter look came back again as he said that, and it troubled Amy, for she did not know what balm to apply.

"I was wrong; I didn't know; I'm very sorry I was so cross, but I can't help wishing you'd bear it better, Teddy, dear."

"Don't! that's her name for me," and Laurie put up his hand with a quick gesture to stop the words spoken in Jo's half-kind, half-reproachful tone. "Wait till you've tried it yourself," he added, in a low voice, as he pulled up the grass by the handful.

"I'd take it manfully, and be respected if I couldn't be loved," cried Amy, with the decision of one who knew nothing about it.

Now Laurie flattered himself that he *had* borne it remarkably well,—making no moan, asking no sympathy, and taking his trouble away to live it down alone. Amy's lecture put the matter in a new light, and for the first time it did look weak and selfish to lose heart at the first failure, and shut himself up in moody indifference. He felt as if suddenly shaken out of a pensive dream, and found it impossible to go to sleep again. Presently he sat up, and asked, slowly,—

"Do you think Jo would despise me as you do?"

"Yes, if she saw you now. She hates lazy people. Why don't you do something splendid, and *make* her love you?"

"I did my best, but it was no use."

"Graduating well, you mean? That was no more than you ought to have done, for your grandfather's sake. It would have been shameful to fail after spending so much time and money, when every one knew you *could* do well."

"I did fail, say what you will, for Jo wouldn't love me," began Laurie, leaning his head on his hand in a despondent attitude.

"No you didn't, and you'll say so in the end,—for it did you good, and proved that you could do something if you tried. If you'd only set about another task of some sort, you'd soon be your hearty, happy self again, and forget your trouble."

"That's impossible!"

"Try it and see. You needn't shrug your shoulders, and think 'Much she knows about such things.' I don't pretend to be wise, but I *am* observing, and I see a great deal more than you'd imagine. I'm interested in other people's experiences and inconsistencies; and, though I can't explain, I remember and use them for my own benefit. Love Jo all your days, if you choose,—but don't let it spoil you,—for it's wicked to throw away so many good gifts because you can't have the one you want. There,—I won't lecture any more, for I know you'll wake up, and be a man in spite of that hard-hearted girl."

Neither spoke for several minutes. Laurie sat turning the little ring on his finger, and Amy put the last touches to the hasty sketch she had been working at while she talked. Presently she put it on his knee, merely saying,—

"How do you like that?"

He looked and then he smiled,—as he could not well help doing, for it was capitally done. The long, lazy figure on the grass, with listless face, half-shut eyes, and one hand holding a cigar, from which came the little wreath of smoke that encircled the dreamer's head.

"How well you draw!" he said, with genuine surprise and pleasure at her skill, adding, with a half-laugh,—

"Yes, that's me."

"As you are,—this is as you were," and Amy laid another sketch beside the one he held.

It was not nearly so well done, but there was a life and spirit in it which atoned for many faults, and it recalled the past so vividly that a sudden change swept over the young man's face as he looked. Only a rough sketch of Laurie taming a horse; hat and coat were off, and every line of the active figure, resolute face, and commanding attitude, was full of energy and meaning. The handsome brute, just subdued, stood arching his neck under the tightly-drawn rein, with one foot impatiently pawing the ground, and ears pricked up as if listening for the voice that had mastered him. In the ruffled mane, the rider's breezy hair and erect attitude, there was a suggestion of suddenly arrested motion, of strength, courage, and youthful buoyancy that contrasted sharply with the supine grace of the *"Dolce far niente"* sketch. Laurie said nothing; but, as his eye went from one to the other, Amy saw him flush up and fold his lips together as if he read and accepted the little lesson she had given him. That satisfied her; and, without waiting for him to speak, she said, in her sprightly way,—

"Don't you remember the day you played 'Rarey' with Puck, and we all looked on? Meg and Beth were frightened, but Jo clapped and pranced, and I sat on the fence and drew you. I found that sketch in my portfolio the other day, touched it up, and kept it to show you."

"Much obliged! You've improved immensely since then, and I

congratulate you. May I venture to suggest in 'a honeymoon Paradise,' that five o'clock is the dinner hour at your hotel?"

Laurie rose as he spoke, returned the pictures with a smile and a bow, and looked at his watch, as if to remind her that even moral lectures should have an end. He tried to resume his former easy, indifferent air, but it *was* an affectation now,—for the rousing had been more efficacious than he would confess. Amy felt the shade of coldness in his manner, and said to herself,—

"Now I've offended him. Well, if it does him good, I'm glad,—if it makes him hate me, I'm sorry; but it's true, and I can't take back a word of it."

They laughed and chatted all the way home; and little Baptiste, up behind, thought that Monsieur and Mademoiselle were in charming spirits. But both felt ill at ease; the friendly frankness was disturbed, the sunshine had a shadow over it, and, despite their apparent gayety, there was a secret discontent in the heart of each.

"Shall we see you this evening, *mon frere?*" asked Amy, as they parted at her aunt's door.

"Unfortunately I have an engagement. *Au revoir, Mademoiselle,*" and Laurie bent as if to kiss her hand, in the foreign fashion, which became him better than many men. Something in his face made Amy say, quickly and warmly,—

"No; be yourself with me, Laurie, and part in the good old way. I'd rather have a hearty English hand-shake than all the sentimental salutations in France."

"Good-by, dear," and, with these words, uttered in the tone she liked, Laurie left her, after a hand-shake almost painful in its heartiness.

Next morning, instead of the usual call, Amy received a note which made her smile at the beginning, and sigh at the end:—

"MY DEAR MENTOR:[9]

"Please make my adieux to your aunt, and exult within yourself, for 'Lazy Laurence' has gone to his grandpa, like the best of boys. A pleasant winter to you, and may the gods grant you a blissful honeymoon at Valrosa. I think Fred would be benefited by a rouser. Tell him so, with my congratulations.

"Yours gratefully, TELEMACHUS."[1]

"Good boy! I'm glad he's gone," said Amy, with an approving smile; the next minute her face fell as she glanced about the empty room, adding, with an involuntary sigh,—

"Yes, I *am* glad,—but how I shall miss him."

9. See p. 167, n. 2 (part 1, chap. 21). Mentor, a trusted friend of Odysseus in Homer's *Odyssey*, watches over his household during his absence.
1. The son of Odysseus, Telemachus must go on his own quest to find his father in Homer's *Odyssey*.

CHAPTER XVII.

THE VALLEY OF THE SHADOW.

WHEN the first bitterness was over, the family accepted the inevitable, and tried to bear it cheerfully, helping one another by the increased affection which comes to bind households tenderly together in times of trouble. They put away their grief, and each did their part toward making that last year a happy one.

The pleasantest room in the house was set apart for Beth, and in it was gathered everything that she most loved—flowers, pictures, her piano, the little work-table, and the beloved pussies. Father's best books found their way there, mother's easy chair, Jo's desk, Amy's loveliest sketches; and every day Meg brought her babies on a loving pilgrimage, to make sunshine for Aunty Beth. John quietly set apart a little sum, that he might enjoy the pleasure of keeping the invalid supplied with the fruit she loved and longed for; old Hannah never wearied of concocting dainty dishes to tempt a capricious appetite, dropping tears as she worked; and, from across the sea, came little gifts and cheerful letters, seeming to bring breaths of warmth and fragrance from lands that know no winter.

Here, cherished like a household saint in its shrine, sat Beth, tranquil and busy as ever; for nothing could change the sweet, unselfish nature; and even while preparing to leave life, she tried to make it happier for those who should remain behind. The feeble fingers were never idle, and one of her pleasures was to make little things for the school children daily passing to and fro. To drop a pair of mittens from her window for a pair of purple hands, a needle-book for some small mother of many dolls, pen-wipers for young penmen toiling through forests of pot-hooks,[2] scrap-books for picture-loving eyes, and all manner of pleasant devices, till the reluctant climbers up the ladder of learning found their way strewn with flowers, as it were, and came to regard the gentle giver as a sort of fairy god-mother, who sat above there, and showered down gifts miraculously suited to their tastes and needs. If Beth had wanted any reward, she found it in the bright little faces always turned up to her window, with nods and smiles, and the droll little letters which came to her, full of blots and gratitude.

The first few months were very happy ones, and Beth often used to look round, and say "How beautiful this is," as they all sat together in her sunny room, the babies kicking and crowing on the floor, mother and sisters working near, and father reading in his pleasant voice, from the wise old books, which seemed rich in good and comfortable words, as applicable now as when written centuries ago—a little chapel, where a paternal priest taught his flock the hard lessons all must learn, trying to show them that hope can comfort love, and faith make resignation possible. Simple sermons, that went straight to the souls of those who listened; for the father's heart was in the minister's reli-

---

2. Curved or hooked strokes in handwriting, usually referring to the marks made by children when learning to write.

gion, and the frequent falter in the voice gave a double eloquence to the words he spoke or read.

It was well for all that this peaceful time was given them as preparation for the sad hours to come; for, by and by, Beth said the needle was "so heavy," and put it down forever; talking wearied her, faces troubled her, pain claimed her for its own, and her tranquil spirit was sorrowfully perturbed by the ills that vexed her feeble flesh. Ah me! such heavy days, such long, long nights, such aching hearts and imploring prayers, when those who loved her best were forced to see the thin hands stretched out to them beseechingly, to hear the bitter cry, "Help me, help me!" and to feel that there was no help. A sad eclipse of the serene soul, a sharp struggle of the young life with death; but both were mercifully brief, and then, the natural rebellion over, the old peace returned more beautiful than ever. With the wreck of her frail body, Beth's soul grew strong; and, though she said little, those about her felt that she was ready, saw that the first pilgrim called was likewise the fittest, and waited with her on the shore, trying to see the Shining Ones coming to receive her when she crossed the river.[3]

Jo never left her for an hour since Beth had said, "I feel stronger when you are here." She slept on a couch in the room, waking often to renew the fire, to feed, lift, or wait upon the patient creature who seldom asked for anything, and "tried not to be a trouble." All day she haunted the room, jealous of any other nurse, and prouder of being chosen then than of any honor her life ever brought her. Precious and helpful hours to Jo, for now her heart received the teaching that it needed; lessons in patience were so sweetly taught her, that she could not fail to learn them; charity for all, the lovely spirit that can forgive and truly forget unkindness, the loyalty to duty that makes the hardest easy, and the sincere faith that fears nothing, but trusts undoubtingly.

Often when she woke, Jo found Beth reading in her well-worn little book, heard her singing softly, to beguile the sleepless night, or saw her lean her face upon her hands, while slow tears dropped through the transparent fingers; and Jo would lie watching her, with thoughts too deep for tears, feeling that Beth, in her simple, unselfish way, was trying to wean herself from the dear old life, and fit herself for the life to come, by sacred words of comfort, quiet prayers, and the music she loved so well.

Seeing this did more for Jo than the wisest sermons, the saintliest hymns, the most fervent prayers that any voice could utter; for, with eyes made clear by many tears, and a heart softened by the tenderest sorrow, she recognized the beauty of her sister's life—uneventful, unambitious, yet full of the genuine virtues which "smell sweet, and blossom in the dust";[4] the self-forgetfulness that makes the humblest on earth remembered soonest in heaven, the true success which is possible to all.

One night, when Beth looked among the books upon her table, to

3. See p. 17, n. 1 (part 1, chap. 1).
4. From scene 3 of *The Contention of Ajax and Ulysses* (1659) by James Shirley. Thoreau includes these lines in his address "The Martyrdom of John Brown" (1860).

find something to make her forget the mortal weariness that was almost as hard to bear as pain, as she turned the leaves of her old favorite Pilgrim's Progress, she found a little paper scribbled over, in Jo's
hand. The name caught her eye, and the blurred look of the lines
made her sure that tears had fallen on it.

"Poor Jo, she's fast asleep, so I won't wake her to ask leave; she
shows me all her things, and I don't think she'll mind if I look at this,"
thought Beth, with a glance at her sister, who lay on the rug, with the
tongs beside her, ready to wake up the minute the log fell apart.

"MY BETH.

"Sitting patient in the shadow
　　Till the blessed light shall come,
A serene and saintly presence
　　Sanctifies our troubled home.
Earthly joys, and hopes, and sorrows,
　　Break like ripples on the strand
Of the deep and solemn river
　　Where her willing feet now stand.

"Oh, my sister, passing from me,
　　Out of human care and strife,
Leave me, as a gift, those virtues
　　Which have beautified your life.
Dear, bequeath me that great patience
　　Which has power to sustain
A cheerful, uncomplaining spirit
　　In its prison-house of pain.

"Give me, for I need it sorely,
　　Of that courage, wise and sweet,
Which has made the path of duty
　　Green beneath your willing feet.
Give me that unselfish nature,
　　That with charity divine
Can pardon wrong for love's dear sake—
　　Meek heart, forgive me mine!

"Thus our parting daily loseth
　　Something of its bitter pain,
And while learning this hard lesson,
　　My great loss becomes my gain.
For the touch of grief will render
　　My wild nature more serene,
Give to life new aspirations—
　　A new trust in the unseen.

"Henceforth, safe across the river,
　　I shall see forever more
A beloved, household spirit

Waiting for me on the shore.
Hope and faith, born of my sorrow,
Guardian angels shall become,
And the sister gone before me,
By their hands shall lead me home."

Blurred and blotted, faulty and feeble as the lines were, they brought a look of inexpressible comfort to Beth's face, for her one regret had been that she had done so little; and this seemed to assure her that her life had not been useless—that her death would not bring the despair she feared. As she sat with the paper folded between her hands, the charred log fell asunder. Jo started up, revived the blaze, and crept to the bedside, hoping Beth slept.

"Not asleep, but so happy, dear. See, I found this and read it; I knew you wouldn't care. Have I been all that to you, Jo?" she asked, with wistful, humble earnestness.

"Oh, Beth, so much, so much!" and Jo's head went down upon the pillow, beside her sister's.

"Then I don't feel as if I'd wasted my life. I'm not so good as you make me, but I *have* tried to do right; and now, when it's too late to begin even to do better, it's such a comfort to know that some one loves me so much, and feels as if I'd helped her."

"More than any one in the world, Beth. I used to think I couldn't let you go; but I'm learning to feel that I don't lose you; that you'll be more to me than ever, and death can't part us, though it seems to."

"I know it cannot, and I don't fear it any longer, for I'm sure I shall be your Beth still, to love and help you more than ever. You must take my place, Jo, and be everything to father and mother when I'm gone. They will turn to you—don't fail them; and if it's hard to work alone, remember that I don't forget you, and that you'll be happier in doing that, than writing splendid books, or seeing all the world; for love is the only thing that we can carry with us when we go, and it makes the end so easy."

"I'll try, Beth;" and then and there Jo renounced her old ambition, pledged herself to a new and better one, acknowledging the poverty of other desires, and feeling the blessed solace of a belief in the immortality of love.

So the spring days came and went, the sky grew clearer, the earth greener, the flowers were up fair and early, and the birds came back in time to say good-by to Beth, who, like a tired but trustful child, clung to the hands that had led her all her life, as father and mother guided her tenderly through the valley of the shadow, and gave her up to God.

Seldom, except in books, do the dying utter memorable words, see visions, or depart with beatified countenances; and those who have sped many parting souls know, that to most the end comes as naturally and simply as sleep. As Beth had hoped, the "tide went out easily"; and in the dark hour before the dawn, on the bosom where she had drawn her first breath, she quietly drew her last, with no farewell but one loving look and a little sigh.

With tears, and prayers, and tender hands, mother and sisters made her ready for the long sleep that pain would never mar again—seeing with grateful eyes the beautiful serenity that soon replaced the pathetic patience that had wrung their hearts so long, and feeling with reverent joy, that to their darling death was a benignant angel—not a phantom full of dread.

When morning came, for the first time in many months the fire was out, Jo's place was empty, and the room was very still. But a bird sang blithely on a budding bough, close by, the snow-drops blossomed freshly at the window, and the spring sunshine streamed in like a benediction over the placid face upon the pillow—a face so full of painless peace, that those who loved it best smiled through their tears, and thanked God that Beth was well at last.

CHAPTER XVIII.

LEARNING TO FORGET.

AMY's lecture did Laurie good, though, of course, he did not own it till long afterward; men seldom do,—for when women are the advisers, the lords of creation don't take the advice till they have persuaded themselves that it is just what they intended to do; then they act upon it, and, if it succeeds, they give the weaker vessel half the credit of it; if it fails, they generously give her the whole. Laurie went back to his grandfather, and was so dutifully devoted for several weeks that the old gentleman declared the climate of Nice had improved him wonderfully, and he had better try it again. There was nothing the young gentleman would have liked better,—but elephants could not have dragged him back after the scolding he had received; pride forbid,— and whenever the longing grew very strong, he fortified his resolution by repeating the words that had made the deepest impression,—"I despise you;" "Go and do something splendid that will *make* her love you."

Laurie turned the matter over in his mind so often that he soon brought himself to confess that he *had* been selfish and lazy; but then when a man has a great sorrow, he should be indulged in all sorts of vagaries till he has lived it down. He felt that his blighted affections were quite dead now; and, though he should never cease to be a faithful mourner, there was no occasion to wear his weeds ostentatiously. Jo *wouldn't* love him, but he might *make* her respect and admire him by doing something which should prove that a girl's "No" had not spoilt his life. He had always meant to do something, and Amy's advice was quite unnecessary. He had only been waiting till the aforesaid blighted affections were decently interred; that being done, he felt that he was ready to "hide his stricken heart, and still toil on."

As Goethe, when he had a joy or a grief, put it into a song, so Laurie resolved to embalm his love-sorrow in music, and compose a Requiem which should harrow up Jo's soul and melt the heart of every hearer. So the next time the old gentleman found him getting restless and moody, and ordered him off, he went to Vienna, where he had musical friends, and fell to work with the firm determination to distinguish himself. But, whether the sorrow was too vast to be embodied in music, or music too ethereal to uplift a mortal woe, he soon discovered that the Requiem was beyond him, just at present. It was evident that his mind was not in working order yet, and his ideas needed clarifying; for often, in the middle of a plaintive strain, he would find himself humming a dancing tune that vividly recalled the Christmas ball at Nice,—especially the stout Frenchman,—and put an effectual stop to tragic composition for the time being.

Then he tried an Opera,—for nothing seemed impossible in the beginning,—but here, again, unforeseen difficulties beset him. He wanted Jo for his heroine, and called upon his memory to supply him with tender recollections and romantic visions of his love. But memory turned traitor; and, as if possessed by the perverse spirit of the girl, would only recall Jo's oddities, faults, and freaks, would only show her in the most unsentimental aspects,—beating mats with her head tied up in a bandanna, barricading herself with the sofa-pillow, or throwing cold water over his passion à la Gummidge,—and an irresistible laugh spoilt the pensive picture he was endeavoring to paint. Jo wouldn't be put into the Opera at any price, and he had to give her up with a "Bless that girl, what a torment she is!" and a clutch at his hair, as became a distracted composer.

When he looked about him for another and a less intractable damsel to immortalize in melody, memory produced one with the most obliging readiness. This phantom wore many faces, but it always had golden hair, was enveloped in a diaphanous cloud, and floated airily before his mind's eye in a pleasing chaos of roses, peacocks, white ponies and blue ribbons. He did not give the complaisant wraith any name, but he took her for his heroine, and grew quite fond of her, as well he might,—for he gifted her with every gift and grace under the sun, and escorted her, unscathed, through trials which would have annihilated any mortal woman.

Thanks to this inspiration, he got on swimmingly for a time, but gradually the work lost its charm, and he forgot to compose, while he sat musing, pen in hand, or roamed about the gay city to get new ideas and refresh his mind, which seemed to be in a somewhat unsettled state that winter. He did not do much, but he thought a great deal, and was conscious of a change of some sort going on in spite of himself. "It's genius simmering, perhaps,—I'll let it simmer, and see what comes of it," he said, with a secret suspicion, all the while, that it wasn't genius, but something far more common. Whatever it was, it simmered to some purpose, for he grew more and more discontented with his desultory life, began to long for some real and earnest work to go at, soul and body, and finally came to the wise conclusion that every one who loved music was not a composer. Returning from one of Mozart's grand Operas, splendidly performed at the Royal Theatre, he looked over his own, played a few of the best parts, sat staring up at the busts of Mendelssohn, Beethoven, and Bach, who stared benignly back again; then suddenly he tore up his music-sheets, one by one, and, as the last fluttered out of his hand, he said soberly, to himself,—

"She is right! talent isn't genius, and you can't make it so. That music has taken the vanity out of me as Rome took it out of her, and I won't be a humbug any longer. Now what shall I do?"

That seemed a hard question to answer, and Laurie began to wish he had to work for his daily bread. Now, if ever, occurred an eligible opportunity for "going to the devil," as he once forcibly expressed it,— for he had plenty of money and nothing to do,—and Satan is proverbially fond of providing employment for full and idle hands. The poor fellow had temptations enough from without and from within, but he withstood them pretty well,—for much as he valued liberty he valued good faith and confidence more,—so his promise to his grandfather, and his desire to be able to look honestly into the eyes of the women who loved him, and say "All's well," kept him safe and steady.

Very likely some Mrs. Grundy will observe, "I don't believe it; boys will be boys, young men must sow their wild oats, and women must not expect miracles." I dare say *you* don't, Mrs. Grundy, but it's true, nevertheless. Women work a good many miracles, and I have a persuasion that they may perform even that of raising the standard of manhood by refusing to echo such sayings. Let the boys be boys,—the longer the better,—and let the young men sow their wild oats if they must,—but mothers, sisters, and friends may help to make the crop a small one, and keep many tares from spoiling the harvest, by believing,—and showing that they believe,—in the possibility of loyalty to the virtues which make men manliest in good women's eyes. If it *is* a feminine delusion, leave us to enjoy it while we may,—for without it half the beauty and the romance of life is lost, and sorrowful forebodings would embitter all our hopes of the brave, tender-hearted little lads, who still love their mothers better than themselves, and are not ashamed to own it.

Laurie thought that the task of forgetting his love for Jo would absorb all his powers for years; but, to his great surprise, he discovered it grew easier every day. He refused to believe it at first,—got angry with himself, and couldn't understand it; but these hearts of ours are curious and contrary things, and time and nature work their will in spite of us. Laurie's heart *wouldn't* ache; the wound persisted in healing with a rapidity that astonished him, and, instead of trying to forget, he found himself trying to remember. He had not foreseen this turn of affairs, and was not prepared for it. He was disgusted with himself, surprised at his own fickleness, and full of a queer mixture of disappointment and relief that he could recover from such a tremendous blow so soon. He carefully stirred up the embers of his lost love, but they refused to burst into a blaze; there was only a comfortable glow that warmed and did him good without putting him into a fever, and he was reluctantly obliged to confess that the boyish passion was slowly subsiding into a more tranquil sentiment,—very tender, a little sad and resentful still,—but that was sure to pass away in time, leaving a brotherly affection which would last unbroken to the end.

As the word "brotherly" passed through his mind in one of these reveries, he smiled, and glanced up at the picture of Mozart that was before him,—

"Well, he was a great man; and when he couldn't have one sister he took the other, and was happy."[5]

Laurie did not utter the words, but he thought them; and the next instant kissed the little old ring, saying to himself,—

"No I won't! I haven't forgotten, I never can. I'll try again, and if that fails, why then—"

Leaving his sentence unfinished, he seized pen and paper and wrote to Jo, telling her that he could not settle to anything while there was the least hope of her changing her mind. Couldn't she, wouldn't she,—and let him come home and be happy? While waiting for an answer he did nothing,—but he did it energetically, for he was in a fever of impatience. It came at last, and settled his mind effectually on one point,—for Jo decidedly couldn't and wouldn't. She was wrapped up in Beth, and never wished to hear the word "love" again. Then she begged him to be happy with somebody else, but always to keep a little corner of his heart for his loving sister Jo. In a post-script she desired him not to tell Amy that Beth was worse; she was coming home in the spring, and there was no need of saddening the remainder of her stay. That would be time enough, please God, but Laurie must write to her often, and not let her feel lonely, homesick, or anxious.

"So I will, at once. Poor little girl; it will be a sad going home for her, I'm afraid;" and Laurie opened his desk, as if writing to Amy had been the proper conclusion of the sentence left unfinished some weeks before.

But he did not write the letter that day; for, as he rummaged out his best paper, he came across something which changed his purpose. Tumbling about in one part of the desk, among bills, passports, and business documents of various kinds, were several of Jo's letters, and in another compartment were three notes from Amy, carefully tied up with one of her blue ribbons, and sweetly suggestive of the little dead roses put away inside. With a half-repentant, half-amused expression, Laurie gathered up all Jo's letters, smoothed, folded, and put them neatly into a small drawer of the desk, stood a minute turning the ring thoughtfully on his finger, then slowly drew it off, laid it with the letters, locked the drawer, and went out to hear High Mass at Saint Stefan's, feeling as if there had been a funeral; and, though not overwhelmed with affliction, this seemed a more proper way to spend the rest of the day, than in writing letters to charming young ladies.

The letter went very soon, however, and was promptly answered, for Amy *was* homesick, and confessed it in the most delightfully confiding manner. The correspondence flourished famously, and letters flew to

5. In 1777, Mozart fell in love with Aloysia Weber, but she left him at the altar on the day of their wedding. He married Aloysia's younger sister Constanze in 1782.

and fro, with unfailing regularity, all through the early spring. Laurie sold his busts, made allumettes⁶ of his opera, and went back to Paris, hoping somebody would arrive before long. He wanted desperately to go to Nice, but would not till he was asked; and Amy would not ask him, for just then she was having little experiences of her own, which made her rather wish to avoid the quizzical eyes of "our boy."

Fred Vaughn had returned, and put the question to which she had once decided to answer "Yes, thank you"; but now she said, "No, thank you," kindly but steadily; for when the time came, her courage failed her, and she found that something more than money and position was needed to satisfy the new longing that filled her heart so full of tender hopes and fears. The words "Fred is a good fellow, but not at all the man I fancied you would ever like," and Laurie's face, when he uttered them, kept returning to her as pertinaciously as her own did, when she said in look, if not in words, "I shall marry for money." It troubled her to remember that now, she wished she could take it back, it sounded so unwomanly. She didn't want Laurie to think her a heartless, worldly creature; she didn't care to be a queen of society now half so much as she did to be a lovable woman; she was so glad he didn't hate her for the dreadful things she said, but took them so beautifully, and was kinder than ever. His letters were such a comfort—for the home letters were very irregular, and were not half so satisfactory as his when they did come. It was not only a pleasure, but a duty to answer them, for the poor fellow was forlorn, and needed petting, since Jo persisted in being stony-hearted. She ought to have made an effort, and tried to love him—it couldn't be very hard—many people would be proud and glad to have such a dear boy care for them; but Jo never would act like other girls, so there was nothing to do but be very kind, and treat him like a brother.

If all brothers were treated as well as Laurie was at this period, they would be a much happier race of beings than they are. Amy never lectured now; she asked his opinion on all subjects; she was interested in everything he did, made charming little presents for him, and sent him two letters a week, full of lively gossip, sisterly confidences, and captivating sketches of the lovely scenes about her. As few brothers are complimented by having their letters carried about in their sisters' pockets, read and re-read diligently, cried over when short, kissed when long, and treasured carefully, we will not hint that Amy did any of these fond and foolish things. But she certainly did grow a little pale and pensive that spring, lost much of her relish for society, and went out sketching alone a good deal. She never had much to show when she came home, but was studying nature, I dare say, while she sat for hours with her hands folded, on the terrace at Valrosa, or absently sketched any fancy that occurred to her—a stalwart knight carved on a tomb, a young man asleep in the grass, with his hat over his eyes, or a curly-haired girl in gorgeous array, promenading down a ball-room, on the arm of a tall gentleman, both faces being left a blurr,

6. Matchsticks.

according to the last fashion in art, which was safe, but not altogether satisfactory.

Her aunt thought that she regretted her answer to Fred; and, finding denials useless, and explanations impossible, Amy left her to think what she liked, taking care that Laurie should know that Fred had gone to Egypt. That was all, but he understood it, and looked relieved, as he said to himself, with a venerable air,—

"I was sure she would think better of it. Poor old fellow, I've been through it all, and I can sympathize."

With that he heaved a great sigh, and then, as if he had discharged his duty to the past, put his feet up on the sofa, and enjoyed Amy's letter luxuriously.

While these changes were going on abroad, trouble had come at home; but the letter telling that Beth was failing, never reached Amy; and when the next found her, the grass was green above her sister. The sad news met her at Vevey, for the heat had driven them from Nice in May, and they had travelled slowly to Switzerland, by way of Genoa and the Italian lakes. She bore it very well, and quietly submitted to the family decree, that she should not shorten her visit, for, since it was too late to say good-by to Beth, she had better stay, and let absence soften her sorrow. But her heart was very heavy—she longed to be at home; and every day looked wistfully across the lake, waiting for Laurie to come and comfort her.

He did come very soon; for the same mail brought letters to them both, but he was in Germany, and it took some days to reach him. The moment he read it, he packed his knapsack, bade adieu to his fellow-pedestrians, and was off to keep his promise, with a heart full of joy and sorrow, hope and suspense.

He knew Vevey well; and as soon as the boat touched the little quay, he hurried along the shore to La Tour, where the Carrols were living *en pension*. The garçon was in despair that the whole family had gone to take a promenade on the lake—but no, the blonde mademoiselle might be in the chateau garden. If *monsieur* would give himself the pain of sitting down, a flash of time should present her. But monsieur could not wait even "a flash of time," and in the middle of the speech, departed to find mademoiselle himself.

A pleasant old garden on the borders of the lovely lake, with chestnuts rustling overhead, ivy climbing everywhere, and the black shadow of the tower falling far across the sunny water. At one corner of the wide, low wall, was a seat, and here Amy often came to read or work, or console herself with the beauty all about her. She was sitting here that day, leaning her head on her hand, with a homesick heart and heavy eyes, thinking of Beth, and wondering why Laurie did not come. She did not hear him cross the court-yard beyond, nor see him pause in the archway that led from the subterranean path into the garden. He stood a minute, looking at her with new eyes, seeing what no one had ever seen before—the tender side of Amy's character. Everything about her mutely suggested love and sorrow; the blotted letters in her lap, the black ribbon that tied up her hair, the womanly pain and patience in her face; even the little ebony cross at her throat seemed pathetic to Laurie, for he had given it to her, and she wore it as her only ornament. If he had any doubts about the reception she would give him, they were set at rest the minute she looked up and saw him; for, dropping everything, she ran to him, exclaiming in a tone of unmistakable love and longing,—

"Oh, Laurie, Laurie! I knew you'd come to me!"

I think everything was said and settled then; for, as they stood together quite silent for a moment, with the dark head bent down protectingly over the light one, Amy felt that no one could comfort and sustain her so well as Laurie, and Laurie decided that Amy was the only woman in the world who could fill Jo's place, and make him happy. He did not tell her so; but she was not disappointed, for both felt the truth, were satisfied, and gladly left the rest to silence.

In a minute Amy went back to her place; and while she dried her tears, Laurie gathered up the scattered papers, finding in the sight of sundry well-worn letters and suggestive sketches, good omens for the future. As he sat down beside her, Amy felt shy again, and turned rosy red at the recollection of her impulsive greeting.

"I couldn't help it; I felt so lonely and sad, and was so very glad to see you. It was such a surprise to look up and find you, just as I was beginning to fear you wouldn't come," she said, trying in vain to speak quite naturally.

"I came the minute I heard. I wish I could say something to comfort you for the loss of dear little Beth, but I can only feel, and—" he could not get any farther, for he, too, turned bashful all of a sudden, and did not quite know what to say. He longed to lay Amy's head down on his shoulder and tell her to have a good cry, but he did not dare, so took her hand instead, and gave it a sympathetic squeeze that was better than words.

"You needn't say anything,—this comforts me," she said, softly. "Beth is well and happy, and I mustn't wish her back,—but I dread the going home, much as I long to see them all. We won't talk about it now, for it makes me cry, and I want to enjoy you while you stay. You needn't go right back, need you?"

"Not if you want me, dear."

"I do, so much! Aunt and Flo are very kind, but you seem like one of the family, and it would be so comfortable to have you for a little while."

Amy spoke and looked so like a homesick child whose heart was full, that Laurie forgot his bashfulness all at once, and gave her just what she wanted,—the petting she was used to, and the cheerful conversation she needed.

"Poor little soul! you look as if you'd grieved yourself half sick. I'm going to take care of you, so don't cry any more, but come and walk about with me,—the wind is too chilly for you to sit still," he said, in the half-caressing, half-commanding way that Amy liked, as he tied on her hat, drew her arm through his, and began to pace up and down the sunny walk, under the new-leaved chestnuts. He felt more at ease upon his legs, and Amy found it very pleasant to have a strong arm to lean upon, a familiar face to smile at her, and a kind voice to talk delightfully for her alone.

The quaint old garden had sheltered many pairs of lovers, and seemed expressly made for them, so sunny and secluded was it, with nothing but the tower to overlook them, and the wide lake to carry away the echo of their words, as it rippled by below. For an hour this new pair walked and talked, or rested on the wall, enjoying the sweet influences which gave such a charm to time and place; and when an unromantic dinner-bell warned them away, Amy felt as if she left her burden of loneliness and sorrow behind her in the Chateau garden.

The moment Mrs. Carrol saw the girl's altered face she was illuminated with a new idea, and exclaimed to herself, "Now I understand it all,—the child has been pining for young Laurence. Bless my heart! I never thought of such a thing!"

With praiseworthy discretion, the good lady said nothing, and betrayed no sign of enlightenment, but cordially urged Laurie to stay, and begged Amy to enjoy his society, for it would do her more good than so much solitude. Amy was a model of docility; and, as her aunt was a good deal occupied with Flo, she was left to entertain her friend, and did it with more than her usual success.

At Nice, Laurie had lounged and Amy had scolded; at Vevey, Laurie was never idle, but always walking, riding, boating, or studying, in the most energetic manner; while Amy admired everything he did, and followed his example as far and as fast as she could. He said the change was owing to the climate, and she did not contradict him, being glad of a like excuse for her own recovered health and spirits.

The invigorating air did them both good, and much exercise worked wholesome changes in minds as well as bodies. They seemed to get clearer views of life and duty up there among the everlasting hills; the fresh winds blew away desponding doubts, delusive fancies and moody mists; the warm spring sunshine brought out all sorts of aspiring ideas, tender hopes and happy thoughts,—the lake seemed to wash away the troubles of the past, and the grand old mountains to look benignly down upon them, saying, "Little children, love one another."[7]

In spite of the new sorrow it was a very happy time,—so happy that Laurie could not bear to disturb it by a word. It took him a little while to recover from his surprise at the rapid cure of his first, and, as he had firmly believed, his last and only love. He consoled himself for the seeming disloyalty by the thought that Jo's sister was almost the same as Jo's self, and the conviction that it would have been impossible to love any other woman but Amy so soon and so well. His first wooing had been of the tempestuous order, and he looked back upon it as if through a long vista of years, with a feeling of compassion blended with regret. He was not ashamed of it, but put it away as one of the bitter-sweet experiences of his life, for which he could be grateful when the pain was over. His second wooing he resolved should be as calm and simple as possible; there was no need of having a scene,—

7. Cf. John 13.34–35.

hardly any need of telling Amy that he loved her; she knew it without words, and had given him his answer long ago. It all came about so naturally that no one could complain, and he knew that everybody would be pleased,—even Jo. But when our first little passion has been crushed, we are apt to be wary and slow in making a second trial; so Laurie let the days pass, enjoying every hour, and leaving to chance the utterance of the word that would put an end to the first and sweetest part of his new romance.

He had rather imagined that the *denouément* would take place in the chateau garden by moonlight, and in the most graceful and decorous manner; but it turned out exactly the reverse,—for the matter was settled on the lake, at noonday, in a few blunt words. They had been floating about all the morning, from gloomy St. Gingolf to sunny Montreux, with the Alps of Savoy on one side, Mont St. Bernard and the Dent du Midi on the other, pretty Vevey in the valley, and Lausanne upon the hill beyond, a cloudless blue sky overhead, and the bluer lake below, dotted with the picturesque boats that look like white-winged gulls.

They had been talking of Bonnivard as they glided past Chillon, and of Rousseau as they looked up at Clarens, where he wrote his Heloise.[8] Neither had read it, but they knew it was a love story, and each privately wondered if it was half as interesting as their own. Amy had been dabbling her hand in the water during the little pause that fell between them, and, when she looked up, Laurie was leaning on his oars, with an expression in his eyes that made her say, hastily,— merely for the sake of saying something,—

"You must be tired,—rest a little, and let me row; it will do me good, for since you came I have been altogether lazy and luxurious."

"I'm not tired, but you may take an oar if you like. There's room enough, though I have to sit nearly in the middle, else the boat won't trim," returned Laurie, as if he rather liked the arrangement.

Feeling that she had not mended matters much, Amy took the offered third of a seat, shook her hair over her face, and accepted an oar. She rowed as well as she did many other things; and, though she used both hands, and Laurie but one, the oars kept time, and the boat went smoothly through the water.

"How well we pull together, don't we?" said Amy, who objected to silence just then.

"So well, that I wish we might always pull in the same boat. Will you, Amy?" very tenderly.

"Yes, Laurie!" very low.

Then they both stopped rowing, and unconsciously added a pretty little *tableau* of human love and happiness to the dissolving views reflected in the lake.

<hr/>

8. François de Bonnivard (c. 1493–1570), Swiss patriot and historian, was detained from 1530 to 1536 in the castle of Chillon, an event romanticized in Lord Byron's poem "The Prisoner of Chillon." The Castle of Chillon, part towered fortress and part stately mansion, is situated on Lake Geneva and dates from the eleventh century. Clarens is a resort village near Montreux where Byron lived for a time; it is the setting for *Julie, or The New Heloise* (1761), an epistolary romance by Jean-Jacques Rousseau (1712–1778).

CHAPTER XIX.

ALL ALONE.

IT was easy to promise self-abnegation when self was wrapt up in another, and heart and soul were purified by a sweet example; but when the helpful voice was silent, the daily lesson over, the beloved presence gone, and nothing remained but loneliness and grief, then Jo found her promise very hard to keep. How could she "comfort father and mother," when her own heart ached with a ceaseless longing for her sister; how could she "make the house cheerful," when all its light, and warmth, and beauty, seemed to have deserted it when Beth left the old home for the new; and where, in all the world, could she "find some useful, happy work to do," that would take the place of the loving service which had been its own reward? She tried in a blind, hopeless way to do her duty, secretly rebelling against it all the while, for it seemed unjust that her few joys should be lessened, her burdens made heavier, and life get harder and harder as she toiled along. Some people seemed to get all sunshine, and some all shadow; it was not fair, for she tried more than Amy to be good, but never got any reward,— only disappointment, trouble, and hard work.

Poor Jo! these were dark days to her, for something like despair came over her when she thought of spending all her life in that quiet house, devoted to humdrum cares, a few poor little pleasures, and the duty that never seemed to grow any easier. "I can't do it. I wasn't meant for a life like this, and I know I shall break away and do something desperate if somebody don't come and help me," she said to herself, when her first efforts failed, and she fell into the moody, miserable state of mind which often comes when strong wills have to yield to the inevitable.

But some one did come and help her, though Jo did not recognize her good angels at once, because they wore familiar shapes, and used the simple spells best fitted to poor humanity. Often she started up at night, thinking Beth called her; and when the sight of the little empty bed made her cry with the bitter cry of an unsubmissive sorrow, "Oh, Beth! come back! come back!" she did not stretch out her yearning arms in vain; for, as quick to hear her sobbing as she had been to hear her sister's faintest whisper, her mother came to comfort her. Not with words only, but the patient tenderness that soothes by a touch, tears that were mute reminders of a greater grief than Jo's, and broken whispers, more eloquent than prayers, because hopeful resignation went hand-in-hand with natural sorrow. Sacred moments! when heart talked to heart in the silence of the night, turning affliction to a blessing, which chastened grief and strengthened love. Feeling this, Jo's burden seemed easier to bear, duty grew sweeter, and life looked more endurable, seen from the safe shelter of her mother's arms.

When aching heart was a little comforted, troubled mind likewise found help; for one day she went to the study, and, leaning over the good gray head lifted to welcome her with a tranquil smile, she said, very humbly,—

"Father, talk to me as you did to Beth. I need it more than she did, for I'm all wrong."

"My dear, nothing can comfort me like this," he answered, with a falter in his voice, and both arms round her, as if he, too, needed help, and did not fear to ask it.

Then, sitting in Beth's little chair close beside him, Jo told her troubles, the resentful sorrow for her loss, the fruitless efforts that discouraged her, the want of faith that made life look so dark, and all the sad bewilderment which we call despair. She gave him entire confidence,—he gave her the help she needed, and both found consolation in the act; for the time had come when they could talk together not only as father and daughter, but as man and woman, able and glad to serve each other with mutual sympathy as well as mutual love. Happy, thoughtful times there in the old study which Jo called "the church of one member," and from which she came with fresh courage, recovered cheerfulness, and a more submissive spirit,—for the parents who had taught one child to meet death without fear, were trying now to teach another to accept life without despondency or distrust, and to use its beautiful opportunities with gratitude and power.

Other helps had Jo, humble, wholesome duties and delights, that would not be denied their part in serving her, and which she slowly learned to see and value. Brooms and dishcloths never could be as distasteful as they once had been, for Beth had presided over both; and something of her housewifely spirit seemed to linger round the little mop and the old brush, that was never thrown away. As she used them, Jo found herself humming the songs Beth used to hum, imitating Beth's orderly ways, and giving the little touches here and there that kept everything fresh and cosy, which was the first step toward making home happy, though she didn't know it, till Hannah said with an approving squeeze of the hand,—

"You thoughtful creter, you're determined we shan't miss that dear lamb ef you can help it. We don't say much, but we see it, and the Lord will bless you for't, see ef He don't."

As they sat sewing together, Jo discovered how much improved her sister Meg was; how well she could talk, how much she knew about good, womanly impulses, thoughts and feelings, how happy she was in husband and children, and how much they were all doing for each other.

"Marriage is an excellent thing after all. I wonder if I should blossom out, half as well as you have, if I tried it, always 'perwisin'' I could," said Jo, as she constructed a kite for Demi, in the topsy-turvy nursery.

"It's just what you need to bring out the tender, womanly half of your nature, Jo. You are like a chestnut burr, prickly outside, but silky-soft within, and a sweet kernel, if one can only get at it. Love will make you show your heart some day, and then the rough burr will fall off."

"Frost opens chestnut burrs, ma'am, and it takes a good shake to bring them down. Boys go nutting, and I don't care to be bagged by them," returned Jo, pasting away at the kite, which no wind that blows would ever carry up, for Daisy had tied herself on as a bob.

Meg laughed, for she was glad to see a glimmer of Jo's old spirit, but she felt it her duty to enforce her opinion by every argument in her power; and the sisterly chats were not wasted, especially as two of Meg's most effective arguments were the babies, whom Jo loved tenderly. Grief is the best opener for some hearts, and Jo's was nearly ready for the bag; a little more sunshine to ripen the nut, then, not a boy's impatient shake, but a man's hand reached up to pick it gently from the burr, and find the kernel sound and sweet. If she had suspected this, she would have shut up tight, and been more prickly than ever; fortunately she wasn't thinking about herself, so, when the time came, down she dropped.

Now, if she had been the heroine of a moral story-book, she ought at this period of her life to have become quite saintly, renounced the world, and gone about doing good in a mortified bonnet, with tracts in her pocket. But you see Jo wasn't a heroine; she was only a struggling human girl, like hundreds of others, and she just acted out her nature, being sad, cross, listless or energetic, as the mood suggested. It's highly virtuous to say we'll be good, but we can't do it all at once, and it takes a long pull, a strong pull, and a pull all together, before some of us even get our feet set in the right way. Jo had got so far, she was learning to do her duty, and to feel unhappy if she did not; but to do it cheerfully—ah, that was another thing! She had often said she wanted to do something splendid, no matter how hard; and now she had her wish,—for what could be more beautiful than to devote her life to father and mother, trying to make home as happy to them as they had to her? And, if difficulties were necessary to increase the splendor of the effort, what could be harder for a restless, ambitious girl, than to give up her own hopes, plans and desires, and cheerfully live for others?

Providence had taken her at her word; here was the task,—not what she had expected, but better, because self had no part in it; now could she do it? She decided that she would try; and, in her first attempt, she found the helps I have suggested. Still another was given her, and she took it,—not as a reward, but as a comfort, as Christian took the refreshment afforded by the little arbor where he rested, as he climbed the hill called Difficulty.[9]

"Why don't you write? that always used to make you happy," said her mother, once, when the desponding fit overshadowed Jo.

"I've no heart to write, and if I had, nobody cares for my things."

"We do; write something for us, and never mind the rest of the world. Try it, dear; I'm sure it would do you good, and please us very much."

"Don't believe I can;" but Jo got out her desk, and began to overhaul her half-finished manuscripts.

An hour afterward her mother peeped in, and there she was scratching away, with her black pinafore on, and an absorbed expression, which caused Mrs. March to smile, and slip away, well pleased with the success of her suggestion. Jo never knew how it happened, but

9. See p. 17, n. 1 (part 1, chap. 1). In *The Pilgrim's Progress*, Christian must ascend the steep and lofty hill of Difficulty to reach the Palace Beautiful.

something got into that story that went straight to the hearts of those who read it; for, when her family had laughed and cried over it, her father sent it, much against her will, to one of the popular magazines, and, to her utter surprise, it was not only paid for, but others requested. Letters from several persons, whose praise was honor, followed the appearance of the little story, newspapers copied it, and strangers as well as friends admired it. For a small thing, it was a great success; and Jo was more astonished than when her novel was commended and condemned all at once.

"I don't understand it; what *can* there be in a simple little story like that, to make people praise it so?" she said, quite bewildered.

"There is truth in it, Jo—that's the secret; humor and pathos make it alive, and you have found your style at last. You wrote with no thought of fame or money, and put your heart into it, my daughter; you have had the bitter, now comes the sweet; do your best, and grow as happy as we are in your success."

"If there *is* anything good or true in what I write, it isn't mine; I owe it all to you and mother, and to Beth," said Jo, more touched by her father's words than by any amount of praise from the world.

So, taught by love and sorrow, Jo wrote her little stories, and sent them away to make friends for themselves and her, finding it a very charitable world to such humble wanderers, for they were kindly welcomed, and sent home comfortable tokens to their mother, like dutiful children, whom good fortune overtakes.

When Amy and Laurie wrote of their engagement, Mrs. March feared that Jo would find it difficult to rejoice over it, but her fears were soon set at rest; for, though Jo looked grave at first, she took it very quietly, and was full of hopes and plans for "the children," before she read the letter twice. It was a sort of written duet, wherein each glorified the other in lover-like fashion, very pleasant to read, and satisfactory to think of, for no one had any objection to make.

"You like it, mother?" said Jo, as they laid down the closely-written sheets, and looked at one another.

"Yes, I hoped it would be so, ever since Amy wrote that she had refused Fred. I felt sure then that something better than what you call 'the mercenary spirit' had come over her, and a hint here and there in her letters made me suspect that love and Laurie would win the day."

"How sharp you are, Marmee, and how silent; you never said a word to me."

"Mothers have need of sharp eyes and discreet tongues, when they have girls to manage. I was half afraid to put the idea into your head, lest you should write, and congratulate them before the thing was settled."

"I'm not the scatter-brain I was; you may trust me, I'm sober and sensible enough for any one's *confidante* now."

"So you are, dear, and I should have made you mine, only I fancied it might pain you to learn that your Teddy loved any one else."

"Now, mother, did you really think I could be so silly and selfish, after I'd refused his love, when it was freshest, if not best?"

"I knew you were sincere then, Jo, but lately I have thought that if he came back, and asked again, you might, perhaps, feel like giving another answer. Forgive me, dear, I can't help seeing that you are very lonely, and sometimes there is a hungry look in your eyes that goes to my heart; so I fancied that your boy might fill the empty place, if he tried now."

"No, mother, it is better as it is, and I'm glad Amy has learned to love him. But you are right in one thing; I *am* lonely, and perhaps if Teddy had tried again, I might have said 'Yes,' not because I love him any more, but because I care more to be loved, than when he went away."

"I'm glad of that, Jo, for it shows that you are getting on. There are plenty to love you, so try to be satisfied with father and mother, sisters and brothers, friends and babies, till the best lover of all comes to give you your reward."

"Mothers are the *best* lovers in the world; but, I don't mind whispering to Marmee, that I'd like to try all kinds. It's very curious, but the more I try to satisfy myself with all sorts of natural affections, the more I seem to want. I'd no idea hearts could take in so many—mine is so elastic, it never seems full now, and I used to be quite contented with my family; I don't understand it."

"I do," and Mrs. March smiled her wise smile, as Jo turned back the leaves to read what Amy said of Laurie.

"It is so beautiful to be loved as Laurie loves me; he isn't sentimental; doesn't say much about it, but I see and feel it in all he says and does, and it makes me so happy and so humble, that I don't seem to be the same girl I was. I never knew how good, and generous, and tender he was till now, for he lets me read his heart, and I find it full of noble impulses, and hopes, and purposes, and am so proud to know it's mine. He says he feels as if he 'could make a prosperous voyage now with me aboard as mate, and lots of love for ballast.' I pray he may, and try to be all he believes me, for I love my gallant captain with all my heart, and soul, and might, and never will desert him, while God lets us be together. Oh, mother, I never knew how much like heaven this world could be, when two people love and live for one another!"

"And that's our cool, reserved, and worldly Amy! Truly love does work miracles. How very, very happy they must be!" and Jo laid the rustling sheets together with a careful hand, as one might shut the covers of a lovely romance, which holds the reader fast till the end comes, and he finds himself alone in the work-a-day world again.

By and by, Jo roamed away upstairs, for it was rainy, and she could not walk. A restless spirit possessed her, and the old feeling came again, not bitter as it once was, but a sorrowfully patient wonder why one sister should have all she asked, the other nothing. It was not true; she knew that, and tried to put it away, but the natural craving for affection was strong, and Amy's happiness woke the hungry longing for some one to "love with heart and soul, and cling to, while God let them be together."

Up in the garret, where Jo's unquiet wanderings ended, stood four little wooden chests in a row, each marked with its owner's name, and each filled with relics of the childhood and girlhood ended now for all. Jo glanced into them, and when she came to her own, leaned her chin on the edge, and stared absently at the chaotic collection, till a bundle of old exercise-books caught her eye. She drew them out, turned them over, and re-lived that pleasant winter at kind Mrs. Kirke's. She had smiled at first, then she looked thoughtful, next sad, and when she came to a little message written in the Professor's hand, her lips began to tremble, the books slid out of her lap, and she sat looking at the friendly words, as if they took a new meaning, and touched a tender spot in her heart.

"Wait for me, my friend, I may be a little late, but I shall surely come."

"Oh, if he only would! So kind, so good, so patient with me always; my dear old Fritz, I didn't value him half enough when I had him, but now how I should love to see him, for every one seems going away from me, and I'm all alone."

And holding the little paper fast, as if it were a promise yet to be fulfilled, Jo laid her head down on a comfortable rag-bag, and cried, as if in opposition to the rain pattering on the roof.

Was it all self-pity, loneliness, or low spirits? or was it the waking up of a sentiment which had bided its time as patiently as its inspirer? Who shall say.

CHAPTER XX.

SURPRISES.

JO was alone in the twilight, lying on the old sofa, looking at the fire, and thinking. It was her favorite way of spending the hour of dusk; no one disturbed her, and she used to lie there on Beth's little red pillow, planning stories, dreaming dreams, or thinking tender thoughts of the sister who never seemed far away. Her face looked tired, grave, and rather sad; for to-morrow was her birthday, and she was thinking how fast the years went by, how old she was getting, and how little she seemed to have accomplished. Almost twenty-five, and nothing to show for it,—Jo was mistaken in that; there was a good deal to show, and by and by she saw, and was grateful for it.

"An old maid—that's what I'm to be. A literary spinster, with a pen for a spouse, a family of stories for children, and twenty years hence a morsel of fame, perhaps; when, like poor Johnson, I'm old, and can't enjoy it[1]—solitary, and can't share it, independent, and don't need it.

1. When Lord Chesterfield tried to claim some credit for sponsoring Samuel Johnson's work on his dictionary, after having given a mere ten pounds to Johnson several years earlier, Johnson wrote a famous letter of rebuttal that included the argument that Chesterfield's attention "has been delayed till I am indifferent and cannot enjoy it."

Well, I needn't be a sour saint nor a selfish sinner; and, I dare say, old maids are very comfortable when they get used to it; but—" and there Jo sighed, as if the prospect was not inviting.

It seldom is, at first, and thirty seems the end of all things to five-and-twenty; but it's not so bad as it looks, and one can get on quite happily if one has something in one's self to fall back upon. At twenty-five, girls begin to talk about being old maids, but secretly resolve that they never will; at thirty, they say nothing about it, but quietly accept the fact; and, if sensible, console themselves by remembering that they have twenty more useful, happy years, in which they may be learning to grow old gracefully. Don't laugh at the spinsters, dear girls, for often very tender, tragical romances are hidden away in the hearts that beat so quietly under the sober gowns, and many silent sacrifices of youth, health, ambition, love itself, make the faded faces beautiful in God's sight. Even the sad, sour sisters should be kindly dealt with, because they have missed the sweetest part of life if for no other reason; and, looking at them with compassion, not contempt, girls in their bloom should remember that they too may miss the blossom time—that rosy cheeks don't last forever, that silver threads will come in the bonnie brown hair, and, that by and by, kindness and respect will be as sweet as love and admiration now.

Gentlemen, which means boys, be courteous to the old maids, no matter how poor and plain and prim, for the only chivalry worth having is that which is the readiest to pay deference to the old, protect the feeble, and serve womankind, regardless of rank, age, or color. Just recollect the good aunts who have not only lectured and fussed, but nursed and petted, too often without thanks—the scrapes they have helped you out of, the "tips" they have given you from their small store, the stitches the patient old fingers have set for you, the steps the willing old feet have taken, and gratefully pay the dear old ladies the little attentions that women love to receive as long as they live. The bright-eyed girls are quick to see such traits, and will like you all the better for them; and, if death, almost the only power that can part mother and son, should rob you of yours, you will be sure to find a tender, welcome, and maternal cherishing from some Aunt Priscilla, who has kept the warmest corner of her lonely old heart for "the best nevvy in the world."

Jo must have fallen asleep (as I dare say my reader has during this little homily), for, suddenly, Laurie's ghost seemed to stand before her. A substantial, lifelike ghost leaning over her, with the very look he used to wear when he felt a good deal, and didn't like to show it. But, like Jenny in the ballad,—

> "She could not think it he,"

and lay staring up at him, in startled silence, till he stooped and kissed her. Then she knew him, and flew up, crying joyfully,—

"Oh my Teddy! Oh my Teddy!"

"Dear Jo, you are glad to see me, then?"

"Glad! my blessed boy, words can't express my gladness. Where's Amy?"

"Your mother has got her, down at Meg's. We stopped there by the way, and there was no getting my wife out of their clutches."

"Your what?" cried Jo—for Laurie uttered those two words with an unconscious pride and satisfaction, which betrayed him.

"Oh, the dickens! now I've done it;" and he looked so guilty that Jo was down upon him like a flash.

"You've gone and got married?"

"Yes, please, but I never will again;" and he went down upon his knees with a penitent clasping of hands, and a face full of mischief, mirth, and triumph.

"Actually married?"

"Very much so, thank you."

"Mercy on us; what dreadful thing will you do next?" and Jo fell into her seat, with a gasp.

"A characteristic, but not exactly complimentary congratulation," returned Laurie, still in an abject attitude, but beaming with satisfaction.

"What can you expect, when you take one's breath away, creeping in like a burglar, and letting cats out of bags like that? Get up, you ridiculous boy, and tell me all about it."

"Not a word, unless you let me come in my old place, and promise not to barricade."

Jo laughed at that as she had not done for many a long day, and patted the sofa invitingly, as she said, in a cordial tone,—

"The old pillow is up garret, and we don't need it now; so, come and 'fess, Teddy."

"How good it sounds to hear you say 'Teddy'; no one ever calls me that but you;" and Laurie sat down with an air of great content.

"What does Amy call you?"

"My lord."

"That's like her—well, you look it;" and Jo's eyes plainly betrayed that she found her boy comelier than ever.

The pillow was gone, but there *was* a barricade, nevertheless; a natural one raised by time, absence, and change of heart. Both felt it, and for a minute looked at one another as if that invisible barrier cast a little shadow over them. It was gone directly, however, for Laurie said, with a vain attempt at dignity,—

"Don't I look like a married man, and the head of a family?"

"Not a bit, and you never will. You've grown bigger and bonnier, but you are the same scapegrace as ever."

"Now, really, Jo, you ought to treat me with more respect," began Laurie, who enjoyed it all immensely.

"How can I, when the mere idea of you, married and settled, is so irresistibly funny that I can't keep sober," answered Jo, smiling all over her face, so infectiously, that they had another laugh, and then settled down for a good talk, quite in the pleasant old fashion.

"It's no use your going out in the cold to get Amy, for they are all coming up, presently; I couldn't wait; I wanted to be the one to tell you the grand surprise, and have 'first skim,' as we used to say, when we squabbled about the cream."

"Of course you did, and spoilt your story by beginning at the wrong end. Now, start right, and tell me how it all happened; I'm pining to know."

"Well, I did it to please Amy," began Laurie, with a twinkle, that made Jo exclaim,—

"Fib number one; Amy did it to please you. Go on, and tell the truth, if you can, sir."

"Now she's beginning to marm it, isn't it jolly to hear her?" said Laurie to the fire, and the fire glowed and sparkled as if it quite agreed. "It's all the same, you know, she and I being one. We planned to come home with the Carrols, a month or more ago, but they suddenly changed their minds, and decided to pass another winter in Paris. But grandpa wanted to come home; he went to please me, and I couldn't let him go alone, neither could I leave Amy; and Mrs. Carrol had got English notions about chaperons, and such nonsense, and wouldn't let Amy come with us. So I just settled the difficulty, by saying, 'Let's be married, and then we can do as we like.'"

"Of course you did; you always have things to suit you."

"Not always;" and something in Laurie's voice made Jo say, hastily,—

"How did you ever get aunt to agree?"

"It was hard work; but, between us, we talked her over, for we had heaps of good reasons on our side. There wasn't time to write and ask leave, but you all liked it, and had consented to it by and by—and it was only 'taking time by the fetlock,' as my wife says."[2]

"Aren't we proud of those two words, and don't we like to say them?" interrupted Jo, addressing the fire in her turn, and watching with delight the happy light it seemed to kindle in the eyes that had been so tragically gloomy when she saw them last.

"A trifle, perhaps; she's such a captivating little woman I can't help being proud of her. Well, then, uncle and aunt were there to play propriety; we were so absorbed in one another we were of no mortal use apart, and that charming arrangement would make everything easy all round; so we did it."

"When, where, how?" asked Jo, in a fever of feminine interest and curiosity, for she could not realize it a particle.

"Six weeks ago, at the American consul's, in Paris—a very quiet wedding, of course; for even in our happiness we didn't forget dear little Beth."

Jo put her hand in his as he said that, and Laurie gently smoothed the little red pillow, which he remembered well.

"Why didn't you let us know afterward?" asked Jo, in a quieter tone, when they had sat quite still a minute.

"We wanted to surprise you; we thought we were coming directly home, at first, but the dear old gentleman, as soon as we were mar-

2. See p. 88, n. 4 (part 1, chap. 10).

ried, found he couldn't be ready under a month, at least, and sent us off to spend our honey-moon wherever we liked. Amy had once called Valrosa a regular honey-moon home, so we went there, and were as happy as people are but once in their lives. My faith, wasn't it love among the roses!"

Laurie seemed to forget Jo, for a minute, and Jo was glad of it; for the fact that he told her these things so freely and naturally, assured her that he had quite forgiven and forgotten. She tried to draw away her hand; but, as if he guessed the thought that prompted the half-involuntary impulse, Laurie held it fast, and said, with a manly gravity she had never seen in him before,—

"Jo, dear, I want to say one thing, and then we'll put it by forever. As I told you, in my letter, when I wrote that Amy had been so kind to me, I never shall stop loving you; but the love is altered, and I have learned to see that it is better as it is. Amy and you change places in my heart, that's all. I think it was meant to be so, and would have come about naturally, if I had waited, as you tried to make me; but I never could be patient, and so I got a heart-ache. I was a boy then— headstrong and violent; and it took a hard lesson to show me my mistake. For it *was* one, Jo, as you said, and I found it out, after making a fool of myself. Upon my word, I was so tumbled up in my mind, at one time, that I didn't know which I loved best—you or Amy, and tried to love both alike; but I couldn't; and when I saw her in Switzerland, everything seemed to clear up all at once. You both got into your right places, and I felt sure that it was well off with the old love, before it was on with the new; that I could honestly share my heart between sister Jo and wife Amy, and love them both dearly. Will you believe it, and go back to the happy old times, when we first knew one another?"

"I'll believe it, with all my heart; but, Teddy, we never can be boy and girl again—the happy old times can't come back, and we mustn't expect it. We are man and woman now, with sober work to do, for play-time is over, and we must give up frolicking. I'm sure you feel this; I see the change in you, and you'll find it in me; I shall miss my boy, but I shall love the man as much, and admire him more, because he means to be what I hoped he would. We can't be little playmates any longer, but we will be brother and sister, to love and help one another all our lives, won't we, Laurie?"

He did not say a word, but took the hand she offered him, and laid his face down on it for a minute, feeling that out of the grave of a boyish passion, there had risen a beautiful, strong friendship to bless them both. Presently Jo said cheerfully, for she didn't want the coming home to be a sad one,—

"I can't make it true that you children are really married, and going to set up housekeeping. Why, it seems only yesterday that I was buttoning Amy's pinafore, and pulling your hair when you teased. Mercy me, how time does fly!"

"As one of the children is older than yourself, you needn't talk so like a grandma. I flatter myself I'm a 'gentleman growed,' as Peggotty said of David;[3] and when you see Amy, you'll find her rather a precocious infant," said Laurie, looking amused at her maternal air.

"You may be a little older in years, but I'm ever so much older in feeling, Teddy. Women always are; and this last year has been such a hard one, that I feel forty."

"Poor Jo! we left you to bear it alone, while we went pleasuring. You *are* older; here's a line, and there's another; unless you smile, your eyes look sad, and when I touched the cushion, just now, I found a tear on it. You've had a great deal to bear, and had to bear it all alone; what a selfish beast I've been!" and Laurie pulled his own hair, with a remorseful look.

But Jo only turned over the traitorous pillow, and answered in a tone which she tried to make quite cheerful,—

"No, I had father and mother to help me, the dear babies to comfort me, and the thought that you and Amy were safe and happy, to make the troubles here easier to bear. I *am* lonely, sometimes, but I dare say it's good for me, and—"

"You never shall be again," broke in Laurie, putting his arm about her, as if to fence out every human ill. "Amy and I can't get on without you, so you must come and teach the children to keep house, and go halves in everything, just as we used to do, and let us pet you, and all be blissfully happy and friendly together."

"If I shouldn't be in the way, it would be very pleasant. I begin to feel quite young already; for, somehow, all my troubles seemed to fly away when you came. You always were a comfort, Teddy;" and Jo leaned her head on his shoulder, just as she did years ago, when Beth lay ill, and Laurie told her to hold on to him.

He looked down at her, wondering if she remembered the time, but Jo was smiling to herself as if, in truth, her troubles *had* all vanished at his coming.

"You are the same Jo still, dropping tears about one minute, and laughing the next. You look a little wicked now; what is it, grandma?"

"I was wondering how you and Amy get on together."

"Like angels!"

"Yes, of course, at first—but which rules?"

"I don't mind telling you that she does, now; at least I let her think so,—it pleases her, you know. By and by we shall take turns, for marriage, they say, halves one's rights and doubles one's duties."

"You'll go on as you begin, and Amy will rule you all the days of your life."

"Well, she does it so imperceptibly that I don't think I shall mind much. She is the sort of woman who knows how to rule well; in fact, I rather like it, for she winds one round her finger as softly and prettily as a skein of silk, and makes you feel as if she was doing you a favor all the while."

3. In *David Copperfield*, Mr. Daniel Peggotty, a fisherman and David's old nurse's brother, welcomes David and refers to him and his classmate Steerforth as "two gent'lmen—gent'lmen growed."

"That ever I should live to see you a henpecked husband and enjoying it!" cried Jo, with uplifted hands.

It was good to see Laurie square his shoulders, and smile with masculine scorn at that insinuation, as he replied, with his "high and mighty" air,—

"Amy is too well-bred for that, and I am not the sort of man to submit to it. My wife and I respect ourselves and one another too much ever to tyrannize or quarrel."

Jo liked that, and thought the new dignity very becoming, but the boy seemed changing very fast into the man, and regret mingled with her pleasure.

"I am sure of that; Amy and you never did quarrel as we used to. She is the sun, and I the wind, in the fable, and the sun managed the man best, you remember."[4]

"She can blow him up as well as shine on him," laughed Laurie. "Such a lecture as I got at Nice! I give you my word it was a deal worse than any of your scoldings. A regular rouser; I'll tell you all about it some time,—*she* never will, because, after telling me that she despised and was ashamed of me, she lost her heart to the despicable party, and married the good-for-nothing."

"What baseness! Well, if she abuses you come to me, and I'll defend you!"

"I look as if I needed it, don't I?" said Laurie, getting up and striking an attitude which suddenly changed from the imposing to the rapturous, as Amy's voice was heard calling,—

"Where is she? where's my dear old Jo?"

In trooped the whole family, and every one was hugged and kissed all over again, and, after several vain attempts, the three wanderers were set down to be looked at and exulted over. Mr. Laurence, hale and hearty as ever, was quite as much improved as the others by his foreign tour,—for the crustiness seemed to be nearly gone, and the old-fashioned courtliness had received a polish which made it kindlier than ever. It was good to see him beam at "my children," as he called the young pair; it was better still to see Amy pay him the daughterly duty and affection which completely won his old heart; and, best of all, to watch Laurie revolve about the two as if never tired of enjoying the pretty picture they made.

The minute she put her eyes upon Amy, Meg became conscious that her own dress hadn't a Parisian air,—that young Mrs. Moffat would be entirely eclipsed by young Mrs. Laurence, and that "her ladyship" was altogether a most elegant and graceful woman. Jo thought, as she watched the pair, "How well they look together! I was right, and Laurie has found the beautiful, accomplished girl who will become his home better than clumsy old Jo, and be a pride, not a torment to him."

---

4. In a fable attributed to Aesop, the sun and the wind have a contest to see who can control a traveler. The wind blows with all its might, but the traveler only wraps his cloak around him more tightly. Then the sun sends its warmth toward the traveler, who responds by removing his cloak altogether, illustrating the idea that gentleness and kind persuasion are superior to force and bluster.

Mrs. March and her husband smiled and nodded at each other with happy faces,—for they saw that their youngest had done well, not only in worldly things, but the better wealth of love, confidence, and happiness.

For Amy's face was full of the soft brightness which betokens a peaceful heart, her voice had a new tenderness in it, and the cool, prim carriage was changed to a gentle dignity, both womanly and winning. No little affectations marred it, and the cordial sweetness of her manner was more charming than the new beauty or the old grace, for it stamped her at once with the unmistakable sign of the true gentlewoman she had hoped to become.

"Love has done much for our little girl," said her mother, softly.

"She has had a good example before her all her life, my dear," Mr. March whispered back, with a loving look at the worn face and gray head beside him.

Daisy found it impossible to keep her eyes off her "pitty aunty," but attached herself like a lap-dog to the wonderful châtelaine full of delightful charms. Demi paused to consider the new relationship before he compromised himself by the rash acceptance of a bribe, which took the tempting form of a family of wooden bears, from Berne. A flank movement produced an unconditional surrender, however, for Laurie knew where to have him:—

"Young man, when I first had the honor of making your acquaintance you hit me in the face; now I demand the satisfaction of a gentleman!" and with that the tall uncle proceeded to toss and tousle the small nephew in a way that damaged his philosophical dignity as much as it delighted his boyish soul.

"Blest if she ain't in silk from head to foot; ain't it a relishin' sight to see her settin' there as fine as a fiddle, and hear folks calling little Amy 'Mis. Laurence!' " muttered old Hannah, who could not resist frequent "peeks" through the slide as she set the table in a most decidedly promiscuous manner.

Mercy on us, how they did talk! first one, then the other, then all burst out together,—trying to tell the history of three years in half an hour. It was fortunate that tea was at hand, to produce a lull and provide refreshment,—for they would have been hoarse and faint if they had gone on much longer. Such a happy procession as filed away into the little dining-room! Mr. March proudly escorted "Mrs. Laurence"; Mrs. March as proudly leaned on the arm of "my son"; the old gentleman took Jo with a whispered "You must be my girl now," and a glance at the empty corner by the fire, that made Jo whisper back, with trembling lips, "I'll try to fill her place, sir."

The twins pranced behind, feeling that the millennium was at hand,—for every one was so busy with the new comers that they were left to revel at their own sweet will, and you may be sure they made the most of the opportunity. Didn't they steal sips of tea, stuff gingerbread *ad libitum*, get a hot biscuit apiece, and, as a crowning trespass, didn't they each whisk a captivating little tart into their tiny pockets, there to stick and crumble treacherously,—teaching them that both human nature and pastry are frail! Burdened with the guilty consciousness of the sequestered tarts, and fearing that Dodo's[5] sharp eyes would pierce the thin disguise of cambric and merino which hid their booty, the little sinners attached themselves to "Dranpa," who hadn't his spectacles on. Amy, who was handed about like refreshments, returned to the parlor on Father Laurence's arm; the others paired off as before, and this arrangement left Jo companionless. She did not mind it at the minute, for she lingered to answer Hannah's eager inquiry,—

"Will Miss Amy ride in her coop (*coupé*), and use all them lovely silver dishes that's stored away over yander?"

"Shouldn't wonder if she drove six white horses, ate off gold plate, and wore diamonds and point-lace every day. Teddy thinks nothing too good for her," returned Jo, with infinite satisfaction.

"No more there is! Will you have hash or fish-balls for breakfast?" asked Hannah, who wisely mingled poetry and prose.

"I don't care," and Jo shut the door, feeling that food was an uncongenial topic just then. She stood a minute looking at the party vanishing above, and, as Demi's short plaid legs toiled up the last stair, a sudden sense of loneliness came over her, so strongly that she looked about her with dim eyes, as if to find something to lean upon,—for even Teddy had deserted her. If she had known what birthday gift was coming every minute nearer and nearer, she would not have said to herself "I'll weep a little weep when I go to bed; it won't do to be dismal now." Then she drew her hand over her eyes,—for one of her boyish habits was never to know where her handkerchief was,—and had just managed to call up a smile, when there came a knock at the porch door.

She opened it with hospitable haste, and started as if another ghost had come to surprise her,—for there stood a stout, bearded gentleman, beaming on her from the darkness like a midnight sun.

"Oh, Mr. Bhaer, I *am* so glad to see you!" cried Jo, with a clutch, as if she feared the night would swallow him up before she could get him in.

"And I to see Miss Marsch,—but no, you haf a party—" and the Professor paused as the sound of voices and the tap of dancing feet came down to them.

"No, we haven't,—only the family. My brother and sister have just come home, and we are all very happy. Come in, and make one of us."

Though a very social man, I think Mr. Bhaer would have gone decorously away, and come again another day; but how could he when Jo shut the door behind him, and bereft him of his hat? Perhaps her face had something to do with it, for she forgot to hide her joy at seeing him, and showed it with a frankness that proved irresistible to the solitary man, whose welcome far exceeded his boldest hopes.

"If I shall not be Monsieur De Trop I will so gladly see them all. You haf been ill, my friend?"

5. A baby-talk nickname for "Jo."

He put the question abruptly, for, as Jo hung up his coat, the light
fell on her face, and he saw a change in it.

"Not ill, but tired and sorrowful; we have had trouble since I saw
you last."

"Ah, yes, I know! my heart was sore for you when I heard that;" and
he shook hands again with such a sympathetic face, that Jo felt as if
no comfort could equal the look of the kind eyes, the grasp of the big,
warm hand.

"Father, mother, this is my friend, Professor Bhaer," she said, with a
face and tone of such irrepressible pride and pleasure, that she might
as well have blown a trumpet and opened the door with a flourish.

If the stranger had had any doubts about his reception, they were
set at rest in a minute by the cordial welcome he received. Every one
greeted him kindly, for Jo's sake, at first, but very soon they liked him
for his own. They could not help it, for he carried the talisman that
opens all hearts, and these simple people warmed to him at once, feeling even the more friendly because he was poor,—for poverty enriches
those who live above it, and is a sure passport to truly hospitable spirits. Mr. Bhaer sat looking about him with the air of a traveller who
knocks at a strange door, and, when it opens, finds himself at home.
The children went to him like bees to a honey-pot; and, establishing
themselves on each knee, proceeded to captivate him by rifling his
pockets, pulling his beard, and investigating his watch, with juvenile
audacity. The women telegraphed their approval to one another, and
Mr. March, feeling that he had got a kindred spirit, opened his choic-
est stores for his guest's benefit, while silent John listened and enjoyed
the talk, but said not a word, and Mr. Laurence found it impossible to
go to sleep.

If Jo had not been otherwise engaged, Laurie's behavior would have
amused her; for a faint twinge, not of jealousy, but something like suspicion, caused that gentleman to stand aloof at first, and observe the
new comer with brotherly circumspection. But it did not last long; he
got interested in spite of himself, and, before he knew it, was drawn
into the circle, for Mr. Bhaer talked well in this genial atmosphere,
and did himself justice. He seldom spoke to Laurie, but he looked at
him often, and a shadow would pass across his face, as if regretting his
own lost youth, as he watched the young man in his prime. Then his
eye would turn to Jo so wistfully, that she would have surely answered
the mute inquiry if she had seen it; but Jo had her own eyes to take
care of, and, feeling that they could not be trusted, she prudently kept
them on the little sock she was knitting, like a model maiden aunt.

A stealthy glance now and then refreshed her like sips of fresh water after a dusty walk, for the sidelong peeps showed her several propitious omens. Mr. Bhaer's face had lost the absent-minded expression,
and looked all alive with interest in the present moment—actually
young and handsome, she thought, forgetting to compare him with
Laurie, as she usually did strange men, to their great detriment. Then
he seemed quite inspired; though the burial customs of the ancients,
to which the conversation had strayed, might not be considered an

exhilarating topic. Jo quite glowed with triumph when Teddy got quenched in an argument, and thought to herself, as she watched her father's absorbed face, "How he would enjoy having such a man as my Professor to talk with every day!" Lastly, Mr. Bhaer was dressed in a spandy-new suit of black, which made him look more like a gentleman than ever. His bushy hair had been cut, and smoothly brushed, but didn't stay in order long, for, in exciting moments, he rumpled it up in the droll way he used to do, and Jo liked it rampantly erect, better than flat, because she thought it gave his fine forehead a Jove-like aspect. Poor Jo! how she did glorify that plain man, as she sat knitting away so quietly, yet letting nothing escape her—not even the fact that Mr. Bhaer actually had gold sleeve-buttons in his immaculate wristbands.

"Dear old fellow; he couldn't have got himself up with more care, if he'd been going a-wooing," said Jo to herself; and then a sudden thought, born of the words, made her blush so dreadfully, that she had to drop her ball, and go down after it, to hide her face.

The manoeuvre did not succeed as well as she expected, however; for, though just in the act of setting fire to a funeral pile, the Professor dropped his torch, metaphorically speaking, and made a dive after the little blue ball. Of course they bumped their heads smartly together, saw stars, and both came up flushed and laughing, without the ball, to resume their seats, wishing they had not left them.

Nobody knew where the evening went to, for Hannah skilfully abstracted the babies at an early hour, nodding like two rosy poppies, and Mr. Laurence went home to rest. The others sat round the fire, talking away, utterly regardless of the lapse of time, till Meg, whose maternal mind was impressed with a firm conviction that Daisy had tumbled out of bed, and Demi set his night-gown afire, studying the structure of matches, made a move to go.

"We must have our sing in the good old way, for we are all together again, once more," said Jo, feeling that a good shout would be a safe and pleasant vent for the jubilant emotions of her soul.

They were not *all* there, but no one found the words thoughtless or untrue; for Beth still seemed among them—a peaceful presence—invisible, but dearer than ever; since death could not break the household league that love made indissoluble. The little chair stood in its old place; the tidy basket, with the bit of work she left unfinished when the needle grew so heavy, was still on its accustomed shelf; the beloved instrument, seldom touched now, had not been moved; and above it, Beth's face, serene and smiling, as in the early days, looked down upon them, seeming to say, "Be happy! I am here."

"Play something, Amy; let them hear how much you have improved," said Laurie, with pardonable pride in his promising pupil.

But Amy whispered, with full eyes, as she twirled the faded stool,—
"Not to-night, dear; I can't show off to-night."

But she did show something better than brilliancy or skill, for she sung Beth's songs, with a tender music in her voice which the best master could not have taught, and touched the listeners' hearts with a sweeter power than any other inspiration could have given her. The room was very still when the clear voice failed suddenly, at the last line of Beth's favorite hymn. It was hard to say,—

"Earth hath no sorrow that heaven cannot heal";[6]

and Amy leaned against her husband, who stood behind her, feeling that her welcome home was not quite perfect without Beth's kiss.

"Now we must finish with Mignon's song, for Mr. Bhaer sings that," said Jo, before the pause grew painful; and Mr. Bhaer cleared his throat with a gratified "hem," as he stepped into the corner where Jo stood, saying,—

"You will sing with me; we go excellently well together."

A pleasing fiction, by the way, for Jo had no more idea of music than a grasshopper; but she would have consented, if he had proposed to sing a whole opera, and warbled away, blissfully regardless of time and tune. It didn't much matter, for Mr. Bhaer sang like a true German, heartily and well; and Jo soon subsided into a subdued hum, that she might listen to the mellow voice that seemed to sing for her alone.

"Know'st thou the land where the citron blooms,"

used to be the Professor's favorite line; for "das land" meant Germany to him; but now he seemed to dwell, with peculiar warmth and melody, upon the words,—

"There, oh there, might I with thee,
Oh my beloved, go";

and one listener was so thrilled by the tender invitation, that she longed to say she did know the land, and would joyfully depart thither, whenever he liked.

The song was considered a great success, and the singer bashfully retired, covered with laurels. But a few minutes afterward, he forgot his manners entirely, and stared at Amy putting on her bonnet—for she had been introduced simply as "my sister," and no one had called her by her new name since he came. He forgot himself still farther, when Laurie said, in his most gracious manner, at parting,—

"My wife and I are very glad to meet you, sir; please remember that there is always a welcome waiting for you, over the way."

Then the Professor thanked him so heartily, and looked so suddenly illuminated with satisfaction, that Laurie thought him the most delightfully-demonstrative old fellow he ever met.

"I too shall go; but I shall gladly come again, if you will gif me leave, dear madame, for a little business in the city will keep me here some days."

He spoke to Mrs. March, but he looked at Jo; and the mother's voice gave as cordial an assent as did the daughter's eyes; for Mrs. March was not so blind to her children's interest as Mrs. Moffat supposed.

6. Cf. Thomas Moore, "Come, Ye Disconsolate," in *Sacred Songs* (1816), line 4.

"I suspect that is a wise man," remarked Mr. March, with placid satisfaction, from the hearth-rug, after the last guest had gone.

"I know he is a good one," added Mrs. March, with decided approval, as she wound up the clock.

"I thought you'd like him," was all Jo said, as she slipped away to her bed.

She wondered what the business was that brought Mr. Bhaer to the city, and finally decided that he had been appointed to some great honor, somewhere, but had been too modest to mention the fact. If she had seen his face when, safe in his own room, he looked at the picture of a severe and rigid young lady, with a good deal of hair, who appeared to be gazing darkly into futurity, it might have thrown some light upon the subject, especially when he turned off the gas, and kissed the picture in the dark.

CHAPTER XXI.

MY LORD AND LADY.

PLEASE, Madam Mother, could you lend me my wife for half an hour? The luggage has come, and I've been making hay of Amy's Paris finery, trying to find some things I want," said Laurie, coming in the next day to find Mrs. Laurence sitting in her mother's lap, as if being made "the baby" again.

"Certainly; go dear; I forget that you have any home but this," and Mrs. March pressed the white hand that wore the wedding-ring, as if asking pardon for her maternal covetousness.

"I shouldn't have come over if I could have helped it; but I can't get on without my little woman any more than a—"

"Weathercock can without wind," suggested Jo, as he paused for a simile; Jo had grown quite her own saucy self again since Teddy came home.

"Exactly; for Amy keeps me pointing due west most of the time, with only an occasional whiffle round to the south, and I haven't had an easterly spell since I was married; don't know anything about the north, but am altogether salubrious and balmy,—hey, my lady?"

"Lovely weather so far; I don't know how long it will last, but I'm not afraid of storms, for I'm learning how to sail my ship. Come home, dear, and I'll find your bootjack; I suppose that's what you are rummaging after among my things. Men are *so* helpless, mother," said Amy, with a matronly air, which delighted her husband.

"What are you going to do with yourselves after you get settled?" asked Jo, buttoning Amy's cloak as she used to button her pinafores.

"We have our plans; we don't mean to say much about them yet, because we are such very new brooms, but we don't intend to be idle. I'm going into business with a devotion that shall delight grandpa, and prove to him that I'm not spoilt. I need something of the sort to keep me steady. I'm tired of dawdling, and mean to work like a man."

"And Amy, what is she going to do?" asked Mrs. March, well pleased at Laurie's decision, and the energy with which he spoke.

"After doing the civil all round, and airing our best bonnet, we shall astonish you by the elegant hospitalities of our mansion, the brilliant society we shall draw about us, and the beneficial influence we shall exert over the world at large. That's about it, isn't it, Madame Récamier?"[7] asked Laurie, with a quizzical look at Amy.

"Time will show. Come away, Impertinence, and don't shock my family by calling me names before their faces," answered Amy, resolving that there should be a home with a good wife in it before she set up a *salon* as a queen of society.

"How happy those children seem together!" observed Mr. March, finding it difficult to become absorbed in his Aristotle after the young couple had gone.

"Yes, and I think it will last," added Mrs. March, with the restful expression of a pilot who has brought a ship safely into port.

"I know it will. Happy Amy!" and Jo sighed, then smiled brightly as Professor Bhaer opened the gate with an impatient push.

Later in the evening, when his mind had been set at rest about the bootjack, Laurie said suddenly to his wife, who was flitting about, arranging her new art treasures,—

"Mrs. Laurence."

"My lord!"

"That man intends to marry our Jo!"

"I hope so; don't you, dear?"

"Well, my love, I consider him a trump, in the fullest sense of that expressive word, but I do wish he was a little younger and a good deal richer."

"Now, Laurie, don't be too fastidious and worldly-minded. If they love one another it doesn't matter a particle how old they are, nor how poor. Women *never* should marry for money—" Amy caught herself up short as the words escaped her, and looked at her husband, who replied, with malicious gravity,—

"Certainly not, though you do hear charming girls say that they intend to do it sometimes. If my memory serves me, you once thought it your duty to make a rich match; that accounts, perhaps, for your marrying a good-for-nothing like me."

"Oh, my dearest boy, don't, don't say that! I forgot you were rich when I said 'Yes.' I'd have married you if you hadn't a penny, and I sometimes wish you *were* poor that I might show how much I love you;" and Amy, who was very dignified in public and very fond in private, gave convincing proofs of the truth of her words.

---

7. The subject of a famous painting (1800) by the French painter Jacques-Louis David, Madame Récamier (1777–1849) was a leader of society and the hostess of a well-known salon in late-eighteenth- and early-nineteenth-century Paris. Renowned for her beauty and charm, she is regarded as a model for de Staël's heroine Corinne.

"You don't really think I am such a mercenary creature as I tried to be once, do you? It would break my heart, if you didn't believe that I'd gladly pull in the same boat with you, even if you had to get your living by rowing on the lake."

"Am I an idiot and a brute? How could I think so, when you refused a richer man for me, and won't let me give you half I want to now, when I have the right? Girls do it every day, poor things, and are taught to think it is their only salvation; but you had better lessons, and, though I trembled for you at one time, I was not disappointed,—for the daughter was true to the mother's teaching. I told mamma so yesterday, and she looked as glad and grateful as if I'd given her a check for a million, to be spent in charity. You are not listening to my moral remarks, Mrs. Laurence,"—and Laurie paused, for Amy's eyes had an absent look, though fixed upon his face.

"Yes I am, and admiring the dimple in your chin at the same time. I don't wish to make you vain, but I must confess that I'm prouder of my handsome husband than of all his money. Don't laugh,—but your nose is *such* a comfort to me," and Amy softly caressed the well-cut feature with artistic satisfaction.

Laurie had received many compliments in his life, but never one that suited him better, as he plainly showed, though he did laugh at his wife's peculiar taste, while she said slowly,—

"May I ask you a question, dear?"

"Of course you may."

"Shall you care if Jo does marry Mr. Bhaer?"

"Oh, that's the trouble, is it? I thought there was something in the dimple that didn't suit you. Not being a dog in the manger[8] but the happiest fellow alive, I assure you I can dance at Jo's wedding with a heart as light as my heels. Do you doubt it, *ma amie?*"

Amy looked up at him, and was satisfied; her last little jealous fear vanished forever, and she thanked him, with a face full of love and confidence.

"I wish we could do something for that capital old Professor. Couldn't we invent a rich relation, who shall obligingly die out there in Germany, and leave him a tidy little fortune?" said Laurie, when they began to pace up and down the long drawing-room, arm-in-arm, as they were fond of doing, in memory of the chateau garden.

"Jo would find us out, and spoil it all; she is very proud of him, just as he is, and said yesterday that she thought poverty was a beautiful thing."

"Bless her dear heart, she won't think so when she has a literary husband, and a dozen little professors and professorins to support. We won't interfere now, but watch our chance, and do them a good turn in spite of themselves. I owe Jo for a part of my education, and she believes in people's paying their honest debts, so I'll get round her in that way."

"How delightful it is to be able to help others, isn't it? That was al-

---

8. In a fable attributed to Aesop, a dog occupies a manger; though he won't eat the hay himself, he won't allow any other animals to eat it either.

ways one of my dreams, to have the power of giving freely; and, thanks to you, the dream has come true."

"Ah, we'll do lots of good, won't we? There's one sort of poverty that I particularly like to help. Out-and-out beggars get taken care of, but poor gentlefolks fare badly, because they won't ask, and people don't dare to offer charity; yet there are a thousand ways of helping them, if one only knows how to do it so delicately that it don't offend. I must say, I like to serve a decayed gentleman better than a blarneying beggar; I suppose it's wrong, but I do, though it is harder."

"Because it takes a gentleman to do it," added the other member of the domestic admiration society.

"Thank you, I'm afraid I don't deserve that pretty compliment. But I was going to say, that while I was dawdling about abroad, I saw a good many talented young fellows making all sorts of sacrifices, and enduring real hardships, that they might realize their dreams. Splendid fellows, some of them, working like heroes, poor and friendless, but so full of courage, patience and ambition, that I was ashamed of myself, and longed to give them a right good lift. Those are people whom it's a satisfaction to help, for if they've got genius, it's an honor to be allowed to serve them, and not let it be lost or delayed for want of fuel to keep the pot boiling; if they haven't, it's a pleasure to comfort the poor souls, and keep them from despair, when they find it out."

"Yes indeed; and there's another class who can't ask, and who suffer in silence; I know something of it, for I belonged to it, before you made a princess of me, as the king does the beggar-maid in the old story.[9] Ambitious girls have a hard time, Laurie, and often have to see youth, health, and precious opportunities go by, just for want of a little help at the right minute. People have been very kind to me, and whenever I see girls struggling along, as we used to do, I want to put out my hand and help them, as I was helped."

"And so you shall, like an angel as you are!" cried Laurie, resolving, with a glow of philanthropic zeal, to found and endow an institution, for the express benefit of young women with artistic tendencies. "Rich people have no right to sit down and enjoy themselves, or let their money accumulate for others to waste. It's not half so sensible to leave a lot of legacies when one dies, as it is to use the money wisely while alive, and enjoy making one's fellow-creatures happy with it. We'll have a good time ourselves, and add an extra relish to our own pleasure, by giving other people a generous taste. Will you be a little Dorcas, going about emptying a big basket of comforts, and filling it up with good deeds?"[1]

"With all my heart, if you will be a brave St. Martin, stopping, as you ride gallantly through the world, to share your cloak with the beggar."[2]

---

9. Reference to the legend of King Cophetua, an African, and the beggar maid Penelophon, a story alluded to by many authors, including Shakespeare in *Romeo and Juliet* and *Love's Labour's Lost*.
1. In the New Testament, Dorcas (also known as Tabitha) is known for her good works, particularly making clothes for the poor. In Acts 9.38–42, Peter raises her from the dead.
2. Saint Martin was a cavalryman who gave half his cloak to a shivering beggar. Later, in a vision, he saw that the beggar was actually Jesus Christ. He left the army and became a Christian; he served as a missionary until 371, when he became the bishop of Tours.

"It's a bargain, and we shall get the best of it!"

So the young pair shook hands upon it, and then paced happily on again, feeling that their pleasant home was more home-like, because they hoped to brighten other homes, believing that their own feet would walk more uprightly along the flowery path before them, if they smoothed rough ways for other feet, and feeling that their hearts were more closely knit together by a love which could tenderly remember those less blest than they.

CHAPTER XXII.

DAISY AND DEMI.

I CANNOT feel that I have done my duty as humble historian of the March family, without devoting at least one chapter to the two most precious and important members of it. Daisy and Demi had now arrived at years of discretion; for in this fast age babies of three or four assert their rights, and get them, too, which is more than many of their elders do. If there ever were a pair of twins in danger of being utterly spoilt by adoration, it was these prattling Brookes. Of course they were the most remarkable children ever born; as will be shown when I mention that they walked at eight months, talked fluently at twelve months, and at two years they took their places at table, and behaved with a propriety which charmed all beholders. At three Daisy demanded a "needler," and actually made a bag with four stitches in it; she likewise set up housekeeping in the side-board, and managed a microscopic cooking-stove with a skill that brought tears of pride to Hannah's eyes, while Demi learned his letters with his grandfather, who invented a new mode of teaching the alphabet by forming the letters with his arms and legs,—thus uniting gymnastics for head and heels. The boy early developed a mechanical genius which delighted his father, and distracted his mother, for he tried to imitate every machine he saw, and kept the nursery in a chaotic condition, with his "sewing-sheen,"—a mysterious structure of string, chairs, clothes-pins and spools, for wheels to go "wound and wound"; also a basket hung over the back of a big chair, in which he vainly tried to hoist his too confiding sister, who, with feminine devotion, allowed her little head to be bumped till rescued, when the young inventor indignantly remarked, "Why, marmar, dats mine lellywaiter, and me's trying to pull her up."

Though utterly unlike in character, the twins got on remarkably well together, and seldom quarrelled more than thrice a day. Of course, Demi tyrannized over Daisy, and gallantly defended her from every other aggressor; while Daisy made a galley-slave of herself, and adored her brother, as the one perfect being in the world. A rosy, chubby, sunshiny little soul was Daisy, who found her way to everybody's heart, and nestled there. One of the captivating children, who seem made to be kissed and cuddled, adorned and adored like little goddesses, and produced for general approval on all festive occasions. Her small virtues were so sweet, that she would have been quite angelic, if a few small naughtinesses had not kept her delightfully human. It was all fair weather in her world, and every morning she scrambled up to the window in her little night-gown to look out, and say, no matter whether it rained or shone, "Oh pitty day, oh pitty day!" Every one was a friend, and she offered kisses to a stranger so confidingly, that the most inveterate bachelor relented and baby-lovers became faithful worshippers.

"Me loves evvybody," she once said, opening her arms, with her spoon in one hand, and her mug in the other, as if eager to embrace and nourish the whole world.

As she grew, her mother began to feel that the Dove-cote would be blest by the presence of an inmate as serene and loving as that which had helped to make the old house home, and to pray that she might be spared a loss like that which had lately taught them how long they had entertained an angel unawares. Her grandfather often called her "Beth," and her grandmother watched over her with untiring devotion, as if trying to atone for some past mistake, which no eye but her own could see.

Demi, like a true Yankee, was of an inquiring turn, wanting to know everything, and often getting much disturbed, because he could not get satisfactory answers to his perpetual "What for?"

He also possessed a philosophic bent, to the great delight of his grandfather, who used to hold Socratic conversations with him, in which the precocious pupil occasionally posed his teacher to the undisguised satisfaction of the women folk.

"What makes my legs go, Dranpa?" asked the young philosopher, surveying those active portions of his frame with a meditative air, while resting after a go-to-bed frolic one night.

"It's your little mind, Demi," replied the sage, stroking the yellow head respectfully.

"What is a little mine?"

"It is something which makes your body move, as the spring made the wheels go in my watch when I showed it to you."

"Open me; I want to see it go wound."

"I can't do that any more than you could open the watch. God winds you up, and you go till He stops you."

"Does I?" and Demi's brown eyes grew big and bright as he took in the new thought. "Is I wounded up like the watch?"

"Yes; but I can't show you how; for it is done when we don't see."

Demi felt of his back, as if expecting to find it like that of the watch, and then gravely remarked,—

"I dess Dod does it when I's asleep."

A careful explanation followed, to which he listened so attentively that his anxious grandmother said,—

"My dear, do you think it wise to talk about such things to that baby? He's getting great bumps over his eyes, and learning to ask the most unanswerable questions."

"If he is old enough to ask the questions he is old enough to receive true answers. I am not putting the thoughts into his head, but helping him unfold those already there. These children are wiser than we are, and I have no doubt the boy understands every word I have said to him. Now, Demi, tell me where you keep your mind?"

If the boy had replied like Alcibiades, "By the gods, Socrates, I cannot tell,"[3] his grandfather would not have been surprised; but when, after standing a moment on one leg, like a meditative young stork, he answered, in a tone of calm conviction, "In my little belly," the old gentleman could only join in grandma's laugh, and dismiss the class in metaphysics.

There might have been cause for maternal anxiety, if Demi had not given convincing proofs that he was a true boy, as well as a budding philosopher; for, often, after a discussion which caused Hannah to prophecy, with ominous nods, "that child ain't long for this world," he would turn about and set her fears at rest by some of the pranks with which dear, dirty, naughty little rascals distract and delight their parents' souls.

Meg made many moral rules, and tried to keep them; but what mother was ever proof against the winning wiles, the ingenious evasions, or the tranquil audacity of the miniature men and women who so early show themselves accomplished Artful Dodgers?[4]

"No more raisins, Demi, they'll make you sick," says mamma to the young person who offers his services in the kitchen with unfailing regularity on plum-pudding day.

"Me likes to be sick."

"I don't want to have you,—so run away and help Daisy make pattycakes."

He reluctantly departs, but his wrongs weigh upon his spirit; and, by and by, when an opportunity comes to redress them, he outwits mamma by a shrewd bargain.

"Now you have been good children, and I'll play anything you like," says Meg, as she leads her assistant cooks upstairs, when the pudding is safely bouncing in the pot.

"Truly, marmar?" asks Demi, with a brilliant idea in his well-powdered head.

"Yes, truly; anything you say," replies the short-sighted parent, preparing herself to sing "The Three Little Kittens" half a dozen times over, or to take her family to "Buy a penny bun," regardless of wind or limb.[5] But Demi corners her by the cool reply,—

"Then we'll go and eat up all the raisins."

Aunt Dodo was chief playmate and *confidante* of both children, and

---

3. Alcibiades was an Athenian citizen and soldier (450–404 B.C.E.). In Plato's *Alcibiades*, he is asked by Socrates how to determine what is just and what is unjust. At length, he responds, "But by the gods, Socrates, I do not know at all what I am saying."
4. In Dickens's *Oliver Twist* (1837–39), Oliver is recruited to be a pickpocket by an older boy, Jack Dawkins, who is known as the Artful Dodger.
5. "The Three Little Kittens" (who lost their mittens), a traditional nursery rhyme, sometimes attributed to Eliza Follen, first appeared in print in *New Nursery Songs for All Good Children* (c. 1843). "Buy a penny bun" may be one of the "To Market" rhymes designed to be used while bouncing a child on one's knee, for example, "To market, to market / To buy a plum bun: / Home again, home again, / Market is done."

the trio turned the little house topsy-turvy. Aunt Amy was as yet only a name to them, Aunt Beth soon faded into a pleasantly vague memory, but Aunt Dodo was a living reality, and they made the most of her,—for which compliment she was deeply grateful. But when Mr. Bhaer came, Jo neglected her playfellows, and dismay and desolation fell upon their little souls. Daisy, who was fond of going about peddling kisses, lost her best customer and became bankrupt; Demi, with infantile penetration, soon discovered that Dodo liked to play with "the bear-man" better than she did with him; but, though hurt, he concealed his anguish, for he hadn't the heart to insult a rival who kept a mine of chocolate drops in his waistcoat pocket, and a watch that could be taken out of its case and freely shaken by ardent admirers.

Some persons might have considered these pleasing liberties as bribes; but Demi didn't see it in that light, and continued to patronize the "bear-man" with pensive affability, while Daisy bestowed her small affections upon him at the third call, and considered his shoulder her throne, his arm her refuge, his gifts treasures of surpassing worth.

Gentlemen are sometimes seized with sudden fits of admiration for the young relatives of ladies whom they honor with their regard; but this counterfeit philoprogenitiveness sits uneasily upon them, and does not deceive anybody a particle. Mr. Bhaer's devotion was sincere, however, likewise effective,—for honesty is the best policy in love as in law; he was one of the men who are at home with children, and looked particularly well when little faces made a pleasant contrast with his manly one. His business, whatever it was, detained him from day to day, but evening seldom failed to bring him out to see—well, he always asked for Mr. March, so I suppose *he* was the attraction. The excellent papa labored under the delusion that he was, and revelled in long discussions with the kindred spirit, till a chance remark of his more observing grandson suddenly enlightened him.

Mr. Bhaer came in one evening to pause on the threshold of the study, astonished by the spectacle that met his eye. Prone upon the floor lay Mr. March, with his respectable legs in the air, and beside him, likewise prone, was Demi, trying to imitate the attitude with his own short, scarlet-stockinged legs, both grovellers so seriously absorbed that they were unconscious of spectators, till Mr. Bhaer laughed his sonorous laugh, and Jo cried out, with a scandalized face,—

"Father, father! here's the Professor!"

Down went the black legs and up came the gray head, as the preceptor said, with undisturbed dignity,—

"Good evening, Mr. Bhaer. Excuse me for a moment,—we are just finishing our lesson. Now, Demi, make the letter and tell its name."

"I knows him," and, after a few convulsive efforts, the red legs took the shape of a pair of compasses, and the intelligent pupil triumphantly shouted "It's a We, Dranpa, it's a We!"

"He's a born Weller," laughed Jo, as her parent gathered himself up, and her nephew tried to stand on his head, as the only mode of expressing his satisfaction that school was over.

"What have you been at to-day, bübchen?" asked Mr. Bhaer, picking up the gymnast.

"Me went to see little Mary."

"And what did you there?"

"I kissed her," began Demi, with artless frankness.

"Prut! thou beginnest early. What did the little Mary say to that?" asked Mr. Bhaer, continuing to confess the young sinner, who stood upon his knee, exploring the waistcoat pocket.

"Oh, she liked it, and she kissed me, and I liked it. *Don't* little boys like little girls?" added Demi, with his mouth full, and an air of bland satisfaction.

"You precocious chick,—who put that into your head?" said Jo, enjoying the innocent revelations as much as the Professor.

"Tisn't in mine head, it's in mine mouf," answered literal Demi, putting out his tongue with a chocolate-drop on it,—thinking she alluded to confectionery, not ideas.

"Thou shouldst save some for the little friend; sweets to the sweet, mannling," and Mr. Bhaer offered Jo some with a look that made her wonder if chocolate was not the nectar drunk by the gods. Demi also saw the smile, was impressed by it, and artlessly inquired,—

"Do great boys like great girls too, 'Fessor?"

Like young Washington, Mr. Bhaer "couldn't tell a lie";[6] so he gave the somewhat vague reply, that he believed they did, sometimes, in a tone that made Mr. March put down his clothes-brush, glance at Jo's retiring face, and then sink into his chair, looking as if the "precocious chick" had put an idea into *his* head that was both sweet and sour.

Why Dodo, when she caught him in the china-closet half an hour afterward, nearly squeezed the breath out of his little body with a tender embrace, instead of shaking him for being there, and why she followed up this novel performance by the unexpected gift of a big slice of bread and jelly, remained one of the problems over which Demi puzzled his small wits, and was forced to leave unsolved forever.

CHAPTER XXIII.

UNDER THE UMBRELLA.

WHILE Laurie and Amy were taking conjugal strolls over velvet carpets, as they set their house in order, and planned a blissful future, Mr. Bhaer and Jo were enjoying promenades of a different sort, along muddy roads and sodden fields.

"I always do take a walk toward evening, and I don't know why I should give it up, just because I often happen to meet the Professor on his way out," said Jo to herself, after two or three encounters; for, though there were two paths to Meg's, whichever one she took

---

6. Allusion to Parson Mason Weems's *The Life and Memorable Actions of George Washington* (1800), in which first appeared the legend about Washington chopping down the cherry tree.

she was sure to meet him, either going or returning. He was always walking rapidly, and never seemed to see her till quite close, when he would look as if his short-sighted eyes had failed to recognize the approaching lady till that moment. Then, if she was going to Meg's, he always had something for the babies; if her face was turned homeward, he had merely strolled down to see the river, and was just about returning, unless they were tired of his frequent calls.

Under the circumstances, what could Jo do but greet him civilly, and invite him in? If she *was* tired of his visits, she concealed her weariness with perfect skill, and took care that there should be coffee for supper, "as Friedrich—I mean Mr. Bhaer—don't like tea."

By the second week, every one knew perfectly well what was going on, yet every one tried to look as if they were stone-blind to the changes in Jo's face—never asked why she sang about her work, did up her hair three times a day, and got so blooming with her evening exercise; and no one seemed to have the slightest suspicion that Professor Bhaer, while talking philosophy with the father, was giving the daughter lessons in love.

Jo couldn't even lose her heart in a decorous manner, but sternly tried to quench her feelings; and, failing to do so, led a somewhat agitated life. She was mortally afraid of being laughed at for surrendering, after her many and vehement declarations of independence. Laurie was her especial dread; but, thanks to the new manager, he behaved with praiseworthy propriety, never called Mr. Bhaer "a capital old fellow" in public, never alluded, in the remotest manner, to Jo's improved appearance, or expressed the least surprise at seeing the Professor's hat on the Marches hall-table, nearly every evening. But he exulted in private, and longed for the time to come when he could give Jo a piece of plate, with a bear and a ragged staff on it as an appropriate coat of arms.

For a fortnight, the Professor came and went with lover-like regularity; then he stayed away for three whole days, and made no sign—a proceeding which caused everybody to look sober, and Jo to become pensive, at first, and then,—alas for romance,—very cross.

"Disgusted, I dare say, and gone home as suddenly as he came. It's nothing to me, of course; but I *should* think he would have come and bid us good-by, like a gentleman," she said to herself, with a despairing look at the gate, as she put on her things for the customary walk, one dull afternoon.

"You'd better take the little umbrella, dear; it looks like rain," said her mother, observing that she had on her new bonnet, but not alluding to the fact.

"Yes, Marmee; do you want anything in town? I've got to run in and get some paper," returned Jo, pulling out the bow under her chin, before the glass, as an excuse for not looking at her mother.

"Yes; I want some twilled silesia,[7] a paper of number nine needles,

7. A fine linen or cotton fabric.

and two yards of narrow lavender ribbon. Have you got your thick boots on, and something warm under your cloak?"

"I believe so," answered Jo, absently.

"If you happen to meet Mr. Bhaer, bring him home to tea; I quite long to see the dear man," added Mrs. March.

Jo heard *that*, but made no answer, except to kiss her mother, and walk rapidly away, thinking with a glow of gratitude, in spite of her heartache,—

"How good she is to me! What *do* girls do who haven't any mothers to help them through their troubles?"

The dry-goods stores were not down among the counting-houses, banks, and wholesale warerooms, where gentlemen most do congregate; but Jo found herself in that part of the city before she did a single errand, loitering along as if waiting for some one, examining engineering instruments in one window, and samples of wool in another, with most unfeminine interest; tumbling over barrels, being half-smothered by descending bales, and hustled unceremoniously by busy men, who looked as if they wondered "how the deuce she got there." A drop of rain on her cheek recalled her thoughts from baffled hopes to ruined ribbons; for the drops continued to fall, and, being a woman as well as a lover, she felt that, though it was too late to save her heart, she might her bonnet. Now she remembered the little umbrella, which she had forgotten to take in her hurry to be off; but regret was unavailing, and nothing could be done but borrow one, or submit to a drenching. She looked up at the lowering sky, down at the crimson bow, already flecked with black, forward along the muddy street, then one long, lingering look behind, at a certain grimy warehouse, with "Hoffman, Swartz & Co." over the door, and said to herself, with a sternly-reproachful air,—

"It serves me right! What business had I to put on all my best things, and come philandering down here, hoping to see the Professor? Jo, I'm ashamed of you! No, you shall *not* go there to borrow an umbrella, or find out where he is, from his friends. You shall slop away, and do your errands in the rain; and if you catch your death, and ruin your bonnet, it's no more than you deserve. Now then!"

With that she rushed across the street so impetuously, that she narrowly escaped annihilation from a passing truck, and precipitated herself into the arms of a stately old gentleman, who said, "I beg pardon, ma'am," and looked mortally offended. Somewhat daunted, Jo righted herself, spread her handkerchief over the devoted ribbons, and putting temptation behind her, hurried on, with increasing dampness about the ankles, and much clashing of umbrellas overhead. The fact that a somewhat dilapidated blue one remained stationary above the unprotected bonnet, attracted her attention; and, looking up, she saw Mr. Bhaer looking down.

"I feel to know the strong-minded lady who goes so bravely under many horse-noses, and so fast through much mud. What do you down here, my friend?"

"I'm shopping."

Mr. Bhaer smiled, as he glanced from the pickle-factory on one side, to the wholesale hide and leather concern on the other; but he only said, politely,—

"You haf no umbrella; may I go also, and take for you the bundles?"

"Yes, thank you."

Jo's cheeks were as red as her ribbon, and she wondered what he thought of her; but she didn't care, for in a minute she found herself walking away, arm-in-arm with her Professor, feeling as if the sun had suddenly burst out with uncommon brilliancy, that the world was all right again, and that one thoroughly happy woman was paddling through the wet that day.

"We thought you had gone," said Jo, hastily, for she knew he was looking at her,—her bonnet wasn't big enough to hide her face, and she feared he might think the joy it betrayed unmaidenly.

"Did you believe that I should go with no farewell to those who haf been so heavenly kind to me?" he asked, so reproachfully, that she felt as if she had insulted him by the suggestion, and answered, heartily,—

"No, *I* didn't; I knew you were busy about your own affairs, but we rather missed you,—father and mother especially."

"And you?"

"I'm always glad to see you, sir."

In her anxiety to keep her voice quite calm, Jo made it rather cool, and the frosty little monosyllable at the end seemed to chill the Professor, for his smile vanished, as he said, gravely,—

"I thank you, and come one time more before I go."

"You *are* going, then?"

"I haf no longer any business here; it is done."

"Successfully, I hope?" said Jo, for the bitterness of disappointment was in that short reply of his.

"I ought to think so, for I haf a way opened to me by which I can make my bread and gif my Jünglings much help."

"Tell me, please! I like to know all about the—the boys," said Jo eagerly.

"That is so kind, I gladly tell you. My friends find for me a place in a college, where I teach as at home, and earn enough to make the way smooth for Franz and Emil. For this I should be grateful, should I not?"

"Indeed you should! How splendid it will be to have you doing what you like, and be able to see you often, and the boys—" cried Jo, clinging to the lads as an excuse for the satisfaction she could not help betraying.

"Ah, but we shall not meet often, I fear; this place is at the West."

"So far away!" and Jo left her skirts to their fate, as if it didn't matter now what became of her clothes or herself.

Mr. Bhaer could read several languages, but he had not learned to read women yet. He flattered himself that he knew Jo pretty well, and was, therefore, much amazed by the contradictions of voice, face, and manner, which she showed him in rapid succession that day,—for she was in half a dozen different moods in the course of half an hour. When she met him she looked surprised, though it was impossible to help suspecting that she had come for that express purpose. When he offered her his arm, she took it with a look that filled him with delight; but when he asked if she missed him, she gave such a chilly, formal reply, that despair fell upon him. On learning his good fortune she almost clapped her hands,—was the joy all for the boys? Then, on hearing his destination, she said, "So far away!" in a tone of despair that lifted him on to a pinnacle of hope; but the next minute she tumbled him down again by observing, like one entirely absorbed in the matter,—

"Here's the place for my errands; will you come in? It won't take long."

Jo rather prided herself upon her shopping capabilities, and particularly wished to impress her escort with the neatness and despatch with which she would accomplish the business. But, owing to the flutter she was in, everything went amiss; she upset the tray of needles, forgot the silesia was to be "twilled" till it was cut off, gave the wrong change, and covered herself with confusion by asking for lavender ribbon at the calico counter. Mr. Bhaer stood by, watching her blush and blunder; and, as he watched, his own bewilderment seemed to subside, for he was beginning to see that on some occasions women, like dreams, go by contraries.

When they came out, he put the parcel under his arm with a more cheerful aspect, and splashed through the puddles as if he rather enjoyed it, on the whole.

"Should we not do a little what you call shopping for the babies, and haf a farewell feast to-night if I go for my last call at your so pleasant home?" he asked, stopping before a window full of fruit and flowers.

"What will we buy?" said Jo, ignoring the latter part of his speech, and sniffing the mingled odors with an affectation of delight, as they went in.

"May they haf oranges and figs?" asked Mr. Bhaer, with a paternal air.

"They eat them when they can get them."

"Do you care for nuts?"

"Like a squirrel."

"Hamburg grapes; yes, we shall surely drink to the Fatherland in those?"

Jo frowned upon that piece of extravagance, and asked why he didn't buy a frail[8] of dates, a cask of raisins, and a bag of almonds, and done with it? Whereat Mr. Bhaer confiscated her purse, produced his own, and finished the marketing by buying several pounds of grapes, a pot of rosy daisies, and a pretty jar of honey, to be regarded in the light of a demijohn. Then, distorting his pockets with the knobby bundles, and giving her the flowers to hold, he put up the old umbrella, and they travelled on again.

8. A basket made of rushes.

"Miss Marsch, I haf a great favor to ask of you," began the Professor, after a moist promenade of half a block.

"Yes, sir," and Jo's heart began to beat so hard she was afraid he would hear it.

"I am bold to say it in spite of the rain, because so short a time remains to me."

"Yes, sir," and Jo nearly smashed the small flowerpot with the sudden squeeze she gave it.

"I wish to get a little dress for my Tina, and I am too stupid to go alone. Will you kindly gif me a word of taste and help?"

"Yes sir," and Jo felt as calm and cool all of a sudden, as if she had stepped into a refrigerator.

"Perhaps also a shawl for Tina's mother, she is so poor and sick, and the husband is such a care,—yes, yes, a thick, warm shawl would be a friendly thing to take the little mother."

"I'll do it with pleasure, Mr. Bhaer. I'm going very fast, and he's getting dearer every minute," added Jo to herself; then, with a mental shake, she entered into the business with an energy which was pleasant to behold.

Mr. Bhaer left it all to her, so she chose a pretty gown for Tina, and then ordered out the shawls. The clerk, being a married man, condescended to take an interest in the couple, who appeared to be shopping for their family.

"Your lady may prefer this; it's a superior article, a most desirable color, quite chaste and genteel," he said, shaking out a comfortable gray shawl, and throwing it over Jo's shoulders.

"Does this suit you, Mr. Bhaer?" she asked, turning her back to him, and feeling deeply grateful for the chance of hiding her face.

"Excellently well, we will haf it," answered the Professor, smiling to himself, as he paid for it, while Jo continued to rummage the counters, like a confirmed bargain-hunter.

"Now shall we go home?" he asked, as if the words were very pleasant to him.

"Yes, it's late, and I'm so tired." Jo's voice was more pathetic than she knew, for now the sun seemed to have gone in as suddenly as it came out, and the world grew muddy and miserable again, and for the first time she discovered that her feet were cold, her head ached, and that her heart was colder than the former, fuller of pain than the latter. Mr. Bhaer was going away; he only cared for her as a friend, it was all a mistake, and the sooner it was over the better. With this idea in her head, she hailed an approaching omnibus with such a hasty gesture that the daisies flew out of the pot, and were badly damaged.

"That is not our omniboos," said the Professor, waving the loaded vehicle away, and stopping to pick up the poor little posies.

"I beg your pardon, I didn't see the name distinctly. Never mind, I can walk, I'm used to plodding in the mud," returned Jo, winking hard, because she would have died rather than openly wipe her eyes.

Mr. Bhaer saw the drops on her cheeks, though she turned her head away; the sight seemed to touch him very much, for suddenly stooping down, he asked in a tone that meant a great deal,—

"Heart's dearest, why do you cry?"

Now if Jo had not been new to this sort of thing she would have said she wasn't crying, had a cold in her head, or told any other feminine fib proper to the occasion; instead of which that undignified creature answered, with an irrepressible sob,—

"Because you are going away."

"Ah, my Gott, that is *so* good!" cried Mr. Bhaer, managing to clasp his hands in spite of the umbrella and the bundles. "Jo, I haf nothing but much love to gif you; I came to see if you could care for it, and I waited to be sure that I was something more than a friend. Am I? Can you make a little place in your heart for old Fritz?" he added, all in one breath.

"Oh yes!" said Jo, and he was quite satisfied, for she folded both hands over his arm, and looked up at him with an expression that plainly showed how happy she would be to walk through life beside him, even though she had no better shelter than the old umbrella, if he carried it.

It was certainly proposing under difficulties, for even if he had desired to do so, Mr. Bhaer could not go down upon his knees, on account of the mud, neither could he offer Jo his hand, except figuratively, for both were full; much less could he indulge in tender demonstrations in the open street, though he was near it; so the only way in which he could express his rapture was to look at her, with an expression which glorified his face to such a degree that there actually seemed to be little rainbows in the drops that sparkled on his beard. If he had not loved Jo very much, I don't think he could have done it *then*, for she looked far from lovely, with her skirts in a deplorable state, her rubber boots splashed to the ankle, and her bonnet a ruin. Fortunately, Mr. Bhaer considered her the most beautiful woman living, and she found him more "Jove-like" than ever, though his hat-brim was quite limp with the little rills trickling thence upon his shoulders (for he held the umbrella all over Jo), and every finger of his gloves needed mending.

Passers-by probably thought them a pair of harmless lunatics, for they entirely forgot to hail a 'bus, and strolled leisurely along, oblivious of deepening dusk and fog. Little they cared what anybody thought, for they were enjoying the happy hour that seldom comes but once in any life—the magical moment which bestows youth on the old, beauty on the plain, wealth on the poor, and gives human hearts a foretaste of heaven. The Professor looked as if he had conquered a kingdom, and the world had nothing more to offer him in the way of bliss, while Jo trudged beside him, feeling as if her place had always been there, and wondering how she ever could have chosen any other lot. Of course, she was the first to speak—intelligibly, I mean, for the emotional remarks which followed her impetuous "Oh yes!" were not of a coherent or reportable character.

"Friedrich, why didn't you—"

"Ah, heaven! she gifs me the name that no one speaks since Minna died!" cried the Professor, pausing in a puddle to regard her with grateful delight.

"I always call you so to myself—I forgot; but I won't, unless you like it."

"Like it! it is more sweet to me than I can tell. Say 'thou,' also, and I shall say your language is almost as beautiful as mine."

"Isn't 'thou' a little sentimental?" asked Jo, privately thinking it a lovely monosyllable.

"Sentimental? yes; thank Gott, we Germans believe in sentiment, and keep ourselves young mit it. Your English 'you' is so cold—say 'thou,' heart's dearest, it means so much to me," pleaded Mr. Bhaer, more like a romantic student than a grave professor.

"Well, then, why didn't thou tell me all this sooner?" asked Jo, bashfully.

"Now I shall haf to show thee all my heart, and I so gladly will, because thou must take care of it hereafter. See, then, my Jo—ah, the dear, funny little name!—I had a wish to tell something the day I said good-by, in New York; but I thought the handsome friend was betrothed to thee, and so I spoke not. Would'st thou have said 'Yes,' then, if I *had* spoken?"

"I don't know; I'm afraid not, for I didn't have any heart, just then."

"Prut! that I do not believe. It was asleep till the fairy prince came through the wood, and waked it up. Ah well, 'Die erste Liebe ist die beste';[9] but that I should not expect."

"Yes, the first love *is* the best; so be contented, for I never had another. Teddy was only a boy, and soon got over his little fancy," said Jo, anxious to correct the Professor's mistake.

"Good! then I shall rest happy, and be sure that thou givest me all. I haf waited so long, I am grown selfish, as thou wilt find, Professorin."

"I like that," cried Jo, delighted with her new name. "Now tell me what brought you, at last, just when I most wanted you?"

"This,"—and Mr. Bhaer took a little worn paper out of his waistcoat pocket.

Jo unfolded it, and looked much abashed, for it was one of her own contributions to a paper that paid for poetry, which accounted for her sending it an occasional attempt.

"How could that bring you?" she asked, wondering what he meant.

"I found it by chance; I knew it by the names and the initials, and in it there was one little verse that seemed to call me. Read and find him; I will see that you go not in the wet."

Jo obeyed, and hastily skimmed through the lines which she had christened—

---

9. A German proverb. Among its variants are "The first love is the best" and "One never forgets the first love."

"IN THE GARRET."

"Four little chests all in a row,
   Dim with dust, and worn by time,
All fashioned and filled, long ago,
   By children now in their prime.
Four little keys hung side by side,
   With faded ribbons, brave and gay,
When fastened there with childish pride,
   Long ago, on a rainy day.
Four little names, one on each lid,
   Carved out by a boyish hand,
And underneath, there lieth hid
   Histories of the happy band
Once playing here, and pausing oft
   To hear the sweet refrain,
That came and went on the roof aloft,
   In the falling summer rain.

"'Meg' on the first lid, smooth and fair,
   I look in with loving eyes,
For folded here, with well-known care,
   A goodly gathering lies—
The record of a peaceful life,
   Gifts to gentle child and girl,
A bridal gown, lines to a wife,
   A tiny shoe, a baby curl.
No toys in this first chest remain,
   For all are carried away,
In their old age, to join again
   In another small Meg's play.
Ah, happy mother! well I know
   You hear like a sweet refrain,
Lullabies ever soft and low,
   In the falling summer rain.

"'Jo' on the next lid, scratched and worn,
   And within a motley store
Of headless dolls, of school-books torn,
   Birds and beasts that speak no more.
Spoils brought home from the fairy ground
   Only trod by youthful feet,
Dreams of a future never found,
   Memories of a past still sweet;
Half-writ poems, stories wild,
   April letters, warm and cold,
Diaries of a wilful child,
   Hints of a woman early old;
A woman in a lonely home,
   Hearing like a sad refrain,—
'Be worthy love, and love will come,'
   In the falling summer rain.

"My 'Beth!' the dust is always swept
   From the lid that bears your name,
As if by loving eyes that wept,
   By careful hands that often came.
Death canonized for us one saint,
   Ever less human than divine,
And still we lay, with tender plaint,
   Relics in this household shrine.
The silver bell, so seldom rung,
   The little cap which last she wore,
The fair, dead Catherine[1] that hung
   By angels borne above her door;
The songs she sang, without lament,
   In her prison-house of pain,
Forever are they sweetly blent
   With the falling summer rain.

"Upon the last lid's polished field—
   Legend now both fair and true—
A gallant knight bears on his shield,
   'Amy,' in letters gold and blue.
Within the snoods that bound her hair,
   Slippers that have danced their last,
Faded flowers laid by with care,
   Fans whose airy toils are past—
Gay valentines all ardent flames,
   Trifles that have borne their part
In girlish hopes, and fears, and shames.
   The record of a maiden heart,
Now learning fairer, truer spells,
   Hearing, like a blithe refrain,
The silver sound of bridal bells
   In the falling summer rain.

"Four little chests all in a row,
   Dim with dust, and worn by time,
Four women, taught by weal and woe,
   To love and labor in their prime.
Four sisters, parted for an hour,—
   None lost, one only gone before,
Made by love's immortal power,
   Nearest and dearest evermore.
Oh, when these hidden stores of ours
   Lie open to the Father's sight,
May they be rich in golden hours,—
   Deeds that show fairer for the light.
Lives whose brave music long shall ring

1. Saint Catherine of Siena (1347–1380), the second youngest child in her family, was known for her spirituality and contentment despite suffering ongoing physical pain. Having influenced Pope Gregory XI to return to Rome and having inspired widespread spiritual revivals throughout Siena, she was canonized in 1461.

> Like a spirit-stirring strain,
> Souls that shall gladly soar and sing
> In the long sunshine, after rain.
>
> "J.M."

"It's very bad poetry, but I felt it when I wrote it one day when I was very lonely, and had a good cry on a rag-bag. I never thought it would go where it could tell tales," said Jo, tearing up the verses the Professor had treasured so long.

"Let it go,—it has done its duty,—and I will haf a fresh one when I read all the brown book in which she keeps her little secrets," said Mr. Bhaer with a smile, as he watched the fragments fly away on the wind. "Yes," he added earnestly, "I read that, and I think to myself, 'She has a sorrow, she is lonely, she would find comfort in true love.' I haf a heart full, full for her; shall I not go and say, 'If this is not too poor a thing to gif for what I shall hope to receive, take it, in Gott's name.'"

"And so you came to find that it was not too poor, but the one precious thing I needed," whispered Jo.

"I had no courage to think that at first, heavenly kind as was your welcome to me. But soon I began to hope, and then I said, 'I will haf her if I die for it,' and so I will!" cried Mr. Bhaer, with a defiant nod, as if the walls of mist closing round them were barriers which he was to surmount or valiantly knock down.

Jo thought that was splendid, and resolved to be worthy of her knight, though he did not come prancing on a charger in gorgeous array.

"What made you stay away so long?" she asked presently, finding it so pleasant to ask confidential questions, and get delightful answers, that she could not keep silent.

"It was not easy, but I could not find the heart to take you from that so happy home until I could haf a prospect of one to give you, after much time perhaps, and hard work. How could I ask you to gif up so much for a poor old fellow, who has no fortune but a little learning?"

"I'm glad you *are* poor; I couldn't bear a rich husband!" said Jo, decidedly, adding, in a softer tone, "Don't fear poverty; I've known it long enough to lose my dread, and be happy working for those I love; and don't call yourself old,—I never think of it,—I couldn't help loving you if you were seventy!"

The Professor found that so touching that he would have been glad of his handkerchief if he could have got at it; as he couldn't, Jo wiped his eyes for him, and said, laughing, as she took away a bundle or two,—

"I may be strong-minded, but no one can say I'm out of my sphere now,—for woman's special mission is supposed to be drying tears and bearing burdens. I'm to carry my share, Friedrich, and help to earn the home. Make up your mind to that, or I'll never go," she added, resolutely, as he tried to reclaim his load.

"We shall see. Haf you patience to wait a long time, Jo? I must go away and do my work alone; I must help my boys first, because even for you I may not break my word to Minna. Can you forgif that, and be happy, while we hope and wait?"

"Yes, I know I can; for we love one another, and that makes all the rest easy to bear. I have my duty also, and my work. I couldn't enjoy myself if I neglected them even for you,—so there's no need of hurry or impatience. You can do your part out West,—I can do mine here,—and both be happy, hoping for the best, and leaving the future to be as God wills."

"Ah! thou gifest me such hope and courage, and I haf nothing to gif back but a full heart and these empty hands," cried the Professor, quite overcome.

Jo never, never would learn to be proper; for when he said that as they stood upon the steps, she just put both hands into his, whispering tenderly, "Not empty now"; and, stooping down, kissed her Friedrich under the umbrella. It was dreadful, but she would have done it if the flock of draggle-tailed sparrows on the hedge had been human beings,—for she was very far gone indeed, and quite regardless of everything but her own happiness. Though it came in such a very simple guise, that was the crowning moment of both their lives, when, turning from the night, and storm, and loneliness, to the household light, and warmth, and peace, waiting to receive them with a glad "Welcome home," Jo led her lover in, and shut the door.

CHAPTER XXIV.

HARVEST TIME.

FOR a year Jo and her Professor worked and waited, hoped and loved; met occasionally, and wrote such voluminous letters, that the rise in the price of paper was accounted for, Laurie said. The second year began rather soberly, for their prospect did not brighten, and Aunt March died suddenly. But when their first sorrow was over,—for they loved the old lady in spite of her sharp tongue,—they found they had cause for rejoicing, for she had left Plumfield to Jo, which made all sorts of joyful things possible.

"It's a fine old place, and will bring a handsome sum, for of course you intend to sell it?" said Laurie, as they were all talking the matter over, some weeks later.

"No, I don't," was Jo's decided answer, as she petted the fat poodle, whom she had adopted, out of respect to his former mistress.

"You don't mean to live there?"

"Yes, I do."

"But, my dear girl, it's an immense house, and will take a power of money to keep it in order. The garden and orchard alone need two or three men, and farming isn't in Bhaer's line, I take it."

"He'll try his hand at it there, if I propose it."

"And you expect to live on the produce of the place? Well, that sounds Paradisiacal, but you'll find it desperate hard work."

"The crop we are going to raise is a profitable one;" and Jo laughed.

"Of what is this fine crop to consist, ma'am?"

"Boys! I want to open a school for little lads—a good, happy, home-like school, with me to take care of them, and Fritz to teach them."

"There's a truly Joian plan for you! Isn't that just like her?" cried Laurie, appealing to the family, who looked as much surprised as he.

"I like it," said Mrs. March, decidedly.

"So do I," added her husband, who welcomed the thought of a chance for trying the Socratic method of education on modern youth.

"It will be an immense care for Jo," said Meg, stroking the head of her one all-absorbing son.

"Jo can do it, and be happy in it. It's a splendid idea—tell us all about it," cried Mr. Laurence, who had been longing to lend the lovers a hand, but knew that they would refuse his help.

"I knew you'd stand by me, sir. Amy does too—I see it in her eyes, though she prudently waits to turn it over in her mind before she speaks. Now, my dear people," continued Jo, earnestly, "just understand that this isn't a new idea of mine, but a long-cherished plan. Before my Fritz came, I used to think how, when I'd made my fortune, and no one needed me at home, I'd hire a big house, and pick up some poor, forlorn little lads, who hadn't any mothers, and take care of them, and make life jolly for them before it was too late. I see so many going to ruin for want of help, at the right minute; I love so to do anything for them; I seem to feel their wants, and sympathize with their troubles; and, oh, I should *so* like to be a mother to them!"

Mrs. March held out her hand to Jo, who took it smiling, with tears in her eyes, and went on in the old enthusiastic way, which they had not seen for a long while.

"I told my plan to Fritz once, and he said it was just what he would like, and agreed to try it when we got rich. Bless his dear heart, he's been doing it all his life,—helping poor boys, I mean,—not getting rich; that he'll never be—money don't stay in his pocket long enough to lay up any. But now, thanks to my good old aunt, who loved me better than I ever deserved, *I'm* rich—at least I feel so, and we can live at Plumfield, perfectly well, if we have a flourishing school. It's just the place for boys—the house is big, and the furniture strong and plain. There's plenty of room for dozens inside, and splendid grounds outside. They could help in the garden and orchard—such work is healthy, isn't it, sir? Then Fritz can train and teach in his own way, and father will help him. I can feed, and nurse, and pet, and scold them; and mother will be my stand-by. I've always longed for lots of boys, and never had enough; now I can fill the house full, and revel in the little dears to my heart's content. Think what luxury; Plumfield my own, and a wilderness of boys to enjoy it with me!"

As Jo waved her hands, and gave a sigh of rapture, the family went off into a gale of merriment, and Mr. Laurence laughed till they thought he'd have an apoplectic fit.

"I don't see anything funny," she said, gravely, when she could be heard. "Nothing could be more natural or proper than for my Professor to open a school, and for me to prefer to reside on my own estate."

"She is putting on airs already," said Laurie, who regarded the idea in the light of a capital joke. "But may I inquire how you intend to support the establishment? If all the pupils are little ragamuffins, I'm afraid your crop won't be profitable, in a worldly sense, Mrs. Bhaer."

"Now don't be a wet-blanket, Teddy. Of course, I shall have rich pupils, also,—perhaps begin with such altogether; then, when I've got a start, I can take a ragamuffin or two, just for a relish. Rich people's children often need care and comfort, as well as poor. I've seen unfortunate little creatures left to servants, or backward ones pushed forward, when it's real cruelty. Some are naughty through mismanagement or neglect, and some lose their mothers. Besides, the best have to get through the hobbledehoy age, and that's the very time they need most patience and kindness. People laugh at them, and hustle them about, try to keep them out of sight, and expect them to turn, all at once, from pretty children into fine young men. They don't complain much,—plucky little souls,—but they feel it. I've been through something of it, and I know all about it. I've a special interest in such young bears, and like to show them that I see the warm, honest, well-meaning boy-hearts, in spite of the clumsy arms and legs, and the topsy-turvy heads. I've had experience, too, for haven't I brought up one boy to be a pride and honor to his family?"

"I'll testify that you tried to do it," said Laurie, with a grateful look.

"And I've succeeded beyond my hopes; for here you are, a steady, sensible, business man, doing lots of good with your money, and laying up the blessings of the poor, instead of dollars. But you aren't merely a business man,—you love good and beautiful things, enjoy them yourself, and let others go halves, as you always did in the old times. I *am* proud of you, Teddy, for you get better every year, and every one feels it, though you won't let them say so. Yes, and when I have my flock, I'll just point to you, and say, 'There's your model, my lads.' "

Poor Laurie didn't know where to look, for, man though he was, something of the old bashfulness came over him, as this burst of praise made all faces turn approvingly upon him.

"I say, Jo, that's rather too much," he began, just in his old boyish way. "You have all done more for me than I can ever thank you for, except by doing my best not to disappoint you. You have rather cast me off lately, Jo, but I've had the best of help, nevertheless; so, if I've got on at all, you may thank these two for it,"—and he laid one hand gently on his grandfather's white head, the other on Amy's golden one, for the three were never far apart.

"I do think that families are the most beautiful things in all the world!" burst out Jo, who was in an unusually uplifted frame of mind, just then. "When I have one of my own, I hope it will be as happy as the three I know and love the best. If John and my Fritz were only here, it would be quite a little heaven on earth," she added more quietly. And that night, when she went to her room, after a blissful evening of family counsels, hopes and plans, her heart was so full of happiness, that she could only calm it by kneeling beside the empty bed always near her own, and thinking tender thoughts of Beth.

It was a very astonishing year, altogether, for things seemed to happen in an unusually rapid and delightful manner. Almost before she knew where she was, Jo found herself married and settled at Plumfield. Then a family of six or seven boys sprung up like mushrooms, and flourished surprisingly. Poor boys, as well as rich,—for Mr. Laurence was continually finding some touching case of destitution, and begging the Bhaers to take pity on the child, and he would gladly pay a trifle for its support. In this way the sly old gentleman got round proud Jo, and furnished her with the style of boy in which she most delighted.

Of course it was up-hill work at first, and Jo made queer mistakes; but the wise Professor steered her safely into calmer waters, and the most rampant ragamuffin was conquered in the end. How Jo did enjoy her "wilderness of boys," and how poor, dear Aunt March would have lamented had she been there to see the sacred precincts of prim, well-ordered Plumfield overrun with Toms, Dicks, and Harrys. There was a sort of poetic justice about it after all,—for the old lady had been the terror of all the boys for miles round; and now the exiles feasted freely on forbidden plums, kicked up the gravel with profane boots unreproved, and played cricket in the big field where the irritable "cow with a crumpled horn"[2] used to invite rash youths to come and be tossed. It became a sort of boys' paradise, and Laurie suggested that it should be called the "Bhaer-garten,"[3] as a compliment to its master, and appropriate to its inhabitants.

It never was a fashionable school, and the Professor did not lay up a fortune, but it *was* just what Jo intended it to be, "a happy, home-like place for boys who needed teaching, care, and kindness." Every room in the big house was soon full, every little plot in the garden soon had its owner, a regular menagerie appeared in barn and shed,—for pet animals were allowed,—and, three times a day, Jo smiled at her Fritz from the head of a long table lined on either side with rows of happy young faces, which all turned to her with affectionate eyes, confiding words, and grateful hearts full of love for "Mother Bhaer." She had boys enough now, and did not tire of them, though they were not angels by any means, and some of them caused both Professor and Professorin much trouble and anxiety. But her faith in the good spot which exists in the heart of the naughtiest, sauciest, most tantalizing little ragamuffin gave her patience, skill, and, in time, success,—for no mortal boy could hold out long with Father Bhaer shining on him as benevolently as the sun, and Mother Bhaer forgiving him seventy times seven. Very precious to Jo was the friendship of the lads, their penitent sniffs and whispers after wrong-doing, their droll or touching little confidences, their pleasant enthusiasms, hopes, and plans; even their misfortunes,—for they only endeared them to her all the more.

2. In the nursery rhyme "The House That Jack Built," first published in *The Pretty Songs of Tommy Thumb* (1744), the cow with the crumpled horn tosses the dog and is milked by the maiden all forlorn.
3. A pun on bear garden, in Elizabethan England, an arena (commonly a theater) wherein bears were baited and tortured. Laurie plays on the roughness and chaotic activity at Plumfield.

There were slow boys and bashful boys, feeble boys and riotous boys, boys that lisped and boys that stuttered, one or two lame ones, and a merry little quadroon, who could not be taken in elsewhere, but who was welcome to the "Bhaer-garten," though some people predicted that his admission would ruin the school.

Yes, Jo was a very happy woman there, in spite of hard work, much anxiety, and a perpetual racket. She enjoyed it heartily, and found the applause of her boys more satisfying than any praise of the world,—for now she told no stories except to her flock of enthusiastic believers and admirers. As the years went on, two little lads of her own came to increase her happiness. Rob, named for grandpa, and Teddy,—a happy-go-lucky baby, who seemed to have inherited his papa's sun-shiny temper as well as his mother's lively spirit. How they ever grew up alive in that whirlpool of boys, was a mystery to their grandma and aunts; but they flourished like dandelions in spring, and their rough nurses loved and served them well.

There were a great many holidays at Plumfield, and one of the most delightful was the yearly apple-picking,—for then the Marches, Lau-rences, Brookeses, and Bhaers turned out in full force, and made a day of it. Five years after Jo's wedding one of these fruitful festivals oc-curred. A mellow October day, when the air was full of an exhilarating freshness which made the spirits rise, and the blood dance healthily in the veins. The old orchard wore its holiday attire; golden-rod and asters fringed the mossy walls; grasshoppers skipped briskly in the sere grass, and crickets chirped like fairy pipers at a feast. Squirrels were busy with their small harvesting, birds twittered their adieux from the alders in the lane, and every tree stood ready to send down its shower of red or yellow apples at the first shake. Everybody was there,—every-body laughed and sang, climbed up and tumbled down; everybody de-clared that there never had been such a perfect day or such a jolly set to enjoy it,—and every one gave themselves up to the simple pleasures of the hour as freely as if there were no such things as care or sorrow in the world.

Mr. March strolled placidly about, quoting Tusser, Cowley, and Columella[4] to Mr. Laurence, while enjoying—

"The gentle apple's winey juice."

The Professor charged up and down the green aisles like a stout Teutonic knight, with a pole for a lance, leading on the boys, who made a hook and ladder company of themselves, and performed wonders in the way of ground and lofty tumbling. Laurie devoted himself to the little ones, rode his small daughter in a bushel basket, took Daisy up among the birds' nests, and kept adventurous Rob from breaking his neck. Mrs. March

---

4. Thomas Tusser (1524?–1580) published verses on Elizabethan farm and country life in *Five Hundreth Pointes of Good Husbandrie* (1557) and other works. Abraham Cowley (1618–1667) was a doctor, poet, and essayist who wrote in "Of Agriculture," "if heraldry were guided by reason, a plough in a field arable would be the most noble and ancient arms." In the first century C.E., Lucius Junius Columella wrote *De Re Rustica*, a treatise on agriculture and gardening.

and Meg sat among the apple piles like a pair of Pomonas,[5] sorting the contributions that kept pouring in; while Amy, with a beautiful motherly expression in her face, sketched the various groups, and watched over one pale lad who sat adoring her with his little crutch beside him.

Jo was in her element that day, and rushed about with her gown pinned up, her hat anywhere but on her head, and her baby tucked under her arm, ready for any lively adventure which might turn up. Little Teddy bore a charmed life, for nothing ever happened to him, and Jo never felt any anxiety when he was whisked up into a tree by one lad, galloped off on the back of another, or supplied with sour russets by his indulgent papa, who labored under the Germanic delusion that babies could digest anything, from pickled cabbage to buttons, nails, and their own small shoes. She knew that little Ted would turn up again in time, safe and rosy, dirty and serene, and she always received him back with a hearty welcome,—for Jo loved her babies tenderly.

At four o'clock a lull took place, and baskets remained empty, while the apple-pickers rested, and compared rents and bruises. Then Jo and Meg, with a detachment of the bigger boys, set forth the supper on the grass,— for an out-of-door tea was always the crowning joy of the day. The land literally flowed with milk and honey on such occasions,—for the lads were not required to sit at table, but allowed to partake of refreshment as they liked,—freedom being the sauce best beloved by the boyish soul. They availed themselves of the rare privilege to the fullest extent, for some tried the pleasing experiment of drinking milk while standing on their heads, others lent a charm to leap-frog by eating pie in the pauses of the game, cookies were sown broadcast over the field, and apple turnovers roosted in the trees like a new style of bird. The little girls had a private tea-party, and Ted roved among the edibles at his own sweet will.

When no one could eat any more, the Professor proposed the first regular toast, which was always drunk at such times,—"Aunt March, God bless her!" A toast heartily given by the good man, who never forgot how much he owed her, and quietly drunk by the boys, who had been taught to keep her memory green.

"Now, grandma's sixtieth birthday! Long life to her, with three times three!"

That was given with a will, as you may well believe; and the cheering once begun, it was hard to stop it. Everybody's health was proposed, from Mr. Laurence, who was considered their special patron, to the astonished guinea-pig, who had strayed from its proper sphere in search of its young master. Demi, as the oldest grandchild, then presented the queen of the day with various gifts, so numerous that they were transported to the festive scene in a wheelbarrow. Funny presents, some of them, but what would have been defects to other eyes were ornaments to grandma's,—for the children's gifts were all their own. Every stitch Daisy's patient little fingers had put into the handkerchiefs she hemmed, was better than embroidery to Mrs. March;

---

5. Symbolized by a pruning knife, Pomona is a wood nymph who loves the garden and the cultivation of fruit, particularly apple trees.

Demi's shoe-box was a miracle of mechanical skill, though the cover wouldn't shut; Rob's footstool had a wiggle in its uneven legs, that she declared was very soothing; and no page of the costly book Amy's child gave her, was so fair as that on which appeared, in tipsy capitals, the words,—"To dear Grandma, from her little Beth."

During this ceremony the boys had mysteriously disappeared; and, when Mrs. March had tried to thank her children, and broken down, while Teddy wiped her eyes on his pinafore, the Professor suddenly began to sing. Then, from above him, voice after voice took up the words, and from tree to tree echoed the music of the unseen choir, as the boys sung, with all their hearts, the little song Jo had written, Laurie set to music, and the Professor trained his lads to give with the best effect. This was something altogether new, and it proved a grand success, for Mrs. March couldn't get over her surprise, and insisted on shaking hands with every one of the featherless birds, from tall Franz and Emil to the little quadroon, who had the sweetest voice of all.

After this, the boys dispersed for a final lark, leaving Mrs. March and her daughters under the festival tree.

"I don't think I ever ought to call myself 'Unlucky Jo' again, when my greatest wish has been so beautifully gratified," said Mrs. Bhaer, taking Teddy's little fist out of the milk pitcher, in which he was rapturously churning.

"And yet your life is very different from the one you pictured so long ago. Do you remember our castles in the air?" asked Amy, smiling as she watched Laurie and John playing cricket with the boys.

"Dear fellows! It does my heart good to see them forget business, and frolic for a day," answered Jo, who now spoke in a maternal way of all mankind. "Yes, I remember; but the life I wanted then seems selfish, lonely and cold to me now. I haven't given up the hope that I may write a good book yet, but I can wait, and I'm sure it will be all the better for such experiences and illustrations as these;" and Jo pointed from the lively lads in the distance to her father, leaning on the Professor's arm, as they walked to and fro in the sunshine, deep in one of the conversations which both enjoyed so much, and then to her mother, sitting enthroned among her daughters, with their children in her lap and at her feet, as if all found help and happiness in the face which never could grow old to them.

"My castle was the most nearly realized of all. I asked for splendid things, to be sure, but in my heart I knew I should be satisfied, if I had a little home, and John, and some dear children like these. I've got them all, thank God, and am the happiest woman in the world;" and Meg laid her hand on her tall boy's head, with a face full of tender and devout content.

"My castle is very different from what I planned, but I would not alter it, though, like Jo, I don't relinquish all my artistic hopes, or confine myself to helping others fulfil their dreams of beauty. I've begun to model a figure of baby, and Laurie says it is the best thing I've ever done. I think so myself, and mean to do it in marble, so that whatever happens, I may at least keep the image of my little angel."

As Amy spoke, a great tear dropped on the golden hair of the sleeping child in her arms; for her one well-beloved daughter was a frail little creature, and the dread of losing her was the shadow over Amy's sunshine. This cross was doing much for both father and mother, for one love and sorrow bound them closely together. Amy's nature was growing sweeter, deeper and more tender; Laurie was growing more serious, strong and firm, and both were learning that beauty, youth, good fortune, even love itself, cannot keep care and pain, loss and sorrow, from the most blest; for—

> "Into each life some rain must fall,
> Some days must be dark, and sad, and dreary."[6]

"She is growing better, I am sure of it, my dear; don't despond, but hope, and keep happy," said Mrs. March, as tender-hearted Daisy stooped from her knee, to lay her rosy cheek against her little cousin's pale one.

"I never ought to, while I have you to cheer me up, Marmee, and Laurie to take more than half of every burden," replied Amy, warmly. "He never lets me see his anxiety, but is so sweet and patient with me, so devoted to Beth, and such a stay and comfort to me always, that I can't love him enough. So, in spite of my one cross, I can say with Meg, 'Thank God, I'm a happy woman.'"

"There's no need for me to say it, for every one can see that I'm far happier than I deserve," added Jo, glancing from her good husband to her chubby children, tumbling on the grass beside her. "Fritz is getting gray and stout, I'm growing as thin as a shadow, and am over thirty; we never shall be rich, and Plumfield may burn up any night, for that incorrigible Tommy Bangs *will* smoke sweet-fern cigars under the bedclothes, though he's set himself afire three times already. But in spite of these unromantic facts, I have nothing to complain of, and never was so jolly in my life. Excuse the remark, but living among boys, I can't help using their expressions now and then."

"Yes, Jo, I think your harvest will be a good one," began Mrs. March, frightening away a big black cricket, that was staring Teddy out of countenance.

"Not half so good as yours, mother. Here it is, and we never can thank you enough for the patient sowing and reaping you have done," cried Jo, with the loving impetuosity which she never could outgrow.

"I hope there will be more wheat and fewer tares every year," said Amy, softly.

"A large sheaf, but I know there's room in your heart for it, Marmee dear," added Meg's tender voice.

Touched to the heart, Mrs. March could only stretch out her arms, as if to gather children and grandchildren to herself, and say, with face and voice full of motherly love, gratitude, and humility,—

"Oh, my girls, however long you may live, I never can wish you a greater happiness than this!"

6. Henry Wadsworth Longfellow, "The Rainy Day," in *Ballads and Other Poems* (1842), lines 14–15.

A Note on the Text

This Norton Critical Edition (NCE) presents the text of the first (1868–69) edition of Louisa M. Alcott's *Little Women, or, Meg, Jo, Beth and Amy*. Roberts Brothers of Boston published the first volume of *Little Women* in early October 1868; this volume went through several printings between 1868 and 1870. The second volume was issued in April 1869 and also saw several printings. In 1870, the two volumes appeared as a set in simultaneous publication. This two-volume version of *Little Women* was reprinted numerous times over the next decade.

In 1880, Roberts Brothers published a revised version of the 1868–69 text. This 1880 revision first appeared as a 586-page quarto volume, the first one-volume version of the novel, with over two hundred illustrations by Frank T. Merrill. In 1881, Roberts Brothers issued what is known as the regular edition of *Little Women*, the revised text of the 1880 illustrated volume but in a smaller format, a single sixteenmo volume of 532 pages, with just four illustrations.

The changes made in the 1880–81, or regular, edition typically involve the modernization of punctuation (fewer semicolons and commas, for instance), the modification of spelling (for example, "cosy" [37.42] becomes "cosey"; references are to the page and line in this NCE), and the alteration of diction and phrasing, including the elimination of slang (see Textual Variants on pp. 386–407). The regular edition revisions also include changes in capitalization (for instance, "Cologne" [22.28] becomes "cologne") and hyphenation ("buttercups" [285.4] becomes "buttercups") as well as paragraphing and chapter numbering (the chapters of both volumes are renumbered consecutively). Although there are no major transformations of the novel's structure or plot, the revisions in wording do modify the characters, the setting, and small elements of the plot, as well as the rhythm of the sentences. These numerous but seemingly slight changes are, however, significant: they result in a more polished, conventional, middle-class narrative. Although Alcott and her editor at Roberts Brothers, Thomas Niles, were certainly aware of these various changes, it has been so far impossible to determine whether either actively contributed to the revision of the text in 1880. Indeed, the available documentary evidence provides little indication of Alcott's view of the changes beyond her hearty approval of Merrill's drawings (see letter to Niles, p. 426). Niles's own opinion was that these changes in "style" or format contributed to a gradual increase in sales for the book in the early 1880s (see letter to Alcott, p. 427).

From 1880 through most of the twentieth century, the text of the regular edition was the version typically reprinted, first in the successive issues by Roberts Brothers and later Little, Brown, and Company (which acquired Roberts Brothers in 1898) and then in the countless versions of the twentieth and twenty-first centuries. Since the 1980s, however, the text of the first edition has gradually received more attention and become the basis for a few of the reprintings currently available.

The text preferred here is that of the first edition of 1868–69. It may be closer to Alcott's authorial intentions, and it is a livelier, more distinctive text. Nevertheless, the differences between the first edition and the regular edition are important to the study of *Little Women*, Alcott's career as a writer, and perhaps other aspects of nineteenth-century American culture (for example, the publishing and marketing of popular books or changes in gender and class expectations in the decades following the Civil War). Thus, this NCE of *Little Women* provides a list of textual variants that will permit students and scholars to examine the changes and determine for themselves the particular significance of the differences and the relative value of each edition.

This NCE of *Little Women* neither modernizes the text of the first edition nor reprints exactly the text of a particular copy of the first edition. Instead the goal has been to use a study of the early documentary forms of the novel to establish as accurate a text of the first edition as possible, a text that includes the correction of obvious errors (even if the obviousness of an error is apparent only after careful study).

The text for this NCE of *Little Women* was established by comparing thirty-one different copies of the two volumes of the first edition of *Little Women*, sixteen copies of the first volume, fifteen of the second. The copies examined include a range of different states, from the first printing of each volume, through successive printings from 1868 to 1870, to the printings of 1870 and 1871, when the volumes were published simultaneously and issued together. The first volume copies that were examined are located at the following libraries: Harvard University's Houghton Library (five copies), the University of Texas's Harry Ransom Humanities Research Center (five copies), Yale University's Sterling Memorial Library, the Cudahy Library of Loyola University Chicago, the Cooper Library at Clemson University, the University of Wisconsin's Memorial Library, Cornell University's Kroch Library, and Kansas State University's Hale Library. The examined copies of the second volume are at Harvard (four copies), Texas (six copies), Yale, Clemson, Wisconsin, Cornell, and Kansas State. Both machine collations and sight collations were used to discover differences among these copies. The first edition text was then twice collated with the text of the regular edition, both to compile a list of textual variants and to complement or complete the textual analysis used to establish the text of the novel for this NCE. Because no set of proofs and no complete manuscript of the novel exist (though a precious few manuscript pages are extant), the text for this NCE is based on the comparison of these printed copies of the novel.

The study of these successive states of the first edition and an examination of the other available documentary evidence—the Alcott-Niles correspondence, the marking of printer's errors on an early copy of the novel—reveal that some care was taken to correct errors that appeared in the earliest printings. The changes made to the first edition from 1868 to at least 1870 suggest deliberate correction of the text. Moreover, we know that Niles conscientiously solicited from Alcott "any corrections" for future printings (see letter to Alcott, p. 419); likewise, he was ready to defend her textual decisions from changes sought by a range of interested parties from printers (see letter p. 418) and outside editors (see pp. 426–27) to Sunday school librarians (see pp. 419, 426–27). Although she did not always fret over issues of spelling and punctuation (see, for instance, *Letters*, 255) and sometimes confessed trouble with grammar (see letter to Higginson, p. 419), Alcott did correct proofs and did communicate her sometimes strong authorial wishes to Niles on a regular basis, as the Alcott-Niles correspondence demonstrates. Although it has not been possible to identify precisely who made which changes, the available evidence suggests that corrections of the first edition were made collaboratively and with Alcott's consent.

Therefore, the emendations to the first edition included in this NCE of *Little Women* fall into two categories: (1) the corrections made by Alcott or her editors at some point during the successive printings of the first edition from 1868 to 1871; and (2) our own corrections of remaining, obvious typographical or printers' errors.

The corrections of the first type are primarily changes in spelling, punctuation, and hyphenation. Examples of spelling changes are numerous: "tarleton" in the earliest printings becomes "tarlatan" (71.30, and six other places); "gipsey" is changed to "gypsy" (101.27) and "tipsey" to "tipsy" (123.44); "gossipped" is corrected to "gossiped" (277.20), "fidgetty" to "fidgety" (312.45), and "Moniaco" to "Monaco" (314.20), among others. Misspelled names—"Joe" (51.2) and "Sally" (223.34)—are also corrected. Many of the changes to punctuation are corrections of clear errors: a missing apostrophe in "dont" (11.21), a misplaced apostrophe in "childrens' " (152.12), a comma where a period should be at "Berne," (349.20), a comma where a question mark should be at "her," (345.10), a misplaced comma at "now and, then just" (53.16), to cite a few examples. Some of the punctuation changes made by Alcott or her editors during the successive printings from 1868 to 1871 are a bit less obvious, but perhaps more significant. For example, the change of "when I spoke, sharply rebuked" to "when I spoke sharply, rebuked" (69.36) does not correct an obvious grammatical mistake, but the change is meaningful: the March children might give their mother a surprised look when she speaks sharply, but it's not plausible that they would give Marmee a look that sharply rebukes her when she simply speaks. Hyphenation is also changed: "sick room" becomes a hyphenated word (149.45), and "book-worm" (38.1) becomes an unhyphenated, single word.

Other changes made shortly after the initial publication of the first edition by Alcott or her editors include corrections of erroneous verb forms ("all that has came lately" [317.30], for example), pronoun agreements ("each doing their share" [99.21–22]), words mistakenly omitted (an omitted "the" in "to ends of the earth" [130.37]), words mistakenly added ("the only only one" [283.32]), italicization ("ought" [194.35]), and capitalization ("Shining ones" [325.18]). Alcott or her editors appear to have also made a few deliberate changes in word choice: "walked" in the earliest states becomes "trampled" (197.19) and an erroneous identification of "Miss Norton" is corrected to "Aunt March" (229.46), to mention two examples.

Except for these corrections made by Alcott or her editors and the correction of remaining typographical errors, the original spelling, punctuation, capitalization, and italicization are not altered. Alcott's spelling, even when inconsistent ("harum-scarum" [40.14], "harem-scarem" [258.4], for example) or irregular ("blurr" [332.47]), is not changed, except for two instances of typographical error (noted below); indeed, her spellings were plausible and often accepted alternates in the nineteenth century ("Sanscrit" [256.15], for example). The irregular but often expressive punctuation is retained, including, for example, the inconsistent use of apostrophes in the plural possessives of proper nouns ("At the Kings" [37.9]). Alcott's rendering of foreign languages is likewise not corrected.

Our own corrections of remaining typographical errors involve chiefly instances of obviously misplaced, missing, mistakenly added, or otherwise incorrect punctuation: the transposed apostrophe in "would'nt" (41.37), or the appearance of a comma where a period should be at "guide-book, I" (101.6), for example. The correction of typographical errors in two passages perhaps merits discussion because the correction changes the sense of each passage.

First, in all first edition copies examined, chapter 9 of part 1 prints the following short paragraph, about Meg's preparations for the party at the Moffats' home, as follows:

> "They are for Miss March," the man said. "And here's a note," put in the maid, holding it to Meg. (73.34).

The arrangement of quotation marks indicates two speakers in this paragraph, including a "man." Because Alcott usually follows the convention elsewhere of marking a change of speaker with a new paragraph and because it does not seem at all likely that Alcott intended an unknown man to be a part of this otherwise private scene among women, the second and third double quotation marks must be a typographical error. This NCE corrects the error to show just one speaker.

Second, in all first edition copies examined, chapter 4 of part 2 prints the following sentence (a small part of a paragraph-long passage in which Jo reads passages from reviews of her work) as follows:

"Another says, 'It's one of the best American novels which has appeared for years' " (I know better than that); "and the next asserts
that 'though it is original, and written with great force and feeling, it is a dangerous book.' " (217.13–16)

The interpolation of a set of double quotation marks before and after
the parenthetical aside does not make sense. They interrupt Jo's
speaking, and they are altogether uncharacteristic of the novel's narrative style: nowhere else does the omniscient third-person narrator shift
into the first-person in such a fashion. It seems clear that Jo is supposed to speak this aside. This NCE removes the quotation marks to
correct the error and make Jo the speaker of the aside.

Corrections of typographical errors besides mistakes in punctuation
include removing a word mistakenly added ("who are they are from"
[73.36]), replacing a word mistakenly dropped ("to go the Hummels"
[141.43]), and fixing two unintended but never corrected spellings
("torquoise" [159.30] and "Freidrich" [271.19]).

This NCE does not alter the text in three places that are probably
typographical mistakes. Where the first edition prints "hero" (15.6), in
reference to the drama the March girls stage on Christmas Day, Alcott
may have intended "villain" instead. Hugo is the villain, not the hero,
of the play. Similarly, "latter," at 25.34, should probably be "letter"—a
servant has just entered with a letter that should provide the happy information. Finally, in the passage where the sisters are preparing a funeral for Beth's bird Pip, "grave" (96.20) is not as satisfying a reading
as "grove." To say that Pip will be "buried in the grave" is redundant
and awkward, and later in the chapter it becomes clear that Pip's final
resting place is "under the ferns in the grove" (98.18). Although it
seems likely that all three instances are typographical errors, the text
as presented in this NCE lets them stand as originally printed for
three reasons: (1) a plausible (though less satisfying) reading is possible; (2) none of the examined copies of the first edition correct these
passages; and (3) each instance is probably, but not conclusively, a typographical error.

Textual Variants

These textual variants allow the reader to compare the 1868–69 first edition of *Little Women* as printed in this NCE and the 1880–81 so-called regular edition. The regular edition revisions include hundreds of changes in capitalization, spelling, italicization, wording, hyphenation, punctuation, paragraphing, and chapter numbering. The list below documents primarily changes in wording but also includes the handful of alterations to italicization and paragraphing. Changes in capitalization, spelling, hyphenation, punctuation, and chapter numbering have not generally been included here, except in a few significant instances.

The first column lists the page and line number where the text can be found in this NCE. The second column presents the text from the first edition as printed in this NCE. The third column presents the text as it appears in the regular edition.

Part I

Chapter 1

Page. line	NCE	1881 Regular Edition
11.5	lots of pretty things,	plenty of pretty things,
11.7	each other, anyhow," said Beth,	each other," said Beth,
11.33	I'm sure we grub hard enough	I'm sure we work hard enough
11.33–34	examining the heels of her boots	examining the heels of her shoes
11.35	teaching those dreadful children	teaching those tiresome children
12.4	fly out of the window or box her ears?"	fly out of the window or cry?"
12.7	I can't practise good a bit."	I can't practise well at all;"
12.25	I guess we are;	I think we are;
12.28–29	put her hands in her apron pockets,	put her hands in her pockets,
12.39	and behave better,	and to behave better,
12.42	"I ain't!	"I'm not!
14.7–8	and lit the lamp,	and lighted the lamp,

386

14.27	some left to buy something for me,"	some left to buy my pencils,"
14.29	"Put 'em on the table,	"Put them on the table,
14.33	with a crown on,	with the crown on,
14.39–40	there is lots to do	there is so much to do
15.6	by the hero of the piece.	by the villain of the piece.
15.15–16	if the audience shout,	if the audience laugh,
15.32	with ma's shoe on it	with mother's shoe on it
15.36	a stout, motherly lady,	a tall, motherly lady,
15.37–39	She wasn't a particularly handsome person, but mothers are always lovely to their children,	She was not elegantly dressed, but a noble-looking woman,
16.4	her hot slippers on,	her warm slippers on,
16.14	regardless of the hot biscuit	regardless of the biscuit
16.21	"Hurry up, and get done.	"Hurry and get done!
16.21–22	and prink over your plate,	and simper over your plate,
17.16	"I *am* a selfish pig!	"I *am* a selfish girl!

Chapter 2

20.20	I guess;	I think;
20.20	do your cakes,	fry your cakes,
21.12	Lots of them!	Many of them!
21.36	the funny party.	the queer party.
21.41–42	cried the poor woman,	said the poor woman,
21.47	and her own shawl.	and her own cloak.
22.4	"Das ist gute!"	"Das ist gut!"
22.4	"Der angel-kinder!"	"Die Engel-kinder!"
22.29–30	pronounced "a perfect fit."	pronounced a "perfect fit."
23.21	a green baize	green baize
24.5	it sung:—	it sang,—
24.10	Oh, use it well!	And use it well,
26.31	and don't like to mix	doesn't like to mix
26.33	study dreadful hard.	study very hard.
26.46–47	Maybe he'll help act;	Perhaps he'll help act;
26.48	"I never had a bouquet before; how pretty it is," and Meg	"I never had such a fine bouquet before! How pretty it is!" And Meg
27.2	sniffing at the half dead posy	smelling the half-dead posy

Chapter 3

| 27.30 | the burn shows horridly, | the burn shows badly, |
| 28.3 | Can't you fix them any way?" | Can't you make them do?" |

28.5	crunched up in my hand,	crumpled up in my hand,
28.15	I'll be as prim as a dish,	I'll be as prim as I can,
28.46–47	I've seen lots of girls do it so,"	I've seen many girls do it so,"
29.9	"quite easy and nice."	"quite easy and fine."
29.10	slippers were dreadfully tight,	slippers were very tight,
29.29–30	wrong, you just remind me	wrong, just remind me
29.36	all the proper quirks?	all the proper ways?
30.21	looked at his boots,	looked at his pumps,
30.35	but I ain't Miss March,	but I am not Miss March,
31.2–3	let Meg do the pretty.	let Meg sail about.
31.5	haven't been about enough	have n't been into company
31.10	Vevey,	Vevay,
31.16	Vevey."	Vevay."
31.18	nom à cette	nom a cette
31.36–37	long nose, nice teeth, little hands and feet, tall as I am;	handsome nose; fine teeth; small hands and feet; taller than I am;
31.46	"Not for two or three years yet;	"Not for a year or two;
32.10	with a queer little French bow.	with a gallant little bow.
32.26	her partner put on.	her partner wore.
32.27	a grand polk,	a grand polka
32.34–35	gave me a horrid wrench.	gave me a sad wrench.
32.37	those silly things.	those silly shoes.
32.44	it's past ten,	It's past nine,
33.9	with the rubbers well hidden,	with rubbers well hidden,
33.12	Making a dive at the table,	Making a dart at the table,
34.32–33	to come home from my party in my carriage,	to come home from the party in a carriage,

Chapter 4

35.7	and drive home in a carriage, and	and drive home, and
35.7	and not grub.	and not work.
35.11	so don't let's grumble,	so don't let us grumble,
35.41–42	kitten, who had swarmed	kitten, which had scrambled
36.3	Hannah, who bounced in,	Hannah, who stalked in,
36.4	and bounced out again.	and stalked out again.
36.9–10	were seldom home before three.	were seldom home before two.

36.21	more ungrateful minxes	more ungrateful wretches
36.22	the slushy road	the snowy walk
36.30–31	*I am neither a rascal nor a minx,*	I am neither a rascal nor a wretch,
37.46	in the big chair,	in the easy-chair,
38.7–8	what it was she had no idea, but left	what it was she had no idea, as yet, but left
39.7	She sung like a little lark	She sang like a little lark
40.16–17	but both took one of the younger into their keeping, and watched over them in their own way;	but each took one of the younger into her keeping, and watched over her in her own way;
41.8	I guess,"	I think,"
41.33	"Didn't the girls shout at the picture?"	"Didn't the girls laugh at the picture?"
41.35	"Laugh! not a one; they sat	"Laugh? Not one! They sat
42.5	wasn't it nice of him?	Was n't it good of him?
42.13–14	with an order for some things.	with an order for some clothes.
43.14	give us a sermon instead of a 'spin,' "	give us a sermon instead of a romance!"

Chapter 5

43.28	clumping through the hall,	tramping through the hall,
44.19–20	but he had not been lately seen,	but he had not been seen lately,
44.24–25	"His grandpa don't know	"His grandpa does not know
44.26	He needs a lot of jolly boys	He needs a party of jolly boys
44.46	I've had a horrid cold,	I've had a bad cold,
45.11	"You know me,"	"You know us,"
45.16	Laurie was in a little flutter	Laurie was in a flutter
45.30	she makes it very nice,	she makes it very nicely,
45.31	I knew you'd shout at them,	I knew you'd laugh at them,
45.46	and the things stood straight	and the things made straight
46.32–33	Her brown face was very friendly,	Her face was very friendly
46.41–42	though he don't look it;	though he does not look so;
46.45	"We ain't strangers,	"We are not strangers,
46.49–47.1	and don't mind much what happens	and does n't mind much what happens
47.1	don't stay here,	does n't stay here,

47.2	no one to go round with me,	no one to go about with me,
47.4	you ought to make a, dive,	You ought to make an effort,
47.5	then you'll have lots of friends,	then you'll have plenty of friends,
47.13–14	I go to wait on my aunt,	I go to wait on my great-aunt,
47.26	"Oh! that does me lots of good;	"Oh! that does me no end of good.
48.1	sinking into the depths of a velvet chair,	sinking into the depth of a velvet chair,
50.34	he don't like to hear me play."	he does n't like to hear me play."
50.37	I ain't a young lady,	I am not a young lady,

Chapter 6

52.27	make it up afterward,"	make it up afterwards,"
55.7	in a twitter of suspense;	in a flutter of suspense.
56.2	they'll think it's killing,"	They'll think it's splendid,"
56.10–11	pressed the shiny pedals.	pressed the bright pedals.

Chapter 7

57.22	for Marmee forbid my having	for Marmee forbade my having
58.27–28	succeeded in banishing gum	succeeded in banishing chewing-gum
59.27–28	to and fro twelve mortal times;	to and fro six dreadful times;
60.14–15	with that pathetic little figure before them.	with that pathetic figure before them.
60.29	the reproachful look Amy gave him,	the reproachful glance Amy gave him,
60.37–38	like this, and Jo wrathfully proposed	like this; Jo wrathfully proposed
60.38–39	while Hannah shook her fist	and Hannah shook her fist
61.17	You are getting to be altogether too conceited and important,	You are getting to be rather conceited,
62.5	that folks may know you've got 'em,"	that folks may know you've got them,"

Chapter 8

62.19–20	for Beth is fussing over her dolls,	for Beth is fussing over her piano,
64.6	"Has any one taken my story?"	"Has any one taken my book?"

64.19–20	you'll never get your silly old story again,"	you'll never see your silly old book again,"

Chapter 9

71.39–40	it looks heavy for spring, don't it? the violet silk	it looks heavy for spring, does n't it? The violet silk
71.44	it don't sweep enough,	it does n't sweep enough,
72.2	my bonnet don't look like Sallie's;	my bonnet does n't look like Sallie's;
72.3	I was dreadfully disappointed	I was sadly disappointed
72.4–5	with an ugly yellowish handle.	with a yellowish handle.
72.12–13	two pairs of spandy gloves	two pairs of new gloves
72.27	the more one wants, don't it?	the more one wants, does n't it?
72.28–29	which I shall leave for mother,"	which I shall leave for mother to pack,"
72.37	a winter of hard work,	a winter of irksome work,
73.23.24	Sallie offered to do her hair,	Sallie offered to dress her hair,
73.27	chattered, prinked, and flew about	chattered, and flew about
73.30–31	heath, and ferns within.	heath, and fern within.
74.10–11	Major Lincoln asked who "the fresh little girl, with the beautiful eyes, was;"	Major Lincoln asked who "the fresh little girl, with the beautiful eyes," was;
74.22	"Mrs. M. has laid her plans,	"Mrs. M. has made her plans,
74.32	I shall ask that Laurence,	I shall ask young Laurence,
74.35	She was proud,	She *was* proud,
74.39	"Mrs. M. has her plans,"	"Mrs. M. has made her plans,"
77.11–13	Put your silver butterfly in the middle of that white barbe, and catch up that long curl	Take your silver butterfly, and catch up that long curl
79.13	"I'm glad you came, for I was afraid you wouldn't,"	"I'm glad you came, I was afraid you wouldn't,"
81.28	"Just say I looked nice,	"Just say I looked pretty well,
81.34	but this sort don't pay,	but this sort does n't pay,
81.47	your mother don't like it,	your mother does n't like it,
82.45	"I told you they rigged me up,	"I told you they dressed me up,

Chapter 10

87.31–32	with a round face and snubby nose,	with a round face and snub nose,
90.13	Up bounced Snodgrass,	Up rose Snodgrass,

Chapter 11

92.10	Plumfield is about as festive	Plumfield is about as gay
92.12	I had a scare	I had a fright
92.16	'Josy-phine,	'Josyphine,
92.23	but it don't matter;	but it does n't matter;
92.31	"Hum!" said Jo;	"No," said Jo;
92.40	if mother don't mind.	if mother does n't mind.
92.41	my children need fixing up	my children need fitting up
93.6	Fun forever, and no grubbage,"	Fun forever, and no grubbing!"
93.10	did not taste good,	did not taste nice,
93.13	and there she sat,	and there Meg sat,
94.25	each acknowledged to herself that they were glad	each acknowledged to herself that she was glad
94.39	she don't act a bit like herself;	she does n't act a bit like herself;
95.19	you be missis,	you be mistress,
95.37	but be clever to him,	but be civil to him,
95.38	if I get stuck,	if I get in a muddle,
95.43	I ain't a fool,"	I'm not a fool,"
96.11–12	or drop left—oh, Pip!	or a drop left. O Pip!
96.20	he shall be buried in the grave;	he shall be buried in the garden;
96.34	Having rekindled it,	Having rekindled the fire,
97.16–17	boiled the asparagus hard for an hour,	boiled the asparagus for an hour,
98.39	one or two bits of sewing were necessary, but neglected till the last minute.	one or two necessary bits of sewing neglected till the last minute.
99.13	"Lounging and larking don't pay,"	"Lounging and larking doesn't pay,"
99.16–17	said Mrs. March, laughing audibly	said Mrs. March, laughing inaudibly
99.27	to bear or forbear,	to bear and forbear,

Chapter 12

100.25–26	I guess Mr. Brooke did it,	I think Mr. Brooke did it,

100.30–31	in her mother's mind, she sewed	in her mother's mind as she sewed
100.31–32	and her mind was busied	and her thoughts were busied
102.18–19	than if it had given her back the rosy roundness	than if it had given back the rosy roundness
103.10	"Oh, oh, Jo! you ain't going to wear that awful hat?	"O Jo, you are not going to wear that awful hat?
103.14	"I just will, though! it's capital;	"I just will, though, for it's capital,—
104.8–9	he was not very wise, but very good-natured and merry, and,	he was not very wise, but very good-natured, and
106.23–24	and tells as long as they please,	and tells as long as he pleases,
106.27–28	with a commanding gesture,	with a commanding air,
107.21–22	got half-way down when ladder broke	got half-way down when the ladder broke,
108.4–6	Of course the British beat—they always do; and, having taken the pirate captain prisoner,	Of course the British beat; they always do." ¶ "No, they don't!" cried Jo, aside. ¶ "Having taken the pirate captain prisoner,
109.29	"What lady do you think prettiest?"	"Which lady here do you think prettiest?"
112.18–19	for he is nearly ready, and as soon as he is off I shall turn soldier."	for he is ready; and as soon as he is off, I shall turn soldier. I am needed."
112.20	"I'm glad of that!"	"I am glad of that!"
112.39	so I put the saddle on it,	so Jo put the saddle on it,
113.17	"My heart! whatever shall I do!	"My heart! what shall I do?
113.21	but I'll never hunt again,	but I can never hunt again,
113.22	so there's no more horses	so there are no more horses

Chapter 13

115.12	Beth a dipper,	Beth a basket,
115.38–39	feeling that he ought to go,	feeling that he ought to go away,
116.1	"I always like your games;	"I always liked your games;
116.1	but if Meg don't want me,	but if Meg does n't want me,
116.2–3	it's against the rule to be idle	it's against the rules to be idle

116.14	"Please, mum, could I inquire	"Please, ma'am, could I inquire
116.28	"No, it was me;	"No, I did;
118.5–6	and moved a brake before her face,	and waved a brake before her face,
118.36	"I have lots of wishes;	"I have ever so many wishes;
119.11	or how much nearer we are them	or how much nearer we are then
119.15	"You and I shall be twenty-six,	"You and I will be twenty-six,
120.3	"Only what your grandpa told mother about him;	"Only what your grandpa told us about him,—
120.49–121.1	(one of which amiable creatures	(one of those amiable creatures

Chapter 14

121.21	Jo was very busy up in the garret,	Jo was very busy in the garret,
121.22–23	the sun lay warmly in at the high window,	the sun lay warmly in the high window,
121.30	If this don't suit	If this won't suit
122.22–23	looking as if she was going	looking as if she were going
122.39	"You got through quick."	"You got through quickly."
124.25	I've been aching to tell this long time.	I've been aching to tell it this long time.
124.43	half the rubbish that's published	half the rubbish that is published
124.45	for it's always pleasant	for it is always pleasant
125.40	for his Atlanta came panting up	for his Atalanta came panting up
126.20	Jo bent over her work	Jo bent over the leaves
126.41–42	that her sisters got quite bewildered.	that her sisters were quite bewildered.
127.11	we never can make her *comme la fo*,"	we never can make her *commy la fo*,"
127.19	don't amount to much, I guess,"	won't amount to much, I guess,"
127.21	"You'd better read it	"You'd better read it aloud;
128.8	loud; triumphantly over the house of March,	triumphantly over the House of March,
128.23–24	and oh—I *am* so happy,	and I *am* so happy,

Chapter 15

129.5	Oh, don't I wish I could fix things	Oh, don't I wish I could manage things

129.27	I've been pegging away at mathematics	I've been working away at mathematics
129.42	and the penny postman hasn't been.	and the postman has n't been.
132.12	I didn't beg, borrow, nor steal it.	I didn't beg, borrow, or steal it.
132.17–18	"She don't look like my Jo any more,	"She does n't look like my Jo any more,
132.46–133.1	I kept thinking *what* I could do,	I kept thinking what I could do,
133.3–4	one black tail, longer, but not so thick as mine,	one black tail, not so thick as mine,
134.37–38	"Be comforted, dear heart! there is always light behind the clouds."	"Be comforted, dear soul! There is always light behind the clouds."

Chapter 16

134.43–44	had come, showing them how rich in sunshine their lives had been. The little books	had come, the little books
135.1–2	they agreed to say good-by cheerfully, hopefully, and send their mother	they agreed to say good-by cheerfully and hopefully, and send their mother
135.12–13	and the little girls' young faces wore a grave, troubled expression,	and the little girls' wore a grave, troubled expression,
137.14	and, touching her hat à la Laurie,	and, touching her hat *à la* Laurie,
138.6	"Three cheers for dear old father!	"Three cheers for dear father!
138.11	and now I can enjoy 'em,	and now I can enjoy them,
139.6	As we busily wield a broom.	As we bravely wield a broom.
140.3	Miss Meg is goin to make a proper good housekeeper;	Miss Meg is going to make a proper good housekeeper;
140.23	"HEAD NURSE OF WARD II.:	"HEAD NURSE OF WARD No. 2,—
140.34–35	Hannah is a model servant, guards pretty Meg like a dragon.	Hannah is a model servant, and guards pretty Meg like a dragon.

Chapter 17

141.11–12	Jo caught a bad cold through neglecting to cover the shorn head enough,	Jo caught a bad cold through neglect to cover the shorn head enough,
141.14–15	subsided on to the sofa	subsided on the sofa
141.17	Meg went daily to her kingdom,	Meg went daily to her pupils,
141.41	"I thought it was most well."	"I thought it was almost well."
142.6–7	I want to finish my story."	I want to finish my writing."
142.26	"You've had scarlet fever, haven't you?"	"You've had the scarlet fever, have n't you?"
142.33	taking her sister in her lap	taking her sister in her arms
143.13–14	so I'm afraid you're going to have it,	so I'm afraid *you* are going to have it,
144.7–8	for I've been with Beth all this time."	for I've been with Beth all the time."
144.11	if it don't entirely,	if it does not entirely,
144.16–17	and I'll be as clever as possible to her,	and I'll be as sweet as possible to her,
144.27	Sing out for Meg, and tell her	Call Meg, and tell her
144.39	There don't seem to be anything	There does n't seem to be anything
144.49	it don't seem quite right to me."	it does n't seem quite right to me.
145.48	"Get along, you're a fright!"	"Get along, you fright!"

Chapter 18

147.38–39	she don't know us, she don't even talk about the flocks of green doves,	she does n't know us, she does n't even talk about the flocks of green doves,
147.39–40	she don't look like my Beth,	she does n't look like my Beth,
148.10	that will help you lots, Jo.	that will help you, Jo.
148.12	now she won't feel bad about leaving	now she won't feel so bad about leaving
148.16	"Don't Meg pull fair?"	"Does n't Meg pull fair?"
148.17	but she don't love Bethy as I do;	but she can't love Bethy as I do;
149.25–26	I never *can* bear to be 'marmed over;'	I never *can* bear to be 'lorded over;'
150.17	and every time the clock struck the sisters,	and every time the clock struck, the sisters

Chapter 19

152.15–16	and she worried Amy most to death with her rules and orders,	and she worried Amy very much with her rules and orders,
153.48	"You seem to take a deal of comfort in your prayers, Esther,	"You seem to take a great deal of comfort in your prayers, Esther,
154.13	and ask the dear God to preserve your sister."	and pray the dear God to preserve your sister."
157.16	her bird to you,	her cats to you,

Chapter 20

158.44	and, when returned, he was stretched out	and, when she returned, he was stretched out
159.10–11	I like it very much, dear," she said, looking from the dusty rosary	I like it very much, dear," looking from the dusty rosary
160.15	"How quick you guessed!	"How quickly you guessed!
160.32	Now Meg don't do anything of the sort;	Now Meg does not do anything of the sort:
160.35–36	but he don't mind me as he ought."	but he does n't mind me as he ought."
160.43	to go petting pa and truckling to you,	to go petting papa and helping you,
161.16–17	and don't think John an ugly name,	and does n't think John an ugly name,
161.18–19	they'll go lovering round the house,	they'll go lovering around the house,
161.22–23	Oh, deary me! why weren't we all boys?	Oh, dear me! why weren't we all boys,
161.28	but all be jolly together	but all be happy together
162.11	"Oh, that don't matter; he's old for his age,	"Only a little; he's old for his age,
162.26	come on, Peggy,"	come, Peggy,"

Chapter 21

163.6	and bid her rest,	and bade her rest,
163.12	he set himself to finding it out,	he set himself to find it out,
163.27	don't eat,	does n't eat,
163.28–29	I caught her singing that song about 'the silver-voiced brook,' and once she said	I caught her singing that song he gave her, and once she said
166.7–9	and Laurie folded his hands together, with such an imploring gesture, and rolled up his	and Laurie folded his hands together with such an imploring gesture, as he spoke

	eyes in such a meekly repentant way, as he spoke	
166.40	Jo immediately pounded again;	Jo immediately knocked again;
167.30–31	and believe me when I say I can't tell him what the row's about."	and believe me when I say I can't tell him what the fuss's about.
168.18	"I knew Meg would wet-blanket such a proposal,	"I know Meg would wet-blanket such a proposal,
169.18	mother forbid it.	mother forbade it.
169.27–28	the irascible old man	the irascible old gentleman
169.32	because he'd promised,	because he promised,
169.34–35	till it looked as if he'd been out in a gale,	till it looked as if he had been out in a gale,
170.36	"If I was you, I'd write him an apology,	"If I were you, I'd write him an apology,
171.6	"No; he was pretty clever, on the whole."	"No; he was pretty mild, on the whole."

Chapter 22

172.8–9	Hannah "felt in her bones that it was going to be an uncommonly plummy day,"	Hannah "felt in her bones" that it was going to be an unusually fine day,
175.22	raisens,	raisins,
176.47–48	she does not fret much, nor prink at the glass,	she does not fret much nor look in the glass,

Chapter 23

177.37	As he sat propped up in the big chair	As he sat propped up in a big chair
178.29–30	and have it over quick,"	and have it over quickly,"
179.3	"I guess not,	"I think not,
179.30	to sidle toward the door,	to sidle towards the door,
179.41–42	holding the small hand fast in both his big ones,	holding the small hand fast in both his own,
181.5	in one of your pa's letters,	in one of your father's letters,
182.3	"Your pa and ma, my dear,	"Your parents, my dear,
182.39	and haven't spirits to see your pa now.	and have n't spirits to see your father now.
185.25–26	to lead him along the peaceful ways she. walked.	to lead him along the peaceful way she walked.

Part 2

Chapter 1

190.20–21	Earnest young men found the gray-headed scholar as earnest and as young at heart as they;	Earnest young men found the gray-headed scholar as young at heart as they;
190.30–31	but the quiet man sitting among his books	but the quiet scholar, sitting among his books,
191.6	the place of under book-keeper,	the place of book-keeper,
191.10	wise in housewifery arts,	wise in housewifely arts,
192.35–36	larches, who looked undecided whether to live or die,	larches, undecided whether to live or die;
194.16	was giving a last polish to the door-handles.	was giving the last polish to the door-handles.
194.35–36	how work *ought* to be done	how work ought to be done
194.39–40	I like this room best of all	I like this room most of all
195.46	a small watchman's rattle	a watchman's rattle
196.13–14	this bran-new bower,	this spick and span new bower,
196.37	"Such as old fellows going to college,	"Such as fellows going to college,
197.19	and Jo trampled on it,	and Jo walked on it,
197.46	"Me! don't be alarmed;	"Don't be alarmed;
198.2–3	if a fellow gets a look at it by accident,	if a fellow gets a peep at it by accident,
198.9–10	I don't wish to get raspy,	I don't wish to get cross,

Chapter 2

199.10	a secret sorrow hidden in the motherly heart,	a secret sorrow hid in the motherly heart
199.17	The curly crop has been lengthened	The curly crop has lengthened
199.19–20	a soft shine in her eyes; only gentle words fall from her sharp tongue	a soft shine in her eyes, and only gentle words fall from her sharp tongue
199.32–33	and having a decided underlip.	and having a decided chin.
199.37	suits of thin, silvery gray	suits of thin silver gray
201.16–17	wine should only be used in illness,	wine should be used only in illness,
201.29	one don't like to refuse, you see."	one doesn't like to refuse, you see."
202.10	galloping down the path	promenading down the path

Chapter 3

203.25–26	to portray "Garrick buying gloves of the grisette,"	to portray Romeo and Juliet
203.36–37	did *not* suggest Murillo;	suggested Murillo;
205.42	and make a little artistic fête	and make a little artistic *fête*
206.10–11	*char-a-banc.*	*char-à-banc.*
207.14	most all accepted,	nearly all accepted,
208.2	it would taste good,	it would taste well,
209.11	"By Jove, she's forgot her dinner!"	"By Jove, she's forgotten her dinner!"
210.9	the unfortunate fête	the unfortunate *fête*
210.22	for the fourth time in two days.	for the second time in two days.

Chapter 4

211.10–11	a black pinafore	a black woollen pinafore
213.24	"I guess you and I could do most as well as that if we tried,"	"I think you and I could do as well as that if we tried,"
213.30	a fellow that works	a fellow who works
213.37–38	while Professor Sands was prosing	while Prof. Sands was prosing
214.13	*denouement.*	*dénouement.*
214.27–29	after years of effort it was *so* pleasant to find that she had learned to do *something*,	after years of effort it was *so* pleasant to find that she had learned to do something,
215.18	"The Curse of the Coventrys"	the "Curse of the Coventrys"
217.4–5	whether I have written a promising book,	whether I've written a promising book
217.12	don't believe in spiritualism,	don't believe in Spiritualism,
217.19–20	for I do hate to be so horridly misjudged."	for I do hate to be so misjudged."

Chapter 5

218.11–12	though she beamed at him from behind the family coffee-pot;	though she beamed at him from behind the familiar coffee-pot;
218.23	as if it was a mathematical exercise,	as if it were a mathematical exercise,
221.47	to flare up and blame him,	to flame up and blame him,
223.49–224.1	she had to scrimp.	she had to economize.

224.11	Meg ached for a new one—	Meg longed for a new one,—
224.24–25	as if it was a thing of no consequence,	as if it were a thing of no consequence,
224.43	and make him guess	and made him guess
225.19	what is 'the dem'd total?'	what is the 'dem'd total,'
225.27–28	with all the furbelows and quinny-dingles you have to have	with all the furbelows and notions you have to have
225.31	"Twenty yards of silk	"Twenty-five yards of silk
226.38	Laurie came creeping	Laurie came sneaking
226.42	"How's the little Ma?	"How's the little mamma?
226.48	bearing a small flannel bundle	bearing a flannel bundle

Chapter 6

228.32	till Amy cornered her	till Amy compelled her
229.24	Take your light kids	Take your light gloves
229.34	tight gloves with two buttons	tight gloves with three buttons
230.14	the Chesters are very elegant	the Chesters consider themselves very elegant
231.25	she don't know what fear is,	she does n't know what fear is,
231.27–28	she can be a pretty horsebreaker,	she can be a horse-breaker,
234.16	and don't speak respectfully	and does n't speak respectfully
234.28	"Not the least, my dear," cut in Jo;	"Not the least, my dear," interrupted Jo;
234.47	to confer a big favor,	to confer a great favor,
234.48	they tell best in the end, I guess."	they tell best in the end, I fancy."
235.7	to be pleasant to them	to be pleasant to him
235.14–15	Preaching don't do any good,	Preaching does not do any good,
236.12	Patronage don't trouble me	Patronage does not trouble me
236.14–15	some don't, and that is trying,"	some do not, and that is trying."

Chapter 7

| 238.7–8 | as she was putting her last touches to her pretty table, | as she was putting the last touches to her pretty table, |
| 239.20 | Beth declared she wouldn't go to the old fair at all, | Beth declared she wouldn't go to the fair at all; |

240.7	and she did what many of us don't always do—	and she did what many of us do not always do,—
243.11–12	when May bid Amy "goodnight,"	when May bade Amy good night,
244.23–24	I'm glad you ain't going quite yet,"	I'm glad you are not going quite yet,"
245.7–8	thoughtfully flattening her nose with her knife.	thoughtfully patting her nose with her knife.
245.25–26	little dreaming how soon he would be called upon	little dreaming that he would be called upon

Chapter 8

247.13	won't we, pa?'	won't we, papa?'
247.20	'See, pa, aren't they pretty!"	'See, papa, are n't they pretty!'
247.27–28	A sweet white hat and blue feather, a distracting muslin to match,	A white hat and blue feather, a muslin dress to match,
247.31	Don't that sound sort of elegant	Does n't that sound sort of elegant
247.40	and whirling round corners,	and whirling around corners
248.1	with a 'Aye, aye, mum,' the old thing made his horse walk,	with an 'Aye, aye, mum,' the man made his horse walk,
249.4–5	What ages ago it seems, don't it?	What ages ago it seems, does n't it?
249.34–35	Uncle don't know ten words,	Uncle does n't know ten words,
250.12	*tres magnifique.*	*très magnifique.*
250.14	but dressed in horrid taste,	but dressed in bad taste,
250.20	Pere la Chaise	Père la Chaise
250.23–24	That is so Frenchy,— *n'est ce pas?*	That is so Frenchy.

Chapter 9

255.12–13	Here's Meg married, and a ma,	Here's Meg married and a mamma,
255.33–34	always having a joke or a frown ready	always having a joke or a smile ready
257.13–14	was seldom seen,	was seldom heard,

Chapter 10

262.3	"NEW YORK, NOV.	"NEW YORK, November.
262.5	for I've got lots to tell,	for I've got heaps to tell,
262.21	rather spoilt, I guess,	rather spoilt, I fancy,

262.38–39	I saw a queer-looking man	I saw a gentleman
263.8	He's most forty,	He's almost forty,
263.31	droll nose,	good nose,
263.33–34	and he hadn't a handsome feature in his face,	and he had n't a really handsome feature in his face,
263.35	his linen was spandy nice,	his linen was very nice,
265.31–32	I guess he has a hard life of it.	I fancy he has a hard life of it.
266.10–11	settling their beavers	settling their hats
266.36–37	in spite of his odd ways.	in spite of his foreign ways.
267.35	don't she, Mr. Bhaer?'	does n't she, Mr. Bhaer?'
268.13	"DEC.	"DECEMBER.
268.28	in such a funny way,	in such a droll way
268.29	To begin at the . beginning Mrs. Kirke called to me,	To begin at the beginning, Mrs. Kirke called to me,
269.20	when he made signs to Tina	while he made signs to Tina
269.26	as red as a beet.	as red as a peony.
269.47–48	as if I'd covered my name with glory:—	as if I'd covered myself with glory.
270.10	'Das ist gute!	'Das ist gut!
270.21	he don't seem tired of it yet,—	he does n't seem tired of it yet,—
270.22–23	for I don't dare offer money.	for I dare not offer money.
270.31	"Jan.	"JANUARY.
270.41	and eat, and laughed	and ate and laughed
271.7–8	for between these two lids	for between these lids
271.15–16	as only Germans can do it.	as only Germans can give it.
271.22–23	a new stand-dish on his table,	a new standish on his table,
271.28–29	an article of *virtu*;	an article of *vertu*;
271.36	I rigged up as Mrs. Malaprop,	I dressed up as Mrs. Malaprop,

Chapter 11

272.23	this delightful *chateau en Espagne*.	this delightful *château en Espagne*.
273.11	she must get through with the matter somehow,	she must get through the matter somehow,
274.6	had all been stricken out.	had been stricken out.
276.11	plain and odd,—	plain and peculiar,

278.11	after they annihilated all the old beliefs.	after they had annihilated all the old beliefs.
278.44	he doesn't prink at his glass	he does n't look in his glass
280.44	and *what should* I do	and what *should* I do
281.11	hadn't been so dreadfully particular about such things."	hadn't been so particular about such things."
281.35–36	who did go, of course, as rewarded	who did go, as rewarded
281.42–43	that's honest, any way;"	that's honest, at least;"

Chapter 12

283.22	Laurie "dug" to some purpose	Laurie studied to some purpose
284.5	wouldn't go and make her hurt his poor little . feelings	wouldn't do anything to make her hurt his poor little feelings.
284.7	for the *tête-a-tête,*	for the *tête-à-tête,*
286.24	for you can make me anything you like!"	for you could make me anything you like."
288.22	he played the "Sonata Pathetique,"	he played the "Sonata Pathétique,"
290.2	than if I were left behind.	than if I was left behind.

Chapter 13

294.28	"I'll try to be willing,"	"I try to be willing,"
294.45	I can't speak out, except to my old Jo.	I can't speak out, except to my Jo.

Chapter 14

279.10	"Mon Dieu! I have so much to say, and don't know where to begin.	"I have so much to say, I don't know where to begin!
297.35–36	Dirty old hole, isn't it?" he added, with a sniff of disgust,	Dirty old hole, is n't it?" he added, with a look of disgust,
298.1–2	and she couldn't find the merry-faced boy	and she could not find the merry-faced boy
301.20	in the long *salle a manger,*	in the long *salle à manger,*
302.22	rather a short Pole to support the steps of	rather a short Pole to support
302.32–33	if he then gave any sign of penitence.	if he then gave any signs of penitence.
303.12–13	and dismaying the garçons	and dismayed the *garçons*

303.37   Balzac's 'Femme piente   Balzac's 'Femme peinte
            par elle même,' "   par elle-même,' "

Chapter 15

304.41   girls early sign a   girls early sign the
            declaration of   declaration of
            independence,   independence,
305.37–38   the sacred precincts of   the sacred precincts of
            Babydom.   Babyland.
306.21   John don't find me   John does n't find me
            interesting   interesting
306.35   I might as well be a   I might as well be
            widow,"   widowed,"
307.8   as if I was little Meg   as if I were little Meg again.
            again.
307.22   He don't see that I want   He does n't see that I want
            him,   him,
307.37–38   just as you do,   just as you are,
309.5   more impressive than all   more impressive than all
            the mother's love pats.   mamma's love-pats.
310.46   he rolled out at the   he rolled out on the other,
            other,
311.43   that tussle with his little that tussle with his son
            son
312.18–19   a pretty little preparation a pretty little preparation of
            of tulle and flowers   lace and flowers
312.26   it was so very small,   it was so small,

Chapter 16

313.38   missed the "muching"   missed the "petting"
315.28–29   said Amy, deftly   said Amy, gathering three of
            gathering three of the   the tiny cream-colored ones
            tiny cream-colored ones
317.12–13   the doubts that had   the doubts that had
            begun   begun
            to worry her lately.   to worry her lately.
318.8   if your tongue don't.   if your tongue won't.
318.9–10   I've heard rumors about   I heard rumors about Fred
            Fred and you   and you
318.11–12   detained so long, that   detained so long, something
            something would have   would have come of it—
            come of it—
321.31–32   if I couldn't be loved,"   if I couldn't be loved," said
            cried Amy,   Amy,
323.17   "Shall we see you this   "Shall we see you this
            evening, *mon frere?*"   evening, *mon frère?*"

Chapter 17

324.6	and each did their part	and each did his or her part
324.11–12	Amy's loveliest sketches;	Amy's finest sketches;
327.21	and feels as if I'd helped her."	and feels as if I'd helped them."
327.41	through the valley of the shadow,	through the Valley of the Shadow,
327.47–48	but one loving look and a little sigh.	but one loving look, one little sigh.

Chapter 18

333.16	Vevey,	Vevay,
333.29	Vevey well;	Vevay
333.31	The garçon was in despair	The *garçon* was in despair
334.25–26	he could not get any farther,	He could not get any further,
335.21	Vevey,	Vevay,
336.9	the *denouément* would take place	the *dénouement* would take place
336.15	pretty Vevey in the valley,	pretty Vevay in the valley,

Chapter 19

337.22	a few poor little pleasures,	a few small pleasures,
338.40	if I tried it, always *'perwisin'* I could," said Jo,	if I tried it?" said Jo,

Chapter 20

343.7–8	but secretly resolve that they never will;	but secretly resolve that they never will be;
345.26	you all liked it, and had consented to it by and by—	you all liked it, had consented to it by and by,
350.30–31	for there stood a stout, bearded gentleman,	for there stood a tall, bearded gentleman,
350.38–39	My brother and sister have just come home,	My sister and friends have just come home,
352.4–5	Mr. Bhaer was dressed in a spandy-new suit of black,	Mr. Bhaer was dressed in a new suit of black.
353.27–28	and the singer bashfully retired, covered with laurels.	and the singer retired covered with laurels.

| 353.31–32 | He forgot himself still farther, when Laurie said, | He forgot himself still further when Laurie said, |

Chapter 21

354.43–44	I'm going into business with a devotion that shall delight grandpa,	I'm going into business with a devotion that shall delight grandfather,
355.8–9	Madame Recamier?"	Madame Récamier?"
356.29	Do you doubt it, *ma amie?*"	Do you doubt it, my darling?"
357.3	"Ah, we'll do lots of good, won't we?	"Ah! we'll do quantities of good, won't we?
357.7	so delicately that it don't offend.	so delicately that it does not offend.
357.35–36	It's not half so sensible to leave a lot of legacies when one dies,	It's not half so sensible to leave legacies when one dies

Chapter 22

| 358.30–31 | with his "sewing-sheen," | with his "sewin-sheen," |
| 358.36 | "Why, marmar, dats mine lellywaiter, | "Why, marmar, dat's my lellywaiter, |

Chapter 23

363.12	"as Friedrich—I mean Mr. Bhaer—don't like tea."	"as Friedrich—I mean Mr. Bhaer—does n't like tea."
363.14–15	to the changes in Jo's face—never asked why she sang	to the changes in Jo's face. They never asked why she sang
364.33	You shall slop away,	You shall trudge away,
367.7	Jo nearly smashed the small flowerpot	Jo nearly crushed the small flower-pot
367.44	"That is not our omniboos,"	"This is not our omniboos,"
367.45	the poor little posies.	the poor little flowers.
368.9	"Ah, my Gott,	"Ach, mein Gott,
371.21	Within the snoods that bound her hair,	Within lie snoods that bound her hair,
372.35	don't call yourself old,— I never think of it,—I couldn't help loving you	don't call yourself old,— forty is the prime of life. I couldn't help loving you

Chapter 24

373.26	for their prospect did not brighten,	for their prospects did not brighten,
374.30	money don't stay in his pocket	money does n't stay in his pocket
375.17–18	well-meaning boy-hearts,	well-meaning boys' hearts,
375.23	doing lots of good with your money,	doing heaps of good with your money,
375.24–25	But you aren't merely a business man,—	But you are not merely a business man:
376.16–17	for the old lady had been the terror of all the boys for miles round;	for the old lady had been the terror of the boys for miles round;
377.19	Brookeses	Brookes,
380.25	I'm growing as thin as a shadow, and am over thirty;	I'm growing as thin as a shadow, and am thirty;

Most of the corrections to the first edition text that appeared in sub-sequent printings of the first edition were retained in the text of the regular edition. In certain instances, however, the regular edition does not use these changes but returns to the uncorrected text of the earli-est printings of the first edition. Thus, there are several places where the text of this NCE differs from the text of the regular edition not be-cause the author or editors made changes while preparing the regular edition but because the author or editors may have relied on an earlier printing of the first edition and/or ignored changes or corrections made in 1869 and 1870. In other words, these discrepancies are not precisely differences between the first edition and the regular edition.

The first column below lists the page and line number where the text appears in this NCE. The second column lists the text from the first edition as printed in this NCE. The third column lists the text as printed in the regular edition, which is identical to the uncorrected text of the earliest printings of the first edition in these thirteen instances.

Page. line	NCE	1881 Regular Edition
129.11	nowadays;	now-a-days;
180.11	mean time,	meantime,
194.35	*ought*	ought
197.19	trampled	walked
218.12	family	familiar
225.31	"Twenty	"Twenty-five
226.38	creeping	sneaking
255.34	frown	smile
290.2	were	was
306.35	be a widow,"	be widowed,"
307.37–38	just as you do,	just as you are,
327.21	helped her."	helped them."
375.18	boy-hearts,	boys' hearts,

BACKGROUNDS
AND CONTEXTS

Journals, Correspondence, and Biography

LOUISA MAY ALCOTT

Journals†

[1855]

* * *

April, 1855.—I am in the garret with my papers round me, and a pile of apples to eat while I write my journal, plan stories, and enjoy the patter of rain on the roof, in peace and quiet.

[Jo in the garret.—L.M.A.][1]

Being behindhand, as usual, I'll make note of the main events up to date, for I don't waste ink in poetry and pages of rubbish now. I've begun to *live*, and have no time for sentimental musing.

* * *

[1856]

* * *

October. * * *
Made plans to go to Boston for the winter, as there is nothing to do here, and there I can support myself and help the family. C. offers 10 dollars a month, and perhaps more. L. W., M. S., and others, have plenty of sewing; the play *may* come out, and Mrs. R. will give me a sky-parlor for $3 a week, with fire and board. I sew for her also.[2]

If I can get A. L. to governess I shall be all right.[3]

I was born with a boy's spirit under my bib and tucker. I *can't wait* when I *can work*; so I took my little talent in my hand and forced the world again, braver than before and wiser for my failures.

[Jo in N. Y.—L. M. A.]

---

† From *Louisa May Alcott: Her Life, Letters, and Journals*, ed. Ednah D. Cheney (Boston: Roberts Brothers, 1889), pp. 80, 85, 121–22, 186, 198–99, 200–201, 202, 207–08, 275, 318.
1. Comments in brackets denote interpolations added by Alcott herself years later [*Editors*].
2. William Warland Clapp (C.), editor of the *Saturday Evening Gazette*, paid Alcott ten dollars for "The Rival Prima Donnas" and published several of her stories during the late 1850s. Louisa Willis (L. W.) and Molly Sewall (M. S.) were Alcott's cousins. Mrs. Mary Ann Reed (R.) ran a boarding house in Boston [*Editors*].
3. Alice Lovering (A. L.) was one of the five children of Mr. and Mrs. Joseph S. Lovering. Alcott worked intermittently as a tutor and governess for this Boston family from 1851 through 1859 [*Editors*].

I don't often pray in words; but when I set out that day with all my wordly goods in the little old trunk, my own earnings ($25) in my pocket, and much hope and resolution in my soul, my heart was very full, and I said to the Lord, "Help us all, and keep us for one another," as I never said it before, while I looked back at the dear faces watching me, so full of love and hope and faith.

* * *

[1860]

* * *

May.—Meg's wedding.[4]

* * *

Saw Anna's honeymoon home at Chelsea,—a little cottage in a blooming apple-orchard. Pretty place, simple and sweet. God bless it!

The dear girl was married on the 23d, the same day as Mother's wedding. A lovely day; the house full of sunshine, flowers, friends, and happiness. Uncle S. J. May married them,[5] with no fuss, but much love; and we all stood round her. She in her silver-gray silk, with lilies of the valley (John's flower) in her bosom and hair. We in gray thin stuff and roses,—sackcloth, I called it, and ashes of roses; for I mourn the loss of my Nan, and am not comforted. We have had a little feast, sent by good Mrs. Judge Shaw;[6] then the old folks danced round the bridal pair on the lawn in the German fashion, making a pretty picture to remember, under our Revolutionary elm.

Then, with tears and kisses, our dear girl, in her little white bonnet, went happily away with her good John; and we ended our first wedding. Mr. Emerson[7] kissed her; and I thought that honor would make even matrimony endurable, for he is the god of my idolatry, and has been for years.

* * *

[1867]

September, 1867.—Niles, partner of Roberts, asked me to write a girls' book. Said I'd try.

F. asked me to be the editor of "Merry's Museum."[8] Said I'd try.

Began at once on both new jobs; but did n't like either.

---

4. Louisa's older sister, Anna Alcott (Meg), married John Bridge Pratt on 23 May 1860. Louisa's parents were married on 23 May 1830 [*Editors*].
5. Samuel Joseph May, the Alcott sisters' uncle, was not a licensed minister but performed the ceremony with the assistance of Ephraim Bull [*Editors*].
6. Hope Savage Shaw, wife of Lemuel Shaw, the Massachusetts Supreme Court chief justice [*Editors*].
7. Ralph Waldo Emerson, the famous American transcendentalist thinker and writer, was a neighbor, sometime financial supporter, and close friend of the Alcotts. Loaning her books and encouraging her reading, he befriended Louisa May Alcott when she was a girl; and throughout her life, she greatly admired him. See Louisa May Alcott, "Reminiscences of Ralph Waldo Emerson," originally printed in *The Youth's Companion*, 25 May 1882; reprinted in *The Sketches of Louisa May Alcott* (New York: Ironweed Press, 2001), 209–14 [*Editors*].
8. Thomas Niles, Alcott's editor at the Boston publishing firm Roberts Brothers. Alcott often refers to him as Mr. N. in her journals. Horace B. Fuller (F.) was the publisher of the children's magazine *Merry's Museum* [*Editors*].

* * **

[*1868*]

* * *

May, 1868.—Father saw Mr. Niles about a fairy book. Mr. N. wants a *girls' story*, and I begin "Little Women." Marmee, Anna, and May all approve my plan. So I plod away, though I don't enjoy this sort of thing. Never liked girls or knew many, except my sisters; but our queer plays and experiences may prove interesting, though I doubt it.

> [Good joke.—L. M. A.]

June.—Sent twelve chapters of "L. W." to Mr. N. He thought it *dull*; so do I. But work away and mean to try the experiment; for lively, simple books are very much needed for girls, and perhaps I can supply the need.

Wrote two tales for Ford, and one for F. L. clamors for more, but must wait.[9]

July 15th.—Have finished "Little Women," and sent it off,—402 pages. May is designing some pictures for it. Hope it will go, for I shall probably get nothing for "Morning Glories."[1]

Very tired, head full of pain from overwork, and heart heavy about Marmee, who is growing feeble.

> [Too much work for one young woman. No wonder she broke down. 1876.—L. M. A.]

August.—Roberts Bros. made an offer for the story, but at the same time advised me to keep the copyright; so I shall.

> [An honest publisher and a lucky author, for the copyright made her fortune, and the "dull book" was the first golden egg of the ugly duckling. 1885.—L. M. A.]

August 26th.—Proof of whole book came. It reads better than I expected. Not a bit sensational, but simple and true, for we really lived most of it; and if it succeeds that will be the reason of it. Mr. N. likes it better now, and says some girls who have read the manuscripts say it is "splendid!" As it is for them, they are the best critics, so I should be satisfied.

* * *

October* * *

* * *

30th.—Saw Mr. N. of Roberts Brothers, and he gave me good news of the book. An order from London for an edition came in. First edition gone and more called for. Expects to sell three or four thousand before the New Year.[2]

---

9. Daniel Ford, editor of *The Youth's Companion*; Horace B. Fuller (F.), publisher of *Merry's Museum*; and Frank Leslie (L.), publisher of several periodicals [*Editors*].
1. For the pictures designed by May, see the four illustrations on pp. 3, 67, 78 and 174. *Morning-Glories, and Other Stories* was a story collection published by Fuller in 1868 [*Editors*].
2. For more detailed information about the printings and sales of *Little Women*, see Joel Myer-

Mr. N. wants a second volume for spring. Pleasant notices and letters arrive, and much interest in my little women, who seem to find friends by their truth to life, as I hoped.

November 1st.—Began the second part of "Little Women." I can do a chapter a day, and in a month I mean to be done. A little success is so inspiring that I now find my "Marches" sober, nice people, and as I can launch into the future, my fancy has more play. Girls write to ask who the little women marry, as if that was the only end and aim of a woman's life. I *won't* marry Jo to Laurie to please any one.

* * *

17th.—Finished my thirteenth chapter. I am so full of my work, I can't stop to eat or sleep, or for anything but a daily run.

* * *

[1869]

January, 1869.— * * * Sent the sequel of "L. W." to Roberts on New Year's Day. Hope it will do as well as the first, which is selling finely, and receives good notices. * * *

* * *

April.— * * * Roberts wants a new book, but am afraid to get into a vortex lest I fall ill.

* * *

People begin to come and stare at the Alcotts. Reporters haunt the place to look at the authoress, who dodges into the woods *à la* Hawthorne,[3] and won't be even a very small lion.

* * *

[1875]

January, 1875.— . . . Father flourishing about the Western cities, "riding in Louisa's chariot, and adored as the grandfather of 'Little Women,' " he says.[4]

* * *

[1879]

* * *

February.— * * *

Went to a dinner, at the Revere House, of the Papyrus Club. Mrs. Burnett and Miss A. were guests of honor.[5] Dr. Holmes took me in, and to my surprise I found myself at the president's right hand, with

---

son and Daniel Shealy, "The Sales of Louisa May Alcott's Books," *Harvard Library Bulletin* 1 (1990): 47–86, esp. 69 [*Editors*].
3. According to nineteenth-century accounts, the novelist Nathaniel Hawthorne often favored a solitary or secluded lifestyle, guarding his privacy and limiting his public contacts [*Editors*].
4. Offering public talks or conversations, Bronson Alcott was on a tour of the Midwest. See his letter to Louisa below, p. 424 [*Editors*].
5. Alcott (Miss A.) and Frances Hodgson Burnett, author of *Little Lord Fauntleroy* (1886), were "guests of honor" at a meeting of the Boston Papyrus Club. Those in attendance included Oliver Wendell Holmes, Sr., Harvard professor and well-known author, and Edmund Clarence Stedman, critic and essayist [*Editors*].

Mrs. B., Holmes, Stedman, and the great ones of the land. Had a gay time. Dr. H. very gallant. "Little Women" often toasted with more praise than was good for me.

* * *

BRONSON ALCOTT

Journals†

[1868]

* * *

October 14

Louisa has letters from Col. Higginson and wife praising her new story as natural and eminently American.[1] This is high praise, and should encourage her to estimate, as I fear she has not properly, her superior gifts as a writer.

* * *

[1869]

March 6

Louisa has good success in her last book *Little Women*, part first, of which four editions have been sold, and her publishers today send her their check for $228.00, as their second payment, having paid her $300.00 last December. They have part second in press, and hope to find as ready a sale for it as for the first. The press generally commends it highly, and the young folks write expressing their admiration.

* * *

April 30

. . . Louisa's *Little Women*, Part II, has been most favorably received and generally praised in the reviews. She has made friends of the New England girls, and is deluged with notes of thanks and admiration by almost every mail. Her publishers are exulting in the pecuniary success, having sold thirteen thousand copies and are now putting a sixth edition to press, confident of selling twenty thousand before Christmas. This is most encouraging. She takes her growing repute modestly, being unwilling to believe her books have all the merit ascribed to them by the public. Her health is by no means yet restored. She writes but little, but has various literary works in thought—among others a novel embodying our family adventures which she entitles *The Cost of an Idea*.[2] If written out with the dramatic genius with which she is gifted, the story will be a taking piece of family biography, as at-

---

† From *The Journals of Bronson Alcott*, ed. Odell Shepard (Boston: Little, Brown, 1938), 391, 393–94, 396, 398, 399–400, 403–4. Reprinted by permission of the Houghton Library, Harvard University, MS Am 1130.12 (38), MS Am 1130.12 (39).
1. See Louisa May Alcott to Mary E. Channing Higginson, p. 419 [*Editors*].
2. Novel based on the life of Bronson Alcott. Louisa planned for many years to write such a book but never finished it [*Editors*].

tractive as any fiction and having the merit of being purely American. She is among the first to draw her characters from New England life and scenes, and is more successful in my judgement, in holding fast to nature, intermingling less of foreign sentiment than any of our novelists. Her culture has been left to nature and the bias of temperament and she comes to her pen taught simply by an experience that few of her age have had the good fortune to enjoy—freedom from the trammels of school and sects, helps that her predecessors in fiction—Hawthorne, Judd, and Mrs. Stowe[3]—had not.

* * *

August 24

* * * My own children, being daughters, and taking their education from the events and experiences of our varied life, have learnt from direct contact with life itself, and, while deficient (as I am) in what the schools profess to give, they have a native strength and grace that schools cannot impart or essentially foster. Louisa is praised for her fine command of the English tongue, and May for the air and expression of her drawings. She is commended by the masters in art. They doubtless owe much to their mother's strength of mind and good spirits.—A good education comes from calling forth the native gifts, and enabling the owner to use these with facility in the callings for which they were intended.

* * *

September 4

I read notices of Louisa's *Little Women* from all parts of the country,[4] and, with one or two exceptions, all are not only highly commendatory but place her in the first rank of writers of fiction. These notices are numerous, coming from all the principle cities and from many of the towns where newspapers are printed.

It is an honor not anticipated, for a daughter of mine to have won so wide a celebrity, and a greater honor that she takes these so modestly, unwilling to believe there is not something unreal in it all. The public has not mistaken, I am persuaded, and if she regains health and strength she will yet justify all her fame. I, indeed, have great reason to rejoice in my children, finding in them so many of their mother's excellencies, and have especially to thank the Friend of families and Giver of good wives that I was led to her acquaintance and fellowship when life and a future opened before me. Our children are our best works—if indeed we may claim them as ours, save in the nurture we bestowed on them.

* * *

December 1   *Cleveland, Ohio*

* * *

As to Louisa, I find I have a pretty dramatic story to tell of her childhood and youth, gaining in interest as she comes up into womanhood and literary note. Yesterday in the schools I was called upon to tell her story,

---

3. Prominent New England authors Nathaniel Hawthorne, Sylvester Judd, and Harriet Beecher Stowe [*Editors*].
4. See the reviews of *Little Women*, pp. 547–53 [*Editors*].

most of the scholars being familiar with her book and curious to learn what I might tell them about her history. I am introduced as the father of Little Women, and am riding in the Chariot of Glory wherever I go.

December 2
. . . Write to Louisa, telling her of the enthusiasm with which her book is here received, and the admiration felt for the author—all of which she will be slow to accept, cannot even comprehend.

LOUISA MAY ALCOTT, THOMAS NILES, AND BRONSON ALCOTT

Correspondence on *Little Women*

Louisa May Alcott to Thomas Niles [*June 1868*]†

* * *

I think "Little Women," had better be the title for No 1. "Young Women," or something of that sort, for No 2, *if* there is a No 2.

Twenty chapters are all that I planned to have & there are but eight more. I dont see how it can be spun out to make twenty four chapters & give you your 400 pages. I will do my best however. I liked the looks of the page which you sent.

* * *

My sister is at work on "Meg in Vanity Fair"—[1]

Thomas Niles to Louisa May Alcott, 16 June 1868‡

* * *

I have read the 12 chapters & am pleased—I ought to be more emphatic & say delighted, so *please* to consider "judgement" as favorable. The 12 chapters make 247 m.s.s. pages which I should think ought to be about the same in type page for page, & the 8 or 10 chapters you have would make the book full large enough. 300 pages or thereabouts, if closely printed, will make a volume to sell at $1.25 or $1.50.

I shall give the copy at once to the printer & when the book is started can make a more accurate calculation. Can you recommend a designer for 4 or 5 cuts—the P.C. voting in Sam Weller, by all means, should be one (the members in costume)

Shall we send you the proofs by mail to Concord

What do you say to this for a title
Little Women.
Meg. Jo Beth, and Amy

---

† From *The Selected Letters of Louisa May Alcott*, Joel Meyerson, Daniel Shealy, and Madeline B. Stern, eds. (Boston: Little, Brown, 1987), p. 116. Reprinted by permission of the Houghton Library, Harvard University, and the literary heirs of Louisa May Alcott. Thomas Niles was Alcott's editor at the Boston publishing firm Roberts Brothers.
1. See illustration p. 78 [*Editors*].
‡ Reprinted by permission of the Houghton Library, Harvard University.

The story of their lives
By
Louisa M. Alcott

First Series.

Boston
Roberts Brothers
1868.

And now while we are about business, wont you be kind enough to set your price on this story, in an outright sum, the succeeding volumes, if this one prospers, to be furnished at the same.

*   *   *

Louisa May Alcott to Thomas Niles [mid-July? 1868]†

*   *   *

I send the proof, corrected, also "Meg at Vanity Fair," admiring herself in the glass.[1] I like it, but the engraver may see many faults, & will please point out such as my sister can mend. I hope whoever engraves the blocks wont spoil the pictures & make Meg cross-eyed, Beth with no nose, or Jo with a double chin. They ruined some of Miss Green's lovely designs & much afflicted me.[2]

I send ten more chapters, making the story 402 pages long. Not having the first half by me was rather a disadvantage, as I dont remember it very well, so may have missed some of the threads. Please "make note on if so be."

I don't care for a Preface, but on one of the first pages, as a sort of motto, we fancy having the lines I send, as they give some clue to the plan of the story.[3]

*   *   *

Thomas Niles to Louisa May Alcott, 25 July 1868‡

*   *   *

I am not sure that it would not be best to add another chapter to "Little Women". I have read the whole of it & I am sure it will "hit", which means I think it will sell well. A chapter could well be added, in which allusions might be made to something in the future.

The m.s.s. is some 12 or more pages less than your number, by mistake in the paging & I am afraid we have not quite matter enough, but we will wait till the whole is in type & then decide.

The printers query if some of your "girls talk" is quite amusing— pray what does he know, or what should he know about it.

---

† From *Letters*, 117. Published courtesy of the Fruitlands Museums, Harvard, Massachusetts, and the literary heirs of Louisa May Alcott.
1. See illustration p. 78 [*Editor*]
2. Elizabeth B. Greene illustrated Alcott's *Morning-Glories, and Other Stories* (1868) and the children's magazine *Merry's Museum* [*Editors*].
3. See Alcott's preface, p. 9 [*Editors*].
‡ Reprinted by permission of the Houghton Library, Harvard University.

*   *   *

Louisa May Alcott to Mary E. Channing Higginson, 18 October [1868]†

*   *   *

I certainly *will* "write you a few lines" to express my thanks for the friendly letter with which you & Col. Higginson lately honored me, & to tell you how encouraging such expressions of interest are from persons whose commendation is of such value.

I am glad my "Little Women" please you, for the book was very hastily written to order & I had many doubts about the success of my first attempt at a girl's book. The characters were drawn from life, which gives them whatever merit they possess; for I find it impossible to invent anything half so true or touching as the simple facts with which every day life supplies me.

I should very gladly write this sort of story altogether, but, unfortunately, it does n't pay as well as rubbish, a mercenary consideration which has weight with persons who write not from the inspiration of genius but of necessity.

Your husband gave me the praise which I value most highly when he said the little story was "good, & American." Please give him my hearty thanks for the compliment; also for the many helpful & encouraging words which his busy & gifted pen finds time to write so kindly to the young beginners who sit on the lowest seats in the great school where he is one of the best & friendliest teachers.

*   *   *

Your husband asks if American children say "no end". They are learning it from English books & college slang. Laurie, who says it, was lived abroad.

Like "Amy" I am often troubled by my parts of speech, especially *whiches* & *thats* for they never *will* get into thier proper places.

Thomas Niles to Louisa May Alcott, 26 October 1868‡

*   *   *

If you have any memo. of errors, or any corrections to make for a new edition of "Little Women" please send them to us.

Some very good & pious people object to the theatrical part of the Merry Christmas chapter and on that acc[ount] object to its introduction into their Sunday School Libraries.

Could you substitute any other matter in [more?] of it & if you could, do you wish to do so?

For my part I think it is about the best part of the whole book. Why will people be so very good.

---

† From *Letters*, 117–18. Reprinted by permission of Berg Collection of English and American Literature, The New York Public Library, Astor, Lenox and Tilden Foundations and the literary heirs of Louisa May Alcott. Born into a prominent Boston family, Mary E. Channing Higginson was a friend of the Alcott family and the wife of Thomas Wentworth Higginson, a well-known reformer, minister, editor, critic, and U.S. Army colonel during the Civil War.

‡ Reprinted by permission of the Houghton Library, Harvard University.

*   *   *

Mr. Higginson makes note of an error in his letter but I cant see it.

Louisa May Alcott to Thomas Niles [early 1869]†

*   *   *

I can only think of the following titles. "Little Women Act Second". "Leaving the Nest. Sequel to Little Women".

Either you like. A jocose friend suggests "Wedding *Marches*" as there is so much pairing off, but I dont approve.

Suggestions gratefully received.

*   *   *

Louisa May Alcott to Alfred Whitman, 6 January 1869‡

*   *   *

I have planned to write to you dozens of times but work prevented, now I really *will*, though piles of Mss. lie waiting for my editorial eye. Dont you ever think old Sophy forgets her Dolphus, why bless your heart I put you into my story as one of the best & dearest lads I ever knew! "Laurie" is you & my Polish boy "jintly". You are the sober half & my Ladislas (whom I met abroad) is the gay whirligig half, he was a perfect dear.[1]

All my little girl-friends are madly in love with Laurie & insist on a sequel, so I've written one which will make you laugh, especially the pairing off part. But I didn't know how to settle my family any other way & I wanted to disappoint the ~~little dears~~ young gossips who vowed that Laurie & Jo *should* marry. Authors take dreadful liberties, but you wont mind being a happy spouse & a proud papa, will you?

*   *   *

Louisa May Alcott to Samuel Joseph May, 22 January [1869]*

*   *   *

I am getting on ver[y] well for a "shiftless Alcott" & after paying up the debts was able to give S.E.S.[1] two hundred out of the three that Roberts gave me for the first 3000 of "Little Women." The fifth thousand is underway I believe,[2] & he says as it goes so well there is no

---

† From *Letters*, 118–19. Reprinted by permission of the Houghton Library, Harvard University, and the literary heirs of Louisa May Alcott.

‡ From *Letters*, 120. Reprinted by permission of the Houghton Library, Harvard University, and the literary heirs of Louisa May Alcott. Originally from Kansas, fifteen-year-old Alf Whitman became a student at Franklin B. Sanborn's school in Concord in 1857. He and Alcott soon became close friends while performing together in the Concord Dramatic Union's stock company. In *The Haunted Man*, an adaptation of a Charles Dickens story, Alcott played the role of Sophy Tetterby and Whitman played Dolphus Tetterby.

1. Ladislas Wisniewski, a young Polish man Alcott met in Vevey, Switzerland, in November 1865 [*Editors*].

* From *Letters*, 121–22. Reprinted by permission of the Houghton Library, Harvard University, and the literary heirs of Louisa May Alcott. Samuel Joseph May was Louisa May Alcott's uncle, the brother of Abba May Alcott.

1. Samuel E. Sewall was Abba May Alcott's cousin and the family's advisor in legal and financial matters [*Editors*].

2. According to Roberts Brothers records, about forty-five hundred copies of part 1 were printed between September and December 1869. The next print run would be a one thou-

reason why it should not run to ten thousand. It is selling in England,[3] & though I get no copy right it helps to make "my works" known.

The sequel is in press, & I often have letters asking [w]hen it will be out. Some [pr]etty little letters from [ch]ildren please me very much, for they are the best critics of such things. I [d]ont like sequels, & dont think No 2 will be as popular as No 1, but publishers are very *perwerse*[4] & wont let authors have thier way so my little women must grow up & be married off in a very stupid style.

*   *   *

Louisa May Alcott to Elizabeth Powell, 20 March [1869]†

Dear Miss Powell.

I feel highly honored that my stupid "Little Women" have been admitted to your College, & hope they will behave themselves in such learned society for the poor things have had few advantages & are rather bashful, like thier Ma. Pray make them useful for the cure of head aches or any other ill which they can lighten, that being the best use that can be made of the little book.

A sequel will be out early in April, & like all sequels will probably disappoint or disgust most readers, for publishers wont let authors finish up as they like but insist on having people married off in a wholesale manner which much afflicts me. "Jo" should have remained a literary spinster but so many enthusiastic young ladies wrote to me clamorously demanding that she should marry Laurie, *or* somebody, that I didnt dare to refuse & out of perversity went & made a funny match for her. I expect vials of wrath to be poured out upon my head, but rather enjoy the prospect.

If you ever come this way remember Concord & pay us a visit. We are all to be at home in the summer, having spent the winter in Boston, & all will be glad to see you, especially father, who considers Miss Powell one of his "fine maids," as he calls his favorites.

With thanks for your kind reception of my daughters I am

yrs truly
L. M. ALCOTT.

---

sand copies in February 1869. See Myerson and Shealy, "The Sales of Louisa May Alcott's Books," 69 [Editors].

3. Published by the London firm Sampson & Low [Editors].

4. See p. 90, n. 8 (part 1, chap. 10) [Editors].

† From *Letters*, 124–25. Reprinted by permission of Friends Historical Library of Swarthmore College and the literary heirs of Louisa May Alcott. Elizabeth Powell was a calisthenics instructor in Concord in the spring of 1865 and at Vassar College from 1866 to 1870. She later became dean of Swarthmore College.

Louisa May Alcott to Elizabeth B. Greene, 1 April [1869]†

* * *

Oh, Betsey! such trials as I have had with that Billings[1] no mortal creter knows! He went & drew Amy a fat girl with a pug of hair, sitting among weedy shrubbery with a light-house under her nose, & a mile or two off a scrubby little boy on his stomach in the grass looking cross, towzly, & about 14 years old! It was a blow, for that picture was to be the gem of the lot. I bundled it right back & blew Niles up to such an extent that I thought he'd never come down again. But he did, oh bless you, yes, as brisk & bland as ever, & set Billings to work again. You will shout when you see the new one for the man followed my directions & made (or tried to) Laurie "a mixture of Apollo, Byron, Tito & Will Greene."[2] Such a baa lamb! hair parted in the middle, big eyes, sweet nose, lovely moustache & cunning hands; straight out of a bandbox & no more like the real Teddy than Ben Franklin.[3] I wailed but let go for the girls are clamoring & the book cant be delayed. Amy is pretty & the scenery good but—my Teddy, oh my Teddy!

* * *

Thomas Niles to Louisa May Alcott, 4 April 1869‡

* * *

I am glad the 2d. part pleases you—I like all the pictures but one, Beth & Joe on the Sea Shore, which is rather a failure.[1]

We start with 3000 copies, which are all sold in advance; the 4th 1000 is printing & the 7th Ed. of the 1st is also printing (5500 sold to date)[2] Pray let this incite you to finish the "New Story by Miss Alcott" (see enclosed circular) & to start another for publication in October or November. "Make hay while the sun shines."

The London Spectator had a notice of "Little Women" which was short but good.[3] I published it in an advertisement, but have not a copy of it to send you.

Shall be glad to give you the notices after a while.

I sold, or thought I had, 750 copies of the 1st pt to Low & Co. of

† From *Letters*, 126. Louisa May Alcott Collection (#6255), Clifton Waller Barrett Library, the Albert and Shirley Small Special Collections Library, University of Virginia Library. Reprinted by permission of the literary heirs of Louisa May Alcott. Elizabeth B. Greene was an illustrator who worked with Alcott on *Merry's Museum* and *Morning-Glories, and Other Stories* (1868).

1. Hammatt Billings was the illustrator for part 2 of *Little Women* (see pp. 186, 212, 264, 292) and provided two new illustrations for part 1 (see pp. 4, 80) when Roberts Brothers issued the novel as a two-volume set [*Editors*].

2. Apollo was the Greek god of music and poetry; Lord Byron was a British Romantic poet of the early nineteenth century; Tito Melema is a character from George Eliot's historical novel *Romola* (1862–63); William Batchelder Greene was a strong, black-haired local minister who had attended Bronson Alcott's Conversations and wondered "has not the demonic man his value?" (see Odell Shepard, *Pedlar's Progress: The Life of Bronson Alcott* [Boston: Little, Brown, 1937], 240) [*Editors*].

3. See illustration, p. 186 [*Editors*].

‡ Reprinted by permission of the Houghton Library, Harvard University.

1. See illustration, p. 292 [*Editors*].

2. For more on the sales of *Little Women*, see Myerson and Shealy, "The Sales of Louisa May Alcott's Books," esp. 69 [*Editors*].

3. See this review on p. 549 [*Editors*].

London but the[y] backed out of 250 copies, that is, they say they bought only 500 & the other 250 copies are in London, unsold.

I have not as yet been able to induce any one to republish it there.

* * *

Thomas Niles to Louisa May Alcott, 29 April 1869†

* * *

"Little Women" continues to sell well & win praises from all—I have not seen the person yet who does not like the second as well or better than the first.

* * *

If you dont send some pictures of Jo March, Concord will be infested with deputations of "little women" & *their* "Lauries"; you have your choice.

* * *

Thomas Niles to Louisa May Alcott, 20 July 1869‡

* * *

I think I never had the supervision of a book, printed from the m.s.s., which required so little alteration or correction in the proof as "Little Women" & judging from this I took it for granted your printed copy was about right.

* * *

Louisa May Alcott to Florence Hilton, 13 March [1874]*

Dear Miss President:

Thanks for the notes and papers telling about your pleasant society and its doings.

I am glad if any thing from my little stories is found worthy of representation, and if you had half as much fun over that immortal play as we did, it has a right to be approved.

The original libretto still exists, written in an old account book, with stage directions, which would convulse any manager, and a list of properties and costumes seldom surpassed.

Did you have russet boots? I would have lent you the genuine articles, for they still adorn my wardrobe, and occasionally my feet.

Did the bed actually shut up? If not, you missed one of the finest stage effects ever seen. When the play was acted here by some Sunday-school children, that crash brought down the house, and I felt myself covered with glory, as the author of this superb idea.

My acting days are over, but I still prance now and then with my boys, for in spite of age, much work, and the proprieties, an occasional

† Reprinted permission of the Houghton Library, Harvard University.
‡ Reprinted permission of the Houghton Library, Harvard University.
* From *Letters*, 181–82. Florence Hilton was the president of the Philocalian Society of Chicago, which had presented a series of short dramatic pieces based on Alcott's work on 1 March 1874.

fit of the old jollity comes over me, and I find I have not forgotten how to romp as in my Joian days.

You may care to know that the Marches are all well, Mr. M. preaching to churches, schools, and divinity students as a peripatetic philosopher should. Marmee sits in her easy arm-chair and makes sunshine for the family. Meg still broods over her babies, doing double duty now that her John is gone.[1] Daisy and Demi are trying school for the first time, and it is unnecessary to say that they are the most remarkable children in America.

Amy, after a year of study in England, is on her way home with such a load of great works that she says "in case of wreck I shall build a raft of my pictures and paddle gaily to shore." Jo is writing, nursing, croaking, and laughing in the old way. Laurie ("my polish boy") is married to a country woman and has "dear little two daughters," as he says.

Hoping this report will prove satisfactory, I am with best wishes to all, Yours truly, L. M. ALCOTT.

Amos Bronson Alcott to Louisa May Alcott, 4 February 1875†

* * *

Such an enthusiastic welcome and salute as your Head of the Little Women folk, received yesterday, from the Young Ladies College here.[1] you would esteem sufficiently dramatic for a new play of the Alcott type.—150 girls all rising and raising hands at the Master's question. "How many have read Miss Alcotts Little Women," and then I need not tell what followed. After my little story of the famous lady was told in plain terms as the subject allowed scores of hands were stretched, arm over arm, by the gathered group, to take that of the "papa." And then as many autographs were inscribe[d] in Albums and little slips extemporized at the moment. What shall poor papa do but bear it gracefully and be himself.

* * *

Louisa May Alcott to Mrs. H. Koorders-Boeke, 7 August 1875‡

* * *

If you want to know something about me, even though there is not much to tell, I would like very much to mention a few little things.

I live with my worthy parents out in the country, just above Boston; they are both old; my father is a minister, my mother is frail. Two sisters still live with me, May ("Amy") a skillful artist, and Anna ("Meg") now a widow with two children, "Daisy and Demi"; and I am the second daughter, an old spinster of 42 years. "Beth" the fourth daughter died a few years past, as in the book.

---

1. The model for John Brooke in *Little Women*, John Bridge Pratt, Louisa May Alcott's brother-in-law and her sister Anna ("Meg") Alcott Pratt's husband, died in 1870 [*Editors*].
† Amos Bronson Alcott Collection (#7052), Clifton Waller Barrett Library, The Albert and Shirley Small Special Collections Library, University of Virginia Library.
1. Milwaukee, Wisconsin [*Editors*].
‡ From *Letters*, 194. H. Koorders-Boeke was the Dutch translator of Alcott's novel *Work* (1873, trans. Dutch 1875).

Many things in my story truly happened; and much of *Little Women* is a reflection of the life led by us four sisters. I am "Jo" in the principal characteristics, not the good ones.

* * *

Louisa May Alcott to Miss Churchill, 25 December [1878?]†

* * *

I can only say to you as I do to the many young writers who ask for advice—There is no *easy* road to successful authorship; it has to be earned by long & patient labor, many disappointments, uncertainties & trials. Success is often a lucky accident, coming to those who may not deserve it, while others who do have to wait & hope till they have *earned* it. That is the best sort & the most enduring.

I worked for twenty years poorly paid, little known, & quite without any ambition but to eke out a living, as I chose to support myself & began to do it at sixteen. This long drill was of use, & when I wrote Hospital Sketches[1] by the beds of my soldier boys in the shape of letters home I had no idea that I was taking the first step toward what is called fame. It nearly cost my life but I discovered the secret of winning the ear & touching the heart of the public by simply telling the comic & pathetic incidents of life.

"Little Women" was written when I was ill, & to prove that I could *not* write books for girls. The publisher thought it *flat*, so did I, & neither hoped much for or from it. We found out our mistake, & since then, though I do not enjoy writing "moral tales" for the young, I do it because it pays well.

But the success I value most was making my dear mother happy in her last years & taking care of my family. The rest soon grows wearisome & seems very poor beside the comfort of being an earthly Providence to those we love.

I hope you will win this joy at least, & think you *will*, for you seem to have got on well so far, & the stories are better than many sent me. I like the short one best. Lively tales of home-life or children go well, & the Youth's Companion[2] is a good paying paper. I do not like Loring[3] as he is neither honest nor polite. I have had dealings with him & know. Try Roberts Brothers 299 Washington St. They are very kind & just & if the book suits will give it a fair chance.

* * *

† From *Letters*, 232–33. Reprinted by permission of Berg Collection of English and American Literature, The New York Public Library, Astor, Lenox and Tilden Foundations. Reprinted by permission of the literary heirs of Louisa May Alcott.
1. *Hospital Sketches* (1863) chronicles Alcott's experiences as a Civil War army nurse; it originally appeared in serial form in the Boston antislavery newspaper the *Commonwealth* [Editors].
2. Popular juvenile periodical, to which Alcott contributed numerous stories and sketches during her career [Editors].
3. A publisher primarily of cheap popular books, Aaron K. Loring published Alcott's *Moods* (1865) and *Three Proverb Stories* (1868). After the financial success of *Little Women*, Loring reissued *Moods* in 1870 without Alcott's consent, a decison that angered Alcott [Editors].

Louisa May Alcott to Thomas Niles, 20 July 1880†

*   *   *

The drawings are all capital, and we had great fun over them down here this rainy day. . . . Mr. Merrill[1] certainly deserves a good penny for his work. Such a fertile fancy and quick hand as his should be well paid, and I shall not begrudge him his well-earned compensation, nor the praise I am sure these illustrations will earn. It is very pleasant to think that the lucky little story has been of use to a fellow-worker, and I am much obliged to him for so improving on my hasty pen-and-ink sketches. What a dear rowdy boy Teddy is with the felt basin on!

*   *   *

Thomas Niles to Louisa May Alcott, 26 July 1881‡

*   *   *

As to the Illus[trate]d Little Women[1] I hope in Dec to make a report on it. We have withdrawn it entirely from the booksellers & are trying to make a success of it by subscription. Thus far we have not done much but I am hoping that the autumn will show better results.

Our new Ed. of the "Little Women Series"[2] in 8 vols. is about ready, and it is about as pretty a set of books as you would wish to look at. I hope we shall sell 1000 sets of it this autumn or 80,000 [sic] vols.

*   *   *

Thomas Niles to Louisa May Alcott [June 1882]*

*   *   *

I send you by mail "The Christian Union" cont[ainin]g the Sunday School Lib[rar]y advertisements & wh[ich] will explain this letter.

I was so *mad*, yes thats that word, that I wrote & told the Editor I was sorry our list was printed.

So, it appears, that
> Louisa M. Alcott
>   (wholly *bad*)
> Mrs. Juliana H. Ewing
>   author of "Jan of the Windmill"
> Jean Ingelow (only partly *good*)

† From *Letters*, 249. Reprinted by permission of the literary heirs of Louisa May Alcott.
1. Frank Merrill, the illustrator of the 1880 edition of *Little Women*, a 586-page one-volume edition with over two hundred sketches [*Editors*].
‡ Reprinted by permission of the Houghton Library, Harvard University.
1. Issued by Roberts Brothers in 1880 as a holiday book, a 586-page, profusely illustrated, one-volume edition [*Editors*].
2. The Roberts Brothers series originally included *Little Women, Hospital Sketches and Camp and Fireside Stories, An Old-Fashioned Girl, Little Men, Eight Cousins, Rose in Bloom, Under the Lilacs,* and *Jack and Jill*. In 1886, *Jo's Boys*, Alcott's last novel, was added to the series and *Hospital Sketches* was dropped [*Editors*].
* Reprinted by permission of the Houghton Library, Harvard University. This handwritten note to Alcott appears at the end of a typed letter from Laurence F. Abbott of the *Christian Union* to Roberts Brothers (6 June 1882). Originally a Baptist periodical, the *Christian Union* became a more general religious, family publication in the 1870s. In 1882, the editors published a list of recommended works from the Roberts Brothers catalog, and Niles objected to the narrowness of the recommendations.

~~Phillip Gilbert Hamerton~~
George L. Chaney
Susan Coolidge (only partly *good*)[1]

and other juvenile writers on our list are wanting in *orthodoxy* & must be tabooo from orthodox s. schools.

* * *

Louisa May Alcott to Mrs. Leavitt [*c. 14 January* 1883][†]

* * *

Many thanks for the honor done me which I gratefully accept, & will try to be a worthy member of "The Little Women Society."

I have no copy of the dramatized scenes, although they have been acted in many places.

It is very easy to arrange a short play by taking the conversation out of the first chapter, ending with the letter & song.

The Operatic Tragedy for the next act, & any other bit that suits the occasion or actors for the third scene. Beth's illness was once done very prettily; the night when the two girls watch, Laurie & Jo send the telegram, & at the pathetic moment Hannah says Beth is better, & Marmee arrives. Another set of young people had the Pickwick Club & read an original paper, full of local hits which was a great success.

If you care for autographs to sell at your fair I will send you "lots" as the girls say when coolly requesting autographs, photographs & autobiographical sketches of your humble servant.

* * *

Thomas Niles to Louisa May Alcott, 5 *January* 1883 [1884?][‡]

* * *

In 1880 we published "Jack & Jill" and we have not had a *new* book by you since. So you will see that the years 81, 82 & '83, beginning with a big jump in '81, exhibit a gradual increase in each year. I attribute this in a great measure to the change in style, putting "Little Women" in 1 volume, and the Illustrated Edition, all combined, with the additional stimulus wh[ich] general advertising gave the "Little Women Series" in 8 vols.

All we want now to make an additional *furore* is "Jo's Boys." The time is ripe for it.

* * *

1. These authors each published with Roberts Brothers. Among them, Juliana H. Ewing wrote *The Brownies* (1870) and *Six to Sixteen* (1875); Jean Ingelow is remembered for *Mopsa the Fairy* (1869); and Susan Coolidge (Sarah Chauncey Woolsey) is noted for *What Katy Did* (1872) and its sequels [*Editors*].

† From *Letters*, 266–67. Published courtesy of the Maine Historical Society and the literary heirs of Louisa May Alcott.

‡ Reprinted by permission of the Houghton Library, Harvard University.

Louisa May Alcott to Mary E. Edie [11 January 1885]†

* * *

Miss Alcott does not usually answer any letters from strangers because she has a lame hand & it is impossible for one busy woman to answer the questions of many curious people.

Having a leisure moment she sends the following replies to the inquiries of Mary Edie.

1. My father only is living.
2. *Laurie* was a real boy.
3. Daisy & Demi were both boys & are both alive, one 20 the other 22.
4. Most of the people & things in Little Women are true.
5. I do not sell my pictures.
6. *Amy's* real daughter *Lulu* is not like me. Amy is dead.[1]
7. Amy or May was in Europe three times, an artist, she married a Swiss gentleman & died in Paris five years ago.
8. We do not live in the old house. It is sold. We live in Boston.
9. Meg is alive & Jo, & Teddy who lives in Paris

* * *

LOUISA M. ALCOTT

Recollections of My Childhood‡

One of my earliest memories is of playing with books in my father's study. Building towers and bridges of the big dictionaries, looking at pictures, pretending to read, and scribbling on blank pages whenever pen or pencil could be found. Many of these first attempts at authorship still exist, and I often wonder if these childish plays did not influence my after life, since books have been my greatest comfort, castle-building a never-failing delight, and scribbling a very profitable amusement.

Another very vivid recollection is of the day when running after my hoop I fell into the Frog Pond and was rescued by a black boy, becoming a friend to the colored race then and there, though my mother always declared that I was an abolitionist at the age of three.

During the Garrison riot in Boston the portrait of George Thompson was hidden under a bed in our house for safe-keeping, and I am told that I used to go and comfort "the good man who helped poor

---

† From *Letters*, 285. Reprinted by permission of Berg Collection of English and American Literature, The New York Public Library, Astor, Lenox and Tilden Foundations, and the literary heirs of Louisa May Alcott.
1. Born in the Paris suburb of Meudon, Louise Marie "Lulu" Nieriker, Louisa May Alcott's niece and namesake, was the daughter of May Alcott Nieriker and her Swiss husband, Ernst Nieriker. When May died in 1879, Lulu was brought to the United States to live with Louisa [*Editors*].
‡ From the *Youth's Companion*, 24 May 1888, 261.

slaves" in his captivity.[1] However that may be, the conversion was genuine, and my greatest pride is in the fact that I have lived to know the brave men and women who did so much for the cause, and that I had a very small share in the war which put an end to a great wrong.

Being born on the birthday of Columbus[2] I seem to have something of my patron saint's spirit of adventure, and running away was one of the delights of my childhood. Many a social lunch have I shared with hospitable Irish beggar children, as we ate our crusts, cold potatoes and salt fish on voyages of discovery among the ash heaps of the waste and that then lay where the Albany station now stands.

Many an impromptu picnic have I had on the dear old Common,[3] with strange boys, pretty babies and friendly dogs, who always seemed to feel that this reckless young person needed looking after.

On one occasion the town-crier found me fast asleep at nine o'clock at night, on a door-step in Bedford Street, with my head pillowed on the curly breast of a big Newfoundland, who was with difficulty persuaded to release the weary little wanderer who had sobbed herself to sleep there.

I often smile as I pass that door, and never forget to give a grateful pat to every big dog I meet, for never have I slept more soundly than on that dusty step, nor found a better friend than the noble animal who watched over the lost baby so faithfully.

My father's school was the only one I ever went to, and when this was broken up because he introduced methods now all the fashion, our lessons went on at home, for he was always sure of four little pupils who firmly believed in their teacher, though they have not done him all the credit he deserved.

I never liked arithmetic or grammar, and dodged these branches on all occasions; but reading, composition, history and geography I enjoyed, as well as the stories read to us with a skill which made the dullest charming and useful.

"Pilgrim's Progress," Krummacher's "Parables," Miss Edgeworth,[4] and the best of the dear old fairy tales made that hour the pleasantest of our day. On Sundays we had a simple service of Bible stories, hymns, and conversation about the state of our little consciences and the conduct of our childish lives which never will be forgotten.

Walks each morning round the Common while in the city, and long tramps over hill and dale when our home was in the country, were a part of our education, as well as every sort of housework, for which I have always been very grateful, since such knowledge makes one inde-

---

1. In October 1835, George Thompson, a prominent English abolitionist who was touring the United States, had come to Boston to speak. A proslavery mob looking for Thompson broke up an antislavery meeting, seized William Lloyd Garrison (a well-known radical abolitionist), and threatened to kill him [Editors].

2. Alcott was born on 29 November 1832; Columbus's exact date of birth is not known [Editors].

3. The Boston Common is one of the oldest and most celebrated parks in the United States. [Editors].

4. John Bunyan, The Pilgrim's Progress (1678, 1684). Friedrich Adolf Krummacher's Parabeln appeared in several nineteenth-century translations and editions, including German Parables (New York, 1833) and Parables (Philadelphia, 1841). Maria Edgeworth (1767–1849) was an Irish author of stories for children [Editors].

pendent in these days of domestic tribulation with the help who are too often only hindrances.

Needle-work began early, and at ten my skilful sister made a linen shirt beautifully, while at twelve I set up as a doll's dress-maker, with my sign out, and wonderful models in my window. All the children employed me, and my turbans were the rage at one time to the great dismay of the neighbors' hens, who were hotly hunted down, that I might tweak out their downiest feathers to adorn the dolls' head-gear.

Active exercise was my delight from the time when a child of six I drove my hoop round the Common without stopping, to the days when I did my twenty miles in five hours and went to a party in the evening.

I always thought I must have been a deer or a horse in some former state, because it was such a joy to run. No boy could be my friend till I had beaten him in a race, and no girl if she refused to climb trees, leap fences and be a tomboy.

My wise mother, anxious to give me a strong body to support a lively brain, turned me loose in the country and let me run wild, learning of nature what no books can teach, and being led, as those who truly love her seldom fail to be,

"Through nature up to nature's God."[5]

I remember running over the hills just at dawn one summer morning, and pausing to rest in the silent woods saw, through an arch of trees, the sun rise over river, hill and wide green meadows as I never saw it before.

Something born of the lovely hour, a happy mood, and the unfolding aspirations of a child's soul seemed to bring me very near to God, and in the hush of that morning hour I always felt that I "got religion" as the phrase goes. A new and vital sense of His presence, tender and sustaining as a father's arms, came to me then, never to change through forty years of life's vicissitudes, but to grow stronger for the sharp discipline of poverty and pain, sorrow and success.

Those Concord days were the happiest of my life, for we had charming playmates in the little Emersons, Channings, Hawthornes and Goodwins,[6] with the illustrious parents and their friends to enjoy our pranks and share our excursions.

Plays in the barn were a favorite amusement, and we dramatized the fairy tales in great style. Our giant came tumbling off a loft when Jack cut down the squash vine running up a ladder to represent the immortal bean. Cinderella rolled away in a vast pumpkin, and a long, black pudding was lowered by invisible hands to fasten itself on the nose of the woman who wasted her three wishes.

Little pilgrims journeyed over the hills with scrip and staff and

5. Alexander Pope, *Essay on Man* (1732–33, 1744), epistle 4, line 331 [*Editors*].
6. The children of Lidian Jackson and Ralph Waldo Emerson, Ellen Fuller and William Ellery Channing (Boston pastor), Sophia Peabody and Nathaniel Hawthorne, and Hersey Bradford Goodwin (Concord minister). Goodwin and his first wife, Lucretia Ann Watson, had one son, William Watson Goodwin (b. 1831); he and his second wife, Amelia Mackey, had two children, a daughter, Amelia, and a son, Hersey Bradford. All three of the Goodwin children were contemporaries of Louisa May Alcott [*Editors*].

cockle-shells in their hats; elves held their pretty revels among the pines, and "Peter Wilkins'" flying ladies came swinging down on the birch tree-tops.[7] Lords and Ladies haunted the garden, and mermaids splashed in the bath-house of woven willows over the brook.

People wondered at our frolics, but enjoyed them, and droll stories are still told of the adventures of those days. Mr. Emerson and Margaret Fuller were visiting my parents one afternoon, and the conversation having turned to the ever interesting subject of education, Miss Fuller said:

"Well, Mr. Alcott, you have been able to carry out your methods in your own family, and I should like to see your model children."

She did in a few moments, for as the guests stood on the door steps, a wild uproar approached and round the corner of the house came a wheelbarrow holding baby May arrayed as a queen. I was the horse, bitted and bridled and driven by my elder sister Anna, while Lizzie played dog and barked as loud as her gentle voice permitted.

All were shouting and wild with fun which, however, came to a sudden end as we espied the stately group before us, for my foot tripped, and down we all went in a laughing heap, while my mother put a climax to the joke by saying with a dramatic wave of the hand:

"Here are the model children, Miss Fuller."

My sentimental period began at fifteen when I fell to writing romances, poems, a "heart journal," and dreaming dreams of a splendid future.

Browsing over Mr. Emerson's library, I found "Goethe's Correspondence with a Child,"[8] and was at once fired with the desire to be a second Bettine, making my father's friend my Goethe. So I wrote letters to him, but was wise enough never to send them, left wildflowers on the door-steps of my "Master," sung Mignon's song in very bad German under his window, and was fond of wandering by moonlight, or sitting in a cherry-tree at midnight till the owls scared me to bed.

The girlish folly did not last long, and the letters were burnt years ago, but Goethe is still my favorite author, and Emerson remained my beloved "Master" while he lived, doing more for me, as for many another young soul, than he ever knew, by the simple beauty of his life, the truth and wisdom of his books, the example of a good, great man untempted and unspoiled by the world which he made nobler while in it, and left the richer when he went.

The trials of life began about this time, and my happy childhood ended. Money is never plentiful in a philosopher's house, and even the maternal pelican could not supply all our wants on the small income which was freely shared with every needy soul who asked for help.

Fugitive slaves were sheltered under our roof, and my first pupil was a very black George Washington whom I taught to write on the hearth with charcoal, his big fingers finding pen and pencil unmanageable.

7. In Robert Paltock's fantastic *The Life and Adventures of Peter Wilkins* (1751), the hero is shipwrecked on an island where he sees a race of flying women known as the Gawrey [Editors].
8. *Goethe's Correspondence with a Child* (1835) is a series of letters between fifteen-year-old Bettina von Arnim and Johann Wolfgang von Goethe. For the text of Mignon's song, see p. 466 of this Norton Critical Edition; see also p. 263, note 6 (part 2, chap. 10) [Editors].

Motherless girls seeking protection were guarded among us; hungry travellers sent on to our door to be fed and warmed, and if the philosopher happened to own two coats the best went to a needy brother, for these were practical Christians who had the most perfect faith in Providence, and never found it betrayed.

In those days the prophets were not honored in their own land, and Concord had not yet discovered her great men. It was a sort of refuge for reformers of all sorts whom the good natives regarded as lunatics, harmless but amusing.

My father went away to hold his classes and conversations, and we women folk began to feel that we also might do something. So one gloomy November day we decided to move to Boston and try our fate again after some years in the wilderness.

My father's prospect was as promising as a philosopher's ever is in a money-making world, my mother's friends offered her a good salary as their missionary to the poor, and my sister and I hoped to teach. It was an anxious council, and always preferring action to discussion, I took a brisk run over the hill and then settled down for "a good think" in my favorite retreat.

It was an old cart-wheel, half hidden in grass under the locusts where I used to sit to wrestle with my sums, and usually forgot them scribbling verses or fairy tales on my slate instead. Perched on the hub I surveyed the prospect and found it rather gloomy, with leafless trees, sere grass, leaden sky and frosty air, but the hopeful heart of fifteen beat warmly under the old red shawl, visions of success gave the gray clouds a silver lining, and I said defiantly, as I shook my fist at fate embodied in a crow cawing dismally on the fence near by,—

"I *will* do something by-and-by. Don't care what, teach, sew, act, write, anything to help the family; and I'll be rich and famous and happy before I die, see if I won't!"

Startled by this audacious outburst the crow flew away, but the old wheel creaked as if it began to turn at that moment, stirred by the intense desire of an ambitious girl to work for those she loved and find some reward when the duty was done.

I did not mind the omen then, and returned to the house cold but resolute. I think I began to shoulder my burden then and there, for when the free country life ended the wild colt soon learned to tug in harness, only breaking loose now and then for a taste of beloved liberty.

My sisters and I had cherished fine dreams of a home in the city, but when we found ourselves in a small house at the South End with not a tree in sight, only a back yard to play in, and no money to buy any of the splendors before us, we all rebelled and longed for the country again.

Anna soon found little pupils, and trudged away each morning to her daily task, pausing at the corner to wave her hand to me in answer to my salute with the duster. My father went to his classes at his room down town, mother to her all-absorbing poor, the little girls to school, and I was left to keep house, feeling like a caged sea-gull as I washed dishes and cooked in the basement kitchen where my prospect was limited to a procession of muddy boots.

Good drill, but very hard, and my only consolation was the evening reunion when all met with such varied reports of the day's adventures, we could not fail to find both amusement and instruction.

Father brought news from the upper world, and the wise, good people who adorned it; mother, usually much dilapidated because she *would* give away her clothes, with sad tales of suffering and sin from the darker side of life; gentle Anna a modest account of her success as teacher, for even at seventeen her sweet nature won all who knew her, and her patience quelled the most rebellious pupil.

My reports were usually a mixture of the tragic and the comic, and the children poured their small joys and woes into the family bosom where comfort and sympathy were always to be found.

Then we youngsters adjourned to the kitchen for our fun, which usually consisted of writing, dressing and acting a series of remarkable plays. In one I remember I took five parts and Anna four, with lightning changes of costume, and characters varying from a Greek prince in silver armor to a murderer in chains.

It was good training for memory and fingers, for we recited pages without a fault, and made every sort of property from a harp to a fairy's spangled wings. Later we acted Shakespeare, and Hamlet was my favorite hero, played with a gloomy glare and a tragic stalk which I have never seen surpassed.

But we were now beginning to play our parts on a real stage, and to know something of the pathetic side of life with its hard facts, irksome duties, many temptations and the daily sacrifice of self. Fortunately we had the truest, tenderest of guides and guards, and so learned the sweet uses of adversity, the value of honest work, the beautiful law of compensation which gives more than it takes, and the real significance of life.

At sixteen I began to teach twenty pupils, and for ten years learned to know and love children. The story writing went on all the while with the usual trials of beginners. Fairy tales told the Emersons made the first printed book, and "Hospital Sketches" the first successful one.[9]

Every experience went into the chauldron to come out as froth, or evaporate in smoke, till time and suffering strengthened and clarified the mixture of truth and fancy, and a wholesome draught for children began to flow pleasantly and profitably.

So the omen proved a true one, and the wheel of fortune turned slowly, till the girl of fifteen found herself a woman of fifty with her prophetic dream beautifully realized, her duty done, her reward far greater than she deserved.

November 22.

---

9. *Flower Fables* (Boston: George W. Briggs & Co., 1854); *Hospital Sketches* (Boston: James Redpath, 1863) [*Editors*].

MADELEINE B. STERN

From Louisa May Alcott: A Biography†

* * *

In May, Father,[1] having consulted Mr. Niles of Roberts Brothers regarding publication of his own *Tablets*, inquired whether the firm would be interested in issuing a fairy book by his daughter. Mr. Niles not only rejected the idea, but repeated the suggestion he had made long since, that Louisa write a girls' story, a domestic novel, for Roberts Brothers. From his office at number 143 Washington Street he had seen vast quantities of books by "Oliver Optic" leaving the rooms of Lee and Shepard at number 149. There must be a similar market for a full-length novel that would be as popular among girls as "Oliver Optic's" narratives were among boys. If Mary Mapes Dodge had been able to write a successful book with a Dutch background called *Hans Brinker or the Silver Skates*, surely Louisa May Alcott could produce as appealing a work about young America. She had proved her ability to report her observations in *Hospital Sketches*; she had indicated her powers of appealing to juvenile readers in her editorship of *Merry's Museum*. Could not Miss Alcott combine both talents in a domestic novel that would reflect American life for the enjoyment of American youth?

Obviously, if she must write a story for girls, she must work her narrative around the only girls she had ever known well, her own sisters. If Mr. Niles had asked for a boys' story, she could have turned to the students of Frank Sanborn's school; but since "Oliver Optic" had flooded the market for boys, Louisa must remain content with a domestic novel about Hillside and the Orchard House.[2] By this time the editor of *Merry's* had established for herself a working method whereby, after stories had simmered in her mind, they wrote themselves out upon paper. She made no alterations and no copies, for the material upon which she lavished the least time seemed the most successful. Any paper, any pen, any quiet room suited her, and at the desk overlooking the Lexington Road she had written, and could still write, from morning till night once the ideas had matured. She sat there now, finding that another story had developed without her realizing it, and that she had relived many an episode of her youth for *Merry's* and could relive more for Mr. Niles. Here was a plot at hand, a plot that she had carried in her mind for years, a plot that four sisters had lived. There was no trick in writing for juvenile readers. She must merely describe life as it actually was. There was no advantage to be gained from making young people do or say what no real young people would ever imagine. The

---

† From Madeleine B. Stern, *Louisa May Alcott: A Biography*, rev. ed. (Boston: Northeastern University Press, 1999), 168–82. Copyright 1950, 1978 by the University of Oklahoma Press; copyright 1996 by Madeleine B. Stern. Reprinted with the permission of the author and Northeastern University Press.
1. Bronson Alcott [*Editors*].
2. Hillside (455 Lexington Road, Concord) was the Alcott family home from 1845 to 1848. The family moved into Orchard House (399 Lexington Road) in 1857 [*Editors*].

writing itself would be simple, for she had learned enough from her experience with *Merry's* to know that she must never use a long word
when a short one would do as well. Perhaps it was for this very moment that her long apprenticeship had been passed. Perhaps it was this
unwritten story, this domestic novel, that would earn the fame and fortune that *Moods*[3] had never brought. Louisa was not sure.

Father had always believed that a happy, kind, and loving family, a
home where peace and gentle quiet abode, were beautiful indeed. Perhaps, if she could paint such a home and such a family, the world
would also find them beautiful. Had he not said years ago that the literature of childhood was not written, that a tale embodying the simple
facts and persons of the family would fill that gap? Mr. Emerson had
called her the poet of children, who knew their angels. He, too, believed that the events that occurred at home were closer to people
than those that were sought in senates and academies. The great facts
were the near ones.

> Tell men what they knew before;
> Paint the prospect from their door.[4]

The door was Hillside's. Could Louisa open it, recover those despised
recollections of childhood, and find in the biography of one foolish
person the miniature paraphrase of the hundred volumes of the universal history?

She had already done so. "The Sisters' Trial" had long ago pictured a
year in the lives of four sisters. "A Modern Cinderella" had painted Anna
and her John, Laura and Di. Her poem, "In the Garret," written for *The
Flag of Our Union*, had centered about the characters of Nan, Lu, Bess,
and May. "A. M. Barnard"[5] could rest from her nightmarish labors, for
Louisa Alcott had known this cast of characters. The sisters were there,
waiting to be reanimated. Anna would turn into Meg, beautified of
course, for there must be one beauty in the book, and after all Anna's
mouth was not so large or her nose so homely as she claimed. Her John
would find a place as John Brooke, for the Pratts had come from Brook
Farm.[6] For a hero she needed only to combine her memories of that very
human boy, Alf Whitman, with those of the gayer whirligig, Ladislas
Wisniewski, to produce—Laurie, since the one name suggested the
other and Alf had made his home in Lawrence, Kansas.[7] The Goddard
donor of ancient relics would emerge as an aunt. The story would write
itself, Louisa knew. By what name would her family be known? Surely
not Alcott, and May was too obvious. But March would do.

Louisa took up her pen, but the Marches wrote her story. May,
transmuted into Amy, afflicted once again with a nose not quite Gre-

3. Alcott's *Moods* (Boston: A. K. Loring, 1864) was neither a financial nor a critical success on
   its initial publication [*Editors*].
4. From Ralph Waldo Emerson's "Fragments on Nature and Life," in *Poems* (Boston and New
   York: Houghton, Mifflin, 1904), 354 [*Editors*].
5. Pseudonym under which Alcott published several thrillers in the mid-1860s [*Editors*].
6. John Brooke was based on Alcott's brother-in-law John Bridge Pratt, who as a child lived at
   Brook Farm with his family. Brook Farm was a well-known transcendentalist commune in
   West Roxbury, Massachusetts, from 1841 to 1847 [*Editors*].
7. See Alcott's letter to Alfred Whitman, 6 January 1869, p. 420 above [*Editors*].

cian enough, struggled in laborious attempts at elegance and decided upon a bottle of cologne for Mother's—Marmee's—Christmas because it would not cost so much and she would have money left to buy pencils. Amy wrote herself into the saga of the Marches, quirking her little finger and simpering over her plate, parading her airs and graces for the amusement if not the edification of the family. Meg could indeed remember better times, and gave a soft, domestic touch to every scene she entered. Louisa would take an easier role than Jarley or Miss Buzzard,[8] the role of herself as Jo, tall and thin and brown, with sharp gray eyes and long thick hair, with odd blunt ways and a hearty understanding of boys. Let Jo, too, write her own story and struggle once more to curb her fiery spirit. Let her love cats and apples again, and books as exciting as *The Heir of Redclyffe*. What family would not love Marmee, tall and motherly, whose gray cloak and unfashionable bonnet adorned a staunch defender of human rights? Father must be muffled, for the author realized that he would be atypical in a book on the American home. Father, with his vegetarianism, his fads, and his reforms, must be a shadow on the Hillside hearth. Laurie would inherit from Ladislas his curly black hair and big black eyes, his musical skill, and his foreign background, while Alf would endow him with high spirits and a sober kind of fascination. Another character remained, for there had been four sisters, not three, and Lizzie must reappear as Beth, glorified a little perhaps, her petty failings glossed over, until she became a cricket on the hearth who sat in corners and lived for others. Beth would be Jo's conscience.

From the moment that Louisa took up her pen, her characters touched themselves off. " 'Christmas won't be Christmas without any presents,' grumbled Jo, lying on the rug." In her choice of a gift, each sister would immediately delineate her own character. Once she had begun, the incidents also wrote themselves. The pen could not fly quickly enough to catch the remembrances. The Alcott birthday celebrations, the love of *Pilgrim's Progress* in four little girls who sped from the City of Destruction to the Celestial City, the plays in the barn—all were waiting in memory for this moment, when she who had joined in the frolics looked up from her desk to see once again four figures from the past spinning out their lives in the present. For the Hillside troupe she would take Hagar from "The Unloved Wife," Hugo from "Norna; or, The Witch's Curse," Zara from "The Captive of Castile," and miraculous potions from "Bianca,"[9] evolving a composite melodrama entitled "The Witch's Curse, an Operatic Tragedy." From the epistles penned by Father at "Concordia" there was material for Mr. March's letters; from Mother's jottings in the children's journals there were suggestions for the room-to-room notes. The Sillig School that Louisa had seen at Vevey would provide Laurie's background. The family post

8. Roles from dramatic pieces Alcott performed: *Mrs. Jarley's Waxworks*, her own adaption of Dickens's *Old Curiosity Shop* (see *Journals*, 335–37), and John Maddison Morton's *Two Buzzards, or, Whitebait at Greenwich* (1850) [Editors].
9. These are the titles of the Alcott girls' early theatricals, which are collected in *Comic Tragedies* (1893) [Editors].

office would hold the messages of the Marches. Louisa's literary career was Jo's now, for "The Pickwick Portfolio" had once upon a time flourished as "The Olive Leaf," and Dr. Blimber and Mr. Snodgrass had not exercised their influence in vain.[1] The poor Hummels would enter the picture from "Living in an Omnibus," and the episode of the breakfast gift be lifted from the pages of "Merry's Monthly Chat."[2]

The chapters were domestic, but Louisa was not sure that they would evolve into a novel. The poverty of the Alcott family must be glossed over and sentimentalized, to appeal to a youthful audience and allow for the introduction of Hannah, the servant. The style, Louisa was sure, was styleless. Good strong words that meant something, unpolished grammar—these would create the mannerless manner that would achieve verisimilitude. The American home was here, Louisa had no doubt. The good times, the plays and tableaux and the sleigh rides and skating frolics, wrote themselves naturally into the story of the Marches, while Louisa raised her eyes from her desk only to see Amy bewailing her pickled limes or Jo pinching Meg's papered locks before the ball. Where did fact end and fiction begin? With Amy's fall through the ice after she had been refused permission to see "The Seven Castles of the Diamond Lake"? With Meg's experience at Annie Moffat's? It scarcely mattered. Fact was embedded in fiction, and a domestic novel begun in which the local and the universal were married, in which adolescents were clothed in flesh and blood.

Still, Louisa was not sure of her ability to spin out the tale. Mr. Niles wanted twenty-four chapters, and she had planned only twenty. When twelve were completed, in June, Louisa sent them to Washington Street along with the suggestion that the book be called "Little Women." Perhaps, if a second volume were demanded, "Young Women" might do for the title. Louisa lived in early memories, completing her manuscript of *Little Women* so that she could send four hundred pages to Mr. Niles. Without the first twelve chapters at hand she was afraid she might miss some of the threads, but the incidents seemed to spin themselves out none the less. Amy proceeded to indite her own will while Beth lay ill; Beth became indeed Jo's conscience; the *Olive Branch* blossomed forth as *The Spread Eagle*, emblazoned with "L. M. A.'s" first story, "The Rival Painters."[3] Louisa's illness became Mr. March's; her loss of her hair was turned into an episode about the selling of her precious tresses.[4] Father's Christmas homecoming, Mother's arrival from Washington, and the fat turkey that graced the table were details domestic enough even for Mr. Niles's de-

---

1. The *Olive Leaf* was the name of an Alcott family newspaper. Doctor Blimber is a character from Dickens's *Dombey and Son* (1846–48); Augustus Snodgrass is a character from Dickens's *Pickwick Papers* (1836–37) [*Editors*].
2. See "Cousin Tribulation" [Louisa May Alcott], "Merry's Monthly Chat," reprinted on pp. 541–43. Alcott's "Living in an Omnibus. A True Story" appeared in *Merry's Museum* (October 1867) [*Editors*].
3. The *Olive Branch* was a Boston paper that published Alcott's first story, "The Rival Painters" (8 May 1852) [*Editors*].
4. During the Civil War, while serving as a U.S. Army nurse in a Washington, D.C., hospital, Alcott contracted typhoid, and the mercury-based calomel used to treat her caused her hair to fall out. These experiences are recounted in *Hospital Sketches* (1863) [*Editors*].

mands. Jo's reactions to Meg's maturity, the desire to know what would happen "ten years hence," Laurie's insistence upon an apology from his grandfather—surely these were characteristic of adolescents.

On July 15, Louisa completed her 402 pages of *Little Women*, rang down the curtain upon what she hoped was only the first act of her domestic drama, and sent the remaining chapters to Mr. Niles. He had thought the first portion dull, and Louisa was not certain that others would not agree with him. While May designed the pictures, Louisa's strength gave out. The two and one-half months during which she had written *Little Women* had left their mark. She had traveled with three sisters from the City of Destruction, but she was not sure whether she had or ever would reach a Celestial City. But the work was done.

> Go then, my little Book, and show to all
> That entertain and bid thee welcome shall,
> What thou dost keep close shut up in thy breast.[5]

For long years she had kept the loving family as a treasure locked in her heart. They were the near facts. Only Time could tell if they were the great ones. The key was turned to release the treasure now. The door to Hillside was opened, and any who would might stroll down the Lexington Road for a visit with the Marches. Had she indeed told men what they knew before, infused into her new book a new spirit?

Neither Louisa nor Mr. Niles was certain. The notes that had come from Roberts Brothers had not been too hopeful. As Louisa had known the letterhead of the firm, she began now to know the cramped and dingy quarters on Washington Street. Lewis A. Roberts still continued his manufacture of photograph albums in cloth and morocco at number 143 at the same time that he was publishing the works of Jean Ingelow, Robert Buchanan, and the Reverend W. R. Alger.[6] Before the dingy signboard that hung opposite the Old South, Louisa stopped and climbed up the stairs. In a corner behind a green curtain she found not Mr. Roberts, but Thomas Niles, the literary representative of the firm. With deep courtesy he received the author of *Little Women* and in a quiet, scholarly manner discussed the arrangements for publishing the new domestic novel. Louisa sat opposite the slender, pale-faced, bright-eyed gentleman, finding him genial and entertaining as he encouraged her and announced that the firm would accept the story. A publisher could never tell in advance whether a book would be successful or not, and he for one could not know whether Louisa M. Alcott would ever rival "Oliver Optic." However, whether he offered three hundred dollars or one thousand dollars outright, Mr. Niles still recommended that Louisa decline the payment and retain, instead, the copyright with royalty privileges of 6.66 percent on each copy sold. Even three hundred dollars could not be scorned, for the story had taken no more than two and one-half months to write, and for her full year's work as editor of

---

5. See the preface to *Little Women*, p. 9 above [*Editors*].
6. Jean Ingelow was a well-known English poet, novelist, and author of children's literature. Robert Buchanan was a British poet, novelist, and playwright. W. R. Alger was a distinguished Unitarian minister in Boston and the author of several religious and inspirational works [*Editors*].

Merry's Louisa received only five hundred dollars. She listened, however, to the advice offered with quiet earnestness, and agreed to accept
the royalty percentage. The book would appear in the fall; Miss Alcott
might anticipate receiving proofs soon. Louisa emerged from behind
the green curtain and walked joyously down the stairs. She looked up
once again at the dingy signboard of Roberts Brothers, hoping that it
would be for her a brighter symbol than any she had yet encountered
upon Boston's Grub Street.

On August 26, the proofs of the whole book arrived along with Mr.
Niles's word that several girls who had read the manuscript had said it
was splendid. His niece, Lillie Almy, had laughed over it at Longwood
till she cried. Since Lillie was a gay and vivacious twenty-year-old, un-
burdened by any deep literary interests, Mr. Niles considered that her
opinion might well foreshadow that of other little women of America.
The house of Alcott might find its fortune in the house of Roberts,
for Father's *Tablets* was in the press as well as his daughter's *Little
Women*. George Bartlett[7] appeared on the Lexington Road to lavish
his attentions upon Louisa and to offer his help in reading the proofs.
Although she rejected the former, claiming that she had decided to
settle down as a chronic old maid, she accepted the latter, and with
the brown-haired, ruddy-faced amateur actor corrected the final gal-
leys of *Little Women*. The book seemed to read better in proof than it
had in manuscript. Here at least there was nothing sensational; truth
and simplicity had taken the place of blood and thunder, and Louisa
knew that if the work did succeed, that would be the reason.

Before the publication of her domestic novel, Louisa took time to help
Jane Austin with *Cipher*, a romance upon which the author of *The Tailor
Boy* and *Outpost* was now working. She was a pleasant companion for
Louisa as they stood together upon the bridge, tossing chip boats into the
river. Eagerly they watched to see which chips would drift ashore, and
which would wreck themselves against the stone pier or remain idle and
motionless in the eddy pool. Louisa had launched, and Mrs. Austin
hoped to launch, a new venture, and both wondered what its fate would
be as they watched the fortunes of their craft upon the Concord River.
Jane Austin had children to turn to for solace if her bark should founder,
but Louisa had none except loving Johnny and philosophic Freddy,[8] and
the shadow children who lived in the pages of her book. Soon they would
come to life, when the curtain was raised upon the March family.

On September 1, 1868, Roberts Brothers sent to the *Publishers' Circular* a list of the books scheduled for appearance during the month.
Besides a new edition of William Morris's *Earthly Paradise* and the
cabinet edition of Jean Ingelow's *Poems*, the company advertised Father's *Tablets* and Louisa's *Little Women*. *Tablets* appeared, delighting
the family with its shiny brown cloth binding and its gilt edges as well
as with its wise and beautiful thoughts. *Little Women; Meg, Jo, Beth,*

---

7. The son of Concord physician Josiah Bartlett and a participant with Alcott in local theatricals.
8. John Sewall Pratt and Frederick Alcott Pratt, Alcott's nephews and the sons of Anna Alcott
Pratt [*Editors*].

and Amy. The Story of Their Lives. A Girls' Book, by Louisa M. Alcott,
promised for September 15 at the price of $1.25, was not ready, how-
ever, until the thirtieth. With the price raised to $1.50 and with three
illustrations and a frontispiece by May, the book, bound in cloth and
destined, according to Mr. Niles, to have a great run during the fall,
made its bow to the public and to the Orchard House. Louisa looked
long at the gilt oval in the center of the front cover and the gilt letters
within the oval. The illustrations unfortunately seemed flat and un-
skillful, but the story still rang true, and Louisa impatiently waited to
discover whether the world would wish the curtain rung up on a second act of her domestic drama.

She was glad that the book had appeared in time for Mother's sixty-
eighth birthday. On October 8 the gifts were placed on a table in the
study, and after breakfast Father escorted Mother to the big red chair,
while Freddy and Johnny pranced ahead blowing their trumpets and
May, Anna, and Louisa marched behind. Louisa could not help feeling
that the decline had begun for her mother, that each new year would
add to the change until feebleness and gentleness replaced the energy
and enthusiasm of old. More than ever she must cherish the mother
who had so long cherished her. More than ever she hoped that the
March family would come to the defense of the Alcotts.

The welcome that the public extended to the new domestic novel
was, for the most part, all that the author had wished. In *The Youth's
Companion*, Roberts Brothers declared that girls who liked good
stories had a rich treat in store for them. *The Nation* implied that
the "agreeable little story" would have a wide appeal, for it might be
read with pleasure by older people. Although things and characters
were painted too much in "local colors," the March girls represented
healthy types and were drawn with a certain cleverness. *The Nation's*
reviewer, however, proceeded to dilate upon the poorly executed illustrations in which Miss May Alcott betrayed not only a want of anatomical knowledge but an indifference to the subtle beauty of the female
figure.[9] A week later, *The Youth's Companion* recommended the work
of "Louise" M. Alcott as an exceedingly sprightly, wide-awake volume
where a graphic account of a year in the lives of four sisters was depicted. The story of their adventures, according to the reviewer, was
sure to interest the class of readers for whom it was designed.[1]

On the whole, the reception, Louisa considered, was favorable. She
felt capable of offering advice on writing to the poets who sent verses
signed with a flourish of initials to *Merry's Museum*, and instructed one
"A. W." to learn to write prose before she attempted poetry. The children at least seemed to read the tale with more excitement than the
critics, for Louisa found a letter from one enthusiast who acknowledged
that she had cried quarts over Beth's sickness and that neither she nor
the girls in her school would ever forgive the author if she did not have
Jo marry Laurie in the second part. Perhaps, after all, there would be a
demand for another act of the March drama. Father, for one, was as

9. See *The Nation's* review, p. 547 [*Editors*].
1. See *The Youth's Companion's* review, p. 547 [*Editors*].

proud of *Little Women* as he had ever been of the prototypes, and was convinced that Laurie was none other than Llewellyn Willis, while Frank Stearns discoursed upon the similarity between the hero and Julian Hawthorne.[2] As long as people speculated, Louisa knew the book would live. Whether its life would be long was as yet uncertain.

In order to continue her editorial work in a more stimulating atmosphere than Concord, Louisa had, on October 26, taken a quiet room on Brookline Street in the new South End. Aaron Powell, editor of the *National Anti-Slavery Standard*, had asked her to send to his paper a report of Mr. Emerson's lecture on the same evening. Determined to forget for a few hours the speculations about Laurie and the possible demand for a second volume of *Little Women*, Louisa left her room for Meionaon Hall under the Tremont Temple. "Historic Notes of Life and Letters in New England" was the subject, and she heard with keen interest Mr. Emerson's remarks about Brook Farm, hung expectantly upon the words, even upon the hesitancies between words, agreeing with Father that the orator did indeed sort his keys to open the cabinet of his mind. Surely she, too, had written her own historic notes of life and letters in New England in the story of four Concord sisters.

Mr. Niles began to agree that the book might have a longer life than he had hoped. Behind the green curtain in his Washington Street office he sat, informing his new author that London had ordered an edition, and that the first two thousand copies were sold. Mr. Niles expected with some assurance to sell three or even four thousand volumes before the new year. Notices and letters had arrived indicating much interest in the four little women, and the publisher demanded a second volume for the spring.

On November 1, after Louisa had prepared *Merry's Museum*, she began work on Part Two of *Little Women*. In her quiet room on Brookline Street she sat, once again tracing the destinies of the March family in ink upon blue-lined paper. The sisters had grown three years older since the curtain had fallen upon Act One, and Meg was ready to marry her John just as Anna had done in that happy May of 1860. Once more, in her room at Brookline Street, Louisa watched her sister don her wedding gown and wear lilies of the valley in her hair. Once more the German was danced around the joyous couple and their happiness relived. May, teaching her drawing classes, developed into an Amy who made a plaster cast of her own foot or held an unfortunate fete graced by only one guest. Jo acted out Louisa's character, sending tales composed in a vortex to a *Flag of Our Union* disguised as the *Blarneystone Banner*. The criticisms that had been given to *Moods* were leveled now upon Jo's first novel, while Amy thrilled to the European voyage that had once been Louisa's, watching the riders on Rotten Row, sailing up the Rhine, and writing Frenchified letters from

2. Frederick Llewellyn Hovey Willis, one of Louisa's childhood friends, had boarded with the Alcotts in 1844. Frank Preston Stearns was a Concord resident and the author of *Sketches from Concord and Appledore: Concord Thirty Years Ago* (1895) and *The Life and Genius of Nathaniel Hawthorne* (1906); Julian Hawthorne was the only son of Nathaniel and Sophia Peabody Hawthorne [*Editors*].

"Votre Amie." The blue-lined papers mounted. Each day one chapter was completed, until Jo sat in Mrs. Kirke's sky parlor, as the author had sat in Mrs. Reed's, dispatching to the *Weekly Volcano* the blood-and-thunder narratives that had emblazoned *Leslie's*.

The gossips who clamored for Jo's marriage with Laurie would be disappointed, for Louisa planned a different destiny for her heroine, a destiny in the shape of Professor Bhaer. Laurie's wheedlesome appeals and boyish love would be rejected, for in his place the author created for Jo a German professor whose traits she mined from her memories of Reinhold Solger and Dr. Rimmer.[3] Professor Bhaer bore striking resemblances also to August Bopp, whom she had long ago delineated in "The King of Clubs."[4] Louisa needed only to develop that sketch to paint her stout German with kind eyes and bushy beard, rusty clothes and gentle understanding.

Her technique, Louisa realized, had been composite, for she had simply amalgamated truth with some little fiction, borrowing her details from life and from her earlier stories. As each day she completed a chapter, she perceived also that her technique was still that of the short-story writer, for each portion concerned one sister, the episode of Meg's married life alternating with Amy's experiences abroad or Jo's struggles with herself at home. The Marches were good New Englanders, and yet their story seemed to Louisa to have a more universal reality than that of a single village. They were human beings also, and the episode of Meg's fifty-dollar silk appeared to her no less valid than the tale of Amy and the pickled limes. The adolescents of memory had emerged into realistic adulthood. As she launched into the future, she had given her fancy freer play, but after twelve more chapters were completed, Louisa knew that she had lived on the whole in the domain of truth. The American countryside of the mid-nineteenth century was unfolded on the blue-lined papers. Historic notes of life and letters in New England were being written at Brookline Street, as they had written themselves into the nation. The American home was here, too, the home that knew no bounds of geography, no limits of time. The latchstring was out, and soon the curtain would be raised upon the second act of her domestic drama. Then the families of the nation might open the door of Hillside to find not the Marches, but themselves waiting within. Under the roof of one New England home, they would see all the homes of America. Perhaps the tale embodying the simple facts and persons of the family was at last being completed, and the literature of childhood written.

On November 16, Louisa left the Marches to visit the Radical Club with Father at the Sargents' on Chestnut Street. Almost every extreme of liberalism would be represented in the commodious parlors at number 13, and Louisa looked forward to John Weiss's lecture on

3. Dr. Reinhold Solger was a German immigrant who lectured in Frank Sanborn's Concord school; Dr. William Rimmer was an artist and drawing instructor who tutored Louisa's sister May Alcott [*Editors*].

4. "The King of Clubs and the Queen of Hearts," a story of the romance between August Bopp and Dolly, was first published in the *Monitor* (19 April–7 June 1862) and then reprinted in *On Picket Duty, and Other Tales* (1864) and *Hospital Sketches and Camp and Fireside Stories* (1869) [*Editors*].

"Woman," after her concentrated work of the past two weeks. Mr. Weiss, steady as a drill sergeant at his post, beamed brightly before his audience. In shrill, penetrating tones he wittily characterized the imperfections of the present political machinery, satirizing the attempts that men had made to give a monopoly of the regulations of public affairs to the rougher half of the human family. With the style of a soldier on dress parade he gave a rose-colored picture of the future, when women would work with men in political matters.

After the clarion call he had sounded in the Chestnut Street parlors, Louisa returned to the blue-lined papers, so full of her work that she could not stop to eat or sleep. It was Beth's secret that consumed her now, Beth like Paul Dombey[5] listening to death's whisper at the seashore, Beth to whom Jo consecrated herself as Louisa had to Lizzie. On and on she wrote, turning from Beth to Amy, who walked, as Louisa had walked, along the Promenade des Anglais, catching a glimpse of the lovely road to Villefranche and that speck out to sea called Corsica. Through Amy she relived her life in a pension, and found for Meg the household happiness that Anna had captured.

Louisa's thirty-sixth birthday was spent alone, with no presents but Father's *Tablets* to divert her from the saga of the Marches. Gradually critics were beginning to find in the first part of *Little Women* a truthful picture of American home life. The sprightly conversation had been remarked upon, and in December Louisa found recommendations of her lively story in *Godey's* and *The Lady's Friend*, while *Arthur's Illustrated Home Magazine* declared it the best Christmas story seen for a long time, originally written, and never commonplace or wearisome though it dealt with the most ordinary everyday life.[6] If *The Ladies' Repository* objected to the lack of Christian religion in *Little Women*, declaring it no good book for the Sunday-school library,[7] still there were enough reviewers who were beginning to find in Miss Alcott the poet of children, who knew their angels. Perhaps the new year would fulfill the uncertain promise of the old.

In December, after Louisa had launched the Christmas *Merry's*, she left Brookline Street to close up the Orchard House for the winter. Father had planned to go west; Mother had moved to Anna's home in Maplewood; and since May intended to live with Louisa in Boston, there seemed no advantage in keeping the Concord house open. Louisa was glad to turn the key on Apple Slump,[8] and in order to indulge her sister's desire for the elegancies of modern life, engaged a room at the new Bellevue Hotel on Beacon Street.

* * *

It was pleasant to live on Beacon Street near the Charles, with its red brick and the worn granite curbstones of the Hill, pleasanter still after Louisa received from Washington Street three hundred dollars as her first royalty on the sale of three thousand copies of *Little Women*.

5. The loving and sensitive but ill son of Paul Dombey in Charles Dickens's *Dombey and Son* (1846–48) [*Editors*].
6. See the reviews on pp. 549, 548, and 548 [*Editors*].
7. See *The Ladies' Repository's* review, p. 549 [*Editors*].
8. Alcott's humorous name for Orchard House [*Editors*].

After paying her debts she was able to give two hundred dollars to Cousin Sam Sewall to invest. The Pathetic Family might emerge right side up after all, for Father was enjoying the success of his book and his Conversations, Mother was happy with Anna, and May was busy with her pupils. Although Louisa did not believe that Part Two of *Little Women* would be as popular as Part One, she determined now to complete the work for spring publication.

In the sky parlor of the Bellevue the blue-lined papers were filled again, until, among the flowers of Valrosa, Laurie learned to pluck the thornless rose that was Amy, until the pain of Lizzie's death was relived and Louisa's poem to the sister passing from her was introduced for a wider audience. In the Vevey where Louisa had wandered, Amy promised to pull always in the same boat with her Laurie. Jo, acting out her nature, had found her style at last, for something entered Jo's story that went straight to the hearts of those who read it. As Louisa had once sung to Mr. Emerson, Professor Bhaer sang to Jo, "Know'st thou the land where the citron blooms?" As Father had taught four little women the alphabet, Grandfather March instructed Demi, sharing Socratic conversations with his new pupil, not putting the thoughts into his head, but helping him unfold those already there. Under the umbrella Jo sallied forth with her professor, thinking of her poem, "In the Garret," and finding, as Louisa had found long since, that families were the most beautiful things in all the world. On the last blue-lined paper the conclusion was written.

> "Yes, Jo, I think your harvest will be a good one," began Mrs. March. . . .
>
> "Not half so good as yours, mother. Here it is, and we never can thank you enough for the patient sowing and reaping you have done," . . .
>
> "I hope there will be more wheat and fewer tares every year," said Amy softly.
>
> "A large sheaf, but I know there's room in your heart for it . . . "

Devoutly Louisa hoped that the new year of 1869 would bring to the Orchard House a happy harvesting from the tears and laughter she had sowed in the book where she had found her style at last.

*   *   *

* * * At the Orchard House Louisa tried to rest, exulting in the knowledge that four editions of *Little Women* had been sold and that the publishers had sent her a second payment of $228. All the debts were settled now, and if the sequel found as ready a sale as the first part, Frank Leslie[9] might no longer advertise Miss Alcott as a regular contributor to his *Illustrated Newspaper*.

In April it appeared that this would come to pass, for on the fourteenth of the month *Little Women* Part Second emerged from the press after four thousand copies had been ordered before publication. The sixth thousand of the first part was now selling, but as the weeks passed, such

---

9. Publisher of several *Frank Leslie* periodicals, to which Alcott had contributed since 1863 [*Editors*].

numbers seemed trifling compared with the sales of the completed work. By the last of the month, Louisa found herself deluged with notes of thanks and admiration from the girls of New England. Grave merchants meeting on Boston's change had begun to compare notes not on their ledgers, but on *Little Women*. The American public had for once forgotten itself, laughing and crying at the will of Louisa M. Alcott. Thirteen thousand copies had been sold, doubling in two weeks the six-months' sale of Part One. The family basked in the knowledge that Louisa had been among the first to draw her characters from New England life and scenes, but she herself took her growing repute modestly, unwilling to believe that her book had all the merit ascribed to it by the public. Still, it was breathtaking to know that the girl who had gone out to service and had modeled her story of "The Rival Prima Donnas" upon her vision of Madame Sontag,[1] that the author who had been advised to stick to her teaching and who had hemmed pillowcases to fill the gaps in the Alcott sinking fund, had not only found her style, but her fortune with it.

Every day fresh reviews arrived to thrill the Orchard House with their contents, the *Anti-Slavery Standard* announcing that Miss Alcott could crave no richer harvest than that which was sure to come from her sowing.[2] *The Nation* smiled upon the Marches, declaring that Miss Alcott's literary success was very like that achieved by Jo.[3] Her book was just such a hearty, unaffected, and genial description of family life as would appeal to the majority of average readers. The general groan of dismay from the young women of the country who had discovered that Miss Alcott had forbidden the banns between Jo and Laurie was almost as loud as the hurrahs that attended the blow upon the last spike of the Union Pacific Railroad.[4] Letter after letter arrived at the Orchard House, begging for pictures, inquiring about Laurie, acclaiming the author as elegant and splendid when she had sat on the rug and whistled in spite of Meg. The long-standing hurts were healed, the reception of the March family into the hearts of New England proving a timely restorative to one who had created that family.

While Mother cut clippings from the papers, while Father pondered upon the genius of the home and the household, and May wondered whether her sister would be as rich as Jay Cooke,[5] reporters haunted Concord to stare at Louisa, who dodged into the woods and refused to be a lion. By the thousands the cloth copies rolled from the press into every bookseller's window and into every reader's hand. "A. M. Barnard" and "L. M. A.," the anonymous author of "Pauline's Passion," "Tribulation Periwinkle," the sewer of sheets, the Dedham housemaid, and the dreamer of dreams at Hillside had taken their places in memory. Out of them all Louisa M. Alcott, author of *Little Women*, had emerged, with fame at one hand and fortune at the other. These were

1. A soprano whom Alcott had seen in concert in 1852 [*Editors*].
2. See *The National Anti-Slavery Standard*'s review, pp. 550–551 [*Editors*].
3. See *The Nation*'s review, p. 551 [*Editors*].
4. In 1869, the completion of the transcontinental railroad, the uniting of the Central and Union Pacific lines, was celebrated by driving a symbolic final gold spike [*Editors*].
5. American financier (1821–1905) who may have been the most prominent banker in the United States from the Civil War until the Panic of 1873 [*Editors*].

sparkling new guests to entertain at the Lexington Road, for they carried in their arms riches and the fulfillment of dreams.

* * *

NOTES ON SOURCES

Niles re a Girls' Book: *Boston Almanac for 1868*, 136; Cheney, 189, 198–99; "T. Niles—In Memoriam," *The Publishers' Weekly*, Vol. XLV, No. 23 (June 9, 1894), 859–60; "Roberts Brothers, Boston," *American Literary Gazette*, Vol. XVII, No. 5 (July 1, 1871), 118; information from Mrs. S. Alice Trickey and Mr. Edmund A. Whitman; J. T. Winterich, *Twenty-three Books and the Stories behind Them* (Philadelphia, 1939), 198–99.

Louisa's Methods of Work: Louisa to Mr. Carpenter, April 1, [1887] (Houghton Library); "Methods of Work" (Orchard House); [Jessie] Bonstelle, [*Little Women Letters from the House of Alcott* (Boston, 1914)], 157ff.; H. Erichsen, "Methods of Authors," *The Writer*, Vol. VI, No. 6 (June, 1893), 115; [Louise] Moulton, "L. M. Alcott," *Our Famous Women* [Hartford, 1883], 52.

Louisa on Juvenile Literature: Lillie, "L. M. Alcott," *The Cosmopolitan*, Vol. V, No. 2 (April, 1888), 163; "Merry's Monthly Chat with His Friends," *Merry's Museum*, Vol. I, No. 5 (May, 1868), 208.

True Incidents and Characterizations in "Little Women": Louisa to Alf Whitman, January 6, 1869 (Houghton Library); L. M. Alcott, *Little Women, passim*; Cheney, 193; "A Letter from Miss Alcott's Sister about 'Little Women,' " *St. Nicholas*, Vol. XXX, No. 7 (May, 1903), 631; A. A. Pratt to Julia and Alice [Lowrie], January 20, 1871; Stern, "L. Alcott, Trouper," *The New England Quarterly*, Vol. XVI, No. 2 (June, 1943), 195; information from Miss Frederika Wendté, Mr. John Pratt Whitman, and Miss K. M. Wilkinson.

Roberts Brothers and Thomas Niles; Niles's Offer for "Little Women": "L. M. Alcott," *The Victoria Magazine*, Vol. V, No. 36 (July, 1880), 7; E. M. Bacon, *The Book of Boston* (Boston, 1916), 56; *Boston Almanac for 1868*, 136, 207; Cheney, 199; Growoll Collection (*Publishers' Weekly*), X, 148; H. Halladay, information re Roberts Brothers in Notebook (*Publishers' Weekly*); information from Mr. Henry Halladay; Little, Brown and Company, *One Hundred Years of Publishing* (Boston, [1937]), 42–43; newspaper reprint in folder (Little, Brown); "T. Niles—In Memoriam," *The Publishers' Weekly*, Vol. XLV, No. 23 (June 9, 1894), 859–60; "Obituary. T. Niles," *The Publishers' Weekly*, Vol. XLV, No. 22 (June 2, 1894), 827–28; "Our Boston Book-Makers," *ibid.*, Vol. XX, No. 13 (September 24, 1881), 399–400; Anna Pratt to Alf Whitman, Concord, August 2, 1868 (Houghton Library); *Publishers and Stationers Trade List for 1868* (Philadelphia, 1868), 542–43; "Lewis A. Roberts," *The Publishers' Weekly*, Vol. LIX, No. 5 (February 2, 1901), 442; "Roberts Brothers, Boston," *American Literary Gazette*, Vol. XVII, No. 5 (July 1, 1871), 117ff.; "Roberts Brothers' Removal," *The Publishers' Weekly*, Vol. XXVII, No. 19 (May 9, 1885), 542; information from Mr. Edmund A. Whitman; percentage rate computed by author on basis of later payments to Louisa on *Little Women*.

Publication and Reception of "Little Women": *Journals of B. Alcott* [ed. Odell Shepard (Boston, 1938)], 391; *American Literary Gazette*, Vol. XI, Nos. 9 and 11 (September 1 and October 1, 1868), 214, 277; *Boston Transcript*, September 30, 1868; *The Independent*, Vol. XX, No. 1034 (September 24, 1868), 6; D. L. Mann, "When the Alcott Books Were New," *The Publishers' Weekly*, Vol. CXVI, No. 13 (September 28, 1929); Moulton, "L. M. Alcott," *Our Famous Women*, 43; "New Books Published by Roberts Brothers," *The Youth's Companion*, Vol. XLI, No. 44 (October 29, 1868); D. A. Randall and J. T. Winterich, "One Hundred Good Novels," *The Publishers' Weekly*, Vol. CXXXV, No. 24 (June 17, 1939), 2183–84; review of *Little Women*, *The Nation*, Vol. VII, No. 173 (October 22, 1868), 335; *The Youth's Companion*, Vol. XLI, No. 43 (October 22, 1868); information from the late Mr. Carroll A. Wilson.

Louisa Starts Work on Part II of "Little Women": Louisa to Alf Whitman, January 6, 1869 (Houghton Library); L. M. Alcott, *Little Women, passim*; information from Miss S. R. Bartlett; Cheney, 201.

Notices of "Little Women," I: Reviews of *Little Women* in *American Literary Gazette*, Vol. XII, No. 1 (November 2, 1868), 16; *Arthur's Illustrated Home Magazine*, December, 1868, p. 375; *Godey's Lady's Book*, Vol. LXXVII, No. 462 (December, 1868), 546; *The Lady's Friend*, Vol. V, No. 12 (December, 1868), 857; *The Ladies' Repository*, Vol. XXVIII (December, 1868), 472; newspaper clipping (Box II, Houghton Library).

Publication and Reception of "Little Women," II: A. B. Alcott to Mrs. Stearns, Concord, May 19, 1869 (Fruitlands); A. B. Alcott, *Concord Days* [Boston, 1872], 83; *Journals of B. Alcott*, 396–97; *Boston Transcript*, April 14, 1869; Cheney, 207–208; T. W. Higginson, *Part of a Man's Life* (Boston and New York, 1905); 31; H. R. Hudson, "Concord Books," *Harper's New Monthly Magazine*, Vol. LI, No. 201 (June, 1875), 27; [Cornelia] Meigs, *Invincible Louisa* [Boston, 1933], 211; E. P. Oberholtzer, *A History of the United States Since the Civil War* (New York, 1917–37, 5 vols.), II, 477–78; V. L. Parrington, *Main Currents in American Thought* (New York, 1927–30, 3 vols.), III, 36; Reviews of *Little Women*, *The Commonwealth*, Vol. VII, No. 34 (April 24, 1869), *National Anti-Slavery Standard*, Vol. XXIX, No. 52 (May 1, 1869), and *The Nation*, Vol. VIII, No. 203 (May 20, 1869); [Frank Preston] Stearns, *Sketches from Concord* [New York, 1895], 82; C. Van Dyke, " 'Little Women' as a Play," *Harper's Bazar*, Vol. XLVI, No. 1 (January, 1912), 24.

Literary Contexts for
Little Women

JOHN BUNYAN

From The Pilgrim's Progress†

[*The Palace Beautiful*]

* * *

* * * Now also he remembered the story that Mistrust and Timorous told him of, how they were frighted with the sight of the lions. Then said Christian to himself again, These beasts range in the night for their prey; and if they should meet with me in the dark, how should I shift them? How should I escape being torn in pieces? Thus he went on his way. But while he was thus bewailing his unhappy miscarriage, he lift up his eyes, and behold there was a very stately palace before him, the name of which was Beautiful; and it stood just by the highway side.

So I saw in my dream that he made haste and went forward, that if possible he might get lodging there. Now, before he had gone far, he entered into a very narrow passage, which was about a furlong from the porter's lodge; and looking very narrowly before him as he went, he espied two lions in the way. Now, thought he, I see the dangers that Mistrust and Timorous were driven back by. (The lions were chained, but he saw not the chains.) Then he was afraid, and thought also himself to go back, for he feared nothing but death was before him. But the porter at the lodge, whose name is Watchful, perceiving that Christian made a halt as if he would go back, cried unto him, saying, Is

† The text for the first five selections, from part 1 of *The Pilgrim's Progress*, is from a nineteenth-century U.S. edition: John Bunyan, *The Pilgrim's Progress* (Philadelphia: Henry Altemus, 1890), 56–81, 94–105, 111–112. This edition, which includes only the more popular part 1, is the kind of version that children in the nineteenth century would have read. It eliminates archaisms and updates spellings, but the text is very similar to Bunyan's original. Many of the quotations in the text are from the Bible. The text for the last two selections, from part 2, is from *Grace Abounding and the Pilgrim's Progress*, ed. John Brown (Cambridge: Cambridge UP, 1907), 287–89, 323.

John Bunyan's *The Pilgrim's Progress* (1678, 1684) was a major influence on and model for *Little Women*. The excerpts here are taken from the passages to which Alcott most directly alludes in the novel. In the narrative, Christian flees the City of Destruction for the Celestial City. Along his way, he travels to a variety of allegorical places: the Palace Beautiful; the Valley of Humiliation, where he battles Apollyon; the Valley of the Shadow of Death; Vanity Fair; and Green Meadows, among others. Often beset by demons, monsters, and other adversaries, Christian also receives aid from various characters, such as Faithful and Hopeful. In part 2, his wife, Christiana, receives similar assistance from Great-heart.

thy strength so small? Fear not the lions, for they are chained, and are placed there for trial of faith where it is, and for discovery of those that had none. Keep in the midst of the path, and no hurt shall come unto thee.

Then he went on, trembling for fear of the lions, but taking good heed to the directions of the porter; he heard them roar, but they did him no harm. Then he clapped his hands, and went on till he came and stood before the gate where the porter was. Then said Christian to the porter, Sir, what house is this? And may I lodge here to-night? The porter answered, This house was built by the Lord of the hill, and he built it for the relief and security of pilgrims. The porter also asked whence he was, and whither he was going.

CHRISTIAN.   I am come from the City of Destruction, and am going to Mount Zion; but because the sun is now set, I desire, if I may, to lodge here to-night.

PORTER.   What is your name?

CHRISTIAN.   My name is now Christian, but my name at the first was Graceless; I came of the race of Japheth, whom God will persuade to dwell in the tents of Shem.

PORTER.   But how doth it happen that you come so late? The sun is set.

CHRISTIAN.   I had been here sooner, but "wretched man that I am!"—I slept in the arbor that stands on the hill-side; I had, notwithstanding that, been here much sooner, but that, in my sleep, I lost my evidence, and came without it to the brow of the hill; and then feeling for it, and finding it not, I was forced with sorrow of heart to go back to the place where I slept my sleep, where I found it, and now I am come.

PORTER.   Well, I will call out one of the virgins of this place, who will, if she likes your talk, bring you in to the rest of the family, according to the rules of the house. So Watchful, the porter, rang a bell, at the sound of which came out at the door of the house a grave and beautiful damsel, named Discretion, and asked why she was called.

The porter answered, This man is on a journey from the City of Destruction to Mount Zion, but being weary and benighted, he asked me if he might lodge here to-night.

Then she asked him whence he was, and whither he was going; and he told her. She asked him also how he got into the way; and he told her. Then she asked him what he had seen and met with in the way; and he told her. And last she asked his name; so he said, It is Christian, and I have so much the more a desire to lodge here to-night, because by what I perceive, this place was built by the Lord of the hill, for the relief and security of pilgrims. So she smiled, but the water stood in her eyes; and after a little pause, she said, I will call forth two or three more of the family. So she ran to the door, and called out Prudence, Piety, and Charity, who, after a little more discourse with him, had him into the family; and many of them, meeting him at the threshold of the house, said, "Come in, thou blessed of the Lord;" this house was built by the Lord of the hill, on purpose to entertain such pilgrims in. Then he bowed his head, and followed them into the house. So when he was come in and set down, they gave him something to drink, and consented together, that until supper was ready, some of them should have some particular discourse with Christian, for the best improvement of time; and they appointed Piety and Prudence and Charity to discourse with him; and thus they began:

PIETY.   Come, good Christian, since we have been so loving to you, to receive you in our house this night, let us talk with you of all things that have happened to you in your pilgrimage. What moved you at first to betake yourself to a pilgrim's life?

CHRISTIAN.   I was driven out of my native country by a dreadful sound that was in mine ears; to wit, that unavoidable destruction did attend me, if I abode in that place where I was.

PIETY.   But how did it happen that you came out of your country this way?

CHRISTIAN.   It was as God would have it; for when I was under the fears of destruction, I did not know whither to go; but by chance there came a man, as I was trembling and weeping, whose name is Evangelist, and he directed me to the wicket-gate, which else I should never have found, and so set me into the way that hath led me directly to this house.

PIETY.   But did you not come by the house of the Interpreter?

CHRISTIAN.   Yes, and did see such things there, the remembrance of which will stick by me as long as I live. The Interpreter took me and showed me a stately palace, and how the people were clad in gold that were in it; and how there came a venturous man, and cut his way through the armed men that stood in the door to keep him out; and how he was bid to come in, and win eternal glory. Methought those things did ravish my heart! I would have stayed at that good man's house a twelvemonth, but that I knew I had further to go.

PIETY.   Why, did you hear him tell his dream?

CHRISTIAN.   Yes, and a dreadful one it was, I thought; it made my heart ache as he was telling of it; but yet I am glad I heard it.

PIETY.   Was that all you saw at the house of the Interpreter? And what saw you else in the way?

CHRISTIAN.   Saw! why, I went but a little further, and I saw one, as I thought in my mind, hang bleeding upon the tree; and the very sight of him made my burden fall off my back (for I groaned under a very heavy burden,) but then it fell down from off me. Yea, and while I stood looking up, for then I could not forbear looking, three Shining Ones came to me. One of them testified that my sins were forgiven me; another stripped me of my rags, and gave me this broidered coat which you see; and the third set the mark which you see in my forehead, and gave me this sealed roll. (And with that he plucked it out of his bosom.)

PIETY.   But you saw more than this, did you not?

CHRISTIAN.   Some other matters I saw, as, namely: three men, Simple, Sloth, and Presumption, lie asleep a little out of the way, as I came, with irons upon their heels; but I could not awake them. Formalist and Hypocrisy also tumbled over the wall, to go, as they pretended, to Zion, but were quickly lost, as I myself did tell them they would be. I found it hard work to get up this hill, and as hard to come by the lions' mouths; and truly if it had not been for the good man, the porter that stands at the gate, I do not know but that after all I might have gone back again; but now, I thank God I am here, and I thank you for receiving me.

Then Prudence thought to ask him a few questions, and desired his answer to them.

PRUDENCE.   Do you not think sometimes of the country from whence you came?

CHRISTIAN.   Yes, but with much shame and detestation.

PRUDENCE.   Do you not yet bear away with you some of the things that then you were conversant withal?

CHRISTIAN.   Yes, but greatly against my will; especially my inward and carnal cogitations, with which all my countrymen, as well as myself, were delighted; but now all those things are my grief.

PRUDENCE.   Do you not find sometimes, as if those things were vanquished, which at other times are your perplexity?

CHRISTIAN.   Yes, but that is seldom; but they are to me golden hours in which such things happen to me.

PRUDENCE.   Can you remember by what means you find your annoyances, at times, as if they were vanquished?

CHRISTIAN.   Yes, when I think what I saw at the cross, that will do it; and when I look upon my broidered coat, that will do it; also when I look into the roll that I carry in my bosom, that will do it; and when my thoughts wax warm about whither I am going, that will do it.

PRUDENCE.   And what is it that makes you so disirous to go to Mount Zion?

CHRISTIAN.   Why, there I hope to see him alive that did hang dead on the cross; and there I hope to be rid of all those things that to this day are in me an annoyance to me; there, they say, there is no death; and there I shall dwell with such company as I like best. I would fain be where I shall die no more, and with the company that shall continually cry, "Holy, Holy, Holy!"

Then said Charity to Christian, Have you a family? Are you a married man?

CHRISTIAN.   I have a wife and four small children.

CHARITY.   And why did you not bring them along with you?

CHRISTIAN.   Then Christian wept, and said, Oh, how willingly would I have done it! but they were all of them utterly averse to my going on pilgrimage.

CHARITY.   But you should have talked to them, and endeavored to have shown them the danger of being behind.

CHRISTIAN.   So I did; and told them also what God had shown to me of the destruction of our city; "but I seemed to them as one that mocked," and they believed me not.

CHARITY.   And did you pray to God that he would bless your counsel to them?

CHRISTIAN.   Yes, and that with such affection; for you must think that my wife and poor children were very dear unto me.

CHARITY.   But did you tell them of your own sorrow and fear of destruction?

CHRISTIAN.   Yes, over, and over, and over. They might also see my fears in my countenance, in my tears, and also in my trembling under the apprehension of the judgment that did hang over our heads; but all was not sufficient to prevail with them to come with me. My wife was afraid of losing this world, and my children were given to the foolish delights of youth; so what by one thing, and what by another, they left me to wander in this manner alone.

CHARITY.   But did you not, with your vain life, damp all that you by words used by way of persuasion to bring them away with you?

CHRISTIAN.   Indeed, I can not commend my life; for I am conscious to myself of many failings therein; I know also, that a man by his conversation may soon overthrow, what by argument or persuasion he doth labor to fasten upon others for their good. Yet this I can say, I was very wary of giving them occasion, by any unseemly action, to make them averse to going on pilgrimage. Yea, for this very thing they would tell me I was too precise, and that I denied myself of things, for their sakes, in which they saw no evil. Nay, I think I may say that, if what they saw in me did hinder them, it was my great tenderness in sinning against God, or of doing any wrong to my neighbor.

Now I saw in my dream, that thus they sat talking together until supper was ready. So when they had made ready, they sat down to meat. Now the table was furnished "with fat things, and with wine that was well refined;" and all their talk at the table was about the Lord of the hill; about what he had done, wherefore he did what he did, and why he had builded that house. And by what they said, I perceived that he had been a great warrior, and had fought with and slain "him that had the power of death," but not without great danger to himself, which made me love him the more. For, as they said, he did it with the loss of much blood; but that which put glory of grace into all he did, was, that he did it out of pure love to his country. And besides, there were some of them of the household that said they had been and spoke with him since he did die on the cross; and they have attested that they had it from his own lips, that he is such a lover of poor pilgrims, that the like is not to be found from the east to the west.

They, moreover, gave an instance of what they affirmed, and that was, he had stripped himself of his glory, that he might do this for the poor; and that they heard him say and affirm "that he would not dwell in the mountain of Zion alone." They said, moreover, that he had made many pilgrims princes, though by nature they were beggars born, and their original had been the dunghill.

Thus they discoursed together till late at night, and after they had committed themselves to their Lord for protection, they betook themselves to rest; the pilgrim they laid in a large upper chamber, whose window opened toward the sun-rising; the name of the chamber was Peace.

So in the morning after some more discourse, they told him that he should not depart till they had shown him the rarities of that place. And first they had him into the study, where they showed him records of the greatest antiquity; in which, as I remember my dream, they showed him first the pedigree of the Lord of the hill, that he was the son of the Ancient of Days, and came by that eternal generation. Here also was more fully recorded the acts that he had done, and the names of many hundreds that he had taken into his service; and how he had placed them in such habitations, that could neither by length of days, nor decays of nature, be dissolved.

Then they read to him some of the worthy acts that some of his servants had done; as, how they had "subdued kingdoms, wrought righteousness, obtained promises, stopped the mouths of lions, quenched the violence of fire, escaped the edge of the sword, out of weakness were made strong, waxed valiant in fight, and turned to flight the armies of the aliens."

They then read again, in another part of the records of the house, where it was showed how willing their Lord was to receive into his favor any, even any though they in time past had offered great affronts to his person and proceedings.

The next day they took him into the armory, where they showed him all manner of furniture, which their Lord had provided for pilgrims, as sword, shield, helmet, breastplate, *all-prayer*, and shoes that would not wear out. And there was here enough of this to harness out as many men for the service of their Lord as there be stars in the heaven for multitude.

They also showed him some of the engines with which some of his servants had done wonderful things. They showed him Moses' rod; the hammer and nail with which Jael slew Sisera;[1] the pitchers, trumpets, and lamps too, with which Gideon put to flight the armies of Midian. Then they showed him the ox's goad wherewith Shamgar slew six hundred men.[2] They showed him also the jaw-bone with which Samson did such mighty feats. They showed him, moreover, the sling and stone with which David slew Goliath of Gath; and the sword, also, with which their Lord will kill the Man of Sin, in the day that he shall rise up to the prey. They showed him, besides, many excellent things, with which Christian was much delighted.

Then I saw in my dream, that on the morrow he got up to go forward; but they desired him to stay till the next day also; and then, said they, we will, if the day be clear, show you the Delectable Mountains, which, they said, would yet further add to his comfort, because they were nearer the desired haven than the place where at present he was; so he consented and stayed. When the morning was up, they had him to the top of the house, and bid him look south; so he did: and behold,

---

1. In Judges 4, Jael, an Israelite, lures Sisera, a leader in the Canaanite army, into her tent, where she provides him with milk and a place to rest. When he falls asleep, Jael drives a tent peg through his head.
2. In Judges 3.31, Shamgar defends Israel by slaying six hundred Philistines with an ox goad, a sharp, pointed herding tool.

at a great distance, he saw a most pleasant mountainous country, beautified with woods, vineyards, fruits of all sorts, flowers also, with springs and fountains, very delectable to behold. Then he asked the name of the country. They said it was Immanuel's Land; and it is as free, said they, as this hill is, to and for all the pilgrims. From thence, said they, thou mayest see to the gate of the Celestial City.

Now he bethought himself of setting forward, and they were willing he should. But first, said they, let us go again into the armory. So they did; and when they came there, they harnessed him from head to foot with what was of proof, lest, perhaps, he should meet with assaults on the way. He being, therefore, thus accoutred, walketh out with his friends to the gate and there he asked the porter if he saw any pilgrim pass by. Then the porter answered, Yes. I asked him his name, and he told me it was Faithful.

CHRISTIAN.   Oh, said Christian, I know him; he is my townsman, my near neighbor. How far do you think he may be before?

PORTER.   He is got by this time below the hill.

CHRISTIAN.   Well, good Porter, the Lord be with thee, and add to all thy blessings much increase, for the kindness that thou hast showed to me.

[The Valley of Humiliation and Apollyon]

Then he began to go forward; but Discretion, Piety, Charity, and Prudence, would accompany him down to the foot of the hill. Then said Christian, As it was difficult coming up, so, so far as I can see, it is dangerous going down. Yes, said Prudence, so it is, for it is a hard matter for a man to go down into the Valley of Humiliation, as thou art now, and to catch no slip by the way; therefore, said they, are we come out to accompany thee down the hill. So he began to go down but very warily; yet he caught a slip or two.

Then I saw in my dream that these good companions, when Christian was gone to the bottom of the hill, gave him a loaf of bread, a bottle of wine, and a cluster of raisins; and then he went on his way.

But now, in this Valley of Humiliation, poor Christian had gone but a little way, before he espied a foul fiend coming over the field to meet him; his name was Apollyon.[3] Then did Christian begin to be afraid, and undecided whether to go back or to stand his ground. But he considered again that he had no armor for his back; and to turn the back to him might give him the greater advantage to pierce him with his darts; so he resolved to stand his ground; for, thought he, had I no more in mine eye than the saving of my life, it would be the best way to stand.

So he went on, and Apollyon met him. Now the monster was hideous to behold; he was clothed with scales, like a fish, he had wings like a dragon, feet like a bear, and out of his belly came fire and smoke, and his mouth was as the mouth of a lion. When he was come

---

3. The name for this dragonlike monster, Apollyon, means "the destroyer." It appears in Revelation 9.11, where Apollyon is the angel of the bottomless pit.

up to Christian, he beheld him with a disdainful countenance, and thus began to question with him.

APOLLYON.   Whence came you? and whither are you bound?

CHRISTIAN.   I am come from the City of Destruction, which is the place of all evil, and am going to the City of Zion.

APOLLYON.   By this I perceive that thou art one of my subjects, for all that country is mine, and I am the prince and god of it. How is it, then, thou hast run away from thy king? Were it not that I hope thou mayest do me more service, I would strike thee now at one blow, to the ground.

CHRISTIAN.   I was born, indeed, in your dominions, but your service was hard, and your wages such as a man could not live on, "for the wages of sin *is* death;" therefore, when I was come to years, I did as other considerate persons do, look out if perhaps I might mend myself.

APOLLYON.   There is no prince that will thus lightly lose his subjects, neither will I as yet lose thee; but since thou complainest of thy service and wages, be content to go back; what our country will afford, I do here promise to give thee.

CHRISTIAN.   But I have let myself to another, even to the King of princes; and how can I, with fairness, go back with thee?

APOLLYON.   Thou hast in this, "Changed a bad for a worse;" but it is ordinary for those that have professed themselves his servants, after a while to give him the slip, and return again to me. Do thou so too, and all shall be well.

CHRISTIAN.   I have given him my faith, and sworn my allegiance to him; how, then, can I go back from this, and not be hanged as a traitor?

APOLLYON.   Thou didst the same to me, and yet I am willing to pass by all, if now thou wilt yet turn again and go back.

CHRISTIAN.   What I promised thee was in my nonage; and, besides, I count the Prince under whose banner now I stand is able to absolve me; yea, and to pardon also what I did as to my compliance with thee; and besides, O thou destroying Apollyon! to speak truth, I like his service, his wages, his servants, his government, his company and country, better than thine; and, therefore, leave off to persuade me further; I am his servant and I will follow him.

APOLLYON.   Consider, again, when thou art in cool blood, what thou art like to meet with in the way that thou goest. Thou knowest that, for the most part, his servants came to an ill end, because they are transgressors against me and my ways. How many of them have been put to shameful deaths; and, besides, thou countest his service better than mine, whereas he never came yet from the place where he is to deliver any that served him out of their hands; but as for me, how many times, as all the world very well knows, have I delivered, either by power, or fraud, those that have faithfully served me, from him and his, though taken by them; and so I will deliver thee.

CHRISTIAN.   His forebearing at present to deliver them is on purpose to try their love, whether they will cleave to him to the end; and as for the ill end thou sayest they come to, that is most glorious in their account; for, for present deliverance, they do not much expect it, for they stay for their glory, and then they shall have it, when their Prince comes in his and the glory of the angels.

APOLLYON.   Thou hast already been unfaithful in thy service to him; and how dost thou think to receive wages of him?

CHRISTIAN.   Wherein, O Apollyon, have I been unfaithful to him?

APOLLYON.   Thou didst faint at first setting out, when thou wast almost choked in the Gulf of Despond; thou didst attempt wrong ways to get rid of thy burden, whereas thou shouldest have stayed till thy Prince had taken it off; thou didst sinfully sleep and lose thy choice thing; thou wast, also, almost persuaded to go back, at the sight of the lions; and when thou talkest of thy journey, and of what thou hast heard and seen, thou art inwardly desirous of vainglory in all that thou sayest or doest.

CHRISTIAN.   All this is true, and much more which thou hast left out! but the Prince whom I serve and honor is merciful, and ready to forgive; but, besides, these infirmities possessed me in thy country, for there I sucked them in; and I have groaned under them, been sorry for them, and have obtained pardon of my Prince.

Then Apollyon broke out into a grievous rage, saying, I am an enemy to this Prince; I hate his person, his laws, and people; I am come out on purpose to withstand thee.

CHRISTIAN.   Apollyon, beware what you do; for I am in the king's highway, the way of holiness; therefore take heed to yourself.

Then Apollyon straddled quite over the whole breadth of the way, and said, I am void of fear in this matter; prepare thyself to die, for I swear by my infernal den, that thou shall go no further; here will I spill thy soul.

And with that he threw a flaming dart at his breast; but Christian had a shield in his hand, with which he caught it, and so prevented the danger of that.

Then did Christian draw, for he saw it was time to bestir him; and Apollyon as fast made at him, throwing darts as thick as hail, by the which, notwithstanding all that Christian could do to avoid it, Apollyon wounded him in his head, his hand, and foot. This made Christian give a little back; Apollyon, therefore, followed his work amain, and Christian again took courage, and resisted as manfully as he could. This sore combat lasted for above half a day, even till Christian was almost quite spent; for you must know that Christian, by reason of his wounds, must needs grow weaker and weaker.

Then Apollyon, espying his opportunity, began to gather up close to Christian, and wrestling with him, gave him a dreadful fall; and with that Christian's sword flew out of his hand. Then said Apollyon, I am sure of thee now. And with that he had almost pressed him to death, so that Christian began to despair of life: but as God would have it, while Apollyon was fetching of his last blow, thereby to make a full end of this good man, Christian nimbly stretched out his hand for his sword and caught it, saying, "Rejoice not against me, O mine enemy:

when I fall I shall arise;" and with that gave him a deadly thrust, which made him give back; as one that had received his mortal wound. Christian perceiving that, made at him again, saying, "Nay, in all these things we are more than conquerors through him that loved us." And with that Apollyon spread forth his dragon's wings and sped him away, that Christian for a season, saw him no more.

In this combat no man can imagine, unless he had seen and heard as I did, what yelling and hideous roaring Apollyon made all the time of the fight—he spake like a dragon; and, on the other side, what sighs and groans burst from Christian's heart. I never saw him all the while give so much as one pleasant look, till he perceived he had wounded Apollyon with his two-edged sword; then indeed, he did smile, and look upward, but it was the dreadfullest sight that ever I saw.

So when the battle was over, Christian said, "I will here give thanks to him that delivered me out of the mouth of the lion, to him that did help me against Apollyon."

Then there came to him a hand, with some of the leaves of the tree of life, the which Christian took, and applied to the wounds that he had received in the battle, and was healed immediately. He also sat down in that place to eat bread, and to drink of the bottle that was given him a little before; so, being refreshed, he addressed himself to his journey, with his sword drawn in his hand; for he said, I know not but some other enemy may be at hand. But he met with no other affront from Apollyon quite through this valley.

[The Valley of the Shadow of Death]

Now, at the end of this valley was another, called the Valley of the Shadow of Death, and Christian must needs go through it, because the way to the Celestial City lay through the midst of it. Now, this valley is a very solitary place, and Christian was worse put to it than in his fight with Apollyon; as you shall see.

I saw then in my dream, that when Christian was got to the borders of the Shadow of Death, there met him two men, children of them that brought up an evil report of the good land, making haste to go back; to whom Christian spake as follows: Whither are you going?

MEN.   Back! back! and we would have you to do so too, if either life or peace is prized by you.

CHRISTIAN.   Why, what's the matter?

MEN.   Matter! we were going that way as you are going, and went as far as we durst; and indeed we were almost past coming back; for had we gone a little further we had not been here to bring the news to thee.

CHRISTIAN.   But what have you met with?

MEN.   Why, we were almost in the Valley of the Shadow of Death; but that, by good hap, we looked before us, and saw the danger before we came to it.

CHRISTIAN.   But what have you seen?

MEN.   Seen! Why, the valley itself, which is as dark as pitch; we also saw there the hobgoblins, satyrs, and dragons of the pit; we heard also in that Valley a continual howling and yelling, as of a people under unutterable misery, who there sat bound in affliction and irons; and over that Valley hangs the discouraging clouds of confusion. Death also doth always spread his wings over it.

Then, said Christian, I perceive that this is my way to the desired haven.

MEN. Be it thy way; we will not choose it for ours. So they parted, and Christian went on his way, but still with his sword drawn in his hand, for fear lest he should be assaulted.

I saw then in my dream so far as this valley reached, there was on the right hand a very deep ditch, into which the blind have led the blind in all ages, and both have there miserably perished. Again, behold on the left hand, there was a very dangerous quag, into which, if even a good man falls, he can find no bottom for his foot to stand on. Into that quag king David once did fall, and had no doubt therein been smothered, had not HE that is able plucked him out.

The pathway was here also exceedingly narrow, and therefore good Christian was the more put to it; for when he sought, in the dark, to shun the ditch on the one hand, he was ready to tip over into the mire on the other; also when he sought to escape the mire, without great carefulness he would be ready to fall into the ditch. Thus he went on, and I heard him here sigh bitterly; for, besides the dangers mentioned above, the pathway was here so dark, that oftimes when he lift up his foot to set forward, he knew not where or upon what he should set it next.

About the midst of this valley, I perceived the mouth of hell to be near by the way-side. Now, thought Christian, what shall I do? And ever and anon the flame and smoke would come out in such abundance, with sparks and hideous noises, (things that cared not for Christian's sword, as did Apollyon before,) that he was forced to put up his sword, and betake himself to another weapon, called All-prayer. So he cried in my hearing, "O Lord, I beseech thee, deliver my soul!" Thus he went on a great while, yet still the flames would be reaching towards him. Also he heard doleful voices, and rushings to and fro, so that sometimes he thought he should be torn in pieces, or trodden down like mire in the streets. This frightful sight was seen and these dreadful noises were heard by him for several miles together; and coming to a place where he thought he heard a company of fiends coming forward to meet him, he stopped, and began to muse what he had best to do. Sometimes he had half a thought to go back; then again he thought he might be half way through the valley; he remembered also how he had already vanquished many a danger, and that the danger of going back might be much more than for to go forward; so he resolved to go on. Yet the fiends seemed to come nearer and nearer; but when they were almost at him, he cried out with a most vehement voice, "I will walk in the strength of the Lord God!" so they gave back and came no further.

One thing I would not let slip; I took notice that now poor Christian was so confounded, that he did not know his own voice; and thus I perceived it. Just when he was come over against the mouth of the burning pit, one of the wicked ones got behind him, and stepped up softly to him, and whisperingly suggested many grievous blasphemies to him, which he verily thought had proceeded from his own mind. This put Christian more to it than anything that he met with before, even to think that he should now blaspheme him that he loved so much before; yet if he could have helped it, he would not have done it; but he had not the discretion either to stop his ears, or to know from whence these blasphemies came.

When Christian had travelled in this disconsolate condition some considerable time, he thought he heard the voice of a man, as going before him, saying, "Though I walk through the valley of the shadow of death, I will fear no evil, for thou *art* with me."

Then he was glad.

By-and-by the day broke; then said Christian, He hath turned "the shadow of death into the morning."

Now morning being come, he looked back, not out of desire to return, but to see, by the light of the day, what hazards he had gone through in the dark. So he saw more perfectly the ditch that was on the one hand, and the quag that was on the other; also how narrow the way was which led betwixt them both; also now he saw the hobgoblins, and satyrs, and dragons of the pit, but all afar off—for after break of day, they came not nigh.

Christian was now much affected with his deliverance from all the dangers of his solitary way. About this time the sun was rising, and this was another mercy to Christian; for though the first part of the Valley of the Shadow of Death was dangerous, yet this second part far more dangerous. From the place where he now stood, even to the end of the valley, the way was all along set so full of "snares, traps, gins, and nets here, and so full of pits, pitfalls, deep holes, and shelvings down there, that, had it now been dark, as it was when he came the first part of the way, had he had a thousand souls, they had in reason been cast away."

* * *

[Vanity Fair]

EVANGELIST.   Peace be with you, dearly beloved; and peace be to your helpers.

Then Christian and Faithful told him of all things that had happened to them in the way; and how, and with what difficulty, they had arrived to that place. Right glad am I, said Evangelist, not that you have met with trials, but that you have been victors; and for that you have, notwithstanding many weaknesses, continued in the way to this very day. I say, right glad am I of this thing, and that for mine own sake and yours. I have sowed, and you have reaped; and the day is coming, when both he that sowed and they that reaped shall rejoice together; that is, if you hold out: "for in due season ye shall reap, if ye faint not." The crown is before you, and it is an incorruptible one; "so run that you may obtain it." Some there be that set out for this crown, and, after they have gone far for it, another comes in, and takes it from them; hold fast, therefore, that you have; let no man take your crown. You are not yet out of the gun-shot of the devil; you have not resisted unto blood, striving against sin; let the kingdom be always before you, and believe steadfastly concerning things that are invisible. Let nothing that is on this side the other world get within you; and above all, look well to your own hearts and to the lusts thereof, "for they are deceitful above all things, and desperately wicked;" set your faces like a flint; you have all power in heaven and earth on your side.

Then Christian thanked him for his exhortation.

Then I saw in my dream, that when they were got out of the wilderness, they saw a town before them, and the name of that town is Vanity; and at the town there is a fair kept, called Vanity Fair; it is kept all the year long; it is so called, because the town where it is kept is lighter than vanity; and also because all that is there sold, or that cometh thither, is vanity. As is the saying of the wise, "all that cometh is vanity."

This fair is no new-erected business, but a thing of ancient standing; I will show you the original of it. Almost five thousand years agone, there were pilgrims walking to the Celestial City, as these two honest persons are; and Beelzebub, Apollyon, and Legion,[4] with their companions, perceiving by the path that the pilgrims made, that their way to the city lay through this town of Vanity, they contrived here to set up a fair; a fair wherein should be sold all sorts of vanity, and that it should last all the year long; therefore at this fair are all such merchandise sold, as houses, lands, trades, places, honors, preferments, titles, countries, kingdoms, lusts, pleasures, and delights of all sorts.

And at all times is to be seen juggling, cheats, games, plays, fools, apes, knaves, and rogues, and that of every kind.

Here are to be seen, too, and that for nothing, thefts, murders, adulteries, false swearers, and that of a bloodred color.

And as in other fairs of less moment, there are several rows and streets, under their proper names, where such and such wares are vended; so here likewise you have the proper places, rows, streets, (viz., countries and kingdoms,) where the wares of this fair are soonest to be found. Here is the Britain Row, the French Row, the Italian Row, the Spanish Row, the German Row, where several sorts of vanities are to be sold. But, as in other fairs, some one commodity is as the chief of all the fair, so the ware of Rome and her merchandise is greatly promoted in this fair; only our English nation, with some others, have taken a dislike thereat.

Now, as I said, the way to the Celestial City lies just through this town where this lusty fair is kept; and he that will go to the City, and yet not go through this town, must needs "go out of the world." The Prince of princes himself, when here, went through this town to his own country, and that upon a fair day too; yea, and as I think, it was

---

4. Legion is the name of a demon (or group of demons) whom Jesus encounters (Mark 5.9).

Beelzebub, the chief lord of this fair, that invited him to buy of his vanities; yea, would have made him lord of the fair, would he but have done him reverence as he went through the town. Yea, because he was such a person of honor, Beelzebub had him from street to street, and showed him all the kingdoms of the world in a little time, that he might, if possible, allure the Blessed One to cheapen and buy some of his vanities; but he had no mind to the merchandise, and therefore left the town without laying out so much as one farthing upon these vanities. This fair, therefore, is an ancient thing of long standing, and a very great fair. Now these pilgrims, as I said, must needs go through this fair. Well, so they did; but behold, even as they entered into the fair, all the people in the fair were moved, and the town itself as it were in a hubbub about them; and that for several reasons; for,

The pilgrims were clothed with such kind of raiment as was diverse from the raiment of any that traded in that fair. The people, therefore, of the fair, made a great gazing upon them; some said they were fools, some they were bedlams, and some they were outlandish men.

And as they wondered at their apparel, so they did likewise at their speech: for few could understand what they said; they naturally spoke the language of Canaan, but they that kept the fair were the men of this world; so that, from one end of the fair to the other they seemed barbarians each to the other.

But that which did not a little amuse the merchandisers was, that these pilgrims set very light by all their wares; they cared not so much as to look upon them, and if they called upon them to buy, they would put their fingers in their ears and cry, "Turn away mine eyes from beholding vanity," and look upwards, signifying that their trade and traffic was in heaven.

One chanced mockingly, beholding the carriage of the men, to say unto them, What will ye buy? But they, looking upon him, answered, "We buy the truth." At that there was an occasion taken to despise the men the more; some mocking, some taunting, some speaking reproachfully, and some calling upon others to smite them. At last things came to a hubbub and a great stir in the fair, insomuch that all order was confounded. Now was word presently brought to the great one of the fair, who quickly came down and deputed some of his most trusty friends to take these men into examination, about whom the fair was almost overturned. So the men were brought to examination; and they that sat upon them, asked them whence they came, whither they went, and what they did there, in such an unusual garb. The men told them that they were pilgrims and strangers in the world, and that they were going to their own country, which was the heavenly Jerusalem, and that they had given no occasion to the men of the town, nor yet to the merchandisers, thus to abuse them, except it was for that, when one asked them what they would buy, they said they would buy the truth. But they that were appointed to examine them did not believe them to be any other than bedlams and mad. Therefore they took them and beat them, and besmeared them with dirt, and put them into the cage, that they might be made a spectacle to all the men of the fair.

There, therefore, they lay for some time, and were made the objects of any man's sport, or malice, or revenge, the great one of the fair laughing still at all that befell them. But the men being patient, and not rendering railing for railing, but contrariwise, blessing, and giving good words for bad, and kindness for injuries done, some men in the fair that were more observing, and less prejudiced than the rest, began to check and blame the baser sort for their continual abuses to the men. They said that for aught they could see, the men were quiet, and sober, and intented nobody any harm; and that there were many that traded in their fair that were more worthy to be put into the cage, yea, and pillory too, than were the men they had abused.

After words had passed on both sides, the men behaving themselves all the while very wisely and soberly, they fell to blows among themselves. Then were these two poor men brought before their examiners again, and there charged as being guilty of the hubbub. So they beat them pitifully, and hanged irons upon them, and led them in chains up and down the fair, for an example and a terror to others, lest any should speak in their behalf, or join themselves unto them. But Christian and Faithful behaved themselves with so much meekness and patience, that it won to their side, though but few in comparison of the rest, several of the men in the fair. This put the other party yet into greater rage, insomuch that they concluded the death of these two men. Wherefore they threatened, that the cage nor irons should serve their turn, but that they should die, for the abuse they had done, and for deluding the men of the fair. Then were they remanded to the cage again, until further order should be taken with them. So they put them in and made their feet fast in the stocks.

Then a convenient time being appointed, they brought them forth to their trial, in order to their condemnation. When the time was come, they were brought before their enemies and arraigned. The judge's name was Lord Hate-good. Their indictment was one and the same in substance, though somewhat varying in form, the contents whereof were this:

"That they were enemies to and disturbers of their trade; that they had made commotions and divisions in the town, and had won a party to their own most dangerous opinions, in contempt of the law of their prince."

Then Faithful began to answer, that he had only set himself against that which hath set itself against him that is higher than the highest. And, said he, as for disturbance, I make none, being myself a man of peace; the parties that were won to us, were won by beholding our truth and innocence, and they are only turned from the worse to the better. And as to the king you talk of, since he is Beelzebub, the enemy of our Lord, I defy him and all his angels.

Then proclamation was made, that they that had aught to say for their lord the king against the prisoner at the bar, should forthwith appear and give in their evidence. So there came in three witnesses, to wit, Envy, Superstition, and Pickthank. They were then asked if they knew the prisoner at the bar, and what they had to say for their lord the king against him.

Then stood forth Envy and Superstition who gave evidence against the prisoner.

Then was Pickthank sworn, and bid say what he knew, in behalf of their lord the king, against the prisoner at the bar.

PICKTHANK.   My Lord, and you gentlemen all, this fellow I have known of a long time, and have heard him speak things that ought not to be spoke; for he hath railed on our noble prince Beelzebub, and hath spoken contemptibly of his honorable friends, whose names are the Lord Old Man, the Lord Carnal Delight, the Lord Luxurious, the Lord Desire of Vain-Glory, my old Lord Lechery, Sir Having Greedy, with all the rest of our nobility; and he hath said, moreover, that if all men were of his mind, if possible, there is not one of these noblemen should have any longer a being in this town. Besides, he hath not been afraid to rail on you, my Lord, who are now appointed to be his judge, calling you an ungodly villain, with many other such like vilifying terms, with which he hath bespattered most of the gentry of our town.

When this Pickthank had told his tale, the Judge directed his speech to the prisoner at the bar, saying, Thou runagate, heretic, and traitor, hast thou heard what these honest gentlemen have witnessed against thee?

FAITHFUL.   May I speak a few words in my own defence?

JUDGE.   Sirrah! Sirrah! thou deservest to live no longer, but to be slain immediately upon the place; yet, that all men may see our gentleness towards thee, let us hear what thou, vile runagate, hast to say.

FAITHFUL.   Then, in answer to what Mr. Envy hath spoken, I never said aught but this, That whatsoever is flat against the Word of God, is diametrically opposite to Christianity. If I have said amiss in this, convince me of my error, and I am ready here before you to make my recantation. As to Mr. Superstition, and his charge against me, I said only this, That in the worship of God there is required a Divine faith; but there can be no Divine faith without a Divine revelation of the will of God. As to what Mr. Pickthank hath said, I say that the prince of this town, with all the rabblement, his attendants, by this gentleman named, are more fit for being in hell than in this town and country; and so, the Lord have mercy upon me!

Then the Judge called to the jury (who all this while stood by, to hear and observe): Gentlemen of the jury, you see this man about whom so great an uproar hath been made in this town. You have also heard what these worthy gentlemen have witnessed against him. Also you have heard his reply and confession. It lieth now in your breasts to hang him or save his life. You see he disputeth against our religion; and for the treason he hath confessed, he deserveth to die the death.

Then went the jury out, whose names were, Mr. Blind-man, Mr. No-good, Mr. Malice, Mr. Love-lust, Mr. Live-loose, Mr. Heady, Mr. High-mind, Mr. Enmity, Mr. Liar, Mr. Cruelty, Mr. Hate-light, and Mr. Implacable; who every one gave in his private verdict against him among themselves, and afterwards unanimously concluded to bring him in guilty before the Judge. And first, among themselves, Mr. Blind-man, the foreman, said, I see clearly that this man is a heretic.

Then said Mr. No-good, Away with such a fellow from the earth. Ay, said Mr. Malice, for I hate the very looks of him. Then said Mr. Love-lust, I could never endure him. Nor I, said Mr. Live-loose, for he would always be condemning my way. Hang him, hang him, said Mr. Heady. A sorry scrub, said Mr. High-mind. My heart riseth against him, said Mr. Enmity. He is a rogue, said Mr. Liar. Hanging is too good for him, said Mr. Cruelty. Let us despatch him out of the way, said Mr. Hate-light. Then said Mr. Implacable, Might I have all the world given me, I could not be reconciled to him; therefore, let us forthwith bring him in guilty of death. And so they did; therefore he was presently condemned to be had from the place where he was, to the place from whence he came, and there to be put to the most cruel death that could be invented.

They, therefore, brought him out first, they scourged him, then they buffeted him, then they lanced his flesh with knives; after that, they stoned him with stones, then pricked him with their swords; and, last of all they burned him to ashes at the stake. Thus came Faithful to his end.

Now I saw that there stood behind the multitude a chariot and a couple of horses, waiting for Faithful, who (so soon as his adversaries had despatched him) was taken up into it; and straightway was carried up through the clouds, with sound of trumpet, the nearest way to the celestial gate.

But Christian had some respite, and was remanded back to prison. So he there remained for a space; but he that overrules all things, having the power of their rage in his own hand, so wrought it about, that Christian for that time escaped them, and went his way.

*   *   *

[Green Meadows]

I saw, then, that they [Christian and his new companion, Hopeful] went on their way to a pleasant river; which David the king called "the river of God," but John, "the river of the water of life."[5] Now their way lay just upon the bank of the river; here, therefore, Christian and his companion walked with great delight; they drank also of the water of the river, which was pleasant and enlivening to their weary spirits; besides, on the banks of this river, on either side, were green trees, that bore all manner of fruit, and the leaves of the trees were good for medicine; with the fruit of these trees they were also much delighted, and the leaves they ate to prevent surfeits and other diseases that are incident to those that heat their blood by travels. On either side of the river was also a meadow, curiously beautified with lilies, and it was green all the year long. In this meadow they lay down and slept; for here they might lie down safely. When they awoke, they gathered again of the fruit of the trees, and drank again of the water of the river,

5. In Psalms 65.9, the poet, presumably King David, speaks of "the river of God" that waters the earth. In Revelation 22.1, the apostle sees a heavenly vision of "a pure river of water of life" flowing from God's throne.

and then lay down again to sleep. Thus they did several days and
nights and when they were disposed to go on, for they were not, as yet,
at their journey's end, they ate and drank, and departed.

*   *   *

[The Author's Way of Sending Forth His Second Part
of the Pilgrim]

*   *   *

Go then, my little Book[6] and shew to all
That entertain, and bid thee welcome shall,
What thou shalt keep close, shut up from the rest,
And wish what thou shalt shew them may be blest
To them for good, may make them chuse to be
Pilgrims, better by far, then thee or me.
   Go then, I say, tell all men who thou art,
Say, I am Christiana, and my part
Is now with my four Sons, to tell you what
It is for men to take a Pilgrims lot;
   Go also tell them who, and what they be,
That now do go on Pilgrimage with thee;
Say, here's my neighbour Mercy, she is one,
That has long-time with me a Pilgrim gone;
Come see her in her Virgin Face, and learn
Twixt Idle ones, and Pilgrims to discern.
Yea let young Damsels learn of her to prize,
The World which is to come, in any wise;
When little Tripping Maidens follow God,
And leave old doting Sinners to his Rod;
'Tis like those Days wherein the young ones cry'd
Hosannah to whom old ones did deride.
   Next tell them of old Honest, who you found
With his white hairs treading the Pilgrims ground;
Yea, tell them how plain hearted this man was,
How after his good Lord he bare his Cross:
Perhaps with some gray Head this may prevail,
With Christ to fall in Love, and Sin bewail.
   Tell them also how Master Fearing went
On Pilgrimage, and how the time he spent
In Solitariness, with Fears and Cries,
And how at last, he won the Joyful Prize.
He was a good man, though much down in Spirit,
He is a good Man, and doth Life inherit.
   Tell them of Master Feeblemind also,
Who, not before, but still behind would go;
Show them also how he had like been slain,
And how one Great-Heart did his life regain:
This man was true of Heart, tho weak in grace,

6. In her preface to *Little Women* (see p. 9), Alcott adopts and revises Bunyan's poetic preface
presented here.

One might true Godliness read in his Face.
    Then tell them of Master Ready-to-halt,
A Man with Crutches, but much without fault:
Tell them how Master Feeblemind, *and he*
Did love, and in Opinions *much agree.*
And let all know, the weakness was their chance,
Yet sometimes one could Sing *the other* Dance.
    Forget not Master Valiant-for-the-Truth,
That Man of courage, tho a very Youth.
Tell every one his Spirit was so stout,
No Man could ever make him face about,
And how Great-Heart, *and he could not forbear*
But put down Doubting Castle, slay Despair.
    Overlook not Master Despondency.
Nor Much-a-fraid, *his Daughter, tho they lye*
Under such Mantles as may make them look
(With some) as if their God had them forsook.
They softly went, but sure, and at the end,
Found that the Lord of Pilgrims *was their Friend.*
When thou hast told the World of all these things,
Then turn about, my book, and touch these strings,
Which, if but touched will such Musick make,
They'l make a Cripple dance, a Gyant quake.
Those Riddles that lie couch't within thy breast,
Freely propound, expound: and for the rest
Of thy mysterious lines, let them remain,
For those whose nimble Fancies shall them gain.
    Now may this little Book a blessing be,
To those that love this little Book and me,
And may its buyer have no cause to say,
His Money is but lost or thrown away,
Yea may this Second Pilgrim *yield that Fruit,*
As may with each good Pilgrims *fancie sute,*
And may it perswade some that go astray,
To turn their Foot and Heart to the right way.

[Great-heart]

* * *

The *Interpreter* then called for a *Manservant* of his, one *Great-heart*, and bid him take *Sword*, and *Helmet* and *Shield*, and take these my Daughters, said he, and conduct them to the House called *Beautiful*, at which place they will rest next. So he took his Weapons, and went before them, and the *Interpreter* said, God speed. * * *

JOHANN WOLFGANG VON GOETHE

From Wilhelm Meister's Apprenticeship†

[*Mignon's Song*]

"Know'st thou the land where citron-apples bloom,
And oranges like gold in leafy gloom,
A gentle wind from deep-blue heaven blows,
The myrtle thick, and high the laurel grows?
Know'st thou it then?
        'T is there! 'T is there!
O my true loved one, thou with me must go!

"Know'st thou the house, its porch with pillars tall?
The rooms do glitter, glitters bright the hall,
And marble statues stand, and look each one:
What's this, poor child, to thee they've done?
Know'st thou it then?
        'T is there! 'T is there!
O my protector, thou with me must go!

"Know'st thou the hill, the bridge that hangs on cloud:
The mules in mist grope o'er the torrent loud,
In caves lie coiled the dragon's ancient brood,
The crag leaps down, and over it the flood:
Know'st thou it then?
        'T is there! 'T is there!
Our way runs; O my father, wilt thou go?"

MARIA EDGEWORTH

The Purple Jar‡

Rosamond, a little girl of about seven years old, was walking with her mother in the streets of London. As she passed along, she looked in at the windows of several shops, and she saw a great variety of different sorts of things, of which she did not know the use, or even the names. She wished to stop to look at them; but there were a great number of people in the streets, and a great many carts, and carriages, and wheelbarrows, and she was afraid to let go her mother's hand.

† From Johann Wolfgang von Goethe, *Wilhelm Meister's Apprenticeship*, trans. Thomas Carlyle (Boston: Ticknor and Fields, 1866), 132. Initially read by Louisa May Alcott at Emerson's suggestion, Goethe's works remained among her favorites throughout her life. This short romantic excerpt from *Wilhelm Meister's Apprenticeship* is twice featured in *Little Women*.
‡ From Maria Edgeworth, *Early Lessons* (London: Routledge, 1801), 1–17. Edgeworth was an author of didactic tales for children and novels for adults; her representation of authoritarian and moralistic mothering differs substantially from the parenting depicted by Alcott, though both authors portray children as moral agents responsible for their own decisions.

"Oh! mother, how happy I should be," said she, as she passed a toy-shop, "if I had all these pretty things!"

"What, all! Do you wish for them all, Rosamond?"

"Yes, mamma, all."

As she spoke, they came to a milliner's shop; the windows were hung with ribands and lace, and festoons of artificial flowers.

"Oh, mamma, what beautiful roses! Won't you buy some of them?"

"No, my dear."

"Why?"

"Because I don't want them, my dear."

They went a little farther, and they came to another shop, which caught Rosamond's eye. It was a jeweller's shop; and there were a great many pretty baubles, ranged in drawers behind glass.

"Mamma, you'll buy some of these."

"Which of them, Rosamond?"

"Which? I don't know which; but any of them, for they are all pretty."

"Yes, they are all pretty; but what use would they be of to me?"

"Use! Oh, I'm sure you could find some use or other, if you would only buy them first."

"But I would rather find out the use first."

"Well, then, mamma, there are buckles: you know buckles are useful things, very useful things."

"I have a pair of buckles, I don't want another pair," said her mother, and walked on. Rosamond was very sorry, that her mother wanted nothing. Presently, however, they came to a shop, which appeared to her far more beautiful than the rest. It was a chemist's shop, but she did not know that.

"Oh, mother! oh!" cried she, pulling her mother's hand; "Look, look; blue, green, red, yellow, and purple! Oh, mamma, what beautiful things! Won't you buy some of these?"

Still her mother answered as before; "What use would they be of to me, Rosamond?"

"You might put flowers in them, mamma, and they would look so pretty on the chimney-piece; I wish I had one of them."

"You have a flower-pot," said her mother; "and that is not a flower-pot."

"But I could use it for a flower-pot, mamma, you know."

"Perhaps, if you were to see it nearer, if you were to examine it, you might be disappointed."

"No, indeed, I'm sure I should not; I should like it exceedingly."

Rosamond kept her head turned to look at the purple vase, till she could see it no longer.

"Then, mother," said she, after a pause, "perhaps you have no money."

"Yes, I have."

"Dear, if I had money, I would buy roses, and boxes, and buckles, and purple flower-pots, and every thing." Rosamond was obliged to pause in the midst of her speech.

"Oh, mamma, would you stop a minute for me; I have got a stone in my shoe, it hurts me very much."

"How comes there to be a stone in your shoe?"

"Because of this great hole, mamma—it comes in there; my shoes are quite worn out; I wish you'd be so very good as to give me another pair."

"Nay, Rosamond, but I have not money enough to buy shoes, and flower-pots, and buckles, and boxes, and every thing."

Rosamond thought, that was a great pity. But now her foot, which had been hurt by the stone, began to give her so much pain, that she was obliged to hop every other step, and she could think of nothing else. They came to a shoemaker's shop soon afterwards.

"There! there! mamma, there are shoes; there are little shoes, that would just fit me; and you know shoes would be really of use to me."

"Yes, so they would, Rosamond. Come in." She followed her mother into the shop.

Mr. Sole, the shoemaker, had a great many customers, and his shop was full, so they were obliged to wait.

"Well, Rosamond," said her mother, "you don't think this shop so pretty as the rest?"

"No, not nearly; it's black and dark, and there are nothing but shoes all round; and, besides, there's a very disagreeable smell."

"That smell is the smell of new leather."

"Is it? Oh!" said Rosamond, looking round, "there is a pair of little shoes; they'll just fit me, I'm sure."

"Perhaps they might, but you cannot be sure, till you have tried them on, any more than you can be quite sure, that you should like the purple vase *exceedingly*, till you have examined it more attentively."

"Why, I don't know, about the shoes, certainly, till I've tried; but, mamma, I'm quite sure, I should like the flower-pot."

"Well, which would you rather have, that jar, or a pair of shoes? I will buy either for you."

"Dear mamma, thank you—but if you could buy both?"

"No, not both."

"Then the jar, if you please."

"But I should tell you, that I shall not give you another pair of shoes this month."

"This month! that's a very long time indeed. You can't think how these hurt me; I believe I'd better have the new shoes—but yet, that purple flower-pot——Oh, indeed, mamma, these shoes are not so very, very bad; I think I might wear them a little longer; and the month will be soon over: I can make them last till the end of the month; can't I? Don't you think so, mamma?"

"Nay, my dear, I want you to think for yourself: you will have time enough to consider about it, whilst I speak to Mr. Sole about my clogs."

Mr. Sole was by this time at leisure; and whilst her mother was speaking to him, Rosamond stood in profound meditation, with one shoe on, and the other in her hand.

"Well, my dear, have you decided?"

"Mamma!—yes—I believe. If you please—I should like the flower-pot; that is, if you won't think me very silly, mamma."

"Why, as to that, I can't promise you, Rosamond; but when you are to judge for yourself, you should choose what will make you the happiest; and then it would not signify who thought you silly."

"Then, mamma, if that's all, I'm sure the flower-pot would make me the happiest," said she, putting on her old shoe again; "so I choose the flower-pot."

"Very well, you shall have it; clasp your shoe and come home."

Rosamond clasped her shoe, and ran after her mother; it was not long before the shoe came down at the heel, and many times was she obliged to stop, to take the stones out of her shoe, and often was she obliged to hop with pain; but still the thoughts of the purple flower-pot prevailed, and she persisted in her choice.

When they came to the shop with the large window, Rosamond felt her joy redouble, upon hearing her mother desire the servant, who was with them, to buy the purple jar, and bring it home. He had other commissions, so he did not return with them. Rosamond, as soon as she got in, ran to gather all her own flowers, which she had in a corner of her mother's garden.

"I'm afraid they'll be dead before the flower-pot comes, Rosamond," said her mother to her, when she was coming in with the flowers in her lap.

"No, indeed, mamma, it will come home very soon, I dare say; and sha'n't I be very happy putting them into the purple flower-pot?"

"I hope so, my dear."

The servant was much longer returning home than Rosamond had expected; but at length he came, and brought with him the long-wished-for jar. The moment it was set down upon the table, Rosamond ran up, with an exclamation of joy: "I may have it now, mamma?" "Yes, my dear, it is yours." Rosamond poured the flowers from her lap, upon the carpet, and seized the purple flower-pot.

"Oh, dear mother!" cried she, as soon as she had taken off the top, "but there's something dark in it—it smells very disagreeably—what is it? I didn't want this black stuff."

"Nor I neither, my dear."

"But what shall I do with it, mamma?"

"That I cannot tell."

"But it will be of no use to me, mamma."

"That I can't help."

"But I must pour it out, and fill the flower-pot with water."

"That's as you please, my dear."

"Will you lend me a bowl to pour it into, mamma?"

"That was more than I promised you, my dear; but I will lend you a bowl."

The bowl was produced, and Rosamond proceeded to empty the purple vase. But what was her surprise and disappointment, when it was entirely empty, to find that it was no longer a *purple* vase. It was a plain white glass jar, which had appeared to have that beautiful colour, merely from the liquor with which it had been filled.

Little Rosamond burst into tears.

"Why should you cry, my dear?" said her mother; "it will be of as much use to you now, as ever, for a flower-pot."

"But it won't look so pretty on the chimney-piece; I am sure, if I had known, that it was not really purple, I should not have wished to have it so much."

"But didn't I tell you, that you had not examined it; and that perhaps you would be disappointed?"

"And so I am disappointed, indeed; I wish I had believed you beforehand. Now I had much rather have the shoes; for I shall not be able to walk all this month: even walking home, that little way, hurt me exceedingly. Mamma, I'll give you the flower-pot back again, and that purple stuff and all, if you'll only give me the shoes."

"No, Rosamond, you must abide by your own choice; and now the best thing you can possibly do is, to bear your disappointment with good humour."

"I will bear it as well as I can," said Rosamond, wiping her eyes; and she began slowly and sorrowfully to fill the vase with flowers.

But Rosamond's disappointment did not end here: many were the difficulties and distresses, into which her imprudent choice brought her, before the end of the month. Every day her shoes grew worse and worse, till, at last, she could neither run, dance, jump, or walk in them. Whenever Rosamond was called to see anything, she was pulling her shoes up at the heels, and was sure to be too late. Whenever her mother was going out to walk, she could not take Rosamond with her, for Rosamond had no soles to her shoes; and, at length, on the very last day of the month, it happened, that her father proposed to take her with her brother to a glass-house, which she had long wished to see. She was very happy; but, when she was quite ready, had her hat and gloves on, and was making haste down stairs to her brother and her father, who were waiting at the hall door for her, the shoe dropped off: she put it on again in a great hurry; but, as she was going across the hall, her father turned round. "Why are you walking slip-shod? no one must walk slip-shod with me; why, Rosamond," said he, looking at her shoes with disgust, "I thought that you were always neat; go, I cannot take you with me."

Rosamond coloured and retired.—"Oh, mamma," said she, as she took off her hat, "how I wish, that I had chosen the shoes—they would have been of so much more use to me than that jar: however, I am sure—no, not quite sure—but, I hope, I shall be wiser another time."

"JO" [LOUISA MAY ALCOTT] AND "MEG" [ANNA B. ALCOTT PRATT]

Norna; or, The Witch's Curse†

CHARACTERS.

COUNT RODOLPHO . . . *A Haughty Noble.*
COUNT LOUIS . . . . *Lover of Leonore.*
ADRIAN . . . . *The Black Mask.*
HUGO . . . . *A Bandit.*
GASPARD . . . . *Captain of the Guard.*
ANGELO . . . . *A Page.*
THERESA . . . . *Wife to Rodolpho.*
LEONORE . . . . *In love with Louis.*
NORNA . . . . *A Witch.*

SCENE FIRST.

[*A room in the castle of* RODOLPHO.
THERESA *discovered alone, and in tears.*]

THERESA. I cannot pray; my aching heart finds rest alone in tears. Ah, what a wretched fate is mine! Forced by a father's will to wed a stranger ere I learned to love, one short year hath taught me what a bitter thing it is to wear a chain that binds me unto one who hath proved himself both jealous and unkind. The fair hopes I once cherished are now gone, and here a captive in my splendid home I dwell forsaken, sorrowing and alone [*weeps*]. [*Three taps upon the wall are heard.*] Ha, my brother's signal! What can bring him hither at this hour? Louis, is it thou? Enter; "all 's well."

[*Enter* COUNT LOUIS *through a secret panel in the wall, hidden by a curtain. He embraces* THERESA.

THERESA. Ah, Louis, what hath chanced? Why art thou here? Some danger must have brought thee; tell me, dear brother. Let me serve thee.

LOUIS. Sister dearest, thy kindly offered aid is useless now. Thou canst not help me; and I must add another sorrow to the many that are thine. I came to say farewell, Theresa.

THERESA. Farewell! Oh, brother, do not leave me! Thy love is all now left to cheer my lonely life. Wherefore must thou go? Tell me, I beseech thee!

LOUIS. Forgive me if I grieve thee. I will tell thee all. Thy husband hates me, for I charged him with neglect and cruelty to thee; and he hath vowed revenge for my bold words. He hath whispered false tales to the king, he hath blighted all my hopes of rank and honor. I

---

† From *Comic Tragedies* (Boston: Roberts Brothers, 1893), 16–94. An example of Alcott's juvenilia, *Norna* is also a model for the March girls' Christmas theatrical in part 1, chap. 2.

am banished from the land, and must leave thee and Leonore, and wander forth an outcast and alone. But—let him beware!—I shall return to take a deep revenge for thy wrongs and my own. Nay, sister, grieve not thus. I have sworn to free thee from his power, and I will keep my vow. Hope on and bear a little longer, dear Theresa, and ere long I will bear thee to a happy home [*noise is heard without*]. Ha! what is that? Who comes?

THERESA.   'T is my lord returning from the court. Fly, Louis, fly! Thou art lost if he discover thee. Heaven bless and watch above thee. Remember poor Theresa, and farewell.

LOUIS.   One last word of Leonore. I have never told my love, yet she hath smiled on me, and I should have won her hand. Ah, tell her this, and bid her to be true to him who in his exile will hope on, and yet return to claim the heart he hath loved so faithfully. Farewell, my sister. Despair not,—I shall return.

[*Exit* LOUIS *through the secret panel; drops his dagger.*]

THERESA.   Thank Heaven, he is safe!—but oh, my husband, this last deed of thine is hard to bear. Poor Louis, parted from Leonore, his fair hopes blighted, all by thy cruel hand. Ah, he comes! I must be calm.

[*Enter* RODOLPHO.

ROD.   What, weeping still? Hast thou no welcome for thy lord save tears and sighs? I'll send thee to a convent if thou art not more gay!

THERESA.   I'll gladly go, my lord. I am weary of the world. Its gayeties but make my heart more sad.

ROD.   Nay, then I will take thee to the court, and there thou *must* be gay. But I am weary; bring me wine, and smile upon me as thou used to do. Dost hear me? Weep no more. [*Seats himself.* THERESA *brings wine and stands beside him. Suddenly he sees the dagger dropped by* LOUIS.] Ha! what is that? 'T is none of mine. How came it hither? Answer, I command thee!

THERESA.   I cannot. I must not, dare not tell thee.

ROD.   Darest thou refuse to answer? Speak! Who hath dared to venture hither? Is it thy brother? As thou lovest life, I bid thee speak.

THERESA.   I am innocent, and will not betray the only one now left me on the earth to love. Oh, pardon me, my lord; I will obey in all but this.

ROD.   Thou *shalt* obey. I 'll take thy life but I will know. Thy brother must be near,—this dagger was not here an hour ago. Thy terror hath betrayed him. I leave thee now to bid them search the castle. But if I find him not, I shall return; and if thou wilt not then confess, I 'll find a way to make thee. Remember, I have vowed,—thy secret or thy life!

[*Exit* RODOLPHO.

THERESA.   My life I freely yield thee, but my secret—never. Oh, Louis, I will gladly die to save thee. Life hath no joy for me; and in the grave this poor heart may forget the bitter sorrows it is burdened with [*sinks down weeping*].

[*Enter* RODOLPHO.

ROD.   The search is vain. He hath escaped. Theresa, rise, and answer me. To whom belonged the dagger I have found? Thy tears avail not; I will be obeyed. Kneel not to me, I will not pardon. Answer, or I swear I'll make thee dumb forever.

THERESA.   No, no! I will not betray. Oh, husband, spare me! Let not the hand that led me to the altar be stained with blood I would so gladly shed for thee. I cannot answer thee.

ROD. [*striking her*].   Then die: thy constancy is useless. I will find thy brother and take a fearful vengeance yet.

THERESA.   I am faithful to the last. Husband, I forgive thee.

[THERESA *dies.*

ROD.   'T is done, and I am rid of her forever; but 't is an ugly deed. Poor fool, there was a time when I could pity thee, but thou hast stood 'twixt me and Lady Leonore, and now I am free. I must conceal the form, and none shall ever know the crime.

[*Exit* RODOLPHO.

[*The panel opens and* NORNA *enters.*]

NORNA.   Heaven shield us! What is this? His cruel hand hath done the deed, and I am powerless to save. Poor, murdered lady, I had hoped to spare thee this, and lead thee to a happier home. Perchance, 't is better so. The dead find rest, and thy sad heart can ache no more. Rest to thy soul, sweet lady. But for *thee*, thou cruel villain, I have in store a deep revenge for all thy sinful deeds. If there be power in spell or charm, I'll conjure fearful dreams upon thy head. I'll follow thee wherever thou mayst go, and haunt thy sleep with evil visions. I'll whisper strange words that shall appall thee; dark phantoms shall rise up before thee, and wild voices ringing in thine ear shall tell thee of thy sins. By all these will I make life like a hideous dream, and death more fearful still. Like a vengeful ghost I will haunt thee to thy grave, and so revenge thy wrongs, poor, murdered lady. Beware, Rodolpho! Old Norna's curse is on thee.

[*She bears away* THERESA'S *body through the secret door, and vanishes.*

CURTAIN.

NOTE TO SCENE SECOND.

The mysterious cave was formed of old furniture, covered with dark draperies, an opening being left at the back wherein the spirits called up by Norna might appear. A kitchen kettle filled with steaming water made an effective caldron over which the sorceress should murmur her incantations; flaming pine-knots cast a lurid glare over the scene;

and large boughs, artfully arranged about the stage, gave it the appearance of a "gloomy wood."

When Louis "retires within," he at once arrays himself in the white robes of the vision, and awaits the witch's call to rise behind the aperture in true dramatic style. He vanishes, quickly resumes his own attire, while Norna continues to weave her spells, till she sees he is ready to appear once more as the disguised Count Louis.

SCENE SECOND.

[*A wood.* Norna's *cave among the rocks.* Enter Louis *masked.*]

Louis. Yes; 't is the spot. How dark and still! She is not here. Ho, Norna, mighty sorceress! I seek thy aid.

Norna [*rising from the cave*]. I am here.

Louis. I seek thee, Norna, to learn tidings of one most dear to me. Dost thou know aught of Count Rodolpho's wife? A strange tale hath reached me that not many nights ago she disappeared, and none know whither she hath gone. Oh, tell me, is this true?

Norna. It is most true.

Louis. And canst thou tell me whither she hath gone? I will reward thee well.

Norna. I can. She lies within her tomb, in the chapel of the castle.

Louis. Dead!—it cannot be! They told me she had fled away with some young lord who had won her love. Was it not true?

Norna. It is false as the villain's heart who framed the tale. *I* bore the murdered lady to her tomb, and laid her there.

Louis. Murdered? How? When? By whom? Oh, tell me I beseech thee!

Norna. Her husband's cruel hand took the life he had made a burden. I heard him swear it ere he dealt the blow.

Louis. Wherefore did he kill her? Oh, answer quickly or I shall go mad with grief and hate.

Norna. I can tell thee little. From my hiding-place I heard her vow never to confess whose dagger had been found in her apartment, and her jealous lord, in his wild anger, murdered her.

Louis. 'T was mine. Would it had been sheathed in mine own breast ere it had caused so dark a deed! Ah, Theresa, why did I leave thee to a fate like this?

Norna. Young man, grieve not; it is too late to save, but there is left to thee a better thing than grief.

Louis. Oh, what?

Norna. Revenge!

Louis. Thou art right. I'll weep no more. Give me thine aid, O mighty wizard, and I will serve thee well.

Norna. Who art thou? The poor lady's lover?

Louis. Ah, no; far nearer and far deeper was the love I bore her, for I am her brother.

Norna. Ha, that's well! Thou wilt join me, for I have made a vow to rest not till that proud, sinful lord hath well atoned for this deep crime. Spirits shall haunt him, and the darkest phantoms that my art can raise shall scare his soul. Wilt thou join me in my work?

LOUIS. I will,—but stay! thou hast spoken of spirits. Dread sorceress, is it in thy power to call them up?

NORNA. It is. Wilt see my skill. Stand back while I call up a phantom which thou canst not doubt.

[LOUIS *retires within the cave.* NORNA *weaves a spell above her caldron.*

NORNA.   O spirit, from thy quiet tomb,
         I bid thee hither through the gloom,
         In winding-sheet, with bloody brow,
         Rise up and hear our solemn vow.
         I bid thee, with my magic power,
         Tell the dark secret of that hour
         When cruel hands, with blood and strife,
         Closed the sad dream of thy young life.
         Hither—appear before our eyes.
         Pale spirit, I command thee *rise.*

                              [*Spirit of* THERESA *rises.*

         Shadowy spirit, I charge thee well,
         By my mystic art's most potent spell,
         To haunt throughout his sinful life,
         The mortal who once called thee wife.
         At midnight hour glide round his bed,
         And lay thy pale hand on his head.
         Whisper wild words in his sleeping ear,
         And chill his heart with a deadly fear.
         Rise at his side in his gayest hour,
         And his guilty soul shall feel thy power.
         Stand thou before him in day and night,
         And cast o'er his life a darksome blight;
         For with all his power and sin and pride,
         He shall ne'er forget his murdered bride.
         Pale, shadowy form, wilt thou obey?

                              [*The spirit bows its head.*

         To thy ghostly work away—away!

                              [*The spirit vanishes.*

         The spell is o'er, the vow is won,
         And, sinful heart, *thy* curse begun.

                              [*Re-enter* LOUIS.

LOUIS.   'T is enough! I own thy power, and by the spirit of my murdered sister I have looked upon, I swear to aid thee in thy dark work.

NORNA.   'T is well; and I will use my power to guard thee from the danger that surrounds thee. And now, farewell. Remember,—thou hast sworn.

[*Exit* Louis.

CURTAIN.

SCENE THIRD.

[*Another part of the wood. Enter* Rodolpho.]

Rod.   They told me that old Norna's cave was 'mong these rocks, and yet I find it not. By her I hope to learn where young Count Louis is concealed. Once in my power, he shall not escape to whisper tales of evil deeds against me. Stay! some one comes. I'll ask my way.

[*Enter* Louis *masked.*

Ho, stand, good sir. Canst guide me to the cell of Norna, the old sorceress?

Louis.   It were little use to tell thee; thou wouldst only win a deeper curse than that she hath already laid upon thee.

Rod.   Hold! who art thou that dare to speak thus to Count Rodolpho?

Louis.   That thou canst never know; but this I tell thee: I am thy deadliest foe, and, aided by the wizard Norna, seek to work thee evil, and bring down upon thy head the fearful doom thy sin deserves. Wouldst thou know more,—then seek the witch, and learn the hate she bears thee.

Rod.   Fool! thinkst thou I fear thee or thy enchantments? Draw, and defend thyself! Thou shalt pay dearly for thine insolence to me!

[*Draws his sword.*

Louis.   I will not stain my weapon with a murderer's blood. I leave thee to the fate that gathers round thee.

[*Exit* Louis.

Rod.   "Murderer," said he. I am betrayed,—yet no one saw the deed. Yet, stay! perchance 't was he who bore Theresa away. He has escaped me, and will spread the tale. Nay, why should I fear? Courage! One blow, and I am safe! [*Rushes forward. Spirit of* Theresa *rises.*] What's that?—her deathlike face,—the wound my hand hath made! Help! help! help!

[*Rushes out. The spirit vanishes.*

CURTAIN.

Scene Fourth.

[*Room in the castle of* RODOLPHO.

RODOLPHO *alone.*]

ROD.   I see no way save that. Were young Count Louis dead she
would forget the love that had just begun, and by sweet words and
gifts I may yet win her. The young lord must die [*a groan behind the
curtain*]. Ha! what is that? 'T is nothing; fie upon my fear! I'll banish
all remembrance of the fearful shape my fancy conjured up within
the forest. I'll not do the deed myself,—I have had enough of blood.
Hugo the bandit: he is just the man,—bold, sure of hand, and secret. I will bribe him well, and when the deed is done, find means to
rid me of him lest he should play me false. I saw him in the court-
yard as I entered. Perchance he is not yet gone. Ho, without there!
Bid Hugo here if he be within the castle.—He is a rough knave, but
gold will make all sure.

[*Enter* HUGO.

HUGO.   What would my lord with me?
ROD.   I ask a favor of thee. Nay, never fear, I'll pay thee well. Wouldst
earn a few gold pieces?
HUGO.   Ay, my lord, most gladly would I.
ROD.   Nay, sit, good Hugo. Here is wine; drink, and refresh thyself.
HUGO.   Thanks, my lord. How can I serve you?

[RODOLPHO *gives wine,* HUGO *sits and drinks.*]

ROD.   Dost thou know Count Louis, whom the king lately banished?
HUGO.   Nay, my lord; I never saw him.
ROD [*aside*].   Ha! that is well. It matters not; 't is not of him I speak.
Take more wine, good Hugo. Listen, there is a certain lord,—one
whom I hate. I seek his life. Here is gold—thou hast a dagger, and
can use it well. Dost understand me?
HUGO.   Ay, my lord, most clearly. Name the place and hour; count
out the gold,—I and my dagger then are thine.
ROD.   'T is well. Now harken. In the forest, near old Norna's cave, there
is a quiet spot. Do thou go there to-night at sunset. Watch well, and
when thou seest a tall figure wrapped in a dark cloak, and masked,
spring forth, and do the deed. Then fling the body down the rocks, or
hide it in some secret place. Here is one half the gold; more shall be
thine when thou shalt show some token that the deed is done.
HUGO.   Thanks, Count; I'll do thy bidding. At sunset in the forest,—
I'll be there, and see he leaves it not alive. Good-even, then, my lord.
ROD.   Hugo, use well thy dagger, and gold awaits thee. Yet, stay! I'll
meet thee in the wood, and pay thee there. They might suspect if
they should see thee here again so soon. I'll meet thee there, and so
farewell.
HUGO.   Adieu, my lord.

[*Exit* HUGO].

Rod.   Yes; all goes well. My rival dead, and Leonore is mine. With
her I may forget the pale face that now seems ever looking into
mine. I can almost think the deep wound shows in her picture yonder. But this is folly! Shame on thee, Rodolpho. I'll think of it no
more. [*Turns to drink.* THERESA'S *face appears within the picture, the
wound upon her brow.*] Ha! what is that? Am I going mad? See the
eyes move,—it is Theresa's face! Nay, I will not look again. Yes, yes;
't is there! Will this sad face haunt me forever?
THERESA.   Forever! Forever!
Rod.   Fiends take me,—'t is her voice! It is no dream. Ah, let me go
away—away!

[RODOLPHO *rushes wildly out.*]

CURTAIN.

NOTE TO SCENE FIFTH.

The apparently impossible transformations of this scene (when played
by two actors only) may be thus explained:—

The costumes of Louis and Norna, being merely loose garments, afford opportunities for rapid change; and the indulgent audience overlooking such minor matters as boots and wigs, it became an easy
matter for Jo to transform herself into either of the four characters
which she assumed on this occasion.

Beneath the flowing robes of the sorceress Jo was fully dressed as
Count Rodolpho. Laid conveniently near were the black cloak, hat,
and mask of Louis,—also the white draperies required for the ghostly
Theresa.

Thus, Norna appears in long, gray robe, to which are attached the
hood and elf-locks of the witch. Seeing Hugo approach she conceals
herself among the trees, thus gaining time to don the costume of
Louis, and appear to Hugo who awaits him.

Hugo stabs and drags him from the stage. Louis then throws off his
disguise and becomes Rodolpho, fully dressed for his entrance a moment later.

As Hugo does not again appear, it is an easy matter to assume the
character of the spectre and produce the sights and sounds which ter-
rify the guilty Count; then slipping on the witch's robe, be ready to
glide forth and close the scene with dramatic effect.

SCENE FIFTH.

[The wood near NORNA'S cave. Enter NORNA.]

NORNA.   It is the hour I bid him come with the letter for Lady
Leonore. Poor youth, his sister slain, his life in danger, and the lady
of his love far from him, 't is a bitter fate. But, if old Norna loses not
her power, he shall yet win his liberty, his love, and his revenge. Ah,

he comes,—nay, 't is the ruffian Hugo. I will conceal myself,—some evil is afoot [*hides among the trees*].

[*Enter* HUGO.

HUGO.   This is the spot. Here will I hide, and bide my time [*conceals himself among the rocks*].

[*Enter* LOUIS.

LOUIS.   She is not here. I'll wait awhile and think of Leonore. How will she receive this letter? Ah, could she know how, 'mid all my grief and danger, her dear face shines in my heart, and cheers me on. [HUGO *steals out, and as he turns, stabs him.*] Ha, villain, thou hast killed me! I am dying! God bless thee, Leonore! Norna, remember, vengeance on Rodolpho! [*Falls.*]

HUGO.   Nay, nay, thou wilt take no revenge; thy days are ended, thanks to this good steel. Now, for the token [*takes letter from* LOUIS's *hand*]. Ah, this he cannot doubt. I will take this ring too; 't is a costly one. I 'll hide the body in the thicket yonder, ere my lord arrives [*drags out the body*].

[*Enter* RODOLPHO.

ROD.   Not here? Can he have failed? Here is blood—it may be his. I'll call. Hugo, good Hugo, art thou here?

HUGO [*stealing from the trees*].   Ay, my lord, I am here. All is safely done: the love-sick boy lies yonder in the thicket, dead as steel can make him. And here is the token if you doubt me, and the ring I just took from his hand [*gives letter*].

ROD.   Nay, nay, I do not doubt thee; keep thou the ring. I am content with this. Tell me, did he struggle with thee when thou dealt the blow?

HUGO.   Nay, my lord; he fell without a groan, and murmuring something of revenge on thee, he died. Hast thou the gold?

ROD.   Yes, yes, I have it. Take it, and remember I can take thy life as easily as thou hast his, if thou shouldst whisper what hath been this day done. Now go; I've done with thee.

HUGO.   And I with thee. Adieu, my lord.

[*Exit* HUGO.

ROD.   Now am I safe,—no mortal knows of Theresa's death by my hand, and Leonore is mine.

VOICE [*within the wood*].   Never—never!

ROD.   Curses on me! Am I bewitched? Surely, I heard a voice; perchance 't was but an echo [*a wild laugh rings through the trees*]. Fiends take the wood! I'll stay no longer! [*Turns to fly.* THERESA'S *spirit rises.*] 'T is there,—help, help— [*Rushes wildly out.*]

[*Enter* NORNA.

NORNA.   Ha, ha! fiends shall haunt thee, thou murderer! Another sin upon thy soul,—another life to be avenged! Poor, murdered youth, now gone to join thy sister. I will lay thee by her side and then to my work. He hath raised another ghost to haunt him. Let him beware!

[*Exit* Norna.

CURTAIN.

SCENE SIXTH.

[*Chamber in the castle of* Lady Leonore. *Enter* Leonore.]

Leonore. Ah, how wearily the days go by. No tidings of Count Louis, and Count Rodolpho urges on his suit so earnestly. I must accept his hand to-day, or refuse his love, and think no more of Louis. I know not how to choose. Rodolpho loves me: I am an orphan and alone, and in his lovely home I may be happy. I have heard it whispered that he is both stern and cruel, yet methinks it cannot be,— he is so tender when with me. Ah, would I could forget Count Louis! He hath never told his love, and doubtless thinks no more of her who treasures up his gentle words, and cannot banish them, even when another offers a heart and home few would refuse. How shall I answer Count Rodolpho when he comes? I do not love him as I should, and yet it were no hard task to learn with so fond a teacher. Shall I accept his love, or shall I reject?

[Norna *suddenly appears.*

Norna. Reject.

Leonore. Who art thou? Leave me, or I call for aid.

Norna. Nay, lady, fear not. I come not here to harm thee, but to save thee from a fate far worse than death. I am old Norna of the forest, and though they call me witch and sorceress, I am a woman yet, and with a heart to pity and to love. I would save thy youth and beauty from the blight I fear will fall upon thee.

Leonore. Save me! from what? How knowest thou I am in danger; and from what wouldst thou save me, Norna?

Norna. From Lord Rodolpho, lady.

Leonore. Ah! and why from him? Tell on, I'll listen to thee now. He hath offered me his heart and hand. Why should I not accept them, Norna?

Norna. That heart is filled with dark and evil passions, and that hand is stained with blood. Ay, lady, well mayst thou start. I will tell thee more. The splendid home he would lead thee to is darkened by a fearful crime, and his fair palace haunted by the spirit of a murdered wife.

[Leonore *starts up.*

Leonore. Wife, sayest thou? He told me he was never wed. Mysterious woman, tell me more! How dost thou know 't is true, and wherefore was it done? I have a right to know. Oh, speak, and tell me all!

Norna. For that have I come hither. He hath been wed to a lady, young and lovely as thyself. He kept her prisoner in his splendid home, and by neglect and cruelty he broke as warm and true a heart as ever beat in woman's breast. Her brother stole unseen to cheer and comfort her, and this aroused her lord's suspicions, and he bid her to confess who was her unknown friend. She would not yield her brother to his hate, and he in his wild anger murdered her. I heard his cruel words, her prayers for mercy, and I stood beside the lifeless form and marked the blow his evil hand had given her. And there I vowed I would avenge the deed, and for this have I come hither to warn thee of thy danger. He loves thee only for thy wealth, and when thou art his, will wrong thee as he hath the meek Theresa.

LEONORE.   How shall I ever thank thee for this escape from sorrow and despair? I did not love him, but I am alone, and his kind words were sweet and tender. I thought with him I might be happy yet, but— Ah, how little did I dream of sin like this! Thank Heaven, 't is not too late!

NORNA.   How wilt thou answer Lord Rodolpho now?

LEONORE.   I will answer him with all the scorn and loathing that I feel. I fear him not, and he shall learn how his false vows are despised, and his sins made known.

NORNA.   'T is well; but stay,—be thou not too proud. Speak fairly, and reject him courteously; for he will stop at nought in his revenge if thou but rouse his hatred. And now, farewell. I 'll watch above thee, and in thy hour of danger old Norna will be nigh. Stay, give me some token, by which thou wilt know the messenger I may find cause to send thee. The fierce Count will seek to win thee, and repay thy scorn by all the evil his cruel heart can bring.

LEONORE.   Take this ring, and I will trust whoever thou mayst send with it. I owe thee much, and, believe me, I am grateful for thy care, and will repay thee by my confidence and truth. Farewell, old Norna; watch thou above the helpless, and thine old age shall be made happy by my care.

NORNA.   Heaven bless thee, gentle lady. Good angels guard thee. Norna will not forget.

[*Exit* NORNA.

LEONORE.   'T is like a dream, so strange, so terrible,—he whom I thought so gentle, and so true is stained with fearful crimes! Poor, murdered lady! Have I escaped a fate like thine? Ah, I hear his step! Now, heart, be firm and he shall enter here no more.

[*Enter* RODOLPHO.

ROD.   Sweet lady, I am here to learn my fate. I have told my love, and thou hast listened; I have asked thy hand, and thou hast not refused it. I have offered all that I possess,—my home, my heart. Again I lay them at thy feet, beloved Leonore. Oh, wilt thou but accept them, poor tho' they be, and in return let me but claim this fair hand as mine own?

[*Takes her hand and kneels before her.*

LEONORE [*withdrawing her hand*].   My lord, forgive me, but I cannot
grant it. When last we met thou didst bid me ask my heart if it could
love thee. It hath answered, "Nay." I grieve I cannot make a fit return for all you offer, but I have no love to give, and without it this
poor hand were worthless. There are others far more fit to grace thy
home than I. Go, win thyself a loving bride, and so forget Leonore.

ROD.   What hath changed thee thus since last we met. Then wert
thou kind, and listened gladly to my love. Now there is a scornful
smile upon thy lips, and a proud light in thine eye. What means
this? Why dost thou look so coldly on me, Leonore? Who has whispered false tales in thine ear? Believe them not. I am as true as
Heaven to thee; then do not cast away the heart so truly thine.
Smile on me, dearest; thou art my first, last, only love.

LEONORE.   'T is false, my lord! Hast thou so soon forgot *Theresa?*

ROD.   What! Who told thee that accursed tale? What dost thou
mean, Leonore?

LEONORE.   I mean thy sinful deeds are known. Thou hast asked me
why I will not wed thee, and I answer, I will not give my hand unto
a murderer.

ROD.   Murderer! No more of this! Thy tale is false; forget it, and I
will forgive the idle words. Now listen; I came hither to receive thy
answer to my suit. Think ere thou decide. Thou art an orphan, unprotected and alone. I am powerful and great. Wilt thou take my
love, and with it honor, wealth, happiness, and ease, or my hate,
which will surely follow thee and bring down desolation on thee and
all thou lovest? Now choose, my hatred, or my love.

LEONORE.   My lord, I scorn thy love, and I defy thy hate. Work thy
will, I fear thee not. I am not so unprotected as thou thinkest. There
are unseen friends around me who will save in every peril, and who
are sworn to take revenge on thee for thy great sins. This is my answer; henceforth we are strangers; now leave me. I would be alone.

ROD.   Not yet, proud lady. If thou will not love, I 'll make thee learn
to fear the heart thou hast so scornfully cast away. Let thy friends
guard thee well; thou wilt need their care when I begin my work of
vengeance. Thou mayst smile, but thou shalt rue the day when
Count Rodolpho asked and was refused. But I will yet win thee, and
then beware! And when thou dost pray for mercy on thy knees, remember the haughty words thou has this day spoken.

LEONORE.   Do thy worst, murderer; spirits will watch above me, and
thou canst not harm. Adieu, my lord.

                                        [*Exit* LEONORE.

ROD.   Foiled again! Some demon works against me. Who could have
told her of Theresa? A little longer, and I should have won a rich
young bride, and now this tale of murder mars it all. But I will win
her yet, and wring her proud heart till she shall bend her haughty
head and sue for mercy.

    How shall it be done? Stay! Ha, I see a way!—the letter Louis
would have sent her ere he died. She knows not of his death, and I

will send this paper bidding her to meet her lover in the forest. She cannot doubt the lines his own hand traced. She will obey,—and I'll be there to lead her to my castle. I'll wed her, and she may scorn, weep, and pray in vain. Ha, ha! proud Leonore, spite of thy guardian spirits thou shalt be mine, and then for my revenge!

[*Exit* RODOLPHO.

CURTAIN.

SCENE SEVENTH.

[LEONORE's *room. Enter* LEONORE *with a letter.*]

LEONORE.   'T is strange; an unknown page thrust this into my hand while kneeling in the chapel. Ah, surely, I should know this hand! 'T is Louis's, and at last he hath returned, and still remembers Leonore [*opens letter and reads*].

DEAREST LADY,—I am banished from the land by Count Rodolpho's false tales to the king; and thus I dare not venture near thee. But by the love my lips have never told, I do conjure thee to bestow one last look, last word, on him whose cruel fate it is to leave all that he most fondly loves. If thou wilt grant this prayer, meet me at twilight in the glen beside old Norna's cave. She will be there to guard thee. Dearest Leonore, before we part, perchance forever, grant this last boon to one who in banishment, in grief and peril, is forever thy devoted LOUIS.

He loves me, and mid danger still remembers. Ah, Louis, there is nothing thou canst ask I will not gladly grant. I 'll go; the sun is well-nigh set, and I can steal away unseen to whisper hope and comfort ere we part forever. Now, Count Rodolpho, thou hast given me another cause for hate. Louis, I can love thee tho' thou art banished and afar.

Hark! 't is the vesper-bell. Now, courage, heart, and thou shalt mourn no longer.

[*Exit* LEONORE.

CURTAIN.

SCENE EIGHTH.

[*Glen near* NORNA'S *cave. Enter* LEONORE.]

LEONORE.   Norna is not here, nor Louis. Why comes he not? Surely 't is the place. Norna! Louis! art thou here?

[*Enter* RODOLPHO, *masked.*

ROD.   I am here, dear lady. Do not fear me; I may not unmask even to thee, for spies may still be near me. Wilt thou pardon, and still trust me tho' thou canst not see how fondly I am looking on thee. See! here is my ring, my dagger. Oh, Leonore, do not doubt me!

LEONORE.   I do trust thee; canst thou doubt it now? Oh, Louis! I
feared thou wert dead. Why didst thou not tell me all before. And
where wilt thou go, and how can I best serve thee? Nought thou
canst ask my love shall leave undone.

ROD.   Wilt thou let me guide thee to yonder tower? I fear to tell thee
here, and old Norna is there waiting for thee. Come, love, for thy
Louis's sake, dare yet a little more, and I will tell thee how thou
canst serve me. Wilt thou not put thy faith in me, Leonore?

LEONORE.   I will. Forgive me, if I seem to fear thee; but thy voice
sounds strangely hollow, and thine eyes look darkly on me from behind this mask. Thou wilt lay it by when we are safe, and then I
shall forget this foolish fear that hangs upon me.

ROD.   Thine own hands shall remove it, love. Come, it is not far.
Would I might guide thee thus through life! Come, dearest!

                                                                                    [*Exit.*

                              CURTAIN.

                        SCENE NINTH.

            [*Castle of* RODOLPHO. *The haunted chamber.*
              Enter RODOLPHO *leading* LEONORE.]

LEONORE.   Where art thou leading me, dear Louis? Thy hiding-place
is a pleasant one, but where is Norna? I thought she waited for us.

ROD.   She will soon be here. Ah, how can I thank thee for this joyful
hour, Leonore. I can forget all danger and all sorrow now.

LEONORE.   Nay, let me cast away this mournful mask! I long to look
upon thy face once more. Wilt thou let me, Louis?

ROD.   Ay, look upon me if thou wilt;—dost like it, lady? [*Drops his
disguise.* LEONORE *shrieks, and rushes to the door, but finds it locked.*]
'T is useless; there are none to answer to thy call. All here are my
slaves, and none dare disobey. Where are thy proud words now? hast
thou no scornful smile for those white lips, no anger in those beseeching eyes? Where are thy friends? Why come they not to aid
thee? Said I not truly my revenge was sure?

LEONORE.   Oh, pardon me, and pity! See, I will kneel to thee, pray,
weep, if thou wilt only let me go. Forgive my careless words! Oh, Count
Rodolpho, take me home, and I will forget this cruel jest [*kneels*].

ROD.   Ha, ha! It is no jest, and thou hast no home but this. Didst
thou not come willingly? I used no force; and all disguise is fair in
love. Nay, kneel not to me. Did I not say thou wouldst bend thy
proud head, and sue for mercy, and I would deny it? Where is thy
defiance now?

LEONORE [*rising*].   I 'll kneel no more to thee. The first wild fear is
past, and thou shalt find me at thy feet no more. As I told thee *then*,
I tell thee *now*,—thine I will never be; and think not I will fail or falter at thy threats. Contempt of thee is too strong for fear.

ROD.   Not conquered yet. Time will teach thee to speak more courteously to thy master. Ah, thou mayst well look upon these bawbles.

They were thy lover's once. This ring was taken from his lifeless hand; this dagger from his bleeding breast, as he lay within the forest whence I led thee. This scroll I found next his heart when it had ceased to beat. I lured thee hither with it, and won my sweet revenge. [LEONORE *sinks down weeping.*] Now rest thee; for when the castle clock strikes ten, I shall come to lead thee to the altar. The priest is there,—this ring shall wed thee. Farewell, fair bride; remember,—there is no escape, and thou art mine forever.

LEONORE [*starting up*].   Never! I shall be free when thou mayst think help past forever. There is a friend to help me, and an arm to save, when earthly aid is lost. Thine I shall never be! Thou mayst seek me; I shall be gone.

ROD.   Thou wilt need thy prayers. I shall return,—remember, when the clock strikes ten, I come to win my bride.

[*Exit.*

LEONORE.   He has gone, and now a few short hours of life are left to me; for if no other help shall come, death can save me from a fate I loathe. Ah, Louis, Louis, thou art gone forever! Norna, where is thy promise now to guard me? Is there no help? Nor tears nor prayers can melt that cruel heart, and I am in his power. Ha! what is that?—*his* dagger, taken from his dying breast. How gladly would he have drawn it forth to save his poor Leonore! Alas, that hand is cold forever! But I must be calm. He shall see how a weak woman's heart can still defy him, and win liberty by death [*takes the dagger; clock strikes ten*]. It is the hour,—the knell of my young life. Hark! they come. Louis, thy Leonore ere long will join thee, never more to part.

[*The secret panel opens.* ADRIAN *enters masked.*]

ADRIAN.   Stay, lady! stay thy hand! I come to save thee. Norna sends me,—see, thy token; doubt not, nor delay; another moment, we are lost. Oh, fly, I do beseech thee!

LEONORE.   Heaven bless thee; I will come. Kind friend, I put a helpless maiden's trust in thee.

ADRIAN.   Stay not! away, away!

[*Exit through the secret panel, which disappears. Enter* RODOLPHO.

ROD.   Is my fair bride ready? Ha! Leonore, where art thou?

VOICE.   Gone,—gone forever!

ROD.   Girl, mock me not; come forth, I say. Thou shalt not escape me. Leonore, answer! Where is my bride?

VOICE [*behind the curtains*].   Here—

ROD.   Why do I fear? She is there concealed [*lifts the curtain; spirit of* THERESA *rises*]. The fiends! what is that? The spirit haunts me still!

VOICE.   Forever, forever—

ROD [*rushes to the door but finds it locked*].   What ho! without there! Beat down the door! Pedro! Carlos! let me come forth! They do not come! Nay, 't is my fancy; I will forget it all. Still, the door is fast; Leonore is gone. *Who* groans so bitterly? Wild voices are sounding in the air, ghastly faces are looking on me as I turn, unseen hands bar the door, and dead men are groaning in mine ears. I'll not look, not listen; 't is some spell set on me. Let it pass!

[*Throws himself down and covers his face.*]

VOICE. The spell will not cease,
   The curse will not fly,
   And spirits shall haunt
   Till the murderer shall die.

ROD. Again, spirit or demon, wherefore dost thou haunt me, and what art thou? [THERESA'S *spirit rises.*] Ha! am I gone mad? Unbar the door! Help! help! [*Falls fainting to the floor.*]

[*Enter* NORNA.

NORNA. Lie there, thou sinful wretch! Old Norna's curse ends but with thy life.

[*Tableau.*

CURTAIN.

SCENE TENTH.

[*A room in the castle of* RODOLPHO. *Enter* RODOLPHO.]

ROD. Dangers seem thickening round me. Some secret spy is watching me unseen,—I fear 't is Hugo, spite the gold I gave him, and the vows he made. A higher bribe may win the secret from him, and then I am undone. Pedro hath told me that a stranger, cloaked and masked, was lurking near the castle on the night when Leonore so strangely vanished [*a laugh*]. Ha!—what's that?—methought I heard that mocking laugh again! I am grown fearful as a child since that most awful night. Well, well, let it pass! If Hugo comes to-night, obedient to the message I have sent, I'll see he goes not hence alive. This cup shalt be thy last, good Hugo! [*Puts poison in the wine-cup.*] He comes,—now for my revenge! [*Enter* HUGO.] Ah, Hugo, welcome! How hath it fared with thee since last we met? Thou lookest weary,—here is wine; sit and refresh thyself.

HUGO. I came not hither, Count Rodolpho, to seek wine, but gold. Hark ye! I am poor; thou art rich, but in my power, for proud and noble though thou art, the low-born Hugo can bring death and dishonor on thy head by whispering one word to the king. Ha!—now give me gold or I will betray thee.

ROD. Thou bold villain, what means this? I paid thee well, and thou didst vow to keep my secret. Threaten me not. Thou art in my power, and shall never leave this room alive. I fear thee not. My menials are at hand,—yield thyself; thou art fairly caught, and cannot now escape me.

HUGO. Nay, not so fast, my lord. One blast upon my horn, and my brave band, concealed below, will answer to my call. Ha! ha! thou art caught, my lord. Thy life is in my hands, and thou must purchase it by fifty good pistoles paid down to me; if not, I will charge thee with the crime thou didst bribe me to perform, and thus win a rich reward. Choose,—thy life is nought to me.

ROD.   Do but listen, Hugo. I have no gold; smile if thou wilt, but I am poor. This castle only is mine own, and I am seeking now a rich young bride whose wealth will hide my poverty. Be just, good Hugo, and forgive the harsh words I have spoken. Wait till I am wed, and I will pay thee well.

HUGO.   That will I not. I'll have no more of thee, false lord! The king will well reward me, and thou mayst keep thy gold. Farewell! Thou wilt see me once again.

ROD.   Stay, Hugo, stay! Give me but time; I may obtain the gold. Wait a little, and it shall be thine. Wilt thou not drink? 'T is the wine thou likest so well. See! I poured it ready for thee.

HUGO.   Nay; I will serve myself. Wine of thy mixing would prove too strong for me [*sits down and drinks*. RODOLPHO *paces up and down waiting a chance to stab him*]. Think quickly, my good lord; I must be gone [*turns his head*. R. *raises his dagger*. HUGO *rising*]. I'll wait no more; 't is growing late, and I care not to meet the spirits which I hear now haunt thy castle. Well, hast thou the gold?

ROD.   Not yet; but if thou wilt wait—

HUGO.   I tell thee I will not. I'll be deceived no longer. Thou art mine, and I'll repay thy scornful words and sinful deeds by a prisoner's cell. And so, adieu, my lord. Escape is useless, for thou wilt be watched. Hugo is the master now!

[*Exit* HUGO.

ROD.   Thou cunning villain, I'll outwit thee yet. I will disguise myself, and watch thee well, and when least thou thinkest it, my dagger shall be at thy breast. And now one thing remains to me, and that is flight. I must leave all and go forth poor, dishonored, and alone; sin on my head, and fear within my heart. Will the sun never set? How slow the hours pass! In the first gloom of night, concealed in yonder old monk's robe, I'll silently glide forth, and fly from Hugo and this haunted house. Courage, Rodolpho, thou shalt yet win a name and fortune for thyself. Now let me rest awhile; I shall need strength for the perils of the night [*lies down and sleeps*].

[*Enter* NORNA.

NORNA.   Poor fool! thy greatest foe is here,—her thou shalt not escape. Hugo shall be warned, and thou alone shalt fall.

[*She makes signs from the window and vanishes.*

ROD [*awakes and rises*].   Ah, what fearful dreams are mine! Theresa—Louis—still they haunt me! Whither shall I turn? Who comes? [*Enter* GASPARD.] Art thou another phantom sent to torture me?

GASP.   'T is I, leader of the king's brave guards, sent hither to arrest thee, my lord; for thou art charged with murder.

ROD.   Who dares to cast so foul a stain on Count Rodolpho's name.

GASP.   My lord, yield thyself. The king may show thee mercy yet—

Rod. I will yield, and prove my innocence, and clear mine honor to the king. Reach me my cloak yonder, and I am ready.

[Gaspard *turns to seek the cloak.* Rodolpho *leaps from the window and disappears.*

Gasp. Ha! he hath escaped,—curses on my carelessness! [*Rushes to the window.*] Ho, there! surround the castle, the prisoner hath fled! We'll have him yet, the blood-stained villain!

[*Exit* Gaspard. *Shouts and clashing of swords heard.*

CURTAIN.

SCENE ELEVENTH.

[Norna's *cave.* Leonore *and* Adrian.]

Adrian. Dear lady, can I do nought to while away the lonely hours? Shall I go forth and bring thee flowers, or seek thy home and bear away thy bird, thy lute, or aught that may beguile thy solitude? It grieves me that I can do so little for thee.

Leonore. Nay, 't is I should grieve that I can find no way to show my gratitude to thee, my brave deliverer. But wilt thou not tell me who thou art? I would fain know to whom I owe my life and liberty.

Adrian. Nay, that I may not tell thee. I have sworn a solemn vow, and till that is fulfilled I may not cast aside this sorrowful disguise. Meanwhile, thou mayst call me Adrian. Wilt thou pardon and trust me still?

Leonore. Canst thou doubt my faith in thee? Thou and old Norna are the only friends now left to poor Leonore. I put my whole heart's trust in thee. But if thou canst not tell me of thyself, wilt tell me why thou hast done so much for me, a friendless maiden?

Adrian. I fear it will cause thee sorrow, lady; and thou hast grief enough to bear.

Leonore. Do not fear. I would so gladly know—

Adrian. Forgive me if I make thee weep: I had a friend,—most dear to me. He loved a gentle lady, but ere he could tell her this, he died, and bid me vow to watch above her whom he loved, and guard her with my life. I took the vow: that lady was thyself, that friend Count Louis.

Leonore. Ah, Louis! Louis! that heart thou feared to ask is buried with thee.

Adrian. Thou didst love him, lady?

Leonore. Love him? Most gladly would I lie down within my grave tonight, could I but call him back to life again.

Adrian. Grieve not; thou hast one friend who cannot change,—one who through joy and sorrow will find his truest happiness in serving thee. Hist! I hear a step: I will see who comes.

[*Exit* Adrian.

Leonore. Kind, watchful friend, how truly do I trust thee!

[*Re-enter* ADRIAN.

ADRIAN.   Conceal thyself, dear lady, with all speed. 'T is Count
Rodolpho. Let me lead thee to the inner cave,—there thou wilt be
safe.

[*They retire within; noise heard without. Enter* RODOLPHO.

ROD.   At last I am safe. Old Norna will conceal me till I can find
means to leave the land. Ha!—voices within there. Ho, there! old
wizard, hither! I have need of thee!

[*Enter* ADRIAN.

ADRIAN.   What wouldst thou?
ROD.   Nought. Get thee hence! I seek old Norna.
ADRIAN.   Thou canst not see her; she is not here.
ROD.   Not here? 'T is false,—I heard a woman's voice within there.
Let me pass!
ADRIAN.   'T is not old Norna, and thou canst not pass.
ROD.   Ah, then, who might it be, my most mysterious sir?
ADRIAN.   The Lady Leonore.
ROD.   Ha!—how came she hither? By my soul, thou liest! Stand back
and let me go. She is mine!
ADRIAN.   Thou canst only enter here above my lifeless body. Leonore
is here, and I am her protector and thy deadliest foe. 'T is for thee
to yield and leave this cell.
ROD.   No more of this,—thou hast escaped me once. Draw and de-
fend thyself, if thou hast courage to meet a brave man's sword!
ADRIAN.   But for Leonore I would not stoop so low, or stain my
sword; but for her sake I'll dare all, and fight thee to the last.

[*They fight their way out. Enter* RODOLPHO.

ROD.   At length fate smiles upon me. I am the victor,—and now for
Leonore! All danger is forgotten in the joy of winning my revenge on
this proud girl! Thou art mine at last, Leonore, and mine forever!
[*Rushes towards the inner cave. Spirit of* THERESA *rises.*] There 't is
again! I will not fly,—I do defy it! [*Attempts to pass. Spirit touches
him; he drops his sword and rushes wildly away.*] 'T is vain: I cannot—dare not pass. It comes, it follows me. Whither shall I fly?

[*Exit. Enter* ADRIAN *wounded.*

ADRIAN.   I have saved her once again,—but oh, this deathlike faint-
ness stealing o'er me robs me of my strength. Thou art safe,
Leonore, and I am content. [*Falls fainting.*]

[*Enter* LEONORE.

LEONORE.   They are gone. Ah, what has chanced? I heard his voice,
and now 't is still as death. Where is my friend? God grant he be not
hurt! I'll venture forth and seek him [*sees* ADRIAN *unconscious before
her*]. Oh, what is this? Adrian, kind friend, dost thou not hear me?

There is blood upon his hand! Can he be dead? No, no! he breathes, he moves; this mask, I will remove it,—surely he will forgive.

[*Attempts to unmask him; he prevents her.*

ADRIAN [*reviving*].   Nay, nay; it must not be. I am better now. The blow but stunned me,—it will pass away. And thou art safe?

LEONORE.   I feared not for myself, but thee. Come, rest thee here, thy wound is bleeding; let me bind it with my kerchief, and bring thee wine. Let me serve thee who hath done so much for me. Art better now! Can I do aught else for thee?

ADRIAN.   No more, dear lady. Think not of me, and listen while I tell thee of the dangers that surround thee. Count Rodolpho knows thou art here, and may return with men and arms to force thee hence. My single arm could then avail not, though I would gladly die for thee. Where then can I lead thee,—no place can be too distant, no task too hard for him whose joy it is to serve thee.

LEONORE.   Alas! I know not. I dare not seek my home while Count Rodolpho is my foe; my servants would be bribed,—they would betray me, and thou wouldst not be there to save. Adrian, I have no friend but thee. Oh, pity and protect me!

ADRIAN.   Most gladly will I, dearest lady. Thou canst never know the joy thy confidence hath wakened in my heart. I will save and guard thee with my life. I will guide thee to a peaceful home where no danger can approach, and only friends surround thee. Thy Louis dwelt there once, and safely mayst thou rest till danger shall be past. Will this please thee?

LEONORE.   Oh, Adrian, thou kind, true friend, how can I tell my gratitude, and where find truer rest than in *his* home, where gentle memories of him will lighten grief. Then take me there, and I will prove my gratitude by woman's fondest friendship, and my life-long trust.

ADRIAN.   Thanks, dear lady. I need no other recompense than the joy 't is in my power to give thee. I will watch faithfully above thee, and when thou needest me no more, I 'll leave thee to the happiness thy gentle heart so well deserves. Now rest, while I seek out old Norna, and prepare all for our flight. The way we have to tread is long and weary. Rest thee, dear lady.

LEONORE.   Adieu, dear friend. I will await thee ready for our pilgrimage, and think not I shall fail or falter, though the path be long, and dangers gather round us. I shall not fear, for thou wilt be there. God bless thee, Adrian.

[*Tableau.*

CURTAIN.

SCENE TWELFTH.

[*Room in the castle of* LOUIS. LEONORE *singing to her lute.*]

The weary bird mid stormy skies,
    Flies home to her quiet nest,

And 'mid the faithful ones she loves,
        Finds shelter and sweet rest.

And thou, my heart, like to tired bird,
        Hath found a peaceful home,
Where love's soft sunlight gently falls,
        And sorrow cannot come.

LEONORE.   'Tis strange that I can sing, but in this peaceful home my
    sorrow seems to change to deep and quiet joy. Louis seems ever
    near, and Adrian's silent acts of tenderness beguile my solitary
    hours, and daily grow more dear to me. He guards me day and
    night, seeking to meet my slightest wish, and gather round me all I
    hold most dear. [*Enter a* PAGE.] Angelo, what wouldst thou?
PAGE.   My master bid me bring these flowers and crave thee to ac-
    cept them lady.
LEONORE.   Bear him my thanks, and tell him that his gift is truly wel-
    come. [*Exit* PAGE.] These are the blossoms he was gathering but
    now upon the balcony; he hath sent the sweetest and the fairest [*a
    letter falls from the nosegay*]. But what is here? He hath never sent
    me aught like this before [*opens and reads the letter*].

DEAREST LADY,—Wilt thou pardon the bold words I here address to
thee, and forgive me if I grieve one on whom I would bestow only the
truest joy. In giving peace to thy heart I have lost mine own. I was thy
guide and comforter, and soon, unknown to thee, thy lover. I love
thee, Leonore, fondly and truly; and here I ask, wilt thou accept the
offering of a heart that will forever cherish thee. If thou canst grant
this blessed boon, fling from the casement the white rose I send thee;
but if thou canst not accept my love, forgive me for avowing it, and
drop the cypress bough I have twined about the rose. I will not pain
thee to refuse in words,—the mournful token is enough. Ask thine
own heart if thou, who hast loved Louis, can feel aught save friendship for the unknown, nameless stranger, who through life and death
is ever
    Thy loving   ADRIAN.

    Oh, how shall I reply to this,—how blight a love so tender and so
true? I have longed to show my gratitude, to prove how I have
revered this noble friend. The hour has come when I may make his
happiness, and prove my trust. And yet my heart belongs to Louis,
and I cannot love another. Adrian was his friend; he loved him, and
confided me to him. Nobly hath he fulfilled that trust, and where
could I find a truer friend than he who hath saved me from danger and from death, and now gives me the power to gladden and
to bless his life. Adrian, if thou wilt accept a sister's love and
friendship, they shall be thine. Louis, forgive me if I wrong thee;
or though I yield my hand, my heart is thine forever. This rose,
Adrian, to thee; this mournful cypress shall be mine in memory of

my blighted hopes [*goes to the window and looks out*]. See! he is waiting yonder by the fountain for the token that shall bring him joy or sorrow. Thou noble friend, thy brave, true heart shall grieve no longer, for thus will Leonore repay the debt of gratitude she owes thee [*flings the rose from the window*]. He hath placed it in his bosom, and is coming hither to pour forth his thanks for the poor gift bestowed. I will tell him all, and if he will accept, then I am his.

[*Enter* ADRIAN *with the rose.*]

ADRIAN.   Dear lady, how can I tell thee the joy thou hast given me. This blessed flower from thy dear hand hath told thy pardon and consent. Oh, Leonore, canst thou love a nameless stranger who is so unworthy the great boon thou givest.

LEONORE.   Listen, Adrian, ere thou dost thank me for a divided heart. Thou hast been told my love for Louis; he was thy friend, and well thou knowest how true and tender was the heart he gave me. He hath gone, and with him rests my first deep love. Thou art my only friend and my protector; thou hast won my gratitude and warmest friendship. I can offer thee a sister's pure affection,—my hand is thine; and here I pledge thee that as thou hast watched o'er me, so now thy happiness shall be my care, thy love my pride and joy. Here is my hand,—wilt thou accept it, Adrian?

ADRIAN.   I will. I would not seek to banish from thy heart the silent love thou bearest Louis. I am content if thou wilt trust me with thy happiness, and give me the sweet right to guide and guard thee through the pilgrimage of life. God bless thee, dearest.

LEONORE.   Dear Adrian, can I do nought for thee? I have now won the right to cheer thy sorrows. Have faith in thy Leonore.

ADRIAN.   Thou hast a right to know all, and ere long thou shalt. My mysterious vow will now soon be fulfilled, and then no doubt shall part us. Thou hast placed thy trust in me, and I have not betrayed it, and now I ask a greater boon of thy confiding heart. Wilt thou consent to wed me ere I cast aside this mask forever? Believe me, thou wilt not regret it,—'t is part of my vow; one last trial, and I will prove to thee thou didst not trust in vain. Forgive if I have asked too much. Nay, thou canst not grant so strange a boon.

LEONORE.   I can—I will. I did but pause, for it seemed strange thou couldst not let me look upon thy face. But think not that I fear to grant thy wish. Thy heart is pure and noble, and that thou canst not mask. As I trusted thee through my despair, so now I trust thee in my joy. Canst thou ask more, dear friend?

ADRIAN.   Ever trust me thus! Ah, Leonore, how can I repay thee? My love, my life, are all I can give thee for the blessed gift thou hast bestowed. A time will come when all this mystery shall cease and we shall part no more. Now must I leave thee, dearest. Farewell! Soon will I return.

[*Exit* ADRIAN.]

LEONORE.   I will strive to be a true and loving wife to thee, dear
Adrian; for I have won a faithful friend in thee forever.

CURTAIN.

SCENE THIRTEENTH.

[*Hall in the castle of* COUNT LOUIS. *Enter* LEONORE, *in bridal robes.*]

LEONORE.   At length the hour hath come, when I shall look upon the
face of him whom I this day have sworn to love and honor as a wife.
I have, perchance, been rash in wedding one I know not, but will
not cast a doubt on him who hath proved the noble heart that beats
within his breast. I am his, and come what may, the vows I have this
day made shall be unbroken. Ah, he comes; and now shall I gaze
upon my husband's face!

[*Enter* ADRIAN.

ADRIAN.   Dearest, fear not. Thou wilt not trust me less when thou
hast looked upon the face so long concealed. My vow is ended, thou
art won. Thy hand is mine; Leonore, I claim thy heart.

[*Unmasks.* LEONORE *screams and falls upon his breast.*

LEONORE.   Louis, Louis! 'T is a blessed dream!
LOUIS.   No dream, my Leonore; it is thy living Louis who hath
watched above thee, and now claims thee for his own. Ah, dearest, I
have tried thee too hardly,—pardon me!
LEONORE.   Oh, Louis, husband, I have nought to pardon; my life, my
liberty, my happiness,—all, all, I owe to thee. How shall I repay
thee? [*Weeps upon his bosom.*]
LOUIS.   By banishing these tears, dear love, and smiling on me as you
used to do. Here, love, sit beside me while I tell thee my most
strange tale, and then no longer shalt thou wonder. Art happy now
thy Adrian hath flung by his mask?
LEONORE.   Happy! What deeper joy can I desire than that of seeing
thy dear face once more? But tell me, Louis, how couldst thou dwell
so long beside me and not cheer my bitter sorrow when I grieved for
thee.
LOUIS.   Ah, Leonore, thou wouldst not reproach me, didst thou know
how hard I struggled with my heart, lest I should by some tender
word, some fond caress, betray myself when thou didst grieve for
me.
LEONORE.   Why didst thou fear to tell thy Leonore? She would have
aided and consoled thee. Why didst thou let me pine in sorrow at
thy side, when but a word had filled my heart with joy?
LOUIS.   Dearest, I dared not. Thou knowest I was banished by the
hate of that fiend Rodolpho. I had a fair and gentle sister, whom he
wed, and after cruelty and coldness that I dread to think of now, he
murdered her. I sought old Norna's aid. She promised it, and well
hath kept her word. When Count Rodolpho's ruffian left me dying

in the forest, she saved, and brought me back to life. She bade me take a solemn vow not to betray myself, and to aid her in her vengeance on the murderer of Theresa. Nor could I own my name and rank, lest it should reach the king who had banished me. The vow I took, and have fulfilled.

LEONORE. And is there no danger now? Art thou safe, dear Louis, from the Count?

LOUIS. Fear not, my love. He will never harm us more; his crimes are known. The king hath pardoned me. I have won thee back. He is an outcast, and old Norna's spells have well-nigh driven him mad. My sister, thou art well avenged! Alas! alas! would I could have saved, and led thee hither to this happy home.

LEONORE. Ah, grieve not, Louis; she is happy now, and thy Leonore will strive to fill her place. Hast thou told me all?

LOUIS. Nay, love. Thou knowest how I watched above thee, but thou canst never know the joy thy faithful love for one thou mourned as dead hath brought me. I longed to cast aside the dark disguise I had vowed to wear, but dared not while Rodolpho was at liberty. Now all is safe. I have tried thy love, and found it true. Oh, may I prove most worthy of it, dearest.

LEONORE. Louis, how can I love too faithfully the friend who, 'mid his own grief and danger, loved and guarded me. I trusted thee as Adrian; as Louis I shall love thee until death.

LOUIS. And I shall prize most tenderly the faithful heart that trusted me through doubt and mystery. Now life is bright and beautiful before us, and may you never sorrow that thou gav'st thy heart to Louis, and thy hand to Adrian the "Black Mask."

CURTAIN.

SCENE FOURTEENTH.

[*A dungeon cell.* RODOLPHO *chained, asleep. Enter* NORNA.]

NORNA. Thy fate is sealed, thy course is run,
And Norna's work is well-nigh done.

[*Vanishes. Enter* HUGO.

ROD [*awaking*]. Mine eyes are bewildered by the forms I have looked upon in sleep. Methought old Norna stood beside me, whispering evil spells, calling fearful phantoms to bear me hence.

HUGO [*coming forward*]. Thy evil conscience gives thee little rest, my lord.

ROD [*starting up*]. Who is there? Stand back! I'll sell my life most dearly. Ah, 't is no dream,—I am fettered! Where is my sword?

HUGO. In my safe keeping, Count Rodolpho, lest in thy rage thou may'st be tempted to add another murder to thy list of sins. [RODOLPHO *sinks down in despair.*] Didst think thou couldst escape? Ah, no; although most swift of foot and secret, Hugo hath watched and followed thee. I swore to win both gold and vengeance. The king hath offered high reward for thy poor head, and it is mine. Methinks it may cheer your solitude my lord, so I came hither on my way to bear thy death warrant to the captain of the guard. What wilt thou give for this? Hark ye! were this destroyed, thou might'st escape ere another were prepared. How dost thou like the plot?

ROD.   And wilt thou save me, Hugo? Give me not up to the king! I'll be thy slave. All I possess is thine. I'll give thee countless gold. Ah, pity, and save me, Hugo!

HUGO.   Ha, ha! I did but jest. Thinkest thou I could forego the joy of seeing thy proud head laid low? Where was thy countless gold when I did ask it of thee? No, no; thou canst not tempt me to forget my vengeance. 'T is Hugo's turn to play the master now. Mayst thou rest well, and so, good even, my lord.

[*Exit* HUGO.

ROD.   Thus end my hopes of freedom. My life is drawing to a close, and all my sins seem rising up before me. The forms of my murdered victims flit before me, and their dying words ring in mine ears,—Leonore praying for mercy at my feet; old Norna whispering curses on my soul. How am I haunted and betrayed! Oh, fool, fool that I have been! My pride, my passion, all end in this! Hated, friendless, and alone, the proud Count Rodolpho dies a felon's death. 'T is just, 't is just! [*Enter* LOUIS *masked.*] What's that? Who spoke? Ah, 't is mine unknown foe. What wouldst thou here?

LOUIS.   Thou didst bribe one Hugo to murder the young Count Louis, whom thou didst hate. He did thy bidding, and thy victim fell; but Norna saved, and healed his wounds. She told him of his murdered sister's fate, and he hath joined her in her work of vengeance, and foiled thee in thy sinful plots. I saved Leonore, and guarded her till I had won her heart and hand, and in her love find solace for the sorrow thou hast caused. Dost doubt the tale? Look on thine unknown foe, and find it true [*unmasks*].

ROD.   Louis, whom I hated, and would kill,—thou here, thou husband of Leonore, happy and beloved! It is too much, too much! If thou lovest life, depart. I'm going mad: I see wild phantoms whirling round me, voices whispering fearful words within mine ears. Touch me not,—there is blood upon my hands! Will this dream last forever?

LOUIS.   May Heaven pity thee! Theresa, thou art avenged.

[*Exit* LOUIS.

ROD.   Ah, these are fearful memories for a dying hour! [*Casts himself upon the floor.*]

[*Enter* NORNA.

NORNA.   Sinful man, didst think thy death-bed could be peaceful? As they have haunted thee in life, so shall spirits darken thy last hour. *I* bore thy murdered wife to a quiet grave, and raised a spirit to affright and haunt thee to thy death. *I* freed the Lady Leonore; *I* mocked and haunted thee in palace, wood, and cell; *I* warned Hugo, and betrayed thee to his power; and *I* brought down this awful doom upon thee. As thou didst refuse all mercy to thy victims, so shall mercy be denied to thee. Remorse and dark despair shall wring thy heart, and thou shalt die unblessed, unpitied, unforgiven. Thy victims are avenged, and Norna's work is done.

[Norna *vanishes.*

Rod.　Ha! ha! 't is gone,—yet stay, 't is Louis' ghost! How darkly his eyes shine on me! See, see,—the demons gather round me! How fast they come! Old Norna is there, muttering her spells. Let me go free! Unbind these chains! Hugo, Louis, Leonore, Theresa,—thou art avenged!

[*Falls dead.* Norna *glides in and stands beside him.*

[*Tableau.*

Curtain.

L. M. A. [LOUISA MAY ALCOTT]

The Masked Marriage†

Chapter First.

The summer moon looked softly down on the silvery waters of the "Arno," whose cool waves washed the marble steps of the noble palaces upon its banks. Rich music pealed from those lighted halls, lovely forms floating in the dance were seen through the open casements, whose heavy curtains were flung back by the cool night wind, which swept in, laden with the perfume of the orange-groves below. Stately knights and fair ladies stood on the balconies, soft words were spoken, tender vows were made; while the quiet stars looked down on many a blushing cheek and downcast eye.

From one of these gay mansions a cavalier emerged, and hastily descending to the waterside, sprang into a light gondola, which darted away through the starlit waves.

On it went, amid drooping boughs and fragrant flowers slumbering in the soft moonlight, that fell so brightly on the countenance of him who looked so sadly at the quiet evening sky. It was a pale and noble face, with nothing of the "Italian" in it, save the dark, lustrous eyes, and the raven hair the night wind flung so freely back, while the unadorned and simple dress told that, though brave and true, a humble fortune must be his.

Meantime, the light boat sped along by lighted palaces and moonlit gardens, till the high, dark walls of the Convent of St. C—— rose be-

---

† From *Dodge's Literary Museum*, 18 December 1852, 26–27. This romance, Alcott's second published short story, is the full and original version of the story published by Meg as S. Pickwick in *The Pickwick Portfolio*.

fore him. The faint, low chant of the evening prayer rose softly on the quiet air, and as the solemn sound of the holy music ceased, the gondola glided into the dark shadow of the walls. A moment more and it was moored beneath a solitary casement, while in a low, sweet voice, these words were sung—

> "The summer wind is sighing
> Across the moonlit sea,
> And bears my bark, dear lady,
> Through whispering waves to thee.
> O, wake! for the evening star
> Casts her soft light o'er me:
> Thou art *my* star, and *I* the wave,
> Reflecting nought but thee."

As the song ceased, the casement opened, and a light female form appeared in the balcony, where the moonlight revealed a young and lovely lady. It was no nun, for the silken robe was clasped with jewels, and no close veil hid the bright locks that fell so softly around the fair, young face, as bending from the balcony, she said—

"Ah, Ferdinand, why hast thou ventured forth to-night? They will miss thee at the palace, and all may be discovered."

"Pardon, dearest Alice, but I could not rest till I had told thee what I this day learned. To-morrow thou wilt leave the convent where till now thy life has flowed along beneath a cloudless sky. The gay world thou wilt enter is too full of sin and sorrow for one so pure and gentle as thou art. O, Alice! my heart is filled with sad forebodings for thee."

"Nay, why fear for me, dear Ferdinand? Amid the sins and follies of the world my heart shall be a holy shrine where all the pure, undying love I bear thee shall be gathered up, and with all a woman's constancy and faith be treasured but for thee."

"That bright dream is over, dearest," replied her lover, and his voice was sad and low. "This is why I could not rest. I would be the first to tell you all our sorrow, and share the grief I bring thy gentle heart. Thy father has betrothed thee to Count Antonio, and by solemn vows hath bound himself to wed thee only unto him, the heir of those rich English lands he so long hath coveted. I knew not of this till it was too late to claim the hand where I had won the heart. I cannot doubt the tidings; our happy visions for the future are no more. Thou must be led a victim to the altar, and I, amid the ruins of my life's fair hopes, will seek for patience to bear this sorrow as I ought."

He ceased, and bowed his head, and the few heavy tears that fell showed how hard a struggle love and honor made within that noble heart.

"How can I free myself from this unholy marriage?" said the gentle girl, while the bright tears fell like summer rain. "I cannot give my hand where my heart can never follow. Ah! save me, Ferdinand, from such a fate."

"Alice, what a heart's best love can do shall not be wanting now. I'll plead as never lover plead before, and if I cannot win my suit, hard as the task may be, we must teach our hearts to share the sorrow nobly, and forget the joy that hath been ours."

"Thou shalt not bear this grief alone; these idle tears shall never dim the light that leads me to my duty. Thy noble words have stilled the deep despair of this poor heart; the happy dream that made my life so bright and beautiful is gone; those hopes and joys have passed away—all but my love and constancy to thee. They may wed me where they list, my heart is ever thine."

"God bless thee, dearest, and reward thee as thy true heart's tenderness deserves. But hark! the convent bell is sounding. I must leave thee, but not yet forever; we shall meet again; till then bear bravely up. And now farewell, dearest; may good angels guard and comfort thee."

"Farewell," said the weeping lady. "If we must part, may you find a heart as true and tender as the one now sorrowing for thee, is the prayer of thy poor Alice."

The boat was gone, the balcony deserted, and the moon's soft light fell only on the bright waves rippling below.

Chapter Second.

The Count de Adelon was a proud and high-born Italian, wedded in his youth to a lovely English lady, who had borne him one fair child, and then, like the sweet but short-lived southern flowers that bloomed around her, faded gently away, and was borne to the tomb of the proud "De Adelons."

Years went by, and the mother's child found a calm and happy home among the gentle nuns of St. C——, and grew up amid the holy sisterhood lovely as a poet's dream, pure and gentle as the saints she worshiped with such pious love.

A father's tenderness and care she had never known; for he had brought another bride to his stately home, and amid the many joys that rank and wealth can bring, forgot the gentle child who was growing into womanhood and beauty in the dim old convent.

At length poverty stole into his luxurious home; for years of careless splendor had brought the proud Count's fortune low. Then, while wandering through the stately halls where no trace of the coming ruin was yet seen, he remembered that a lovely daughter yet unknown to the gay world dwelt within the gloomy convent. She might wed some lord, whose wealth would well repay the honor done him by the noble house of Adelon.

He sought the daughter he had so long neglected, and with wondering delight beheld a form and face that well might grace the proudest home in Italy. Tender memories rose in his cold heart, and with kind and loving words he won his daughter's love, and from time to time had taken her to his splendid home, that others might see the loveliness of his fair child.

'Twas there she had seen and learned to love Ferdinand de Vere. Young, brave, and rich in manly virtues, he soon won the heart he longed for, and amid the proud and high-born guests who thronged her father's halls, the English stranger was the only one whose image did not fade like a bright dream, when in the silent convent she forgot the gay scenes that had passed before her. And thus ere long the loving hearts were joined, and the bright waves rippling by St. C—— bore on their bosom the happy lover to the little cell where all his earthly happiness was found.

Little dreaming of the tender scenes the moon looked down on through those long summer nights, the Count de Adelon was winning for his child the hand of Count Antonio, an Italian noble, whose unbounded wealth would build up the broken fortunes of the bride's father.

And at length the young lord, won by the daughter's beauty and the father's rank, besought the Count's leave to bring her from the convent to his own noble palace, as his wife. That leave was given, and the lovers' happy dream was broken by the summons of the gentle Alice home.

Chapter Third.

The setting sun stole with a softened light through the curtains of a humbly furnished chamber, where sat Ferdinand de Vere, pale and sad, struggling to calm the bitter sorrow of a hopeless love.

A low tap broke the deep silence, and a servant entered, saying—

"Signor, a stranger waits below, entreating you to see her. Shall I admit her?"

"Nay, Bertoni, I can see no stranger now; yet, if she is poor, or in sorrow, it were cruel to refuse. I will see her, whoever it be."

A light step sounded on the stair, and a young girl stood before him, wrapped in a dark mantle, but the veil so closely folded ill concealed the bright dark eyes and clustering hair.

"Signor, I come on a strange errand," she said, "but to me a sad one. My mother lies upon her death-bed, and cannot die in peace till she has revealed to thee a secret which will bring thee wealth and honor. Wilt thou trust me as thy guide, and follow quickly?"

" 'Tis a strange summons," said the young man. "How can I, a stranger here, be known to thy mother? Nay, do not weep, poor child— I will follow thee, if my presence can bring comfort to a suffering spirit."

And with his unknown guide he passed into the silent streets.

Twilight shadows were deepening, and the soft light had faded away, as the young girl stopped before a ruined gate; then passing in, she led the way through a deserted garden to a low door, which was opened by an old servant, who said—

"The Virgin be praised, you are not too late! Come quickly—she is with the priest."

Up a flight of narrow stairs they went, into a darkened room, where on a low couch lay a woman in whose pale and haggard face traces of great beauty still were seen. Beside her stood a gray-haired priest holding a golden crucifix before her fading eyes.

"Mother, he is here," said the young girl, kneeling beside the couch, while her tears fell thick and fast.

"Ah!" said the dying woman; "lift me higher, Rosalie, and do thou, holy father, bear witness to the last words of this sinful heart. Young man, draw nearer. Is thy name Ferdinand de Vere?"

"It is," replied he, wondering at the strange scene before him.

"Then listen while I unfold to thee the tale of sin I could not carry to the grave with me.

"Thy father, years ago, when he was gay and young, wooed and won a simple village maiden's heart. It was her only wealth, and she gave it freely, asking for no return but constancy and truth. She knew not that her humble lover was a rich and noble knight. He vowed to love and wed her, and she believed him. Happy days passed, and then she was left to sigh in lonely sorrow. He was wedded to a noble lady, and forgot the warm heart he had won. I was that poor maiden, and in the bitter hour of agony and grief I vowed a fierce revenge.

"That vow I kept. Years rolled away, and I was wedded to a wild mountain robber, and sought in the stirring scenes of a wandering life to still the voice that whispered of forgiveness; but an evil demon drove me on, and my vow was at length fulfilled. Thy father's life had been a long bright dream of happiness and love; wealth such as few possess was his, and 'twas all gathered up for thee. Thou wert a fair, unconscious child, and often did I wander to thy home to look upon thy mother bending over thee, and with all her heart's love blessing thee as mothers only can. Her life seemed all bound up in thine, and I hated her for possessing the joy I could not win.

"At length thy father died. Thou canst not remember thy mother's grief, nor her wonder and alarm, when no will was found, and thus all the wealth so hoarded up for thee passed to thy kinsman, Count Antonio. Thou wert left fatherless and poor.

"My revenge was gained. I had stolen the will that left all to thee, and thou and thy mother were penniless. Death took her hence, and thou hast made thyself loved and honored for thy nobleness and truth. My cruel work was done, and for years I wandered over the earth a sinful, sorrowing outcast.

"Think not, young man, I called thee hither to learn this sad and simple story for no purpose. I can give thee *now* thy father's wealth. My life is well nigh spent, and I would perform one good deed ere I depart. My child, bring hither the ivory casket; thou knowest the secret hiding-place."

The weeping girl stole out, and a deep silence followed.

No words can tell the wonder, joy, and tender grief the dying woman's tale had stirred within the breast of the young listener. Thoughts of Alice, golden dreams of wealth and happiness, and sad memories of the mother who had so deeply suffered for the sins of the wild, revengeful woman, who now, long years after, lay dying here before him—these came crowding to his mind like a troubled dream, till the silence was broken by the return of Rosalie, bearing the casket in her hand.

"Unclasp it, love," said the dying woman, faintly; "my strength fails, and my work is yet undone. These papers," she continued, in broken accents, "will prove thy right to all thy father's wealth. Would it could buy this poor soul its pardon and forgiveness!

"Now, farewell. I cannot die in peace with a face so like thy father's bending over me. I have told all. This good priest will counsel thee. Now go, and may this last deed repay thee for the great wrong this sinful heart hath done thee."

"May God forgive thee as freely as I do, and grant thee peace," whispered the young man, and with a few words to the old priest, he stole softly out into the silent night.

Chapter Fourth.

Days had passed; the dead was buried, and Rosalie in a safe home. Long and anxious were the counsels of the priest and young De Vere. The strange discovery had brought many difficulties; those who had witnessed the will were to be found. After a long and careful search they were at length traced to Rome. Messengers were dispatched to bring them secretly to F——.

Amid all these wearisome duties, one thought still cheered the happy lover on—thought of the hour when he might claim Alice as his own, and this he could not hope to do until his right to all the English wealth was clear.

So he eagerly hurried on the work, and thus the weeks rolled on, when tidings reached him that in three days the nuptials of the Count Antonio would take place. Then in the wildest haste he sought the priest, for comfort and advice.

"My son," said the old man, "there is but one way left thee. Go to thy lady's father and ask her hand. Thou hast virtue, and an honorable name. She loves thee, and if he bear a father's heart within his breast, he will never sell her for the Count Antonio's gold when her heart is given to thee. Say nothing of the strange tale thou hast lately heard, for if he makes his daughter's happiness by giving up his worldly hopes, then it will be a fit reward when he shall learn that the fortune he so coveted is thine."

He went, and plead his love with all his heart's deep devotion, but in vain. The ambitious Count had set his worldly heart on the wealth of Lord Antonio, and with haughty coldness answered the young lover's prayers, saying, as he turned to go—

"My daughter is the last of her noble name, and whoso wins her hand must possess the wealth and rank befitting such an honor."

"My lord," replied the young man, while the light shone in his dark eyes, "the name of De Vere is noble as your own. I am not poor, and can give your daughter a happy home, and a heart whose only care shall be to spare her every sorrow. Count Antonio's wealth may pass away. Where then will be the happiness you now seek for your child in paltry gold and a titled name?"

"Enough, young man," exclaimed the Count. "When you can boast a name and fortune noble as the Count's, I will yield my daughter when and where you please to claim her."

And with a scornful smile he turned away.

"Stay! my lord," cried Ferdinand. "Did I hear aright, and will you give your daughter's hand when I shall bring you wealth like that Antonio now possesses? I take you at your word. Remember it is pledged. Three days hence I will claim my bride."

And with a proud, triumphant smile he passed out.

"Three days, sayest thou?" muttered the Count. "Thy bride shall then be another's, and thou wilt claim her then in vain. 'Tis a strange vow I have made; I fear I have said too much. But no, it cannot be; no mortal could in three days gather up such boundless wealth as Count Antonio brings my child. 'Tis a foolish fear; I'll think of it no more."

And in dreams of grandeur yet to come, the haughty noble thought not of the sorrowing heart that beat so sadly in the bosom of his gentle child.

The three days were nearly spent, and well had the old priest done his work. The witnesses were come, all was proved, and Ferdinand de Vere was lord of the English wealth.

Count Antonio had yielded all his generous rival would accept, and secretly left Italy.

The morning of the third day came, and proudly went the Count de Adelon through his lordly home; for that night would the barter of his fair young daughter bring all the wealth he coveted.

As thus he mused, a paper was placed in his hand; it was in the writing of Count Antonio, and thus it ran:—

"MY LORD:—This night, according to my promise, your daughter shall wed the heir of Lord Devereux's unbounded wealth. Pardon whatever mystery may appear when next we meet. Ask nothing, and all shall be explained when the ceremony is over."

"Some romantic folly," thought the Count; "I care not what. He shall have no cause to chide me, for not a word will I speak till all is over. And now to Alice; she must know of this new whim."

And he passed on to where his daughter sat, pale, and still striving to banish the tender thoughts as they rose in her sorrowing heart.

Chapter Fifth.

Gondola after gondola swept up to the marble steps, and deposited its light-hearted occupants to swell the brilliant throng that filled the stately halls of the Count de Adelon.

Plumes and gay hearts fluttered, jewels and bright eyes flashed, soft words were spoken, tender glances given, and jests went around. Knights and ladies, elves and pages, kings and flower-girls all mingled gaily in the dance; sweet voices and rich melody filled the air; and so with mirth and music the masquerade went on.

"Has your highness seen the Lady Alice?" asked a stately knight of the fairy queen who stood beside him. "Lovely she has ever been, but to-night her beauty is beyond aught I have ever seen."

"Her dress is well chosen," replied his gay companion; "that bridal robe is but a token of the one she will shortly wear, for Count Antonio claims her hand, and if I do not err, the next time we tread these halls it will be to dance at the sweet lady's bridal. But look! yonder comes the Count Antonio. I know him in spite of his mask, by the star of the Devereux upon his breast."

"He too is attired as for a bridal," said the knight, "but never did I see him bear himself so nobly as to-night. Did you mark that whisper, as he offered Lady Alice yon white rose she seems so proud of?"

"That I did," answered the lady, with a gay laugh. "I wish all knights grew as strangely graceful and gallant when a fair lady smiles on their suit. I must ask Alice for the charm she has used to change the awkward, rude Antonio into yon graceful cavalier in the white velvet doublet. The music sounds; do you dance?"

And knight and lady passed away through the flower-decked halls.

Many were the wondering remarks at the bridal dress of Alice and her lover, and ere long it was whispered through the crowd that the proud Count de Adelon had drawn them hither to celebrate the nuptials of his fair daughter with the young lord so many hearts had tried to win; not for his bravery or love, but for the name and fortune he possessed. And when at length the priest appeared, a low murmur passed through the crowd.

Then the Count de Adelon stepped proudly forth, saying—

"My friends, pardon this little plot, but I desired to show all honor to the noble Count who this night weds my child, and where can they more fitly pledge their faith than here, amid festivity and joy, surrounded by happy hearts and loving friends. Father, we wait your services."

A deep stillness fell upon the throng as the bridal party stood before the priest, but a murmur of astonishment was heard when the bridegroom took his place, for the mask he had so carefully worn was not removed. All had wondered at the unbroken silence of the young Count. To none but Alice had he spoken; all others he had carefully avoided, and many had noticed the graceful ease of the once uncouth Count.

Curiosity and wonder were at their height, but respect restrained all questions till the solemn words were spoken. Then the eager crowd gathered round the Count de Adelon, and poured forth their unbounded astonishment at the strange scene they had witnessed.

"Gladly will I tell you when I am told myself, my lord," he said, turning to the bridegroom; "patiently have I borne my part in this strange masquerade of yours. The bridal is now over, and I claim your promise of revealing your reason for so mysterious an act."

"It shall be given," replied the bridegroom; and the next moment the mask was off, and the noble face of Ferdinand de Vere appeared, glowing with joy and manly beauty, his stately form drawn proudly up, the brilliant star of an English Earl flashing upon his breast, and Alice, radiant with happiness, leaning on his arm.

Not a sound broke the stillness that followed after the first low murmur of astonishment, till the tones of his musical voice sounded through the long hall, saying—

"My lord, you bid me claim your daughter when I could show as high a name, as boundless wealth as Count Antonio. I can do more, and even your ambitious heart can find naught to wish for, when the son of the Earl of Devereux, with all the English wealth you covet, and his own fair fortune, is the happy husband of the child you would have sold for the worthless gold that cannot buy a noble woman's love.

"My right is proved, and Count Antonio has left Italy; and now, my lord, no longer as a simple knight, but Ferdinand Earl of Devereux and De Vere, I claim this hand, dearer than aught the earth can give, for with it comes a heart wealth could not buy, nor titles tempt. Kind friends," continued he, turning gaily to those knights who gathered warmly around him, "my best wish is that you may gain as fair a fortune and as true a bride as I have won by this MASKED MARRIAGE."

M. L. A. [LOUISA MAY ALCOTT]

The Sisters' Trial†

Four sisters sat together round a cheerful fire on New Year's Eve. The shadow of a recent sorrow lay on the young faces over which the red flames flickered brightly as they lit up every nook of the quiet room, whose simple furniture and scanty decorations plainly showed that Poverty had entered there hand in hand with her sister, grief.

The deep silence that had lasted long as each sat lost in sad memories of the past, or anxious thought for the future, was at length broken by Leonore, the eldest, a dark haired, dark eyed woman whose proud, energetic face was softened by a tender smile as she looked upon the young girls, saying cheerily:

"Come, sisters, we must not sit brooding gloomily over our troubles when we should be up and doing. To-night, you know we must decide what work we will each choose by which to earn our bread, for this home will soon be ours no longer and we must find some other place to shelter us, and some honest labor to maintain ourselves by, that we may not be dependant on the charity of relatives, till our own exertions fail. Tell me what after your separate search you have each decided to do. Agnes, you come first. What among the few pursuits left open to us have *you* chosen?"

The color deepened in Agnes' cheek and the restless light burned brighter in her large eyes as she hastily replied, "*I* will be an actress. Nay do not start and look so troubled, Nora. I am fixed, and when you hear all, you will not oppose me, I feel sure. You know this has been the one wish of my life, growing with my growth, strengthening with my strength; haunting my thoughts by day, my dreams by night. I have longed for it, planned for it, studied for it secretly, for years, always hoping a time might come when I could prove to you that it was no idle fancy, but a real desire, and satisfy myself whether I have in truth

---

† From the *Saturday Evening Gazette*, 26 January 1856, 2. This short story, with its depiction of the artistic and economic struggles of four sisters, anticipates the compelling characters and relationships portrayed in *Little Women*.

the power to succeed, or whether I have cherished a false hope and been deluded by my vanity. I have thought of it seriously and earnestly during my search for employment, and see but one thing else that I can do. I *will* not chain myself to a needle and sew my own shroud for a scanty livelihood. Teaching, therefore, is all that remains. I dislike it, am unfitted for it, in every way, and cannot try it till everything else has failed.

"*You*, Nora, have your pen, Ella her music, Amy her painting; you all *love* them and can support yourselves well by them. *I* have only this one eager longing that haunts me like a shadow and seems to beckon me away to the beautiful brilliant life I feel that I was born to enjoy."

"Set yourself resolutely about some humbler work and this longing will fade away if you do not cherish it," said Leonore earnestly.

"It will not. I have tried in vain and now I will follow it over every obstacle till I have made the trial I desire.

"You are calm and cold, Nora, and cannot understand my feelings, therefore do not try to dissuade me, for an actress I must and *will* be," answered Agnes resolutely.

A look of sudden pain crossed Leonore's face at her sister's words, but it quickly passed and looking into her excited countenance she said gently, "How will you manage this? It is no easy thing for a young and unknown girl to take such a step alone; have you thought of this? and what are your plans!"

"Listen and I will tell you, for all is ready though you seem inclined to doubt it," replied Agnes, meeting her sisters' wondering glances with a look of triumph as she went on.

"Mrs. Vernon, whom our mother loved and respected, (actress though she is,) has known us long and been a friend to us in our misfortunes. I remembered this; after seeking vainly for some employment that I did not hate, I went to her, and telling all my hopes and wishes asked for her advice.

"She listened kindly and after questioning me closely and trying what little skill I have acquired, she said that if you consented she would take me with her to the West, train and teach me, and then try what I can do. There is an opening for me there, and under her protection and motherly care what need I fear? I should have told you this before but you bade us each to look and judge for ourselves before we asked for your advice, making this our first lesson in self-reliance which now is all we can depend on for support and guidance.

"Now what is your answer? Shall I go as I *wish* safely and properly with Mrs. Vernon, or as I *will*, alone and unprotected if you deny me your consent? Ah! do say yes, and you will make my life so beautiful and pleasant that I shall love and bless you forever."

As Agnes spoke, Leonore had thought rapidly of her sister's restless and unsatisfied life. Her unfitness for the drudgery she would be forced to if denied her wish. Of their mother's confidence in the kind friend who would be a faithful guardian to her, and looking in the eager imploring face lifted to her own and reading there the real unconquerable passion that filled her sister's heart she felt that hard experience alone could teach her wisdom, and that time only could dispell her dream or fix and strengthen it forever. So she replied simply and seriously. "Yes, Agnes, you may go."

Agnes, prepared for argument and denial seemed bewildered by this ready acquiescence, till meeting Leonore's troubled glance fixed anxiously upon her, she saw there all the silent sorrow and reproach she would not speak, and coming to her side, Agnes said gratefully and with a fond caress, "You never shall have cause to repent your goodness to me, Nora, for I will be true to you and to myself whatever else may happen. So do not fear for me, the memory of *home* and *you*, dear girls, will keep me safe amid the trials and temptations of my future life."

Leonore did not answer but drew her nearer as if to cherish and protect her for the little time they yet could be together, and with dim eyes but a cheerful voice bade Ella tell *her* plans.

"*I*," said the third sister, turning her placid face from the fire whose pleasant glow seemed shining from it, as if attracted there by kindred light and warmth, "I shall go to the South as governess to three motherless little girls. Aunt Elliott, who told me of it, assured me it would prove a happy home, and with my salary which is large I shall so gladly help you, and mite by mite lay by a little store that may in time grow large enough to buy our dear old home again. This is my future lot and I am truly grateful it is such a pleasant one."

"How can you be content with such a dreary life?" cried Agnes.

"Because it is my duty, and in doing that I know I shall find happiness," replied Ella. "For twenty years I have been shielded from the rough winds that visit so many, I have had my share of rest and pleasure and I trust they have done well their work of sweetening and softening my nature. Now life's harder lessons are to be learned and I am trying to receive them as I ought. Like you I will not be dependant on relations rich in all but love to us, and so must endeavor to go bravely out into the world to meet whatever fate God sends me."

The light of a pure unselfish heart beamed in the speaker's gentle face and her simple child-like faith seemed to rebuke her sister's restless doubts and longings.

"I come next," said Amy, a slender graceful girl of eighteen, "and my search has been most successful. While looking for pupils, I met again my dear friend Annie L——, who when she learned my troubles bade me look no farther but come and make my home with her. That I would not do till she agreed that I should take the place of her attendant and companion (for she is lame you know), and go with her to Europe for a year. Think how beautiful it will be to live in those lands I have so longed to see, and pass my days sketching, painting and taking care of Annie, who is alone in the world and needs an affectionate friend to cheer the many weary hours that must come to one rich, talented, and young, but a cripple for life. I shall thus support myself by my own labor though it is one of love, and gain skill and knowledge in my art in the only school that can give it me. This is my choice. Have I not done well, sisters?"

"You have indeed, but how can we let you go so far from us, dear

Amy?" said Leonore as they all looked fondly at her for she had been the pet and sunbeam of the household all her life and their hearts clung to her fearing to send her out so young to strive and struggle with the selfish world.

But she met their anxious gaze with a brave smile, saying: "Fear nothing for me, it is what I need, for I shall never know my own strength if it is never tried and with you it will not be, for you cherish me like a delicate flower. Now I shall be blown about and made to think and judge for myself as it's time I should. I shall not seem so far away as you now think for my letters will come to you like my voice from over the sea and it shall always be loving and merry that nothing may be changed as the year rolls on, and I may ever seem your own fond, foolish little Amy.

"Now, Nora, last not least, let us know in what part of the globe you will bestow yourself."

"I shall stay here, Amy," answered Leonore.

"Here!" echoed the sisters. "How can you when the house is sold and the gentleman coming to take possession so soon?"

"Just before our mother died," replied Leonore in a reverent voice, "she said to me in the silence of the night, 'Nora you are the guardian of your sisters now, be a watchful mother to them, and if you separate, as I fear you must, try to secure some little spot, no matter how poor, where you may sometimes meet and feel that you have a *home*. Promise me that, for I cannot rest in peace feeling that all the sweet ties that now bind you tenderly together are broken, and that you are growing up as strangers to each other, scattered far apart.'

"I promised her, and this is why I longed so much to have you all remain in B——, that we might often meet and cheer each other on.

"But, as it cannot be, I have decided to remain here, for Mr. Morton is a kind old man, with no family but a maiden sister. They need few apartments, and when I told him how things were, and that I desired to hire one room, he willingly consented, and naming those they wished left the rest to me. I chose this one, and here, surrounded by the few familiar things now left us, I shall live and by my pen support myself, or if that fails seek for needlework or teaching.

"It will be a quiet, solitary life, but tidings of *you* all will come to cheer me, and when another New Year shall come round, let us, if we can, meet here again to tell our wanderings and to spend it on the spot where have passed so many happy ones.

"This is my decision, here I shall live, and remember, dear girls, wherever you may be, that there is one nook in the dear old home where in sickness or sorrow you can freely come, ever sure of a joyful welcome, and in this troubled world one heart that is always open to take you in, one friend that never can desert you."

The sisters gathered silently about her as Leonore rose, and taking from a case three delicately painted miniatures of their mother, in a faltering voice, said, as she threw the simply woven chains of her own dark hair about their necks:

"This is my parting gift to you, and may the dear face Amy's hand has given us so freshly, prove a talisman to keep you ever worthy of our mother's love. God bless and bring us all together once again, better and wiser for our first lesson in the school of life."

The fire leaped up with a sudden glow, and from the hearthstone where a tenderly united family once had gathered fell now like a warm, bright blessing on the orphan sisters folded in each other's arms for the last time in the shelter of their home.

The year was gone, and Leonore sat waiting for the wanderers to come with a shadow on her face, and a secret sorrow at her heart.

The once poor room now wore an air of perfect comfort. Flowers bloomed in the deep windows sheltered from the outer cold by the warm folds of graceful curtains, green wreaths framed the picture faces on the walls, and a generous blaze burned red upon the hearth, flashing brightly over old familiar objects beautified and freshened by a tasteful hand.

A pleasant change seemed to have fallen on all there but the thoughtful woman, in whose troubled face passion and pride seemed struggling with softer, nobler feelings as she sat there pale and silent in the cheerful room. As the twilight deepened, the inward storm passed silently away, leaving only a slight cloud behind as she paced anxiously to and fro, till well known footsteps sounded without, and Ella and Amy came hastening in.

They had returned a week before, but though much with Leonore in her pleasant home they had playfully refused to answer any questions till the appointed night arrived.

Time seemed to have passed lightly over Ella, for her face was bright and tranquil as of old, while some secret joy seemed treasured in her heart, which, though it found no vent in words, shone in the clear light of her quiet eyes, sounded in the music of her voice, and deepened the sweet seriousness of her whole gentle nature.

Amy's single year of travel had brought with its culture and experience fresh grace and bloom to the slender girl who had blossomed suddenly into a lovely woman, frank and generous as ever, but softened and refined by the simple charms of early womanhood.

Gathered in their old places, the sisters talking cheerfully waited long for Agnes. But at length she came slowly, and faintly her footsteps sounded on the stair, and when she entered such a change had fallen on her they could scarce believe it was the same bright creature who had left them but a year ago.

Worn and wasted, with dim eyes and pallid cheeks, she came back but a shadow of her former self.

Her sisters knew she had been ill, and guessed she had been unhappy, for a gradual change had taken place in her letters; from being full of overflowing hope and happiness, they had grown sad, desponding, and short. But she had never spoken of the cause, and now, though grieved and startled, they breathed not a word of questioning, but, concealing their alarm, tenderly welcomed her, and tried to banish her gloom.

Agnes endeavored with forced gayety to join them, but it soon deserted her, and after the first affectionate greetings, seemed to sink unconsciously into a deep and painful reverie.

The sisters glanced silently and anxiously at one another as they heard her heavy sighs, and saw the feverish color that now burned on her thin cheek as she sat gazing absently into the glowing embers.

None seemed willing to break the silence that had fallen on them till Amy said, with a pleasant laugh:

"As I probably have the least to tell I will begin. My life, since we parted, has been one of rich experience and real happiness; with friends and labor that I loved how could it well be otherwise?

"I have fared better in my trial than I ever hoped to, and have been blessed with health of body and peace of heart to enjoy the many pleasant things about me. A home in Italy more beautiful than I can tell you, a faithful friend in Annie, cultivated minds around me, and time to study and improve myself in the things that I most love,—all these I have had, and hope I have improved them well. I have gained courage, strength, and knowledge, and armed with these I have the will and power to earn with my pencil and brush an honest livelihood, and make my own way in this busy world which has always been a friendly one to me.

"I shall stay with Annie till her marriage with the artist whom we met abroad, about whom I have already told you. Then I shall find some quiet nook, and there sit down to live, love, and labor, while waiting what the future may bring forth for me."

"May it bring you all the happiness you so well deserve, my cheerful-hearted Amy," said Leonore, looking fondly and proudly at her young sister. "Your cheerful courage is a richer fortune to you than money can ever be, while your contented mind will brighten life with the truest happiness for one who can find sunshine everywhere.

"Now, Ella, let us know how you have fared, and what your future is?" continued Leonore.

"The past year has been one of mingled joy and sorrow," answered Ella. "The sorrow was the sudden loss of little Effie, the youngest and the dearest of my pupils. It was a heavy grief to us all, and her father mourned most bitterly, till a new love, as strong and pure as that he bore the lost child, came to cheer and comfort him when he most needed it." Here, in the sudden glow on Ella's cheek, and the radiant smile that lit her face with a tenderer beauty, the sisters read the secret she had hidden from them until now, as in a low, glad voice she said:

"The joy I spoke of was that this love, so generous and deep, he offered to the humble girl who had tried to be a mother to his little child, and sorrowed like one when she went. Freely, gratefully did I receive it, for his silent kindness and the simple beauty of his life had long made him very dear to me, and I felt I had the power to be to him a true and loving friend.

"And now, no longer poor and solitary, I shall journey back to fill the place, not of the humble governess, but of a happy wife and mother in my beautiful southern home. Ah, sisters, this has been a rich and blessed year to me, far more than I have deserved."

And Ella bent her head upon her folded hands, too full of happiness for words.

Agnes had been strongly moved while Ella spoke, and when she ceased broke into bitter weeping, while her sisters gathered round her, vainly trying to compose and comfort her. But she did not heed them till her sudden grief had wept itself calm, then speaking like one in a dream, she said, abruptly:

"My year has been one of brilliant, bitter sorrow, such another I could not live through.

"When I first began my new life all seemed bright and pleasant to me. I studied hard, learned fast, and at last made the wished for trial, you know how successfully. For awhile I was in a dream of joy and triumph, and fancied all was smooth and sure before me. I had done much, I would do more, and not content to rise slowly and surely, I longed to be at once what years of patient labor alone can make me, I struggled on through the daily trials that thickened round me, often disheartened and disgusted at the selfishness and injustice of those around me, and the thousand petty annoyances that tried my proud, ambitious spirit.

"It was a hard life, and but for the great love I still cherished for the better part of it I should have left it long ago. But there were moments, hours, when I forgot my real cares and troubles in the false ones of the fair creations I was called upon to personate. Then I seemed to move in an enchanted world of my own, and *was* the creature that I *seemed*. Ah! that was glorious to feel that, my power, small as it was, could call forth tears and smiles and fill strange hearts with pity, joy, or fear.

"So time went on, and I was just beginning to feel that at last I was rising from my humble place, lifted by my own power and the kind favor I had won, when between me and my brightening fortune there came a friend, who brought me the happiest and bitterest hours of my whole life."

Here Agnes paused, and putting back her fallen hair from her wet cheek, looked wistfully into the anxious faces around her, and then, after a moment's pause, with an effort and in a hurried voice, went on,

"Among the many friends who admired and respected Mrs. Vernon and often visited her pleasant home, none was more welcome than the rich, accomplished Mr. Butler, (whose name you may remember in my letters). None came oftener, or stayed longer, he was with us at the theatre and paid a thousand kind attentions to my good friend and to me, in whom he seemed to take an interest from the first moment we met. Do not think me weak and vain, how could I help discovering it, when among many who looked coldly on me, or treated me with careless freedom, I found *him* always just, respectful, and ah! how kind? He had read and travelled much, and with his knowledge of the world, he taught, encouraged and advised me, making my hard life beautiful by his generous friendship.

"You know my nature, frank, and quick to love, touched by a gentle word or a friendly deed. I was deeply grateful for his many silent acts of kindness and the true regard he seemed to feel for me, and slowly, half unconsciously, my gratitude warmed into love. I never knew how strong and deep, until I learned too late that it was all in vain.

"One night (how well I can remember its least circumstance!) I was playing one of my best parts, and never had I played it better, for *he* was there, and I thought only of *his* approbation then. Toward the close of the evening I was waiting for my cue, when Mr. Butler and friend passed near the spot where I was standing, partially concealed by a deep shadow; I caught the sound of my own name, and then in a low, pained voice, as if replying to some questions, Mr. Butler said,

" 'I respect, admire, yes, love her too far deeply, willfully to destroy her peace, but I am of a proud race and cannot make an *actress* my wife. Therefore I shall leave to-morrow before she can discover what I have lately learned, and although we shall never meet again, I shall always be her friend.'

"They passed on and the next moment I was on the stage, laughing merrily with a dizzy brain and an aching heart. Pride nerved me to control my wandering thoughts and to play out mechanically my part in the comedy that had so suddenly become the deepest tragedy to me.

"Actress as I thought myself, it needed all my skill to hide beneath a smiling face the pang that wrung my heart, and but for the many eyes upon us and the false bloom on my cheek I should have betrayed all, when he came to take his leave that night. Little dreaming what I suffered, he kindly, seriously said farewell, and so we parted forever. For days I struggled to conceal the secret grief that preyed upon me until it laid me on a sick bed, from which I rose as you now see me, broken in health and spirit, saddened by the disappointed hopes and dreams that lie in ruins round me, distrustful of myself, and weary of life."

With a desponding sigh Agnes laid her head on Leonore's bosom, as if she never cared to lift it up again.

Ella knew why she had wept so sadly while listening to the story of *her* happy love, and bending over her she spoke gently of the past and cheerfully of the future till the desponding gloom was banished and Agnes looked up with a face brightened by earnest feeling as she said in answer to Leonore's whispered question, "You will stay with us now, dearest?"

"Yes; I shall never tread the stage again, for though I love it with a lingering memory of the many happy hours spent there, the misery of that one night has taught me what a hollow mockery the life I had chosen *may* become. I have neither health nor spirit for it now, and its glare and glitter have lost their charms. I shall find some humble work and quietly pursuing it, endeavor to become what *he* would have me: not an actress, but a simple woman, trying to play well her part in life's great drama. And though we shall never meet again, he may one day learn that, no longer mistaking the shadow for the substance, I have left the fair, false life and taken up the real and true."

"Thank heaven for this change," cried Leonore. "Dear Agnes, this shall henceforth be your home, and here we will lead a cheerful, busy life, sharing joy and sorrow together as in our childhood, and journeying hand in hand thro' light and darkness to a happy, calm old age."

"Leonore, you must tell us your experiences now, or our histories are not complete," said Amy, after a little time.

"I have nothing to relate but what you already know," replied her sister. "My book was well received and made for me a place among these writers who have the power to please and touch the hearts of many. I have earned much with my pen, and have a little store laid by for future need. My life has been a quiet, busy one. I have won many friends whose kindness and affection have cheered my solitude and helped me on. What more can I say but that I heartily rejoice that all has gone so well with us, and we have proved that we possess the power to make our own way in the world and need ask charity of none. Our talismans have kept us safe from harm, and God has let us meet again without one gone."

"Leonore," said Agnes, looking earnestly into her sister's face, "you have not told us *all*; nay, do not turn away, there is some hidden heart-sorrow that you are silent of. I read it in the secret trouble of your eye, the pallor of your cheek, and most of all, in your quick sympathy for me. We have given you our confidence, ah! give us yours as freely, dearest Nora."

"I cannot, do not ask me," murmured Leonore, averting her face.

"Let nothing break the sweet ties that now bind you together, and do not be as strangers to each other when you should be closest friends," whispered Ella from the low seat at her knee.

Leonore seemed to struggle with herself, and many contending emotions swept across her face, but she longed for sympathy and her proud heart melted at the mild echo of her mother's words. So holding Agnes's hand fast in her own, as if their sorrow drew them nearer to each other, she replied with a regretful sigh, "Yes, I will tell you, for your quick eyes have discovered what I hoped to have hidden from your sight forever. It *is* a heart-sorrow, Agnes, deeper than your own, for you still can reverence and trust the friend you have lost, but I can only feel contempt for what I have so truly loved. You well remember cousin Walter, the frank, generous-hearted boy who was our dearest playmate and companion years ago? Soon after we had separated he returned from India with his parents, and though *they* took no heed of me, *he* sought me out, and simply, naturally took the place of friend and brother to me, as of old. I needed help just then, he gave it freely, and by his wise counsel and generous kindness, banished my cares and cheered me when most solitary and forlorn.

"I always loved him, and pleasant memories of the happy past have kept his image fresh within my heart. Through the long years of his absence I have sighed for his return, longing to know if the promise of a noble manhood I remembered in the boy had been fulfilled. He came at last when most I wished him, and with secret pride and joy I found him all I had hoped, brave, generous, and sincere. Ah! I was very happy then, and as our friendship grew, slowly and silently the frank affection of the girl deepened into the woman's earnest love.

"I knew it was returned, for in every look and deed the sweet, protecting tenderness that had guarded me in my childish days, now showed itself more plainly still, and at length found vent in words, which few and simple as they were seemed to fill my life with a strange happiness and beauty.

"Agnes, you have called me cold, but if you knew the deep and fervent passion that has stirred my heart, softening and sweetening my stern nature, you could never wrong me so again. Unhappy as that love has been, its short experience has made me wiser, and when its first sharp disappointment has passed away, the memory of it will linger like the warm glow of a fire whose brightness has departed.

"Two months ago a change came over Walter; he was kind as ever, coming often to cheer my lonely life, filling my home with lovely things, and more than all with his own dear presence, but a cloud was on him and I could not banish it.

"At length a week passed and he did not come, but in his place a letter from his father saying 'that he disapproved of his son's love for me and had persuaded him to relinquish me for a wife more suited to his rank in life; therefore at his request he wrote to spare us the pain of parting.' I cannot tell what more was in that cold, insulting letter, for I burned it, saving only two faintly written words in Walter's well known hand, 'Farewell, Leonore;' that was enough for me; by what magic the great change was wrought I cared not to discover. All I thought or felt was that he had left me without a word of explanation, breaking his plighted word, and like a coward fearing to tell me freely and openly that he no longer loved me.

"I have not seen or heard from him since; though rumors of his approaching marriage, his departure for Europe and a sudden illness, have reached my ears, I believe none of them and struggling sternly to conceal my sorrow have passed silently on leaving him without one word of entreaty or reproach to the keen regret his cruelty will one day cause him."

A proud indignant light burned in Leonore's eye and flushed her cheek as with a bitter smile she met her sisters' troubled glances saying:

"You need not pity *me*, *he* wants it most, for money can buy his truth and cast an evil spell on him, and a sordid father has the power to tempt and win him from his duty. None but *you* will ever know the secret sorrow that now bows my spirit but shall never break it; I shall soon banish the tender memories that haunt me, and hiding the deep wound he has caused me, be again the calm, cold Leonore.

"Oh! Walter! Walter! you have made the patient love that should have been the blessing of my life, its heaviest sorrow; may God forgive you as I try to do."

And as these words broke from her lips, Leonore clasped her hands before her face and hot tears fell like rain on Ella's head bent down upon her knee.

Agnes and Amy, blinded by the dimness of their own eyes, had not seen a tall dark man who had entered silently as Leonore last spoke and had stood spell bound till she ceased, then coming to her side the stranger said in a low eager voice,

"Nora, will you hear me?"

With a quick start Leonore dashed away her tears and rose up pale and stately, looking full into the earnest, manly face before her and plainly reading there all she had doubted. Truth in the frank, reproachful eyes that freely met her own, tender sorrow in the trembling lips, and over all the light of the faithful, generous love which never had deserted her.

Her stern glance softened as she bowed a silent reply, and fell before his own as standing close beside her and looking steadily into her changing countenance, her cousin Walter laid his thin hand on her own saying in the friendly voice she had so longed to hear,

"Leonore, from the sick bed where I have lain through these long weary weeks, I have come to prove my truth, which had your pride allowed you to inquire into you never would have doubted, knowing me as I fondly hoped you did."

With a sudden motion Leonore drew a little worn and blistered paper from her bosom and laid it in his hand from which she coldly drew her own and fixed a keen look on his face, where not a shadow of shame or fear appeared, as he read it, silently glancing from the tear-stains to the eyes that looked so proudly on him with a quiet smile that brought a hot glow to her cheek as she asked quickly,

"Did *you* write those cruel words?"

"I did; nay, listen patiently before you judge me, Nora," he replied as she turned to leave him.

"Two months ago my father questioned me of *you*. I told him freely that I loved you and soon hoped to gladden his home with a daughter's gentle presence. But his anger knew no bounds and commanding me to beware how I thwarted his wishes, he bade me choose between utter poverty and you, or all his Indian wealth and my cousin Clara; I told him that my choice was already made, but he would not listen to me and bade me consider it well for one whole week and then decide before I saw you again. I yielded to calm his anger and for a week tried to win him to a wiser and kinder course, but all in vain: his will was iron and mine was no less firm, for, high above all selfish doubts and fears, all lures of rank and wealth, rose up my faithful love for you and nothing else could tempt me. That needed no golden fetters to render it more true, no idle show to make it richer, fonder than it is and ever will be.

"It was no virtue in me to resist, for nothing great enough was offered in exchange for that: poverty was wealth with *you* and who would waver between a false, vain girl and a true hearted woman?

"Ah, Nora, you will learn to know me now and see how deep a wrong you have done me. But to finish. When at the week's close I told my father that my purpose was unbroken he bade me leave his house forever and would have cursed me but his passion choked the sinful words ere they were spoken and he is saved that sorrow, when he thinks more kindly of me hereafter.

"I silently prepared to leave his house, which since my own mother's death has never been like home to me, and should have hastened joyfully to you, had not the fever already burning in my veins, augmented by anxiety and grief, laid me on my bed from which I am just risen, and where through those long nights and days I have been haunted even in delirium by your image, and the one longing wish to tell you why I did not come.

"When better, I sent messages and letters, but they were never delivered, for my father thinking sickness might have changed me, was still at my side to watch my actions and to tempt me to revoke my words. I have since learned that he wrote to you and guiding my unconscious hand traced the words that gave you the right to doubt me. But now I am strong again; nothing can separate us more, and I am here to bury the past and win your pardon for the sorrow I could not spare you. Now, Leonore, I am poor and friendless as yourself, with my fortune to make by the labor of my hands as you have done. You once wished this and said you never would receive the wealth I longed to give you; your wish is granted; I have nothing now to offer but a hand to work untiringly for you, and a heart to love and cherish you most tenderly forever. Will you take them, Nora?"

Leonore's proud head had sunk lower and lower as he spoke and when he ceased it rested on his shoulder, and her hand lay with an earnest, loving clasp in his as she whispered in a broken voice,

"Forgive me, Walter, for the wrong I have done you and teach me to be worthy the great sacrifice you have made for me."

The clock struck twelve and as its silvery echoes sounded through the quiet room, the old year with its joys and sorrows, hopes and fears floated away into the shadowing past bearing among its many records the simple one of the Sisters' Trial.

[LOUISA MAY ALCOTT]

A Modern Cinderella: or, The Little Old Shoe†

HOW IT WAS LOST.

Among green New England hills stood an ancient house, many-gabled, mossy-roofed, and quaintly built, but picturesque and pleasant to the eye; for a brook ran babbling through the orchard that encompassed it about, a garden-plot stretched upward to the whispering birches on the slope, and patriarchal elms stood sentinel upon the lawn, as they had stood almost a century ago, when the Revolution rolled that way and found them young.

---

† From the *Atlantic Monthly* 6 (1860): 425–41. Inspired by Anna Alcott and John Bridge Pratt's courtship, this work of fiction for middlebrow and highbrow adult audiences is another early example of Alcott's blending of fiction and autobiography.

One summer morning, when the air was full of country sounds, of mowers in the meadow, blackbirds by the brook, and the low of kine upon the hill-side, the old house wore its cheeriest aspect, and a certain humble history began.

"Nan!"

"Yes, Di."

And a head, brown-locked, blue-eyed, soft-featured, looked in at the open door in answer to the call.

"Just bring me the third volume of 'Wilhelm Meister,'[1]—there's a dear. It's hardly worth while to rouse such a restless ghost as I, when I'm once fairly laid."

As she spoke, Di pushed up her black braids, thumped the pillow of the couch where she was lying, and with eager eyes went down the last page of her book.

"Nan!"

"Yes, Laura," replied the girl, coming back with the third volume for the literary cormorant, who took it with a nod, still too intent upon the "Confessions of a Fair Saint" to remember the failings of a certain plain sinner.

"Don't forget the Italian cream for dinner. I depend upon it; for it's the only thing fit for me this hot weather."

And Laura, the cool blonde, disposed the folds of her white gown more gracefully about her, and touched up the eyebrow of the Minerva she was drawing.

"Little daughter!"

"Yes, father."

"Let me have plenty of clean collars in my bag, for I must go at three; and some of you bring me a glass of cider in about an hour;—I shall be in the lower garden."

The old man went away into his imaginary paradise, and Nan into that domestic purgatory on a summer day,—the kitchen. There were vines about the windows, sunshine on the floor, and order everywhere; but it was haunted by a cooking-stove, that family altar whence such varied incense rises to appease the appetite of household gods, before which such dire incantations are pronounced to ease the wrath and woe of the priestess of the fire, and about which often linger saddest memories of wasted temper, time, and toil.

Nan was tired, having risen with the birds,—hurried, having many cares those happy little housewives never know,—and disappointed in a hope that hourly "dwindled, peaked, and pined." She was too young to make the anxious lines upon her forehead seem at home there, too patient to be burdened with the labor others should have shared, too light of heart to be pent up when earth and sky were keeping a blithe holiday. But she was one of that meek sisterhood who, thinking humbly of themselves, believe they are honored by being spent in the service of less conscientious souls, whose careless thanks seem quite reward enough.

---

1. See Johann Wolfgang von Goethe, "Confessions of a Fair Saint," in *Wilhelm Meister's Apprenticeship*, trans. Thomas Carlyle (Boston: Ticknor and Fields, 1866), book 6 [*Editors*].

To and fro she went, silent and diligent, giving the grace of willing-ness to every humble or distasteful task the day had brought her; but some malignant sprite seemed to have taken possession of her king-dom, for rebellion broke out everywhere. The kettles would boil over most obstreperously,—the mutton refused to cook with the meek alacrity to be expected from the nature of a sheep,—the stove, with unnecessary warmth of temper, would glow like a fiery furnace,—the irons would scorch,—the linens would dry,—and spirits would fail, though patience never.

Nan tugged on, growing hotter and wearier, more hurried and more hopeless, till at last the crisis came; for in one fell moment she tore her gown, burnt her hand, and smutched the collar she was preparing to finish in the most unexceptionable style. Then, if she had been a nervous woman, she would have scolded; being a gentle girl, she only "lifted up her voice and wept."

"Behold, she watereth her linen with salt tears, and bewaileth her-self because of much tribulation. But, lo! help cometh from afar: a strong man bringeth lettuce wherewith to stay her, plucketh berries to comfort her withal, and clasheth cymbals that she may dance for joy."

The voice came from the porch, and, with her hope fulfilled, Nan looked up to greet John Lord, the house-friend, who stood there with a basket on his arm; and as she saw his honest eyes, kind lips, and helpful hands, the girl thought this plain young man the comeliest, most welcome sight she had beheld that day.

"How good of you, to come through all this heat, and not to laugh at my despair!" she said, looking up like a grateful child, as she led him in.

"I only obeyed orders, Nan; for a certain dear old lady had a moth-erly presentiment that you had got into a domestic whirlpool, and sent me as a sort of life-preserver. So I took the basket of consolation, and came to fold my feet upon the carpet of contentment in the tent of friendship."

As he spoke, John gave his own gift in his mother's name, and be-stowed himself in the wide window-seat, where morning-glories nod-ded at him, and the old butternut sent pleasant shadows dancing to and fro.

His advent, like that of Orpheus[2] in Hades, seemed to soothe all un-propitious powers with a sudden spell. The fire began to slacken, the kettles began to lull, the meat began to cook, the irons began to cool, the clothes began to behave, the spirits began to rise, and the collar was finished off with most triumphant success. John watched the change, and, though a lord of creation, abased himself to take com-passion on the weaker vessel, and was seized with a great desire to lighten the homely tasks that tried her strength of body and soul. He took a comprehensive glance about the room; then, extracting a dish from the closet, proceeded to imbrue his hands in the strawberries' blood.

2. See p. 277, n. 2 (part 2, chap. 11) [*Editors*].

"Oh, John, you needn't do that; I shall have time when I've turned the meat, made the pudding, and done these things. See, I'm getting on finely now;—you're a judge of such matters; isn't that nice?"

As she spoke, Nan offered the polished absurdity for inspection with innocent pride.

"Oh that I were a collar, to sit upon that hand!" sighed John,—adding, argumentatively, "As to the berry question, I might answer it with a gem from Dr. Watts, relative to 'Satan' and 'idle hands,'[3] but will merely say, that, as a matter of public safety, you'd better leave me alone; for such is the destructiveness of my nature, that I shall certainly eat something hurtful, break something valuable, or sit upon something crushable, unless you let me concentrate my energies by knocking off these young fellows' hats, and preparing them for their doom."

Looking at the matter in a charitable light, Nan consented, and went cheerfully on with her work, wondering how she could have thought ironing an infliction, and been so ungrateful for the blessings of her lot.

"Where's Sally?" asked John, looking vainly for the energetic functionary who usually pervaded that region like a domestic police-woman, a terror to cats, dogs, and men.

"She has gone to her cousin's funeral, and won't be back till Monday. There seems to be a great fatality among her relations; for one dies, or comes to grief in some way, about once a month. But I don't blame poor Sally for wanting to get away from this place now and then. I think I could find it in my heart to murder an imaginary friend or two, if I had to stay here long."

And Nan laughed so blithely, it was a pleasure to hear her.

"Where's Di?" asked John, seized with a most unmasculine curiosity all at once.

"She is in Germany with 'Wilhelm Meister'; but, though 'lost to sight, to memory dear';[4] for I was just thinking, as I did her things, how clever she is to like all kinds of books that I don't understand at all, and to write things that make me cry with pride and delight. Yes, she's a talented dear, though she hardly knows a needle from a crow-bar, and will make herself one great blot some of these days, when the 'divine afflatus' descends upon her, I'm afraid."

And Nan rubbed away with sisterly zeal at Di's forlorn hose and inky pocket-handkerchiefs.

"Where is Laura?" proceeded the inquisitor.

"Well, I might say that *she* was in Italy; for she is copying some fine thing of Raphael's, or Michael Angelo's, or some great creature's or other; and she looks so picturesque in her pretty gown, sitting before her easel, that it's really a sight to behold, and I've peeped two or three times to see how she gets on."

---

3. Reference to Isaac Watts's poem "Against Idleness and Mischief," lines 9–12 of which read, "In works of labour or of skill, / I would be busy too; / For Satan finds some mischief still / For idle hands to do" [*Editors*].
4. See George Linley, "Song" (c. 1830), line 1 [*Editors*].

And Nan bestirred herself to prepare the dish wherewith her pictur-esque sister desired to prolong her artistic existence.

"Where is your father?" John asked again, checking off each answer with a nod and a little frown.

"He is down in the garden, deep in some plan about melons, the be-ginning of which seems to consist in stamping the first proposition in Euclid all over the bed, and then poking a few seeds into the middle of each. Why bless the dear man! I forgot it was time for the cider. Wouldn't you like to take it to him, John? He'd love to consult you; and the lane is so cool, it does one's heart good to look at it."

John glanced from the steamy kitchen to the shadowy path, and an-swered with a sudden assumption of immense industry,—

"I couldn't possibly go, Nan,—I've so much on my hands. You'll have to do it yourself. 'Mr. Robert of Lincoln' has something for your pri-vate ear;[5] and the lane is so cool, it will do one's heart good to see you in it. Give my regards to your father, and, in the words of 'Little Ma-bel's' mother, with slight variations,—

> 'Tell the dear old body
> This day I cannot run,
> For the pots are boiling over
> And the mutton isn't done.' "[6]

"I will; but please, John, go in to the girls and be comfortable; for I don't like to leave you here," said Nan.

"You insinuate that I should pick at the pudding or invade the cream, do you? Ungrateful girl, leave me!" And, with melodramatic sternness, John extinguished her in his broad-brimmed hat, and of-fered the glass like a poisoned goblet.

Nan took it, and went smiling away. But the lane might have been the Desert of Sahara, for all she knew of it; and she would have passed her father as unconcernedly as if he had been an apple-tree, had he not called out,—

"Stand and deliver, little woman!"

She obeyed the venerable highwayman, and followed him to and fro, listening to his plans and directions with a mute attention that quite won his heart.

"That hop-pole is really an ornament now, Nan; this sage-bed needs weeding,—that's good work for you girls; and, now I think of it, you'd better water the lettuce in the cool of the evening, after I'm gone."

To all of which remarks Nan gave her assent; though the hop-pole took the likeness of a tall figure she had seen in the porch, the sage-bed, curiously enough, suggested a strawberry ditto, the lettuce vividly reminded her of certain vegetable productions a basket had brought, and the bob-o-link only sung in his cheeriest voice, "Go home, go home! he is there!"

5. Cf. William Cullen Bryant, "Robert of Lincoln" (1864), lines 13–14: "Hear him call in his merry note: / Bob-o'-link, bob-o'-link." John tells Nan to get some fresh air and listen to the birds singing before she continues her domestic labor [*Editors*].
6. See Mary Botham Howitt, "Mabel on Midsummer Day: A Story of the Olden Time," in *Marien's Pilgrimage; A Fire-Side Story, and Other Poems* (1859), lines 13–16 [*Editors*].

She found John—he having made a freemason of himself, by assuming her little apron[7]—meditating over the partially spread table, lost in amaze at its desolate appearance; one half its proper paraphernalia having been forgotten, and the other half put on awry. Nan laughed till the tears ran over her cheeks, and John was gratified at the efficacy of his treatment; for her face had brought a whole harvest of sunshine from the garden, and all her cares seemed to have been lost in the windings of the lane.

"Nan, are you in hysterics?" cried Di, appearing, book in hand. "John, you absurd man, what are you doing?"

"I'm helpin' the maid of all work, please marm." And John dropped a curtsy with his limited apron.

Di looked ruffled, for the merry words were a covert reproach; and with her usual energy of manner and freedom of speech she tossed "Wilhelm" out of the window, exclaiming, irefully,—

"That's always the way; I'm never where I ought to be, and never think of anything till it's too late; but it's all Goethe's fault. What does he write books full of smart 'Phillinas' and interesting 'Meisters' for? How can I be expected to remember that Sally's away, and people must eat, when I'm hearing the 'Harper' and little 'Mignon'?[8] John, how dare you come here and do my work, instead of shaking me and telling me to do it myself? Take that toasted child away, and fan her like a Chinese mandarin, while I dish up this dreadful dinner."

John and Nan fled like chaff before the wind, while Di, full of remorseful zeal, charged at the kettles, and wrenched off the potatoes' jackets, as if she were revengefully pulling her own hair. Laura had a vague intention of going to assist; but, getting lost among the lights and shadows of Minerva's helmet, forgot to appear till dinner had been evoked from chaos and peace was restored.

At three o'clock, Di performed the coronation-ceremony with her father's best hat; Laura re-tied his old-fashioned neckcloth, and arranged his white locks with an eye to saintly effect; Nan appeared with a beautifully written sermon, and suspicious ink-stains on the fingers that slipped it into his pocket; John attached himself to the bag; and the patriarch was escorted to the door of his tent with the triumphal procession which usually attended his out-goings and incomings. Having kissed the female portion of his tribe, he ascended the venerable chariot, which received him with audible lamentation, as its rheumatic joints swayed to and fro.

"Good-bye, my dears! I shall be back early on Monday morning; so take care of yourselves, and be sure you all go and hear Mr. Emerboy[9] preach to-morrow. My regards to your mother, John. Come, Solon!"

But Solon merely cocked one ear, and remained a fixed fact; for long experience had induced the philosophic beast to take for his

7. Members of the Free and Accepted Order of Masons wore sheepskin aprons in connection with their secret rituals [*Editors*].
8. Characters in *Wilhelm Meister's Apprenticeship* [*Editors*].
9. A play on Emer*son* [*Editors*].

motto the Yankee maxim, "Be sure you're right, then go ahead!" He knew things were not right; therefore he did not go ahead.

"Oh, by-the-way, girls, don't forget to pay Tommy Mullein for bringing up the cow: he expects it to-night. And, Di, don't sit up till daylight, nor let Laura stay out in the dew. Now, I believe, I'm off. Come, Solon!"

But Solon only cocked the other ear, gently agitated his mortified tail, as premonitory symptoms of departure, and never stirred a hoof, being well aware that it always took three "comes" to make a "go."

"Bless me! I've forgotten my spectacles. They are probably shut up in that volume of Herbert[1] on my table. Very awkward to find myself without them ten miles away. Thank you, John. Don't neglect to water the lettuce, Nan, and don't overwork yourself, my little Martha.'[2] Come"—

At this juncture, Solon suddenly went off, like "Mrs. Gamp,"[3] in a sort of walking swoon, apparently deaf and blind to all mundane matters, except the refreshments awaiting him ten miles away; and the benign old pastor disappeared, humming "Hebron"[4] to the creaking accompaniment of the bulgy chaise.

Laura retired to take her *siesta*; Nan made a small *carbonaro*[5] of herself by sharpening her sister's crayons, and Di, as a sort of penance for past sins, tried her patience over a piece of knitting, in which she soon originated a somewhat remarkable pattern, by dropping every third stitch, and seaming *ad libitum*. If John had been a gentlemanly creature, with refined tastes, he would have elevated his feet and made a nuisance of himself by indulging in a "weed"; but being only an uncultivated youth, with a rustic regard for pure air and womankind in general, he kept his head uppermost, and talked like a man, instead of smoking like a chimney.

"It will probably be six months before I sit here again, tangling your threads and maltreating your needles, Nan. How glad you must feel to hear it!" he said, looking up from a thoughtful examination of the hard-working little citizens of the Industrial Community settled in Nan's work-basket.

"No, I'm very sorry; for I like to see you coming and going as you used to, years ago, and I miss you very much when you are gone, John," answered truthful Nan, whittling away in a sadly wasteful manner, as her thoughts flew back to the happy times when a little lad rode a little lass in the big wheelbarrow, and never spilt his load,— when two brown heads bobbed daily side by side to school, and the favorite play was "Babes in the Wood,"[6] with Di for a somewhat peckish robin to cover the small martyrs with any vegetable substance that lay

---

1. George Herbert (1593–1633), English minister, writer, and poet. His "A Priest to the Temple" (1652) contains "plain, prudent, useful rules for the country parson" [*Editors*].
2. See p. 218, n. 8 (part 2, chap. 5) [*Editors*].
3. See p. 93, n. 1 (part 1, chap. 11) [*Editors*].
4. A hymn with lyrics by Isaac Watts (1707) and music by Lowell Mason (1823) [*Editors*].
5. Coal man (Italian) [*Editors*].
6. A traditional English ballad in which two children are abandoned in a wood and die in each other's arms.

at hand. Nan sighed, as she thought of these things, and John regarded the battered thimble on his fingertip with increased benignity of aspect as he heard the sound.

"When are you going to make your fortune, John, and get out of that disagreeable hardware concern?" demanded Di, pausing after an exciting "round," and looking almost as much exhausted as if it had been a veritable pugilistic encounter.

"I intend to make it by plunging still deeper into 'that disagreeable hardware concern'; for, next year, if the world keeps rolling, and John Lord is alive, he will become a partner, and then—and then"—

The color sprang up into the young man's cheek, his eyes looked out with a sudden shine, and his hand seemed involuntarily to close, as if he saw and seized some invisible delight.

"What will happen then, John?" asked Nan, with a wondering glance.

"I'll tell you in a year, Nan,—wait till then." And John's strong hand unclosed, as if the desired good were not to be his yet.

Di looked at him, with a knitting-needle stuck into her hair, saying, like a sarcastic unicorn,—

"I really thought you had a soul above pots and kettles, but I see you haven't; and I beg your pardon for the injustice I have done you."

Not a whit disturbed, John smiled, as if at some mighty pleasant fancy of his own, as he replied,—

"Thank you, Di; and as a further proof of the utter depravity of my nature, let me tell you that I have the greatest possible respect for those articles of ironmongery. Some of the happiest hours of my life have been spent in their society; some of my pleasantest associations are connected with them; some of my best lessons have come to me from among them; and when my fortune is made, I intend to show my gratitude by taking three flat-irons rampant for my coat of arms."

Nan laughed merrily, as she looked at the burns on her hand; but Di elevated the most prominent feature of her brown countenance, and sighed despondingly,—

"Dear, dear, what a disappointing world this is! I no sooner build a nice castle in Spain, and settle a smart young knight therein, than down it comes about my ears; and the ungrateful youth, who might fight dragons, if he chose, insists on quenching his energies in a saucepan, and making a Saint Lawrence of himself by wasting his life on a series of gridirons.[7] Ah, if *I* were only a man, I would do something better than that, and prove that heroes are not all dead yet. But, instead of that, I'm only a woman, and must sit rasping my temper with absurdities like this." And Di wrestled with her knitting as if it were Fate, and she were paying off the grudge she owed it.

John leaned toward her, saying, with a look that made his plain face handsome,—

"Di, my father began the world as I begin it, and left it the richer for the useful years he spent here,—as I hope I may leave it some half-

7. See p. 320, n. 7 (part 2, chap. 16) [*Editors*].

century hence. His memory makes that dingy shop a pleasant place to me; for there he made an honest name, led an honest life, and bequeathed to me his reverence for honest work. That is a sort of hardware, Di, that no rust can corrupt, and which will always prove a better fortune than any your knights can achieve with sword and shield. I think I am not quite a clod, or quite without some aspirations above money-getting; for I sincerely desire that courage which makes daily life heroic by self-denial and cheerfulness of heart; I am eager to conquer my own rebellious nature, and earn the confidence of innocent and upright souls; I have a great ambition to become as good a man and leave as green a memory behind me as old John Lord."

Di winked violently, and seamed five times in perfect silence; but quiet Nan had the gift of knowing when to speak, and by a timely word saved her sister from a thunder-shower and her stocking from destruction.

"John, have you seen Philip since you wrote about your last meeting with him?"

The question was for John, but the soothing tone was for Di, who gratefully accepted it, and perked up again with speed.

"Yes; and I meant to have told you about it," answered John, plunging into the subject at once. "I saw him a few days before I came home, and found him more disconsolate than ever,—'just ready to go to the Devil,' as he forcibly expressed himself. I consoled the poor lad as well as I could, telling him his wisest plan was to defer his proposed expedition, and go on as steadily as he had begun,—thereby proving the injustice of your father's prediction concerning his want of perseverance, and the sincerity of his affection. I told him the change in Laura's health and spirits was silently working in his favor, and that a few more months of persistent endeavor would conquer your father's prejudice against him, and make him a stronger man for the trial and the pain. I read him bits about Laura from your own and Di's letters, and he went away at last as patient as Jacob, ready to serve another 'seven years' for his beloved Rachel."[8]

"God bless you for it, John!" cried a fervent voice; and, looking up, they saw the cold, listless Laura transformed into a tender girl, all aglow with love and longing, as she dropped her mask, and showed a living countenance eloquent with the first passion and softened by the first grief of her life.

John rose involuntarily in the presence of an innocent nature whose sorrow needed no interpreter to him. The girl read sympathy in his brotherly regard, and found comfort in the friendly voice that asked, half playfully, half seriously,—

"Shall I tell him that he is not forgotten, even for an Apollo? that Laura the artist has not conquered Laura the woman? and predict that the good daughter will yet prove the happy wife?"

With a gesture full of energy, Laura tore her Minerva from top to

8. See Genesis 29.18–30 [Editors].

bottom, while two great tears rolled down the checks grown wan with hope deferred.

"Tell him I believe all things, hope all things, and that I never can forget."

Nan went to her and held her fast, leaving the prints of two loving, but grimy hands upon her shoulders; Di looked on approvingly, for, though rather stony-hearted regarding the cause, she fully appreciated the effect; and John, turning to the window, received the commendations of a robin swaying on an elm-bough with sunshine on its ruddy breast.

The clock struck five, and John declared that he must go; for, being an old-fashioned soul, he fancied that his mother had a better right to his last hour than any younger woman in the land,—always remembering that "she was a widow, and he her only son."[9]

Nan ran away to wash her hands, and came back with the appearance of one who had washed her face also: and so she had; but there was a difference in the water.

"Play I'm your father, girls, and remember it will be six months before 'that John' will trouble you again."

With which preface the young man kissed his former playfellows as heartily as the boy had been wont to do, when stern parents banished him to distant schools, and three little maids bemoaned his fate. But times were changed now; for Di grew alarmingly rigid during the ceremony; Laura received the salute like a grateful queen; and Nan returned it with heart and eyes and tender lips, making such an improvement on the childish fashion of the thing, that John was moved to support his paternal character by softly echoing her father's words,—"Take care of yourself, my little 'Martha.'"

Then they all streamed after him along the garden-path, with the endless messages and warnings girls are so prone to give; and the young man, with a great softness at his heart, went away, as many another John has gone, feeling better for the companionship of innocent maidenhood, and stronger to wrestle with temptation, to wait and hope and work.

"Let's throw a shoe after him for luck, as dear old 'Mrs. Gummage' did after 'David' and the 'willin' Barkis!'[1] Quick, Nan! you always have old shoes on; toss one, and shout, 'Good luck!'" cried Di, with one of her eccentric inspirations.

Nan tore off her shoe, and threw it far along the dusty road, with a sudden longing to become that auspicious article of apparel, that the omen might not fail.

Looking backward from the hill-top, John answered the meek shout cheerily, and took in the group with a lingering glance: Laura in the shadow of the elms, Di perched on the fence, and Nan leaning far over the gate with her hand above her eyes and the sunshine touching her brown hair with gold. He waved his hat and turned away; but the

---

9. See "Clarian's Picture," *Atlantic Monthly* 5 (June 1860): 709.
1. In Charles Dickens's *David Copperfield* (1850), Mrs. Gummidge is pressured to throw a shoe for good luck at Clara Peggotty and Barkis's wedding [*Editors*].

music seemed to die out of the blackbird's song, and in all the summer landscape his eye saw nothing but the little figure at the gate.

"Bless and save us! here's a flock of people coming; my hair is in a toss, and Nan's without her shoe; run! fly, girls! or the Philistines will be upon us!" cried Di, tumbling off her perch in sudden alarm.

Three agitated young ladies, with flying draperies and countenances of mingled mirth and dismay, might have been seen precipitating themselves into a respectable mansion with unbecoming haste; but the squirrels were the only witnesses of this "vision of sudden flight," and, being used to ground-and-lofty tumbling, didn't mind it.

When the pedestrians passed, the door was decorously closed, and no one visible but a young man, who snatched something out of the road, and marched away again, whistling with more vigor of tone than accuracy of tune, "Only that, and nothing more."[2]

HOW IT WAS FOUND.

Summer ripened into autumn, and something fairer than

> "Sweet-peas and mignonette
> In Annie's garden grew."[3]

Her nature was the counterpart of the hill-side grove, where as a child she had read her fairy tales, and now as a woman turned the first pages of a more wondrous legend still. Lifted above the many-gabled roof, yet not cut off from the echo of human speech, the little grove seemed a green sanctuary, fringed about with violets, and full of summer melody and bloom. Gentle creatures haunted it, and there was none to make afraid; wood-pigeons cooed and crickets chirped their shrill roundelays, anemones and lady-ferns looked up from the moss that kissed the wanderer's feet. Warm airs were all afloat, full of vernal odors for the grateful sense, silvery birches shimmered like spirits of the wood, larches gave their green tassels to the wind, and pines made airy music sweet and solemn, as they stood looking heavenward through veils of summer sunshine or shrouds of wintry snow.

Nan never felt alone now in this charmed wood; for when she came into its precincts, once so full of solitude, all things seemed to wear one shape, familiar eyes looked at her from the violets in the grass, familiar words sounded in the whisper of the leaves, and she grew conscious that an unseen influence filled the air with new delights, and touched earth and sky with a beauty never seen before. Slowly these May-flowers budded in her maiden heart, rosily they bloomed, and silently they waited till some lover of such lowly herbs should catch their fresh aroma, should brush away the fallen leaves, and lift them to the sun.

Though the eldest of the three, she had long been overtopped by the more aspiring maids. But though she meekly yielded the reins of government, whenever they chose to drive, they were soon restored to her

2. See Edgar Allan Poe, "The Raven," in *The Raven and Other Poems* (1845), line 6 [*Editors*].
3. Cf. Eliza Lee Follen, "Annie's Garden," in *Little Songs* (1832), lines 3–8 [*Editors*].

again; for Di fell into literature, and Laura into love. Thus engrossed, these two forgot many duties which even blue-stockings and *in-namoratas* are expected to perform, and slowly all the homely hum-drum cares that housewives know became Nan's daily life, and she accepted it without a thought of discontent. Noiseless and cheerful as the sunshine, she went to and fro, doing the tasks that mothers do, but without a mother's sweet reward, holding fast the numberless slight threads that bind a household tenderly together, and making each day a beautiful success.

Di, being tired of running, riding, climbing, and boating, decided at last to let her body rest and put her equally active mind through what classical collegians term "a course of sprouts." Having undertaken to read and know *everything*, she devoted herself to the task with great en-ergy, going from Sue to Swedenborg with perfect impartiality, and hav-ing different authors as children have sundry distempers, being fractious while they lasted, but all the better for them when once over. Carlyle ap-peared like scarlet-fever, and raged violently for a time; for, being any-thing but a "passive bucket," Di became prophetic with Mahomet, belligerent with Cromwell, and made the French Revolution a veritable Reign of Terror to her family. Goethe and Schiller alternated like fever and ague; Mephistopheles became her hero, Joan of Arc her model, and she turned her black eyes red over Egmont and Wallenstein. A mild at-tack of Emerson followed, during which she was lost in a fog, and her sisters rejoiced inwardly when she emerged informing them that

> "The Sphinx was drowsy,
> Her wings were furled."[4]

Poor Di was floundering slowly to her proper place; but she splashed up a good deal of foam by getting out of her depth, and rather exhausted herself by trying to drink the ocean dry.

Laura, after the "midsummer night's dream" that often comes to girls of seventeen, woke up to find that youth and love were no match for age and common sense. Philip had been flying about the world like a thistle-down for five-and-twenty years, generous-hearted, frank, and kind, but with never an idea of the serious side of life in his handsome head. Great, therefore, were the wrath and dismay of the enamored thistle-down, when the father of his love mildly objected to seeing her begin the world in a balloon with a very tender but very inexperienced aëronaut for a guide.

"Laura is too young to 'play house' yet, and you are too unstable to assume the part of lord and master, Philip. Go and prove that you have prudence, patience, energy, and enterprise, and I will give you my girl,—but not before. I must seem cruel, that I may be truly kind; be-lieve this, and let a little pain lead you to great happiness, or show you where you would have made a bitter blunder."

The lovers listened, owned the truth of the old man's words, be-wailed their fate, and—yielded,—Laura for love of her father, Philip

4. See Emerson, "The Sphinx," in *Poems* (1847), lines 1–2 [*Editors*].

for love of her. He went away to build a firm foundation for his castle in the air, and Laura retired into an invisible convent, where she cast off the world, and regarded her sympathizing sisters through a grate of superior knowledge and unsharable grief. Like a devout nun, she worshipped "St. Philip," and firmly believed in his miraculous powers. She fancied that her woes set her apart from common cares, and slowly fell into a dreamy state, professing no interest in any mundane matter, but the art that first attracted Philip. Crayons, bread-crusts, and gray paper became glorified in Laura's eyes; and her one pleasure was to sit pale and still before her easel, day after day, filling her portfolios with the faces he had once admired. Her sisters observed that every Bacchus, Piping Faun, or Dying Gladiator bore some likeness to a comely countenance that heathen god or hero never owned; and seeing this, they privately rejoiced that she had found such solace for her grief.

Mrs. Lord's keen eye had read a certain newly written page in her son's heart,—his first chapter of that romance, begun in Paradise, whose interest never flags, whose beauty never fades, whose end can never come till Love lies dead. With womanly skill she divined the secret, with motherly discretion she counselled patience, and her son accepted her advice, feeling, that, like many a healthful herb, its worth lay in its bitterness.

"Love like a man, John, not like a boy, and learn to know yourself before you take a woman's happiness into your keeping. You and Nan have known each other all your lives; yet, till this last visit, you never thought you loved her more than any other childish friend. It is too soon to say the words so often spoken hastily,—so hard to be recalled. Go back to your work, dear, for another year; think of Nan in the light of this new hope; compare her with comelier, gayer girls; and by absence prove the truth of your belief. Then, if distance only makes her dearer, if time only strengthens your affection, and no doubt of your own worthiness disturbs you, come back and offer her what any woman should be glad to take,—my boy's true heart."

John smiled at the motherly pride of her words, but answered with a wistful look.

"It seems very long to wait, mother. If I could just ask her for a word of hope, I could be very patient then."

"Ah, my dear, better bear one year of impatience now than a lifetime of regret hereafter. Nan is happy; why disturb her by a word which will bring the tender cares and troubles that come soon enough to such conscientious creatures as herself? If she loves you, time will prove it; therefore let the new affection spring and ripen as your early friendship has done, and it will be all the stronger for a summer's growth. Philip was rash, and has to bear his trial now, and Laura shares it with him. Be more generous, John; make *your* trial, bear *your* doubts alone, and give Nan the happiness without the pain. Promise me this, dear,—promise me to hope and wait."

The young man's eye kindled, and in his heart there rose a better chivalry, a truer valor, than any Di's knights had ever known.

"I'll try, mother," was all he said; but she was satisfied, for John seldom tried in vain.

"Oh, girls, how splendid you are! It does my heart good to see my handsome sisters in their best array," cried Nan, one mild October night, as she put the last touches to certain airy raiment fashioned by her own skilful hands, and then fell back to survey the grand effect.

Di and Laura were preparing to assist at an "event of the season," and Nan, with her own locks fallen on her shoulders, for want of sundry combs promoted to her sisters' heads, and her dress in unwonted disorder, for lack of the many pins extracted in exciting crises of the toilet, hovered like an affectionate bee about two very full-blown flowers.

"Laura looks like a cool Undine,[5] with the ivy-wreaths in her shining hair; and Di has illuminated herself to such an extent with those scarlet leaves, that I don't know what great creature she resembles most," said Nan, beaming with sisterly admiration.

"Like Juno, Zenobia, and Cleopatra simmered into one, with a touch of Xantippe by way of spice. But, to my eye, the finest woman of the three is the dishevelled young person embracing the bed-post; for she stays at home herself, and gives her time and taste to making homely people fine,—which is a waste of good material, and an imposition on the public."

As Di spoke, both the fashion-plates looked affectionately at the gray-gowned figure; but, being works of art, they were obliged to nip their feelings in the bud, and reserve their caresses till they returned to common life.

"Put on your bonnet, and we'll leave you at Mrs. Lord's on our way. It will do you good, Nan; and perhaps there may be news from John," added Di, as she bore down upon the door like a man-of-war under full sail.

"Or from Philip," sighed Laura, with a wistful look.

Whereupon Nan persuaded herself that her strong inclination to sit down was owing to want of exercise, and the heaviness of her eyelids a freak of imagination; so, speedily smoothing her ruffled plumage, she ran down to tell her father of the new arrangement.

"Go, my dear, by all means. I shall be writing; and you will be lonely, if you stay. But I must see my girls; for I caught glimpses of certain surprising phantoms flitting by the door."

Nan led the way, and the two pyramids revolved before him with the rigidity of lay-figures, much to the good man's edification; for with his fatherly pleasure there was mingled much mild wonderment at the amplitude of array.

"Yes, I see my geese are really swans, though there is such a cloud between us that I feel a long way off, and hardly know them. But this little daughter is always available, always my 'cricket on the hearth.' "[6]

5. See p. 11, n. 3 (part 1, chap. 1) [Editors].
6. See p. 39, n. 6 (part 1, chap. 4) [Editors].

As he spoke, her father drew Nan closer, kissed her tranquil face, and smiled content.

"Well, if ever I see picters, I see 'em now, and I declare to goodness it's as interestin' as play-actin', every bit. Miss Di, with all them boughs in her head, looks like the Queen of Sheby, when she went a-visitin' What's-his-name; and if Miss Laura a'n't as sweet as a lally-barster figger, I should like to know what is."

In her enthusiasm, Sally gambolled about the girls, flourishing her milk-pan like a modern Miriam[7] about to sound her timbrel for excess of joy.

Laughing merrily, the two Mont Blancs bestowed themselves in the family ark, Nan hopped up beside Patrick, and Solon, roused from his lawful slumbers, morosely trundled them away. But, looking backward with a last "Good night!" Nan saw her father still standing at the door with smiling countenance, and the moonlight falling like a benediction on his silver hair.

"Betsey shall go up the hill with you, my dear, and here's a basket of eggs for your father. Give him my love, and be sure you let me know the next time he is poorly," Mrs. Lord said, when her guest rose to depart, after an hour of pleasant chat.

But Nan never got the gift; for, to her great dismay, her hostess dropped the basket with a crash, and flew across the room to meet a tall shape pausing in the shadow of the door. There was no need to ask who the new-comer was; for, even in his mother's arms, John looked over her shoulder with an eager nod to Nan, who stood among the ruins with never a sign of weariness in her face, nor the memory of a care at her heart,—for they all went out when John came in.

"Now tell us how and why and when you came. Take off your coat, my dear! And here are the old slippers. Why didn't you let us know you were coming so soon? How have you been? and what makes you so late to-night? Betsey, you needn't put on your bonnet. And—oh, my dear boy, *have* you been to supper yet?"

Mrs. Lord was a quiet soul, and her flood of questions was purred softly in her son's ear; for, being a woman, she *must* talk, and, being a mother, *must* pet the one delight of her life, and make a little festival when the lord of the manor came home. A whole drove of fatted calves were metaphorically killed, and a banquet appeared with speed.

John was not one of those romantic heroes who can go through three volumes of hairbreadth escapes without the faintest hint of that blessed institution, dinner; therefore, like "Lady Leatherbridge,"[8] he "partook copiously of everything," while the two women beamed over each mouthful with an interest that enhanced its flavor, and urged upon him cold meat and cheese, pickles and pie, as if dyspepsia and nightmare were among the lost arts.

Then he opened his budget of news and fed *them*.

7. See Exodus 15.20 [*Editors*].
8. Character in John Maddison Morton and Thomas Morton's comedy *All That Glitters Is Not Gold* (1851) [*Editors*].

530 [Louisa May Alcott]

"I was coming next month, according to custom; but Philip fell upon and so tempted me, that I was driven to sacrifice myself to the cause of friendship, and up we came to-night. He would not let me come here till we had seen your father, Nan; for the poor lad was pining for Laura, and hoped his good behavior for the past year would satisfy his judge and secure his recall. We had a fine talk with your father; and, upon my life, Phil seemed to have received the gift of tongues, for he made a most eloquent plea, which I've stored away for future use, I assure you. The dear old gentleman was very kind, told Phil he was satisfied with the success of his probation, that he should see Laura when he liked, and, if all went well, should receive his reward in the spring. It must be a delightful sensation to know you have made a fellow-creature as happy as those words made Phil to-night."

John paused, and looked musingly at the matronly tea-pot, as if he saw a wondrous future in its shine.

Nan twinkled off the drops that rose at the thought of Laura's joy, and said, with grateful warmth,—

"You say nothing of your own share in the making of that happiness, John; but we know it, for Philip has told Laura in his letters all that you have been to him, and I am sure there was other eloquence beside his own before father granted all you say he has. Oh, John, I thank you very much for this!"

Mrs. Lord beamed a whole midsummer of delight upon her son, as she saw the pleasure these words gave him, though he answered simply,—

"I only tried to be a brother to him, Nan; for he has been most kind to me. Yes, I said my little say to-night, and gave my testimony in behalf of the prisoner at the bar, a most merciful judge pronounced his sentence, and he rushed straight to Mrs. Leigh's to tell Laura the blissful news. Just imagine the scene when he appears, and how Di will open her wicked eyes and enjoy the spectacle of the dishevelled lover, the bride-elect's tears, the stir, and the romance of the thing. She'll cry over it to-night, and caricature it to-morrow."

And John led the laugh at the picture he had conjured up, to turn the thoughts of Di's dangerous sister from himself.

At ten Nan retired into the depths of her old bonnet with a far different face from the one she brought out of it, and John, resuming his hat, mounted guard.

"Don't stay late, remember, John!" And in Mrs. Lord's voice there was a warning tone that her son interpreted aright.

"I'll not forget, mother."

And he kept his word; for though Philip's happiness floated temptingly before him, and the little figure at his side had never seemed so dear, he ignored the bland winds, the tender night, and set a seal upon his lips, thinking manfully within himself, "I see many signs of promise in her happy face; but I will wait and hope a little longer for her sake."

"Where is father, Sally?" asked Nan, as that functionary appeared, blinking owlishly, but utterly repudiating the idea of sleep.

"He went down the garding, miss, when the gentlemen cleared, bein' a little flustered by the goin's on. Shall I fetch him in?" asked Sally, as irreverently as if her master were a bag of meal.

"No, we will go ourselves." And slowly the two paced down the leaf-strewn walk.

Fields of yellow grain were waving on the hill-side, and sere corn-blades rustled in the wind, from the orchard came the scent of ripening fruit, and all the garden-plots lay ready to yield up their humble offer-ings to their master's hand. But in the silence of the night a greater Reaper had passed by, gathering in the harvest of a righteous life, and leaving only tender memories for the gleaners who had come so late.

The old man sat in the shadow of the tree his own hands planted; its fruitful boughs shone ruddily, and its leaves still whispered the low lullaby that hushed him to his rest.

"How fast he sleeps! Poor father! I should have come before and made it pleasant for him."

As she spoke, Nan lifted up the head bent down upon his breast, and kissed his pallid cheek.

"Oh, John, this is not sleep!"

"Yes, dear, the happiest he will ever know."

For a moment the shadows flickered over three white faces and the silence deepened solemnly. Then John reverently bore the pale shape in, and Nan dropped down beside it, saying, with a rain of grateful tears,—

"He kissed me when I went, and said a last 'good night!' "

For an hour steps went to and fro about her, many voices whispered near her, and skilful hands touched the beloved clay she held so fast; but one by one the busy feet passed out, one by one the voices died away, and human skill proved vain. Then Mrs. Lord drew the orphan to the shelter of her arms, soothing her with the mute solace of that motherly embrace.

"Nan, Nan! here's Philip! come and see!"

The happy call reëchoed through the house, and Nan sprang up as if her time for grief were past.

"I must tell them. Oh, my poor girls, how will they bear it?—they have known so little sorrow!"

But there was no need for her to speak; other lips had spared her the hard task. For, as she stirred to meet them, a sharp cry rent the air, steps rang upon the stairs, and two wild-eyed creatures came into the hush of that familiar room, for the first time meeting with no welcome from their father's voice.

With one impulse, Di and Laura fled to Nan, and the sisters clung together in a silent embrace, far more eloquent than words. John took his mother by the hand, and led her from the room, closing the door upon the sacredness of grief.

"Yes, we are poorer than we thought; but when everything is settled, we shall get on very well. We can let a part of this great house, and live quietly together until spring; then Laura will be married, and Di can go on their travels with them, as Philip wishes her to do. We shall be cared for; so never fear for us, John."

Nan said this, as her friend parted from her a week later, after the saddest holiday he had ever known.

"And what becomes of you, Nan?" he asked, watching the patient eyes that smiled when others would have wept.

"I shall stay in the dear old house; for no other place would seem like home to me. I shall find some little child to love and care for, and be quite happy till the girls come back and want me."

John nodded wisely, as he listened, and went away prophesying within himself,—

"She shall find something more than a child to love; and, God willing, shall be very happy till the girls come home and—cannot have her."

Nan's plan was carried into effect. Slowly the divided waters closed again, and the three fell back into their old life. But the touch of sorrow drew them closer; and, though invisible, a beloved presence still moved among them, a familiar voice still spoke to them in the silence of their softened hearts. Thus the soil was made ready, and in the depth of winter the good seed was sown, was watered with many tears, and soon sprang up green with the promise of a harvest for their after years.

Di and Laura consoled themselves with their favorite employments, unconscious that Nan was growing paler, thinner, and more silent, as the weeks went by, till one day she dropped quietly before them, and it suddenly became manifest that she was utterly worn out with many cares and the secret suffering of a tender heart bereft of the paternal love which had been its strength and stay.

"I'm only tired, dear girls. Don't be troubled, for I shall be up to-morrow," she said cheerily, as she looked into the anxious faces bending over her.

But the weariness was of many months' growth, and it was weeks before that "tomorrow" came.

Laura installed herself as nurse, and her devotion was repaid four-fold; for, sitting at her sister's bedside, she learned a finer art than that she had left. Her eye grew clear to see the beauty of a self-denying life, and in the depths of Nan's meek nature she found the strong, sweet virtues that made her what she was.

Then remembering that these womanly attributes were a bride's best dowry, Laura gave herself to their attainment, that she might become to another household the blessing Nan had been to her own; and turning from the worship of the goddess Beauty, she gave her hand to that humbler and more human teacher, Duty,—learning her lessons with a willing heart, for Philip's sake.

Di corked her inkstand, locked her bookcase, and went at house-work as if it were a five-barred gate; of course she missed the leap, but scrambled bravely through, and appeared much sobered by the exercise. Sally had departed to sit under a vine and fig-tree of her own, so

Di had undisputed sway; but if dish-pans and dusters had tongues, direful would have been the history of that crusade against frost and fire, indolence and inexperience. But they were dumb, and Di scorned to complain, though her struggles were pathetic to behold, and her sisters went through a series of messes equal to a course of "Prince Benreddin's" peppery tarts.[9] Reality turned Romance out of doors; for, unlike her favorite heroines in satin and tears, or helmet and shield, Di met her fate in a big checked apron and dust-cap, wonderful to see; yet she wielded her broom as stoutly as "Moll Pitcher" shouldered her gun,[1] and marched to her daily martyrdom in the kitchen with as heroic a heart as the "Maid of Orleans"[2] took to her stake.

Mind won the victory over matter in the end, and Di was better all her days for the tribulations and the triumphs of that time; for she drowned her idle fancies in her wash-tub, made burnt-offerings of selfishness and pride, and learned the worth of self-denial, as she sang with happy voice among the pots and kettles of her conquered realm.

Nan thought of John, and in the stillness of her sleepless nights prayed Heaven to keep him safe, and make her worthy to receive and strong enough to bear the blessedness or pain of love.

Snow fell without, and keen winds howled among the leafless elms, but "herbs of grace"[3] were blooming beautifully in the sunshine of sincere endeavor, and this dreariest season proved the most fruitful of the year; for love taught Laura, labor chastened Di, and patience fitted Nan for the blessing of her life.

Nature, that stillest, yet most diligent of housewives, began at last that "spring-cleaning" which she makes so pleasant that none find the heart to grumble as they do when other matrons set their premises a-dust. Her handmaids, wind and rain and sun, swept, washed, and garnished busily, green carpets were unrolled, apple-boughs were hung with draperies of bloom, and dandelions, pet nurslings of the year, came out to play upon the sward.

From the South returned that opera troupe whose manager is never in despair, whose tenor never sulks, whose prima donna never fails, and in the orchard *bonâ fide* matinées were held, to which buttercups and clovers crowded in their prettiest spring hats, and verdant young blades twinkled their dewy lorgnettes, as they bowed and made way for the floral belles.

May was bidding June good-morrow, and the roses were just dreaming that it was almost time to wake, when John came again into the quiet room which now seemed the Eden that contained his Eve. Of course there was a jubilee; but something seemed to have befallen the whole group, for never had they all appeared in such odd frames of

9. See "Prince Bedreddin's Tarts; or, The Consequences of an Indigestion," *United States Magazine and Democratic Review* 16 (1845): 446–55; a comic romance on "the necessity of introducing the study of cookery in the education of women" (455) [*Editors*].
1. Mary Hays McCauly (1754?–1832), the American Revolutionary hero, was known as Molly Pitcher because she carried water to the tired and wounded soldiers at the battle of Monmouth; when her husband was overcome by heat, she manned his cannon through the rest of the battle [*Editors*].
2. Joan of Arc [*Editors*].
3. See Emerson, "Beauty," in *The Conduct of Life* (1860) [*Editors*].

mind. John was restless, and wore an excited look, most unlike his usual serenity of aspect.

Nan the cheerful had fallen into a well of silence and was not to be extracted by any hydraulic power, though she smiled like the June sky over her head. Di's peculiarities were out in full force, and she looked as if she would go off like a torpedo at a touch; but through all her moods there was a half-triumphant, half-remorseful expression in the glance she fixed on John. And Laura, once so silent, now sang like a blackbird, as she flitted to and fro; but her fitful song was always, "Philip, my king."

John felt that there had come a change upon the three, and silently divined whose unconscious influence had wrought the miracle. The embargo was off his tongue, and he was in a fever to ask that question which brings a flutter to the stoutest heart; but though the "man" had come, the "hour" had not. So, by way of steadying his nerves, he paced the room, pausing often to take notes of his companions, and each pause seemed to increase his wonder and content.

He looked at Nan. She was in her usual place, the rigid little chair she loved, because it once was large enough to hold a curly-headed playmate and herself. The old work-basket was at her side, and the battered thimble busily at work; but her lips wore a smile they had never worn before, the color of the unblown roses touched her cheek, and her downcast eyes were full of light.

He looked at Di. The inevitable book was on her knee, but its leaves were uncut; the strong-minded knob of hair still asserted its supremacy aloft upon her head, and the triangular jacket still adorned her shoulders in defiance of all fashions, past, present, or to come; but the expression of her brown countenance had grown softer, her tongue had found a curb, and in her hand lay a card with "Potts, Kettel, & Co." inscribed thereon, which she regarded with never a scornful word for the "Co."

He looked at Laura. She was before her easel, as of old; but the pale nun had given place to a blooming girl, who sang at her work, which was no prim Pallas, but a Clytie turning her human face to meet the sun.[4]

"John, what are you thinking of?"

He stirred as if Di's voice had disturbed his fancy at some pleasant pastime, but answered with his usual sincerity,—

"I was thinking of a certain dear old fairy tale called 'Cinderella.'"

"Oh!" said Di; and her "Oh" was a most impressive monosyllable. "I see the meaning of your smile now; and though the application of the story is not very complimentary to all parties concerned, it is very just and very true."

She paused a moment, then went on with softened voice and earnest mien:—

---

4. The daughter of Triton and playmate of Athena, Pallas was accidentally killed by Athena, who erected a monument (the Palladium) to honor her slain friend. Clytie, a nymph who pines for Apollo (the god of the sun), is transformed into a sunflower whose face follows Apollo's trajectory across the sky [*Editors*].

"You think I am a blind and selfish creature. So I am, but not so blind and selfish as I have been; for many tears have cleared my eyes, and much sincere regret has made me humbler than I was. I have found a better book than any father's library can give me, and I have read it with a love and admiration that grew stronger as I turned the leaves. Henceforth I take it for my guide and gospel, and, looking back upon the selfish and neglectful past, can only say, Heaven bless your dear heart, Nan!"

Laura echoed Di's last words; for, with eyes as full of tenderness, she looked down upon the sister she had lately learned to know, saying, warmly,—

"Yes, 'Heaven bless your dear heart, Nan!' I never can forget all you have been to me; and when I am far away with Philip, there will always be one countenance more beautiful to me than any pictured face I may discover, there will be one place more dear to me than Rome. The face will be yours, Nan,—always so patient, always so serene; and the dearer place will be this home of ours, which you have made so pleasant to me all these years by kindnesses as numberless and noiseless as the drops of dew."

"Dear girls, what have I ever done, that you should love me so?" cried Nan, with happy wonderment, as the tall heads, black and golden, bent to meet the lowly brown one, and her sisters' mute lips answered her.

Then Laura looked up, saying, playfully,—

"Here are the good and wicked sisters;—where shall we find the Prince?"

"There!" cried Di, pointing to John; and then her secret went off like a rocket; for, with her old impetuosity, she said,—

"I have found you out, John, and am ashamed to look you in the face, remembering the past. Girls, you know, when father died, John sent us money, which he said Mr. Owen had long owed us and had paid at last? It was a kind lie, John, and a generous thing to do; for we needed it, but never would have taken it as a gift. I know you meant that we should never find this out; but yesterday I met Mr. Owen returning from the West, and when I thanked him for a piece of justice we had not expected of him, he gruffly told me he had never paid the debt, never meant to pay it, for it was outlawed, and we could not claim a farthing. John, I have laughed at you, thought you stupid, treated you unkindly; but I know you now, and never shall forget the lesson you have taught me. I am proud as Lucifer, but I ask you to forgive me, and I seal my real repentance so—and so."

With tragic countenance, Di rushed across the room, threw both arms about the astonished young man's neck and dropped an energetic kiss upon his cheek. There was a momentary silence; for Di finely illustrated her strong-minded theories by crying like the weakest of her sex. Laura, with "the ruling passion strong in death," still tried to draw, but broke her pet crayon, and endowed her Clytie with a supplementary orb, owing to the dimness of her own. And Nan sat with drooping eyes, that shone upon her work, thinking with tender pride,—

"They know him now, and love him for his generous heart."

Di spoke first, rallying to her colors, though a little daunted by her loss of self-control.

"Don't laugh, John,—I couldn't help it; and don't think I'm not sincere, for I am,—I am; and I will prove it by growing good enough to be your friend. That debt must all be paid, and I shall do it; for I'll turn my books and pen to some account, and write stories full of dear old souls like you and Nan; and some one, I know, will like and buy them, though they are not 'works of Shakespeare.' I've thought of this before, have felt I had the power in me; *now* I have the motive, and *now* I'll do it."

If Di had proposed to translate the Koran, or build a new Saint Paul's, there would have been many chances of success; for, once moved, her will, like a battering-ram, would knock down the obstacles her wits could not surmount. John believed in her most heartily, and showed it, as he answered, looking into her resolute face,—

"I know you will, and yet make us very proud of our 'Chaos,' Di. Let the money lie, and when you have made a fortune, I'll claim it with enormous interest; but, believe me, I feel already doubly repaid by the esteem so generously confessed, so cordially bestowed, and can only say, as we used to years ago,—'Now let's forgive and so forget.'"

But proud Di would not let him add to her obligation, even by returning her impetuous salute; she slipped away, and, shaking off the last drops, answered with a curious mixture of old freedom and new respect,—

"No more sentiment, please, John. We know each other now; and when I find a friend, I never let him go. We have smoked the pipe of peace; so let us go back to our wigwams and bury the feud. Where were we when I lost my head? and what were we talking about?"

"Cinderella and the Prince."

As he spoke, John's eye kindled, and, turning, he looked down at Nan, who sat diligently ornamenting with microscopic stitches a great patch going on, the wrong side out.

"Yes,—so we were; and now taking pussy for the godmother, the characters of the story are well personated,—all but the slipper," said Di, laughing, as she thought of the many times they had played it together years ago.

A sudden movement stirred John's frame, a sudden purpose shone in his countenance, and a sudden change befell his voice, as he said, producing from some hiding-place a little worn-out shoe,—

"I can supply the slipper,—who will try it first?"

Di's black eyes opened wide, as they fell on the familiar object; then her romance-loving nature saw the whole plot of that drama which needs but two to act it. A great delight flushed up into her face, as she promptly took her cue, saying,—

"No need for us to try it, Laura; for it wouldn't fit us, if our feet were as small as Chinese dolls';—our parts are played out; therefore 'Exeunt wicked sisters to the music of the wedding-bells.'" And pouncing upon the dismayed artist, she swept her out and closed the door with a triumphant bang.

John went to Nan, and, dropping on his knee as reverently as the herald of the fairy tale, he asked, still smiling, but with lips grown tremulous,—

"Will Cinderella try the little shoe, and—if it fits—go with the Prince?"

But Nan only covered up her face, weeping happy tears, while all the weary work strayed down upon the floor, as if it knew her holiday had come.

John drew the hidden face still closer, and while she listened to his eager words, Nan heard the beating of the strong man's heart, and knew it spoke the truth.

"Nan, I promised mother to be silent till I was sure I loved you wholly,—sure that the knowledge would give no pain when I should tell it, as I am trying to tell it now. This little shoe has been my comforter through this long year, and I have kept it as other lovers keep their fairer favors. It has been a talisman more eloquent to me than flower or ring; for, when I saw how worn it was, I always thought of the willing feet that came and went for others' comfort all day long; when I saw the little bow you tied, I always thought of the hands so diligent in serving any one who knew a want or felt a pain; and when I recalled the gentle creature who had worn it last, I always saw her patient, tender, and devout,—and tried to grow more worthy of her, that I might one day dare to ask if she would walk beside me all my life and be my 'angel in the house.' Will you, dear? Believe me, you shall never know a weariness or grief I have the power to shield you from."

Then Nan, as simple in her love as in her life, laid her arms about his neck, her happy face against his own, and answered softly,—

"Oh, John, I never can be sad or tired any more!"

L. M. ALCOTT

Tilly's Christmas†

"I'm so glad to-morrow is Christmas, because I'm going to have lots of presents."

"So am I glad, though I don't expect any presents but a pair of mittens."

"And so am I; but I sha'n't have any presents at all."

As the three little girls trudged home from school they said these things, and as Tilly spoke, both the others looked at her with pity and some surprise, for she spoke cheerfully, and they wondered how she

† From *Merry's Museum* 1 (1868): 1–5. This children's story is a precursor of the opening Christmas scenes in *Little Women*.

could be happy when she was so poor she could have no presents on Christmas.

"Don't you wish you could find a purse full of money right here in the path?" said Kate, the child who was going to have "lots of presents."

"Oh, don't I, if I could keep it honestly!" and Tilly's eyes shone at the very thought.

"What would you buy?" asked Bessy, rubbing her cold hands, and longing for her mittens.

"I'd buy a pair of large, warm blankets, a load of wood, a shawl for mother, and a pair of shoes for me; and if there was enough left, I'd give Bessy a new hat, and then she needn't wear Ben's old felt one," answered Tilly.

The girls laughed at that; but Bessy pulled the funny hat over her ears, and said she was much obliged, but she'd rather have candy.

"Let's look, and may be we *can* find a purse. People are always going about with money at Christmas-time, and some one may lose it here," said Kate.

So, as they went along the snowy road, they looked about them, half in earnest, half in fun. Suddenly, Tilly sprang forward, exclaiming,—

"I see it! I've found it!"

The others followed, but all stopped disappointed; for it wasn't a purse, it was only a little bird. It lay upon the snow with its wings spread and feebly fluttering, as if too weak to fly. Its little feet were benumbed with cold; its once bright eyes were dull with pain, and instead of a blithe song, it could only utter a faint chirp, now and then, as if crying for help.

"Nothing but a stupid old robin. How provoking!" cried Kate, sitting down to rest.

"I sha'n't touch it; I found one once, and took care of it, and the ungrateful thing flew away the minute it was well," said Bessy, creeping under Kate's shawl, and putting her hands under her chin to warm them.

"Poor little birdie! How pitiful he looks, and how glad he must be to see some one coming to help him. I'll take him up gently, and carry him home to mother. Don't be frightened, dear, I'm your friend;" and Tilly knelt down in the snow, stretching her hand to the bird with the tenderest pity in her face.

Kate and Bessy laughed.

"Don't stop for that thing; it's getting late and cold: let's go on and look for the purse," they said, moving away.

"You wouldn't leave it to die!" cried Tilly. "I'd rather have the bird than the money; so I sha'n't look any more. The purse wouldn't be mine, and I should only be tempted to keep it; but this poor thing will thank and love me, and I'm *so* glad I came in time."

Gently lifting the bird, Tilly felt its tiny cold claws cling to her hand, and saw its dim eyes brighten as it nestled down with a grateful chirp.

"Now I've got a Christmas present after all," she said, smiling, as they walked on. "I always wanted a bird, and this one will be such a pretty pet for me."

"He'll fly away the first chance he gets, and die anyhow; so you'd better not waste your time over him," said Bessy.

"He can't pay you for taking care of him, and my mother says it isn't worth while to help folks that can't help us," added Kate.

"My mother says, 'Do as you'd be done by;'[1] and I'm sure I'd like any one to help me, if I was dying of cold and hunger. 'Love your neighbor as yourself,'[2] is another of her sayings. This bird is my little neighbor, and I'll love him and care for him, as I often wish our rich neighbor would love and care for us," answered Tilly, breathing her warm breath over the benumbed bird, who looked up at her with confiding eyes, quick to feel and know a friend.

"What a funny girl you are," said Kate, "caring for that silly bird, and talking about loving your neighbor in that sober way. Mr. King don't care a bit for you, and never will, though he knows how poor you are; so I don't think your plan amounts to much."

"I believe it, though; and shall do my part anyway. Good-night. I hope you'll have a merry Christmas, and lots of pretty things," answered Tilly, as they parted.

Her eyes were full, and she felt *so* poor as she went on alone toward the little old house where she lived. It would have been so pleasant to know that she was going to have some of the pretty things all children love to find in their full stockings on Christmas morning. And pleasanter still to have been able to give her mother something nice. So many comforts were needed, and there was no hope of getting them; for they could barely get food and fire.

"Never mind, birdie, we'll make the best of what we have, and be merry in spite of everything. *You* shall have a happy Christmas, anyway; and I know God wont forget us, if every one else does."

She stopped a minute to wipe her eyes, and lean her cheek against the bird's soft breast, finding great comfort in the little creature, though it could only love her, nothing more.

"See, mother, what a nice present I've found," she cried, going in with a cheery face that was like sunshine in the dark room.

"I'm glad of that, deary; for I haven't been able to get my little girl anything but a rosy apple. Poor bird! Give it some of your warm bread and milk."

"Why, mother, what a big bowlful! I'm afraid you gave me all the milk," said Tilly, smiling over the nice steaming supper that stood ready for her.

"I've had plenty, dear. Sit down and dry your wet feet, and put the bird in my basket on this warm flannel."

Tilly peeped into the closet and saw nothing there but dry bread.

"Mother's given me all the milk, and is going without her tea, 'cause

1. Cf. Luke 6.31 [*Editors*].
2. Cf. Mark 12.31 [*Editors*].

she knows I'm hungry. Now I'll surprise her, and she shall have a good supper too. She is going to split wood, and I'll fix it while she's gone."

So Tilly put down the old tea-pot, carefully poured out a part of the milk, and from her pocket produced a great plummy bun, that one of the school-children had given her, and she had saved for her mother. A slice of the dry bread was nicely toasted, and the bit of butter set by for her put on it. When her mother came in there was the table drawn up in a warm place, a hot cup of tea ready, and Tilly and birdie waiting for her.

Such a poor little supper, and yet such a happy one; for love, charity, and contentment were guests there, and that Christmas eve was a blither one than that up at the great house, where lights shone, fires blazed, a great tree glittered, and music sounded, as the children danced and played.

"We must go to bed early, for we've only wood enough to last over to-morrow. I shall be paid for my work the day after, and then we can get some," said Tilly's mother, as they sat by the fire.

"If my bird was only a fairy bird, and would give us three wishes, how nice it would be! Poor dear, he can't give me anything; but it's no matter," answered Tilly, looking at the robin, who lay in the basket with his head under his wing, a mere little feathery bunch.

"He can give you one thing, Tilly,—the pleasure of doing good. That is one of the sweetest things in life; and the poor can enjoy it as well as the rich."

As her mother spoke, with her tired hand softly stroking her little daughter's hair, Tilly suddenly started and pointed to the window, saying, in a frightened whisper,—

"I saw a face,—a man's face, looking in! It's gone now; but I truly saw it."

"Some traveller attracted by the light, perhaps; I'll go and see." And Tilly's mother went to the door.

No one was there. The wind blew cold, the stars shone, the snow lay white on field and wood, and the Christmas moon was glittering in the sky.

"What sort of a face was it?" asked Tilly's mother, coming back.

"A pleasant sort of face, I think; but I was so startled, I don't quite know what it was like. I wish we had a curtain there," said Tilly.

"I like to have our light shine out in the evening; for the road is dark and lonely just here, and the twinkle of our lamp is pleasant to people's eyes as they go by. We can do so little for our neighbors, I am glad to cheer the way for them. Now put these poor old shoes to dry, and go to bed, deary; I'll come soon."

Tilly went, taking her bird with her to sleep in his basket near by, lest he should be lonely in the night.

Soon the little house was dark and still, and no one saw the Christmas spirits at their work that night.

When Tilly opened the door next morning, she gave a loud cry, clapped her hands, and then stood still, quite speechless with wonder and delight. There, before the door, lay a great pile of wood, all ready to burn, a big bundle and a basket, with a lovely nosegay of winter roses, holly, and evergreen tied to the handle.

"Oh, mother, did the fairies do it?" cried Tilly, pale with her happiness, as she seized the basket while her mother took in the bundle.

"Yes, dear, the best and dearest fairy in the world, called 'Charity.' She walks abroad at Christmas-time, does beautiful deeds like this, and does not stay to be thanked," answered her mother with full eyes, as she undid the parcel.

There they were,—the warm, thick blankets, the comfortable shawl, the new shoes, and, best of all, a pretty winter hat for Bessy. The basket was full of good things to eat, and on the flowers lay a paper saying,—

"For the little girl who loves her neighbor as herself."

"Mother, I really think my bird is a fairy bird, and all these splendid things come from him," said Tilly, laughing and crying with joy.

It really did seem so, for, as she spoke, the robin flew to the table, hopped to the nosegay, and perching among the roses, began to chirp with all his little might. The sun streamed in on flowers, bird, and happy child, and no one saw a shadow glide away from the window; no one ever knew that Mr. King had seen and heard the little girls the night before, or dreamed that the rich neighbor had learned a lesson from the poor neighbor.

And Tilly's bird *was* a fairy bird; for by her love and tenderness to the helpless thing, she brought good gifts to herself, happiness to the unknown giver of them, and a faithful little friend who did not fly away, but stayed with her till the snow was gone, making summer for her in the winter-time.

COUSIN TRIBULATION [LOUISA MAY ALCOTT]

Merry's Monthly Chat with His Friends†

A Happy New Year all round, and best wishes to every one, especially those who give old Merry a welcome in his new dress. Those who knew him years ago will, we hope, lend him a hand for old acquaintance sake; and the young folks will find him such a pleasant companion, that they will open their doors to him, and make a little place on their library shelves for Uncle Merry, who, in spite of time, keeps his heart young, and dearly loves the children.

A new friend wishes to be admitted to the circle, and cousin Tribulation shall have a place.

DEAR MERRYS:—As a subject appropriate to the season, I want to tell you about a New Year's breakfast which I had when I was a little

† From *Merry's Museum* 1 (1868): 35–36. This children's story, written shortly before Alcott began to draft *Little Women*, provides an early depiction of the Hummels and the March girls' philanthropic efforts.

girl. What do you think it was? A slice of dry bread and an apple. This is how it happened, and it is a true story, every word.

As we came down to breakfast that morning, with very shiny faces and spandy clean aprons, we found father alone in the dining-room.

"Happy New Year, papa! Where is mother?" we cried.

"A little boy came begging and said they were starving at home, so your mother went to see and—ah, here she is."

As papa spoke, in came mamma, looking very cold, rather sad, and very much excited.

"Children, don't begin till you hear what I have to say," she cried; and we sat staring at her, with the breakfast untouched before us.

"Not far away from here, lies a poor woman with a little new-born baby. Six children are huddled into one bed to keep from freezing, for they have no fire. There is nothing to eat over there; and the oldest boy came here to tell me they were starving this bitter cold day. My little girls, will you give them your breakfast, as a New Year's gift?"

We sat silent a minute, and looked at the nice, hot porridge, creamy milk, and good bread and butter; for we were brought up like English children, and never drank tea or coffee, or ate anything but porridge for our breakfast.

"I wish we'd eaten it up," thought I, for I was rather a selfish child, and very hungry.

"I'm so glad you come before we began," said Nan, cheerfully.

"May I go and help carry it to the poor, little children?" asked Beth, who had the tenderest heart that ever beat under a pinafore.

"I can carry the lassy pot," said little May, proudly giving the thing she loved best.

"And I shall take *all* the porridge," I burst in, heartily ashamed of my first feeling.

"You shall put on your things and help me, and when we come back, we'll get something to eat," said mother, beginning to pile the bread and butter into a big basket.

We were soon ready, and the procession set out. First, papa, with a basket of wood on one arm and coal on the other; mamma next, with a bundle of warm things and the teapot; Nan and I carried a pail of hot porridge between us, and each a pitcher of milk; Beth brought some cold meat. May the "lassy pot," and her old hood and boots; and Betsy, the girl, brought up the rear with a bag of potatoes and some meal.

Fortunately it was early, and we went along back streets, so few people saw us, and no one laughed at the funny party.

What a poor, bare, miserable place it was, to be sure,—broken windows, no fire, ragged clothes, wailing baby, sick mother, and a pile of pale, hungry children cuddled under one quilt, trying to keep warm. How the big eyes stared and the blue lips smiled as we came in!

"Ah, mein Gott! it is the good angels that come to us!" cried the poor woman, with tears of joy.

"Funny angels, in woollen hoods and red mittens," said I; and they all laughed.

Then we fell to work, and in fifteen minutes, it really did seem as if fairies had been at work there. Papa made a splendid fire in the old fireplace and stopped up the broken window with his own hat and coat. Mamma set the shivering children round the fire, and wrapped the poor woman in warm things. Betsey and the rest of us spread the table, and fed the starving little ones.

"Das ist gute!" "Oh, nice!" "Der angel-Kinder!" cried the poor things as they ate and smiled and basked in the warm blaze. We had never been called "angel-children" before, and we thought it very charming, especially I who had often been told I was "a regular Sancho." What fun it was! Papa, with a towel for an apron, fed the smallest child; mamma dressed the poor little new-born baby as tenderly as if it had been her own. Betsey gave the mother gruel and tea, and comforted her with assurance of better days for all. Nan, Lu, Beth, and May flew about among the seven children, talking and laughing and trying to understand their funny, broken English. It was a very happy breakfast, though we didn't get any of it; and when we came away, leaving them all so comfortable, and promising to bring clothes and food by and by, I think there were not in all the city four merrier children than the hungry little girls who gave away their breakfast, and contented themselves with a bit of bread and an apple on New Year's day.

COUSIN TRIBULATION.

CRITICISM

CRITICISM

Nineteenth-Century Reviews

From *The Nation*†

Miss Alcott's new juvenile is an agreeable little story, which is not only very well adapted to the readers for whom it is especially intended, but may also be read with pleasure by older people. The girls depicted all belong to healthy types, and are drawn with a certain cleverness, although there is in the book a lack of what painters call atmosphere—things and people being painted too much in "local colors," and remaining, under all circumstances, somewhat too persistently themselves. The letterpress is accompanied by four or five indifferently executed illustrations, in which Miss May Alcott betrays not only a want of anatomical knowledge, and that indifference to or non-recognition of the subtle beauty of the lines of the female figure which so generally marks women artists, but also the fact that she has not closely studied the text which she illustrates.

From the *Albany Evening Journal*‡

The girls who like good stories have a rich treat in store for them in Miss Louisa M. Alcott's new book, which she calls *Little Women, or Meg., Jo., Beth. and Amy*. In it Miss Alcott displays her great abilities as a good story teller in a remarkable manner, and the book is full of striking and pleasing incidents. We know one "little woman" who laughed over it till she cried, and declares it to be the nicest book she ever read. It will have a great run with the "little women" of America. Roberts Brothers are the publishers.

From *The Youth's Companion**

An exceedingly sprightly, wide-awake volume. Miss Alcott excels in writing for young people, and in this book she gives a very graphic account of a year in the life of four sisters, during the absence of their father, who was a chaplain in the army. The four girls were totally unlike in their character and manners, and the story of their adventures and misadventures is sure to interest the class of readers for whom it is designed.

† From *The Nation*, 22 October 1868, 335.
‡ From *The Albany Evening Journal*, quoted in the *Youth's Companion*, 22 October 1868, 172.
* From *The Youth's Companion*, 29 October 1868, 176.

From the *American Literary Gazette and Publishers' Circular*†

There is plenty of incident and of sprightly conversation in this story, and it cannot fail to please young people, especially the little school girls.

From *Arthur's Illustrated Home Magazine*‡

This is decidedly the best Christmas story which we have seen for a long time. The heroines (there are four of them) are the "little women" of the title, ranging from twelve to sixteen years of age, each interesting in her way, and together enacting the most comical scenes and achieving most gratifying results. The father is in the army, and it is to please him that his daughters make an effort of a year to correct certain faults in their dispositions. In this they are quite successful, and the father comes home, after many sad war scenes, to find his little ones greatly improved in many respects, a comfort and joy to both their parents. The book is most originally written. It never gets commonplace or wearisome, though it deals with the most ordinary everyday life. Parents desiring a Christmas book for a girl from ten to sixteen years, cannot do better than to purchase this.

The writer almost promises, as the story is concluded, to follow this volume with others of similar character. We sincerely hope she will.

From *The Lady's Friend**

A capital story for girls—sure to please them, and sure to influence them for good. "Illustrated by May Alcott:" looks as if one sister had written the book, and another designed for it. We do not know that it is so, but it suggests what a pretty employment for women is this designing for books, and another employment, wood-engraving, both in great and increasing demand. Mothers should encourage in their little ones the amusement of drawing. This early culture of eye and hand may much facilitate the acquisition of a valuable art. It is said, that the best illustrations in the English magazines are the work of young ladies who have adopted drawing as a profession. Some of the most amusing sporting pictures in *Punch*[1] are from the pencil of a lady, and several of our American magazines are illustrated by lady artists.

---

† From the *American Literary Gazette and Publishers' Circular*, 2 November 1868, 16.
‡ From *Arthur's Illustrated Home Magazine*, December 1868, 375.
* From *The Lady's Friend*, December 1868, 857.
1. British illustrated periodical, popular in the nineteenth century [*Editors*].

From *The Ladies' Repository*†

This is a very readable juvenile book. It is beautifully printed and bound, and well illustrated. The story of four lively girls is vivaciously told. But it is not a Christian book. It is religion without spirituality, and salvation without Christ. It is not a good book for the Sunday school library.

From *Godey's Lady's Book*‡

Miss Alcott has written a lively story for the young, as its title indicates. Its heroines are four young girls ranging in ages from twelve to sixteen years. Their experiences and adventures, as narrated by the authoress, make an exceedingly interesting story.

From *The Galaxy**

GOOD books for children are so rare that we welcome one which is so marked an exception to the general rule as Louisa M. Alcott's "Little Women," published, with several good illustrations, by Roberts Brothers. The incidents are those of everyday child-life; the talk is natural and childlike; the narrative is lively, and the moral teaching conveyed in a manner to make a lasting impression on the children who read the book.

From *The Spectator***

Miss Alcott is * * * entirely at home with her subject. She takes us to the other side of the Atlantic, and gives us some pictures from the home life of the four daughters of a family gently bred, but poor, the head of which is fighting in the Northern ranks. These are given with a genuine humour and pathos. The writer's strength is principally given to the portraiture of Jo, *alias* Josephine, a boy, we may call her, who by some misadventure finds himself or herself in the shape of a girl. She is, indeed, a person to be remembered. The character is not an easy one to draw, but it is managed without a shade of vulgarity or rudeness. Jo is always a young lady. The story of how she sells her hair, her one beauty, to have something to send to her father at the camp, and is woman enough to wake in the night and cry over it, is singularly good. Miss Alcott hints that she has something more to tell about her young heroines; by all means let us have it.

---

† From *The Ladies' Repository*, December 1868, 472.
‡ From *Godey's Lady's Book*, December 1868, 546.
* From *The Galaxy*, January 1869, 137.
** From *The Spectator* (London), 13 March 1869, 332.

From *The Commonwealth*†

No reader of Miss Alcott's *Little Women*, published some months since by Roberts Brothers, but will desire to possess the "second part" of the charming sketches which she has just given to the public through the same publishers. The first series was one of the most successful ventures to delineate juvenile womanhood ever attempted; there was a charm and attractiveness, a naturalness and grace, about both characters and narrative, that caused the volume to become a prime favorite with everybody. This issue continues the delight—it is the same fascinating tale, extended without weakening, loading the palate without sickishness. The varied emotions of the young heart are here caught and transfixed so that we almost note the expression of the face upon the printed page. Surely Miss Alcott has wonderful genius for the portraiture, as, years ago, we knew she had for the entertainment, of children.

From *The National Anti-Slavery Standard*‡

The second part of this charming story is out, and all who followed the four sisters and their brother-friend through their childish years, will be eager to follow their various experiences through maidenhood, in college, abroad, and later, in the new home centres they all, save one, helped to make. It would not be fair to those who will read the book, and whose eyes may fall upon this notice to tell any of the story. It is enough to say that the second part perfectly fulfills the promise of the first, and one leaves it with the sincere wish that there were to be a third and a fourth part; indeed he wishes he need never part company, with these earnest, delightful people.

One thought ought to be sown broadcast, till it supplants the heresy that "boys *must* have wild oats to sow," with the truth that purity and virtue are not less the birthright of the brother than of the sister. Of Laurie she says "The poor fellow had temptations enough from without and from within, but he withstood them pretty well,—for much as he valued liberty he valued good faith and confidence more,—so his promise to his grandfather, and his desire to be able to look honestly into the eyes of the women who loved him, and say 'All's well,' kept him safe and steady.

"Very likely some Mrs. Grundy[1] will observe, 'I don't believe it; boys will be boys, young men must sow their wild oats, and women must not expect miracles.' I dare say *you* don't, Mrs. Grundy, but its true, nevertheless. Women work a good many miracles, and I have a persuasion that they may perform even that of raising the standard of manhood by refusing to echo such sayings. Let the boys be boys,—the longer the better—and let the young men sow their wild oats if they

† From *The Commonwealth*, 24 April 1869, 1.
‡ From *The National Anti-Slavery Standard*, 1 May 1869, 3.
1. See p. 207, n. 8 (part 2, chap. 3) [*Editors*].

must,—but mothers, sisters, and friends may help to make the crop a small one, and keep many tares from spoiling the harvest, by believing,—and showing that they believe,—in the possibility of loyalty to the virtues which make men manliest in good women's eyes. If it *is* a feminine delusion, leave us to enjoy it while we may—for without it half the beauty and the romance of life is lost, and sorrowful forebodings would embitter all our hopes of the brave, tender-hearted little lads, who still love their mothers better than themselves, and are not ashamed to own it."[2]

Miss Alcott could crave no richer harvest than that which is sure to come from her sowing. Thousands of young people will read her story of these healthy, happy homes, and their standard of home and happiness must in many cases be raised. This is a blessed thing to accomplish in these days of extravagance, when the highest ideal of home is more and more seldom realized.

From *The Nation*†

Miss Alcott's literary success seems to be very like that achieved by her favorite, "Jo," in this pleasant little story. She has not endangered her popularity by any excessive refinement, nor by too hard a struggle after ideal excellence in her work. Her book is just such a hearty, unaffected, and "genial" description of family life as will appeal to the majority of average readers, and is as certain to attain a kind of success which is apt enough fatally to endanger its author's pretensions to do better work in future. Meantime, "Little Women" is entertaining reading, and, as far as its moral lesson goes, may safely be put into the hands of young people, and will be likely, too, to give their elders a certain pleasure.

From the *Hartford Courant*‡

Simply one of the most charming little books that have fallen into our hands for many a day. There is just enough of sadness in it to make it true to life, while it is so full of honest work and whole-souled fun, paints so lively a picture of a home in which contentment, energy, high spirits and real goodness make up for the lack of money, that it will do good wherever it finds its way. Few will read it without lasting profit.

---

2. See p. 330 (part 2, chap. 18) [*Editors*].
† From *The Nation*, 20 May 1869, 400.
‡ From the *Hartford Courant*, quoted in *Appleton's Journal*, 10 July 1869, 479.

From *Catholic World*†

This is a charming story, full of life, full of fun, full of human nature, and therefore full of interest. The little women play at being pilgrims when they are children, and resolve to be true pilgrims as they grow older. Life to them was earnest; it had its duties, and they did not overlook them or despise them. Directed by the wise teachings and beautiful example of a good mother, they became in the end true and noble women. Make their acquaintance; for Amy will be found delightful, Beth very lovely, Meg beautiful, and Jo splendid; that there is a real Jo somewhere we have not the slightest doubt.

From *Putnam's Magazine*‡

The second part of LOUISA M. ALCOTT'S domestic study, *Little Women; or, Meg, Jo, Beth and May*, is issued by Roberts Brothers, Boston. Miss Alcott's work is always that of a thoughtful and cultured woman, and shows delicate feeling and taste. There is, perhaps, a slight dullness, or lack of interesting action, in the progress of the present tale.

From *The Galaxy**

MISS ALCOTT'S dear "Little Women," Meg, Jo, Beth, and Amy, are already bosom friends to hundreds of other little women, who find in their experiences the very mirror of their own lives. In Part First we find them four natural, sweet girls, with well-defined characters, which, in Part Second, are developed to womanhood through such truthful and lifelike scenes as prove Miss Alcott to be a faithful student of nature. It isn't *à la mode* now to be moved over stories, but we pity the reader who can repress a few tears as well as many hearty laughs over the lives of these little women. We are glad to hear that Miss Alcott is to give us some "Little Men," too. She has struck a vein that will bear working.

From *The Ladies' Repository***

Miss Alcott is a very sprightly writer, fresh and truthful to nature and character, producing books that are sufficiently entertaining to sustain the interest of those who feel they have the time to read them.

---

†   From *Catholic World*, July 1869, 576.
‡   From *Putnam's Magazine*, July 1869, 124.
*   From *The Galaxy*, July 1869, 141.
** From *The Ladies' Repository*, August 1869, 157.

From *Harper's New Monthly Magazine*†

Little Women, Part II., by LOUISE M. ALCOTT, is a rather mature book for the little women, but a capital one for their elders. It is natural, and free from that false sentiment which pervades too much of juvenile literature. Autobiographies, if genuine, are generally interesting, and it is shrewdly suspected that Joe's experience as an author photographs some of Miss Alcott's own literary mistakes and misadventures. But do not her children grow rather rapidly? They are little children in Part First, at the breaking out of the civil war. They are married, settled, and with two or three children of their own before they get through Part Second.

From the *London Graphic*‡

The critic of the London *Graphic* calls Miss Alcott's "Little Women" "an excellent description of American family life among the poorer gentry."

---

† From *Harper's New Monthly Magazine*, August 1869, 455–56.
‡ From the *London Graphic*, quoted in *Appleton's Journal*, 28 January 1871, 119.

Modern Critical Views

ELIZABETH VINCENT

Subversive Miss Alcott†

It is a humorous reflection that Louisa M. Alcott did not like girls. When her publishers asked her to write a book for girls she complied reluctantly, with more of an eye to the price than the pleasure, though of course she did not slight her duty to be a wholesome influence. "I plod away, though I don't like this sort of thing. I never liked girls or knew many," she wrote. Whereupon Little Women became a best seller before it was a week off the press, and a classic before its second half was written. When the second half did come out, and it appeared that Jo had turned down Laurie, and that the minx Amy had caught him on the rebound, there was such great excitement that several young persons are said to have gone to bed with a fever. Miss Alcott feared at one time that her book contained too much "lovering," but this the young folks denied, and even their elders did not feel called upon to disapprove. "No mother fears," wrote a feminine critic, "that Miss Alcott's books will brush the bloom of modesty from the faces of her young men or maidens,"—an assertion anyone will support who has read Professor Bhaer's proposal to Jo under the umbrella, or Laurie's to Amy in the rowboat.

"'How well we pull together, don't we?' said Amy . . .

"'So well, that I wish we might always pull in the same boat. Will you, Amy?' very tenderly.

"'Yes, Laurie!' very low.

"Then they both stopped rowing, and unconsciously added a pretty little tableau of human love and happiness to the dissolving views reflected in the lake."

Now there is a young girl—I might almost say a young woman—of thirteen among my acquaintance, who is not by any means old-fashioned. She dances whatever is latest and talks the fashionable divorce and likes to get sermons over the radio because they sound so silly. Yet I found her once sunk in a chair, her long legs bridging the gap to a table, with an ancient battered Little Women in her lap.

"I read it every year," she said.

There you are. Miss Alcott didn't like girls, but she wrote a book that was immediately read—laughed and cried over is the proper way

† From the *New Republic*, 22 October 1924, 204.

of saying it, I believe—by every little girl in America. Our insurgent age has discarded nineteenth century New England with a great fanfare, yet here is our hopeful youth addicted to the double distilled essence of New England, to the very thing we were at such great pains to get rid of for their sakes. The fact is that Little Women and Little Men, those late classics, are classics still. "They touch," Miss Cheney says, "the universal heart deeply."[1] And so it would appear, for here are Little, Brown and Company bringing out a brand new edition.

The question is Why? Why do people republish these books? Why do small girls with the freedom of Sheik fiction and the films[2] read them? Take Little Women. The characters are perfectly categorical— each patterned on a simple formula like this: Mr. March, father, philosopher and friend; Mrs. March, Mother and All That Stands For; Meg, fastidious womanliness; Amy, a perfect little lady; Beth, angel in the house. Even Jo is not the person to cut much ice with the current 'teens. At least you'd not think so. She is a tom-boy according to her lights:

"'We are a pretty jolly set, as Jo would say,' said Meg.

"'Jo does use such slangwords!' observed Amy . . . Jo immediately sat up, put her hands in her pockets and began to whistle,"—not such a tomboy as would take the breath of a first-team forward. And look at Meg married to her steadfast John and safely on the shelf,—"the sort of shelf on which young wives and mothers may consent to be laid, safe from the restless fret and fever of the world . . . and learning, as Meg learned, that a woman's happiest kingdom is her home, her highest honor the art of ruling it,"—a fine popular doctrine for the age of equality and economic independence.

The so-called plot holds few apparent thrills for a generation raised on Fairbanks.[3] Miss Alcott herself admitted it was not "sensational," and at that she exaggerated. Except for the uncomplicated chronicle of their loves and marriages the Marches have really nothing to offer in the way of plot at all. The structure of the book is largely segmental, each chapter a neatly rounded episode, loaded with its lesson, and capped with repentance and tears and a few words of comfort from Mrs. March.

And yet—and yet: one does have to admit that these impossible Marches are real people. The children who get so absorbed in them are not wrong in finding them alive and true. The only wonder is that any child raised this side of 1900 has been able to put up with the things they do and the things they say, these all too real people. Of course the Marches were real people. Except for the trussing up of episodes and the simplification of character which passes for Miss Al-

---

1. Cf. Cheney, 190 [Editors].
2. Edith Maude Hull's The Sheik (1919) appeared on lists of American best-sellers through 1922. The motion picture starring Rudolph Valentino came out in 1921 and caused women to faint in the aisles. Often taking place in a desert, a jungle, or some other exotic setting, "Sheik fiction" is characterized by romance and sensationalism [Editors].
3. Douglas Fairbanks, the idealized image of the American male in early motion pictures, was the star of numerous adventure films, including The Three Musketeers (1921) and Robin Hood (1922) [Editors].

cott's art, she has merely reported her own family. The searching of consciences and amateur theatricals and domestic trials which went on in the March family all happened to the Alcotts. It is not the people in the book who are unreal, but the people who lived. The Alcott's flourished on transcendental truth. But the truth of their day, the simple faith of our fathers, we have seen thinned and worn, until it has become the bandwagon drool and pulpit hypocrisy of ours. Can this be what our modern small daughters like?

The sort of thing that used to be said was that Miss Alcott's books have been a greater force for good among the girls and boys of this country than any other one etc., etc. Then rose a Modern—from New England, too—who cried out that Miss Alcott's books have done incalculable harm in all the nurseries of the land by implanting in young minds a false and priggish picture. I think Miss Alcott, with her conscientious little morals, turned over in her grave at that point. But I confess that that statement holds the best explanation I can see of why little girls still read her books. They are bad for them of course. Could any but pernicious influence hold such a fascination for so long? The fact is that little girls have a natural depraved taste for moralizing. They like to see virtue rewarded and evil punished. They like good resolutions. They like tears and quarrels and loving reconciliations. They believe in the ultimate triumph of good, in moral justice, and honeymoons in Valarosa. And Miss Alcott panders to these passions!

Let modern mothers bob their hair and talk the neopsychic talk. Let children spell by drawing rabbits; let them study the city water works. Yet it will not avail. For unless we take to censorship to protect them against the subversions of the past, little girls will read Little Women still.

ANNE DALKE

"The House-Band": The Education of Men in
Little Women†

Seven years ago, Nina Auerbach elevated *Little Women* from children's classic to a place on the college syllabus. She did so by re-visioning the book, by instructing us, as we in turn gleefully instructed our students, in the "plenitude" and "primacy" of the sisterhood set forth in the novel's first half. The "world of the March girls," Auerbach told us, is "rich enough to complete itself" (*Communities* 58, 61, 55).

In Auerbach's vision of the fiction, the happy marriages at the end of *Little Women* are irrelevant. Auerbach not only exalted the novel's

---

† From *College English* 47 (1985): 571–78. Copyright © 1985 by The National Council of Teachers of English. Reprinted by permission of The National Council of Teachers of English. Page references to this Norton Critical Edition are given in brackets following Dalke's original citations.

first half at the expense of the second, but offered an alternative ending. She described Alcott's article on "Happy Women," published in
The New York Ledger at the time she was writing the book, as offering
"the idyll lying behind Marmee's new wives' training school: a community of new women, whose sisterhood is not an apprenticeship making
them worthy of appropriation by father-husbands, but a bond whose
value is itself" (64).

Auerbach's reading of *Little Women* excited me when it first appeared, and continues to do so today. But I have come increasingly to
feel that it is false to Alcott's intention and achievement. To re-write
the novel into a forum for the autonomous development of women is,
I think, to do violence to Alcott's fiction. To embrace only half the
book, and to dismiss the rest as compromised, is to misread the whole.
Like *Pilgrim's Process*, on which she drew so heavily, Alcott's novel offers a "stereoscopic" view of two journeys: the first individual and the
second communal (cf. Frye 97). The second journey is the appropriate
culmination of the first. Auerbach observes that the "March girls had
to relinquish the art they all aspired toward" (66); Judith Fetterley has
charted in some detail the subjugation of the artistic ambitions of both
Jo and Amy into family service. But at the same time that Alcott creates, in the novel's second half, a balance for the female ambitions expressed and sought after in the first, she gives the males in the family
the opportunity to participate in a new, expanded family life.

The strength of the novel lies in the combination of its parts. In the
first section, Alcott acknowledges "the opportunity her all-girl family
had provided for her own development" (Heilbrun, "Influence" 22). In
the novel's second half, she envisions the entire March family, most
insistently including the men who are incorporated into it, in a non-
patriarchal arrangement.

The fascination *Little Women* holds for me now lies less in Jo's ease
in adopting male manners and behavior (cf. Heilbrun, "Influence" 23),
than in the facility with which her whole family restructures itself on
a female pattern. Auerbach argues that the sisterhood of the March
girls is "dissolved by marriage" (68). But the book does not fall apart
when Meg, Jo, Beth and Amy leave the family. It reaches a climax
when Father, John, Friedrich and Laurie join their ranks. Ultimately,
the novel celebrates less Jo's reinvention of girlhood (Heilbrun, *Reinventing* 212) than the opportunities provided by the strength and
stability of the March matriarchy for reinventing manhood. The sons,
husbands, and fathers of Alcott's fiction are reeducated by the women
they love. They slowly discover new ways of being men: affectionate,
expressive and nurturing (cf. Rich 209–211). With the help of their
female associates, they rework masculinity on a female model. Love
becomes, by the novel's end, not the power play described by Fetterley,
but rather an act of service performed mutually by both sexes.

In her selective adaptation of a preface from John Bunyan, Alcott
makes it very clear that her primary focus is on the pilgrimage to be
undertaken by the "young damsels" in her story. The "tripping maids"
are aided in their stumbling progress by a number of older, seemingly

wiser, males (Fetterley 381–382; Spacks 95–101). Certainly the March girls' initial resolve to play Pilgrim's Progress in earnest is prompted by a desire to please their absent parent with their improvement, or, as Marmee says, to "see how far you can get before Father comes home" (*Little Women* 11) [18].

The girls are assisted in that attempt by a male closer to their own age, whom they acknowledge as "a remarkable boy" (278) [235], and whom they use as a standard to measure both other young men and their own behavior. Vain Meg first realizes the extent of her misconduct when she meets Laurie's disapproval in "Vanity Fair" (87) [79]; angry Jo's ill temper is certified when "even good-natured Laurie had a quarrel with her" (104) [94]; shy Beth [the reference here is actually to Amy] is offered Laurie as a model of accomplishment without conceit (67) [61]; and selfish Amy is saved from thin ice by his self-possession, from dull Aunt March by his powers of entertainment, and from an inappropriate marriage by his reproof (74, 180, 397) [66, 152, 318].

Laurie offers the girls reward as well as censure. His home becomes the "Palace Beautiful" for them all: it allows Meg the pleasures of a garden, Jo a library, Beth a piano, and Amy art. If his house is a metaphoric heavenly retreat, Laurie himself fulfills the role of substitute deity. Jo, for example, finds him a great comfort when " 'God seems so far away I can't find Him' " (173) [147].

Laurie satisfies more mundane needs as well. His sociability saves a dismal dinner party, and his appetite a poorly attended one. He is bodyguard to the girls in their mother's absence; his initiative brings her back. He names Meg's son, and even after he leaves for college, provides, with his "weekly visit . . . an important event in their quiet lives" (229) [195].

Auerbach and Carolyn Heilbrun have both made much of Laurie's initial, wistful solicitation of entrance into the happy community of women next door (*Communities* 57–58; "Influence" 22). But both critics dismiss Laurie, along with all the other men in the novel, as essentially "peripheral" to the rich March household (Auerbach, Afterword 463). Neither acknowledges that self-fulfillment, in Alcott's world, is discovered in relations with others, and that Laurie's eventual admission into the closed circle of women is testimony both to their achievement and to his own.

The relationship between Laurie and the March girl is very much a reciprocal one. He helps them in their journey toward self-improvement, but needs and receives instruction himself in return. Anne Hollander is right to identify Laurie "as a student of the March way of life" (34). Indeed, a major subplot to the story of the four pilgrims' progresses is the *bildungsroman* of their "fifth sister" (Hoyt; cf. Auerbach, *Communities* 60), a young man who goes on a journey much longer and harder than the ones they must undertake, a journey which is incomplete even when the young women exult, at Harvest Time, over their own accomplishments.

Laurie's pilgrimage differs from that of his neighbors, and is correspondingly longer, both because he is wealthy and because he is male.

Jo worries about the temptations and amusements usually associated with affluence: billiards, gambling, and drink (140) [123]. But Laurie's worst failing is passivity. Poverty provides for the Marches an impetus to occupation; for Laurie, prosperity has the opposite effect.

Like each of his neighbors, Laurie has a central fault. Although his solitary state is soon remedied by his inclusion in the activities of the March family, it requires the length of the novel for him to conquer his indolence. The juxtaposition of the single male against the group of women is succeeded by the juxtaposition of his laziness with their vigor, and that juxtaposition lasts.

On his first encounter with the Marches, Laurie finds that "their busy, lively ways made him ashamed of the indolent life he led" (55) [52]. Ashamed, perhaps, but not shamed into action. Months after he has made friends with the girls, he lounges "luxuriously swinging to and fro in his hammock . . . wondering what his neighbors were about, but too lazy to go and find out" (130) [114]. When he does pursue them on an expedition, he is admitted to their group only on the condition that he " 'do something; it's against the rules to be idle' " (131) [116]. Although full of "gratitude for the favor of admission into the 'Busy Bee Society' " (132) [116], Laurie's employment there, as subsequently in college, is only intermittent; he does not learn to emulate the directed energy of the sisters. His visit to Amy, five years later in Nice, is chronicled in a chapter entitled "Lazy Laurence," in which he lives up to his name: "Laurie made no effort of any kind, but just let himself drift along as comfortably as possible" (374) [314].

Not until Amy reproves him directly, and harshly, for his "dreadful . . . indolence" (376) [316] does Laurie consider reform. It takes Amy's denunciation to provoke him to activity: " 'you are faulty . . . and miserable. . . . you have grown abominably lazy. . . . and waste time. . . . you can do nothing but dawdle' " (380–381) [319–20]. When Laurie departs to prove Amy wrong, he addresses her as his "dear Mentor," and signs himself off as "Telemachus" (385) [323]. The appellations he chooses are fitting. Amy's role is not unlike that of Athena, who in *The Odyssey* assumes the disguise of Mentor and encourages Telemachus to action. The journey of the nineteenth-century Telemachus leads him not in search of a father figure, however, but back to the instructor who with her scolding has proved herself an appropriate match for the erring boy.

Laurie has been posited as a potential suitor for each of the March sisters in turn, and till now found wanting in each case (Auerbach, *Communities* 61). His final mating with Amy is apt because they can learn the most from each other. Fetterley describes the marriages in the novel as "excessively hierarchical" (381–382), but the term is inappropriate as a description of Laurie and Amy's match. She is his best educator, as he is hers. Their bethrothal takes place as they are rowing together, and they pledge in their marriage to always "pull in the same boat" (403) [336].

Amy claims that Laurie "made a princess of me, as the king does the beggar-maid" (429) [357], but his transformation by marriage is even greater than hers. Like Jo, he finds that his heart "was asleep til the fairy prince came through the wood, and waked it up" (445) [369]. It is Amy who exhorts Laurie to "wake up and be a man" (384) [322], and he himself speaks with a great deal of decision and energy about his intentions to act on his newly acquired "manly" virtues (395) [330]: " 'I'm going into business with a devotion . . . and prove . . . that I'm not spoiled. I need something of the sort to keep me steady. I'm tired of dawdling, and mean to work like a man' " (426) [354–55].

But we never see a demonstration of such work. For marriage to Amy liberates Laurie into another form of activity entirely, not working like a man, but loving like a woman. He does not appear at the office, for example, but instead is deeply involved in family matters: "Laurie devoted himself to the little ones, rode his small daughter in a bushel basket, took Daisy up among the birds' nests, and kept adventurous Rob from breaking his neck" (455) [377].

Laurie is too vigorously engaged in such romps to take part in the final summing up of the novel, in which his wife and her sisters compare their earlier "castles in the air" with their present lives. But Amy reports that she has " 'Laurie to take more than half of every burden. . . . He . . . is so sweet and patient with me, so devoted to Beth, and such a stay and comfort to me always that I can't love him enough' " (458) [380]. The comparison with Laurie's early hopes to " 'just enjoy myself and live for what I like' " (134) [118] is here implicit.

Laurie had been right to predict that his arrival, in the married life that constitutes the this-worldly paradise of the novel's conclusion, would be delayed: " 'I shall have to do a good deal of traveling, before I come in sight of your celestial city' " (133) [117]. But he eventually earns his place in the March family, a place denied him at first because of his wealth, his indolence, and his sex. With Amy's help, he learns to put the first to good use, to overcome the second, and to subjugate the customary prerogatives of the third to those of the female.

Ironically, his masculinity first attracted Jo to Laurie. She gave him a nickname more masculine than the one he gave himself, and solicited his entrance into the "P.C." (a "ladies' club" in which the March girls assumed male personae), because he would restrain their sentimentality (99) [90]. But the primary lesson that his neighbors have to teach Laurie is the same one which Jo learns: the value of female occupation, the worth not only to others, but to the self, of the traditional female virtue of "taking care."

Laurie is taught by the March girls how to respond to women, children, and to other men. Fetterley emphasizes Alcott's portrayal of "the love that exists between women" (379); such love also serves as a model for male relationships. The interaction of Laurie and his grandfather, for example, is carefully coached by Jo. She suggests a course of apology and reconciliation when the two strong-willed men quarrel (*Little Women* 198–203) [167–171]. When she herself refuses Laurie's offer of marriage, she prepares Mr. Laurence to be kind to his grandson. Her preparation enables the older man to handle the situation in a motherly mode: " 'I can't stand this,' muttered the old gentleman. Up he got, groped his way to the piano, laid a kind hand on either of the broad shoulders, and said, as gently as a woman, 'I know, my boy, I know' " (344) [288].

As the result of such instruction, Laurie acknowledges that he owes Jo "for a part of my education" (429) [356]. But his finishing comes from Amy. The structure of the final quarter of the novel, in which chapters alternate between Jo's experience at home and Laurie's abroad, suggests that the two erstwhile companions are simultaneously undergoing similar learning experiences, for which they will receive similar rewards. Jo discovers in Beth's example the "solace of a belief in . . . love," and acknowledges finally the concomitant "poverty of other desires" (391) [327]. With less pathos, Laurie learns the same lessons from Amy. She teaches him the emptiness of ambition; he comes to accept not the limitations of the conventional act of nurturing, but rather the limits of male autonomy and striving.

Laurie is not the only man in the novel to move past the egocentric self to an appreciation of, and involvement in, the family. All of the men in the novel long for home, all of them solicit access to the circle formed by the March women. Compelled to express such desires, each of them thinks himself "unmanly" for doing so. Laurie is visibly emotional in his plea for admission to the March family circle: his voice "*would* get choky now and then in spite of manful efforts to keep it steady," while his lashes were "still wet with the bitter drop or two her hardness of heart had wrung from them" (339–341) [284–86]. Professor Bhaer's tears come when Jo gives him a different answer, but that experience of happiness is preceded by one of solitary gloom: "he sat long before his fire, with the tired look on his face and . . . homesickness lying heavy at his heart. . . . He did his best and did it manfully, but . . . [didn't find] a pair of rampant boys, a pipe, or even the divine Plato . . . a satisfactory substitute for wife and child and home" (337) [282–83].

Admission to the family group comes easier to John Brooke than to Laurie or the Professor, but even John shows himself a "domestic man" (363) [305] at a time when the March girls are dreaming dreams which are explicitly not home-bound. When Meg teases him, "Poor Mr. Brooke looked as if his lovely castle in the air was tumbling about his ears" (214) [180].

The girls' father, like their prospective husbands, is distinguished less for activity in the outside world than for his role within the family. Father spends his service in Washington longing to return home. Once arrived, he resumes the function of "household conscience, anchor and comforter . . . in the truest sense of those sacred words, husband and father" (223) [190]. His position in the family, like the "unmanful" roles assumed by his sons-in-law, is emphatically female: "Like bees swarming after their queen, mother and daughters hovered about Mr. March" (211) [177].

The men in Alcott's novel participate little more than the women in the world outside of the family. All significant activity is located in the home. Auerbach is mistaken in her conclusion that the March girls

are unable to accomplish "the final amalgamation of their matriar-
chate with the history it tries to subdue. . . . history remains where we
found it at the beginning of *Little Women*: 'far away, where the fighting was' " (*Communities* 73). Rather history has been refocused, by Alcott, on the family. Like the homes described by Jane Tompkins in her
discussion of *Uncle Tom's Cabin*, the household in *Little Women* is
"the center of all meaningful activity . . . physical and spiritual, economic and moral, whose influence spreads out in ever-widening
circles." The family offers a blueprint for revising the world, for
reforming the human race (95–98). Alcott offers the March home as
an alternative to the fashionable and pugnacious activity conducted
outside its boundaries.

Men are not incidental to this endeavor (cf. Tompkins 98 and
Marsella 9, 130). Both they and the women spend the novel learning
to understand the central role of the male in this new scheme. Boys
are "almost unknown creatures" to the March girls at the novel's beginning (28) [31], and the young women are perfectly satisfied not to
include men in their group. Meg reports, in fact, that she is " 'rather
glad I hadn't any wild brothers to do wicked things and disgrace the
family' " (40) [41]. But just as Laurie must learn not to be wild and
wicked, his neighbors must learn that men have the capacity for fulfilling other functions. The March family is slowly educated on the necessity of including men in their circle, slowly taught that marriage will
not, as Jo claims, "make a hole in the family" (191) [161], but rather
fill in the gaps which already exist. Meg is only the first to discover the
"treasuries of . . . mutual helpfulness. . . . walking side by side, through
fair and stormy weather, with a faithful friend, who is, in the true
sense of the good old Saxon word, the 'house band' " (373) [313].

The stewards who join the group bring with them wisdom and
wealth, but most emphatically a refusal to abide by the traditional separation between love and work. There is no "Two-Person Career," no
"Dual-Career Family" in *Little Women* (cf. Heilbrun, *Reinventing*
193). The novel offers instead a family unit in which husband and
wife share the economic and, more significantly, the emotional re-
sponsibilities of group existence. John, Friedrich and Laurie all learn
to participate in the pattern established by Father March. As Marmee
tells Meg,

> "don't shut [your husband] out of the nursery, but teach him how
> to help in it. His place is there as well as yours, and the children
> need him; let him feel that he has his part to do . . . . and it will be
> better for you all. . . . That is the secret of our home happiness:
> [Father] does not let business wean him from the little cares and
> duties that affect us all. . . . Each do our part alone in many
> things, but at home we work together, always." (366) [307]

Marmee's plea for the equal involvement of both partners in the demands of family life is put into increasingly successful practice by
each of her sons-in-law in turn. Meg is house-bound while John goes
out to work. Laurie and Amy have a more equitable arrangement: both

stay at home. But it is Jo's marriage which is most explicitly made over on the matriarchal pattern. She chooses the life work for herself and her partner, and provides the setting for their new school. She and her professor enlarge the family beyond the ties of blood, putting women's traditional strengths to work in an arena wider than that of the immediate household. As Jo says, " 'no one can say I'm out of my sphere now, for women's special mission is supposed to be drying tears and bearing burdens. I'm to carry my share, Friedrich, and help to earn the home' " (449) [372]. He learns to carry his share as well, in making that home.

As the male characters enter the family, they are successively remodeled on the female mode. The family which incorporates them is not dead (cf. Auerbach, Afterword 466–467), but thriving, growing, and ever more influential. The "wholehearted antagonism to traditional family life" that so many feminist critics have observed in *Little Women* (Auerbach, "Feminist Criticism" 267) thus finds its locus in the role men are taught to play in the novel.

Little Women is the first book in a trilogy. The next two novels both focus clearly on the education of men. What is subplot in *Little Women* becomes main plot in *Little Men* and *Jo's Boys*: the need to reeducate young men for a new world, one that demands their active participation in those activities conventionally reserved for women. Heilbrun suggests that Jo takes in motherless boys because she has no interest in insignificant girls (*Reinventing* 190). I would suggest instead that she does so as a vehement assertion of Alcott's belief in the salvation available to males through the power of motherly love. Jo does not need to make fighting and business accessible to women. Her real work involves remaking men on a female pattern, by granting them admission to female activities, and by teaching them the values of nurturance.

WORKS CITED

Alcott, Louisa May. *Little Women*. 1868–69. New York: Bantam, 1983.
Auerbach, Nina. Afterword. *Little Women*. By Louisa May Alcott. New York: Bantam, 1983. 461–470.
———. *Communities of Women: An Idea in Fiction*. Cambridge: Harvard UP, 1978.
———. "Feminist Criticism Reviewed." *Gender and Literary Voice: Women and Literature* 1 n.s. (1980): 258–268.
Fetterley, Judith. "*Little Women*: Alcott's Civil War." *Feminist Studies* 5 (1979): 369–383.
Frye, Roland Mushat. *God, Man and Satan: Patterns of Christian Thought and Life in Paradise Lost, Pilgrim's Progress and the Great Theologians*. Princeton: Princeton UP, 1960.
Heilbrun, Carolyn. "The Influence of *Little Women*." *Women, the Arts, and the 1920s in Paris and New York*. Ed. Kenneth W. Wheeler and Virginia Lee Lussier. New Brunswick, NJ: Transaction Books, 1982. 20–26.
———. *Reinventing Womanhood*. New York: Norton, 1979.
Hollander, Anne. "Reflections on *Little Women*." *Children's Literature* 9 (1981): 28–39.
Hoyt, Sarita. "The Fifth Sister." Unpublished essay, English 015.01, Bryn Mawr College, Fall 1983.
Marsella, Joy. *The Promise of Destiny: Children and Women in the Short Stories of Louisa May Alcott*. Westport, CT: Greenwood, 1983.
Rich, Adrienne. *Of Woman Born: Motherhood as Experience and Institution*. New York: Bantam, 1976.
Spacks, Patricia Meyer. *The Female Imagination*. New York: Knopf, 1975.
Tompkins, Jane P. "Sentimental Power: *Uncle Tom's Cabin* and the Politics of Literary History." *Glyph* 8 (1981): 79–102.

ANGELA M. ESTES AND
KATHLEEN MARGARET LANT

Dismembering the Text: The Horror of
Louisa May Alcott's Little Women†

Me from Myself—to banish—
Had I Art—
Impregnable my Fortress
Unto All Heart—

But since myself—assault Me—
How have I peace
Except by subjugating
Consciousness?

And since We're mutual Monarch
How this be
Except by Abdication—
Me—of Me?
                              —Emily Dickinson

On the floor of an attic room slumps a thirty-year-old woman, strip-ping off her disguise as a submissive seventeen-year-old governess; re-moving her false teeth, she takes another swig from a flask and plots a scheme to undermine and conquer an entire family. In another room sits a young girl, laboriously—albeit resentfully—stitching together small remnants of fabric as she learns simultaneously the practical art of patchwork and the womanly virtues of patience, perseverance, and restraint. What possible connection could exist between these two women?

These two scenes—the first from Louisa May Alcott's thriller "Behind a Mask" and the second from her children's story "Patty's Patchwork"—exemplify the apparent extremes that characterize the heroines and plots of Alcott's works. Traditionally, Alcott has been con-sidered a writer of inoffensive, sometimes mildly rebellious children's fiction, but the discovery and republication in 1975 and 1976[1] of Al-cott's anonymous and pseudonymous adult thrillers (first published between 1863 and 1869) and the emergence of more thoughtful re-cent critical approaches to her children's stories have raised significant questions for Alcott scholars: How is the Alcott canon to be reenvi-sioned to explain the existence of her hidden fictional efforts? How do

† From Children's Literature 17 (1989): 98–123. [Epigraph reprinted by permission of the publishers and the Trustees of Amherst College from The Poems of Emily Dickinson, edited by Thomas H. Johnson, Cambridge, Mass.: The Belknap Press of Harvard University Press, copyright 1951, © 1955, 1979, 1983 by the President and Fellows of Harvard College. By permission also of Little, Brown and Company, from The Complete Poems of Emily Dickin-son, edited by Thomas H. Johnson, copyright 1929 by Martha Dickinson Bianchi; copyright © renewed 1957 by Mary L. Hampson (Estes and Lant's acknowledgment).] Page references to this Norton Critical Edition are given in brackets following Estes and Lant's original cita-tions. Footnotes are the authors' except where followed by [Editors].
1. Alcott's adult thrillers were discovered by Madeleine Stern and Leona Rostenberg and pub-lished by Stern in Behind a Mask (1975) and Plots and Counterplots (1976).

we account for Alcott's fascination with the lurid, the wild, the unacceptable and untrammeled heroines of the thrillers when we remember the little girls—at least superficially docile—of the children's short stories and the ultimately tamed Jo of *Little Women?* And, most importantly, how do these thrillers, characterized by violence, deceit, infidelity, and licentiousness of every kind imaginable, reshape or enrich our understanding of Alcott's classic children's novel *Little Women* (1868)?[2]

I

The seemingly contradictory aspects of Alcott's fiction can be better understood when we place her in a personal and historical context. She was intimately involved in the transcendental circle of her father and his friends, the literati of Concord, including, of course, its leader Ralph Waldo Emerson. Alcott embraced the transcendental ideals of self-expression, self-reliance, and self-exploration as espoused by both Emerson and her father, Bronson Alcott. In a journal entry (27 April 1882), Alcott affirms Emerson's pervasive influence on her life and thought: "Mr. Emerson died at 9 P.M. suddenly. Our best and greatest American gone. The nearest and dearest friend Father has ever had, and the man who has helped me most by his life, his books, his society. I can never tell all he has been to me . . . his essays on Self-reliance, Character, Compensation, Love, and Friendship helped me to understand myself and life, and God and Nature" (Cheney 345). Alcott insisted, moreover, that the self-reliance and self-awareness so vaunted by the transcendentalists be extended to women as well as men. In a letter to Maria S. Porter, she asserts woman's right to an identity and a life of her own by calling for an exploration and redefinition of "woman's sphere": "In future let woman do whatever she can do; let men place no more impediments in the way; above all things let's have fair play,—let *simple justice* be done, say I. Let us hear no more of 'woman's sphere' either from our wise (?) legislators beneath the gilded dome, or from our clergymen in their pulpits." Alcott goes

---

2. *Little Women* has been both assaulted and acclaimed by contemporary critics. Eugenia Kaledin writes that Alcott's "acceptance of the creed of womanly self-denial as much as her willingness to buy success by catering to middle class ideals aborted the promise of her art and led her to betray her most deeply felt values" (251).

Most recent critics of *Little Women*, however, have found more to admire in Alcott's fiction. Their critical responses to *Little Women* have generally been of two kinds. Some emphasize the independence, autonomy, and rebelliousness of Jo March (Janeway, Russ), while others perceive in the novel a matriarchal "reigning feminist sisterhood" (Auerbach). Historian Sarah Elbert finds Jo's development in the novel to be "the only fully complete one" and views Jo's marriage to Professor Bhaer as a "democratic domestic union" (207).

Other critics focus on the tensions and conflicts inherent in the novel. Alma Payne, for example, views Jo as an embodiment of the struggle between "a sense of duty" and "a strong self" (261). Ann Douglas finds that *Little Women* embodies the conflicts which Alcott inherited from her mother's and father's opposing natures ("Mysteries"). And Elizabeth Keyser argues that in *Little Women* Alcott undercuts the domestic values she seems to assert. Finally, Judith Fetterley, perhaps the most insightful critic of Alcott, finds a conflict within the text of *Little Women* between overt and covert messages "which provide evidence of Alcott's ambivalence" on "the subject of what it means to be a little woman" (370–71, 382).

In contrast to these critics, we argue here that in *Little Women* there is not only evidence of ambivalence but also covert manipulation of the text by Alcott in order to disguise the fate of her experimental, self-reliant heroine.

on to insist that woman be allowed to "find out her own limitations" (Porter 13–14).

But Alcott, well educated in the proprieties of her own time, realized the dangers for a woman of nineteenth-century America in advocating such potentially liberating attitudes too openly. In fact, Alcott seemed to sense the ambiguities inherent, at least for women, in Emerson's position, for it is Emerson, the man from whom she learned the value of self-reliance, whose censure she fears when creating (in the adult thrillers) her most self-reliant and self-assertive female characters:

> I think my natural ambition is for the lurid style. I indulge in gorgeous fancies and wish that I dared inscribe them upon my pages and set them before the public. . . . How should I dare to interfere with the proper grayness of old Concord? The dear old town has never known a startling hue since the redcoats were there. Far be it from me to inject an inharmonious color into the neutral tint. And my favorite characters! Suppose they went to cavorting at their own sweet will, to the infinite horror of dear Mr. Emerson, who never imagined a Concord person as walking off a plumb line stretched between two pearly clouds in the empyrean. [Pickett 107–08]

Alcott was, moreover, reticent about openly advocating self-reliance and assertiveness in her works for children; she was aware of the responsibility she bore her young readers in that they so fully identified with and followed the careers of such characters as Jo. In fact, after the publication of *Little Women*, Alcott seemed quite moved by her young readers' responses to her works: "Over a hundred letters from boys & girls . . . & many from teachers & parents assure me that my little books are read & valued in a way I never dreamed of seeing them" (quoted by Stern in her introduction to Myerson and Shealy, xxxiii). And in a letter of 1872 to William Henry Venable, Alcott expresses gratitude that her stories are "considered worthy to be used for the instruction as well as the amusement of young people" (Myerson and Shealy 172).[3]

In the final analysis, however, it seems clear that Alcott was not unambivalently committed to the creation of "innocent" entertainments (Myerson and Shealy 172) for the young. In fact, her impatience with such works becomes obvious in her more candid moments: she claims in a letter probably written in 1878 that she wrote what she refers to as "moral tales for the young" because she felt pressure from her publishers and because such tales provided her with a much needed income. "I do it," she admits, "because it pays well" (Myerson and Shealy 232).

Louisa Alcott found herself, then, confronted with conflicting impulses: on the one hand, Alcott—educated under the tutelage of

---

3. In her study of Alcott's short stories Joy Marsella observes that Alcott acknowledged the socializing effect stories had upon children and that she wrote her own in a way that "formed minds, prepared hearts, and molded characters" in a manner fully acceptable to the conservative editors of children's periodicals (xxi).

Emerson and Bronson Alcott—craves freedom and the power of self-assertion for both herself and her characters; on the other hand, she feels strongly the pressure to meet the needs of her young readers and the demands of her publishers. In Alcott's most famous novel for children, therefore, woman's development toward membership in the acceptable female sphere is rendered in a surface narrative; to reveal the complex, dangerous truths of female experience, the self-assertive drives toward womanly independence, Alcott (resorting to one of the ploys she uses frequently in the thrillers—disguise) must incorporate a subtext. Thus, in *Little Women*, Alcott, employing both a surface narrative and a subtext to disclose an extended vision of feminine conflict, presents a vision of female experience at once innocuous and deadly. What appears at first to be a conventional and somewhat sentimental tale of the innocent trials of girlhood—what we have mistaken for a "feminine" novel of domestic education—is, on closer examination, another of Alcott's lurid, violent sensation stories. For in presenting the conflict between appropriate womanly behavior and the human desire for assertiveness and fulfillment, Alcott finds herself forced to wage war upon her protagonist, Jo. Young Jo—fiery, angry, assertive—represents all that adult Jo can never be, and for this reason young Jo must be destroyed. Thus, while the surface narrative achieves some closure, while it implies a moderately "normal," well-integrated future for Jo, the horrifying subtext of *Little Women* reveals that for an independent, self-determined Jo, no future is possible.

II

The horrors that lurk at the heart of Alcott's novel are, surprisingly, least obvious to those who cherish her work most. Even today, women who as children read *Little Women* remember Jo at her best, that is to say, at her most liberated. Elizabeth Janeway, for example, praises the novel's heroine as "the one young woman in 19th-century fiction who maintains her individual independence, who gives up no part of her autonomy as payment for being born a woman—and who gets away with it" (Janeway 42). Janeway seems to repress her awareness that Jo—who never wants to marry, who values her writing above all else—*does* finally marry and abandon the writing she cherishes, taking up the kinds of writing her family and husband deem suitable for her.

However, two of the most hostile readers of *Little Women*, Leslie Fiedler and James Baldwin, have sensed a certain horror and duplicity in it, and despite their patent distaste for Alcott's novel, their unsympathetic readings of *Little Women* illuminate the work. In comparing Alcott's work to Harriet Beecher Stowe's *Uncle Tom's Cabin*, Baldwin and Fiedler denigrate *both* works, terming them sentimental, self-righteous, dishonest, and inhumane—among other harsh criticisms. Both imply, too, that a secret crime or perversion hides at the center of these two novels. Fiedler finds the "chief pleasures" of *Uncle Tom's Cabin* "rooted not in the moral indignation of the reformer but in the more devious titillations of the sadist" (114). And at the center of these "titillations of the sadist" is Little Eva, "the pre-pubescent corpse as heroine" (114). Fiedler compares Stowe's "orgy of approved pathos" to that created by Alcott in *Little Women*: "Little Eva is the classic case in America, melting the obdurate though kindly St. Clare from skepticism to faith. What an orgy of approved pathos such scenes provided in the hands of a master like Harriet Beecher Stowe, or the late Louisa May Alcott, who in *Little Women* reworked the prototype of Mrs. Stowe into a kind of fiction specifically directed at young girls!" (114). James Baldwin also sees a kind of orgy of "sentimentality" in *Uncle Tom's Cabin*, which he condemns by comparing it with *Little Women*: "*Uncle Tom's Cabin* is a very bad novel, having, in its self-righteous, virtuous sentimentality, much in common with *Little Women*. Sentimentality, the ostentatious parading of excessive and spurious emotion, is the mark of dishonesty, the inability to feel; the wet eyes of the sentimentalist betray his aversion to experience, his fear of life, his arid heart; and it is always, therefore, the signal of secret and violent inhumanity, the mask of cruelty. *Uncle Tom's Cabin*—like its multitudinous, hard-boiled descendants—is a catalogue of violence" (92).

Baldwin and Fiedler have sensed—perhaps because of their antagonism toward these novels and their lack of sympathy with the characters who inhabit these two works by women—the doubleness of *Uncle Tom's Cabin* and *Little Women*. As masculinist critics, however, neither seems capable of sufficiently disengaging himself from the prejudices of his culture to understand or elucidate the complexities of the two novels. For it is true that both novels mask secret crimes and enact hidden violence, and the more open-minded reader must inevitably ask herself why Alcott and Stowe resort to hidden abuses to resolve the conflicts their novels present. And also, if *Little Women* has "much in common" with *Uncle Tom's Cabin*; if Alcott's novel is, in Baldwin's terms, replete with a "dishonesty" that masks some "secret and violent inhumanity," some act of "cruelty," then the reader must ask the nature and source of the novel's "dishonesty," she must discover the act of "inhumanity" and "cruelty" the novel perpetrates.[4]

The answers to these questions begin to surface only when we disinter the protagonist of *Little Women*, Jo March, from the text of the novel. For Jo is an experimental heroine through whom Alcott can explore the tensions of female experience in nineteenth-century America: between being a dutiful member of woman's sphere and being an independent, self-reliant woman. In the surface narrative of *Little Women*, the story suitable for Alcott's young readers, Jo March begins as an unruly, self-assertive girl and gradually learns to become a proper "little woman." But when Leslie Fiedler asserts that Little Eva is the "model for all the protagonists of a literature at once juvenile and genteelly gothic" (114), he again inadvertently points by implication to the true design of *Little Women*, revealed in the novel's dis-

---

4. For a discussion of the "crime" hidden at the center of *Uncle Tom's Cabin*, see Kathleen Margaret Lant's "The Unsung Hero of *Uncle Tom's Cabin*."

guised text. For the experimental transformation of Jo March into a proper "little woman"—performed and delineated in a textual laboratory which masquerades as an informative and supportive guidebook for children—turns out to be, in fact, a "gothic" study in horror, the very kind of story Alcott so longed to write but which she renounced, or tried to, for the sake of her young, impressionable readers.

In order for Jo to live fictionally, to maintain her position within the narrative framework Alcott has constructed, Alcott must murder Jo spiritually. Given Jo's lust for independence, her devotion to her own power and development, Alcott could *never* have allowed her to marry for love—in other words, to love and marry Laurie—for, as the novel demonstrates with Meg's marriage to John Brooke, marriage for love reduces woman to "submission" (*Little Women* 209) [183]. Alcott was vehement in her refusal to allow this to happen to Jo. In a letter to Thomas Niles (1869), she deplores the numerous "pairing[s] off" in *Little Women*, asserting "I don't approve" (Myerson and Shealy 119), and in a letter to Samuel Joseph May (1869), she bitterly complains that "publishers are very *perverse* & wont let authors have their way so my little women must grow up & be married off in a very stupid style" (Myerson and Shealy 121–22).

Tragically, Alcott's reluctance to sacrifice Jo to convention through marriage ultimately results in Alcott's violence against this very character. In a letter to Elizabeth Powell, Alcott is quite clear on her own desires for Jo and on the conflicting demands she feels from her readers. Alcott's solution is to subject Jo to certain violent narrative abuses: " 'Jo' should have remained a literary spinster but so many enthusiastic young ladies wrote to me clamorously demanding that she should marry Laurie, *or* somebody, that I didn't dare to refuse & out of perversity went & made a funny match for her. I expect vials of wrath to be poured out upon my head, but rather enjoy the prospect" (Myerson and Shealy 125).

Like Cassy, the horribly abused slave woman of *Uncle Tom's Cabin*, and like Sethe, the equally besieged black woman of Toni Morrison's *Beloved*, Alcott chooses to murder her dearest child rather than force that child to live in a world hostile to her. Alcott's murder of Jo, then, is the secret violence at the center of *Little Women*. Alcott's response to her fiction seems characteristic of the woman or the woman writer beset by irreconcilable conflicts and demands: Jo finds herself among the good who must die young. In order that she not be corrupted by the adult world of heterosexuality, Jo must be killed while at her zenith of eager and fiery independence.

III

From the beginning of *Little Women*, fifteen-year-old Jo March rebels and refuses to be a "young lady": " 'I'm not! And if turning up my hair makes me one, I'll wear it in two tails till I'm twenty,' cried Jo, pulling off her net and shaking down a chestnut mane" (5) [12]. Jo's behavior is entirely inappropriate for a proper young female. Her "quick temper, sharp tongue, and restless spirit" are "always getting her into scrapes" (36) [38]. And although Jo is devoted to and loves the female community she shares with her mother and sisters—Meg, Beth, and Amy— she acts "in a gentlemanly manner," uses "slang words," and constantly defies her sisters' attempts to admonish and reform her:

> "Don't Jo; it's so boyish!"
> "That's why I do it."
> "I detest rude, unladylike girls!"
> "I hate affected, niminy-piminy chits!" [4–5] [12]

In her arrogation of masculine mannerisms, language, and roles, Jo instinctively and correctly identifies the opportunities for independence, self-reliance, adventure, and assertion as those conventionally reserved for men. Jo realizes, in fact, the awful dichotomy between her own impulses and the expectations held out to her: "I can't get over my disappointment in not being a boy" (5) [13].

Jo March is, thus, a nineteenth-century female caught between the requisite role of the domesticated "little woman," represented by her given, imposed name, Josephine, and her own self-guided impulses, represented by her "masculine" chosen name, Jo. Her conflict is so intense that she has renamed, redefined herself. In spite of Jo's self-reliant acts, however—"I'm the man of the family now Papa is away" (6) [14]—she receives continual reminders from her sisters of her inevitable fate: "you must try to be contented with making your name boyish and playing brother to us girls" (5) [13]. But for a brief moment at the beginning of *Little Women*, Jo March resides in an idyllic female community of which she is the "male" head. She is a heroic figure—a young woman intent on maintaining the female community of "woman's sphere" while still acting in accordance with her own self-reliant impulses.

And Jo's heroic balancing act works as long as this "woman's sphere," the matriarchal community of Jo's family, remains entirely self-contained and entirely female. But once a male character—the young boy next door, Laurie, who has been longing to enter this female utopia—successfully penetrates the female community, the plot of *Little Women* and the destiny of Jo are immutably altered.

Laurie, a rich but orphaned young boy, is warmly welcomed into the March family, and at first—with the children still inhabiting a prelapsarian Eden—life appears to go on as before. Because the children are presexual in the early parts of the novel, Laurie (as his name suggests) becomes in effect "one of the girls." He is accepted into the female community and poses no threat to Jo or to the female world she loves. Nevertheless, planted in this female garden now, with the arrival of a male, are the seeds of its own destruction. But before these seeds sprout and take root, Alcott seizes the opportunity provided by this idyllic lull in sexual development; she begins, in a subtext, to reveal the causes of both the disintegration of this female community and Jo's fall from self-reliance.

By using Laurie, a male, as a foil for Jo, Alcott underscores the na-

ture of the conflicts which Jo, as a female, must experience and the
fate to which she—unlike Laurie—must ultimately acquiesce. In
many ways Jo and Laurie are twins: they are the same age, they are
both characterized as untamed animals—Jo as a horse (5, 6, 25) [13,
29] and Laurie as a centaur (59) [57]—and both, hating their given
names, have renamed themselves. Even Jo's mother remarks that Jo
and Laurie would not be "suited" to each other for marriage because
they are "too much alike" (299) [260]. And Laurie's grandfather, seeing the influence of Jo on Laurie, thinks how Jo "seemed to understand the boy almost as well as if she had been one herself" (50) [49].
So identical are Jo and Laurie, in fact, that in their presexual relationship, even as Laurie becomes "one of the girls," so Jo becomes with
Laurie just "one of the boys."

Despite the masculine similarities between Jo and Laurie, however,
Alcott emphatically reveals that Jo's fate in life—because Jo is, inescapably, female—will be different from Laurie's. Our recognition of
the similar natures, attitudes, and feelings that Jo and Laurie share
serves, moreover, only to intensify our awareness of the conflicts Jo
must endure. Although both Laurie and Jo hate their given names and
rename themselves, only Laurie can actively "thrash" and challenge
those who would force a false name and thus a false role on him. Jo
must passively "bear it":

> "My first name is Theodore but I don't like it, for the fellows
> called me Dora, so I made them say Laurie instead."
> "I hate my name, too—so sentimental! I wish everyone would
> say Jo instead of Josephine. How did you make the boys stop call-
> ing you Dora?"
> "I thrashed 'em."
> "I can't thrash Aunt March, so I suppose I shall have to bear
> it"; and Jo resigned herself with a sigh. [27] [30]

Not only can Laurie, because he is male, actively alter reality in accordance with his own will, but he can also, should his self-reliant acts
fail, simply leave those situations which limit him; as Huck Finn, the
archetypal masculine hero of nineteenth-century American literature,
puts it, he can "light out for the Territory." But when Laurie, angry at
his grandfather, proposes to Jo that they run away from home together,
Jo, although filled with the same impulses of flight and freedom, must
resign herself to captivity:

> For a moment Jo looked as if she would agree, for wild as the
> plan was, it just suited her. She was tired of care and confine-
> ment, longed for change. . . . Her eyes kindled as they turned
> wistfully toward the window, but they fell on the old house oppo-
> site and she shook her head with sorrowful decision.
> "If I was a boy, we'd run away together and have a capital time;
> but as I'm a miserable girl, I must be proper and stop at home.
> Don't tempt me, Teddy, it's a crazy plan."
> "That's the fun of it," began Laurie, who had got a willful fit on
> him and was possessed to break out of bounds in some way.

"Hold your tongue!" cried Jo, covering her ears. " 'Prunes and prisms' are my doom, and I may as well make up my mind to it." [191] [168]

Interestingly, Jo's frustrations and lack of freedom are characterized specifically in terms of her femaleness and in terms of her relationship as a female to language. Jo, the writer, longs to control language, to make herself independent and her family secure with her use of language. But as a woman, "prunes and prisms" are her lot: her relationship to language *should* be characterized by her desire for beauty. As Nancy Baker points out in *The Beauty Trap*, her study of the American woman's obsession with appearance, women of the nineteenth century, reluctant to wear too much makeup, "pinched their cheeks to make them pinker and . . . practiced repeating sequences of words beginning with the letter p—prunes, peas, potatoes, papa, prisms—in order to effect the small, puckered mouth that was so popular" (Baker 21).

Even within the presexual Eden of childhood, then, Jo's stream of impulses is dammed and divided. Were *Little Women* one of Alcott's short stories for children, this is how we would remember Jo: a young female destined sooner or later to come to terms with being a proper "little woman," but a young female alive with rebellion and wildness, intent on having her own way. Because *Little Women* is a novel, though, an extended fiction, the children—including Jo—*do* grow up, they *do* (at least offstage) become sexual. And each sexual coming-of-age is a blow to the foundations of the female community which has become essential to Jo's self-assertion and sense of self-worth. Only as the reigning "patriarch" and caretaker of this female family—"if anything is amiss at home, I'm your man" (292) [254]—does Jo enjoy any power: that power of self-reliantly protecting and providing for one's family, traditionally reserved for the family's highest-ranking male. Jo's solution to the problems her sisters face in finding worthy husbands is a simple one—"Then we'll be old maids" (90) [84]—and as her sisters are drawn closer and closer to marriage, Jo vehemently protests the usurpation of her power and the fall of her female domain: "I think it's dreadful to break up families so" (225) [198].

Jo's power begins to dwindle as a result of the first sexual coming-of-age in *Little Women*—Meg's attraction and marriage to John Brooke. Jo immediately perceives that her weakened position is a direct result of being female and that this challenge to her territory and power is the inevitable manifestation of male privilege: " 'She'll go and fall in love, and there's an end of peace and fun, and cosy times together. I see it all! They'll go lovering around the house, and we shall have to dodge; Meg will be absorbed and no good to me any more; Brooke will scratch up a fortune somehow, carry her off, and make a hole in the family; and I shall break my heart, and everything will be abominably uncomfortable. Oh, dear me! Why weren't we all boys; then there wouldn't be any bother' " (183) [161]. As Meg's attraction to John Brooke becomes more certain, Jo grows increasingly anxious, lamenting her feminine powerlessness and asserting a desire to usurp masculine sexual as well as social privilege: "I knew there was mischief brewing; I felt it; and now it's worse than I imagined. I just wish I could marry Meg myself, and keep her safe in the family" (182) [161]. Finally, when Jo unexpectedly encounters the "spectacle" of the just-engaged lovers in the parlor, she is overcome with revulsion: "Oh, *do* somebody go down quick; John Brooke is acting dreadfully, and Meg likes it!" (209) [183]. The scene of the "strong-minded sister," whom Jo had hoped would reject her suitor, now "enthroned" upon the knee of Jo's "enemy" and wearing "an expression of the most abject submission" (209) [183] is intolerable for Jo.

Jo's "shock" (209) [183] and horror at her sister's transformation suggest that Amy, Beth, and Meg function for Jo as more than mere sisters.[5] They embody experimental alter egos of Jo; they represent the versions of female experience—the ways of reconciling a woman's dual impulses—possible for Jo herself. Meg, in her completely acquiescent marriage and motherhood, manifests the total repression of self-reliant impulses. Through her marriage to John Brooke she learns "that a woman's happiest kingdom is home, her highest honor the art of ruling it not as a queen, but as a wise wife and mother" (361) [313]. Meg thus represents for Jo the successful, dutiful member of woman's sphere. But as this first sister departs from Jo's female realm, Jo vehemently rejects the example of submission and marriage which Meg offers: "I'm not one of the agreeable sort. . . . There should always be one old maid in a family" (224) [197]. Jo insists that she will never marry—" 'I'd like to see anyone try it,' cried Jo fiercely" (138) [125]—and is, in fact, "alarmed at the thought" (203) [179].

At this point in the novel, Jo is still defiantly independent and assertive. She proudly claims that she belongs to the "new" set and that she admires "reformers": "and I shall be one if I can" (269) [235]. Thus, when Jo and Amy visit their Aunt March and Aunt Carrol, unaware that her aunt is considering taking her on a trip to Europe, Jo boasts, "I don't like favors; they oppress and make me feel like a slave. I'd rather do everything for myself and be perfectly independent" (270) [236]. But the consequences of self-reliant behavior continue to impose themselves on Jo, for her "revolutionary" (269) [235] outburst costs her the trip. Jo is deprived because she has a "too independent spirit" rather than an acquiescent and "docile" (280) [244] nature like that of Amy, who is chosen to accompany her aunt to Europe.

Jo gradually adjusts to her misfortune, to Amy's departure, and to the first assault upon her female community, Meg's marriage, only to be confronted with what for Jo is one of the ultimate horrors in the novel: Laurie reveals to Jo that he loves her—as a lover, not as a buddy. When it is first hinted to Jo that Laurie loves her, she rejects the possibility: she "wouldn't hear a word upon the subject and scolded violently if anyone dared to suggest it" (293) [255]. And when

5. For other discussions of Jo's sisters and their responses to the demands and conflicts of becoming "little women," see Nina Auerbach, Sarah Elbert, Judith Fetterley, Anne Hollander, Elizabeth Keyser, and Patricia Meyer Spacks. Several of these essays and other critical works on Alcott have been collected by Madeleine Stern in *Critical Essays on Louisa May Alcott*.

Laurie does confess his love, Jo decidedly rejects him and all potential suitors: "I haven't the least idea of loving him or anybody else. . . . I don't believe I shall ever marry. I'm happy as I am, and love my liberty too well to be in any hurry to give it up for any mortal man" (329, 330) [285, 287].

Alcott's nineteenth-century readers, who clamored for Jo to marry Laurie, found Jo's rejection—and outright horror and dismissal—of marriage to the handsome and wealthy Laurie inconceivable. Jo's revulsion from marriage to Laurie is not so puzzling, however, if we remember that throughout the novel Jo and Laurie have, in effect, been "brothers," even doubles of the same self. Jo categorically rejects Laurie, then, in part because marriage to Laurie would be tantamount to incest. As Jo confides to Laurie, "I don't believe it's the right sort of love, and I'd rather not try it" (328) [285].

Jo also refuses Laurie because marriage to him would render Jo completely powerless. Jo has already witnessed the self-sacrifice, repression, and submission required of Meg in her marriage to John Brooke, and Jo realizes that she, herself, is eminently unsuited to such a role. Jo's mother, too, astutely observes that Laurie and Jo "would both rebel" in a marriage to each other because both are "too fond of freedom" and both have "hot tempers and strong wills" (299) [260]. In other words, a marriage between Laurie and Jo would not work because both are, in conventional terms, masculine. Even more important to Jo, therefore, marrying Laurie would entail the absurd paradox of relinquishing her power to the only male with whom—in her relationship as just "one of the boys"—she has ever had power. To retain any remnant of control over her own life, Jo must refuse to marry Laurie. In an identical act of rebellion and self-assertion Jo's creator, Louisa Alcott, concurs: "Girls write to ask who the little women marry, as if that was the only end and aim of a woman's life. I *won't* marry Jo to Laurie to please any one" (Cheney 201). Despite the repressive and conservative message conveyed in *Little Women*, Jo's refusal to marry Laurie remains—for both Jo and her author—the one act of self-assertion which neither can quell.

When Laurie eventually falls in love with and marries Jo's sister Amy, the relief of being freed from the possibility of marriage to Laurie attenuates Jo's grief over the loss of a second member of her female community. Amy, in her marriage to Laurie, represents another of Jo's alter egos—an additional way of reconciling a woman's divided impulses toward self-reliance and woman's appropriate sphere of activity. As Laurie thinks to himself, "Jo's sister was almost the same as Jo's self" (388) [335]. Amy is an especially important alter ego for Jo because she, like Jo, wants to be an artist. At the end of the novel Amy as a wife and mother attempts to combine her "artistic hopes" with life in woman's sphere: "I don't relinquish all my artistic hopes or confine myself to helping others fulfill their dreams of duty [the text actually says "beauty"]" (442) [379]. Amy's declaration seems to suggest the possibility of balancing a life of art and a life of appropriate feminine behavior.

Although a wife and mother, Amy has "begun to model" again, but her ability to balance the self-expressive demands of art and the self-expressive demands of marriage and motherhood is undermined by what she models. For Amy creates not out of a fresh encounter of her own self with the world; rather, she repeats, imitates, what is now for her the primary act of creation, biological creation, as she models "a figure of baby." And according to both Amy and Laurie, this "figure of baby" is her ultimate achievement: "Laurie says it is the best thing I've ever done. I think so myself." (442) [379]. Amy's ability to balance successfully the demands of art and womanhood becomes even more doubtful when we recall that from the beginning Amy has resolved to be "an attractive and accomplished woman, even if she never became a great artist" (233) [204]. Amy is interested in her own art, but is more concerned with what people think of her. By her own admission to Jo, Amy intends to follow "the way of the world": "people who set themselves against it only get laughed at for their pains. I don't like reformers, and I hope you will never try to be one" (269) [235]. Thus, although Amy seems to represent a possible alternative for Jo—as both artist and "little woman"—Amy, in fact, follows Meg's example in her willing suppression of self-reliant impulses. But Jo's response to Amy's condemnation of "reformers" is typically undaunted: "We can't agree about that, for you belong to the old set, and I to the new" (269) [235].

Jo's commitment to the "new" has been clear from the novel's beginning; she devotes herself rebelliously to her life-long passion: writing. As she sits in her "favorite refuge" (22) [27]—the "garret" (133) [121]—and writes, Jo embodies a version of Sandra Gilbert and Susan Gubar's "madwoman in the attic," attempting to empower and define herself by engaging in the forbidden (for women) act of writing. Jo's goal, her "favorite dream," is to do something "splendid" and "heroic or wonderful that won't be forgotten after I'm dead" (129) [118]. Her chief desire, in short, is to write: "I think I shall write books and get rich and famous: that would suit me, so that is *my* favorite dream" (129) [118]. Thus, when Jo publishes her first story and receives both the praise of her family and the promise of payment for future stories, she is ecstatically happy: "I shall write more . . . and I *am* so happy, for in time I may be able to support myself and help the girls" (141) [128]. Alcott clearly discloses here that writing is the "key" (130) [118] to a successful life for Jo: "for to be independent and earn the praise of those she loved were the dearest wishes of her heart, and this seemed to be the first step toward the happy end" (141–42) [128].

Jo herself is aware, however, that there may never be a "happy end," a successful merging of her dual impulses toward independence and appropriate feminine behavior: " 'I've got the key to my castle in the air, but whether I can unlock the door remains to be seen,' observed Jo mysteriously" (130) [118]. And in fact, along with Jo's success as a writer comes a warning to Jo of the dangers, even the impossibility, of committing herself entirely to a self-reliant life of writing. For when Jo proudly sends her first novel out to publishers, she finds that she will have to "chop it up to suit purchasers" (245) [215]. Consequently, Jo performs a deed that foreshadows the fate—at the hands of her "authoress," Alcott—of her own self-reliant being: "With Spartan firmness, the young authoress laid her firstborn on her table and chopped it up as ruthlessly as any ogre" (246) [216]. Finally, Jo receives one further indication that writing (now Jo's primary self-assertive act) and duty toward woman's sphere may not be compatible. Absorbed in her writing, Jo lets her sister Beth nurse their sick neighbors, and when Beth contracts scarlet fever, Jo is filled with remorse: "serves me right, selfish pig, to let you go and stay writing rubbish myself!" (160) [143]. As a result of Beth's illness—caused by Jo's devotion to her writing— Beth's already frail nature is weakened, and she eventually dies. And with Beth dies the last member of Jo's female community.

Even before Beth's death, however, and despite Jo's success as an author, Jo suffers from the shock of recognition that Laurie's proposal of marriage has forced upon her. His proposal makes Jo realize that she must now confront not only the loss of her female community through the marriage of her sisters but also the assault on her own self-reliant autonomy. In short, Jo is forced into the realization that she is inescapably female. This realization marks a turning point in the novel, after which Jo as we know her mysteriously begins to disappear—or to be erased—from the story. Just as Jo finds it necessary to mutilate her works to satisfy her publishers, so Alcott must destroy Jo to appease her audience.

From the time that Beth becomes ill, Jo's vibrant personality begins to fade, to weaken, to undergo some horrifying transformation. Just as Alcott has referred to Jo's book as Jo's own offspring, just as Alcott is aware that—to please her readers—Jo must mutilate that offspring, now Alcott herself begins inexorably to mutilate her own text, her own character—Jo. The comparison between Jo as author/parent to her books and Alcott as author/parent of *Little Women* (as well as to her other works) becomes convincingly clear in Alcott's correspondence. In a letter to Lucy Larcom, Alcott refers to some lost manuscripts as "waifs of mine" (Myerson and Shealy 119), and to Elizabeth Powell she writes that she herself is the "Ma" of her "stupid 'Little Women' " (Myerson and Shealy 124). Perhaps Alcott—in the very act of mutilating the energetic and irrepressible Jo—felt some kinship with Jo as Jo bowdlerized her own book.

Jo's growing awareness of what it means to be female is confirmed when her sister Beth dies. Through Beth's death, Alcott depicts a further possible response from another of Jo's alter egos to the female predicament. Beth, who has not even sufficient self-reliant impulses to stay alive, becomes for Jo—and by extension for Alcott—the example of what all women are required by custom to be, the completely perfect woman—passive, acquiescent, dead.[6] Ironically, however, Beth's death is also the sole way to maintain Jo's idyllic female community, for only in death can Beth remain inviolably Jo's. When Beth

6. Fetterley thoroughly delineates this point in "Alcott's Civil War": "Beth's history carries out the implication of being a little woman to its logical conclusion: to be a little woman is to be dead" (380).

dies, she is "well at last" (379) [328], and her death discloses one sure way of curing a woman's problems. In contrast to Leslie Fiedler's contention that the "pre-pubescent corpse" functions to provide the "titillations of the sadist," it seems much more likely that for a nineteenth-century woman writer and her audience, a "dead woman" would indeed be the only "safe woman" (Fiedler 114). Fiedler asserts that at the death of Little Eva in *Uncle Tom's Cabin*, "death becomes the supreme rapist" (114). But in *Little Women*, death is the only thing, at least in Jo's eyes, that can save a female from the psychological rape—the violation of self-direction and the disintegration of female community—that await her if she grows up and takes her proper feminine place in the heterosexual world. For Jo, then, and for Alcott as well, the dead woman and the perfect woman become synonymous.

From this point in the novel, Jo's response to her own femaleness in many ways parallels Beth's. But because of the intensity of her self-assertive impulses, Jo cannot simply die. Rather, she is forced to be an accomplice to a crime, to participate actively in her own demise. From its beginning, the text of *Little Women* thoroughly documents the enormous influence that Beth—as an alter ego embodying devotion to woman's sphere—exerts over Jo: "by some strange attraction of opposites, Jo was gentle Beth's. . . . Over her big harum-scarum sister, Beth unconsciously exercised more influence than anyone in the family" (38) [40] Indeed it is through Beth that Jo learns the virtues of woman's sphere:[7] "Then it was that Jo, living in the darkened room with that suffering little sister always before her eyes and that pathetic voice sounding in her ears, learned to see the beauty and the sweetness of Beth's nature, to feel how deep and tender a place she filled in all hearts, and to acknowledge the worth of Beth's unselfish ambition to live for others and make home happy by the exercise of those simple virtues which all may possess and which all should love and value more than talent, wealth, or beauty" (164–65) [146]. Beth, in fact, increasingly appears to become a part of Jo as her "submissive spirit" seems "to enter into Jo" (167) [148]. And in her sickbed, Beth constantly keeps Jo's cast-off "invalid" (56) [38] doll, "Joanna"—symbolic of Jo's divided and therefore crippled self—at "her side" (165) [147]. Even independent Jo finally becomes aware of her affinity with Beth: "Beth is my conscience, and I *can't* give her up. I can't! I can't!" (166) [148].

As Beth grows closer to death, her influence over Jo intensifies, and Jo increasingly identifies with Beth: " 'More than anyone in the world, Beth. I used to think I couldn't let you go, but I'm learning to feel that I don't lose you; that you'll be more to me than ever, and death can't part us, though it seems to' " (378) [327]. Just before her death, Beth's influence over Jo and her affinity with Jo are so powerful, in fact, that Beth tells Jo that she must replace her: "You must take my place, Jo" (378) [327]. And sure enough, on the morning after Beth finally dies,

---

7. Fetterley supports this reading of Beth's role in the novel: "One can say that Beth's primary function in *Little Women* is to be a lesson to Jo" (381). In contrast to our thesis here, however, Fetterley argues for Jo's "ultimate acceptance of the doctrines of *Little Women*" (382).

Jo is gone: "Jo's place was empty" (379) [328]. Unlike selfless Beth, strong-willed and defiant Jo must go on living, but—in a children's novel—not as Jo.

IV

Through Beth's death, Alcott performs a literary feat of escape rivaling the marvels of Houdini. By this point in the novel, the character of Jo March has become intensely problematic for Alcott. Because Jo inhabits a fictional environment inhospitable to a fully liberated woman, she can have no radically independent life of her own, but because of the spirited self-reliant nature given to her by her creator, she will not submit to repression. Since the perfect woman, the "true woman" is—as Alcott's experiment reveals—a dead woman, and since Alcott's novel demands the showcasing of a "true woman," Alcott can develop the character of Jo, that intractably independent and *alive* female, no further. Jo can only be replaced. In other words, Alcott discovers through the character of Jo March what, according to Ann Douglas, many other women writers toward the end of the nineteenth century were realizing: that there was no place for a self-aware woman to go, that women were "strangely superannuated as a sex" ("Impoverishment" 17). Thus, having stretched the character of Jo March as far as she can on a rack fastened at one end by Jo's independent impulses and secured at the other end by her need to be a proper member of the female community of "little women," Alcott witnesses the final snap of her experimental creation. But by a fascinating sleight of hand, Alcott hides the failed experimental corpse of Jo and switches the identity of her victim.

In *Little Women*, Alcott (with the help of Jo and her writing) kills Beth and then forces Jo to assume a kind of death in life, to impersonate the dead Beth. And this is why Jo, after the death of Beth, displays none of her former willful and self-reliant behavior and all the selflessness of a zombie. Ultimately, then, deep in the macabre subtext of *Little Women*, Alcott's true victim is Jo; Alcott has, in fact, killed the self-celebratory Jo and replaced her with the self-effacing Beth. And the horror of this corpse switching, this premature burial of the living and impersonation of the dead, is accentuated by the fact that not a scream or moan is uttered. All is executed in this novel for children under the pleasant guise of a young girl's gently guided growth into a "little woman."

Alcott's creation of the new zombielike Jo also helps to explain the incredible change in Jo's character following Beth's death. For Jo's transformation in the final chapters of *Little Women* into the blushing, halting maiden and the dutiful wife and mother are otherwise completely implausible. In hiding the evidence of her fictional crime, the longer form of the novel actually works in Alcott's favor. The length of *Little Women* indeed helps to obscure the reader's memory of the youthful Jo, the girl who vehemently proclaimed that she was "not one of the agreeable sort" and preferred therefore to be an "old maid"

(224) [197], the Jo who was "alarmed at the thought" (203) [179] of marriage. Because the reader's memory of young Jo who "carried her love of liberty and hate of conventionalities to such an unlimited extent" (235) [207] is apt to have dimmed towards the end of the novel, that reader may be more likely to accept the authenticity of the new Jo, who is "thrilled" by the possibility of a "tender invitation" to "joyfully depart" with her suitor, the much older Professor Bhaer, "whenever he liked" (410) [353]. Confronted with such schizophrenic behavior, however, the reader with a good memory is incredulous.

V

The alert reader's sense of discontinuity results from Alcott's deliberate and somewhat desperate mutilation of both her protagonist and her text. Not only has Jo been dismembered and then reformed as a less threatening version of herself, but the text also has been dismantled, reshaped, and disguised. What was originally a story of Jo's refusal to accede to a repressive feminine role now becomes a story of courtship and marriage. But this courtship and marriage mask the horror tale that lies at the center of the novel—the murder of Jo. At this point Jo, like the speaker in Emily Dickinson's poem, has been forced to abdicate herself. Banished from her own consciousness, Jo finds herself alienated and alone.

The kind old German professor thus shines "like a midnight sun" on Jo in her "darkness" (406) [350], and Jo desperately reaches out to him: " 'Oh Mr. Bhaer, I *am* so glad to see you!' cried Jo, with a clutch, as if she feared the night would swallow him up before she could get him in" (406) [350]. Through the power of love—Alcott's useful tool for altering her stubborn heroines—Jo is required to embrace the accomplice to her own murder. Although Jo's figurative death is alluded to by Laurie—when he transfers his love from Jo to Amy, he feels "as if there had been a funeral" (383) [331] and later responds to Jo out of the "grave" of his "boyish passion" (402) [346]—the subtext discloses that it is Professor Bhaer who is instrumental in effecting Alcott's scheme. For while Professor Bhaer and Jo covertly admire each other from across the room, Bhaer is discussing "the burial customs of the ancients" (408) [351], and he impulsively moves toward Jo, the text tells us, "just in the act of setting fire to a funeral pile" (409) [352]. It is significant, then, that Alcott presents Professor Bhaer as a "birthday gift" (406) [350] to the murdered Jo, for out of the death of her old self, Jo must now enact a new birth, a grisly resurrection.

Since the beginning of Beth's illness, Alcott has stealthily but inexorably erased the authentic Jo from the text. Jo first begins to "take lessons" (308) [268] from Professor Bhaer and then, in an act of self-abdication, forgoes even her own intellectual and moral vision: "Now she seemed to have got on the Professor's mental or moral spectacles also" (322) [280]. Through Professor Bhaer, Alcott systematically strips Jo of all vestiges of self until she is indeed "Bhaer," or bare—ready to be clothed and defined by someone else, her husband. When

Jo finally agrees to marry Professor Bhaer, the professor looks "as if he had conquered a kingdom" and tells Jo, "be sure that thou givest me all. I haf waited so long, I am grown selfish, as thou wilt find, Professorin" (429) [369]. Even the feminized German title chosen for Jo by the professor reveals the extent to which Jo has acquiesced to her proper role and become a female version of the professor himself. Most important, Professor Bhaer—in preparing Jo for her resurrection as Beth—has succeeded in destroying Jo's one authentic means of self-assertion—her writing.

We recall that for the young Jo, writing seemed the key to her independence, success, and happiness, the "first step toward the happy end" (142) [128]. And when Jo realized that she could write and sell "sensation" stories (243) [214], she "began to feel herself a power in the house" (244) [215], to regain some of the ascendancy she lost as her female kingdom was destroyed. But the surface narrative clearly indicates that a "sensation" story, the melodramatic but authentic inscription of her autonomous female self, is in opposition to the virtues of woman's sphere: "Unconsciously, she was beginning to desecrate some of the womanliest attributes of a woman's character" (316) [275]. Professor Bhaer, therefore—the upholder of social proprieties and agent of Alcott's surface narrative—disapproves of Jo's writing, insists that she stop writing sensation stories, and thereby takes away Jo's power, ensuring that there will be no "happy end" to her story: " 'I wish these papers did not come in the house; they are not for children to see nor young people to read. It is not well, and I haf no patience with those who make this harm. . . . They haf no right to put poison in the sugarplum and let the small ones eat it. No, they should think a little, and sweep mud in the street before they do this thing' " (321–22) [279–80]. Jo, now internalizing Professor Bhaer's "short-sighted" (322) [280] moral vision, watches Bhaer burn one of the newspapers which publish sensation stories and moments later imitates his act, destroying all of her writing:

> "They *are* trash, and will soon be worse trash if I go on, for each is more sensational than the last. . . . I know it's so, for I can't read this stuff in sober earnest without being horribly ashamed of it; and what *should* I do if they were seen at home or Mr. Bhaer got hold of them?"
> Jo turned hot at the bare idea and stuffed the whole bundle into her stove, nearly setting the chimney afire with the blaze. [322] [280]

Blazing up the chimney along with Jo's writings go the remnants of Jo's independent self. Jo burns her stories to please Professor Bhaer, and henceforth not even a memory of the early self-reliant Jo exists.

Ironically, Jo's last self-assertive act is the burning of her writings, the destroying of her own self—her self-reliant, self-expressive, and self-authenticating being. This ultimate act of self-annihilation comes as no surprise, however, to the reader who has been alert to the subtext of the novel. For this alternate text has foreshadowed the enforced self-mutilation that is Jo's fate. One of Jo's first acts of self-effacement in order to become a proper "little woman" occurs early in the novel when Jo cuts off her cherished long hair, selling it to obtain money for her mother to visit her sick father in the army. Jo's comments about her sacrifice reveal that it is much more than a noble act of charity. For the shearing of her hair is Jo's attempt to atone for her selfish acts—"I felt wicked" (147) [132]—and to curb her self-assertive behavior: "It will be good for my vanity" (146) [132]. The subtext reveals, however, the destructive consequences of the attempt to suppress a woman's self-reliant impulses, as Jo relates her feelings after cutting off her hair: "It almost seemed as if I'd an arm or leg off" (148) [133].

Jo is repeatedly associated in the novel, in fact, with self-mutilation. Throughout the novel, Beth cares for Jo's cast-off "invalid" doll—appropriately named "Joanna" (56) [54]—a lobotomized amputee symbolic of the fate of the "tempestuous" Jo herself: "One forlorn fragment of *dollanity* had belonged to Jo, and having led a tempestuous life, was left a wreck in the ragbag, from which dreary poorhouse it was rescued by Beth and taken to her refuge. Having no top to its head, she tied on a neat little cap, and as both arms and legs were gone, she hid these deficiencies by folding it in a blanket and devoting her best bed to this chronic invalid" (36) [38]. Here Beth hides the "deficiencies" of "Joanna" even as Alcott later uses the persona of Beth to "hide" the "deficiencies" of the incorrigible Jo. And twice in the novel Jo must mutilate her writing—the sole means she has to express her true self—in order to conform to the demands of others. First she mutilates her works, her "children," to please her editors, "feeling as a tender parent might on being asked to cut off her baby's legs in order that it might fit into a new cradle" (314) [274]. Then she completely destroys her works for Professor Bhaer.

Forced to efface and divorce herself from herself, Jo tries now to write moral children's stories. These products of an impersonating self, however, these "masquerading" (323) [281] stories fail. Since Jo no longer writes her beloved thrillers ("Jo corked up her inkstand," 323) [281], she has finally passed the "test" set up for her by the surface narrative's assistant, Professor Bhaer: "He did it so quietly that Jo never knew he was watching to see if she would accept and profit by his reproof; but she stood the test and he was satisfied; for, though no words passed between them, he knew that she had given up writing" (324) [282]. Jo now refrains from writing until after Beth's death when—at her mother's suggestion—she attempts a "simple little story" to relieve her depression and to please her family. Jo creates a surprisingly successful and moving work but a work which is more the result of compliance than creativity. By her own admission, certain aspects of the story—for all its "truth . . . humor and pathos"—are not hers: "If there is anything good or true in what I write, it isn't mine; I owe it all to you and Mother and to Beth" (394) [340]. Even in her act of creativity, Jo has, to a certain extent, internalized the values of those around her.

By the end of the novel Jo has no rebellion, no self, left. Jo's mind,

earlier filled with divided but vital and authentic impulses, is now—
like the doll Joanna's head—vacuumed out and replaced with Beth's
one-dimensional, selfless personality. Alcott can finally resolve the
problems and conflicts engendered by the clash of Jo's independent
personality with her required role in woman's sphere only by excising
and replacing Jo's character.

Careful to leave no trace of blood in this children's novel, Alcott
quietly substitutes for Jo an impersonation of the perfect "little
woman," the dead and selfless Beth. And when Jo agrees to marry Professor Bhaer, her words affirm the success of Alcott's endeavor: "I may
be strong-minded, but no one can say I'm out of my sphere now"
(433–34) [372]. Jo has indeed been forced into her proper "sphere,"
but to do so, Alcott has had to perform a lobotomy on her. While in
the surface narrative Jo seems to learn the lessons of little womanhood, the subtext of the novel reveals Alcott's Procrustean intent: Jo
may begin life as a young "madwoman in the attic," but Alcott kills off
this madwoman, leaving only the "angel in the house" (217) [191].

Early in the novel, when Jo writes to her absent mother to report on
the progress of the children, Jo writes of herself, "I—well, I'm Jo, and
never shall be anything else" (154) [138]. The horror of *Little Women*
is that Jo does stop being Jo. She has been replaced by a false Jo, a
broken doll, a compliant Beth. This, then, is the act of "cruelty," of
"secret and violent inhumanity," which according to James Baldwin
lurks behind the "sentimentality" of *Little Women*. In reworking
Stowe's "prototype"—as Leslie Fiedler suggests Alcott does—Alcott
has transformed "the pre-pubescent corpse as heroine" into the pu-
bescent heroine as corpse.

Thus, *Little Women* hides a secret crime. And like many crimes
against women, this one is frequently ignored, overlooked, or dismissed as irrelevant. Even readers respectful of Alcott's novel—as
Fiedler and Baldwin are not—disregard the horror perpetrated on Jo,
insisting that Jo grows smoothly into the woman she was destined to
become; in this way, Anne Hollander can observe: "A satisfying continuity informs all the lives in *Little Women*. Alcott creates a world
where a deep 'natural piety' indeed effortlessly binds the child to the
woman she becomes. The novel shows that as a young girl grows up,
she may rely with comfort on being the same person, whatever mysterious and difficult changes must be undergone in order to become an
older and wiser one. Readers can turn again and again to Alcott's book
solely for a gratifying taste of her simple, stable vision of feminine
completeness" (28). The tragedy of *Little Women* is, of course, that Jo
is no longer Jo when she reaches maturity, for the real Jo never could
reach maturity.

Torn between her personal loyalty to the original Jo—a lovely, vibrant, lively "New Woman" (as Janeway calls her, 44)—and her commitment to those readers who demanded a sufficiently traditional or
comfortable narrative pattern, Alcott faced irreconcilable demands.
The crime in *Little Women* is Alcott's brutal resolution of this conflict,
and its real horrors emerge when we become aware of Alcott's willing-

ness to finish Jo off (in *Jo's Boys*) as "a literary nursery-maid providing moral pap for the young" (42).[8] Alcott has, at this moment, lost even her own fervid joy in the young woman who promised so much, who shone so brightly for so many readers young and old, but who could not grow into adulthood as herself, as Jo.

WORKS CITED

Alcott, Louisa May. "Behind a Mask, *or* A Woman's Power." In *Behind a Mask: The Unknown Thrillers of Louisa May Alcott*, ed. Madeleine Stern. New York: William Morrow, 1975. 1–104.

———. *Jo's Boys: A Sequel to "Little Men."* New York: Grosset and Dunlap, 1949.

———. *Little Women, or Meg, Jo, Beth and Amy*. Boston: Little, Brown, 1968.

———. "Patty's Patchwork." In *Aunt Jo's Scrap-Bag*. Vol. 1. Boston: Roberts, 1872. 193–215.

Auerbach, Nina. *Communities of Women: An Idea in Fiction*. Cambridge: Harvard Univ. Press, 1978.

Baker, Nancy C. *The Beauty Trap: Exploring Woman's Greatest Obsession*. New York: Franklin Watts, 1984.

Baldwin, James. "Everybody's Protest Novel." In *Critical Essays on Harriet Beecher Stowe*, ed. Elizabeth Ammons. Boston: G. K. Hall, 1980. 92–97.

Cheney, Ednah D. *Louisa May Alcott: Her Life, Letters, and Journals*. Boston: Roberts, 1889.

Dickinson, Emily. *The Poems of Emily Dickinson*. Ed. Thomas H. Johnson. Cambridge: Belknap, 1955.

Douglas (Wood), Ann. "The Literature of Impoverishment: The Women Local Colorists in America, 1865–1914." *Women's Studies* 1 (1972): 3–45.

———. "Mysteries of Louisa May Alcott." Review of *Louisa May: A Modern Biography of Louisa May Alcott*, by Martha Saxton, and *Work: A Story of Experience*, by Louisa May Alcott. *The New York Review of Books* 28 Sept. 1978: 60–63.

Elbert, Sarah. *A Hunger for Home: Louisa May Alcott's Place in American Culture*. New Brunswick: Rutgers Univ. Press, 1987.

Fetterley, Judith. "*Little Women*: Alcott's Civil War." *Feminist Studies* 5 (1979): 369–83.

Fiedler, Leslie. "Harriet Beecher Stowe's Novel of Sentimental Protest." In *Critical Essays on Harriet Beecher Stowe*, ed. Elizabeth Ammons. Boston: G. K. Hall, 1980. 112–16.

Gilbert, Sandra M., and Susan Gubar. *The Madwoman in the Attic: The Woman Writer and the Nineteenth-Century Literary Imagination*. New Haven: Yale Univ. Press, 1979.

Hollander, Anne. "Reflections on Little Women." *Children's Literature* 9 (1981): 28–39.

Janeway, Elizabeth. "Meg, Jo, Beth, Amy and Louisa." *New York Times Book Review* 29 Sept. 1968: 42–46.

Kaledin, Eugenia. "Louisa May Alcott: Success and the Sorrow of Self-Denial." *Women's Studies* 5 (1978): 251–63.

Keyser, Elizabeth. "Alcott's Portraits of the Artist as Little Woman." *International Journal of Women's Studies* 5 (1982): 445–59.

———. "Women and Girls in Louisa May Alcott's *Jo's Boys*." *International Journal of Women's Studies* 6 (1983): 457–71.

Lant, Kathleen Margaret. "The Unsung Hero of *Uncle Tom's Cabin*." *American Studies* 28 (1987): 47–71.

Marsella, Joy A. *The Promise of Destiny: Children and Women in the Short Stories of Louisa May Alcott*, Westport, Conn.: Greenwood, 1983.

Myerson, Joel, and Daniel Shealy, eds. Madeleine B. Stern, assoc. ed. *Selected Letters of Louisa May Alcott*. Boston: Little, Brown, 1987.

Payne, Alma S. "Duty's Child: Louisa May Alcott." *American Literary Realism* 6 (1973): 260–61.

Pickett, LaSalle Corbell. "Louisa May Alcott." In *Across My Path: Memories of People I Have Known*. Freeport, N.Y.: Books for Libraries, 1970. 105–11.

Porter, Maria S. "Recollections of Louisa May Alcott." *New England Magazine* 6 (1892): 2–19.

Russ, Lavinia. "Not To Be Read on Sunday." *Horn Book* 44 (1968): 521–26.

Spacks, Patricia Meyer. *The Female Imagination*. New York: Avon, 1972.

Stern, Madeleine B. *Critical Essays on Louisa May Alcott*. Boston: G. K. Hall, 1984.

8. See Elizabeth Keyser's "Women and Girls in Louisa May Alcott's *Jo's Boys*" for an illuminating discussion of the adult Jo's continuing frustration and resentment arising from her conflicts between "self-assertion and self-sacrifice" (463). Keyser delineates "the broken fragments of Jo's inconsistent ideology" in the "first layer" of the text of *Jo's Boys* and brilliantly suggests how Alcott's "disposing of her characters—most of them in conventional 'happy' marriages" approximates the "act of violence" Alcott contemplated in her temptation to "engulf Plumfield and its environs so deeply in the bowels of the earth that no youthful Schliemann could ever find a vestige of it" (469–70).

CATHARINE R. STIMPSON

Reading for Love: Canons, Paracanons, and Whistling Jo March†

I

The "canon": that superego of literary culture, that bedraggled, resilient sign. Like others, I have believed that the bore of canons has been dangerously narrow. Like others, I have proposed that societies first construct a canon and then their canon instructs them. Like others, I have encouraged the "disestablishment of consensus."[1] Such arguments throw cold water on the yawny dream of an immutable curriculum that reflects human universals.[2]

† From *New Literary History* 21 (1990): 957–76. Copyright © The University of Virginia. Reprinted by permission of the Johns Hopkins University Press. [I have read versions and portions of this essay at a Gauss Colloquium, Princeton University, April, 1988; a conference on feminist theory in Dubrovnik, May, 1988; the Midwest Modern Language Association, St. Louis, November, 1988; the University of Montana, January, 1989; and the University of California, Santa Barbara, February, 1989. I am grateful for the comments of my listeners and for the responses of Joseph Carroll, Margaret Ferguson, Kathy Gentile, Domna C. Stanton, and Judith Fetterley (Stimpson's acknowledgment).] Page references to this Norton Critical Edition are given in brackets following Stimpson's original citations. Footnotes are the author's except where followed by [*Editors*].

1. I take the phrase from John Guillory, "The Ideology of Canon-Formation: T. S. Eliot and Cleanth Brooks," *Critical Inquiry*, 10, No. 1 (1983), 195. Gerald Graff (*Professing Literature: An Institutional History* [Chicago, 1987]) surveys shifts in the meaning and formation of the canon in the United States. Feminist criticism, which has influenced me, offers four potentially contradictory assemblages of ideas about the canon. Like Nina Baym in "Melodramas of Beset Manhood: How Theories of American Fiction Exclude Women Authors" (in *Feminist Criticism*, ed. Elaine Showalter [New York, 1985], pp. 63–80), the first assemblage protests against the exclusion of women, as authors and as cultural authorizers, from existing canons and asks why exclusion tends to be the melancholy, irritating case. Next, critics such as Barbara Christian or Sandra M. Gilbert and Susan Gubar excavate a women's tradition. They carry forward Gertrude Stein's *The Geographical History of America* (1936; rpt. New York, 1973). Stein broods about both the "masterpiece" and the "mater-piece." Knowing the mater-piece is a necessary part of the process of knowing everything, including the masterpiece. Even as the excavation of women's traditions redeems the previously noncanonical woman author, such as Harriet Wilson, it can, however, reconstitute the idea of a canon. Most provoked by *The Norton Anthology of Literature by Women: The Tradition in English* (ed. Sandra M. Gilbert and Susan Gubar [New York, 1985]), this accusation is now common. For example, Draine worries that courses about contemporary fiction by women have already enshrined a canon, which primarily reflects only middle- or upper-middle-class women as writers and readers. (Betsy Draine, "Academic Feminists Must Make Sure Their Commitments Are Not Self-Serving," *Chronicle of Higher Education* [10 Aug. 1988], A-40). Third, like Jane Tompkins, feminist critics have proposed alternative canons that enfold and include women. (Jane Tompkins, *Sensational Designs: The Cultural Work of American Fiction 1790–1860* [New York, 1985].) Fourth and finally, like Christine Froula, feminist critics have debunked all cultural hierarchy. Reread the traditional canon, Froula urges, in order to "expose the deeper structures of authority" (343). (Christine Froula, "When Eve Reads Milton: Undoing the Canonical Economy," *Critical Inquiry*, 10, No. 2 [1983], 321–47.) Kutzinski places feminist criticism within a systematic process of suspicion of cultural authority. (Vera M. Kutzinski, *Against the American Grain: Myth and History in William Carlos Williams, Jay Wright, and Nicolas Guillen* [Baltimore, 1987], pp. 244–50.) Guillory offers a succinct critique of the various responses of feminist criticism to the canon. He finds them incomplete because they seek to "open up" rather than abandon the canon; because they do not fully confront the question of values; because they insufficiently connect changes in a curriculum, in educational institutions, and in society. (John Guillory, "Canonical and Non-Canonical: A Critique of the Current Debate," *English Literary History*, 54, No. 3 [1987], 478–91, 497, 521.)

2. Catharine R. Stimpson, "Is There a Core in This Curriculum?" *Change*, 20, No. 2 (March/April 1988), 26–31, and *Where the Meanings Are: Feminism and Cultural Spaces* (New York, 1988). The spins of the publishing industry intensify instability. In 1949–50,

Canons, however, are tenacious.[3] Today, they persist in part because the managers of modern literary culture need some principles of order. So do the consumers. Our jobs as teachers, critics, and editors demand that we apply some reasonable criteria of selection as we hustle, bustle, and rustle up anthologies, textbooks, syllabi, library collections, and computer programs. Nota bene. Thinking about canons, then, creates an unruly tension. On the one hand, beyond a reasonable doubt, canons are guilty of ideological complicities and tautological self-definitions. What is "the best"? Well, the best is the best.[4] On the other hand, being with literature demands making some judgments about texts, some choices among them, much of the time.

To ease this tension, I wish to introduce the concept of the "paracanon." A paracanon recognizes our need for some cultural shelter, a tidy site. Simultaneously, a paracanon finds "the canon" both a house of orthodoxy and a house of cards. To mediate between these two perceptions, the paracanon is a tenet that neither ranks cultural works nor travels a compromised *via media*[5] among them. Instead, it negotiates a particular lease on the life of their commonalities and differences. How can a text join the paracanon? Texts are paracanonical if some people have loved and do love them.

II

No matter how difficult or accessible, how "high" or "low," any text is eligible for inclusion in a paracanon if it is beloved. Camp sensibility is one source. In her profound essay about its apparent superficialities, Susan Sontag writes that camp begins in love—of a still photo of the shoulders of a movie star, of the neck of a pink flamingo lawn statue. She writes that "the essence of Camp is its love of the unnatural: of artifice and exaggeration."[6] Being loved is the way into a paracanon of the present, having been loved the way into those of the past. A paracanonical work may or may not have "literary value," however critics define that term. Its worth exists in its capacity to inspire love. The paracanon asks that we systematically expand our theoretical investigations of "the good" to include "the lovable."

When we love a book, we read energetically. We believe that if a beloved book were human, it would embrace us. Our feeling is more intense than easy pleasure, more dashing and ferocious than delight, more gorgeous than distraction. We are grateful to the beloved text

---

8,000 new listings emerged; in 1987–88, 90,000. About 800,000 different titles were then available. In a mass consumer society, they have a short shelf life. 50,000 to 60,000 titles go out of print each year. The number of publishers has also grown. Their influence, however, is uneven, their power concentrated among a few. Of perhaps 21,000 publishers, 14 percent control about 90 percent of all titles. Figures from "Awash in an Ever-Deepening Sea of Print," *Newsweek*, 11 July 1988, p. 66.

3. I am indebted to Smith for her theory about the "continuity of circulation" of canonical works. See Barbara Herrnstein Smith, *Contingencies of Value: Alternative Perspectives for Critical Theory* (Cambridge, 1988), esp. pp. 30–53.

4. Guillory, in "The Ideology of Canon-Formation," 174, writes of "the massively resistant tautology of literary history: the works *ought* to be canonized because they *are* good."

5. Middle course [*Editors*].

6. Susan Sontag, "Notes on 'Camp' " in *Against Interpretation* (New York, 1966), p. 275.

for being there. If it were not, how might we connect with it? Even cathect to it? In our gratitude, we treasure the books we love. We may even become addicted to them. For they provide some of love's relational and terrifying thrills: its ecstasies; the threat of the loss, the closure, of these ecstasies; union with a different being; the threat of the loss, the closure, of this union; the sensation of inhabiting a world apart from the world that normally inhibits one; an oscillation between control and self-abandonment; a dance with the partners of amusement and of consolation; the gratification of needs that a reader has concealed.

So described, the conventions of paracanonical love might seem to resemble those of Western romance. A couple, bound by each other's spell, quiver and burn within a deliriously separate space.[7] Certainly, one virtue of passionate reading is that it creates the psychological sensation of being within such a space, except that the couple is a text and a reader, not a person and a person. When a reader feels crowded or harassed by other people (on a rush hour subway, for example), the isolation of reading is a relief, a coping mechanism, an escape. The individuality of readers' wants and needs cooks up an illusion that the paracanon is a wildly archaic collection of texts rubbing against each other. Readers may want and need anything. Think of the riotous host of texts people freely choose for a trip on a subway or an airplane.[8]

However, to describe paracanonical love only as a private transaction is completely inadequate. For social and cultural forces do have a hand in the structuring of subjectivity and the intricate domains of desire, intimacy, and love. The history of homosexuality—as word, category of behavior, value, and act—is but one demonstration of this truism. To enter into the paracanon a text should have a number of loving readers. This number need not be big enough to have turned a book in the mass market into a best-seller. This number does need to be big enough to be proof that a candidate for paracanonicity has more support than the whim of a handful of readers. Although paracanonical is not synonymous with popular, popularity is one sign that love is more than a singular obsession. Nor is asking for a collectivity of readers a methodological device to prevent the paracanon from degenerating into a list of individual preferences. Rather, it is a method of showing how the strong feelings that some cultural works provoke are the result of an interplay among individual preferences, larger forces that assign membership cards in social groups to individuals, and sign systems that give these assignments meaning.[9]

---

7. For an exploration of the psychology of romantic love, see Ethel Spector Person, *Dreams of Love and Fateful Encounters: The Power of Romantic Passion* (New York, 1988).
8. I recognize how important it is to place a paracanon within emotive theories about art as transport, theories about art as sweetness and delight, and theories of aesthetic pleasure. Such a task is beyond the scope of this essay.
9. One example: A mass-circulation women's magazine in the United States asked its readers to write in about their favorite books, what they read "for fun." One choice was *Lives on the Boundary: The Struggles and Achievements of America's Underprepared* by Mike Rose (New York, 1989). One individual, Deborah J. Fox from Champaign, Ill., said it was "An optimistic, hopeful story about real people struggling to succeed economically and educationally in American society." Fox's attraction to the story combines her temperament, place in social

Moreover, paracanonical love can beautifully enhance the relationship between a text, be it written or oral, and a specific community of readers. When this is the case, the community's love aids in ensuring the survival of a text. In turn, a text sustains the group's identity. This process, surely, has characterized African American culture.[1] Obviously, African American culture has incorporated conventionally canonical texts. Think, for example, of the *Narrative of the Life of Frederick Douglass*.[2] Here, at enormous risk, some slaves break the law that forbids them to learn to read. Their love of reading is inseparable from their desire for freedom and self-empowerment. They gain access to canonical works, especially to the Bible. Teaching it to other slaves, whom he also loves, Douglass sees the difference between the Christianity of the Land, which defends slavery, and the Christianity of Christ, which opposes it. Douglass also teaches himself the discourse of liberty and slavery through reading classical orations in an anthology he finds, *The Columbian Orator*. After he escapes from slavery and goes North, he takes the name "Douglass" from Sir Walter Scott's "The Lady of the Lake." This loving outlaw of a reader uses authoritative texts to defy a brutally authoritarian society.

As obviously, African American culture has created paracanonical texts. Think, for example, of *Mules and Men* by Zora Neale Hurston, the narrative of a young black woman anthropologist who returns to her birthplace, the American South, to "collect Negro folk-lore."[3] Here, paracanonical love flows through three channels. First, the community enjoys its culture: its songs, tales, prayers, poems, and rituals. Significantly, it hides them from the dominant, overweeningly domineering culture. The community's paracanonical love for *its* nonauthoritative texts mingles with its defiance of a brutally authoritarian society that would despise and exploit them. Hurston explains: "The theory behind our tactics: 'The white man is always trying to know into somebody else's business. All right, I'll set something outside the door of my mind for him to play with and handle. He can read my writing but he sho' can't read my mind. I'll put this play toy in his hand, and he will seize it and go away. Then I'll say my say and sing my song'" (18–19). Next, Hurston records the "vivid imagination" of her community joyously. Anthropologist, historian, curator, teacher, she engages in a labor of love. Third and finally, as the conventional canon of the late twentieth-century United States is opening up, African American texts are entering in, including those of Hurston in general and *Mules and Men* in particular, especially if we accept anthropology as literature. For many,

class, and a national ideology that encourages both the celebration of struggle against the odds rather than rage against them, and optimism about the future rather than resignation to the present. See Laura Mathews, "Word on Books," *Glamour*, Aug. 1989, p. 170.

1. Anne McClintock, "'Azikwelwa' (We Will Not Ride): Politics and Value in Black South African Poetry," *Critical Inquiry*, 13, No. 3 (1987), 597–623. McClintock shows a community (black South Africa) preserving and creating its own texts, while struggling against both an existing political order, *apartheid*, and an existing cultural order, which includes a literary canon based on English literature.

2. Frederick Douglass, *Narrative of the Life of Frederick Douglass* (1845; rpt. New York, 1968).

3. Zora Neale Hurston, *Mules and Men: Negro Folktales and Voodoo Practices in the South* (1935; rpt. New York, 1970), p. 17; hereafter cited in text.

guaranteeing Hurston's passage into a revised canon is another labor of love that builds on the paracanonical love that her texts originally inspired before they were so respectably reputable. In 1978, in a "Dedication" to her edition of Hurston's writing, Alice Walker was forthright, "for all her contrariness, her 'chaos,' her ability to stir up dislike that is as strong today as it was fifty years ago, many of us love Zora Neale Hurston. . . . We love [her] for her work . . . first."[4]

Too few critics now proclaim their love for a book. Wayne Booth has commented on the decline of friendship as a "serious subject of inquiry" in the past century and on the even sharper decline of talk about "books as friends."[5] He has contrasted readers of the past century to a Leigh Hunt who openly adores the authors in his library (171). For Booth, the "fullest friendship" between reader and book is ethical. It offers "shared aspirations and loves of a kind that makes life together worth having as an end in itself" (174). The various causes of the repressed and repressive decorum Booth deplores might include the desire of critics to push criticism closer towards science; the strength of cognitive traditions of criticism that prize philological skills or interpretative performances; the cult of the impersonal and conceptualizing literary voice; the influence of psychoanalytic theories about desire, in which loving a book might be the outward and visible sign of sublimation or fetishism; and, finally, the movement of criticism into academic departments that reward uptight writing and thinking.

Whatever the cause, a routine distinction exists between the text that provokes official respect and the text that provokes unofficial love. In *Lost in a Book: The Psychology of Reading for Pleasure*, Victor Nell studies such a group. He adapts the concept of "ludic reading," which is playful, private, unproductive, and absorbing. It so influences the consciousness of the reader that s/he experiences a sense of sovereignty, domination, and autonomy. Nell suggests, "one of the delights of reading for pleasure is that it is a truly response-free activity, pursued in the quiet certainty that no authoritative voice will call me to account for passages I skimmed or from which my attention wandered . . ."[6] However, the ludic reader, no matter how sophisticated or unsophisticated, distinguishes between a book that gives pleasure and a book that has merit, between a "good read" and a "good book," between a love object and a candidate for the canon. Michener is no Melville. The good book is hard. Nell suggests, "The close association between difficulty and merit rankings supports the notion that the value systems of many readers will be under the sway of Protestant Ethic convictions, such as that pain and virtue are constant companions" (164).

For several reasons, *Lost in a Book* is disturbing. It tries hard to bal-

---

4. Alice Walker, *I Love Myself When I Am Laughing . . . And Then Again When I Am Looking Mean and Impressive: A Zora Neale Hurston Reader*, ed. Alice Walker (Old Westbury, N.Y., 1979), pp. 1–2.
5. Wayne C. Booth, *The Company We Keep: An Ethics of Fiction* (Berkeley, 1988), pp. 170–71; hereafter cited in text.
6. Victor Nell, *Lost in a Book: The Psychology of Reading for Pleasure* (New Haven, 1988), p. 88; hereafter cited in text.

ance the humanities and the social sciences. It both cites William Gass and manipulates chi squares. Yet, as if their growth were beyond control, the more dehumanizing methods of the social sciences take over. Their ugliest signifier is the photograph of a white, male subject. He is wearing goggles and listening to white noise, with electrodes attached to earlobe, cheeks, and jowl. Despite the trappings of positivism, *Lost in a Book* uses a problematic sample. The subjects are South Africans. Given the realities of contemporary South Africa, are they as "universal" in their reading experiences as they seem to be meant to be? Nell, too, distinguishes them by gender and by language community (English or Afrikaans), but rarely, if ever, by race. Are they, then, all white, or is race not to matter in a study in South Africa?

These difficulties may diminish, if not destroy, Nell's description of a divorce between the admiring and the affectionate reading; between the book we praise publicly and the book we crave privately. Yet, if his analysis survives his method, *Lost in a Book* warns us that we have separated our studied measurements of the culturally valuable from our passionate engagements with the culturally accessible. We have severed authority from dearness. The middle managers of culture have edited feeling from criticism. So doing, we/they have also replicated the ideological and social division between a formal, rational, public domain (yes, masculine) and an informal, emotional, private domain (yes, feminine) that is a feature of modernity. Such polarities are commensurate with a gap between high and popular culture.

The concept of the paracanon reclaims love and pleasure for criticism. Aiding and abetting the restoration are two regiments of professional readers. Surging within and about them both are the several forces, such as African American or feminist criticism, that question "the canon." These forces use a reader's alienation from the canon as a seed of skepticism about its universality. Now large enough to be a division, or even a corps, the first regiment of professional readers practices reception theory and reader response criticism. It has reconnected texts to potentially besotted readers. Janice A. Radway's *Reading the Romance* studies women who often love popular romances and take them as their textual preference. She confesses that she had to relearn her critical methodology. She had to expand her focus from text to the drama between text and reader.[7]

These processes have permitted academic critics to infuse literary studies with autobiography, to fuse "reader" and "self." First-person accounts, then, both name a theory about reading and illustrate its practice. Demonstrating "transactive reading," Norman N. Holland enters into an association with "The Purloined Letter." He wittily represents himself as a two-fold reader, an identity that shows up in his teaching as well. He is a knowing reader, in competition with Derrida and Lacan, who objectifies a text, and a feeling reader, free from the strains of competition, who emotionally relates to that text. Showing both selves in his etymology of "purloined," he cracks, "Norman

---

7. Janice A. Radway, *Reading the Romance* (Chapel Hill, N.C., 1984), p. 86.

French or, if you like Norm's French."[8] Midway through his analysis, Holland bursts out, "I love this story, as I love the Holmes stories, because I can be both the Dupin[9] one admires and the relater who loves and is loved of Dupin" (359).

Because he eroticizes the grammar and syntax of reading, Holland belongs to the second regiment of professional readers as well: those who pitch a literary aesthetic back into the magnetic field of the body. In effect, they remind us that readers have retinas. Influentially, in 1964, Susan Sontag published, not only "Notes on Camp," but "Against Interpretation." Sontag writes as if it were possible to erase any mediating structure between art work and observer and to enjoy a pure aesthetic experience. Nevertheless, her argument anticipates the notion of a paracanon. Sontag suspects representational theories of art because they lead us down the primrose path of stressing the content of a work. Content is not the articulation of universal truths, but "a hindrance, a nuisance, a subtle or not so subtle philistinism."[1] Content demands narrow interpretation, mere translation, technocratic skills. Romantically, she affirms, "In a culture whose already classical dilemma is the hypertrophy of the intellect at the expense of energy and sensual capability, interpretation is the revenge of the intellect upon art" (7). She calls for a criticism that would come to its senses and replace hermeneutics with "an erotics of art" (14).

In *The Pleasure of the Text*, Roland Barthes answers Sontag's call. If Booth is a *magister*[2] of an ethics of reading, Barthes is a *magister* of an "erotics of reading."[3] As writer, text, and reader upend each other in the circulation of bliss, those prissy distinctions between the "good book" and the "good read" disappear, like lines on a sun-washed sea-washed beach. Barthes instead distinguishes between the texts of pleasure (the sun?), which submit themselves to the language of criticism and, perhaps, eventually to ethical interrogation, and the texts of bliss (the sea?), which defy language. If the text of pleasure seems to inspire the equivalent of conjugal or familial love, the text of bliss is a *coup de foudre*.[4] "Text of pleasure: the text that contents, fills, grants euphoria; the text that comes from culture and does not break with it, is linked to a comfortable practice of reading. Text of bliss: the text that imposes a state of loss, the text that discomforts (perhaps to the point of a certain boredom), unsettles the reader's historical, cultural, psychological assumptions, the consistency of his tastes, values, memories, brings to a crisis his relation with language."[5]

8. Norman N. Holland, "Re-covering 'The Purloined Letter': Reading as a Personal Transaction," in *The Reader in the Text*, ed. Susan R. Suleiman and Inge Crossman (Princeton, N.J., 1980), pp. 350–70.

9. The clever, rational, and imaginative detective from Edgar Allan Poe's "The Purloined Letter" and "The Murders in the Rue Morgue" [*Editors*].

1. Susan Sontag, "Against Interpretation," in *Against Interpretation*, p. 5; hereafter cited in text.

2. Master [*Editors*].

3. Richard Howard, "A Note on the Text," in Roland Barthes, *The Pleasure of the Text*, tr. Richard Miller (New York, 1975), p. viii.

4. Thunderbolt [*Editors*].

5. Roland Barthes, *The Pleasure of the Text*, p. 14; hereafter cited in text as *PT*. Lawrence D. Kritzman, "Roland Barthes: The Discourse of Desire and the Question of Gender," *MLN*,

To contemplate loving in Barthes's lanes (one fast, one closer to the security of the shoulder) is to approach the first of two difficulties with the concept of the paracanon: the shambles of the sentence "I(we) love this book." This disarray has at least three sources. First, in contemporary English, the words "I love" can mean the most profound, passionate commitment to a person, place, or thing, or the sweetly pastel approval of a person, place, or thing—a sushi bar, for example. (Similarly, the word *tragedy* has degenerated until it now refers tritely to the sad and/or unpleasant, a fire in an apartment house, for example.) Next, accompanying the spread of references of the verb "to love" is the wide array of disparate theoretical explanations, from sociobiological to theological, of the human capacities for love. We lack a consensus about the causes of love. Third, the direct object "book" can include an even greater disparity of titles, that "riotous host" I mentioned earlier, from *Lord Jim* to *Soldier of Fortune* magazine, from *To the Lighthouse* to *Watchtower*, that publication of the Jehovah's Witnesses. The variety of beloved texts guarantees that some people will love a text that others will find hateful.[6]

This very shambles is, however, significant. First, it is a symptom of postmodern society. Our culture is a network of intersecting systems and cross-cutting lines of force. To collate the meanings of the verb "to love" is to write a story of contemporary emotions, that nexus of a wry somatics; psychology; hierarchies of age, class, race, religion, and gender; and a mass consumer economy. One meaning of love, of course, is the promise of escape from a mass consumer society into the rosy authenticity of a coupled body and soul. To collate the theories about love is to write a contemporary intellectual history. To collate the beloved titles, with their odd admixtures, is to write a story of contemporary literacy and culture. Next, what can be done for the present can be done for the past. Mapping a paracanon is a historiographical project that can lead to narratives about a period that tell of the connections among its emotions, its libraries and classrooms, its literacies and illiteracies.[7]

The Pleasure of the Text anticipates such a labor of love. At three points, Barthes fantasizes what the collectivity of pleasured readers might be like. At each, he unfolds his condition of textual bliss, a seam at which contradictions meet. He cunningly delights in dramatizing a

103 (1988), 848, uses a quote from "Against Interpretation" as the epigraph for an essay about Barthes. Drawing on the work of Domna Stanton, among others, Kritzman explores Barthes's theory of the text as maternal body. See, too, Jane Gallop, "Feminist Criticism and the Pleasure of the Text," *North Dakota Quarterly*, 54 (1986), 119–34.

6. Doubtless Senator Jesse Helms fixes his eye on camp artifacts with dismay, but doubtless some of his rhetoric is, if unwittingly, campy.

7. Guillory, "Canonical and Non-Canonical." I agree with him that the story of literacy is the history of "the systematic regulation of reading and writing" (p. 489). My suggestion that the history of the paracanon can be a guide to that of social, cultural, and psychological formations is similar to Guillory's proposal that the history of canon formation is a guide to that of education. He writes, "The canon does not accrete over time like a pyramid built by invisible hands, nor does it act directly and irresistibly upon social relations, like a chemical reagent; it is a discursive instrument of transmission situated historically with a specific institution of reproduction: the school. The latter is a more or less formal arrangement for undertaking intensively educational functions also distributed extensively across the institutional breadth of any social formation" (pp. 494–95).

mild contradiction between the ahistorical and the historical. He first imagines a "Society of the Friends of the Text." Its members would have nothing in common "but their enemies: fools of all kinds, who decree foreclosure of the text and of its pleasure" (*PT* 14–15). Such a society would have no site. It could function only in "total atopia." Yet, it would also be "a kind of phalanstery," that site of nineteenth-century yearnings, which would acknowledge differences but purge them of painful conflict. Secondly, Barthes plays, if skeptically, with the possibility of harvesting all the texts *"which have given pleasure to someone"* (*PT* 34). Displaying this textual body would parallel the way in which psychoanalysis has displayed our erotic body. Finally, he sketches an aesthetic based "entirely . . . on the pleasure of the consumer," no matter what the class, group, culture. He sighs, happily, "the consequences would be huge, perhaps even harrowing" (*PT* 59).

The second of the two difficulties with the concept of the paracanon lies in the lexical genetics of my neologism: canon is the parent word of paracanon. Though invented in a recurrent workshop suspicious of canonical practices, "paracanon" nevertheless takes its meaning from "canon." It lies beside the canon as a medicine bottle does a sick man or woman. So doing, "paracanon" may be another incorrigible example of the difficulty of current debates that John Guillory persuasively analyzes. Such arguments set up a binary opposition between the "canonical" and the "noncanonical" that is meant to reflect still another binary opposition, between included and excluded social groups. Indeed, being out of the canon *signifies* being out of social prestige and power. Getting near to the canon has two risks: being pacified within or becoming an imitation without. Guillory writes that the difficulty of annexing "non-canonical works to a hegemonic tradition" lies in the "phenomenon of cooptation." He goes on, "It may be possible to defer this impasse by the establishment of alternative canons—canons of the non-canonical—but these pedagogic constructions also do not escape the formal features of canonicity. Rather, they suffer the deuterocanonical fate of 'ghettoized' programs."[8]

The paracanon, however, embraces both "canonical" and "noncanonical" works. In this respect, it is like a "women's tradition," which, in English, includes both a George Eliot and the silly female novelists she despised. The principle of inclusion in the paracanon is neither the official approval by a culture's schools, nor official indifference; neither authorship by a powerful social group, nor authorship by an excluded social group. On the contrary. The principle of inclusion is the ability to inspire any reader's love. So constructed, the paracanon has at least two potential relationships to an existing canon. First, if schools construct and maintain such a cultural formation, the paracanon will subvert it, as the id does ego and superego, as "illicit" love does order, as "camp" does high modernism. A paracanon serves, in these situations, as a jumble of works that float beside, beneath, and around any canonical arrangements that a culture might have in

8. Guillory, pp. 483–84.

place to hoard and board up art, literature, and the media. Next, if a society has no single canon, if it has a number of ways of organizing and evaluating cultural works, the "paracanon" can be but one way among several. Its last two syllables will be but a reminder of a recorded time. Similarly, the contemporary bearer of a well-known family name (Washington, Lee, Rockefeller, Guggenheim) evokes history even if he or she rejects every other family heirloom.

III

My example of a paracanonical text is *Little Women* by Louisa May Alcott, which I choose because I once worshipped it. Appearing on the verge of a youthful breakdown, I walked to third grade, a white, middle-class, provincial girl, reciting entire chapters to myself. This book was my friend, and I was more than half-right to delight in Jo March, that bolt of desire, who put salt on the strawberries, read with rats in the attic, fought murderously with her sisters, and turned down the rich boy next door. Rude and unladylike though it was, she whistled too.

Other readers have shared my passion. Jo March has been much beloved, in the United States and elsewhere. In 1927, United States high school students voted *Little Women* the book that had "interested" them the most, more than the Bible or *Ben Hur*. An essay contest accompanied the poll, which Mildred Childs, of Gray, Ga., won with a piece on the Book of Jo.[9] By 1968, a century after publication, *Little Women* had sold 6,000,000 copies in the United States alone. Its narrative has been supple enough to charm and seduce a number of boys and men. A grown man confesses in *Mademoiselle*, a magazine for adolescent and postadolescent women, that he fell "irrevocably" in love with the totality of *Little Women*. It was a grand American, Americanizing fable. "[T]o me, a first generation American, raised in an Orthodox Jewish household where more Yiddish was spoken than English, everything about *Little Women* was exotic. It was all so American, so full of life I did not know but desperately hoped to be part of, an America full of promises, hopes, optimisms, an America where everyone had a chance to become somebody wonderful like Jo March—Louisa May Alcott who . . . did become, with this story book that I adored, world famous."[1]

Moreover, its narrative and characters have been appealing enough to cross over into other media: theater, film, television, and comic strip. In February, 1988, *Ms.* magazine (for which Louisa May Alcott would surely have written had she been alive) began a serialized cartoon: "Little Women: Meg, Amy, Beth, Jo, and Marmee Face Life in the '80s."[2] Meg has too few designer outfits, Amy too few chances for

9. Anonymous, "*Little Women* Leads Poll: Novel Rated Ahead of Bible for Influence on High School Pupils," rpt. from *New York Times* in Madeleine B. Stern, *Critical Essays on Louisa May Alcott* (Boston, 1984), p. 84.

1. Leo Lerman, "Little Women: Who's in Love with Miss Louisa May Alcott? I Am," in *Critical Essays on Louisa May Alcott*, p. 113.

2. Victoria Roberts is the author/illustrator. In 1989, *Ms.* dropped the series, which hints at a diminishing love for *Little Women*.

cosmetic surgery. Beth wants a Bosendorf piano. Jo cannot write without a computer.

Possibly, the ethical standards of *Little Women* have subconsciously influenced my invention of the paracanon. Alcott testifies to the morality of love. Setting up the ability to inspire readerly love as the gateway to the paracanon transfers her judgments about behavior to my judgments about texts. Unfortunately, at their most strenuous, her judgments flatten *Little Women* as a text of bliss into a text of pleasure; as a text of pleasure into a text of duty. Moreover, her morality of unlimited love has its limits. *Little Women* seeks to be radical about race and class, but it is the radicalism of philanthropy. Its benevolence demands the needy, lesser other to justify its existence. How could Mother March, the "Marmee" who would prefer to be marred than to mar, succor the poor if there were no poor? The pastoral idyll of Plumfield, the school that is paradise regained, includes naughty, saucy little ragamuffins, "feeble boys and riotous boys, boys that lisped and boys that stuttered, one or two lame ones, and a merry little quadroon, who could not be taken in elsewhere. . . ."[3] How could Plumfield be so open-hearted if there were not the developmentally and racially different to scamper into its waiting chambers? Eventually, we must sober up and temper our love for the paracanonical with critical self-consciousness. Re-tooling ourselves as lover/readers, we school ourselves as ophthalmologists for the blindnesses of bliss.

In yet another example of the gap between love and power, the passion of her readers has been unable to guarantee Alcott's place in the United States canon. Nina Baym compares her fall to that of Harriet Beecher Stowe.[4] Both were quick in the nineteenth-century canon and dead in the twentieth. At least five activities might account for Alcott's loss of critical currency: first, a misreading that reduced *Little Women*, a text that mixes genres and messages, to but one genre, an ideologically purified and strained realism; next, a misreading of Alcott that reduced her to that deflated *Little Women*; next, a belittling of its vision of women and women's culture; next, the shelving of *Little Women* as children's literature (however, in a self-contradictory move inseparable from the trashing of a commitment to women, was the bestowing of honor upon some children's literature, especially upon some "boy's books"[5]); fifth and finally, as Jane Tompkins shows, a snubbing of popular texts, because popularity seemed, a priori, incompatible with the rigors of interpretive strategists.

Though some readers favor Beth or Amy, most readers love *Little Women* because they love Jo March. The appeal of Jo to readers who resist the cult of true womanhood is such that some commentators mistakenly detach her from the history that has bred and buttered up

---

3. Louisa May Alcott, *Little Women* (1868; rpt. New York, 1983), p. 597 [377] hereafter cited in text as *LW*.
4. Nina Baym, *Women's Fiction: A Guide to Novels by and about Women in America 1820–1870* (Ithaca, 1978), p. 23.
5. Critics most often compare *Little Women* to *Huck Finn*, which the Concord Library Committee barred in 1885. See John W. Crowley, "*Little Women* and the Boy-Book," *New England Quarterly*, 58, No. 3 (1985), 384–99.

such a cult. These readers then attach Jo to putatively ahistorical narratives. Madelon Bedell, for example, discerns in her introduction a "quality of universality" and suggests that *Little Women* may be "*the* American female myth, its subject the primordial one of the passage from childhood, from girl to woman" (*LW* xi, italics hers). Although *Little Women* can sweetly condescend to the needy, it never condescends to Jo—no matter how lame a pilgrim she might be or how dependent on her mother's approval. Jo is too tough. She wants independence and power. When she finds her sister Meg on John Brooke's lap, looking gaga and "wearing an expression of the most abject submission," Jo rages. In angry shock, she sobs and cries (*LW* 286) [183]. Crucially, she is an active reader and writer who initially claims power over language. Much of *Little Women* consists of her writing: letters, poems, journals, a family newspaper. Writing elevates Jo as blissfully as reading does the lover-reader: "She did not think herself a genius by any means; but when the writing fit came on, she gave herself up to it with entire abandon, and led a blissful life, unconscious of want, care, or bad weather, while she sat safe and happy in an imaginary world . . ." (*LW* 329) [211].

Writing permits Jo to support her family as a surrogate man. When she marries a "real" man, she seems to give it up. However, a first-person narrative voice controls *Little Women*. In part, the voice is that of a sententious moralizer, affirming the value of the feminine and domestic. In part, the voice is that of a gossipy historian of the March family, inscribing Jo March's progress toward the citadel of Jo Bhaerdom. Despite this, the voice can support Jo March. Coming home from a party, where all the merrymakers have been richer than the Marches, Jo defiantly declares, " 'I don't believe that fine young ladies enjoy themselves a bit more than we do, in spite of our burnt hair, old gowns, one glove apiece, and tight slippers.' " The narrator retrospectively adds, "And I think that Jo was quite right" (*LW* 45) [34]. An echo of Jo March whistles on.

In the reciprocity of love, *Little Women* has some gifts for a reader to carry away after the reading party. Because of them, the text provides an "afferent" as well as an "aesthetic" experience.[6] Jo as character and *Little Women* as narrative offer models of behavior to integrate into autobiography. Feminist critics have exposed a problem with *Little Women* as moral and behavioral polemic: the untamed Jo in the beginning of *Little Women* seems more lovable than the tamed Jo at the end.[7] The boyish, temperamental mode of activity that Jo struggles to discard is more appealing than the womanly, genial mode of activity she at last adopts. Largely, Alcott distinguishes early Jo from late, Jo March from Jo Bhaer, in their capacities for love. Both love, but Jo March loves her freedom, her mother, and her family of origin. More-

---

6. I obviously borrow the terms from Louise M. Rosenblatt, *The Reader, the Text, the Poem: The Transactional Theory of the Literary Work* (Carbondale, Ill., 1978), pp. 22–47.
7. See, for example, Judith Fetterley, "*Little Women*: Alcott's Civil War," *Feminist Studies*, 5, No. 2 (1979), 369–83, or Elaine Showalter, "Introduction," in *Alternative Alcott* (New Brunswick, N.J., 1988), pp. ix–xliii.

over, she is angry, impetuous, and, in fantasy, sadistic. Jo Bhaer loves her boy students' freedom, her mother, her family of origin, and its organic extensions. She is no longer angry, less impetuous, and cleansed of sadism.

Nevertheless, a grumpy tension remains between the softening of gender categories, which tomboy Jo March emblemizes, and the hardening of an ideology of a happy family that clings to those very gender categories, a belief system that *Little Women* valorizes. To keep this conflict from tearing the story apart, *Little Women* shows both Jo March and Jo Bhaer needing and enjoying a happy family. It also advances an explicit nationalism that is capacious enough to contain gender contradictions. Tactically and tactfully, the novel metamorphoses Jo's strong-willed love of personal freedom into a patriotic love of national freedom and purpose that includes a more refined and unselfish maintenance of personal freedom. *Little Women* slides away from the 1848 Seneca Falls Declaration, which revised the Declaration of Independence by mentioning women, and glides towards the Declaration's original text, which does not.[8]

So doing, *Little Women* celebrates life, liberty (in degrees), and, most valuably, happiness. Marmee has the last word. She wishes her daughters the flowers of joy her patient sacrifices cultivated. "Oh, my girls, however long you may live, I never can wish you a greater happiness than this!" (*LW* 603) [380]. Gooey and sappy though she might seem, this is nevertheless a speaking mother. The novel's end marries, not groom and bride, not father and mother, but language and mother. Both are objects of desire for a reading daughter who loves Jo, a reading, writing, whistling ego ideal.

A bonus of loving Jo, for girls and boys, is the safety of the feeling. Like the perfect mother, she offers the heart a haven. First, one's love is unrequited, but only the zaniest, neediest, and most jejune reader would expect requited love from a literary character. For how could a Jo, except in a reader's self-authored delusions, spurn one's affections? How could she speak? Or refuse to speak? Answer a letter? Or refuse to answer a letter? Next, Jo is this way because Jo is bodiless. As a result, how could loving her, again except in a self-authored delusion, ever be consummated? The anxieties of actually having to be erotic, whether as heterosexual or homosexual, fade away—like film exposed to sunlight.

Generations of female readers, lucky enough to have books, have maneuvered themselves around Alcott's most obviously constrictive maneuvers. They have continued to tutor themselves in unfeminine will through choosing which parts of *Little Women* and which Jo they will imitate, or, at the very least, find enchanting. Recidivists of reading, they return again and again to the far naughtier beginning and middle of the narrative. In a graceful essay about Jo's influence on readers, Carolyn Heilbrun states, ". . . Jo was a miracle. She may have been the single female model continuously available after 1868 to girls dreaming beyond the confines of a constricted family destiny to the

---

8. Modeled on the Declaration of Independence, the Declaration of Sentiments from the Seneca Falls Convention of 1848 demanded civic and human rights for women [*Editors*].

possibility of autonomy and experience initiated by one's self."[9] For a female reader, then, much of the joy of Little Women exists because one part of the text encourages rebellion. When the novel falls into parts, she can choose which part to love, even (or especially) a rebellious part. Possibly, though, both female and male readers love any text that gives an experience of division and self-division. Barthes writes, "pleasure of the text does not prefer one ideology to another . . . this impertinence does not proceed from liberalism but from perversion: the text, its reading, are split. What is overcome, split, is the *moral unity* that society demands of every human product" (PT 31). If so, the female reader's love of Little Women becomes a synecdoche for both a female and male love of a textual escape from any psychological and ethical coherence that seems as pre-formed as a slab of concrete.

Men and women alike prove and improve their love of paracanonical texts, not through an expert's interpretative flurries, but through self-willed, self-authorized rereadings. Assigned a story about Little Women in 1968, the centennial of its publication, a reviewer denies the possibility of objectivity. For she knows too little and has loved too much: ". . . I am no authority on children's literature, am not equipped by degrees to evaluate Little Women academically, nor by temperament—I loved it too much when I was young to evaluate it dispassionately."[1] Often, the love affair with a paracanonical text begins when a reader is young and a text is officially "children's literature." Meant for girls, Little Women was published after children's literature had become, first, a genre, and, next, a gender-marked genre.[2] Thomas Niles, a partner in the publishing firm that was considering Little Women, was dubious about the promise of the early chapters that he saw. In a primitive gesture of market research, he gave the manuscript to a niece, Lila Almy. According to a witness, Lila laughed, cried, was engrossed. This little girl-child's reaction reassured Niles that he should cut a deal. However, cross-reading could, and did, occur. Often discontent with the sugar and no-spice of their own, girls took up boys' books; to a lesser degree, in a sign of downward literary mobility, boys took up books consigned to girls. In part because Jo prefers boys to girls, Little Women was a cross-over text.[3] Such transgressions cast the young as mini-guerillas against modern ideologies of gender. What

9. Carolyn G. Heilbrun, "Louisa May Alcott: The Influence of Little Women," in Women, the Arts, and the 1920s in Paris and New York, ed. Kenneth W. Wheeler and Virginia Lee Lussier (New Brunswick, N.J., 1982), p. 21.
1. Lavinia Russ, "Not to Be Read on Sunday," in Critical Essays on Louisa May Alcott, p. 99.
2. Baym argues that Alcott shows the transmutation of women's fiction into girls' fiction: "The story of feminine heroism now becomes a didactic instrument for little girls; as an adult genre, woman's fiction becomes the gothic romance" (Baym, Women's Fiction, p. 296). In a complementary move, Elbert finds Little Women combining the sentimental novel with romantic children's fiction, in which a child's "vision of the world seems particularly honest and sincere" (Sarah Elbert, A Hunger for Home [New Brunswick, N.J., 1987]), pp. 198–99). Moers stresses the importance of work throughout Alcott's writing. In contrast to Tom Sawyer, where work is to be avoided, work in Alcott "is something real, lasting, serious, necessary, and inescapable as Monday morning" (Ellen Moers, Literary Women: The Great Writers [Garden City, N.Y., 1976], p. 89). The thematics of work guarantees that Little Women will not be an escape into a childish fantasy of a prelapsarian world free from toil.
3. Elizabeth Segal, " 'As the Twig Is Bent . . .': Gender and Childhood Reading," in Gender and Reading: Essays on Readers, Texts, and Contexts, ed. Elizabeth A. Flynn and Patrocinio P. Schweickart (Baltimore, 1986), pp. 176–77.

Nancy K. Miller writes of the woman reader might serve for the young as well: "[T]he power and the pleasure of the weak derive from circumventing the laws of contingency and circulation."[4]

Now *Little Women* is canonical children's literature. At first, children have very little say about the canons of their literature. Institutions (libraries, schools, families) impose texts upon children. So do individual gift-givers, whom both institutions and personal histories influence. My first copy of *Little Women* was a birthday present. Only later can children shape a canon—through their choices of what to reread or rehear or, now, to rerun on the VCR. In a commercial society, the choice of rereading or rehearing is parallel to buying the same product brand again and again, of sticking with Fords or Wheaties or Ivory. The rereadings that maintain a children's canon rehearse the rereadings that buttress an adult paracanon. Moreover, behind the latter are the memories of the former. Like the canon, then, the paracanon can be a conserving, preserving force.[5]

Ironically, as paracanonical text, *Little Women* saves and solidifies the memory of a girl's blasphemy, fierce negativities, and chaotic, indeterminate striving. Jo March has desires, but no fixed goal; energies, but no fixed post. Alcott writes: "Jo's ambition was to do something very splendid; what it was she had no idea, but left it for time to tell her; and, meanwhile, found her greatest affliction in the fact that she couldn't read, run, and ride as much as she liked" (*LW* 51) [38]. As ironically, the passage of *Little Women*, over the life span of a reader, from the status of children's canonical text to that of adult's paracanonical text, inverts the passage of clever, coltish Jo March, our trope of the girl as *de trop*,[6] to wise, brood mare Jo Bhaer, our trope of the woman as trooper. For grown-ups, the text loses a cultural respectability. Within the text, once grown-up, Jo gains social respectability.

One person did not always express love for *Little Women*: Louisa May Alcott. Pressed by financial worries, publisher, and father, she plugged away to fuse autobiographical materials with a genre. Martha Saxton suggests that it "was only rarely a labor of love."[7] Exaggerated though this comment may be, Alcott was later to downplay the importance of *Little Women*. Who was Alcott, the literary nursemaid, compared to Whittier and Emerson? Or to the canon as she construed it? In *Little Women*, Jo, making a career in New York, writes home to Boston about Professor Bhaer. Rebuking her for her popular writing, making her feel guilty about her professional talents, he upholds the canon. His New Year's present to Jo is his own "fine Shakespeare." His

---

4. Nancy K. Miller, "Emphasis Added: Plots and Plausibilities in Women's Fiction," in *Feminist Criticism*, ed. Elaine Showalter (New York, 1985), p. 349.
5. See Gail Mazur, "Growing Up With Jo," *Boston Review*, Feb. 1988, pp. 17–18. This is a parable of reading Jo and *Little Women*, in its various generic manifestations, throughout her life, including a period as parent in which she taught *Little Women* to her children. Elbert describes the adult woman rereading *Little Women* as a time traveler, going "backward to recover toys in the attic" (Elbert, *A Hunger for Home*, pp. 199–200).
6. Too much [*Editors*].
7. Martha Saxton, *Louisa May: A Modern Biography of Louisa May Alcott* (New York, 1978), p. 4.

other valued books are a "German Bible, Plato, Homer, and Milton" (*LW* 422–23) [271].

Yet, even as Alcott labels her own worth counterfeit and banks instead with a masculinized canon, she counters herself and asserts her value. As critic and self-critic, she is divided about the value of the canon and about her canonical worth as a literary producer. In *Jo's Boys*, she writes of her surrogate, Mrs. Jo, as a literary nursemaid who "provides moral pap for the young."[8] Pap may be soft or semi-liquid food. However, pap is also a nipple, the fount of maternal nourishment. Brazenly, Alcott claims virtues for the woman writer that she once stole away from her. Moreover, "pap" can be the paternal Pap. Even more brazenly, Alcott melds maternal and paternal in the blender of the pun. Finally, despite *his* many virtues, Professor Bhaer softens and fumbles away much of his authority. In the amateur theatricals in New York on New Year's Eve, before giving Jo his Shakespeare, he plays that Shakespearean ass, Nick Bottom. The flag Alcott has been weaving for the canon becomes a shroud as well.

IV

As noun, *paracanon* is an offering to the office that stores matériel for the customs officers of culture. They pass on some objects, rummage through others, reject still others. The paracanon might give some coherence to such gestures. Though noun, a paracanon summons up verbs: to read, to love what we read, to codify and judge what we read by what we love to read, to write a history of emotions and of literacy by noting what people have loved to read and how. So construed, the notion of the paracanon can be a pedagogical tool, a way of organizing the classroom and a syllabus. Using it, a teacher can foreground the experiences of reading that teacher and students actually have. The teacher can then assist the class in placing these experiences within larger cultural patterns. Why was *this* text loved? By whom? Was *this* text not loved, but hated, love's demonic other? Why? By whom? And did *this* text find only indifference? Did it look for love in all the wrong places? In contemporary classrooms, these discussions will doubtless show a greater passion for reading TV than for reading a book.[9] Ironically, we brood about literary canons as TV sprawls out like the megaburbs and literature tends to remain in the older neighborhoods. Fortunately, as we can apply the notion of the paracanon to both written and oral texts, so we can also apply it to TV and the other visual media. It is not whistling in the dark to remember that love has more than one object choice.

---

8. Louisa May Alcott, *Jo's Boys, and How They Turned Out* (1886; Boston, 1914), p. 50.
9. In a thoughtful personal communication, April 6, 1989, Richard Keller Simon observes that few of his students at Cal Poly in San Luis Obispo, Calif., admit to loving stories. He estimates that only about twenty-five percent of his classes report having read a book without having been told to do so and without having to worry about the possibility of being tested on it. Most of this twenty-five percent is female. However, everyone enthusiastically talks about the TV programs they loved as children.

ELIZABETH KEYSER

"Portrait(s) of the Artist": *Little Women*†

> It was all very well to insist that art was art and had no sex, but the
> fact was that the days of men were not in the same way fragmented,
> atomized by indefinite small tasks. There was such a thing as woman's
> work and it consisted chiefly . . . in being able to stand constant in-
> terruption and keep your temper. Each single day she fought a war to
> get to her desk before her little bundle of energy had been dissipated,
> to push aside or cut through an intricate web of slight threads pulling
> her in a thousand directions.
>
> May Sarton,
Mrs. Stevens Hears the Mermaids Singing (18)

> My ideals of art are those with which marriage is perfectly incompat-
> ible. Success—for a woman—means absolute surrender, in whatever
> direction. Whether she paints a picture, or loves a man, there is no
> division of labor possible in her economy. To the attainment of any
> end worth living for, a symmetrical sacrifice of her nature is compul-
> sory upon her. I do not say that this was meant to be so. I do not
> think we know what was meant for women. It is enough that it *is* so.
>
> Elizabeth Stuart Phelps,
The Story of Avis (69–70)

Jean Muir's ability to ingratiate herself with the adolescent Bella and
her mother[1] anticipates Alcott's phenomenal success in *Little Women*
(1868–69), the book that has kept her reputation alive throughout the
twentieth century. Paid to educate, edify, and entertain the daughter
of the household, Jean transforms dull lessons into lively fun, gently
corrects breaches of propriety, and encourages plenty of fresh air and
exercise as well as conventional occupations such as needlework. In
the evenings she captivates the whole family by singing, playing, reading aloud, and telling stories. Little wonder that Bella "soon adored
her" and Mrs. Coventry comes to trust her (25); together they enable
Jean to infiltrate the patriarchal family, disruption of which has been
her object from the outset. Mrs. Coventry at last comes to understand
her purpose, for as Edward reads aloud Jean's letters, she "clasped her
daughter in her arms, as if Jean Muir would burst in to annihilate the
whole family" (102). Yet despite this understanding, she, no more than
Bella, can wholly condemn Jean. After the governess's exposure, "Bella
half put out her hand, and Mrs. Coventry sobbed as if some regret
mingled with her resentment" (104). Bella's previous admiration for
Jean as Judith—"Oh, isn't she splendid?" (61)—suggests that she extends her hand not to the defrocked governess but to the daring insur-

---

† From Elizabeth Lennox Keyser, *Whispers in the Dark: The Fiction of Louisa May Alcott*
(Knoxville: U of Tennessee P, 1993), 59–82. Copyright © 1993 by The University of Tennessee Press. Reprinted by permission of The University of Tennessee Press. Page references
to this Norton Critical Edition are given in brackets following Keyser's original citations and
following two quotations for which Keyser does not give page references. Footnotes are the
author's except where followed by [*Editors*].
1. Jean Muir is the femme fatale protagonist of Alcott's "Behind a Mask," a thriller published
in 1866, about two years before *Little Women* [*Editors*].

gent. Alcott's splendor as a juvenile writer, I would argue, derives from just such insurgency.

Jean Muir provided Alcott with a model when, two years later, she was asked by Thomas Niles of Roberts Brothers to produce a "girls' story," but *Little Women* had other precursors.[2] "A Modern Cinderella" (1860) and "Psyche's Art" (1868), both based on the Alcott family, also deal with the conflict between art (or some other fulfilling occupation) and life as constituted by romantic love and domestic responsibility.[3] *Little Women*, though it finally becomes Jo's story, contains portraits of all four Alcott sisters: Meg March, like Anna Alcott, is domestic; Jo, like Louisa, is a tomboy and writer; Beth, like Elizabeth, is frail; and Amy, like May, is charming and artistic. "A Modern Cinderella" seems to have been written as a tribute to Anna Alcott, for the self-centered literary and artistic sisters, Diana and Laura, are subordinated to Nan, called "little woman" and "Martha" by her father and "my 'angel in the house' " by the hero, modeled on Anna's husband, John Pratt. "Psyche's Art" was perhaps designed as a similar tribute to May Alcott, though her name is given to the dying sister of the heroine, who is called Psyche, Bronson's name for Elizabeth.[4]

Although the number of sisters in these stories varies from two to four, certain elements remain constant: in each a sister (Beth, Nan, Psyche) sacrifices her own interests to those of her family; in each one or more sisters (Jo, Diana and Laura, Psyche) learns to put "that humbler and more human teacher, Duty" before "the goddess Beauty" ("Cinderella" 286); in each a sister (Beth, Nan, May) sickens, Nan and Beth as a result of their sacrifices. Finally, as the artists learn to subordinate their needs to those of their families, their art becomes less heroic and ambitious, more domestic and humble: Diana resolves to "turn my books and pen to some account, and write stories of dear old souls like you [the hero] and Nan" (292); Jo likewise writes homely stories about ordinary people, and like Psyche, whose sister also dies, she resumes her art at the urging of the family, finding in it solace for

2. Although at first reluctant to undertake the task, Alcott was actually well prepared to do so. As the editor of the children's magazine *Merry's Museum* and as a writer of occasional verse and fairy tales for children, she was familiar with the juvenile literary market. Her May 1868 journal entry reads: "Father saw Mr. Niles about a fairy book. Mr. N. wants a *girls' story*, and I begin 'Little Women.' Marmee, Anna, and May all approve my plan. So I plod away, though I don't enjoy this sort of thing. Never liked girls or knew many, except my sisters; but our queer plays and experiences may prove interesting, though I doubt it" (Alcott, *Journals*, 165–66).

3. In "Louisa Alcott, Trouper," Madeleine Stern identifies an earlier sketch for *Little Women*, "The Sisters' Trial" (1856) (195). Still another is the fantasy story "The Rose Family" (1864), in which the three oldest daughters all suffer from some character flaw: Moss is indolent, Briar is passionate and willful, and Blush is vain. They are sent to a fairy, Star, who gives each a talisman—a drop from a magic fountain in which, no matter where they are, they can see their mother's face. Thus the drops function much like the notes from Marmee that Meg and Jo fasten inside their clothes. Each rose is then forced, like Psyche, to perform labors until, aided by the talisman drop, she is ready to return home, cured of her indolence, passion, or vanity.

4. Bronson Alcott kept a journal on the growth of each of his daughters. His journal for his third daughter, Elizabeth, was entitled "Psyche, or The Breath of Childhood" (M. Bedell 1980, 101). Janice Alberghene, in "Alcott's Psyche and Kate," believes it possible to read "Psyche's Art" as "a specific response to Elizabeth's death" but prefers to "see the story as a more general expression of Alcott's view of the artist's proper balancing of her relationship to her art and to her family" (38).

her grief.[5] The lesson of these female artists, then, appears to be the lesson that Alcott supposedly learned: to subordinate their needs for artistic expression to the needs of their families and to use their artistic talents for the benefit not only of their own families but of the family as an institution.

The lesson in "Psyche's Art," however, is ambiguous. As though anticipating the furor over her refusal in *Little Women* to marry Jo to Laurie, Alcott equivocates as to the fate of Psyche and her fellow sculptor, Paul Gage: "Those who prefer the good old fashion may believe that the hero and heroine fell in love, were married and lived happily ever afterward. But those who can conceive of a world outside of a wedding-ring may believe that the friends remained faithful friends all their lives, while Paul won fame and fortune, and Psyche grew beautiful with the beauty of a serene and sunny nature, happy in duties which became pleasures, rich in the art which made life lovely to herself and others" (226). Of course one might argue that the ending Alcott obviously prefers is itself ambiguous. Is Psyche's art—"the art which made life lovely to herself and others"—her sculpture or merely the feminine art of pleasing and serving?[6] From what Psyche tells Paul in the final scene, the latter appears unlikely. Although her mother believes that she has forsaken sculpture, Psyche assures Paul that "when my leisure does come I shall know how to use it, for my head is full of ambitious plans, and I feel that I can do something now" (225). In other words, a year's devotion to domestic responsibility has served to confirm her commitment to her art. But what then do we make of the disparity between Paul's career and Psyche's? Is hers a minor talent exercised for the pleasure of a private audience—domestic, decorative, gratifying in its modesty and lack of pretension? Is Psyche resigned to view her art as an extension of the domestic sphere rather than as an alternative to it?

Psyche learns that a life of artistic achievement cannot be gracefully combined with a life of domestic responsibility. But she also learns that domestic life can offer a humanizing vision as well as legitimate subjects for art. At first she tries to employ her sister May as a model, but the dying child's fretfulness soon forces Psyche to acknowledge the opposition between her role as artist and that of caregiver. But while May obstructs Psyche's progress in one way, she facilitates it in another, for her inability to pose, to become an object, forces Psyche to see her more clearly than she has seen anything before. When, after May's death, Psyche resumes her work, she produces something "lovely in its simple grace and truth." This figure, "a child looking upward as if watching the airy flight of some butterfly which had evi-

5. For a discussion of this pattern see Veronica Bassil's "The Artist at Home: The Domestication of Louisa May Alcott." Still another example in *Little Women* is Amy March, who at the end of the book is modeling a bust of her frail daughter, Beth, with the encouragement of her husband, Laurie. Also, in "Patty's Patchwork" Aunt Pen encourages Patty to finish the quilt as a tribute to the baby sister who has just died.

6. In *Little Women* Mr. March tells Amy that "though I should be very proud of a graceful statue made by her, I shall be infinitely prouder of a lovable daughter, with a talent for making life beautiful to herself and others" (275) [177].

dently escaped from the chrysalis still lying in the little hand" (222), is most obviously a tribute to May and represents her soul's release. On another level, however, it represents the release of Psyche's creative spirit from its uneasy alliance with domesticity, though she has learned from domestic experience to see things whole.[7] "Psyche's Art," then, shows how temporary immersion in family life, such as Alcott herself often experienced, can serve to warn the female artist of the dangers of lifelong commitment to that sphere.[8] At the same time, it suggests how the traditional experiences of women can enrich their art.

"Psyche's Art" begins "once upon a time," as does a brilliant self-reflexive passage in *Little Women*. In an early chapter entitled "Burdens," Mrs. March, or Marmee, tells her girls a story that is the book in microcosm:

> "Once upon a time there were four girls, who had enough to eat, and drink, and wear; a good many comforts and pleasures, kind friends and parents, who loved them dearly, and yet they were not contented." (Here the listeners stole sly looks at one another, and began to sew diligently.) "These girls were anxious to be good, and made many excellent resolutions, but somehow they did not keep them very well, and were constantly saying, 'If only we had this,' or 'if we could only do that,' quite forgetting how much they already had, and how many pleasant things they actually could do; so they asked an old woman what spell they could use to make them happy, and she said, "When you feel discontented, think over your blessings, and be grateful.' " (Here Jo looked up quickly, as if about to speak, but changed her mind, seeing that the story was not done yet.)
>
> "Being sensible girls, they decided to try her advice, and soon were surprised to see how well off they were. One discovered that money couldn't keep shame and sorrow out of rich people's houses; another that though she was poor, she was a great deal happier with her youth, health, and good spirits, than a certain fretful, feeble old lady, who couldn't enjoy her comforts; a third, that, disagreeable as it was to help get dinner, it was harder still to have to go begging for it; and the fourth, that even carnelian rings were not so valuable as good behavior. So they agreed to stop complaining, to enjoy the blessings already possessed, and try to deserve them, lest they should be taken away entirely, instead of

7. Psyche's sculpture recalls the jeweled butterfly in Hawthorne's story "The Artist of the Beautiful." In contrast to Psyche, Hawthorne's artist produces through minute observation and exhaustive analysis a "mechanism" of metallic brilliance. Eventually it is destroyed by a malevolent child, but one wonders if it was not the bitterness of the artist's nature, projected onto the child, that doomed his art. Although Psyche actually molds only the chrysalis, her love for the child who holds it succeeds in creating the illusion of "airy life." In fact, by portraying only the chrysalis, Psyche solves on a small scale the problem Hawthorne attributed to sculpture—that of rendering life and motion through the lifeless immobility of stone.

8. Alcott was no stranger to the conflict that Psyche experiences. For example, she wrote to her sister Anna some years earlier, "You ask what I am writing. Well, two books half done, nine stories simmering, and stacks of fairy stories moulding on the shelf. I can't do much, as I have no time to get into a real good vortex. It unfits me for work, worries Ma to see me look pale, eat nothing, and ply by night. These extinguishers keep genius from burning as I could wish. . . ." ([Alcott, *Letters*,] 59).

increased; and I believe they were never disappointed, or sorry that they took the old woman's advice."

"Now, Marmee, that is very cunning of you to turn our own stories against us, and give us a sermon instead of a 'spin,' " cried Meg.

"I like that kind of sermon; it's the sort father used to tell us," said Beth, thoughtfully, putting the needles straight on Jo's cushion.

"I don't complain near as much as the others do, and I shall be more careful than ever now, for I've had warning from Susie's downfall," said Amy, morally.

"We needed that lesson, and we won't forget it. If we do, you just say to us as Old Chloe did in Uncle Tom,—'Tink ob yer marcies, chillen, tink ob yer marcies,' " added Jo, who could not for the life of her help getting a morsel of fun out of the little sermon, though she took it to heart as much as any of them. (58–59) [42–43]

Marmee's story incorporates the experiences that her daughters have already related and thus recapitulates the chapter it concludes. It also embodies the same theme and employs the same method as the book as a whole: as *Little Women* continues, the four girls learn, under Marmee's tutelage, to moderate their longings and aspirations, to resign themselves to or content themselves with the choices available to them; and just as Marmee moves from the girls as individuals to the girls as a group and back again, so Alcott devotes a chapter to each in turn, then a chapter to the entire family, and so on throughout the book. Finally, Marmee's story and her daughters' responses to it suggest Alcott's relationship with her audience. It engages the girls' attention because, for all its "spin" or fairy-tale elements, it recognizably depicts the teller's and the listeners' lives. But their different reactions to it indicate different ways of reading the larger story. Simple Beth is content with what she takes to be a patriarchal sermon. Pleasure-loving Meg feels somewhat betrayed to find an exemplum masquerading as entertainment. Rebellious Jo attempts to subvert the sermon with blackface humor but, by alluding to *Uncle Tom's Cabin*, she inadvertently likens the girls and their mother to slaves. Thereby, Alcott invites at least some among her readers to transform the larger story into a different kind of sermon, a vehement protest against servitude and oppression.[9]

9. As one would expect, critical opinions of *Little Women* vary widely. Eugenia Kaledin, Judith Fetterley, Karen Halttunen, Beverly Lyon Clark, and Lynda Zwinger believe that the book, by advocating women's self-abnegation (or at least the semblance of it), marked the end of Alcott's attempt to subvert traditional values for women; Elizabeth Langland and Nina Auerbach see an unacknowledged conflict between "female self-realization in marriage to a man" and "female fulfillment in a community of women" (Langland 112); Sarah Elbert sees the novel as a feminist utopia in which women's traditional values are celebrated and promise to transform the world. Different as their opinions are, all of these feminist critics, with the possible exception of Kaledin, recognize with Madelon Bedell that *Little Women* is "not about 'being good,' nor even about growing up, but about the complexities of female power and the struggle to maintain it in a male-dominated society" (1983, xv). For a brief but comprehensive survey of the last twenty years of *Little Women* scholarship, see Ann Murphy's "The Borders of Ethical, Erotic, and Artistic Possibilities in *Little Women*."

As Amy Lang writes of *Uncle Tom's Cabin*, "home [or the domestic sphere] fails as a *viable* alternative to this world because it is, finally, a contingent sphere, shaping itself in response to the male world outside it" (53). From the very first page of *Little Women*, Alcott makes clear the contingent nature of the March home. The novel opens with the March sisters preparing to sacrifice Christmas presents for themselves in order to purchase gifts for their mother, Marmee. But this sacrifice is not entirely self-initiated; it is prompted by Marmee's belief that "we ought not to spend money for pleasure, when our men are suffering so in the army" (7) [11]. In other words, this sacrifice within the home is exacted by the actions of men outside it. Later in the chapter the girls receive a letter from their absent father, a Union army chaplain, exhorting them to "fight their bosom enemies bravely, and conquer themselves so beautifully, that when I come back to them I may be fonder and prouder than ever of my little women" (16) [17]. This letter prompts Marmee to recommend that the girls play in earnest their childhood game of Pilgrim's Progress. She reminds them of how they used to "travel through the house from the cellar, which was the City of Destruction, up, up, to the housetop, where you had all the lovely things you could collect to make a Celestial City" (17) [17]. When twelve-year-old Amy claims to be too old for such games, Marmee reproves her: "We never are too old for this, my dear, because it is a game we are playing all the time in one way or another. . . . see how far on you can get before father comes home" (18) [18]. Marmee's words imply not only that life is a spiritual journey but that women's pilgrimage is merely a game, an imitation of men's, and that it takes place within the confines of the home for the purpose of winning male approval. Women can expand their constricted sphere only through the exercise of their imaginations, as when the March girls divide the sheets they are sewing into continents and "talked about the different countries as they stitched their way through them" (19) [18].

Playing, pretending, acting—these activities loom large in the lives of the March girls and would seem to offer compensation for and temporary liberation from poverty, irksome tasks, and, above all, the constricting roles of little women.[1] Jo complains, "I can't get over my

---

1. For extended discussions of the theater in Alcott's life and art see Madeleine Stern's "Louisa Alcott, Trouper," Nina Auerbach's afterword to *Little Women*, and Karen Halttunen's "The Domestic Drama of Louisa May Alcott." As early as 1943 Stern gave a detailed account of Alcott's youthful dramatic activities in Walpole, between 1855 and 1857, and in Concord, between 1857 and 1860. Stern perceived that the "thrillers that she launched across the pages of the penny dreadfuls had their source in the writer's early dramatic career" (194) and observed that "Whenever she wrote a story that contained any autobiographical elements, one theme was sure to concern the drama" (195). Auerbach and Halttunen both comment on how theatricals frame the March novels—*Little Women, Little Men,* and *Jo's Boys.* As Auerbach puts it, "The March trilogy begins with a play; once it produces an actress, it can let 'the curtain fall forever on the March family' " (465). Halttunen argues that Bronson Alcott encouraged theatricals as a means of teaching children "how to control every aspect of their self-expression" (237), but that Louisa May Alcott's melodramas "not only moved beyond Bronson's use of allegorical drama, but actually subverted it" (238). She believes, however, that in *Little Women* Alcott "left behind not only her Gothic period, but also her use of theatricality to undermine the cult of domesticity" (242). Sharon O'Brien, in "Tomboyism and Adolescent Conflict," sees Alcott's adolescent plays as foreshadowing her inability to reconcile "the energetic, assertive self represented by her tomboy period with an adult female identity" (365).

disappointment in not being a boy" (10) [13], but her dramas allow her to play "male parts to her heart's content" (25) [23]. Even Jo's plays, however, serve to suggest the girls' entrapment. In "The Witch's Curse" Jo plays both the hero and the villain, an indication not only of her longing for male freedom and her major role in the larger drama of *Little Women* but also of her self-divided nature. Meg, the most conventional of the girls and the quickest to reprove Jo, plays both the witch, whose curse destroys the villain, and Don Pedro, "the cruel sire," [24] whose patriarchal authority would thwart the hero. The casting of the youngest, Amy, as the heroine and her wooden performance in that role indicate its unchallenging and stultifying nature. Finally, Beth plays a "stout little retainer" (29) [24], the part she habitually assumes in the March household, but also an ugly black imp, which implies a darker side to the retainer role. The futility of Jo's efforts to simulate the male world from which she is excluded becomes apparent at a meeting of the girls' Pickwick Club. When Jo recommends admitting Laurie, the boy next door, Meg and Amy object: "We don't wish any boys; they only joke and bounce about. This is a ladies' club, and we wish to be private and proper" (131) [90].

By learning to make believe and play various parts, the girls are rehearsing for the games and roles they will, as Marmee says, be playing all their lives. Significantly, conventional Meg, not passionate Jo or stubborn Amy, is described as the most accomplished actress. Although she professes to be too grown-up to continue acting in Jo's productions, she is simply ready to play the part in life assigned her, a part for which, more than her self-assertive sisters, she has a talent. Yet all the girls, whether reluctantly or enthusiastically, must rehearse their lines in a domestic script. In a sense they are always on stage, performing for a male audience, for as Laurie tells Jo, "sometimes you forget to put down the curtain . . . and, when the lamps are lighted, it's like looking at a picture to see the fire, and you all round the table with your mother" (65) [46].

A party scene early in *Little Women* points up both the opposition between Meg and Jo, implied by their adversarial roles in "The Witch's Curse," and the nature of the part that Meg is eager to play—that of "a real lady." Meg, concerned that Jo's party dress is scorched in back from standing too close to the fire, warns her to "sit still all you can, and keep your back out of sight" (34) [27]. Because Jo has soiled her gloves, and because, according to Meg, "a real lady is always known by neat boots, gloves, and handkerchief" (37) [29], she must wear one of Meg's, even though her hand is larger and will stretch it, while carrying one of her own. Girls like Jo, who burn their frocks and soil their gloves, who, in other words, are too full of passion and life, must acquire the art of concealment. But that art, uncomfortable in itself, can lead to further suffering. Meg, whose "tight slippers tripped about so briskly that none would have guessed the pain their wearer suffered smilingly" (38) [30], pays for her dubious pleasure with a sprained ankle. Before Meg's accident, however, Jo meets Laurie, forgets the need to conceal her dress, and dances a spirited polka. But her few moments of exhilaration simply sharpen the images of pain, concealment, and constriction. Thus her comment on the evening, "I don't believe fine young ladies enjoy themselves a bit more than we do," can be read ironically, as can the narrator's aside, "And I think Jo was quite right" (45) [34].

Such ambiguity is typical of Alcott's narrator even when she seems to be affirming the life of selfless service and patient, silent suffering. In one of the many passages that have been read as "a sweet sermon on self-sacrifice," the narrator seems to glorify Beth's passive, retainer role: "There are many Beths in the world, shy and quiet, sitting in corners till needed, and living for others so cheerfully, that no one sees the sacrifices till the little cricket on the hearth stops chirping, and the sweet, sunshiny presence vanishes, leaving silence and shadow behind" (53) [39]. Yet "silence and shadow" seems as much a description of the living Beth, the black imp, as of the void left by her dying. Marmee's moralistic judgments are similarly undercut by the situations that prompt them. The chapter "Burdens," which culminates in Marmee's "sermon," contains stories of women's ignorance, passivity, vulnerability, and dependence. Jo discovers that she is lucky, because, unlike her crotchety Aunt March, she can appreciate the magnificent library "left to dust and spiders" since her uncle's death [37]. Meg concludes that she is luckier than the wealthy family she serves as governess because she hasn't "any wild brothers to do wicked things, and disgrace the family" (56) [41]. Amy stops envying a friend when that friend is punished in a most humiliating way for having made a caricature of the schoolmaster. And Beth marvels at the goodness of Mr. Laurence, who presented a big fish to a poor woman unable to feed her family. Each girl recognizes her comparative good fortune, and Marmee, by emphasizing their blessings, reinforces their complacency. But the stories themselves tell of women's intellectual and economic deprivation and their vulnerability to disgrace and humiliation. Thus in a sense Marmee's "sermon" can be read as a "spin," a glossing over of women's plight that, as Meg suggests, turns their own stories against them.[2]

While Jo is privileged compared with her Aunt March, her very privilege—her ability to penetrate male preserves such as her uncle's library—leads to conflict between her androgynous nature as mirrored by Laurie and her feminine role as modeled by Meg and Marmee. Confined, almost imprisoned, in the big house next door, Laurie is freed by Jo in a reversal of the Sleeping Beauty tale. In boldly entering the house that she regards as "a kind of enchanted palace, full of splendors and delights" [44], and by confronting gruff old Mr. Lau-

2. In an early scene the March girls sacrifice their Christmas breakfast to an impoverished family. The narrator's editorial emphasis seems to be on the goodness of the girls, called "angelkinder" by the Hummel children, and their satisfaction in self-sacrifice. But the stark description of the Hummels' living conditions—"A poor, bare, miserable room . . . with broken windows, no fire, ragged bed-clothes, a sick mother, wailing baby, and a group of pale, hungry children cuddled under one old quilt, trying to keep warm" (23–24) [21]—reveals the helplessness of women who have lost or been abandoned by their men. Significantly, Mrs. March believes that they too would be "lonely and helpless" should anything happen to Mr. March (57) [42].

rence, Jo seems to be appropriating male power and freeing a part of her own nature. In fact, the shabby old brown house containing the five women—what Mr. Laurence calls "that little nunnery over there" (75) [52]—and the stately but lifeless stone mansion containing Laurie, his grandfather, and his tutor, John Brooke, can be seen as representing feminine and masculine spheres. Jo and Laurie, whose friendship brings the spheres into contact and thus enlarges both of them, seem to make up a whole, androgynous person; Jo's nickname expresses her longing for masculine freedom and independence, whereas Laurie's nickname, "Dora," and even "Laurie" itself suggest the feminine in his nature, the kinship with his artist mother. Although Jo draws him into the March girls' charmed circle,[3] she also brings out the manliness in "Teddy," as she alone calls him, for as Mr. Laurence observes, "she seemed to understand the boy almost as well as if she had been one herself" (70) [49].

Androgynous as he is, Laurie, like Jo, finds his entrapment in gender-role stereotypes especially galling. Laurie's "castle in the air" is "to be a famous musician . . . never to be bothered about money or business" (177) [118]. But Laurie's grandfather equates business with masculinity and Laurie's interest in art and music with effeminacy. Ironically, Mr. Laurence's efforts to ensure that his grandson prove his manhood by taking over the family business keep Laurie as sheltered from the world as any girl. In a sense Laurie, like Guy in "A Whisper in the Dark" and the Coventry brothers in "Behind a Mask," exemplifies (as the reversal of the Sleeping Beauty tale suggests) not only the masculine plight but the feminine. Like a woman, he is dependent on and subservient to a patriarchal figure, who in turn depends upon his subject for love. As Meg tells Laurie when he is encouraged by Jo to rebel: "you should do just what your grandfather wishes. . . . As you say, there is no one else to stay with and love him." We are told that Laurie "had a young man's hatred of subjection" (180) [119], and we are left to infer that it is no more natural or legitimate than Jo's.

Laurie and Jo enable each other to temporarily escape entrapment in gender-role stereotypes. From their first meeting Laurie allows Jo to be her full self and offers her the male camaraderie for which she has always longed. In nominating Laurie for membership in the Pickwick Club, Jo argues that he will "give a tone to our contributions, and keep us from being sentimental" (132) [90], and once admitted he inspires her to revise "her own works with good effect" (134) [91]. Laurie not only accepts, encourages, and provides a model for the development of Jo's masculine side; he also elicits and nurtures the feminine. On Jo's first visit to the "enchanted palace," she enters like a male hero but presents herself to Laurie as a nurse. Later, when Beth lies critically ill, Jo, despite her belief that "tears were an unmanly weakness" (97) [65], allows herself to break down in Laurie's presence and be com-

---

3. In an argument similar to Sarah Elbert's, Anne Dalke, in " 'The House-Band': The Education of Men in *Little Women*" [reprinted in this Norton Critical Edition on pp. 556–63] discusses how the feminine sphere, represented by the March women, transforms the men who are allowed to enter it.

forted by him. And though Jo's bracing companionship has tended to make him more manly, Laurie has learned, through contact with the feminine household, how to offer maternal support. In words that recall Marmee's on another occasion, he says, "I'm here, hold on to me, Jo, dear," and silently strokes "her bent head as her mother used to do" (228) [148]. In short, the friendship of Jo and Laurie seems to provide the best of both spheres—masculine strength and freedom from sentimentality with feminine sympathy. Later, when Jo, for reasons she finds difficult to explain, rejects Laurie's proposal of marriage, she feels "as if she had stabbed her dearest friend; and when he left her, without a look behind him, she knew that the boy Laurie never would come again" (455) [291]. The description of this parting makes it clear that Jo has betrayed not only a friend but a crucial part of herself that she cannot hope to recover. In refusing to marry Jo to Laurie, Alcott conveys her recognition that in society as it was then constituted such androgynous wholeness as would have been theirs—and as she had symbolically envisioned in *Moods* and "A Marble Woman"—was impossible.

The boy in Jo, as represented by Laurie, is successfully opposed by Meg, Beth, and Marmee. Meg and Jo, as the two eldest sisters, have a special relationship rather like that of Jane and Elizabeth Bennet in *Pride and Prejudice*, But unlike Austen's heroines, Alcott's are always at odds. Jo's "good, strong words, that mean something" are "dreadful expressions" to Meg (48) [36]; Jo enters the "enchanted palace" for the first time partly because she loves "scandalizing Meg by her queer performances" (61) [44]. Jo in turn is scandalized rather than delighted when, breaking in on Meg and her suitor John Brooke, she finds "the strong-minded sister enthroned upon his knee, and wearing an expression of the most abject submission" (286) [183]. In Jo's play, we remember, Meg plays the witch and Don Pedro, the symbol of patriarchal authority. In her unquestioning submission to that authority and in her affinity for the traditional female role, she does represent a curse and a threat. Like the benign witch in the play, Meg opposes what to her seems villainous or shocking in Jo, but, like Don Pedro, she also opposes what is heroic and creative. She does not realize that to subdue the one is to stifle the other. As the model lady, wife, and finally mother, Meg embodies the patriarchal pattern imposed on women that Jo wants desperately to escape.

Meg, while much tamer than Sybil, Sylvia, and Cecil,[4] is akin to those adolescent heroines. The description of her simultaneously enthroned and submissive after accepting John's proposal reminds us of the illusory sense of power that Sybil sought in courtship, and the image of her perched upon his knee suggests that marriage will perpetuate her childhood as it did Sylvia's and Cecil's. Just as Sylvia "seemed most like a child" when "learning to be a woman," so Meg's initiation into womanhood coincides with a retreat into childhood. As a house

---

4. Sybil is the narrator of Alcott's thriller "A Whisper in the Dark" (1863); Sylvia Yule is the protagonist of *Moods* (1864); and Cecil, or Cecilia, Stein, is the ingenue heroine of "A Marble Woman" (1865) [*Editors*].

guest of the worldly Moffats, Meg suddenly finds herself regarded as a marriageable young woman. In order to deny rumors about her and Laurie, she protests that he "is only a little boy" and that "it is quite natural that we children should play together" (112) [75]. Trying to decline the offer of a low-cut gown, Meg claims that "my old dress . . . does well enough for a little girl like me" (113) [76]. Forced to wear the sophisticated and revealing costume, Meg survives the evening by imagining herself "acting the new part of fine lady" (116) [77]. Like Cecil after the ball at which she impersonates a radiant bride, Meg goes to bed "feeling as if she had been to a masquerade" (120) [82]. Afterward a chastened Meg confesses to Marmee that she has been "a silly little girl," but Jo rightly recognizes that, compromised, contrite, and childlike as she is, "during that fortnight her sister had grown up amazingly, and was drifting away from her into a world where she could not follow" (122) [84].

Jo wishes that "wearing flatirons on our heads could keep us from growing up" (252) [162], but the only apparent alternative to adult womanhood and the childlike submission it entails is to remain genuinely childlike, as Beth does. Lacking both Meg's willingness to conform and Jo's will to resist, Beth simply remains fixed in her roles as "Little Faithful." In one of the many significant juxtapositions in *Little Women*, Beth enters the "Palace Beautiful" shortly after Jo's first visit to the "enchanted palace." But whereas Jo enters boldly, without a formal invitation, Beth creeps in only after being assured that no one will see her. She is as drawn to the grand piano as Jo is to the library, but Mr. Laurence, recognizing that her timidity almost cancels out her pleasure, provides her with a "cabinet piano" so that she can remain at home. Yet, despite her meekness, "over her big, harum-scarum sister Beth unconsciously exercised more influence than anyone in the family" (54) [40]. Jo refers to Beth as her "conscience," and when she rests her head on Beth's hood "the submissive spirit of its gentle owner seemed to enter into Jo" (229) [148]. As Jo's conscience, Beth, as in the play, is both Jo's retainer and her black imp. Her model of submissiveness is more subtle and insidious than Meg's because Jo is not aware of a need to struggle against it.

Marmee, who admits to being "angry nearly every day of my life" (101) [68] and who has "never enjoyed housekeeping" (141) [95], teaches, ironically, the self-repression that Beth alone has completely achieved, as well as the feminine and domestic virtues so easily acquired by Meg. When Jo asks how she has learned to "keep still" when angered, Marmee explains that Jo's father made "it easy to be good" (101–2) [69]. But Marmee's later advice to Meg on the necessity of controlling her temper so as not to provoke her husband's suggests that men do not so much make it easy to be good as demand it.[5] Despite her tacit admission of women's subordinate position in marriage, Marmee insists that "To be loved and chosen by a good man is the best

5. As Fetterley points out in "Alcott's Civil War," female anger in the novel produces, or threatens to produce, dire consequences for its female subject, whereas male anger threatens its female object (376, 380).

and sweetest thing which can happen to a woman" (123) [84].[6] By virtually denying her daughters other choices and by repressing the parts
of themselves that would make other choices available, Marmee keeps
her daughters dependent, undeveloped, diminutive—like Beth, who
literally fails to attain adulthood.

Marmee allows, even encourages, the girls' childish dependency, but
she would deny the child who seeks her own gratification. Amy, the
"spoiled" baby of the family, is to Jo's chagrin the most insistent in her
claim to adult privileges.[7] When Amy wheedles Meg and Jo to let her
accompany them to the theater, Jo refuses, calling her a little girl and
a baby. Amy warns that Jo will be sorry and promptly destroys Jo's "loving work of several years" (96) [64]. Jo is unable to forgive her and
later, when Amy tags after her and Laurie, spitefully neglects to warn
her of the thin ice through which she falls. In excluding, punishing,
and nearly killing Amy, Jo seems trying to rid herself of the needy,
greedy, demanding, and childish nature that nonetheless drives one to
adult achievement and the achievement of adulthood. The destruction
of Jo's book and her agony of remorse after the accident suggest, like
Bazil Yorke's attempts to banish Germain,[8] the futility and danger of
denying one's natural impulses.[9] Just as Amy was the heroine in Jo's
play, the issue at stake between the hero and the villain, so she seems
to represent something crucial in Jo's nature, something toward which
Jo is deeply ambivalent. Unfortunately, Jo and Marmee see this
episode as calling for more repression rather than for a recognition of
the feelings that prompted it.

Jo, unlike her sisters, consciously aspires to independence, but she
internalizes her mother's values to the point that she cannot seek it
without guilt. Jo views the publication of her first story as the first step
in realizing "the dearest wishes of her heart"—"to be independent, and
earn the praise of those she loved" (194) [128]. But the two wishes are
conflicting, if not incompatible: to achieve independence she will have
to assert herself in such a way as to incur blame; and to win the praise
of those she loves best, she will have to curtail, or at least modify, her
striving for independence. When Meg is staying with the Moffats, she
slips Marmee's note "into her pocket as a sort of talisman against envy,
vanity, and false pride" (109) [73]. Similarly, Jo pins Marmee's note
"inside her frock, as a shield and reminder, lest she be taken unaware"
(151) [101]. Jo must guard against her emotions at all times; otherwise she will disappoint her mother and, through her, her father.
When, upon his return, Mr. March praises Jo, causing her to blush
with pleasure, it is for having become "a young lady who pins her collar straight, laces her boots neatly, and neither whistles, talks slang,

6. Auerbach argues in *Communities of Women* that Marmee allows "her girls a great freedom
. . . the freedom to remain children and, for a woman, the more precious freedom *not* to fall
in love" (62). But how can the girls appreciate the latter freedom if, as Marmee implies, it
means missing out on the most fulfilling experience a woman can know?
7. Anne Hollander, in "Reflections on *Little Women*," views the younger Amy as unlike the
other March girls in that she is unpleasant, selfish, and genuinely bad.
8. In "A Marble Woman," Basil and Germain are rival suitors for Cecilia [*Editors*].
9. Fetterley remarks that Amy's accident is part of a "pattern of maximum possible consequences for a minimal degree of self-absorption and selfishness" (1979, 381).

nor lies on the rug, as she used to do" (274) [176]—in short, a lady as defined earlier by Meg.

Meg's marriage, as described in part 2 (originally entitled "Good Wives"), exemplifies the constriction—physical, mental, and emotional—to which even Jo finally adapts. The lawn of Meg's home, which she calls "my baby-house," is "about as big as a pocket-handkerchief," and her dining room is described as a "tight fit" (301, 297) [194, 192]. Just as Meg earlier had to smile although her slippers pinched her feet, so now she must gracefully, even gratefully, accept her cramped and narrow lot in life. While John takes "the cares of the head of a family upon his shoulders" (338) [218], Meg's greatest challenge is the making of jelly. Her failure touches off the one quarrel we witness between John and Meg, during which she declares, "I'm away—sick, dead, anything" (343) [221]. Rash as these words sound, the imagery surrounding Meg's marriage does indeed suggest a living death. After the birth of her twins, Daisy and Demi, Meg complains to Marmee that she is "on the shelf." Marmee, as an exemplar of "real womanhood," exhorts Meg not to "shut yourself up in a bandbox because you are a woman" (482) [308] but to enter, at least through reading and conversation, her husband's sphere and teach him how to help in her own. Although John succeeds in teaching *her* how to cope with their son, Demi, years of little womanhood have ill prepared Meg to share John's world of ideas, and she soon decides "that politics were as bad as mathematics" (489) [312]. After a few such "domestic experiments," Meg learns "that a woman's happiest kingdom is home"— "the sort of shelf on which young wives and mothers may consent to be laid, safe from the restless fret and fever of the world, finding loyal lovers in the little sons and daughters who cling to them" (491) [313]. The image of the shelf, the passive verb "laid," and the idea that children are the most appropriate lovers for women all imply that marriage arrests female development.[1] Just as the title of part 1, "Little Women," suggests that adolescent girls should be miniature adults, so the eventual extension of that title to part 2 suggests that "good wives" should remain little women or girls.

Meg's "loyal lovers," Daisy and Demi, perpetuate the gender stereotypes Jo tries in vain to escape.[2] At three, Daisy begins to sew and "managed a microscopic cooking-stove with a skill that brought tears of pride to Hannah's [the Marches' servant's] eyes, while Demi learned his letters with his grandfather" and "developed a mechanical genius which delighted his father" (566) [358]. Whereas Daisy demands a "needler," Demi actually tries to construct a sewing machine. Furthermore, in their relationship to each other they reflect the age-old stereotypes: "Demi tyrannized over Daisy . . . while Daisy made a galley-slave of herself, and adored her brother, as the one perfect be-

---

1. Jane Van Buren sees Alcott's "suffusion of florid prose" as recommending an "idealized version" of marriage (297–98).
2. Carolyn Heilbrun writes in *Reinventing Womanhood*, "Perhaps only in America, with its worship of 'manliness,' could boy-girl twins, elsewhere universally a literary phenomenon characterized by their resemblance to one another, be so sharply defined and differentiated by sex roles" (191).

ing in the world" (567) [358]. Daisy is so angelic, such a perfect little woman, that she reminds her family of Beth. "Her grandfather often called her Beth,' and her grandmother watched over her with untiring devotion, as if trying to atone for some past mistake, which no eye but her own could see" (568) [359]. Her eye fails to detect that in rewarding Beth, and now Daisy, for angelic or slavish, self-abnegating behavior the family fails to prepare them for full participation in the adult world. Ironically, it is Jo, not Daisy, who eventually succeeds Beth as "angel in the house," for in evading Laurie, she walks into the very domestic trap she had sought to avoid. Encouraged by Marmee, who believes that Jo and Laurie "are too much alike, and too fond of freedom" (407) [260], Jo goes to New York, where, just as she is getting a taste of independence, she finds in Professor Bhaer that "something sweeter" than freedom that Marmee had wished for her (408) [261].

Whereas Laurie had always encouraged Jo's writing without attempting to direct it, Jo's parents and, later, Professor Bhaer, are as ruthless as her opportunistic editors. While still at home Jo frequently falls into a "vortex" of creativity and, after earning several checks for her stories, begins "to feel herself a power in the house" (333) [215]. But although she enjoys both the process and the proceeds of her writing, it does not, as she had hoped, bring her the unqualified praise of those she loves. The process disturbs Marmee, who always "looked a little anxious when 'genius took to burning,' "[3] and when her sensation story wins a cash prize, her father says, "You can do better than this, Jo. Aim at the highest, and never mind the money" (332) [214]. Perhaps Jo's earnings disturb her father for the very reason they delight her: "She saw that money conferred power." But she tries to reconcile her unwomanly desire for power with her duty, as a woman, to be selfless: "money and power, therefore, she resolved to have, not to be used for herself alone, but for those she loved more than self" (425) [272]. Not content to dictate Jo's attitude toward her writing, her parents intervene in the writing process itself. In order to accommodate their criticisms of her first serious novel, Jo "laid her first-born on her table, and chopped it up as ruthlessly as any ogre" (335) [216]. Later the newspaper to which she takes her sensation stories asks her to edit out all moral reflections, causing her to feel "as a tender parent might on being asked to cut off her baby's legs in order that it might fit into a new cradle" (428) [274]. Jo's work, no less than Meg's life, must adjust itself to a "tight fit," and the strikingly similar passages equate her parents' moral with her publisher's amoral influence.

Although Professor Bhaer is described as a "genial fire" (431) [276], he too throws a damper on Jo's creative powers. Bhaer, like John Brooke, is a tutor, and his relationship with Jo, like John's with Meg, begins in German lessons, a return for Jo's mending of his socks. For Christmas, Bhaer gives Jo what he calls a "library" between two "lids," an edition of Shakespeare, which he takes from its "place of honor, with his German Bible, Plato, Homer, and Milton"—patriarchal works

---

3. See note 8 [on p. 603], above.

and authors all. Bhaer, in giving her Shakespeare, professes to hope that "the study of character in this book will help you to read it in the world and paint it with your pen" (422–23) [271]. But as Virginia Woolf points out in *A Room of One's Own*, women cannot write like Shakespeare until, freed from the fetish of chastity, they are allowed to experience life as Shakespeare and other male authors have done (48–52).[4] Jo, under the stimulus of her sensation writing, has begun to free herself and to experience life, at least vicariously: "as thrills could not be produced except by harrowing up the souls of the readers, history and romance, land and sea, science and art, police records and lunatic asylums, had to be ransacked for the purpose" (430) [275]. As a result, Jo begins to catch "glimpses of the tragic world which underlies society," but the narrator, like Professor Bhaer, reproves her for "beginning to desecrate some of the womanliest attributes of a woman's character" (430) [275]. After Bhaer, in disgust, burns a sheet of the *Weekly Volcano* for which Jo writes,[5] she rereads her work, feeling as though she is wearing "the Professor's mental or moral spectacles" (438) [280]. He is soon satisfied to see that Jo has "stood the test" and "given up writing" (440) [282].

Professor Bhaer saves Jo from "the frothy sea of sensational literature" (429) [274] only to plunge her into a slough of creative and personal despond. Having sacrificed the *Weekly Volcano* and the vortex of creativity to Bhaer's "genial fire," Jo goes on to sacrifice "my boy," as she calls Laurie, to "my Beth" and, later, "my Professor." Her reasoning—"you'd hate my scribbling, and I couldn't get on without it" (449) [287]—seems disingenuous, for Laurie, who greeted the sale of her first story with a "Hurrah for Miss March, the celebrated American authoress!" (188) [124], has always championed her writing. Indeed, in rejecting Laurie, Jo feels much as she did when editing her work against her better judgment—"as if she had murdered some innocent young thing, and buried it under the leaves" (450) [287]. And in turning from Laurie to her dying sister, it is as though she chooses to wed death rather than life. Jo and Beth's time together at the shore is described as a honeymoon: they are "all in all to each other . . . quite unconscious of the interest they excited in those about them" (457) [291]. Beth lies with her head in Jo's lap, and Jo's arms "instinctively tightened their hold upon the dearest treasure she possessed" (458) [293]. Before returning home, Jo, with "a silent kiss," "dedicated herself soul and body to Beth" (462) [295], and later in a poem she asks Beth to "Give me that unselfish nature" (512) [326]. Gradually, Jo begins to feel "that I don't lose you; that you'll be more to me than ever,

4. Alcott's contemporary, Elizabeth Stuart Phelps, has the heroine of *The Story of Avis* wonder, "Was that what the work of women lacked?—high stimulant, rough virtues, strong vices, all the great peril and power of exuberant, exposed life?" (79). As we have seen, Hawthorne praised Fanny Fern for writing "as if the devil was in her." He goes on to say that "Generally women write like emasculated men, and are only distinguished from male authors by greater feebleness and folly; but when they throw off the restraints of decency, and come before the public stark naked, as it were—then their books are sure to possess character and value" (xxxv).

5. Bhaer actually burns a story paper similar to the *Weekly Volcano*, not the *Weekly Volcano* itself. See p. 280 (part 2, chap. 11) [*Editors*].

and death can't part us." Beth promises, "I shall be your Beth, still" and urges Jo to take her place, assuring her, "you'll be happier in doing that, than writing splendid books, or seeing all the world." In response, "then and there Jo renounced her old ambition" and "pledged herself to a new and better one" (513) [327].

Just as Germain's death (and in *Moods* Warwick's death) symbolized the internalization of the values he represents, so Beth's indicates that Jo has internalized the values of little womanhood.[6] After Beth dies, Jo assumes her role: she takes shelter in her mother's arms, sits in Beth's little chair close beside her father, and assumes Beth's housekeeping duties with her implements. Turning to Meg for comfort, Jo is urged to consider marriage and domesticity as a means of bringing out "the tender, womanly half" of her nature (533) [338]. Marmee, realizing it is now safe to do so, encourages Jo to "write something for us, and never mind the rest of the world" (535) [339]. After she has done so, her father mails the piece to a popular magazine, where it is accepted and much acclaimed. Jo wonders, "what *can* there be in a simple little story like that, to make people praise it so?" Her father tells her, "you have found your style at last"; but Jo demurs: "If there *is* anything good or true in what I write, it isn't mine; I owe it all to you and mother, and to Beth" (535) [340]. Jo's stories now, rather than letting "the passions have a holiday" (330) [213], are "little stories," "humble wanderers," received by a "charitable world" and sending back "comfortable tokens to their mother, like dutiful children" (535–36) [340]. The image of the female artist as mother, her works as dutiful children, and their reception as charitable suggests Jo's withdrawal into the domestic and dependent sphere from which she had sought escape. As we have seen, illness or death of a sister affects the art of Diana in "A Modern Cinderella" and Psyche in "Psyche's Art." But Diana, in a burst of penitence, only *says* that she will modify her aspirations; Psyche, despite the commemorative nature of her bust of May, does not, like Jo, disavow her own role in creating it and, further, renews her dedication to art. Jo, in contrast, alters both her present practice and future plans, for love and approval now mean more to her than anything else in the world.[7]

More subversive than Jo, and potentially the more successful artist,

---

6. Cheri Register, in "Letting the Angel Die," views Beth as Jo's "shadow," but argues that "Jo does not really come into her own until she learns how to practice Beth's patience, kindness, and self-forgetfulness" (3). On the other hand, Angela Estes and Kathleen Lant [their essay is reprinted in this Norton Critical Edition on pp. 564–83] see Jo as stretched to the snapping point between her "independent impulses" and "her need to be a proper member of the female community of 'little women.' " Alcott, in order to disguise "the final snap of her experimental creation," replaces the "corpse" of the "self-celebratory Jo . . . with the self-effacing Beth" (115).

7. Fetterley writes in "Alcott's Civil War," "Good writing for women is not the product of ambition or even enthusiasm, nor does it seek worldly recognition. Rather it is the product of a mind seeking solace for private pain, that scarcely knows what it is doing and that seeks only to please others and, more specifically, those few others who constitute the immediate family. Jo has gone from burning genius to a state where what she writes isn't even hers" (374). Lynda Zwinger adds, "Jo's relation to her text is now neither physical nor direct. She may have written it, but she can't read it" (56). Beverly Lyon Clark identifies the chastened Jo with her creator: "Alcott may have espoused women's rights, including suffrage, but in her books as in her life the greatest good was not individual rights and self-fulfillment but loyalty and service to the Family" (93).

is Amy, for she is not afraid to assert herself, take risks, and appear selfish or foolish. As the pampered baby of the family, she does not feel Jo's need to earn its love or avoid its disapproval. Therefore, from the beginning of the book, she is the least willing to engage in self-sacrifice. When her sisters decide to spend their Christmas dollars on presents for Marmee, Amy resolves to spend but a part of hers. (She later weakens but only for the purpose of making the most impressive display!) The most worldly of the sisters, she is also the most eager to venture out into the world or, something the others never try to do, bridge the gap between world and home. Thus Amy attends school while Beth stays home, teases to accompany the older girls on their grown-up outings, and braves their ridicule by planning a luncheon for her wealthy classmates. The only one to invite outsiders (apart from the Laurences) into the family circle, Amy is removed from that circle in times of crisis. When Beth is ill, Amy stays with Aunt March; when Beth is dying, Amy remains in Europe, where she, not Jo, satisfies a lifelong ambition to study art abroad. Even Amy's marriage to Laurie takes place there rather than in the bosom of the family as Meg's does. Perhaps most significant, in the family tableaux that end both parts of *Little Women*, Amy is a figure somewhat apart, and it is she, not Jo, who is portrayed as the artist, engaged herself in portraying the family. At the end of part 1, a scene in which everyone else is paired, "Amy was drawing the lovers" (289) [185]; at the end of part 2, Amy, albeit "with a beautiful motherly expression in her face, sketched the various groups" (598) [378]. It is as though Amy's comparative detachment from the family and its self-denying ethos frees her to record it.

Amy's subversiveness, like that of *Little Women* itself, is easy to overlook because, as in Jo's play, she appears the conventional heroine, Jo the hero. Always ladylike, Amy shrewdly defines Jo's version of independence as a desire to "go through the world with your elbows out and your nose in the air" (321) [207]. Jo's unconventionality, while genuine, is, as Amy implies, a matter of appearance and manners; she is only independent of those for whom she cares nothing. Amy, on the other hand, moderates her behavior so as to please those who can help her, but she is truly independent of her family's judgment, as when she plans her luncheon party. While Jo would flaunt her unconventionality, Amy conceals hers in order to preserve and foster her genuine independence and what would appear to be the rudiments of a feminist consciousness. Like Jean Muir, Amy recognizes women's vulnerability. As she tells Jo in preparing to pay some social calls, "Women should learn to be agreeable, particularly poor ones; for they have no other way of repaying the kindnesses they receive" (366) [235]. Not only does Amy recognize that poor women are dependent solely upon their power of pleasing; she depreciates the power so often attributed to them—the power of moral influence. Whereas Jo would show her disapproval of fast young men in an attempt to curb them, Amy denies that it would have "a particle of effect" (366) [235]. She later tells Laurie, "You men tell us we are angels, and say we can make you what we will; but the instant we honestly try to do you good, you laugh at us, and won't listen, which proves how much your flattery is worth" (502) [320]. Amy's willingness to forgo asserting her independence and to practice the art of pleasing pays dividends for her art. During a call on Aunt March and Aunt Carrol, Jo blurts out, "I don't like favors; they oppress and make me feel like a slave; I'd rather do everything for myself, and be perfectly independent" (368) [236]. Amy, by accepting patronage "when it is well meant," earns the trip to Europe that Jo has coveted.

Amy's early "artistic attempts" are treated mockingly, but even these suggest her artistic independence. For example, Amy casts her own foot and has to have it dug out of the plaster by Jo, who "was so over-come with laughter while she excavated, that her knife went too far" and "cut the poor foot" (317) [204]. The image implies that Amy puts herself into her work and that Jo, in an attempt to extricate life from art, does injury to both. Further, at the end of a long passage that seems to disparage Amy's art, the narrator adds that Amy "persevered in spite of all obstacles, failures, and discouragements, firmly believing that in time she should do something worthy to be called 'high art' " (317) [204]. Unlike Jo, Amy does not give up or modify her art in re-sponse to male criticism. By the time she again meets Laurie, who is impressed with her artistic progress, Amy has independently discov-ered that "talent isn't genius." As she tells him, "Rome took all the vanity out of me" (498) [317]. While Jo subjects her work to Professor Bhaer's "moral spectacles," Amy uses the gauge of superior work, in this case the greatest masterpieces. Perhaps a still more independent female artist might have questioned the appropriateness of the gauge, for its use recalls Bhaer's advice to Jo—that she learn from Shake-speare how to develop her characters. Nonetheless, Amy does not al-low external authority or fear of impropriety to determine the course of her career. Even after surrendering her ambitions, Amy continues working for her own pleasure; she does not need parental encourage-ment—or permission—to resume a proscribed activity.[8]

Amy's courtship and marriage reflect her greater independence but also point up its limitations. During courtship, she is assertive: when driving with Laurie, she holds the reins, and, unlike her sisters, who marry their tutors, she plays Mentor to Laurie's Telemachus as well as the Prince to his Sleeping Beauty. While Laurie is still languishing for Jo, looking like "the effigy of a young knight asleep on his tomb" (497) [317], Amy wakes him up as he had thought only Jo could do. As Lau-rie later tells Jo, Amy's lecture was "a deal worse than any of your scoldings" (549) [348]. It is Amy, then, who makes a man of Laurie, whereas Jo would keep him "her boy." As Amy says, "I know you'll wake up, and be a man in spite of that hard-hearted girl" (505) [322]. Laurie's manhood seems achieved and traditional gender roles re-stored when, just prior to his proposal, he rows while Amy rests. But the proposal itself is prompted when Amy relieves him of an oar, and

8. Patricia Meyer Spacks contends that Amy's desire to paint is "narcissistic" (126), but Hol-lander discerns that Amy is artistically more ambitious than Jo; Jo wants to be successful and to make money, whereas Amy wants to achieve greatness (33).

the two pull smoothly together through the water. And the letter they send home to announce their engagement is described as a "duet." Theirs is the one joyous, seemingly egalitarian marriage in the book. Thus Amy playfully allows herself to regress upon their return home. Once there Laurie calls her "little woman," Jo buttons her cloak as though she were a child, and Marmee holds her on her lap "as if being made 'the baby' again" (559–60) [354]. Yet when we think of Meg "enthroned" on John's knee, then laid on the shelf, and when we think of Jo in "Beth's little chair close beside" her father (not to mention the regressions of Sylvia Yule both after marriage and after separation from her husband), we have to wonder whether Amy has truly succeeded where Jo failed.

The very qualities that exempt Amy from the most painful restrictions of little womanhood—unwillingness to suffer and adaptability to circumstances—prevent her from escaping them altogether. Or to put it another way, Amy, like Jean Muir, is only clever enough to transform the liabilities of her condition into assets. Just as the sacrifice of her Christmas dollar becomes an occasion for display, so Amy consistently converts female suffering into aesthetic pleasure. During Beth's first illness, Amy, with the help of Aunt March's Catholic maid, fits up a closet as a little shrine in which she thinks "good thoughts" and prays for Beth's recovery. At the same time, however, she delights in the careful disposition of her few treasures, and her "beauty-loving eyes were never tired of looking up" at "a very valuable copy of one of the famous pictures of the world" (239–40) [154]. Similarly, after Beth dies, Amy's gentle melancholy, especially when compared with Jo's raw grief, takes on an aesthetic quality. When Laurie finds Amy mourning in a château garden, "Everything about her mutely suggested love and sorrow; the blotted letters in her lap, the black ribbon that tied up her hair, the womanly pain and patience in her face; even the little ebony cross at her throat seemed pathetic to Laurie, for he had given it to her, and she wore it as her only ornament" (524) [333–34].

Amy's greatest art, we begin to suspect, is not her painting or sculpture but rather the graceful way in which she, like Jean, exploits her little womanhood. The incident in which Amy tries to cast her own foot is again instructive: Amy gives herself to art by becoming an art object. Unlike Cecil Stein, Amy molds herself, but she nonetheless conforms to a male model of femininity. In a passage that allies Amy with the sensation heroines Sybil, Cecil, and Jean, Alcott describes Amy awaiting Laurie. Like Sybil awaiting Guy, Amy "once arranged herself under the chandelier, which had a good effect upon her hair." Unlike Sybil, Amy thinks better of her ploy, but she removes herself from under the chandelier only to place her "slender, white figure against the red curtains," where Laurie finds her "as effective as a well-placed statue" (470) [300]. On this occasion, Amy's simple dress is covered "with a cloud of fresh illusion" (469) [300], and Laurie's play on the word further suggests that Amy, like Jean, is a mistress of effects. Combining the plasticity of the actress with the immobility of the statue, Amy has in one sense lost, in another retained, the stiffness that prevented her from being a convincing heroine in Jo's play. Amy can now *play* the role to perfection, but in her conscious playing of it and in her inability to break out of it, she is both more than a conventional heroine and less than a true hero.

Jo, in the dark chapter "All Alone," bitterly compares herself to Amy: "Some people seemed to get all sunshine, and some all shadow; it was not fair, for she tried more than Amy to be good, but never got any reward,—only disappointment, trouble, and hard work" (530) [337]. Amy, as Jo dimly recognizes, manipulates the forms of little womanhood but rejects their self-sacrificial essence; thus she avoids the painful sacrifices incumbent upon most women. Jo resents the forms but, having long accepted their underlying principle, is unable to escape them. Later in this chapter, the narrator denies that Jo becomes "the heroine of a moral storybook": "if she had been . . . she ought at this period of her life to have become quite saintly, renounced the world, and gone about doing good in a mortified bonnet, with tracts in her pocket. But you see Jo wasn't a heroine; she was only a struggling human girl, like hundreds of others" (534) [339]. But this denial, while ostensibly distinguishing Jo's—and normal women's—behavior from that of morbid martyrs and ridiculous fanatics, serves rather to confound them. The narrator goes on to vindicate Jo's self-immolation or to show how she vindicates herself: "She had often said she wanted to do something splendid, no matter how hard; and now she had her wish,—for what could be more beautiful than to devote her life to father and mother, trying to make home as happy to them as they had to her? And, if difficulties were necessary to increase the splendor of the effort, what could be harder for a restless, ambitious girl, than to give up her own hopes, plans and desires, and cheerfully live for others?" (534) [339]. The narrator's first question implies that nothing could be more splendid than for Jo to repay her parents, but, if their teachings have brought her to this pass, for what is she repaying them? And even if she does owe them a debt of gratitude, could she not repay them better by making something of herself? If they have devoted themselves to her happiness, can they be happy in her sacrifice? The narrator's second question implies that "nothing" could be harder, but, if so, then why should this hardship be imposed? The narrator's rhetorical questions thus provoke real questions, questions that the book as a whole seems designed to raise.

According to the narrator, self-immolation prepares a woman for marriage: "Grief is the best opener for some hearts, and Jo's was nearly ready for the bag; a little more sunshine to ripen the nut, then, not a boy's impatient shake, but a man's hand reached up to pick it gently from the burr, and find the kernel sound and sweet. If she had suspected this, she would have shut up tight, and been more prickly than ever; fortunately she wasn't thinking about herself, so, when the time came, down she dropped" (533) [339]. Jo's self-oblivion, reflected in her newly selfless writing, brings Professor Bhaer to her. At the end of the chapter "All Alone," Jo, having just heard of Amy and Laurie's engagement, wanders up to the garret where genius used to burn. There she peruses "four little wooden chests in a row, each marked with its owner's name, and each filled with relics of the childhood and girl-hood ended now for all" (538) [342]. This burial ground of all the sisters' hopes and aspirations prompts a poem that recapitulates (just as Marmee's sermon anticipated) the movement of *Little Women*. As described by Jo, the lids of the "four little chests" bear the stamp of their owners' personalities: Meg's is "smooth and fair," Jo's "scratched and worn," Beth's "always swept," and Amy's "polished." The stanza Jo devotes to herself, her epitaph, as it were, alludes to "Dreams of a future never found" and "Half-writ poems, stories wild." The lines "Diaries of a wilful child, / Hints of a woman early old" compress into a few words the fate of "wilful" female children in a patriarchal society. The lines that draw the Professor are doubtless the next ones: "A woman in a lonely home, / Hearing like a sad refrain,— / 'Be worthy love, and love will come'" (586) [370–37]. While to him the lines may suggest ripening, to some readers (and perhaps to Jo, who hastily destroys his copy of the poem) they suggest the culture's insistence on marriage as a woman's only alternative to confinement in a lonely home. And the context of the lines is suggestive not of ripening but of decay.

Self-immolation prepares a woman for marriage in part because it unfits her for a satisfying life outside marriage. Spinsterhood, as the unmarried Alcott well knew, provided no sure escape from unremu-nerated domestic service. In fact, the prospect of spinsterhood is so forbidding that it can hasten ripening and "harvest time," as the final chapter is called. As Jo approaches her twenty-fifth birthday, she anticipates life as a "literary spinster, with a pen for a spouse, a family of stories for children, and twenty years hence a morsel of fame, perhaps" (540) [342]. As though to correct Jo's bleak vision, the narrator supplies a lengthy passage to the effect that spinsters can lead "useful, happy" lives (542) [343]. But spinsters, as described by the narrator, sound like superannuated Beths. Girls are urged to appreciate their "many silent sacrifices of youth, health, ambition, love itself," and boys are exhorted to chivalrous regard for "the good aunts who have not only lectured and fussed, but nursed and petted, too often without thanks" (541) [343]. The word *old* recurs throughout the passage, and the narrator ends by tacitly admitting the ineffectuality of her argument: "Jo must have fallen asleep (as I dare say my reader has during this little homily)" (542) [343]. At this point, Laurie breaks in, to enliven Jo temporarily but also to remind her of what she has lost—her youthful exuberance and spontaneity. As she tells him, "You may be a little older in years, but I'm ever so much older in feeling, Teddy. Women always are; and this last year has been such a hard one, that I feel forty" (547) [347] Little wonder, then, that Jo, so ripened, drops at once into the matrimonial bag extended by Professor Bhaer. Breaking into the newly re-formed family circle, Bhaer immediately creates a masculine circle around him. The "burial customs of the ancients, to which the conversation had strayed" (555) [351], spells the death of our hopes for Jo.

Because Professor Bhaer represents the patriarchal values around which the March circle ultimately revolves, his seeming disruption of that circle serves rather to perpetuate it and to preserve Jo's place in it. Jo, by establishing with her husband a school for boys at Plumfield, the estate that she inherits from her Aunt March, remains what Beth was—a retainer—only on a much larger scale. As Jo predicts, a strict division of labor by gender will obtain at Plumfield: "Fritz [Bhaer] can train and teach in his own way, and father will help him. I [like the maiden aunts?] can feed, and nurse, and pet, and scold them; and mother will be my stand-by" (593) [374]. Among Bhaer's trainees is Jo herself, much as Marmee was her husband's: "Jo made queer mistakes; but the wise Professor steered her safely into calmer waters" (595) [376] just as he earlier rescued her from "the frothy sea of sensational literature." But Jo now finds "the applause of her boys more satisfying than any praise of the world—for now she told no stories except to her flock of enthusiastic believers and admirers" (597) [377]. Comparing the end of part 1 with the end of part 2, we can appreciate Jo's reluctance to look into the future for fear of seeing "something sad" (289) [185]. Not only is her literary silence sad; so too are the gender-segregated groups of the final family tableau. Although Marmee, stretching out her arms to embrace the scene, can wish no "greater happiness" for her "girls," Alcott has allowed us to question whether it be happiness at all. Alcott's contemporary readers were disappointed by her refusal to marry Jo to Laurie; modern readers are disappointed that Alcott, supposedly succumbing to the demands that Jo marry someone, married her to Professor Bhaer. But just this sense of disappointment, even outrage, this reluctance to accept the traditional happy ending as a happy one, attests to the subversive power of Alcott's design.

In "A Whisper in the Dark" and "Behind a Mask," Alcott's madwoman and bad woman expose, however cryptically, women's wrongs and wounds. In *Moods* and "A Marble Woman," the death of a male character signifies that, with the death of patriarchy, such wrongs could be rectified, such wounds healed, divided selves made whole, and unmated pairs well matched. In *Little Women* the androgynous natures of Jo and Laurie, and their mutually sustaining friendship, suggest the realization of that possibility. But for all its sprightly tone, *Little Women* is among the most pessimistic of these early fictions. The imagery of death surrounding Jo's rejection of Laurie and acceptance of Professor Bhaer conveys a tragic loss of opportunity. In *Moods* and "A Marble Woman," Warwick and Germain die; in *Little Women* Beth dies but is reborn, not only in Jo but as Amy's daughter of that name, the "shadow over Amy's sunshine" and the "cross" for both parents (601) [380]. In the earlier and seemingly more somber works, Alcott predicts, at least symbolically, a new order; in *Little Women* she documents the persistence and pernicious effects of the old. In "Psyche's Art" Alcott warned of the dangers of "duty" or domesticity for the female artist but also celebrated its legitimate place in art. She further hinted at spinsterhood as a desirable alternative to marriage for women artists, allowing them to draw on their experiences as sisters and daughters but to escape the demands on wives and mothers. But in *Little Women*, as we have seen, the domestic exploitation and entrapment of even single women is unsparingly presented. Even were Jo to escape from family obligations, her hunger for "all kinds" of love, as she confides to Marmee, would go unsatisfied. However much we may deplore Jo's "absolute surrender" to conventional marriage, we would regret an equivalent "sacrifice of her nature" to her art.

Jo, in the last chapter of *Little Women*, exclaims in a burst of enthusiasm, "I do think that families are the most beautiful things in all the world!" (595) [375]. And *Little Women* has long been taken as an argument, more or less convincing, for that assertion. But Jo "was in an unusually uplifted frame of mind, just then" (595) [375]. Even Jean Muir is capable of writing to her friend Hortense, "Something in the atmosphere of this happy home has made me wish I was anything but what I am." The next moment she declares, "Bah! how I hate sentiment!" (99). Jean's sense of exclusion and estrangement from an institution that she knows to be far other than its sentimentalized image nonetheless has power to threaten her identity. Rather than surrender that identity, however, Jean resolves to humble "an intensely proud family" by first creating, then dispelling, the idyllic family scenes that exist only in the sentimental imagination. Alcott, in her preface to *Little Women*, instructs her "little Book" to "show to all / That entertain, and bid thee welcome shall, / What thou dost keep close shut up in thy breast." What we find there are cozy scenes, theatrical performances, and many "a sweet sermon upon self-sacrifice" ("Mask" 68) such as Jean delivers. But we also find what Jean discloses when she bares *her* breast—the self-inflicted wounds that are a woman's price for her well-nigh obligatory membership in the patriarchal family.[9] Thus Alcott, in her guise of mentor to girl readers, replicates Jean's lessons to Bella Conventry: that behind the charming model of little womanhood lurks a figure "early old" but with the power to detonate that model.

WORKS CITED
WORKS BY LOUISA MAY ALCOTT

Alternative Alcott. Edited by Elaine Showalter. American Women Writers Series. New Brunswick: Rutgers Univ. Press, 1988.
"Behind a Mask or A Woman's Power." In *The Hidden Louisa May Alcott*. Edited by Madeleine Stern, 3–104. New York: Avenel, 1984.
The Journals of Louisa May Alcott. Edited by Joel Myerson and Daniel Shealy with Madeleine B. Stern. Introduction by Stern. Boston: Little, Brown, 1989.
Little Women. Introduction by Madelon Bedell. New York: Modern Library, 1983.
"A Marble Woman or The Mysterious Model." In *The Hidden Louisa May Alcott*, 407–511.
"A Modern Cinderella; or, The Little Old Shoe." In *Hospital Sketches and Camp and Fireside Stories*, 257–94. Boston: Roberts, 1869.
Moods. Edited by Sarah Elbert. American Women Writers Series. New Brunswick: Rutgers Univ. Press, 1991.
"Patty's Patchwork." In *My Boys, Etc.*, 193–215. Vol. 1 of *Aunt Jo's Scrap-Bag*. Boston: Roberts, 1872.
"Psyche's Art." In *Alternative Alcott*, 207–26.

9. In "Behind a Mask," Jean Muir disguises the scar of a recent knife wound, one that she has reportedly inflicted on herself in a dramatic and desperate attempt to pressure a lover to marry her [*Editors*].

"The Rose Family." In *Morning Glories and Other Stories*, 45–71. Boston: Fuller, 1868.
The Selected Letters of Louisa May Alcott. Edited by Joel Myerson and Daniel Shealy with Madeleine B. Stern. Introduction by Madeleine B. Stern. Boston: Little, Brown, 1987.
"A Whisper in the Dark." In *The Hidden Louisa May Alcott*, 537–75.

OTHER WORKS CITED

Alberghene, Janice M. "Alcott's Psyche and Kate: Self-Portraits, Sunny-side Up." In *Proceedings of the Eighth Annual Conference of the Children's Literature Association*, 37–43. Univ. of Minnesota, Mar. 1981. Boston: Children's Literature Association, 1982.
Auerbach, Nina. Afterword to *Little Women*, by Louisa May Alcott. Toronto: Bantam, 1983.
——. *Communities of Women.* Cambridge, Mass.: Harvard Univ. Press, 1978.
Bassil, Veronica. "The Artist at Home: The Domestication of Louisa May Alcott." *Studies in American Fiction* 15 (1987): 187–97.
Bedell, Madelon. *The Alcotts: Biography of a Family.* New York: Potter, 1980.
——. Introduction to *Little Women*, by Louisa M. Alcott. New York: Modern Library, 1983.
Clark, Beverly Lyon. "A Portrait of the Artist as a Little Woman." *Children's Literature* 17 (1989): 81–97.
Dalke, Anne. " 'The House-Band': The Education of Men in *Little Women*." *College English* 47 (1985): 571–78.
Elbert, Sarah. *A Hunger for Home: Louisa May Alcott and* Little Women. Philadelphia: Temple Univ. Press, 1984.
Estes, Angela M., and Kathleen Margaret Lant. "Dismembering the Text: The Horror of Louisa May Alcott's *Little Women*." *Children's Literature* 17 (1989): 98–123.
Fetterley, Judith. "*Little Women*: Alcott's Civil War." *Feminist Studies* 5 (1979): 369–83.
Halttunen, Karen. "The Domestic Drama of Louisa May Alcott." *Feminist Studies* 10 (1984): 233–54.
Hawthorne, Nathaniel. *Tales and Sketches.* The Library of America. New York: Viking, 1982.
Heilbrun, Carolyn G. *Reinventing Womanhood.* New York: Norton, 1979.
Hollander, Anne. "Reflections on *Little Women*." *Children's Literature* 9 (1981): 28–39.
Kaledin, Eugenia. "Louisa May Alcott: Success and the Sorrow of Self-Denial." *Women's Studies* 5 (1978): 251–63.
Keyser, Elizabeth Lennox. " 'The Most Beautiful Things in All the World'? Families in *Little Women*." In *Stories and Society: Children's Literature in Its Social Context.* Edited by Dennis Butts, 50–64. London: Macmillan, 1992.
Lang, Amy Schrager. "Slavery and Sentimentalism: The Strange Career of Augustine St. Clare." *Women's Studies* 12 (1986): 31–54.
Langland, Elizabeth. "Female Stories of Exerience: Alcott's *Little Women* in Light of *Work*." In *The Voyage In: Fiction of Female Development.* Edited by Elizabeth Abel, Marianne Hirsch, and Elizabeth Langland, 112–27. Hanover, N.H.: Univ. Press of New England, 1983.
Murphy, Ann B. "The Borders of Ethical, Erotic, and Artistic Possibilities in *Little Women*." *Signs* 15 (1990): 562–85.
O'Brien, Sharon. "Tomboyism and Adolescent Conflict: Three Nineteenth-Century Case Studies." In *Woman's Being, Woman's Place: Female Identity and Vocation in American History.* Edited by Mary Kelley, 351–72. Boston: Hall, 1979.
Phelps, Elizabeth Stuart. *The Story of Avis.* Edited by Carol Farley Kessler. American Women Writers Series. New Brunswick: Rutgers Univ. Press, 1985.
Register, Cheri. "Letting the Angel Die." *Hurricane Alice* 3, no. 2 (1986): 1–4.
Sarton, May. *Mrs. Stevens Hears the Mermaids Singing.* Introduction by Carolyn G. Heilbrun. New York: Norton, 1975.
Spacks, Patricia Meyer. *The Female Imagination.* New York: Avon, 1972.
Stern, Madeleine B. "Louisa Alcott, Trouper: Experiences in Theatricals, 1848–1880." *New England Quarterly* 16 (1943): 175–97.
Van Buren, Jane. "Louisa May Alcott: A Study in Persona and Idealization." *Psychohistory Review* 9 (1981): 282–99.
Woolf, Virginia. *A Room of One's Own.* New York: Harcourt, n.d.
Zwinger, Lynda. *Daughters, Fathers, and the Novel: The Sentimental Romance of Heterosexuality.* Madison: Univ. of Wisconsin Press, 1991.

RICHARD H. BRODHEAD

Starting Out in the 1860s: Alcott, Authorship, and the Postbellum Literary Field†

* * *

* * * [I]f much in *Little Women* is familiar from the previous generation's domestic fiction, some things have changed, and one change is a new liberality of tone. Without departing from highly traditional conceptions of women's character formation, *Little Women* brings a mirth to the plot of female domestication not found in the novels of the 1850s. Fun has a license in the March family unknown to Ellen Montgomery:[1] any reader of Warner's dour novel will note by contrast how game-filled and play-oriented Alcott's novel is. More, while this book is always moving toward a quite conventional character ideal as its end—its truant girls are on their way to becoming little women, and its little women on their way to becoming (in the second volume's title) good wives—Alcott makes a new allowance for, and takes a new pleasure in, the phase where such goals are not yet achieved. Girls must be girls at the end of Alcott's book, but meanwhile they are allowed to be boys: *Little Women* tolerates deviations from normative gender identities unknown to earlier works in the domestic genre. These same girls must eventually become good housekeepers, but before that happens they regularly—how else to put it?—mess up: spill salad dressing on their clean dresses, swamp their kitchens with batches of failed jelly, and so on.

The new liberality that sees the humanness, even the fun, in otherwise-censurable error travels together with a new relaxation on the part of authority-figures in *Little Women*. Unlike Susan Warner's Mrs. Montgomery, who is always there in force with an arsenal of parental sanctions, Alcott's Marmee backs off from the children in her charge, leaving them unprecedentedly free. The mother has left the daughters home alone in *Little Women*'s opening chapter. When Meg wants to engage in social climbing at the home of the wealthy Moffats, Marmee lets her. When Amy wants to impress the high-toned girls in her drawing class, Marmee helps her prepare an absurdly pretentious luncheon. When the four daughters decide to live totally idly during their vacation, the mother not only tolerates their idleness but joins their abdication of household chores. The softened or humanized authority

---

† From *Cultures of Letters: Scenes of Reading and Writing in Nineteenth-Century America* (Chicago: U of Chicago P, 1993), 92–103. Copyright 1993 by The University of Chicago Press. Reprinted by permission of Richard H. Brodhead and The University of Chicago Press. All of Brodhead's quotations from *Little Women* are from the 1983 Bantam Classic (New York) edition and are cited by page number within the text. Page references to this Norton Critical Edition are given in brackets following Brodhead's original citations. Footnotes are the author's except where followed by [*Editors*].

1. The pious, lachrymose heroine of Susan B. Warner's *The Wide, Wide World* (1850). Emphasizing self-denial and self-control, the novel follows Ellen through her childhood, her grief over the death of her mother and her abandonment by her father, the hardships she experiences in the rural household of her guardian aunt (Miss Fortune Emerson), and her eventual marriage [*Editors*].

of antebellum domesticity has permuted itself, here, into an astonishing permissiveness; but Marmee pursues highly regulatory goals through this strategy of nonauthoritarianism. She allows her daughters their free experience on the understanding that it will teach them the lessons she might have enforced—as, allowed her folly, Amy learns that she has been a fool about her luncheon; and left in idleness, the girls learn the misery of idleness and reinvent the domestic work ethic for themselves. Marmee does not abdicate the work of maternal tutelage so much as she relocates its agency—makes experience teach what was once parentally enjoined.

This reinvestment of authority characterizes the book quite as much as the mother within the book. For the prose of *Little Women* has made its own mitigations of traditional maternal sway. Alcott called juvenile-domestic fiction the "heavy moral" mode, but "heavy moral" is what her own writing is not. Her text has dropped the habit of mustering high-voltage ethical charges around the rules of everyday conduct that made life in earlier domestic novels one long risk of transgression: what the doctor tells Ellen early in *The Wide, Wide World*—don't burn the toast or your mother will die—is a kind of thinking Alcott has largely relaxed. (Not entirely of course: "be angry or selfish and your sister will die" is a rule this book still enforces.) In particular, *Little Women* has put in abeyance the ultimate enforcer of the 1850s literary generation: the threat of divine displeasure and promise of heavenly reward. Except for rare moments—the proscription of anger in chapter eight [of part 1] and Beth's death in chapter forty [part 2, chapter 17, in this Norton Critical Edition]—whose transcendent importance is indicated just by the invocation of religion, *Little Women* is a remarkably secular text, a de-evangelized domestic text, so to speak. The book's deactivation of such older authority systems is what creates the possibility for its brand of domestic realism. The foibles of everyday life can be caught in their funny human familiarity here because they are not being nailed to heavily sanctioned moral meanings. (Amy's irritable-charitable disposal of her failed luncheon—"Bundle everything into a basket and send it to the Hummels: Germans like messes" [248] [210]—would be something else than laughable in a more authority-haunted book.) But this textual leniency does not mean that Alcott has given up the cult of domesticity's tutelary program. Rather, the book, like Marmee, has licensed a now-"free" experience to teach requisite lessons in authority's apparent absence.[2]

The new liberality of a book like *Little Women* has been taken as a sign of a more general liberalization of middle-class culture in the postbellum nineteenth century. Behind this book it is possible to read the history of a social class now socially established, and so not needing to insist on the group values it had used to define and justify itself in its insurgent phase. Bernard Wishy and Daniel Rodgers have sug-

---

2. The collusion of "free" experience in the supporting of authority is extremely clear in *Little Men*, where Jo's charges are allowed a weekly pillow fight in exchange for their pledge of orderly behavior the rest of the week.

gested that such children's writing marks a further reorientation in nineteenth-century middle-class culture from the highly disciplined self-denials of the work ethic to the now-tolerated (even mandated) indulgences of an emerging ethic of consumption.* * *[3] But to think *Little Women* back into its historical world is also to have another salient feature of the book come into strong focus: namely, the new way it charts the geography of adjacent social space.

The domestic value system that informs *Little Women* has, as always in the domestic tradition, a quite definite social base. Meg's life ties the book to the single-family household in which the man goes out to work at a white-collar job and the wife stays home to run the house (with help), with both parents earnestly involved in the drama of child rearing—ties it in short to the idealized norms of middle-class life, domestic fiction's traditional ground. But the historical group that projected this idyll of insular family privacy did not live by itself in reality. It lived in sight of other social formations and experienced itself in relation to them; and a major function of its group literature was imaginatively to specify its relation to neighboring groups. The older domestic novel typically situates its ideal family over against a schematically represented lower class, often of immigrant origin, that is domestically disorganized and an object of social welfare. (The Phelans fill this role in Sedgwick's *Home*;[4] the equally minimally-sketched Hummels, objects of charity and sources of infection, are the Phelans of *Little Women*.) This class is usually balanced, at the other side of middle-class self-definition, by an equally alien upper class seen as idle, luxuriously wasteful, and devoid of proper virtues of self-control—like the business partner-speculator of *Home*, whose bankrupt home is awash in champagne bottles. But the social adjacency that most deeply interests 1850s domestic fiction is the older household economy based on domestic production and unsentimentalized family bonds. The rustic life so intricately recorded in the Aunt Fortune chapters of *The Wide, Wide World* shows this older order as a menacing proximity to that book's ideal domesticity, which in Ellen's case collapses back upon and must win its way out from this "world we have lost." The nightmare in-laws of Fanny Fern's *Ruth Hall*,[5] also affiliated with an older culture of multigenerational families, homemade commodities, nonsentimental bonds, and indifference to privacy, pursue the model couple Ruth and Harry and criticize their private life—testimony again to a new social order's anguished sense of interinvolvement with an earlier form from which it has not yet managed to separate fully.

In *Little Women* the household economy still so vividly present to

---

3. See [Bernard] Wishy, *The Child and the Republic* [(Philadelphia: University of Pennsylvania Press, 1968)], pp. 81–104, and Daniel T. Rodgers, *The Work Ethic in Industrial America, 1850–1920* (Chicago: University of Chicago Press, 1978), pp. 125–52.
4. Catharine Maria Sedgwick, *Home* (1835) [*Editors*].
5. A comic, autobiographical novel (1854) by Sara Payson Willis Parton, a novelist and columnist who used the pen name Fanny Fern. When her much-loved husband Harry dies, Ruth's relatives and in-laws are unsupportive, and Ruth becomes an independent working woman (eventually becoming a writer) in order to support her children and herself [*Editors*].

these mid-century books has largely vanished. But now another social rival has become comparably absorbing. A different culture of greater affluence and status is always right at hand in Alcott's book, so close that when her little women go out they are at once in its midst. When Amy goes to school, she is immersed in the lime-exchange cult of more free-spending girls. When Jo and Meg go to a dance, it is to a house where people wear expensive and showy clothes. Meg's principal contacts outside the home are the Moffats, walking embodiments of conspicuous consumption. Amy later mixes with the well-to-do Chesters; Laurie's well-heeled college chums (who are rich enough to buy out the Chesters' fair); the fabulously wealthy Fred; and the luxury set she meets in her art class. I take this change to mean that by 1868 the middle-class audience no longer needs to differentiate itself from the household economic order it was once imperfectly separated from but now needs to deploy its tools of self-definition against another threatening adjacency—the emerging leisure-class world of the postbellum years. Alcott's work, at this obsessively revisited social juncture, is to write a boundary-maintaining moral difference between the "right" world of Marmee and this more affluent surround. When Meg (for instance) falls, in the positively Dreiserian chapter "Domestic Experiences," into such a fit of fashion-envy and consumeristic desire that she buys a dress she cannot afford, the experience teaches her (and us) the necessity of family frugality. But at the same time that it is erecting an ethic of poor but honest virtue against the temptations of affluence, *Little Women* opens an unobtrusive commerce between old-style virtuous domesticity and a new-style lavishness. The Laurence mansion is right next door to the March house (so proximate are these orders in *Little Women*), and the daughters who learn homely virtues at one place nevertheless receive covert aid—luxuries like pianos and ice cream—from the other. Having ritually reasserted the reign of traditional values, similarly, this book indulges in its own version of upward mobility. Amy March renounces the plutocrat Fred only to land the quite sufficiently wealthy Laurie. Wielding a mother-like character-making power, she convinces Laurie to work for a living rather than live off his income; but the industrious idyll they look forward to is full of upper-class consciousness: Amy becomes at last a "true gentlewoman" (418) [349]; she and Laurie contemplate the special pleasures of altruism on behalf of "poor gentle folk" (429) [357]; and Jo's school looks forward to including "rich pupils" as well as "a ragamuffin or two" (it sounds like a prep school with a scholarship plan), since "rich people's children often need care and comfort, as well as poor" (452) [375].

In the Amy plot especially, *Little Women* is profoundly concerned to negotiate between an older, more heavily moralized version of middle-class life and the more affluent and enjoyment-oriented version of that life becoming socially pressing at the book's time. But Amy's path is toward not just a new social situation but specifically a new base for cultural activity. In the primitive distribution of March family gifts, Amy is marked as the artistic child or "Little Raphael" (38) [39]. Her castle in the air is to "go to Rome, and do fine pictures, and be the best artist in the whole world" (134) [118], and her selfish wish, on the book's opening page, is for art materials—Faber's drawing pencils. Adept at the arts of pleasing, specifically those who are socially above her, Amy wins her way not just into a wealthy or classy milieu but into a space with profound relevance to her art. What Amy most essentially wins, through her winning ways, is Europe—a long stay in Europe at someone else's expense.* * *

In *Little Women*, Amy does not attain to an artistic career. Approached with the hierarchical plan of aesthetic value she brings from home, Europe shows Amy the difference between "talent" like hers and "genius" (378) [317] like the great masters', and like the Hilda of Hawthorne's *The Marble Faun* or the Rowland Mallet of James's *Roderick Hudson*,[6] she renounces her own ambitions as a tribute to the artistically great. She becomes, instead, a patron of the arts, putting her wealth and trained taste to the service of supporting fine art's cultural presence—her "white pillared mansion," the Mount Parnassus of *Jo's Boys*, is "full . . . of music, beauty, and the culture young hearts and fancies long for."[7] What Alcott images in Amy is a contemporaneous development * * * from the author's side. Her plot figures the emergence, to one side of the old-style domestic world, of a new social support for artistic activity, the high-cultural world stabilized after 1860 with leisure-class or owner-class backing (she and Laurie must have subscribed to the *Atlantic*);[8] and her plot suggests how this new world's boundary mechanism works. In *Little Women*, Amy gets out of the world of domesticity and self-denial because she gets to go to Europe, and she gets to go to Europe because she curries favor with her wealthy Aunt. As this book understands it the new high culture organized around nondomestic values accepts and even seeks recruits from the middling orders, but it requires them to have had certain formative "experiences"—like European travel—only open to the well-to-do and their adherents: to the upward-looking Amy, but not the favor-shunning Jo; in real life to self-gentrifiers like William Dean Howells or Bernard Berenson[9] or even Mark Twain, but not to Louisa May Alcott. (Alcott first went to Europe as a paid companion to a neurotic invalid—as an extension of female servitude, in other words, not an adventure in leisure and privilege.)

If I am right here, one project of *Little Women* is charting the field

6. Hilda is a young, innocent, and somewhat cold painter in Nathaniel Hawthorne's Italian novel, *The Marble Faun* (1860). In Henry James's *Roderick Hudson* (1876), also set in Italy, Rowland Mallet is the American patron of the title character, a young and talented sculptor [*Editors*].

7. Alcott, *Jo's Boys* [1886; rpt. New York: Puffin Books, 1983], pp. 8–9. Amy, Laurie, and Meg have moved out to the suburban Plumfield to avoid creeping urbanization and industrialization: "when the rapid growth of the city shut in the old house, spoilt Meg's nest, and dared to put a soap-factory under Mr. Laurence's indignant nose, our friends emigrated to Plumfield, and the great changes began" (ibid., p. 8)

8. Founded in 1857, *The Atlantic Monthly* identified itself as a high-cultural literary magazine devoted to artistic and cosmopolitan values [*Editors*].

9. A Lithuanian-born immigrant to the United States, Bernard Berenson (1865–1959) became a distinguished art connoisseur, critic, and historian. Like Mark Twain and William Dean Howells, Berenson had modest beginnings but eventually established himself as a key figure within artistic high culture [*Editors*].

of specifically artistic spaces that have opened up at the time of its writing. What makes this hunch more plausible is the fact that the book attends much more overtly to another new literary economy: the reading culture centered on the story-paper. Jo is a publishing author in *Little Women* and in the chapter "Literary Lessons" she finds a new outlet for her work, which the book characterizes rather complexly. At a public lecture Jo sees someone reading "a pictorial sheet" illustrated with "an Indian in full war costume, tumbling over a precipice with a wolf at his throat, while two infuriated young gentlemen, with unnaturally small feet and big eyes, were stabbing each other close by, and a disheveled female was flying away in the background with her mouth wide open" (251) [213]: unmistakably, a story-paper. The story-paper, Jo apprehends, features a certain "style" of writing (252) [214]—the exotic and elaborately melodramatic "sensational story" (253) [214]. But it also binds such writing to a particular system of literary production, centered in a business office—a nondomestic space and very much a men's world—where sharp-eyed editors freely alter work with an eye to its popular sale. It ties writing as well to a certain economics of authorship—Mrs. S. L. A. N. G. Northbury, Alcott's rendition of the staple producer for the *New York Ledger*, Mrs. E. D. E. N. South-worth,[1] is known to "make a good living out of such stories." It ties writing to a socially differentiated audience—it is notably a "lad" (251) [213], not the feminine reader of domestic fiction, whom Jo sees reading the *Blarneystone Banner*. And it ties writing as well to a highly particular social ethos. This journal's productions "belong to that class of light literature in which the passions have a holiday"—conspicuously not, in other words, to the literary culture of self-control and self-restraint. Its editor mercilessly cuts "all the moral reflections" (326) [274] Jo has put in her work: edification, staple and end of middle-class fiction, has no place in this differently conceived prose entertainment.

The story-paper is grasped as a literary-social institution in *Little Women*, an organized place for writing that enmeshes writing in a definite set of social relations. This socially structured writing world is another of the new presences *Little Women* knows to be adjacent to itself; and another work of this novel is to bound its world off from this newly encroaching neighbor.

This bounding is enacted through an extraordinarily elaborate textual activity in *Little Women*. Story-paper writing first appears in the book simply as an available career, a kind of work that is open to Jo. But the book then manufactures a strongly negative ethical charge around this apparently indifferent activity. The proscription of such writing is performed first through the narrative voice. Usually tolerant and bemused, Alcott becomes for once intrusively moralistic and heavy-handedly censorious when she approaches this subject: "the means [Jo] took to gain her end were not the best" (324) [272], she

---

1. A popular, mid-nineteenth-century American writer, whose most famous work, *The Hidden Hand*, originally appeared in the *New York Ledger* in 1859 [*Editors*].

writes; and again: "wrongdoing always brings its own punishment, and when Jo most needed hers, she got it" (328) [275]. The narrator's exposition of the "wrong" of such writing runs as follows:

> Mr. Dashwood rejected any but thrilling tales, and as thrills could not be produced except by harrowing up the souls of the readers, history and romance, land and sea, science and art, police records and lunatic asylums, had to be ransacked for the purpose. Jo soon found that her innocent experience had given her but few glimpses of the tragic world which underlies society, so regarding it in a business light, she set about supplying her deficiencies with characteristic energy. Eager to find material for stories, and bent on making them original in plot, if not masterly in execution, she searched newspapers for accidents, incidents, and crimes; she excited the suspicions of public librarians by asking for works on poisons; she studied faces in the street, and characters, good, bad, and indifferent, all about her; she delved into the dust of ancient times for facts or fictions so old that they were as good as new, and introduced herself to folly, sin, and misery, as well as her limited opportunities allowed. She thought she was prospering finely, but unconsciously she was beginning to desecrate some of the womanliest attributes of a woman's character. She was living in bad society, and imaginary though it was, its influence affected her, for she was feeding heart and fancy on dangerous and unsubstantial food, and was fast brushing the innocent bloom from her nature by a premature acquaintance with the darker side of life, which comes soon enough to all of us. [327–28] [275]

The genres of story-papers require certain forms of knowledge of their would-be writers, the experience needed to project their generic "reality." This experiential horizon is "dark," a "tragic" dimension, Alcott's last phrase implies, that characterizes all human life. But her prose also suggests that this "darker" life corresponds specifically to the life of a lower, and a fearfully lower, social stratum: a social "underside" characterized by crime, sexual license and the nonprotection of women's "innocent bloom," poor nutritional habits, "folly, sin, and misery." Alcott presumes, here, that story-papers are the literary emanation of lower-class culture, such that to "enter into" such writing even imaginatively is tantamount to going into "bad society." A woman can cross over into this genre and social culture, but not without violating the shieldedness from indecent knowledge that establishes the proper "women" of middle-class society. For a woman to write such work, in short, is to become unwomanly: to desecrate "some of the womanliest attributes of a woman's character."

In this paragraph an apparently universal term in fact linked to the norms of one social group gets deployed against a literary form known to belong to a different social group. The very idea of the decently domestic "little woman," the concept on which the ethos of middle-class domesticity is founded, is mobilized against story-paper fiction here; and the subsequent narrative reinforces this effect. As Alcott continues her story, Jo's secret writing career turns out to have been detected—by Professor Bhaer, the husband destined for this "good wife." Generations of readers have groaned over this final match. But the disappointment Bhaer engenders is just what makes him right for Jo, within the thinking of the book's dominant ethos. In an ethos that sets the transcendence of untutored personal desire as a primary value for women, Bhaer's nonattractions—his poverty, his age—become positive qualifications in a husband. (Jo knows better than to accept the proposal of Laurie, who is wrong for her just because he is so right for her: so young, so wealthy, so high-spirited, so much fun.) Bhaer's further "attractiveness" lies in his moral superiority, and even more in the confident authority with which he projects it. In the nineteenth-century culture of domesticity, the insistence that the child take a morally authoritative parent as its love-object strongly disposes the child to find its lovers in parentlike figures: it is not accident but the fulfillment of her upbringing that Ellen Montgomery finds her adult love in John Humphreys, who stands to her as older to younger, teacher to pupil, and moral regulator to morally regulated.[2] This is just the relation Professor Bhaer occupies toward Jo; but to fit him for the role of love-object the book needs to let him assert himself toward her in a morally authoritative form.

This is what happens in the story-paper subplot. Bhaer is only a teacher in the same house with Jo, a learned man known to be in need of a good wife (Jo's peeping has taught her that he darns his own socks) and known as a public defender of old-time religion, until the scene where he weighs in against her writing. Story-paper fiction, he informs her here, is "bad trash" (333) [280], not just a vacuous entertainment of innocent manufacture but an active agent of social debasement. When Jo tells him that "many very respectable people make an honest living out of what are called sensation stories," he turns on her and takes higher ground: "If the respectable people knew what harm they did, they would not feel that the living *was* honest. They haf no right to put poison in the sugarplum, and let the small ones eat it" (333) [280]. In taking this high tone, Bhaer associates himself with "that Father and Mother" whose moral insistences laid "sure foundations" for Jo "to build character upon in womanhood" (334) [281]; and the narrative organization of *Little Women* gives this otherwise unrelated development extraordinary literary implications. For as the story is constructed, Professor Bhaer qualifies himself as parent substitute and potential beloved through his censure of story-papers; and Jo attains to her mature womanly life by accepting his lesson, renouncing her sensation-fiction writing, and converting to a more morally acceptable genre. The juvenile-domestic writing she turns to now, exemplified in the text by the *Little Women*-like poem "In the Garret," brings Jo to her husband and her own married self.

2. For a more extensive discussion of the child-woman/mentor couple in sentimental fiction, see Alfred Habegger, "Precocious Incest: First Novels by Louisa May Alcott and Henry James," *Massachusetts Review* 26 (Summer 1985):233–62, reprinted in Habegger's *Henry James and the "Woman Business"* (Cambridge: Cambridge University Press, 1989). This book offers evidence of James's early involvement with the domestic writing from which criticism has detached him.

If more evidence were needed, this sequence shows how little the social situation of Alcott's authorship is external to her work. *Little Women* is a book written in full awareness of the places for writers and writing structured in its surrounding culture, and weighing their different meanings and accessibilities is one of its chief imaginative projects. The way Alcott differentiates among writing worlds within *Little Women* sheds considerable light on her own choice of literary position. But the book's great interest is that it affords a glimpse, as well, of a larger process of cultural discrimination.

* * *

BARBARA SICHERMAN

Reading *Little Women*: The Many Lives of a Text†

"I have read and re-read 'Little Women' and *it* never seems to grow old," fifteen-year-old Jane Addams confided to a friend.[1] Writing in 1876, Addams did not say why she liked *Little Women*. But her partiality was by no means unusual among women, and even some men, of her generation. Louisa May Alcott's tale of growing up female was an unexpected success when it appeared in the fall of 1868. Already a classic when Addams wrote, the book has been called "the most popular girls' story in American literature"; a century and a quarter after publication, there are twenty editions in print.[2]

The early history of this publishing phenomenon is full of ironies. Not the least of them is the author's expressed distaste for the project. When Thomas Niles Jr., literary editor of the respected Boston firm of Roberts Brothers, asked Alcott to write a "*girls' story*," the author tartly observed in her journal: "I plod away, though I don't enjoy this sort of thing. Never liked girls or knew many, except my sisters, but our queer plays and experiences may prove interesting, though I doubt it."[3] After

† From *U.S. History as Women's History: New Feminist Essays*, ed. Linda K. Kerber, Alice Kessler-Harris, and Kathryn Kish Sklar (Chapel Hill: U of North Carolina P, 1995), 245–66, 414–24. Copyright © 1995 by the University of North Carolina Press. Reprinted by permission of the publisher. [I thank Joan Jacobs Brumberg, Marlene Fisher, Linda K. Kerber, Alice Kessler-Harris, Elizabeth Young, and members of my writing group—Ann duCille, Joan Hedrick, Gertrude Hughes, Indira Karemcheti, and Laura Wexler—for reading earlier drafts of this essay; Ann Morrissey and Janet Murphy for research assistance; the Watkinson Library, Patricia Bunker, and Mary Curry for reference and interlibrary loan assistance; Trinity College for a sabbatical leave; and the William R. Kenan Jr. Professorship of American Institutions and Values for research funds. Joan Hedrick, who read several versions, deserves special mention. Citations from the Little, Brown and Co. Papers (*87M-113) and the Alcott Family Papers (bMS Am 1130.8 and bMS Am 800.23) are by permission of the Houghton Library, Harvard University (Sicherman's acknowledgment).] Page references to this Norton Critical Edition are given in brackets following Sicherman's original citations. Footnotes are the author's except where followed by [*Editors.*].

1. Addams to Vallie Beck, March 16, 1876, *The Jane Addams Papers*, edited by Mary Lynn McCree Bryan (Ann Arbor: University Microfilms International, 1984) (hereafter cited as *Addams Papers*), reel 1.
2. Frank Luther Mott, *Golden Multitudes: The Story of Best Sellers in the United States* (New York: Macmillan, 1947), p. 102; *Books in Print, 1992–93.*
3. May 1868, *The Journals of Louisa May Alcott*, edited by Joel Myerson and Daniel Shealy, associate ed. Madeleine B. Stern (Boston: Little, Brown, 1989), pp. 165–66 (hereafter cited as *Journals*). On rereading this entry in later years, Alcott quipped: "Good joke." Niles first re-

delivering twelve chapters in June 1868, she claimed that both she and her editor found them "*dull*."[4] Niles assured her that he was "pleased—I ought to be more emphatic & say delighted,—so *please* to consider 'judgement' as favorable"; the following month he predicted that the book would " 'hit.' "[5] Influenced perhaps by the verdict of "some girls" who had pronounced the manuscript " 'splendid!' " Alcott reconsidered while correcting proof: "It reads better than I expected. Not a bit sensational, but simple and true, for we really lived most of it." Of the youngsters who liked it, she observed: "As it is for them, they are the best critics, so I should be satisfied."[6]

The informal "readers' report" was right on target. Published in early October 1868, the first printing (2,000 copies) of *Little Women, or, Meg, Jo, Beth and Amy* sold out within the month. A sequel appeared the following April, with only the designation *Part Second* differentiating it from the original. By the end of the year some 38,000 copies (of both parts) were in print, with another 32,000 in 1870. Nearly 200,000 copies had been printed by Roberts Brothers by January 1888, two months before Alcott's death.[7] Like it or not, with this book Alcott established her niche in the expanding market for juvenile literature.

Perhaps even more remarkable than *Little Women*'s initial success has been its longevity. It topped a list of forty books compiled by the Federal Bureau of Education in 1925 that "all children should read before they are sixteen."[8] Two years later—in response to the question "What book has influenced you most?"—high school students ranked it first, ahead

---

quested a girls' book in 1867; Alcott says she "[b]egan at once . . . but didn't like" it. September [1867], *Journals*, p. 158.

4. June [1868], *Journals*, p. 166.

5. Niles to Alcott, June 16, 1868 (#1) and July 25, 1868 (#2), bMS Am 1130.8, Alcott Family Papers, Houghton Library, Harvard University (all citations from Niles's letters are from this collection). On Alcott's publishing history, see Raymond L. Kilgour, *Messrs. Roberts Brothers Publishers* (Ann Arbor: University of Michigan Press, 1952), and Daniel Lester Shealy, "The Author-Publisher Relationships of Louisa May Alcott" (Ph.D. diss, University of South Carolina, 1985). I am grateful to Michael Winship for the last reference.

6. August 26 [1868], *Journals*, p. 166. According to most sources, Niles tested the manuscript on his niece, whose age is variously given.

7. For an account of Alcott's sales through 1909, by which time nearly 598,000 copies of *Little Women* had been printed by Roberts Brothers, see Joel Myerson and Daniel Shealy, "The Sales of Louisa May Alcott's Books," *Harvard Library Bulletin*, n.s., 1 (Spring 1990), esp. pp. 69–71, 86. I am grateful to Michael Winship for this reference. See also Roberts Brothers Cost Book D, [i], *87M-113, Little, Brown and Co. Papers, Houghton Library, Harvard University (hereafter cited as Little, Brown Papers). These figures do not include foreign sales. Although *Little Women* was not published in a single volume until 1880, I will refer to it in the singular except when one volume is specifically intended.

   Sales figures are unreliable for the twentieth century, in part because of foreign sales and the proliferation of editions after the expiration of copyright. Dorothea Lawrence Mann, "When the Alcott Books Were New," *Publishers' Weekly* 116 (September 28, 1929): 1619, claimed sales of nearly three million. According to an account published three years later, Little, Brown and Co., which had absorbed Roberts Brothers, reported that over 1.5 million copies of *Little Women* had been sold in the United States. "Louisa M. Alcott Centenary Year," *Publishers' Weekly* 122 (July 2, 1932): 23–24. Charles A. Madison, *Book Publishing in America* (New York: McGraw-Hill, 1966), p. 134, cites sales of 3 million but gives no sources.

   Sales, of course, are only part of the story: library use was high at the outset and remained so. Niles to Alcott (#18), undated fragment [1870? but probably about August 1869] and "Popularity of 'Little Women,' " December 12, 1912, "Press [illegible] Albany," in bMS Am 800.23 (newspaper clippings, reviews, and articles about Louisa May Alcott and her family), Alcott Family Papers.

8. Mann, "When the Alcott Books Were New."

of the Bible and *Pilgrim's Progress*.[9] On a bicentennial list of the best eleven American children's books, *Little Women, The Adventures of Tom Sawyer*, and *The Adventures of Huckleberry Finn* were the only nineteenth-century titles. Like most iconic works, *Little Women* has been transmuted into other media, into song and opera, theater, radio, and film. A comic strip even surfaced briefly in 1988 in the revamped *Ms.*[1]

Polls and statistics do not begin to do justice to the *Little Women* phenomenon. Reading the book has been a rite of passage for generations of adolescent and preadolescent females of the comfortable classes. It still elicits powerful narratives of love and passion.[2] In a 1982 essay on how she became a writer, Cynthia Ozick declared: "I read 'Little Women' a thousand times. Ten thousand. I am no longer incognito, not even to myself. I am Jo in her 'vortex'; not Jo exactly, but some Jo-of-the-future. I am under an enchantment: Who I truly am must be deferred, waited for and waited for."[3] Ozick's avowal encapsulates recurrent themes in readers' accounts: the deep, almost inexplicable emotions engendered by the novel; the passionate identification with Jo March, the feisty tomboy heroine who publishes stories in her teens; and—allowing for exaggeration—a pattern of multiple readings. Numerous women who grew up in the 1940s and 1950s report that they read the book yearly or more during their teens or earlier; some confide that they continue to read it as adults, though less frequently. Presumably for them, as for Jane Addams, the story did not grow old.

One of many intriguing questions about *Little Women* is how and why the "dull" book, the girls' story by a woman who claimed she never liked girls, captivated so many readers. An added irony is that Alcott, the product of an unconventional upbringing, whose eccentric transcendentalist father self-consciously tested his child-rearing theories on his daughters, took them to live in a commune, and failed utterly as a breadwinner, should write what many contemporaries considered the definitive story of American family life.[4]

My concern here, however, is with *Little Women* as a cultural phenomenon and what it can tell us about the relationship between reading and female identity. A cultural profile of the book and its readers casts light on *Little Women's* emergence as the classic story of American girlhood and why, in the words of a recent critic, it has remained "a kind of miracle of preservation" when most other works of its era

9. " 'Little Women' Leads Poll," *New York Times*, March 22, 1927, p. 7, reprinted in Madeleine B. Stern, ed., *Critical Essays on Louisa May Alcott* (Boston: G. K. Hall, 1984), p. 84.
1. See Gloria T. Delamar, *Louisa May Alcott and 'Little Women': Biography, Critique, Publications, Poems, Songs, and Contemporary Relevance* (Jefferson, N.C.: McFarland and Co., 1990), p. 167 and passim. I am grateful to Joan Jacobs Brumberg for this reference.
2. For an intriguing analysis of well-loved texts that takes *Little Women* as a point of departure, see Catharine R. Stimpson, "Reading for Love: Canons, Paracanons, and Whistling Jo March," *New Literary History* 21 (Autumn 1990): 957–76 [reprinted in this Norton Critical Edition on pp. 584–99].
3. "Spells, Wishes, Goldfish, Old School Hurts," *New York Times Book Review*, January 31, 1982, p. 24.
4. The classic biography is still Madeleine B. Stern, *Louisa May Alcott* (Norman: University of Oklahoma Press, 1950), which should be supplemented by Stern's extensive criticism on Alcott. See also Sarah Elbert, *A Hunger for Home: Louisa May Alcott and "Little Women"* (Philadelphia: Temple University Press, 1984), and Martha Saxton, *Louisa May: A Modern Biography of Louisa May Alcott* (New York: Avon Books, 1978).

have long since disappeared from the juvenile canon.[5] Building on recent work in cultural criticism and history, this study also examines the "cultural work" *Little Women* performed for diverse reading communities.[6] Such an approach challenges traditional assumptions about the universality of texts. It also demonstrates the importance of reading for the construction of female identity.

Little Women was commissioned because the publisher believed a market existed for a "girls' story," a relatively new genre still in the process of being defined. The book's success suggests that this assumption was correct, although there is also evidence that its readership extended beyond the targeted group. Two unusual features affected the book's production and early reception. First, its two-stage publication gave readers unusual influence in constructing the plot, an important element in its long-term appeal. Second, the book was marketed in ways that elicited reader identification with author as well as heroine, an author, moreover, who was not only astonishingly successful but whose connections with Ralph Waldo Emerson (her intellectual mentor) and Nathaniel Hawthorne (her neighbor) were widely known. Enjoying considerable popularity from the outset, *Little Women* became part of the prescribed reading of an American girlhood, as did Alcott's own life.

Knowing how a book is promoted is not the same as knowing how it is read, however. *Little Women* has been interpreted in many ways, by ordinary readers as well as critics.[7] Initially praised by readers and reviewers as a realistic story of family life, by the time of its successful stage adaptation in 1912–14 it seemed "quaint" to some.[8] In the twentieth century, Jo, always the most admired sister, was for many the only one who mattered.

With its origin as a girls' story—by definition a domestic story—and a plot in which the sisters overcome their personal failings as they move from adolescence to womanhood, *Little Women* has been viewed by some recent critics as exacting discipline from its readers as well as its heroines.[9] This interpretative line recognizes only one way of read-

5. Richard H. Brodhead, "Starting Out in the 1860s: Alcott, Authorship, and the Postbellum Literary Field," chap. 3 in *Cultures of Letters: Scenes of Reading and Writing in Nineteenth-Century America* (Chicago: University of Chicago Press, 1993), p. 89 [an excerpt is reprinted in this Norton Critical Edition on pp. 624–32].
6. On cultural work, see Jane Tompkins, *Sensational Designs: The Cultural Work of American Fiction, 1790–1860* (New York: Oxford University Press, 1985). Two theoretically sophisticated, historically based studies of readers are Janice A. Radway, *Reading the Romance: Women, Patriarchy, and Popular Literature* (1984; reprint, with a new introduction by the author, Chapel Hill: University of North Carolina Press, 1991), and Roger Chartier, "Texts, Printing, Readings," in *The New Cultural History*, edited by Lynn Hunt (Berkeley: University of California Press, 1989), pp. 154–75.
7. The critical literature on *Little Women* is immense and growing. Useful starting points are Stern, *Critical Essays*; Alma J. Payne, *Louisa May Alcott: A Reference Guide* (Boston: G. K. Hall, 1980); and Judith C. Ullom, *Louisa May Alcott: A Centennial for Little Women: An Annotated Selected Bibliography* (Washington, D.C.: Library of Congress, 1969).
8. For nineteenth- and early twentieth-century reviews, mainly in newspapers, see bMS Am 800.23, Alcott Family Papers, and Janet S. Zehr, "The Response of Nineteenth-Century Audiences to Louisa May Alcott's Fiction," *American Transcendental Quarterly*, n.s., 1 (December 1987): 323–42, which draws on this mostly undated collection.
9. For Foucauldian approaches, see Steven Mailloux, "The Rhetorical Use and Abuse of Fiction: Eating Books in Late Nineteenth-Century America," *boundary 2* 17 (Spring 1990): 133–57, and Brodhead, "Starting Out in the 1860s," pp. 69–106.

ing the story—a conservative one. Feminist explications have for the most part focused on Jo, who has been variously read as "the one young woman in 19th-century fiction who maintains her individual independence, who gives up no part of her autonomy as payment for being born a woman—and who gets away with it" and as a character who is betrayed and even murdered by her creator, who allows her to be tamed and married.[1]

Whether they discern negative or positive messages, critics agree on the importance of the story. *Little Women* has been called "*the* American female myth," Jo "the most influential figure of the independent and creative American woman."[2] To read the book in this way, even as a failed bildungsroman, as do critics who view Jo's marriage as a surrender of autonomy and a capitulation to traditional femininity, assumes an individualistic outlook on the part of readers, a belief that a woman could aspire to and even attain personal success outside the family claim.

The formulation of *Little Women* as "*the* American female myth" is a distinctly middle-class reading, one that assumes both a universality of female experience and a single mode of reading Alcott's text that transcends class, race, ethnicity, and historical era. While adolescents from diverse backgrounds *can* interpret *Little Women* as a search for personal autonomy—and have in fact done so—this is by no means a universal reading. The female quest plot is inflected by class and culture as well as gender. The story has appealed primarily to an audience that is white and middle class. Historical evidence from working-class sources is scarce and is often filtered through middle-class observers. What we have suggests that working-class women did not necessarily have access to "the simple, every-day classics that the school-boy and -girl are supposed to have read," among them *Little Women*, and that many had a penchant for less "realistic" fiction of the sort usually dismissed as "escapist."[3] For some Jewish working-class immigrant women early in the twentieth century, Alcott's story provided a model for becoming American and middle-class rather than for removing themselves from women's domestic lot, as was the case with the

---

1. Elizabeth Janeway, "Meg, Jo, Beth, Amy and Louisa," *New York Times Book Review*, September 29, 1968, p. 42; Angela M. Estes and Kathleen Margaret Lant, "Dismembering the Text: The Horror of Louisa May Alcott's *Little Women*," *Children's Literature* 17 (1989): 98–123 [reprinted in the Norton Critical Edition on pp. 564–83]. See also Judith Fetterley, "*Little Women*: Alcott's Civil War," *Feminist Studies* 5 (Summer 1979): 369–83, and Linda K. Kerber, "Can a Woman Be an Individual?: The Limits of Puritan Tradition in the Early Republic," *Texas Studies in Literature and Language* 25 (Spring 1983): 165–78.
2. Madelon Bedell, "Introduction," *Little Women* (New York: Modern Library, 1983), p. xi, and Elaine Showalter, "*Little Women*: The American Female Myth," chap. 3 in *Sister's Choice: Tradition and Change in Women's Writing* (Oxford: Clarendon Press, 1991), p. 42. All quotations from *Little Women* are from the Modern Library edition, which is taken from 1869 printings of parts one and two.
3. Dorothy Richardson, *The Long Day: The Story of a New York Working Girl as Told by Herself* (1905; reprint, New York: Quadrangle Books, 1972), pp. 84–85. Alcott's juvenile fiction did not appear in the story papers most likely to be found in working-class homes; nor was it available in the Sunday school libraries to which some poor children had access. The latter might encounter Alcott in middle-class sites. In the late 1880s, for example, she was one of the three most popular authors at the reading room for "deprived" girls run by the United Workers and Woman's Exchange in Hartford; the others were Mrs. A. D. T. Whitney and Edgar Allan Poe. *Annual Report* 1 (1888): 8.

native-born writers and intellectuals to whom *Little Women*'s appeal is better known. In this reading, *Little Women* was still a success story—but of a different kind.

Dissimilar though they are, in both interpretations women readers found in *Little Women* a sense of future possibility. Gerda Lerner has demonstrated that access to learning has been central to the creation of feminist consciousness over the centuries.[4] I would add that literature in general and fiction in particular have been critically important in the construction of female identity, although not always a feminist one. The scarcity in life of models for nontraditional womanhood has prompted women more often than men to turn to fiction for self-authorization.[5]

Little Women's long-lived popularity permits examination of the ways in which adolescent girls of diverse class, culture, and historical era have read the text. Where critics have debated the meaning of the novel, in particular whether Jo is a symbol of independent or resigned womanhood, I hope to show that meaning resides in the social location, interpretive conventions, and perceived needs of disparate communities of readers.[6] But the story of *Little Women* is one of continuity as well as difference, particularly in the common interpretive stance of white, middle-class women readers for more than a century. This persistence can perhaps best be understood as a consequence of the snail-like pace of change for women and the dearth of models for such a quest—in fiction and in life. In this context, Jo March was unique.[7]

Early Publishing and Marketing History

Alcott claimed that she kept on with *Little Women* because "lively, simple books are very much needed for girls, and perhaps I can supply the need."[8] She subsequently redirected her energies as a writer away from adult fiction—some of it considered sensational and published anonymously or pseudonymously—to become not only a successful author of "juveniles," but one of the most popular writers of the era.

4. Lerner, *The Creation of Feminist Consciousness: From the Middle Ages to Eighteen-seventy* (New York: Oxford University Press, 1993).

5. Lewis M. Terman and Margaret Lima, *Children's Reading: A Guide for Parents and Teachers*, 2d ed. (New York: Appleton, 1931), pp. 68–84, found that "at every age girls read more than boys" (p. 68) and read more fiction. Half the adult female respondents in one study named *Little Women* as one of ten books read in childhood that they could recall most easily. Men's choices were far more varied.

6. By reading communities, I adopt the definition proposed by Janice Radway for those who, without necessarily constituting a formal group, "share certain assumptions about reading as well as preferences for reading material" based on their social location or, I would add, the position to which they aspired. "Interpretive Communities and Variable Literacies: The Functions of Romance Reading," *Daedalus* 113 (Summer 1984): 54. This essay builds on my earlier work on the interpretive conventions of specific reading communities in "Sense and Sensibility: A Case Study of Women's Reading in Late Victorian America," in *Reading in America: Literature and Social History*, edited by Cathy N. Davidson (Baltimore: Johns Hopkins University Press, 1989), pp. 201–25, and "Reading and Ambition: M. Carey Thomas and Female Heroism," *American Quarterly* 45 (March 1993): 73–103.

7. Carolyn G. Heilbrun emphasizes the lack of autonomous female models in literature and the exceptional nature of Jo in *Reinventing Womanhood* (New York: Norton, 1979), pp. 190–91, 212. See also Heilbrun, *Writing a Woman's Life* (New York: Norton, 1988).

8. June [1868], *Journals*, p. 166.

Alcott may have regretted being channeled into one type of literature, but she was extremely well paid for her efforts, a source of considerable pride to a woman whose father was so feckless about money.[9]

Juvenile literature was entering a new phase in the 1860s at the very time Alcott was refashioning her career. This literature was more secular and on the whole less pietistic than its antebellum precursors, the characterizations more apt; children, even "bad boys," might be basically good, whatever mischievous stages they went through.[1] An expanding middle class, eager to provide its young with cultural as well as moral training, underwrote the new juvenile market that included genteel literary magazines paralleling those read by adults. So seriously was this literature taken that even journals that embraced "high culture" devoted as much space to reviewing children's as adult fiction; thus the seeming anomaly of a review of Alcott's *Eight Cousins* in the *Nation* by the young Henry James.[2]

In contrast to the overtly religious antebellum stories, in which both sexes were expected to be good and domesticated, the new juvenile market was becoming increasingly segmented by gender. An exciting new adventure literature for boys developed after 1850, featuring escape from domesticity and female authority. Seeking to tap into a new market, Niles asked Alcott to write a "girls' story" after he observed the hefty sales of boys' adventure stories by "Oliver Optic," pseudonym of William Taylor Adams.[3] Since prevailing gender ideology defined tales for girls as domestic, it is understandable why Alcott, who idolized her Concord mentor Emerson, adored Goethe, and loved to run with boys, would be disinclined to write one. The designation "girls' story" connoted classification by age as well as gender. Although people of all ages and both sexes read *Little Women*, the book evolved for the

9. Niles told Alcott that her royalties were higher than any other Roberts Brothers author, including Harriet Beecher Stowe, whom he considered the American writer who could command the highest fees (Alcott possibly excepted). Niles to Alcott, June 7, 1871 (#25), February 17, 1873 (#39). Whether or not this was the case, Alcott was the firm's best-selling author, an awareness registered in a poem she wrote and sent Niles entitled "The Lay of a Golden Goose." Myerson and Shealy, "The Sales of Louisa May Alcott's Books," p. 67, settle on $103,375 as the most accurate estimate of Alcott's earnings with Roberts Brothers between 1868 and 1886; this figure does not include foreign sales or magazine earnings.
1. Other "juvenile" classics that appeared about the same time were *Hans Brinker; or, The Silver Skates* (1865) by Mary Mapes Dodge and *The Story of a Bad Boy* (1869) by Thomas Bailey Aldrich. A 1947 source claims that these titles, along with *Little Women*, "initiated the modern juvenile." *One Hundred Influential American Books Printed before 1900: Catalogue and Addresses: Exhibition at The Grolier Club* (New York: The Grolier Club, 1947), p. 106. Also of the period, though less highly esteemed, were *Elsie Dinsmore* (1867) by Martha Finley and Horatio Alger Jr.'s *Ragged Dick* (1868).
2. See Richard L. Darling, *The Rise of Children's Book Reviewing in America, 1865–1881* (New York: Bowker, 1968). Though he compared Alcott as a satirist to William Makepeace Thackeray and Anthony Trollope and thought her "extremely clever," James took her to task for her "rather vulgar prose" and her "private understanding with the youngsters she depicts, at the expense of their pastors and masters." *Nation*, October 14, 1875, pp. 250–51, reprinted in Stern, *Critical Essays*, pp. 165–66.
3. Elizabeth Segel, " 'As the Twig Is Bent . . .': Gender and Childhood Reading," in *Gender and Reading: Essays on Readers, Texts, and Contexts*, edited by Elizabeth A. Flynn and Patrocinio P. Schweickart (Baltimore: Johns Hopkins University Press, 1986), pp. 165–86, is a useful brief analysis. See also Daniel T. Rodgers, *The Work Ethic in Industrial America, 1850–1920* (Chicago: University of Chicago Press, 1978), pp. 125–52, and R. Gordon Kelly, ed., *Children's Periodicals of the United States* (Westport, Conn.: Greenwood Press, 1984) [William Taylor Adams (1822–1891) was a schoolteacher and an author of children's stories under the pseudonym Oliver Optic (*Editors*).]

emerging female youth market, the "young adults" in the transitional period between childhood and adulthood that would soon be labeled adolescence.[4]

These readers had an unusual say in determining Jo's fate. Eager to capitalize on his experiment, Niles urged Alcott to add a chapter "in which allusions might be made to something in the future."[5] Employing a metaphor well suited to a writer who engaged in theatrical performances most of her life, the volume concludes: "So grouped the curtain falls upon Meg, Jo, Beth and Amy. Whether it ever rises again, depends upon the reception given to the first act of the domestic drama, called 'LITTLE WOMEN.' "[6] Reader response to Alcott's floater was positive but complicated her task. Reluctant to depart from autobiography, Alcott insisted that by rights Jo should remain a "literary spinster." But she felt pressured by readers to imagine a different fate for her heroine. The day she began work on the sequel, she observed: "Girls write to ask who the little women marry, as if that was the only end and aim of a woman's life. I *won't* marry Jo to Laurie to please anyone." To foil her readers, she created a "funny match" for Jo—the middle-aged, bumbling German professor, Friedrich Bhaer.[7]

The aspect of the book that has frustrated generations of readers—the foreclosing of marriage between Jo and Laurie—thus represents a compromise between Alcott and her initial audience. Paradoxically, this seeming misstep has probably been a major factor in the story's enduring success. If Jo had remained a spinster, as Alcott wished, or if she had married the attractive and wealthy hero, as readers hoped, it is unlikely that the book would have had such a wide appeal. Rather, the problematic ending contributed to *Little Women's* popularity, the lack of satisfying closure helping to keep the story alive, something to ponder, return to, reread, perhaps with the hope of a different resolution. Alcott's refusal of the conventionally happy ending represented by a pairing of Jo and Laurie and her insistence on a "funny match" to the rumpled and much older professor effectively subvert adolescent romantic ideals. The absence of a compelling love plot has also made it easier for generations of readers to ignore the novel's ending when Jo becomes Mother Bhaer and to retain the image of Jo as the questing teenage tomboy.[8]

4. See Edward G. Salmon, "What Girls Read," *Nineteenth Century* 20 (October 1886): 515–29, and the ad for a series of "Books for Girls" whose intended audience was those "between eight and eighteen. . . . for growing-up girls, the mothers of the next generation." *American Literary Gazette and Publishers' Circular* (ALG) 17 (June 1, 1871): 88.
5. Niles to Alcott, July 25, 1868 (#2).
6. *Little Women*, p. 290 [185].
7. November 1, [1868], *Journals*, p. 167; Alcott to Elizabeth Powell, March 20, [1869], in *The Selected Letters of Louisa May Alcott*, edited by Joel Myerson and Daniel Shealy, associate ed. Madeleine B. Stern (Boston: Little, Brown, 1987), p. 125 (hereafter cited as SL). Erin Graham, "Books That Girls Have Loved," *Lippincott's Monthly Magazine*, September 1897, pp. 428–32, makes much of Bhaer's foreignness and ungainliness. The author recalls reading Alcott after the age of thirteen, when more "lachrymose" heroines had "palled" and she and her friends "did not take kindly to the romantic passion."
8. Jo's standing as a tomboy was recognized—and even respected; an ad for *Little Men* noted that "when a girl, [Jo] was half a boy herself." ALG 17 (May 15, 1871): 49. For girls in early adolescence and/or lesbian readers, the young Jo may have been the primary romantic interest.

At the same time, an adolescent reader, struggling with her appearance and unruly impulses while contemplating the burdens of future womanhood, might find it reassuring that her fictional counterpart emerges happily, if not perhaps ideally, from similar circumstances. For Jo is loved. And she has choices. She turns down the charming but erratic hero, who consoles himself by marrying her pretty and vain younger sister, Amy. Professor Bhaer is no schoolgirl's hero, but Jo believes that he is better suited to her than Laurie. The crucial point is that the choice is hers, its quirkiness another sign of her much-prized individuality.[9] Jo gives up writing sensation stories because her prospective husband considers them unworthy, but she makes it clear that she intends to contribute to the support of their future family.

By marrying off the sisters in the second part, Alcott bowed to young women's interest in romance. The addition of the marriage to the quest plot enabled Little Women to touch the essential bases for middle-class female readers in the late nineteenth century. In this regard, it was unusual for its time. In adult fiction, marriage and quest plots were rarely combined; success in the former precluded attainment of the latter.[1] The inclusion of a marriage plot in a book for a nonadult audience was also unusual. Even though critics noted the need for literature for the in-between stage, variously designated as eight to eighteen and fourteen to twenty, Harper's New Monthly Magazine judged the sequel "a rather mature book for the little women, but a capital one for their elders."[2] The conjunction of quest and marriage plots helps to account for the book's staying power: it is difficult to imagine large numbers of adolescent female readers in the twentieth century gravitating to a book in which the heroine remained single.[3]

Little Women took off with the publication of the second part in April 1869. A Concord neighbor called it "the rage in '69 as 'Pinafore' was in '68."[4] A savvy judge of the market, Niles urged Alcott to " 'Make hay while the Sun-shines' " and did everything he could to keep her name before the public.[5] Shortly after the appearance of Little Women, Part Second, Roberts Brothers brought out an augmented edition of her first critical success under the title, Hospital Sketches and Camp and Fireside Stories, and in succeeding years published An Old-Fashioned Girl (1870) and Little Men (1871), a sequel to Little Women. Niles encouraged publicity about books and author, whom he kept informed about her extensive press coverage while she traveled

---

9. A conversation with Dolores Kreisman contributed to this analysis.
1. See Rachel Blau DuPlessis, Writing beyond the Ending: Narrative Strategies of Twentieth-Century Women Writers (Bloomington: Indiana University Press, 1985).
2. Harper's New Monthly Magazine, August 1869, pp. 455–56, reprinted in Stern, Critical Essays, p. 83.
3. For an analysis of changes in girls' stories as the heterosexual imperative became stronger, see Martha Vicinus, "What Makes a Heroine?: Nineteenth-Century Girls' Biographies," Genre 20 (Summer 1987): 171–87.
4. Frank Preston Stearns, Sketches from Concord and Appledore (New York: Putnam, 1895), p. 82.
5. Niles to Alcott, April 14, 1869 (#4). On advertising techniques of the era, see Susan Geary, "The Domestic Novel as a Commercial Commodity: Making a Best Seller in the 1850s," Papers of the Bibliographical Society of America 70 (1976): 365–93.

abroad. Alcott was then at the peak of her popularity; between October 1868 and July 1871 Roberts Brothers sold some 166,000 volumes of her juvenile fiction.[6]

The well-publicized autobiographical status of *Little Women*, together with Alcott's realistic subject matter and direct style, encouraged identification by middle-class readers.[7] Reviewers stressed the realism of her characters and scenes; readers recognized themselves in her work. Thirteen-year-old Annie Adams of Fair Haven, Vermont, wrote *St. Nicholas*, the most prestigious of the new children's magazines, that she and her three sisters each resembled one of the March sisters (she was Jo): "So, you see, I was greatly interested in 'Little Women,' as I could appreciate it so well; and it seemed to me as if Miss Alcott must have seen us four girls before she wrote the story."[8] Girls not only read themselves into *Little Women*, they elaborated on it and incorporated the story into their lives. In 1872 the five Lukens sisters from Brinton, Pennsylvania, sent Alcott a copy of their home newspaper, "Little Things," which was modeled after "The Pickwick Portfolio" produced by the March sisters. Alcott responded with encouragement, asked for further details, and subscribed to the paper; subsequently she offered advice about reading, writing, and religion and even sent a story for publication. She took their aspirations seriously, providing frank, practical advice about magazines, publishers, and authors' fees to these budding literary women.[9]

There was, then, a reciprocal relationship between the characters and home life depicted in *Little Women* and the lives of middle-class American girls. An unusual feature of this identification was the perception that author and heroine were interchangeable. Alcott's work was marketed to encourage the illusion not only that Jo was Alcott but that Alcott was Jo. When Alcott traveled in Europe in 1870, Niles encouraged her to send for publication " 'Jo's Letters from Abroad to the March's [*sic*] at Home' "; the following year he asked her to select "from the million or less letters" some that could be published in a volume entitled "Little Women and Little Men Letters or Letters to 'Jo'

6. "Roberts Brothers, Boston," *ALG* 17 (July 1, 1871): 118. Led by *Little Women, An Old-Fashioned Girl*, and *Little Men*, Alcott's fiction for younger readers continued to sell. Her adult books, including *Hospital Sketches* which received excellent reviews, did not do as well. In general, sales fell off in the late 1870s but picked up again in the 1880s with the repackaging of *Little Women* as a single volume and publication of eight titles in a " 'Little Women' Series." Roberts Brothers Cost Books, including summary in Cost Book D [i], *87M-113, Little, Brown Papers, and Myerson and Shealy, "The Sales of Louisa May Alcott's Books."

7. An early ad called *Little Women* a "history of actual life" (*Boston Evening Transcript*, September 30, 1868, p. 3), while an undated source claimed: "It was known to friends and acknowledged by Miss Alcott herself that 'Little Women' is the transcript, more or less literal, of her own and her sisters['] girlhood" (torn clipping, probably an obituary, bMS Am 800.23, Alcott Family Papers). See also [Franklin B. Sanborn], "The Author of 'Little Women,' " *Hearth and Home*, July 16, 1870.

8. Letter in *St. Nicholas*, February 1878, p. 300.

9. "Little Things," at first handwritten, then typeset on a small press, was part of a national phenomenon. See Paula Petrik, "The Youngest Fourth Estate: The Novelty Toy Printing Press and Adolescence, 1870–1886," in *Small Worlds: Children and Adolescents in America, 1850–1950*, edited by Elliott West and Paula Petrik (Lawrence: University Press of Kansas, 1992), pp. 125–42. Alcott's correspondence with the Lukens sisters, which extended over fourteen years, is reprinted in *SL*; it was published earlier in the *Ladies' Home Journal*, April 1896, pp. 1–2. The Alcott sisters had their own Pickwick Club in 1849.

by 'Little Women' and 'Little Men.' "[1] Neither book materialized, but *Shawl-Straps*, a humorous account of Alcott's European trip, appeared in 1872 as the second volume in the *Aunt Jo's Scrap-Bag* series. Niles sometimes addressed his leading author as "Jo," "Jo March," or "Aunt Jo." Alcott often substituted the names of the March sisters for her own when she answered fans; on occasion, she inserted them into her journal. The equation of author and character continued after Alcott's death. When her sister Anna Pratt supervised publication of *Comic Tragedies* (1893), a volume of childhood plays, she wrote the foreword as "Meg," and the title page read "Written By 'Jo' and 'Meg' and Acted by the 'Little Women.' "

Readers responded in kind. An ad for *Little Women* quotes a letter written by "Nelly" addressed to "Dear Jo, or Miss Alcott": "We have all been reading 'Little Women,' and we liked it so much I could not help wanting to write to you. We think *you* are perfectly splendid; I like you better every time I read it. We were all so disappointed about your not marrying Laurie; I cried over that part,—I could not help it. We all liked Laurie ever so much, and almost killed ourselves laughing over the funny things you and he said." Blurring the lines between author and character, the writer also requested a picture, wished the recipient improved health, and invited her to visit.[2]

The illusion that she was the youthful and unconventional Jo made Alcott a more approachable author. But the conflation of author and character had its risks. Young readers who formed an image of the author as Jo, a teenager for most of the novel, were startled by Alcott's appearance. When the Lukens sisters informed her that some "friends" had been disappointed in her picture, Alcott replied that she could not understand why people insisted Jo was young "when she is said to be 30 at the end of the book . . . After seeing the photograph it is hardly necessary to say that Jo and L.M.A. are *not* one, & that the latter is a tired out old lady of 42."[3]

With the publication of *Little Women, Part Second*, Alcott became a celebrity. Correspondents demanded her photograph and autograph seekers descended on her home while she "dodge[d] into the woods *à la* Hawthorne."[4] Customarily shunning the limelight, she was mobbed by fans on her rare public appearances. After a meeting of the Woman's Congress in 1875, she reported, "the stage filled . . . with beaming girls all armed with Albums and cards and begging to speak to Miss A. . . . 'Do put up your veil so we can see how you really look' said one. 'Will you kiss me please,' said another. . . . I finally had to run for my life with more girls all along the way, and Ma's clawing me

1. Niles to Alcott, August 30, 1870 (#16), August 14, 1871 (#29). Unfortunately, only a few letters from Alcott's fans survive.
2. Letter from "Nelly," dated March 12, 1870, reproduced in Delamar, *Louisa May Alcott*, p. 146.
3. Alcott to the Lukens Sisters, October 2, 1874, *SL*, pp. 185–86. Readers' disappointment with her appearance is a recurrent subject in Alcott's letters. Alice Stone Blackwell, who knew the writer, found her "positively unpleasant looking." See Marlene Deahl Merrill, ed., *Growing Up in Boston's Gilded Age: The Journal of Alice Stone Blackwell, 1872–1874* (New Haven: Yale University Press, 1990), p. 174.
4. April [1869], *Journals*, p. 171.

as I went." Things were somewhat more decorous at Vassar, but even college students insisted on kissing Alcott and obtaining her autograph.[5] She avenged herself with a devastating portrait of celebrity hounds in *Jo's Boys* (1886), the sequel to *Little Men*.[6]

Alcott also drew more serious admirers, some of whom, like the Lukens sisters, sought her literary advice. In the 1860s and 1870s authorship was the most respected female vocation—and the best paid. Before the consolidation of the American literary canon later in the century, women writers had an acknowledged, though not unchallenged, place in the world of letters. Feminist critics and historians have recently been documenting women's presence, but Alcott has been largely left out of this reassessment, in large part because of her status as a writer of "juvenile fiction."[7]

Alcott was a well-respected writer during her lifetime, an era of relatively inclusive and nonhierarchical definitions of literature. An American literature course taken by Jane Addams at Rockford Female Seminary in 1878–79 covered authors of domestic fiction, Alcott among them.[8] But her literary reputation transcended the category. A review of *Little Men* pronounced: "Even thus early in her brief history as a country and a nation, America can boast a long list of classics—Prescott, Irving, Hawthorne, Longfellow—and Time, the great sculptor will one day carve Miss Alcott's name among them."[9] Alcott received nearly a page to Hawthorne's page and a half in James S. Hart's *A Manual of American Literature: A Text-Book for Schools and Colleges* (1873); both were listed under the category "Novels and Tales." She was compared with her former neighbor on more than one occasion; a younger Concord resident proclaimed: "In American fiction 'Little Women' holds the next place to the 'Scarlet Letter' and 'Marble Faun.' " Since Hawthorne stood at the pinnacle of American literature, this was high praise.[1]

A teenage girl contemplating a literary career could dream of becoming a published author who, like Alcott, might produce a beloved and immortal work. At a time when young women were encouraged, even expected, to take part in the literary activities that suffused middle-class domestic life, such success was not beyond imagining.

5. Louisa May Alcott to Amos Bronson Alcott, [October 18, 1875], *SL*, p. 198; see also September–October 1875, *Journals*, pp. 196–97. It is an interesting commentary on changing sex and gender expectations that Alcott had the kind of fan appeal for teenage girls that in the twentieth century has been reserved for male pop singers.
6. "Jo's Last Scrape," pp. 45–65.
7. See, however, Richard H. Brodhead's stimulating discussion of Alcott's professional options in "Starting Out in the 1860s." An earlier, more amateur mode of "starting out" is analyzed by Joan D. Hedrick, "Parlor Literature: Harriet Beecher Stowe and the Question of 'Great Women Artists,' " *Signs* 17 (Winter 1992): 275–303. For an analysis of efforts to make "high culture" a safe space for men, see Hedrick, *Harriet Beecher Stowe: A Life* (New York: Oxford University Press, 1994); on the literary marketplace, see Susan Coultrap-McQuin, *Doing Literary Business: American Women Writers in the Nineteenth Century* (Chapel Hill: University of North Carolina Press, 1990).
8. "American Literature," [1878–79], *Addams Papers*, reel 27, frames 239–95.
9. Undated review of *Little Men* ("Capital" penciled in), bMS Am 800.23, Alcott Family Papers.
1. Stearns, *Sketches from Concord and Appledore*, p. 84. Nina Baym claims that Alcott and Stowe were the only women included in the American literary canon at the end of the century. Baym, *Woman's Fiction: A Guide to Novels by and about Women in America, 1820–1870* (Ithaca: Cornell University Press, 1978), p. 23.

From Hart's manual a reader could learn that Alcott began writing for publication at sixteen and, by hard work and perseverance, became both famous and self-supporting by her pen in her late thirties.[2] The real female American success story was Alcott's, not Jo's.

There were, then, many reasons why a young woman seeking a literary career in the 1870s and early 1880s would look to Alcott as a model. Most important was the story that brought pleasure to so many. Despite claims that *Little Women* is a text about disciplining girls into proper womanhood, a comparison with other "girls' books" marks it as a text that opened up new avenues of experience for readers.[3] The contrast with Martha Finley's *Elsie Dinsmore* (1867), a story in which strict obedience is exacted from children—to the point of whipping—is striking. In this first of many volumes, the lachrymose and devoutly religious heroine is put upon by relatives and by her father, who punishes her for refusing to play the piano on the Sabbath. Elsie holds fast to her principles but is otherwise self-abnegating in the extreme: it is difficult to imagine her even trying to have fun.[4] *Faith Gartney's Girlhood* (1863) by Mrs. A. D. T. Whitney, a forgotten but once highly acclaimed writer with whom Alcott was often compared, was the story of a girl's emergence into serious and self-affirming womanhood. Written for a female audience between fourteen and twenty to show "what is noblest and truest," the book is more complex than *Elsie Dinsmore*, the tone less charged. But Whitney relies heavily on didactic narrative and fails to exploit the emotional potential of her plot: the authorial voice is moralistic and the religion conspicuous.[5]

The fictional world of *Little Women* is strikingly different. Despite the use of John Bunyan's *Pilgrim's Progress* as a framing device, an older Calvinist worldview that emphasized sin and obedience to the deity has been replaced by a moral outlook in which self-discipline and doing good to others come first.[6] Consonant with *Little Women*'s new moral tone, so congenial to an expanding middle class, are its informal style and rollicking escapades. Aided by her love of the theater and influenced as well by her youthful idol, Charles Dickens, Alcott

2. See, e.g., Louise Chandler Moulton, "Louisa May Alcott," *Our Famous Women* (1883; reprint, Hartford: A. D. Worthington, 1884), pp. 29–52, which was prepared with Alcott's assistance. Reports of Alcott's financial success appeared frequently in the press. An obituary estimated her earnings for *Little Women* alone at $200,000. "Death of Miss Alcott," *Ladies' Home Journal*, May 1888, p. 3. The figure is high, but it attests to belief in her success.

3. In this sense, *Little Women* may be considered a book that extends readers' "horizons of expectations," to use Hans Robert Jauss's term. Jauss, "Literary History as a Challenge to Literary Theory," *New Directions in Literary History*, edited by Ralph Cohen (Baltimore: Johns Hopkins University Press), pp. 11–41.

4. It is a sign of the changing times that the Elsie books were banned from some libraries on the grounds that they were commonplace and not true to life. Esther Jane Carrier, *Fiction in Public Libraries, 1876–1900* (New York: Scarecrow Press, 1965), pp. 356–60.

5. For comparisons of the two authors, see the review of *An Old-Fashioned Girl* in *Nation*, July 14, 1870, p. 30, and Niles to Alcott, January 13, 1871 (#20). Niles reported that Stowe wanted to know why Alcott's books were "so much more popular" than Mrs. Whitney's, which she considered "equally as good." *Faith Gartney's Girlhood* had a long run in the Sunday school libraries.

6. *The Ladies' Repository* ([December 1868], p. 472), while finding *Little Women* "very readable," pointedly observed that it was "not a Christian book. It is religion without spirituality, and salvation without Christ."

was a wonderful painter of dramatic scenes; some were heartbreaking, but many were high-spirited depictions of frolics, games, and theatrical productions.[7] She also had an ear for young people's language: her substitution of dialogue for the long passages of moralizing narrative that characterized most girls' books gave her story a compelling sense of immediacy. So did her use of slang, for which critics often faulted her, but which must have endeared her to young readers. Finally, the beautifully realized portrait of Jo March as tomboy, one of the first of its kind, spoke to changing standards of girlhood. Beginning in the 1860s, tomboys were not only tolerated but even admired—up to a point, the point at which they were expected to become women.[8] Perhaps it was fitting after all that it was Alcott, writing of her idiosyncratic childhood in the 1840s, who identified a new type of American girlhood for the 1870s.[9]

Why Alcott? Why *Little Women*? The questions were asked during the author's lifetime and after. *Little Women* was strategically placed within the new market for secular juvenile books as well as the more specialized category of "girls' books." A fortuitous combination of author, heroine, subject, and style, along with shrewd marketing, helped propel the book to popularity and its author to celebrity. Alcott, neighbor and friend of writers who were increasingly enshrined in the nation's literary pantheon, partook of their glory. But she had a luster of her own. Although often considered a "New England writer," she was also praised as a quintessentially "American" writer, a sign both of New England's dominance in the American literary tradition and of Alcott's prominent place within it.[1]

Jo as a Literary and Intellectual Model

Reading Alcott became a necessary ritual for children of the comfortable classes. Growing up at a time and in a class that conferred leisure on its young, children devoted considerable time and energy to literary pursuits. *Little Women* was a way station en route to more adult

7. Alcott's depiction of home theatricals drew the wrath of some evangelicals. Niles to Alcott, October 26, 1868 (#3). *The Christian Union*, edited by Henry Ward Beecher, evidently did not include her books on its Sunday school list, to Niles's great irritation. Lawrence F. Abbott to Roberts Brothers, June 6, 1882, with appended note by Niles to Alcott (#128).

8. On tomboys, see Sharon O'Brien, "Tomboyism and Adolescent Conflict: Three Nineteenth-Century Case Studies," in *Woman's Being, Woman's Place: Female Identity and Vocation in American History*, edited by Mary Kelley (Boston: G. K. Hall, 1979), pp. 351–72, which includes a section on Alcott, and Alfred Habegger, "Funny Tomboys," in *Gender, Fantasy, and Realism in American Literature* (New York: Columbia University Press, 1982), pp. 172–83. Habegger claims that although remembered today only in the figure of Jo March, the tomboy became a major literary type in the 1860s (pp. 172–73).

9. The Katy books of "Susan Coolidge," pen name of Sarah Chauncey Woolsey, another Roberts Brothers author, are perhaps closest to Alcott's. But even Katy Carr, who begins as another Jo, an ambitious, harumscarum, and fun-loving girl, is severely punished for disobedience; only after suffering a broken back and several years of invalidism does she emerge as a thoughtful girl who will grow into "true womanhood."

1. By the early twentieth century Franklin B. Sanborn, a New England writer and reformer, claimed that Alcott was more widely read than any other of the " 'Concord Authors,' so-called." Sanborn, *Recollections of Seventy Years* (Boston: Richard G. Badger, 1909), 2:342, 338. He had earlier deemed her very American in "her humor, her tastes, her aspirations, her piety." [Sanborn], "The Author of 'Little Women.' " English reviews emphasized Alcott's Americanness.

books. But it was also a text that acquired its own cachet. Alcott was such an accepted part of childhood that even Theodore Roosevelt declared, "at the cost of being deemed effeminate," that he "worshiped" *Little Men, Little Women*, and *An Old-Fashioned Girl*.[2]

Readers' explanations of their fondness for Alcott constitute a trope for personal preferences. Not all of Alcott's early readers focused on Jo; some were taken with the saga of the entire March family, which invited comparisons with their own. Charlotte Perkins Gilman,[3] for example, who grew up in genteel poverty after her father abandoned the family, liked the fact that in Alcott, as in Whitney, "the heroes and heroines were almost always poor, and good, while the rich people were generally bad."[4] S. Josephine Baker,[5] for her part, considered Alcott "the unattainable ideal of a great woman." A tomboy who became a prominent physician and wore ties to downplay her gender, "Jo" Baker not only claimed Jo March as her "favorite character in all fiction" but pointedly dissociated herself from Elsie Dinsmore.[6]

Jo March also fueled the literary aspirations of M. Carey Thomas, one of Alcott's early readers, during the critical years of early adolescence.[7] In the fall of 1869, the year of *Little Women*'s great success, Thomas and her cousin Frank Smith adopted the personae of Jo and Laurie, although as Quakers they should not have been reading fiction at all. At the ages of twelve and fifteen respectively, Thomas and Smith began addressing each other and signing their letters as Jo and Laurie; they meted out other roles to friends and relatives. When Bessie King, Thomas's closest female companion, made a bid to be Jo, Frank wrote his cousin that Bessie must choose another part "if she won't be Jo 2., or Meg, or Beth, or Amy; or Daisy, or anybody besides Jo 1. since *thou will* be the latter." Since Jo was the only acceptable heroine of *Little Women*, Bessie chose Polly, heroine of *An Old-Fashioned Girl*, Alcott's latest.[8]

When Thomas began a journal in 1870 at age thirteen, she did so in Jo's name. Declaring at the outset: "Ain't going to be sentimental / 'No no not for Jo' (not Joe)," she had much in common with Alcott's heroine.[9] Both were "bookworms" and tomboys; both desired independence. Like Jo, Thomas wished to do something "splendid." In early adolescence her ambitions were still diffuse, but they centered on becoming a famous writer, a famous *woman* writer—"Jo (not Joe)." Her life was suffused with literature, with writing as well as reading: in ad-

2. Roosevelt, *An Autobiography* (1913; reprint, New York: De Capo Press, 1985), p. 17.
3. Prolific American author and women's rights advocate (1860–1935), perhaps best known for her short story "The Yellow Wall-Paper" (1892) [*Editors*].
4. Gilman, *The Living of Charlotte Perkins Gilman* (1935; reprint, New York: Harper and Row, 1975), p. 35.
5. Sara Josephine Baker (1873–1945) was a medical doctor, writer, and public health care researcher and advocate.
6. Baker, *Fighting for Life* (New York: Macmillan, 1939), pp. 17, 9.
7. Martha Carey Thomas (1857–1935) was an educator, president of Bryn Mawr College from 1894 to 1922), and a women's rights activist [*Editors*].
8. Franklin Whitall Smith to Thomas, February 20, 1870, *The Papers of M. Carey Thomas in the Bryn Mawr College Archives*, edited by Lucy Fisher West (Woodbridge, Conn.: Research Publications, 1982) (hereafter cited as MCTP), reel 58. Thomas's reading is analyzed more fully in Sicherman, "Reading and Ambition"; on *Little Women*, see pp. 80–83.
9. M. Carey Thomas Journal, June 20, 1870, MCTP, reel 1.

dition to keeping a journal, she wrote poetry, kept a commonplace book, and compiled lists of favorite books and poems, some of them annotated. As she gravitated to such champions of aestheticism as Algernon Charles Swinburne and Dante Gabriel Rossetti, by her early twenties she had outgrown Alcott and other writers who upheld morality in their art. But Bessie King acknowledged the importance of their childhood play in 1879, when Thomas took the audacious step of starting graduate study in Germany: "Somehow today I went back to those early days when our horizon was so limited yet so full of light & our path lay as plain before us. It all came of reading over Miss Alcott's books now the quintescence [*sic*] of Philistinism then a Bible. . . . Doesn't thee remember when to turn out a 'Jo' was the height of ambition"?[1]

At the time Thomas was so engaged with *Little Women*, she was already a feminist. Sensitive to any gender restriction or slight, whether from people she knew or from biblical or scientific sources, she resolved at fifteen to disprove female inferiority by advancing her own education.[2] Despite its inception as a domestic story, then, Thomas read *Little Women* as a female bildungsroman, as did many women after her. This has in many ways been the most important reading, the one that has made the book such a phenomenon for so many years.

With its secular recasting of *Pilgrim's Progress*, *Little Women* transforms Christian's allegorical search for the Celestial City into the quintessential female quest plot. In a chapter entitled "Castles in the Air," each of the March sisters reveals her deepest ambition. In its loving depictions of the sisters' struggles to attain their goals (Jo to be a famous writer, Amy an artist, and Meg mistress of a lovely house), *Little Women* succeeds in authorizing female vocation and individuality. Nor did Alcott rule out the possibility of future artistic creativity: although married and managing a large household and school, Jo has not entirely given up her literary dreams, nor Amy her artistic ones. Beth, who has no ambition other than "to stay at home safe with father and mother, and help take care of the family," dies because she can find no way of growing up; her mysterious illness may be read as a failure of imagination, her inability to build castles in the air.[3]

In Jo, Alcott creates a portrait of female creativity that was not traditionally available to women:

> Every few weeks she would shut herself up in her room, put on her scribbling suit, and "fall into a vortex," as she expressed it, writing away at her novel with all her heart and soul, for till that was finished she could find no peace. . . .
> She did not think herself a genius by any means; but when the writing fit came on, she gave herself up to it with entire abandon, and led a blissful life, unconscious of want, care, or bad weather, while she sat safe and happy in an imaginary world, full of friends

1. Elizabeth King Ellicott to Thomas, November 23, [1879], MCTP, reel 39.
2. See Marjorie Housepian Dobkin, ed., *The Making of a Feminist: Early Journals and Letters of M. Carey Thomas* (N.p.: Kent State University Press, 1979), pp. 66–67 and passim.
3. These remarks draw on Sicherman, "Reading and Ambition," pp. 82–83.

almost as real and dear to her as any in the flesh. Sleep forsook her eyes, meals stood untasted, day and night were all too short to enjoy the happiness which blessed her only at such times, and made these hours worth living, even if they bore no other fruit. The divine afflatus usually lasted a week or two, and then she emerged from her "vortex" hungry, sleepy, cross, or despondent.[4]

Alcott's portrait of concentrated purpose—which describes her own creative practice—is as far removed as it could be from the ordinary lot of women, at least any adult woman. Jo not only has a room of her own; she also has the leisure—and the license—to remove herself from all obligation to others. Jo was important to young women like Thomas because there were so few of her—in literature or in life. One need only recall the example of Margaret Fuller, a generation older than Alcott, who suffered nightmares and delirium from her hothouse education and often felt isolated as the exceptional woman. By contrast, Jo is enmeshed in a family that constitutes a sustaining community of women.[5]

More conventional readers of Thomas's era could find in *Little Women* practical advice on two subjects of growing concern to women: economic opportunities and marriage. Alcott was well qualified to advise on the former because of her long years of struggle in the marketplace. Though portrayed more starkly in *Work* (1873), an autobiographical novel for the adult market, middle-class women's need to be able to earn a living is a central motif in *Little Women*, as it was in Alcott's life. The novel can be read as a defining text on this subject, at a time when even conservative critics were beginning to concede the point. Mr. March's economic setback, like Bronson Alcott's, forces his daughters into the labor market. Their jobs (as governess and companion) are depicted as mainly unrewarding, although Jo's literary career is described with loving particularity. As we have seen, to please her readers, Alcott compromised her belief that "liberty [was] a better husband." But although the March sisters marry, Marmee March, who wishes no greater joy for her daughters than a happy marriage, declares that it is better to remain single than to marry without love. Opportunities for self-respecting singlehood and women's employment went hand in hand, as Alcott knew.[6]

If Alcott articulated issues highly pertinent to young women of her era, Jo's continued appeal suggests not only the dearth of fictional heroines to foster dreams of glory but the continued absence of real-life models. Perhaps that is why Simone de Beauvoir was so attracted to *Little Women*, in which she thought she "caught a glimpse of my future self":

---

4. *Little Women*, pp. 328–29 [211].
5. See Nina Auerbach, *Communities of Women: An Idea in Fiction* (Cambridge: Harvard University Press, 1978), pp. 55–73.
6. On this subject, see Lee Virginia Chambers-Schiller, *Liberty, a Better Husband: Single Women in America: The Generations of 1780–1840* (New Haven: Yale University Press, 1984). In her next book, *An Old-Fashioned Girl*, Alcott ventures much further in envisioning a life of singlehood and lovingly depicts a community of self-supporting women artists.

I identified passionately with Jo, the intellectual. . . . She wrote: in order to imitate her more completely, I composed two or three short stories. . . . [T]he relationship between Jo and Laurie touched me to the heart. Later, I had no doubt, they would marry one another; so it was possible for maturity to bring the promises made in childhood to fruition instead of denying them: this thought filled me with renewed hope. But the thing that delighted me most of all was the marked partiality which Louisa Alcott manifested for Jo. . . . [I]n *Little Women* Jo was superior to her sisters, who were either more virtuous or more beautiful than she, because of her passion for knowledge and the vigor of her thinking; her superiority was as outstanding as that of certain adults, and guaranteed that she would have an unusual life: she was marked by fate. I, too, felt I was entitled to consider my taste in reading and my scholastic success as tokens of a personal superiority which would be borne out by the future. I became in my own eyes a character out of a novel.[7]

De Beauvoir found in Jo a model of authentic selfhood, someone she could emulate in the present and through whom she could read—and invent—her own destiny. It was a future full of possibility, open rather than closed, intellectual and literary rather than domestic. By fictionalizing her own life, de Beauvoir could more readily contemplate a career as a writer and an intellectual, no matter how improbable such an outcome seemed to her family. She could also rationalize her sense of superiority to her environment and to her own sister. Although de Beauvoir later claimed that she first learned from *Little Women* that "marriage was not necessary," she responded to the romance as well as the quest plot.[8] Far from interfering with her enjoyment, her disappointment that Jo did not marry Laurie prompted her to rework the story to her own satisfaction. Her conviction that Jo and Laurie would marry some day and the "renewed hope" this belief gave her suggest the power of wish fulfillment and the reader's capacity to create her own text. There is no textual basis for this belief: Jo and Laurie each marry someone else; each is a parent by the end of the story. De Beauvoir's reading is therefore not just a matter of filling in gaps but of rewriting the text. Her powerful commentary suggests the creativity of the reading experience and the permeability of boundaries between life and art: lives can be fictionalized, texts can be rewritten, art can become life and life art.

Not all women read with the intensity of Thomas or de Beauvoir.

---

7. Simone de Beauvoir, *Memoirs of a Dutiful Daughter*, translated by James Kirkup (1949; reprint, Cleveland: World Publishing Co., 1959), pp. 94–95. Despite differences in culture and religion, de Beauvoir found many parallels between the March family and her own, in particular the belief "that a cultivated mind and moral righteousness were better than money" (p. 94). According to Deirdre Bair, de Beauvoir had read *Little Women* by the time she was ten. Bair, *Simone de Beauvoir: A Biography* (New York: Summit Books, 1990), pp. 68–71.

8. Bair, *Simone de Beauvoir*, p. 69. Shirley Abbott, who grew up in Arkansas in the 1940s and 1950s, was also dismayed by Jo's rejection of Laurie: "I took a page in my notebook and began: / JO AND LAURIE / by Louisa May Abbott"; she literally rewrote the ending to suit herself. Shirley Abbott, *The Bookmaker's Daughter: A Memory Unbound* (New York: Ticknor and Fields, 1991), pp. 133–34.

But there is considerable evidence that, from the time of her creation until the recent past, Jo March provided for young women of the comfortable classes a model of female independence and of intellectual and literary achievement. This is not the only way of reading *Little Women*, but it constitutes a major interpretive strand, particularly in the twentieth century. Testimony on this point began as soon as the book was published and persists today among women who grew up in the 1940s and 1950s.[9] Thomas, whose love relations were with women, never mentions the marriage plot, but for de Beauvoir, writing in the twentieth century, it was both important and compatible with a quest plot.

Inflections of Class and Culture

Not everyone has access to the same cultural resources, wishes to engage the same texts, or interprets them in identical ways. Although class is by no means the sole determinant of what or how much is read, it is a critical variable in determining basic literacy and educational levels. These in turn, in conjunction with the aspirations of group, family, or individual, influence reading practices and preferences.[1]

For African American women, in the nineteenth century at least, class rather than race was probably the primary determinant of reading practices. Both Mary Church Terrell, a graduate of Oberlin College, and Ida B. Wells, the slave-born daughter of a carpenter and "a famous cook" who became a journalist and reformer, read Alcott. Terrell claimed that her books "were received with an acclaim among the young people of this country which has rarely if ever been equaled and never surpassed," while Wells observed: "I had formed my ideals on the best of Dickens's stories, Louisa May Alcott's, Mrs. A.D.T. Whitney's, and Charlotte Brontë's books, and Oliver Optic's stories for boys." Neither singled out *Little Women*; both seem to have read Alcott as part of the standard fare of an American middle-class childhood.[2]

For African American writer Ann Petry, now in her eighties, *Little Women* was much more than that. On the occasion of her induction into the Connecticut Women's Hall of Fame, she noted her admiration for women writers who had preceded and set the stage for her— "'Think of Louisa May Alcott.'" *Little Women* was the first book Petry

9. These conclusions emerge from my reading and from discussions of *Little Women* with more than a dozen women. They were highly educated for the most part and mainly over fifty, but some women under thirty also felt passionately about the book. Most of my informants were white, but see n. 3 below [on p. 651].

1. On the relation of class and education to cultural preferences, see Pierre Bourdieu, *Distinction: A Social Critique of the Judgement of Taste,* translated by Richard Nice (Cambridge: Harvard University Press, 1984). There was greater overlap in cultural tastes in the nineteenth-century United States than Bourdieu's analysis of late-twentieth-century France allows.

2. Mary Church Terrell, *A Colored Woman in a White World* (1940; reprint, New York: Arno Press, 1980), p. 26; Alfreda M. Duster, ed., *Crusade for Justice: The Autobiography of Ida B. Wells* (Chicago: University of Chicago Press, 1970), pp. 7, 21–22. Wells observed that in her early years, she "never read a Negro book or anything about Negroes."

"read on her own as a child." Her comments are reminiscent of those of de Beauvoir and other writers: "I couldn't stop reading because I had encountered Jo March. I felt as though I was part of Jo and she was part of me. I, too, was a tomboy and a misfit and kept a secret diary. . . . She said things like 'I wish I was a horse, then I could run for miles in this splendid air and not lose my breath.' I found myself wishing the same thing whenever I ran for the sheer joy of running. She was a would-be writer—and so was I."[3]

Two contrasting responses to *Little Women* from up and down the class ladder suggest the essentially middle-class and perhaps also middle-brow nature of the book's appeal. Edith Wharton, who drops the names of famous books and authors in an autobiography dominated by upper-class and high-culture values, noted that her mother would not let her read popular American children's books because "the children spoke bad English *without the author's knowing it*." She claimed that when she was finally permitted to read *Little Women* and *Little Men* because everyone else did, "[M]y ears, trained to the fresh racy English of 'Alice in Wonderland,' 'The Water Babies' and 'The Princess and the Goblin,' were exasperated by the laxities of the great Louisa."[4]

Like Wharton, though for different reasons, some working-class women also found *Little Women* too banal. Dorothy Richardson, a journalist, suggests as much in *The Long Day*, an account of her life among the working class. In an arresting episode, Richardson ridicules the reading preferences of her fellow workers in a paper box factory. The plot of a favorite novel, Laura Jean Libbey's *Little Rosebud's Lovers; or, A Cruel Revenge*, is recounted by one of the workers as a tale of a woman's triumph over all sorts of adversity, including abductions and a false marriage to one of the villains. When Richardson summarizes *Little Women*, a coworker dismisses it: " '[T]hat's no story—that's just everyday happenings. I don't see what's the use of putting things like that in books. I'll bet any money that lady what wrote it knew all them boys and girls. They just sound like real, live people; and when you was telling about them I could just see them as plain as plain could be. . . . I suppose farmer folks likes them kind of stories. . . . They ain't used to the same styles of anything that us city folks are.' "[5]

3. *The Middletown Press*, June 1, 1994, p. B1, and Ann Petry to author, letter postmarked July 23, 1994; I am grateful to Farah Jasmine Griffin for the *Middletown Press* reference. *Little Women* continues to play an important role in the lives of some young black women. A high school student in Jamaica, for example, rewrote the story to fit a local setting. And a young, African American academic felt so strongly about *Little Women* that, on learning about my project, she contended with some heat that Aunt March was unfair in taking Amy rather than Jo to Europe; she seemed to be picking up a conversation she had just left off. Comments like these and Petry's suggest the need for research on the interaction between race and class in African American women's reading practices. A conversation with James A. Miller was helpful on this point.
4. Edith Wharton, *A Backward Glance* (New York: Appleton-Century, 1934), p. 51. Annie Nathan Meyer, a member of New York's German-Jewish elite who describes the authors in the family library as "impeccable," claims that Alcott was the only writer of children's books she could "endure." Meyer, *It's Been Fun: An Autobiography* (New York: Henry Schuman, 1951), pp. 32–33.
5. Richardson, *The Long Day*, pp. 75–86 (quotation, p. 86); I am grateful to Michael Denning for pointing out this episode. *The Long Day*, which purports to be the story of an educated woman forced by circumstances to do manual labor, must be used with caution. It was ini-

The box makers found the characters in *Little Women* "real"—an interesting point in itself—but did not care to enter its narrative framework. Though they were not class conscious in a political sense, their awareness of their class position may account at least in part for their disinterest in a story whose heroines, despite economic reverses, had the leisure to pursue their interests in art, music, and literature and could expect to live in suburban cottages, conditions out of reach for most working-class women. Since *their* "everyday happenings" were poverty and exhausting work, the attraction of fictions about working girls who preserved their virtue and came into great wealth, either through marriage or disclosure of their middle- or upper-class origins, is understandable. Such denouements would have seemed just as likely—or unlikely—as a future in a suburban cottage. In the absence, in story or in life, of a female success tradition of moving up the occupational ladder, the "Cinderella tale" of marrying up was the nearest thing to a Horatio Alger story for working-class women.[6]

Reading practices depend on cultural as well as class location. It is a telling commentary on class in America that some Jewish immigrant women, who would be defined as working class on the basis of family income and occupation, not only enjoyed *Little Women* but also found in it a vehicle for envisioning a new and higher status.[7] For them, Alcott's classic provided a model for transcending their status as ethnic outsiders and for gaining access to American life and culture. It was a first step into the kind of middle-class family life rejected by Thomas and de Beauvoir. These immigrants found the book liberating and read it as a success story—but of a different kind.

In *My Mother and I*, Elizabeth G. Stern (1889–1954) charts the cultural distance a Jewish immigrant woman traveled from Russia and a midwestern urban ghetto to the American mainstream: she graduates from college, studies social work, marries a professional man, and becomes a social worker and writer.[8] *Little Women* occupies a crucial

---

tially published anonymously, and many scenes read like sensational fiction. Leonora O'Reilly, a feminist trade unionist, was so outraged at the book's condescension and its insinuations that working-class women were immoral that she drafted a blazing indictment. Leonora O'Reilly Papers, edited by Edward T. James, *Papers of the Women's Trade Union League and Its Principal Leaders* (Woodbridge, Conn.: Research Publications, 1981), reel 9.

6. Michael Denning, *Mechanic Accents: Dime Novels and Working-Class Culture in America* (London: Verso, 1987), pp. 197–200, analyzes *Little Rosebud's Lovers* as a "Cinderella tale." He suggests that stories read by the middle class tended to depict working-class women as victims (of seduction and poverty) rather than as triumphant. Joyce Shaw Peterson, "Working Girls and Millionaires: The Melodramatic Romances of Laura Jean Libbey," *American Studies* 24 (Spring 1983): 19–35, also views Libbey's stories as a "success myth for women." There were other sorts of female working-class traditions than the one suggested here, particularly among the politically aware. These included reading circles, some with a particular political or philosophical slant, and various efforts at "self-improvement." See, e.g., n. 5 [on pp. 651–52].

7. I have discussed Jewish immigrants at some length because of the abundance of evidence, not because I view them as the only model for an alternative reading of *Little Women*.

8. *My Mother and I* (New York: Macmillan, 1917) is a problematic book. Some contemporaries reviewed it as autobiographical fiction, but recent critics have tended to view it as autobiography. Theodore Roosevelt must have considered it the latter when he lauded it as a "really noteworthy story" of Americanization in the foreword. (A shorter version appeared in the *Ladies' Home Journal*, October 1916, as "My Mother and I: The Story of How I Became an American Woman, with an Appreciation by Theodore Roosevelt, to Whom the Manuscript Was Sent.") Moreover, the facts Stern gave out about her early life—including her status as an Eastern European Jewish immigrant—correspond with the narrator's history. Stern's

place in the story. After the narrator comes across it in a stack of newspapers in a rag shop, the book utterly engrosses her: "I sat in the dim light of the rag shop and read the browned pages of that ragged copy of 'Little Women.' . . . [N]o book I have opened has meant as much to me as did that small volume telling in simple words such as I myself spoke, the story of an American childhood in New England. I had found a new literature, the literature of childhood." She had also found the literature of America: "I no longer read the little paper-bound Yiddish novelettes which father then sold. In the old rag shop loft I devoured the English magazines and newspapers." Of the books her teachers brought her from the public library, she writes:

> Far more marvellous than the fairy stories were to me in the ghetto street the stories of American child life, all the Alcott and the Pepper books. The pretty mothers, the childish ideals, the open gardens, the homes of many rooms were as unreal to me as the fairy stories. But reading of them made my aspirations beautiful.
>
> My books were doors that gave me entrance into another world. Often I think that I did not grow up in the ghetto but in the books I read as a child in the ghetto. The life in Soho passed me by and did not touch me, once I began to read.[9]

Stern's testimony to the importance of reading in reconfiguring aspiration is not unlike de Beauvoir's, although the context is entirely different, as is the nature of the desire elicited by her reading. In American books, the ghetto fell away and the protagonist discovered both childhood and beauty. Far from being realistic, *Little Women* was an American fairy tale. Indeed, some of the narrator's "precocious" thirteen-year-old school friends "scoffingly averred that there were 'no such peoples like Jo and Beth.' " As she climbs the educational ladder, she discovers that such people do exist and that a life of beauty is possible, even for those of humble origin. With its emphasis on middle-class domesticity, *My Mother and I* is a story of Americanization with a female twist.[1]

Stern was not unique in reading *Little Women* as a vehicle for assimilation into American middle-class life or in conflating "American"

---

older son, however, maintains that his mother was native born and Protestant and claimed her Jewish foster parents as her biological parents to hide her out-of-wedlock birth. T[homas] Noel Stern, *Secret Family* (South Dartmouth, Mass.: T. Noel Stern, 1988). Ellen M. Umansky, who generously shared her research materials with me, concludes in "Representations of Jewish Women in the Works and Life of Elizabeth Stern," *Modern Judaism* 13 (1993): 165–76: "[I]t may be difficult if not impossible to ever determine which of Stern's literary self representations reflected her own experiences" (p. 174). Sources that appear to substantiate Elizabeth Stern's foreign and Jewish birth are the U.S. Census for 1900 and for 1910, which both list her birthplace as Russia; the certificate of her marriage, which was performed by a prominent Orthodox rabbi in Pittsburgh; and Aaron Levin's will, which lists Stern as his oldest child.

Despite its contested status, I have drawn on *My Mother and I* because Stern's choice of *Little Women* as a critical marker of American aspirations is consistent with other evidence. The narrative's emphasis on the differences between immigrant and American culture comports with representations in less problematic works by Jewish immigrant writers. Moreover, whatever the facts of Stern's birth, she lived with the Jewish Levin family for many years.

9. *My Mother and I*, pp. 69–71.
1. Ibid., pp. 71–72.

and "middle class." More than half a century later, a Jewish male writer explored the novel's appeal as an "American" book:

[T]o me, a first generation American, raised in an Orthodox Jewish household where more Yiddish was spoken than English, everything about *Little Women* was exotic. It was all so American, so full of a life I did not know but desperately hoped to be part of, an America full of promises, hopes, optimisms, an America where everyone had a chance to become somebody wonderful like Jo March—Louisa May Alcott who (I had discovered that the Marches and the Alcotts were almost identical) did become, with this story book that I adored, world famous."[2]

What had been realistic to the early middle- and upper-middle-class WASP readers of *Little Women* was "exotic" to Jewish immigrants a generation or two later. Could there be a better illustration of the importance of historical location in determining meaning?

Teachers, librarians, and other cultural mediators encouraged Jewish immigrant women to read what many viewed as the archetypal American female story. Book and author became enshrined in popular legend, especially after publication of *Louisa May Alcott: Her Life, Letters, and Journals* (1889), the year after the author's death, by her friend Ednah Dow Cheney. Interest in Alcott remained high in the early twentieth century. There was a 1909 biography by Belle Moses and a dramatization in 1912 that received rave reviews and toured the country. Alcott's books were sometimes assigned in public schools.[3] Jews themselves often served as cultural intermediaries between native and immigrant communities. When Rose Cohen, an immigrant affiliated with the Nurses' (later Henry Street) Settlement, found *Julius Caesar* too difficult, she asked the librarian at the Educational Alliance, a Jewish agency that assisted recent Eastern European immigrants, for a book "any book—like for a child. She brought me 'Little Women.' "[4]

Cohen was offered *Little Women* as a less taxing vehicle for learning English than Shakespeare. But Alcott was often prescribed as a safe and even salutary writer. Librarians had long debated the effects of reading on those who were young, female, and impressionable. They were echoed by some members of the working class, including Rose Pastor Stokes, an immigrant from Eastern Europe via England. Contending that "*all* girls are what they read," Stokes, writing as "Zelda" for the English page of the *Yiddishes Tageblatt*, admonished her readers to avoid "crazy phantasies from the imbecile brains" of writers like

2. Leo Lerman, "Little Women: Who's in Love with Miss Louisa May Alcott? I Am," *Mademoiselle*, December 1973, reprinted in Stern, *Critical Essays*, p. 113. See also Stephan F. Brumberg, *Going to America, Going to School: The Jewish Immigrant Public School Encounter in Turn-of-the-Century New York City* (New York: Praeger, 1986), pp. 121–22, 141.
3. See, e.g., *The Louisa Alcott Reader: A Supplementary Reader for the Fourth Year of School* (1885; reprint, Boston: Little, Brown, 1910) and Fanny E. Coe, ed., *The Louisa Alcott Story Book* (Boston: Little, Brown, 1910). The former included fairy tales, the latter, more realistic stories, with the moral printed beneath the title in the table of contents, e.g. "Kindness to horses" and "Wilfulness is punished." In Philadelphia in the 1930s, *Little Women* was on a list from which seventh graders could choose books for reports.
4. Rose Cohen, *Out of the Shadow* (New York: Doran, 1918), p. 253.

Laura Jean Libbey. She urged those sixteen and under to read Alcott, a writer known for her "excellent teachings" and one from whom "discriminating or indiscriminating" readers alike derived pleasure. Zelda also recommended Cheney, claiming that "the biographies of some writers are far more interesting, even, than the stories they have written."[5]

One of the Jewish immigrants for whom Alcott's success proved inspiring was Mary Antin, a fervent advocate of assimilation into American life. Alcott's were the children's books she "remember[ed] with the greatest delight" (followed by boys' adventure books, especially Alger's). Antin, who published poems in English in her teens and contemplated a literary career, lingered over the biographical entries she found in an encyclopedia. She "could not resist the temptation to study out the exact place . . . where my name would belong. I saw that it would come not far from 'Alcott, Louisa M.'; and I covered my face with my hands, to hide the silly, baseless joy in it."[6] We have come full circle. Eager to assimilate, Antin responded in ways reminiscent of Alcott's early native-born and middle-class readers who admired her success as an author. Antin, too, could imagine a successful American career for herself, a career for which Alcott was still the model.

Conclusion

Not all readers of *Little Women* read the same text. This is literally the case, since the story went through many editions. Not until 1880 did it appear in one volume, illustrated in this case and purged of some of its slang.[7] Since then there have been numerous editions and many publishers. I have been concerned here with the changing meaning of the story for different audiences and with historical continuities as well. For many middle-class readers, early and later, *Little Women* provided a model of womanhood that deviated from conventional gender norms, a continuity that suggests how little these norms changed in their essentials from the late 1860s to the 1960s. Reading individualistically, they viewed Jo as an intellectual and a writer, the liberated woman they sought to become. No matter that Jo marries and raises a family; such readers remember the young Jo, the teenager who is far from beautiful, struggles with her temper, is both a bookworm and the center of action, and dreams of literary glory while helping to support her family with her pen. These readers for the most part took for granted their right to a long and privileged childhood, largely exempt from the labor market. Jewish women who immigrated to the United States in their youth could not assume such a childhood. Nor were

5. " 'Zelda' on Books," English Department, *Jewish Daily News* (New York), August 4, 1903; see also "Just Between Ourselves, Girls," ibid., July 12, 1903. Stokes also recommended the novels of Charles Dickens, George Eliot, Charlotte Brontë, and Grace Aguilar, an English Jewish writer, as well as Jewish and general history. I am grateful to Harriet Sigerman for the references.
6. Mary Antin, *The Promised Land* (Boston: Houghton Mifflin, 1912), pp. 257, 258–59.
7. Showalter, "*Little Women*," pp. 55–56; Madeleine B. Stern to author, July 31, 1993. The English edition continued to be published in two volumes, the second under the title *Good Wives*.

those raised in Orthodox Jewish households brought up on an individualistic philosophy. Their school experiences and reading—American
books like *Little Women*—made them aware of different standards of
decorum and material life that we tend to associate with class, but
that are cultural as well. For some of these readers, *Little Women* offered a fascinating glimpse into an American world. Of course we
know, as they did not, that the world Alcott depicted was vanishing,
even as she wrote. Nevertheless, that fictional world, along with their
school encounters, provided a vision of what life, American life, could
be.

Can readers do whatever they like with texts? Yes and no. As we
have seen, *Little Women* has been read in many ways, depending not
only on when and by whom it was read but also on readers' experiences and aspirations. It has been read as a romance or as a quest, or
both. It has been read as a family drama that validates virtue over
wealth. It has been read as a how-to manual by immigrants who
wanted to assimilate into American, middle-class life and as a means
of escaping that life by women who knew its gender constraints too
well. For many, especially in the early years, *Little Women* was read
through the life of the author, whose literary success exceeded that of
her fictional persona.

At the same time, both the passion *Little Women* has engendered in
diverse readers and its ability to survive its era and transcend its genre
point to a text of unusual permeability. The compromise Alcott ef-
fected with her readers in constructing a more problematic plot than
is usual in fiction for the young has enhanced the story's appeal. If *Little Women* is not exactly a "problem novel," it is a work that lingers in
readers' minds in ways that allow for imaginative elaboration. The frequent rereadings reported by women in their fifties also hint at nostal-
gia for lost youth and for a past that seems more secure than the
present, perhaps even an imagined re-creation of idealized love between mothers and daughters.[8] Most important, readers' testimony in
the nineteenth and twentieth centuries points to *Little Women* as a
text that opens up possibilities rather than foreclosing them. With its
multiple reference points and voices (four sisters, each distinct and
recognizable), its depictions of joy as well as sorrow, its fresh and un-
labored speech, Alcott's classic has something for almost everyone. For
readers on the threshold of adulthood, the text's authorizing of female
ambition has been a significant counterweight to more habitual gender prescriptions.

Little Women is such a harbinger of modern life, of consumer culture and new freedom for middle-class children, it is easy to forget
that it was written just a few years after the Civil War, in the midst of
Reconstruction and at a time of economic dislocation. For the most
part, Alcott left such contemporary markers out of her story, another

---

8. Paradoxically, in view of the sanctity of Victorian motherhood, *Little Women* is one of the
few books of its era (adult or juvenile) that depicts a strong maternal figure; mothers are often dead, ill, or powerless. See Baym, *Woman's Fiction*. The female-dominated March
household and the figure of Marmee may, in consequence, have had a special appeal to Alcott's early readers.

sign of the text's openness. The Civil War provides an important back-drop and a spur to heroism at home as well as on the battlefield, but it is primarily a plot device to remove Mr. March from the scene. Despite her family's support of John Brown, Alcott does not press a particular interpretation of the war. A final reason *Little Women* has survived so well, despite the chasm that separates Alcott's era from ours, is the virtual absence of references to outside events that would date her story and make it grow old.[9] That way each generation can invent it anew.

---

9. Elizabeth Young, "Embodied Politics: Fictions of the American Civil War" (Ph.D. diss., University of California, Berkeley, 1993), reading *Little Women* in conjunction with *Hospital Sketches*, views it as a "war novel" (p. 108).

Louisa May Alcott: A Chronology

1832   Louisa May Alcott (LMA), the second of four daughters, born to Amos Bronson Alcott and Abigail "Abba" May Alcott on 29 November in Germantown, Pennsylvania. First daughter, Anna Bronson Alcott, born 1831.

1834   Alcotts move to Boston. Bronson opens school in Masonic Temple building.

1835   Alcotts' third daughter, Elizabeth "Lizzie" Sewall Alcott, born.

1838   Temple School closes.

1840   Alcotts move to Hosmer Cottage in Concord. Abby May "May" Alcott born.

1842   Bronson travels to England; returns to United States accompanied by Charles Lane and Henry Wright, British reformers and avid advocates of Bronson's educational principles.

1843   Alcotts along with Lane and Wright move to Fruitlands. LMA starts journal and begins writing poems.

1844   Alcott family moves to Still River, Massachusetts. LMA and Anna attend district school. With Anna and LMA writing and directing, Alcott children produce own plays. Alcotts return to Concord and board with Hosmer family.

1845   Abba purchases house in Concord. Bronson names it Hillside. Sophia Foord tutors Alcott children. LMA and Anna attend John Hosmer's school.

1846   LMA reads avidly, especially Dickens; composes journal entries, plays, stories, and poems. Sisters stage dramatic performances in barn at Hillside.

1847   With access to Emerson's library, LMA begins reading Goethe and later Carlyle, Dante, and Shakespeare.

1848   LMA writes "The Rival Painters." Alcotts move to Boston, where Abba takes paid position as charity worker.

1849   Alcotts move in with Samuel Joseph May, Abba's brother. Alcott sisters produce first issue of family newspaper "The Olive Leaf."

1850   Alcotts move to Groton Street, Boston. LMA assists Anna at her school. Family contracts smallpox, but all recover.

1851   LMA attends rally protesting Fugitive Slave Law; works as governess; publishes poem "Sunlight" under pseudonym "Flora Fairfield" in *Peterson's Magazine*; works unhappily as servant in Dedham, Massachusetts, home of lawyer James Richardson.

1852   *Olive Branch* publishes LMA's "The Rival Painters." LMA and

Anna start small school. LMA hears Theodore Parker, a radical Unitarian minister and reformer, preach a sermon about working women.

1853   LMA teaches school. Anna moves to Syracuse. Bronson begins first lecture tour of the Midwest.

1854   Bronson returns. James T. Fields, a partner in the Boston publishing firm Ticknor and Fields, turns down story submitted by LMA and advises her to give up writing. She teaches school. *Saturday Evening Gazette* publishes LMA's "The Rival Prima Donnas." LMA's first book, *Flower Fables*, a collection of fairy tales, published.

1855   LMA moves to Walpole, New Hampshire, and works with Walpole Dramatic Company; returns to Boston and teaches school.

1856   LMA returns to Walpole. Lizzie and May contract scarlet fever. LMA lives as boarder with Mary Ann Reed in Boston; tutors Alice Lovering.

1857   LMA returns to Walpole for summer. Alcotts buy house in Concord and name it Orchard House. Lizzie's health declines. LMA joins Concord Dramatic Union.

1858   Lizzie dies. Anna and John Bridge Pratt announce engagement. LMA returns to Boston, where she tutors Alice Lovering.

1859   LMA teaches, tutors, and writes in Boston. Bronson becomes superintendent of Concord's schools. LMA returns to Concord.

1860   *Atlantic Monthly* publishes LMA's "Love and Self-Love." Anna and John Bridge Pratt marry. LMA writes *Moods*; returns to Boston.

1861   LMA begins novel called "Success" and revises *Moods*. Civil War begins. LMA visits relatives in Gorham, New Hampshire.

1862   LMA moves to Boston and boards with James T. Fields; teaches kindergarten; submits "Pauline's Passion and Punishment" to *Frank Leslie's Illustrated Newspaper* competition; applies for nursing position in Washington, D.C.; travels to Washington to start work at Union Hotel Hospital; wins *Leslie's* one-hundred-dollar prize.

1863   "Pauline's Passion and Punishment" appears in *Frank Leslie's Illustrated Newspaper*. LMA contracts typhoid pneumonia; calomel treatments exacerbate her condition. Bronson travels to Washington to bring LMA back to Concord. She remains ill throughout winter. Frederick Alcott Pratt, Anna's first son, born. *Hospital Sketches* appears in the *Commonwealth*; Boston reformer and sometime publisher James Redpath then reprints it in book form. LMA writes and publishes short fiction, thrillers, fairy tales, and fantasy stories; dramatic adaptation of Dickens's works premieres in Boston.

1864   LMA reedits *Moods*. "Enigmas" appears in *Frank Leslie's Illustrated Newspaper*. *Moods* published.

1865   LMA continues to publish thrillers. Civil War ends, and Pres-
        ident Lincoln is assassinated. Anna gives birth to a second
        son, John Sewall Pratt. LMA travels to Europe with invalid
        Anna Weld; meets Ladislas Wisniewski, a Polish soldier, in
        Vevey, Switzerland.

1866   LMA spends winter in Nice; travels to Paris, where Wis-
        niewski spends time with her sightseeing; moves on to Lon-
        don; returns to the United States and writes about a dozen
        stories in three months. *Moods* published in England. "Behind
        a Mask" serialized in *The Flag of Our Union*.

1867   LMA suffers illness; writes *Morning Glories, and Other Sto-
        ries*. Thomas Niles of Roberts Brothers asks her to write girls'
        book; she agrees to try. Fuller invites her to edit *Merry's Mu-
        seum*. She moves to Boston to concentrate on writing.

1868   *Morning Glories, and Other Stories* published; first issue of
        Merry's Museum appears. She returns to Orchard House; be-
        gins writing *Little Women*; finishes part 1 in mid-July and
        sends it to Niles. *Little Women*, part 1, published in early Oc-
        tober. She moves back to Boston and starts *Little Women*,
        part 2.

1869   LMA completes *Little Women*, part 2, and sends it to Roberts
        Brothers. LMA sick but continues to write; returns to Con-
        cord. *Little Women*, part 2, published in April. LMA visits
        Canada. *An Old-Fashioned Girl* begins serial run in *Merry's
        Museum*. LMA visits Maine. *Hospital Sketches and Camp and
        Fireside Stories* published. LMA moves to Boston.

1870   Roberts Brothers publishes *An Old-Fashioned Girl*. LMA visits
        Europe with sister May and May's friend Alice Bartlett. John
        Bridge Pratt dies.

1871   LMA begins writing *Little Men*, which is published later in the
        year. LMA returns to United States, but May stays in Europe
        to study and paint.

1872   *My Boys* published. Harriet Beecher Stowe asks LMA to con-
        tribute to the *Christian Union*. LMA revises "Success" and
        retitles it *Work*. *Shawl-Straps* published. *Work* begins to ap-
        pear in installments in the *Christian Union*.

1873   LMA finishes *Work*, which is published as a book. *Cupid and
        Chow-Chow* published.

1874   May returns from London. LMA travels to Conway, New
        Hampshire, with Anna and her two boys. LMA and May move
        to Bellevue Hotel, Boston. LMA completes *Eight Cousins*.

1875   *Eight Cousins* serialized in *St. Nicholas* and then published as
        a book. LMA visits Vassar College and New York City; returns
        to Concord; attends Woman's Congress in Syracuse; revisits
        New York City.

1876   LMA visits Philadelphia. *Silver Pitchers* published. LMA
        writes *Rose in Bloom*. May goes back to Europe. Roberts
        Brothers publishes *Rose in Bloom*.

1877   LMA moves back to Bellevue Hotel; writes *A Modern*

Mephistopheles. Anna and LMA buy Thoreau House. LMA
writes *Under the Lilacs.* Abba's health declines. Alcotts close
Orchard House and open Thoreau House. Abba dies. *My Girls*
published; first installments of *Under the Lilacs* appear in *St.
Nicholas.*

1878   May and Ernst Nieriker marry. LMA attempts but fails to
write memoir about her mother. *Under the Lilacs* published.

1879   Bronson opens Concord School of Philosophy. LMA registers
to vote, first woman in Concord to do so. LMA writes *Jack and
Jill*; *Jimmy's Cruise in the Pinafore* published. Louise Marie
"Lulu" Nieriker born. Serialization of *Jack and Jill* begins in
St. Nicholas. May dies.

1880   LMA mourns May's death; struggles to finish *Jack and Jill*;
moves back to old room at Bellevue Hotel; vacations in Maine
with nephews Fred and John Pratt; moves back to Concord.
Lulu arrives from Europe. Roberts Brothers publishes *Jack
and Jill.* LMA and Lulu move into cousin Elizabeth Sewall
Willis Wells's house on Louisburg Square in Boston.

1881   LMA returns to to Concord. LMA and Lulu visit Nonquitt,
Massachusetts. LMA meets Walt Whitman; works on develop-
ing suffrage organization; writes preface for new edition of
Moods.

1882   LMA helps organize temperance society. Emerson dies. LMA
visits Nonquitt; returns to Boston; begins writing *Jo's Boys*;
publishes *An Old-Fashioned Thanksgiving.* Bronson suffers
stroke. LMA moves back to Concord.

1883   LMA and Lulu move to Boston, then Concord, then Nonquitt, and then back to Boston.

1884   Lulu begins kindergarten. LMA sells Orchard House and buys
cottage in Nonquitt; returns to Concord; moves to Boston.
Spinning-Wheel Stories published. LMA works again on *Jo's
Boys* but is too ill to continue.

1885   LMA tries mind-cure treatments. First volume of *Lulu's Library* published.

1886   LMA begins treatment by Dr. Rhoda Ashley Lawrence. *Jo's
Boys* finished and published. LMA moves to Lawrence's nursing home in Roxbury, Massachusetts.

1887   LMA ill; works on *A Garland for Girls*; makes will. Second
volume of *Lulu's Library* published. *A Garland for Girls* published.

1888   Fred Pratt marries Jessica L. Cate. Bronson dies. LMA dies
two days later, 6 March; buried in Concord.

Selected Bibliography

• indicates work included or excerpted in this Norton Critical Edition.

Alberghene, Janice M., and Beverly Lyon Clark, eds. Little Women *and the Feminist Imagination: Criticism, Controversy, Personal Essays*. New York and London: Garland, 1999.

Armstrong, Frances. " 'Here Little, and Hereafter Bliss': *Little Women* and the Deferral of Greatness." *American Literature* 64 (1992): 453–74.

Auerbach, Nina. *Communities of Women: An Idea in Fiction*. Cambridge: Harvard UP, 1978. 55–75.

Avery, Gillian. "Classic Family Stories." *Behold the Child: American Children and Their Books, 1621–1922*. Baltimore: Johns Hopkins UP, 1994. 168–73.

Bassil, Veronica. "The Artist at Home: The Domestication of Louisa May Alcott." *Studies in American Fiction* 15 (1987): 187–97.

Bedell, Madelon. *The Alcotts: Biography of a Family*. New York: Clarkson N. Potter, 1980.

Beegel, Susan F. " 'Bernice Bobs Her Hair': Fitzgerald's Jazz Elegy for 'Little Women.' " *New Essays on F. Scott Fitzgerald's Neglected Stories*. Ed. R. Bryer-Jackson. Columbia: U of Missouri P, 1996. 58–73.

Berman, Ruth. "No Jo Marches!" *Children's Literature in Education* 29 (1998): 237–47.

Bernstein, Susan Naomi. "Writing and *Little Women*: Alcott's Rhetoric of Subversion." *American Transcendental Quarterly* 7 (1993): 25–43.

• Brodhead, Richard H. "Starting Out in the 1860s: Alcott, Authorship, and the Postbellum Literary Field." *Cultures of Letters: Scenes of Reading and Writing in Nineteenth-Century America*. Chicago: U of Chicago P, 1993. 69–106.

Brophy, Brigid. "A Masterpiece, and Dreadful." *New York Times Book Review*, 17 January 1965, 1, 44.

Campbell, Donna M. "Sentimental Conventions and Self-Protection: *Little Women* and *The Wide, Wide World*." *Legacy* 11 (1994): 118–29.

Clark, Beverly Lyon. "A Portrait of the Artist as a Little Woman." *Children's Literature* 17 (1989): 81–97.

Crisler, Jesse S. "Alcott's Reading in *Little Women*: Shaping the Autobiographical Self." *Resources for American Literary Study* 20 (1994): 27–36.

Crowley, John W. "*Little Women* and the Boy-Book." *New England Quarterly* 58 (1985): 384–89.

• Dalke, Anne. " 'The House-Band': The Education of Men in *Little Women*." *College English* 47 (1985): 571–78.

Delamar, Gloria T. *Louisa May Alcott and* Little Women: *Biography, Critique, Publications, Poems, Songs and Contemporary Relevance*. Jefferson, NC: McFarland & Company, 1990.

Donovan, Ellen. "Reading for Profit and Pleasure: *Little Women* and *The Story of a Bad Boy*." *The Lion and the Unicorn* 18 (1994): 143–53.

Doyle, Christine. *Louisa May Alcott and Charlotte Brontë: Transatlantic Translations*. Knoxville: U of Tennessee P, 2000.

Eiselein, Gregory, and Anne K. Phillips, eds. *The Louisa May Alcott Encyclopedia*. Westport, CT: Greenwood P, 2001.

Elbert, Sarah. *A Hunger for Home: Louisa May Alcott's Place in American Culture*. Rev. ed. New Brunswick: Rutgers UP, 1987.

Ellis, Kate. "Life with Marmee: Three Versions." *The Classic American Novel and the Movies*. Ed. Gerald Peary and Roger Shatzkin. New York: Ungar, 1977. 62–77.

Englund, Sheryl A. Reading the Author in *Little Women*: A Biography of a Book." *American Transcendentalist Quarterly* 12 (1998): 199–219.

• Estes, Angela M., and Kathleen Margaret Lant. "Dismembering the Text: The Horror of Louisa May Alcott's *Little Women*." *Children's Literature* 17 (1989): 98–123.

Fetterley, Judith. "Impersonating 'Little Women': The Radicalism of Alcott's *Behind a Mask*." *Women's Studies* 10 (1983): 1–14.

———. "*Little Women*: Alcott's Civil War." *Feminist Studies* 5 (1979): 369–83.

Foster, Shirley, and Judy Simons. "Louisa May Alcott: *Little Women*." *What Katy Read: Feminist Re-Readings of "Classic" Stories for Girls*. Iowa City: U of Iowa P, 1995. 85–106.

Gaard, Greta. " 'Self-Denial Was All the Fashion': Repressing Anger in *Little Women*." *Papers on Language and Literature* 27 (1991): 3–19.

Gay, Carol. "*Little Women* at the Movies." *Children's Novels and the Movies*. Ed. Douglas Street. New York: Frederick Ungar, 1983. 28–38.

Grasso, Linda. "Louisa May Alcott's 'Magic Inkstand': *Little Women*, Feminism, and the Myth of Regeneration." *Frontiers* 19 (1998): 177–92.

Griswold, Jerry. "Bosom Enemies: *Little Women*." *Audacious Kids: Coming of Age in America's Classic Children's Books*. New York: Oxford UP, 1992. 156–66.

Halttunen, Karen. "The Domestic Drama of Louisa May Alcott." *Feminist Studies* 10 (1984): 233–54.

Hamblen, Abigail Ann. "The Divided World of Louisa May Alcott." *Webs and Wardrobes: Humanist and Religious World Views in Children's Literature*. Ed. Joseph O'Beirne Milner and Lucy Floyd Morcock Milner. Lanham, MD: UP of America, 1987. 57–64.

Heilbrun, Carolyn G. "Louisa May Alcott: The Influence of *Little Women*." *Women, the Arts, and the 1920s in Paris and New York*. Ed. Kenneth W. Wheeler and Virginia Lee Lussier. New Brunswick: Transaction Books, 1982. 20–26. Reprinted as "Alcott's *Little Women*." *Hamlet's Mother and Other Women*. New York: Columbia UP, 1990. 140–47.

Hollander, Anne. "Portraying *Little Women* through the Ages." *New York Times*, 15 January 1995, sec. 2, pp. 11, 21.

———. "Reflections on *Little Women*." *Children's Literature* 9 (1981): 28–39.

Hollinger, Karen, and Teresa Winterhalter. "A Feminist Romance: Adapting *Little Women* to the Screen." *Tulsa Studies in Women's Literature* 18 (1999): 173–92.

James, Caryn. "Amy Had Golden Curls; Jo Had a Rat. Who Would You Rather Be?" *New York Times Book Review*, 25 December 1994, 3, 17.

Janeway, Elizabeth. "Meg, Jo, Beth, Amy, and Louisa." *New York Times Book Review*, 29 September 1968, 42–46.

Kaledin, Eugenia. "Louisa May Alcott: Success and the Sorrow of Self-Denial." *Women's Studies* 5 (1978): 251–63.

Kerber, Linda K. "Can a Woman Be an Individual? The Limits of Puritan Tradition in the Early Republic." *Texas Studies in Literature and Language* 25 (1983): 165–78.

Keyser, Elizabeth Lennox. "Alcott's Portraits of the Artist as Little Woman." *International Journal of Women's Studies* 5 (1982): 445–59.

———. *Little Women: A Family Romance*. New York: Twayne, 1999.

• ———. *Whispers in the Dark: The Fiction of Louisa May Alcott*. Knoxville: U of Tennessee P, 1993.

Kirkham, Pat, and Sarah Warren. "Four Little Women: Three Films and a Novel." *Adaptations: From Text to Screen, Screen to Text*. Ed. Deborah Cartmell and Imelda Whelehan. London: Routledge, 1999. 81–97.

Klass, Perri. "Stories for Girls about Girls Who Write Stories." *New York Times Book Review*, 17 May 1992, 1, 36–39.

Kornfield, Eve, and Susan Jackson. "The Female Bildungsroman in Nineteenth-Century America: Parameters of a Vision." *Journal of American Culture* 10 (1987): 69–75.

Langland, Elizabeth. "Female Stories of Experience: Alcott's *Little Women* in Light of *Work*." *The Voyage In: Fictions of Female Development*. Ed. Elizabeth Abel, Marianne Hirsch, and Elizabeth Langland. Hanover, NH: U P of New England, 1983. 112–27.

MacDonald, Ruth K. *Christian's Children: The Influence of John Bunyan's* The Pilgrim's Progress *on American Children's Literature*. New York: Lang, 1989. 68–78.

———. *Louisa May Alcott*. Boston: Twayne, 1983.

———. "Louisa May Alcott's *Little Women*: Who Is Still Reading Miss Alcott and Why." *Touchstones: Reflections on the Best in Children's Literature*. Vol 1. Ed. Perry Nodelman. West Lafayette, IN: Children's Literature Association, 1985. 13–20.

Mackey, Margaret. "*Little Women* Go to Market: Shifting Texts and Changing Readers." *Children's Literature in Education* 29 (1998): 153–73.

Mailloux, Steven. "The Rhetorical Use and Abuse of Fiction: Eating Books in Late Nineteenth-Century America." *Reconceptualizing American Literary/Cultural Studies: Rhetoric, History, and Politics in the Humanities*. Ed. William E. Cain. New York: Garland, 1996. 21–33.

Marchalonis, Shirley. "Filming the Nineteenth Century: *The Secret Garden* and *Little Women*." *American Transcendental Quarterly* 10 (1996): 273–92.

May, Jill P. "Feminism and Children's Literature: Fitting *Little Women* into the American Literary Canon." *CEA Critic* 56 (1994): 19–27.

Meigs, Cornelia. *Invincible Louisa: The Story of the Author of* Little Women. Boston: Little, Brown, 1933.

Minadeo, Christy Rishoi. "*Little Women* in the Twenty-first Century." *Images of the Child*. Ed. Harry Eiss. Bowling Green: Bowling Green State U Popular P, 1994. 199–214.

Murphy, Ann B. "The Borders of Ethical, Erotic, and Artistic Possibilities in *Little Women*." *Signs* 15 (1990): 562–85.

Myerson, Joel, and Daniel Shealy. "The Sales of Louisa May Alcott's Books." *Harvard Library Bulletin* 1 (1990): 47–86.

Nelson, Michael C. "Writing during Wartime: Gender and Literacy in the American Civil War." *Journal of American Studies* 31 (1997): 43–68.

O'Brien, Sharon. "Tomboyism and Adolescent Conflict: Three Nineteenth-Century Case Studies." *Woman's Being, Woman's Place: Female Identity and Vocation in American History*. Ed. Mary Kelley. Boston: G.K. Hall, 1979. 351–72.

Paul, Lissa. "Reading *Little Women*." *Reading Otherways*. Stroud, Gloucestershire, U.K.: Thimble Press, 1998. 40–55.

Pauly, Thomas H. "*Ragged Dick* and *Little Women*: Idealized Homes and Unwanted Marriages." *Journal of Popular Culture* 9 (1975): 583–92.

Payne, Alma J. *Louisa May Alcott: A Reference Guide*. Boston: G.K. Hall, 1980.

Phillips, Anne K. "The Prophets and the Martyrs: Pilgrims and Missionaries in *Little Women* and *Jack and Jill*." In Alberghene and Clark. 213–36.

Reardon, Colleen. "Music as Leitmotif in Louisa May Alcott's *Little Women*." *Children's Literature* 24 (1996): 74–85.

Russ, Lavinia. "Not to Be Read on Sunday." *Horn Book* 44 (1968): 521–26.

Sands-O'Connor, Karen. "Why Jo Didn't Marry Laurie: Louisa May Alcott and *The Heir of Redclyffe*." *American Transcendental Quarterly* 15 (2001): 23–41.

Saxton, Martha. *Louisa May: A Modern Biography of Louisa May Alcott*. Boston: Houghton Mifflin, 1977.

Shealy, Daniel. "The Author-Publisher Relationships of Louisa May Alcott." *Book Research Quarterly* 3 (1987): 63–74.

———. " 'Families Are the Most Beautiful Things': The Myths and Facts of Louisa Alcott's March Family in *Little Women*." *The Child and the Family: Selected Papers from the 1988 International Conference of the Children's Literature Association, College of Charleston, Charleston, South Carolina, May 19–22, 1988*. Ed. Susan R. Gannon and Ruth Anne Thompson. [New York]: Pace University, [1990]. 65–69.

Sherman, Sarah Way. "Sacramental Shopping: *Little Women* and the Spirit of Modern Consumerism." *Prospects* 26 (2001): 183–237.

Showalter, Elaine. "*Little Women*: The American Female Myth." *Sister's Choice: Tradition and Change in American Women's Writing*. Oxford: Clarendon Press, 1991. 42–64.

• Sicherman, Barbara. "Reading *Little Women*: The Many Lives of a Text." *U.S. History as Women's History: New Feminist Essays*. Ed. Linda K. Kerber, Alice Kessler-Harris, and Kathryn Kish Sklar. Chapel Hill: U of North Carolina P, 1995. 245–66.

Skabarnicki, Anne M. "Dear Little Women: Down-Sizing the Feminine in Carlyle and Dickens." *Carlyle Studies Annual* 14 (1994): 33–42.

• Stern, Madeleine B. *Louisa May Alcott: A Biography*. Rev. ed. Boston: Northeastern UP, 1999.

———, ed. *Critical Essays on Louisa May Alcott*. Boston: G.K. Hall, 1984.

• Stimpson, Catharine R. "Reading for Love: Canons, Paracanons, and Whistling Jo March." *New Literary History* 21 (1990): 957–76.

Ullom, Judith C., comp. *Louisa May Alcott: A Centennial for* Little Women, *An Annotated, Selected Bibliography*. Washington, D.C.: Library of Congress, 1969.

Vallone, Lynne. "The Daughter of the Republic: Girls' Play in Nineteenth-Century American Juvenile Fiction." *Disciplines of Virtue: Girls' Culture in the Eighteenth and Nineteenth Centuries*. New Haven: Yale UP, 1995. 106–34.

Van Buren, Jane. "*Little Women*: A Study in Adolescence and Alter Egos." *The Modernist Madonna: Semiotics of the Maternal Methaphor*. Bloomington: Indiana UP, 1989. 96–123.

• Vincent, Elizabeth. "Subversive Miss Alcott." *New Republic*, 22 October 1924, 204.

Walters, Karla. "Seeking Home: Secularizing the Quest for the Celestial City in *Little Women* and *The Wonderful Wizard of Oz*." *Reform and Counterreform: Dialectics of the Word in Western Christianity since Luther*. Ed. John C. Hawley. Berlin: Mouton de Gruyter, 1994. 153–71.

Zehr, Janet S. "The Response of Nineteenth-Century Audiences to Louisa May Alcott's Fiction." *American Transcendental Quarterly* 1 (1987): 321–42.

Zwinger, Lynda. "*Little Women*: The Legend of Good Daughters." *Daughters, Fathers, and the Novel: The Sentimental Romance of Heterosexuality*. Madison: U of Wisconsin P, 1991. 46–75.